GLOAMIN' BRIDGE

(A Civil War Remembrance)

Thomas McCabe

Gloamin' Bridge (A Civil War Remembrance)

Published by Zaveair Press
tkmccabe@comcast.net
Copyright © 2009 by Thomas McCabe

Printed in the United States of America

Library of Congress Catalog-in-Publication data

Library of Congress Control Number: 2001012345

McCabe, Thomas Keith

Gloamin' Bridge (A Civil War Remembrance) / Thomas McCabe

ISBN - 13: 978-0-9842624-0-3
ISBN - 10: 0-9842624-0-7

United States--History--Civil War, 1861-1865 Historical Fiction

Cover drawing – Jim Meehan, Chicago

Author's photograph – Megan Beyer

They were affectionately called the Six Micks while growing up in Naperville, Illinois: Don McCabe, Keith "Pete" McCabe, Bob McCabe, Ben McCabe, Jack McCabe and Bill McCabe. All six left Naperville and headed overseas to fight in World War Two. Gloamin' Bridge *is dedicated to the memory of those brave, loving and unassuming men, and to their wives. It is also dedicated to their parents, Benjamin and Grace McCabe, whose huge presence stayed with their sons during the darkest hours of their individual ordeals.*

GLOAMIN' BRIDGE

(A Civil War Remembrance)

Billy McCabe told no one he was going for a walk as he made his way out the front door of his stately Italianate in Naperville. It was a cloudy afternoon, not too cold for a December day in northeastern Illinois, but at ninety-four he was past the time in life when heading out on his own was acceptable to those who looked after him. Billy understood their concern and tolerated their benign ignorance.

He wasn't going far, just down to the timeworn walking bridge that spanned the DuPage River below the old dam. There wasn't much to the dam. It was only six feet high at best, but inconvenienced the generally lazy river enough to discourage it from doing much other than ease over the old limestone and mortar barrier, keeping the river shallow below the dam. It was no more than knee-deep in most spots, unless spring thaws or heavy rains held sway. The gravel river bed created an ideal cattle crossing, although it hadn't been used as such since before the turn of the century.

After leaving his home at 221 West Jefferson Avenue, Billy continued to make his way the half block to Eagle Street then south one block to the bridge. It was well constructed, having been built from the highest quality timber by men who had taken pride in their craftsmanship and reputations, expecting both to continue after they were long dead as irrefutable affirmations of their skill and devotion. Attributes that foreshadowed their expectations to be sure, since the last amongst them had been laid to rest one year before President Lincoln's assassination, and less than a month after the bridge had been completed.

The good citizens of Naperville, of whom there were more than a few when it seemed to matter, had always made it a priority to maintain the structure. By 1941 however, there was some speculation that after nearly eighty years perhaps the bridge's time was, if not at hand, focused in that direction. Those concerned with historical preservation didn't subscribe to that notion and their influence had thus far remained intact.

Billy hadn't been down there in quite a while because he never expected the historic bridge to disappear, comforted as he was with its eternally quiet strength. It was a valued part of his past. It transcended vulnerability as if the bridge held fast an invincible stability, not unlike a stalwart lake of impressive depths whose primary purpose was to hold fast Billy's affirmation; a lake that could not be drained or altered no more than Billy's entire history could be, nor the history of his once large family whose strength, courage and love could never be erased or successfully challenged in any way.

***

IT HAD been the news on the radio that had prompted Billy to take his walk, the news that Pearl Harbor had been bombed by the Japanese. United States entry into World War II was imminent, a war that would indeed engulf nearly the entire world; just as Billy McCabe's world had been engulfed when he was barely fourteen.

It hadn't been as far off as Hawaii, and it had been a much smaller island than Oahu, but when the cannonades fired upon Fort Sumter the effect had been the same; and Billy, his parents, and what remained of his five older brothers would live the rest of their days ever mindful of what all of it had come to represent. And the new bridge, completed in 1864, would stand sentinel for the duration and beyond - as it had for the Reckoning so many years before.

IN 1861, fourteen-year-old Billy McCabe watched his older brothers leave the farm and head off to war, first Don and Ben Jr., then a few months later Jackie and Robert. Pete, age twenty-two, was the second oldest and most able farmer amongst them. He had been the last to go, having held off until the crops had been harvested before fall collapsed into winter.

Pete's Christian name was Keith, but years before when he was in his early teens he went to work part-time for a new arrival to the Naperville area, a farmer who had recently emigrated from Europe. He pronounced his young worker's first name Keat. When Keith's brothers got wind of the mispronunciation his nickname became Pete, and had stuck there ever since except as far as his parents were concerned. Father Benjamin and Mother Grace always called him Kee, which prompted some folks to joke about why they had bothered to name him Keith to begin with, since it was apparent no one ever got around to using the name.

***

PETE'S DEPARTURE made the void nearly complete, and that stark reality was the reason all pretenses had been abandoned, why the tears had flowed so freely, at least from Mother Grace. Father Benjamin's tears stood their ground until he had made his way to the far end of the High Hayloft, well out of sight, or so he believed. Billy had quietly followed his father to the large barn though, watching until he saw the rhythmic heaving of his father's shoulders and heard the deep-throated sobs, at least the few that had managed to escape. Young Billy retreated down the ladder he had ascended as quickly as stealth and mercy would allow.

***

SUPPER THAT night was a lonely and quiet affair, except for the sounds of flatware against plates, an occasional cough or slight throat clearing. The sounds struck Billy as odd, especially the sound of his parents chewing their food. He had never heard it before, or more like it never noticed. There had always been his five older brothers crowded next and across from him upon the wooden benches that ran the length of the large, rectangular butternut table. Other than during grace at the beginning of each meal, silence had been the last thing to be found at the McCabe family's warm and generous table.

Even when Pete had been the only one left, save Billy, there had almost always been conversation. With Pete's departure talk of crops, weather, situations on neighboring farms and other happenings both local and national had suddenly disappeared. It was as if all the topics had vanished down the dirt road along with Pete and the rest of the boys who had turned into young men with each fading, dusty footstep; their Yankee blue uniforms concealing their individuality, at least for the time being, as they marched towards the Southern horizon.

"Thank the dear Lord at least one of our boys is too young to march away," Mother Grace said as she placed her hand on top of Billy's, breaking the supper table silence. He wanted to pull away but didn't have the heart. "Am I selfish to feel this way, Benjamin?" She inquired of her husband, squeezing her youngest child's hand harder still. Her gaze was steady – Father Benjamin felt it even before his eyes met hers.

"Our boys will be fighting so a mother may no longer fear losing ownership of her child," he said, paraphrasing a Michigan abolitionist whose name he did not recall, softening his words as he spoke. "Your sacrifice would have been generous had only one of our boys marched away. Mr. Lincoln can preserve the Union to his heart's content. To my mind, thwarting the atrocity of selling a mother's child to the highest bidder is the true call to arms."

"And a father's child, Benjamin?" Mother Grace added, her gaze warming into a familiar acceptance that bonded them without need of another word. Father Benjamin spoke anyway.

"And a father's." He wasn't conscious of the wistful smile that stayed on his lips as he basked in the glow of his wife's enduring gaze, one that had consistently reinvented itself in so many enchanting ways during the twenty-five years of their marriage. Father Benjamin never tired of looking into his wife's eyes that were nearly the same shade of blue as his.

Mother Grace was a somewhat tall woman. Even after the birth of six sons she remained slender and firm. She wasn't plain or beautiful, although her soft facial features mirrored a loveliness her fifty years had been unable to diminish. When her brown and silver hair was down, nearly to the small of her back, Father Benjamin swore she was as lovely as the day he married her.

He wasn't a tall man, and at almost five foot nine was about the same height as his wife. His hair was thinning, especially in the front. He was broad shouldered, and although he didn't appear fat, his thick waist was a testament to his prodigious appetite. He was a farmer by trade but had the look and demeanor of a college professor, or so some folks said, especially when he wore his spectacles which was usually the case.

Silenced conversation again stole over the supper table but Billy had stopped listening to the remaining sounds. He instead envisaged someone approaching his mother and father with a legal document in hand, telling them their six sons had just been sold and would soon be off to a sugar plantation somewhere very hot, and so very far away that when they departed it would be the last view of their boys by either parent until God fulfilled his promise to them all with His Final Reward.

And what if the selling had occurred when the boys were mere adolescents, crippled as they would have been by their lack of knowledge of the world, their vulnerability laid bare? And what if they had all been girls? Billy had girl cousins, plus the daughters of close family friends as well as other girls he knew from the Naper Academy where he sometimes attended school in town on Eagle Street, unless he was attending classes at the smaller country school over in Copenhagen Corners. For some reason the thought of girls being led away in shackles, never to be seen again, seemed even more chilling to the youth. Chilling and morally reprehensible, so much so he could even justify stopping such abominations at the point of a gun, although squeezing a trigger, any trigger attached to a gun pointed at any living thing, was something others seriously doubted Billy could do. He knew his brothers could though; hadn't they set out to do that very thing?

In his desire to emulate his older brothers he had attempted to convince them he could as well, but only with words. Billy felt the words rang true when he spoke them since gaining their approval meant so much to him, but his true nature was something they already admired, although at fourteen, amidst all the clashing philosophies the times were generating, that was lost on the youth.

His brothers had never teased Billy about his nature, not really. It was understood Billy had found their mother's deep-seated religion or whatever spirituality that flowed continuously within and from the boy since before he could talk. Even so, his inner being contained a few inexplicable realities that were difficult to fathom. When he was but a baby it was not uncommon to see butterflies land upon him, slowly fluttering their wings as if they had discovered the ultimate haven if not a taste of heaven itself, or so Mother Grace believed.

The wonderment continued throughout his adolescence and not once, to no one's surprise, did young Billy shoo them away. All he ever did, every single time, was warm up and smile. The glow would remain even after the delicate travelers determined his arms, hands, even his cheeks and lips weren't heaven after all, but apparently close enough because they always seemed to hesitate before leaving. More than a few always returned, as if uncertainty didn't have to confine them to continuing their search after all.

Once when he was three and had wandered off, the whole family came running from various places when Billy's shrieks, coming from the Purple Meadow thus named for its abundance of clover, could be heard even in the barn a quarter mile away. When everyone arrived, spaced apart within a few minutes of each other, it was all euphoria. There must have been over a hundred snow-white butterflies upon him. He looked as if a down pillow had been emptied over his head after he'd been dipped in black strap molasses. Maybe the butterflies hadn't found heaven, but they had sure enough created it for young Billy. He cooed and giggled himself to sleep that night, the last one to drift off.

Billy never missed Sunday services with his mother, not once in all his fourteen years unless the weather was brutal. His father felt obliged to attend services from time to time, although his true places of worship were the meadows, streams and especially the forests that hugged both banks of the west branch of the DuPage River that ran just a few miles east of the farm, located on the north side of a dirt road south of Naperville that decades later would be called 75th Street. His older brothers, except Jackie, fell in step with their father's feelings. Jackie was also a church regular and at two years his senior closest in age to Billy.

Father Benjamin saw to it his two youngest boys could handle a horse and buggy at a very young age, younger by two years than any of their brothers had been allowed to enjoy. None of the McCabe boys were irresponsible, but Billy and Jackie had always demonstrated a thoughtful maturity so well beyond their years it seemed natural for them to head out on a Sunday morning with Mother Grace, guiding Black Hat along the roads the coal black mare knew so well.

Studs and Rivet, Black Hat's stable mates, snorted contemptuously at the attention the impressive mare received most Sunday mornings. It was assumed any jealousy the two draft horses harbored would soon be nullified since Sundays, for much of the year, also meant the heavy labor they performed all week would be replaced with wandering aimlessly about the Purple Meadow, eating the delectable clover to their hearts' content, hauling or pulling along nothing heavier than themselves.

***

BENJAMIN RETIRED to the front porch after supper, pipe in hand. Billy helped his mother with what few dishes, comparatively speaking, there were then headed out to the barn. Black Hat, Studs and Rivet would be expecting their evening rations of crisp fall Jonathan apples from the North Orchard. Besides, the new goat they had recently acquired and promptly named President Davis had shown signs of a disagreeable bowel condition whose prodigious discharges, Father Benjamin had insisted, more than justified the goat's new moniker. Perhaps, Billy hoped, a generous helping of North Orchard apples would also serve to quiet that malady for their new dignitary as well as please the horses he felt compelled to pamper. Billy loved helping the sick and infirm, regardless of how many legs they had or what life form they took. When he was a young boy even injured insects became recipients of his care, although few survived their benefactor's good intentions.

His deep-seated concerns for all living things had evolved into more effective applications as the years passed, thanks to Dr. Silas Wygant. Billy was delighted, but not surprised to find Doc Wygant checking on President Davis when the boy made his way to the barn that night, lantern in hand. The old man had a way of appearing when ailments were present, whether humans or other animals were doing the suffering, and more often than not without the good doctor having been notified or summoned by any conventional means the town and country folk had ever been able to ascertain. It was a wonderment, and more than a little unsettling to those who needed their strict religious interpretations to help them cope. It was rumored the town's only avowed atheist, Colin McSwede, found it especially perturbing if not downright frightening.

Although as a youth Doc Wygant had apprenticed with a local doctor and afterwards spent a year at the Medical College of Ohio in the 1820's, Silas wasn't technically a doctor if providing evidence of a medical degree was required. He knew, however, as much as fifty-odd years of experience could teach any person as committed to helping others as he. Animal husbandry was another of his specialties as was dentistry, but unless one could afford the loss of a tooth or two it was a good idea not to admit to pain in that particular area unless it was so unbearable the added agony of the ultimate cure was unavoidable.

For whatever reason, old Doc Wygant, tongs in hand, was known to go after toothaches with a curious determination. Most folks felt it was a very good idea to insist the first tooth pulled was indeed the culprit regardless of how much whiskey or laudanum was promised if further exploration would be allowed. Besides, Doc Wygant was seldom wrong when it came to teeth, even if he did tend to get a little carried away with pulling out an extra tooth or two he thought might be a problem later on. If he was wrong, had somehow missed another culprit, he would reappear in a day or two anyway. He had most of his teeth, but for whatever reason didn't seem overly concerned if others didn't share his luxury.

He was a good and highly respected man, although his sometimes mysterious ways gave pause to those who especially feared what they couldn't understand. Once in a while even those folks fantasized about garnering Doc's respect when the notion caught them off guard. By the time Billy was twelve, Doc Wygant had taught him a good deal and was the only person Billy had confided in concerning the youth's future plans.

"I'd head there myself even if I am gettin' on in years," Doc Wygant told Billy on several previous occasions, "but for the life of me I don't know what would become of the two thousand or so folks and their fellow animals here at home. There were only six of us to begin with, and four of the younger doctors from around here's already enlisted. That leaves just me and old Doc Daniels, unless you want to count "Doctor" Gilbert Van Craig over in Wheaton, 'cept he's not worth a tinker's damn drunk or sober, although I suppose he's at least consistent in that regard."

Billy had believed him the first time Doc Wygant had brought up his reasons for not being able to go off to war. He didn't understand why the old man insisted upon getting that particular point out of the way almost each time the subject was raised, especially if Doc's whiskey bottle was lighter than when he'd left home, although that rarely occurred. Billy knew Doc was a brave man, even if the rail-thin, white-haired doctor, especially at his age, wouldn't be able to thwart a determined enemy in hand-to hand combat. He wouldn't be expected to, but Billy thought that may have been the reason Doc Wygant mentioned it, as if he needed to assure the youth his old friend's advanced years, lack of size and physical prowess weren't capable of disaffirming his willingness and bravery.

"Heading off to war at fourteen shows sand, but not as much common sense as I've grown accustomed to hearing from you, Billy boy."

"I know Doc," Billy said, "but look at all the help I could bring to those wounded men out there, and all the horses and shot up livestock too. Might even be one of my brothers I'd be saving. That would do Mother Grace proud, don't you think?"

"Don't ply me with that, Billy. What you *want* to do doesn't yet square with what you *can* do. I know you could be of help, but I also know how fast you're picking up on things. In two years I'll have taught you how to use a scalpel, hemostat and bullet probe in ways that can repair wounds a damn sight more serious than lancing pus from a boil. Then you'd really be an asset, keeping grief away from more mothers than merely your own. Just two more years, Billy boy. Hell, you'll only be sixteen."

Billy knew the old man was right. It seemed Dr. Silas Wygant was always right, about most things anyway. Besides, even if Billy did run off and join, the very heart he wanted to make so proud would not only be broken but betrayed in ways he could only pretend not to imagine. No, if he was going to go it could only be after telling his parents to their faces, like his brothers had done. Sixteen would be old enough even if just barely, but he'd have the training Doc Wygant had always promised and with it he would no doubt be assigned away from the fighting, for the most part. That's what he'd tell his mother at any rate, although he saw himself being the first to arrive after the bullet, bayonet, or canister struck.

His biggest concern was the war would be over before he could enlist. Most folks said the Rebels would be trounced good and proper in a matter of months, not years.

That was a good thing of course and Billy knew it, but if he ended up being the only McCabe son who hadn't answered the Call, especially when he had so much to offer those who Providence or its antithesis placed in harm's way, he would never forgive himself; he just knew it.

He couldn't help but wonder if an early end to the war was on Doc Wygant's mind as well. Billy loved Doc, but knew the old man could play both ends from the middle - borne to it if ever a soul had such a calling. It was more than possible the two years of training Doc referred to should take only months, but Billy knew he'd never get an unequivocal answer to that question until the training and subsequent application of his new skills were completed and he could answer that question himself. According to Doc, he couldn't teach much without patients to work on or whose field hospital operations, such as they would be, could be explained in detail. Some of the returning wounded would fill that bill, Doc insisted, perhaps sooner than later. Regardless, Billy gave his word he would wait until turning sixteen, if Doc would promise to accompany him when he approached Mother Grace and Father Benjamin with the plan. With that, their deal was struck.

Inwardly, Doc Wygant did have qualms about Billy going off to war, at least if the youth ended up in battle. Unlike his large, strapping brothers, especially Pete, Billy was slight of build even for his tender age - barely five feet tall and not a hundred twenty pounds. His soft blue eyes and corn silk hair didn't paint an imposing picture either, although the girls thereabouts had certainly taken notice of his striking good looks. He wasn't a coward, far from it, which in battle could easily get him killed if the fighting was hand-to-hand. Still, Doc had his two year deal and fully intended to hold his young protégé to it, whether by conformity to truth or guile.

***

THE APPLES, along with one of Doc Wygant's concoctions did indeed offer much relief to President Davis. After Billy shoveled out the soon-to-be grateful goat's stall and Doc had departed, the youth made his way around the house to the front porch where he extinguished his lantern.

Father Benjamin was working on his second bowl, the smoke curling upwards on the windless, waxing-moon night. They watched Doc Wygant's buggy move down the narrow dirt road, his gray mare clip-clopping at a steady gait, a soft scurry of dust trailing in the faint moonlight as the buggy headed east. The air was ambrosial and crisp, as only the fall season could muster so delectably. The recent chill felt welcome after so many warm summer evenings, and a few downright hot ones that were even more of a nuisance when they insisted upon intruding well into September.

"How far you s'pect Pete's made it, Pa?" Billy asked as he patiently waited for his father's reply, somewhat concerned his question had intruded upon other musings.

"Well, if the train was close to on time out of Wheaton yesterday, and Kee made his connection with the one leaving Chicago, he should be in Indianapolis by now. A ways south of there is where your brother said the 1st Naperville Cavalry was to do its initial training. Kee sure hoped he'd make that train in time to hook up with those boys."

"They should wait the whole train for him," Billy said in the way younger brothers and sisters are prone to do when defending the infallibility of an older sibling they admired to a fault. "There's not a one of them comes close to Pete on a horse, least of all that no-account Clifton Janeway."

"Well son, that boy always was a handful, but in times like these it's best we all band together much as possible I suppose. Remember, it was his pa that put out the money to equip those boys, brand new Spencer rifles and all, which was no mean feat. Even their horses and tack. Abe Lincoln only had to come up with the uniforms."

Billy fell silent after his father's admonition. As mild as it had been it still stung the boy. Mother Grace always said he was the sensitive one, although never when Billy was within earshot.

"I'll grant you," Father Benjamin continued, when his boy's silence alerted his own sensibilities as it pertained to his son, as well as the fact Billy was no longer a little boy, "the apple didn't fall far from the tree, and was just as rotten when it landed I'll be bound. Buford Janeway was a handful himself years back. I know my nights would be fitful if I had a fortune secured the way his was."

"Is it true he was a robber, Pa?"

"Not so much with a gun, Billy boy, but I wouldn't put that past him either, least ways a few decades back. It's enough to know he will gladly ruin the life work of an honest man for a mere pittance, although *his* pocket would not recognize it to be such. Least ways that's his history. Some of his plunder and influence are finally being put to good use, but I s'pect it's more to lift his own stature and that of his boy's more than anything else. Least of all some noble cause is behind it to be sure, and I suspect his true motive is more'n likely corrupt in nature."

Billy was thoroughly enjoying the conversation with his father. It was the first time he was being talked to directly as an adult, and although it occurred to him it may have been because his older brothers were away, he appreciated it anyway.

"Why," Father Benjamin continued, "I recall the time Buford tried to keep a slave he bought in Mississippi, telling everyone hereabouts she was a free girl brought here as a maid for Mrs. Janeway. One day Cortance came home unexpectedly and found out the real reason her "devoted" husband had acquired a teenaged Negro girl. After that, the young gal wasn't long for Naperville. To Mrs. Janeway's credit she sent the girl to Canada, but my guess is Buford figured out a way to make that more of a story to calm Cortance's sensitivities and the truth went begging. He never could stomach losing anything, especially money, and that handsome little gal had cost him a pretty penny."

"What *was* the real reason he brought that Negro girl here, Pa?" That stopped Father Benjamin cold, but just for a moment.

"Oh, slave work of some kind. Go check on your mother, William. She no doubt needs the company of at least one of her boys."

William. When Billy heard that he knew their conversation was over. He headed inside to find his mother, but his mind wandered back to his original question. Although he loved them all, where, exactly, was the brother he most admired? Where was Pete?

II

As much as he tried to focus on what was ahead, it was what he had left behind that occupied Pete McCabe. His parents, young Billy and his concerns about how the home folks could possibly manage the farm without him held sway over his more immediate considerations. Concerns over his other four brothers hovered, and he wondered if any of them had been in the thick of it yet.

One constant sensation never seemed to dim or change. It had been radiating from his depths as long as he could remember. Its essence was myriad personifications involving Delicia Annice O'Darcy. In Pete's mind she was the epitome of everything profoundly beautiful, a conduit to all things worth seeking. Every decision he made was a continuation, regardless of its duration, complexity or direction, of something to do with her. They had known each other since childhood and even then he had been in love with her, to whatever heightened degree of intensity could be afforded any child.

Their fathers had been good friends since serving together during the Black Hawk War decades before, when Naperville was barely a village along the banks of the DuPage River. The bond between the two men carried over, affording the two families numerous opportunities to socialize as the years went by. Both men had prospered. Father Benjamin was a successful farmer, as was Hezekiah O'Darcy who also owned two limestone quarries near the banks of the DuPage, not far from his home just south, and a little west of town.

Hezekiah had built an impressive twelve room brick and stone Victorian Eclectic on a rise located close to his property's northwest corner, not a quarter mile south of the river. He referred to the rise as a craig, a Scottish-Welsh term, and after his older daughters had planted a number of pine trees upon the rise the house itself was given the name Pinecraig.

Summer picnics at their respective farms were Pete's favorite times. Hezekiah and his wife Annice had a large family of their own with five daughters and two sons. When the McCabe and O'Darcy families gathered it was always a big affair, with games, hayrides and of course the food. The gatherings started off with fresh produce from the gardens along with hams and other delicacies from the smokehouse. There were always meat pies, fried chicken, potatoes served in a variety of ways and fresh baked bread along with plenty of apple cider. The bountiful meals were topped off with fruit pies, cakes, homemade ice cream and other desserts, especially Mother Grace's famous strawberry rhubarb preserves that went with just about anything. Father Benjamin swore he could enjoy it spread upon a cloth napkin.

Pete and Delicia were born within a year of each other, and their relationship had always been different from the ones Pete had developed with the other O'Darcy girls. The same was true for Delicia and her relationship with Pete's brothers. As much as Pete was, and had always been in love with Delicia, her feelings for him were the full measure of his. Ever since they were old enough to crawl, seeing them apart by choice had seldom been witnessed by anyone.

As the two of them approached adulthood there were some parental concerns and more than a little town and country gossip about their yearning to be together so often, even if their engagement appeared inevitable. Delicia had become such a fine-figured and beautiful young lady males of all ages were hard pressed not to stare, with the bold, confident or foolish attempting to engage her in conversation at every opportunity.

Pete had grown to be the largest and most athletic McCabe brother and most other young men in the general Naperville area as well. All the McCabe boys were fine looking young men, but only young Billy was considered better looking than Pete by those who coveted, or at least paid attention to such things.

So many memories, especially those wonderful times with Delicia, just wouldn't leave Pete alone as the train continued to chug from Chicago's Central Depot towards Indianapolis. He had never been farther from home than Chicago, and even then just a few times. The more distance that accumulated between him and Naperville, and more specifically Delicia, the more his thoughts and feelings wanted to daydream him back home. He found it to be a very easy thing to do, even if he was embarking upon an adventure that would be the defining moment in the lives of thousands of farm and city boys in the North and South, as well as so many others. Those memories of Delicia though, and the ones yet to be created, were always close by.

The other young, soon-to-be cavalrymen on the train talked excitedly about what was in their immediate future, but Pete's thoughts traveled beyond bravado and their naïve assumptions about the glories of battle. His mind's eye saw him after the war, on a proud chestnut roan, heading down the narrow dirt road south of town that led to the McCabe farm. The O'Darcy property wasn't three miles northeast of the McCabe spread, so in his fantasy Delicia was there waiting for him as well. Actually, she spots him first, long before the others know he is approaching, or at least long enough for the two of them to share a lingering embrace…

On that dreamscape day after the war Pete and Delicia are strolling about hand-in-hand, re-exploring each other as they move about on the McCabe farm. They first wander around and within the white, two story house itself, affectionately named Tin

Pan Alley by Pete's father when it was built. It had always been such an elegant place for a farmhouse, with porches on both the first and second floors that stretched along the entire length of the structure's front. Mother Grace's pride was the narrow windows that went from nearly the floor to the ceilings, at least on the first floor. Most of the rooms were large, and at a little over three thousand square feet so was the entire house by 1860's Naperville farmhouse standards.

Pete's favorite room, not surprisingly, had always been the spacious kitchen, and that's where the two reunited lovers take a seat next to each other at the large, rectangular table that had been made from an old butternut tree a spring storm had felled decades before. A delicious lunch is ready but in Pete's mind they are the only two souls in the room. They decide to pack a picnic basket and head over near Brook Creek that runs along the east side of the Purple Meadow.

It is such a gorgeous summer's day, and Pete finds himself mesmerized by the simplicities and intricacies of Delicia's beauty as the angled rays of sun dance through her flowing, light brown hair as one soft breeze after another haphazardly lifts and caresses first one lock, then another. Her eyes, an astonishing shade of pronounced blue, lighten each time she smiles, almost matching the intensity of the Purple Meadow's blossoms. In his fantasy he doesn't recall having made the nearly half mile stroll to get there.

They had to have passed the large, white barn a little northeast from the rear of the house and beyond that the corral, chicken coup and smokehouse, not to mention traversing the eastern side of the North Orchard before arriving at the Purple Meadow, but no matter. They are alone amidst their favorite place, near the narrow bend in Brook Creek, and if ever a time had arrived for a first kiss that was surely the moment; a first lovers' kiss so passionate all but the necessary inhibitions would immediately fade away…

"Pete, upon my soul! Is this really you?" The young major said, shattering Pete's daydream beyond any hope of immediate repair.

"Sackett!" Pete said, quickly regaining his composure, "I had no idea you were on this train." They shook hands as the other recruits watched amidst the din of conversation that hadn't let up.

"Wasn't supposed to be, but when I received the wire finally granting my request to command the 1st Naperville Cavalry, I was on it like a shot! It's good to see you, Pete. How's my family?"

"They were all in good health when I left, Sackett."

"Including Delicia I assume," Sackett O'Darcy added with a teasing grin.

"Your sister is in especially fine form, in every way." Pete said, returning Sackett's smile. "Here, take a seat. I'll bring you up to date on home and you can return the favor with the latest news about the 1st Naperville. Most of these boys seem content with rumors, not that I know any better."

"I'm not sure I do either, at least not as much as I'd like," Sackett said as he let out a barely perceptible sigh. "But I can attest to their hearts, as can you. I suppose their courage will follow whatever natural course such things take, but I had hoped for more time to prepare them for what's ahead."

"Is there something about that I need to know?" Pete asked, realizing his friend would have such information before the rest of the new recruits, if not everyone else on the train and points beyond.

Sackett O'Darcy had received his West Point recommendation from none other than Abraham Lincoln himself, in 1854. Lincoln had been elected to the Illinois State Legislature. Although he had declined the seat to run for the U.S. Senate, Lincoln had nonetheless used his influence to see that the eldest son of his old acquaintance and fellow militiaman during the Black Hawk War, Sackett's father Hezekiah, received an appointment to West Point.

Sackett had done himself and his family proud, graduating close to the top of his class. Like Pete and most other Naperville youths while growing up, Sackett had received an excellent education at the local schools. Although any number of communities in mid 19th century Illinois had other priorities, the mostly German immigrants who had settled in or near Naperville considered education paramount for their offspring. The end result was apparent in speech, overall knowledge and comportment as it pertained to most Naperville youths and young adults.

Sackett had remained in Washington until the war had exploded, serving with distinction until his recent transfer to Chicago. He had been a captain, but was now a major whose responsibilities included command of the 1st Naperville Cavalry even though he had not raised the unit. Moreover, since he had been promoted to the rank of major, it took some maneuvering on his part to command a cavalry troop of roughly a hundred men, a task that usually fell within the province of a captain.

Due to the lack of military experience of the Naperville volunteers who could benefit greatly from Major Sackett O'Darcy's expertise, coupled with the fact they would be operating in the less crucial Western Theater of the war, his superiors had relented to Major O'Darcy's repeated requests to train and lead the men from his hometown. Later on, if it was determined his service was needed elsewhere it could be arranged easily enough.

"I don't know all that much myself, Pete, but I imagine we'll be in the thick of things sooner than later. Too soon I fear, perhaps less than four weeks. Tending farms takes hard work and perseverance, but is a sorry substitute for the type of training needed for this task."

Pete pondered his friend's words in silence, causing Sackett to wonder if he had possibly offended his long time friend. He knew Pete was up to the challenge but a distance of five years stood between them. A person's temperament can alter after so many years apart.

"What I meant to say, Pete, is that -"

"No need to explain yourself to me, Sackett," Pete replied, as calm as Sackett remembered his friend to have almost always been. "You've had my respect for as long as I can remember. There's no doubt in my mind we all need to learn what you can teach. I guess Southern boys are at least as good with a horse and a gun as us, from a farmer's perspective at least, and just as green when it comes to war. It could be yours is the most difficult job."

"Thanks, Pete. I can't help but look around at these young men and brood about where my guidance will lead them. Their fate may be in the hands of Providence, but I can't help but feel Providence expects more from me than I can deliver."

"Then I guess Providence has placed all of us in an unenviable position," Pete responded with a smile that erased concerns of their nearly five year separation with ease. "Not unlike that time in Aurora. I seem to recall your sand and leadership was evident even then."

That recollection brought a vague smile to Sackett's face that was as revealing as the memory itself...

***

IT HAD been intended as a dual celebration, Pete's seventeenth birthday and the letter that Sackett had been accepted to West Point. It had occurred five years ago to the month as they sat in the train, although it didn't seem that long ago to either man. Apparently time did grow impatient after all, just like the old folks claimed. The older the pontificator the more intolerant time appeared to be with dallying.

Sackett, his younger brother James, Pete and his younger brother Robert had convinced themselves, if not initially their fathers, they had stepped far enough into manhood to test their mettle in the unshaven town of Aurora twelve miles due west of Naperville. Their fathers knew such a time was inevitable, and also realized they were the ones who would have to answer to their wives if a night or two of youthful frivolity ended up justifying the oldsters' worst fears. It almost did that very thing.

Aurora was a decent enough town, but not in every quarter, and certainly not in the part of town where the boys had eventually set their sights. Their fathers knew the validity of that concept despite the unpersuasive promises their sons had attempted to convey. Still, their sons weren't planning to embark on anything Father Benjamin and Hezekiah hadn't undertaken in their day. Boys, to be sure, would be boys their fathers agreed, but the time had to come when they must become men or at least begin the journey.

The first night had mirrored the youths' promises, so much so any concerns to forego a second night had been easily dismissed. Had they not ventured from the relative safety of Elk Hill Tavern and its boarding house on Stolp Island, the decision would have indeed mirrored their declarations, but the allure of the La Salle Street District on the near east side of town had helped confirm the opposite. It wasn't by accident they had chosen a tavern whose reputation generally kept the faint hearted away, although it wasn't just the timorous who avoided the establishment.

"So beer is the only drink a wet-behind-the-ears *plowboy* from Naperville can handle, then?" The large, ruddy-faced man all but shouted over the din of the noisy tavern when Pete had declined for a second time the man's dubious offer to share whiskey with him as they stood next to each other at the bar, as long as Pete paid. His tone could have been taken in jest, for someone accustomed to rationalizing away insult.

"If it is, why would I need to prove otherwise to a drunkard who needs hard liquor to boost his courage enough to say I can't?" Pete had replied with a smile that had not appeared in his eyes.

Within moments the ruddy-faced man had several of his companions, local ne'er-do-wells to a man, at or near his side. His reply, bolstered by their apparent support, soon followed. "Big words for a *plowboy* beer sipper from Naperville! Didn't your ma teach you no manners, or was it your pa, assumin' his identity is knowed?"

Unlike his tormentor Pete hadn't bothered to see if his cohorts were close by, not when he had first spoken or when he smashed his fist flush into the ruddy-faced man's yellow teeth. Sackett and his brother James, as well as Pete's brother Robert were in the adjacent room, engrossed in a game of billiards.

Pete's blow had sent the ruddy-faced man backwards into the bar, shattering glasses as well as several front teeth. Although initially taken aback by the seventeen-year-old boy's audacity, the others were soon on him. The ensuing uproar had riveted the entire establishment's attention; even the piano player had stopped to witness the commotion. The ruddy-faced man had grabbed the neck of a whiskey bottle as his group wrestled Pete's arms behind his back and forced his head upward to receive the impending blow.

"You God damned whelp!" The enraged man hollered as he spat out blood and shards of what moments before had been a front row of teeth, sorry as they had been. "I'll wager yer face will fare worse'n mine!"

Sackett's initial approach, with the two brothers following behind, hadn't even been noticed, nor had the pool cue he held at his side. His six foot, two hundred pound frame of tensed muscle could have easily caused at least one homicide, a prospect not lost on two of the men still holding Pete. They let go immediately. The third one hesitated and ended up groveling on the floor with a four inch gash across the top of his skull, caused by a well placed blow from Sackett.

"Drop the God damned bottle or use it," Sackett told the ruddy-faced man, his tone pure conviction.

The other two moved just far enough away to indicate they'd seen enough blood for one night, unless their unofficial leader demonstrated otherwise. The ruddy-faced man wished he could join them but too many eyes were on him. Aurora was a broad shouldered town, but not big enough for a newly discovered coward's reputation to go unnoticed. He came at Sackett, all but his face that stayed where the butt of the pool cue had stopped it with a furious forward jab. That ended the ownership of his lower front teeth as well, but at least the ruddy-faced man had displayed grit. He joined his friend on the sawdust covered floor, and although Sackett's blow hadn't rendered the man unconscious, the bleeding fellow knew enough to pretend it had.

The bartender demanded the Naperville contingent leave immediately, in a voice filled with as much venom as the chambers of the double barreled 8 gauge he had finally produced from under the bar. It was entirely possible he had done so in order to protect the Naperville farm boys from the gathering crowd. The ruddy-faced man and his group had never been the bartender's favorite patrons, but he had to put up a show for the few locals who weren't thus disposed.

Once outside, a scuffle with some local toughs had ensued, and although the boys had held their own it was apparent to the folks back in Naperville the next day their local heroes had definitely been in a fight. They would have fared worse than the assortment of blackened eyes and two broken noses indicated, but Sackett alone had put enough of a hurt on four otherwise capable Aurora men to discourage the rest of the local tormentors. The other three Naperville boys had held their own as well, but there was no doubt the outcome would have been much different had Sackett not been along.

***

"THAT WAS an evening to remember," Sackett said to Pete, a pensive smile on his face as the train chugged towards Indianapolis. *If only that could end up being the extent of our battles*...that much Sackett kept to himself.

He knew the resolve of his former comrades at West Point, his former compatriots from the South who had left to fight for their sovereignty. To view those men as enemies was difficult and alarmingly unnatural for Sackett; an anomalistic reversal of world order so profound it defied reality to an extreme degree. No, as incredulous as it all felt to Sackett he didn't doubt their determination, their *devotion* any more than his own. By itself that was enough to convince him the struggle wouldn't be resolved in a matter of months. That devotion, he was convinced, could result in the dissolution of the Union - the successful outcome of the second and arguably most important American Revolution, as his former comrades referred to their cause, and with it the very real destruction of everything, if not everyone, Sackett and so many others from his side of the conflict held dear. His former comrades, some of them close friends, struggled with similar concerns. Their devotion was no less heartfelt than Sackett's, their resolve no less entrenched than his own. Any number of fuses had been ignited, impossible to extinguish, racing towards the powder.

***

AS SOON as the troop train steamed to a halt at the depot in Indianapolis it was understood Sackett was from then on to be addressed by Pete as Major O'Darcy, at least in the company of others. To his credit, Pete was aware of that without any reminder, implied or otherwise, being necessary.

It wasn't total bedlam but it might as well have been as the men filed from the train and attempted to follow the commands of their superiors, including the assignment of mounts that were already in Indianapolis. For virtually all of them, including most of the officers, the entire military experience made them feel as if they were actors preparing for a performance, a vague resemblance of what they had been taught in country and small town schools by schoolmarms and a few male teachers who were usually not as delicate as they appeared.

All that the young men on both sides had at their disposal were events obscured by time; the American War of Independence against the still distrusted British, the War of 1812 which continued, amongst other things, to perpetrate that distrust and of course the Mexican War the young republic had endured. It was as if a terrible, yawing tide were in motion, but during that moment in time only hypothetically so. War, especially the yet to be realized carnage of unspeakable proportions, remained an abstraction to all but the most ardent skeptics. There would be bullets, blood and mayhem, but those calamities would prove to be of greater concern to the other side. The combatants from both sides held that concept dear, since unwavering resolve coupled with hope forged the core of their fiber.

***

HOPE, EXPECTATION and resolve are fickle and illusive companions as virtually all soldiers, especially combat soldiers, eventually realize. A capricious nature eventually shows itself, and for Major Sackett O'Darcy and later his newly appointed adjutant, Corporal Pete McCabe, the arbitrary realities of military life had shown itself a week before Pete's arrival:

"Since Captain Clifton Janeway hails from your small burg," Lieutenant General Phineas Smithington had said to his underling Major O'Darcy that week as if he were the bearer of good news, "I can only assume his appointment will be greeted with as much enthusiasm with which it is delivered."

Sackett had offered an exasperated glance before responding. "With all due respect General Smithington, I was under the impression appointments of this magnitude would be voted on by the men. At the very least, I had expected it would have been left to my discretion."

"Your discretion, sir, or any variations thereof," General Smithington had replied, leaving no doubt in Sackett's mind who was in charge, "does not afford you the luxury of countermanding or even questioning any decisions by your superiors without permission. Are we clear on that point?"

"Indeed we are sir," Sackett had replied, glaring steadily at the portly, aging general.

***

"AT LEAST they didn't place that dandy above me, Pete." Sackett said as the two of them began to ride out with the others from the train station. They were en route to where the Union division was bivouacked, and as he spoke Sackett made sure no one else was in earshot.

"How could something like that occur, Sackett - I mean Major O'Darcy?"

"Sackett will do, if no one's listening. As to your question, welcome to a wartime army. Clifton is no doubt the beneficiary of his father's so-called patriotic generosity. War and politics not only makes strange bedfellows, but all too often we must rely upon them. A sorry state of affairs to be sure, but no less necessary."

"I'd rather take Studs or Rivet into battle with nothing but my squirrel gun than accept anything from Buford Janeway, if taking orders from that no-account son of his is the price I have to pay," Pete replied. He wondered if he had over stepped his bounds. He hadn't, for the most part.

"I admire your sand, Pete, but make no mistake - the horse you're riding and the new Spencer repeating rifles the elder Janeway's money secured will make a few "yes sirs" to that pimple Clifton well worth it when the fighting ensues. Turns out old man Janeway had an in with a Mr. Luke Wheelock, Christopher Spencer's gunsmith.

"Some think those new Spencer's are a tad heavy for cavalry use, but I don't. They're accurate as hell - you ever fired one? I suspect not, no offense intended. I know you're an excellent marksman. Fires off seven rounds as fast as you can work the lever, cock the hammer and squeeze the trigger before you have to re-load, which takes hardly any time at all. They don't have sling rings so you have to be careful not to drop them, but they fire a .56-56 rim fire cartridge and believe me, when that bullet hits most anything within range all hell breaks loose. Rather smoky when the wind is down, but deadly nonetheless. After you're trained to shoot from a moving horse that problem generally corrects itself, although most of our fighting will be done after we have dismounted.

"I can't imagine any cavalry unit on either side that wouldn't make them their weapon of choice if only they could, all things considered. Weapons of that quality and enough ammunition are hard to come by, let alone for a troop of cavalry from Illinois. Those rifles are a big plus, I'll give old man Janeway credit for that. Tough as hell to come by new as they are, but by Jesus he did it. I heard that Spencer fellow also has a new carbine in the works and Janeway has dibs on the first batch of those as well, if they get around to making them in time. Shorter, more lightweight, and those will supposedly have sling rings. I can't emphasize enough the importance of having such an advantage, Pete, even if it means we'll have to put up with Clifton. I hope he's bright enough, or cunning enough to realize what's in store for him if he tries to pull any of his shenanigans on you."

Pete believed his friend about Clifton Janeway but still had reservations. Having been away for so many years, Sackett was only aware of the bad blood between Clifton and Pete as it pertained to their boyhood altercations. As the two men rode on in silence, pretending to appreciate the predictable Indiana landscape, Pete pondered the more recent confrontations between himself and Clifton. He almost started to speak of one in particular then decided, for the time being anyway, that it was better left unsaid. He didn't want to give the appearance of someone in need of assistance, especially where Clifton Janeway was concerned. He decided not to speak, but as they continued to ride along the memories took hold and weren't about to let go…

***

PETE HAD accepted the fact males of all ages were attracted to Delicia, and had enough confidence in himself as well as her to realize the absurdity of jealous behavior on either of their parts. If Delicia was engaged in conversation with another male, he knew her well enough to determine whether any intrusion on his part would be appreciated or not. The same held true during social events like the dances held on an occasional basis at various locations. The Pre-Emption House located on the northeast corner of Main and Water Streets was the most desirable in-town location. Other venues farther from town were also used, weather permitting.

It was not uncommon for the two of them to dance with other partners, young and older people they had known all their lives. Nothing untoward was implied, certainly not expected, for the most part. There were exceptions of course, especially if Clifton Janeway and his small group of miscreants were in attendance. The only time that generally occurred was when the dances were held at the Schmidt farm. Helmit

Schmidt had the most impressive barn in DuPage County, up on Swallowtail Hill. Except for its southern slope it wasn't much of a hill really, but the swallowtails were in such abundance in that area the name was a natural fit.

Buford Janeway had given Schmidt what had been considered a very good bargain for the lumber and timbers to build such an impressive structure as well as furnishing the manpower for its construction, but as with all of Janeway's business proposals there was more to it. In Schmidt's case, it had arrived in the form of mineral rights on a forty acre tract Schmidt owned along the DuPage River southeast of town, a tract Janeway coveted. The deal had been struck so the two men ended up partners, if the ultimately one-sided arrangement could be called such, on a stone and gravel quarry. Later on that also meant Clifton and his small group had standing invitations to attend any dances held in the spacious, multi-purposed Swallowtail Hill barn.

Despite his wealth, the only invitations his son and only child ever received were due to whatever influence, undo or otherwise, Buford Janeway could bring to bear on a given situation. Clifton Janeway, rather than feeling slighted in any way or so he let on, seemed to revel in his outcast status. His sense of entitlement was so entrenched there was virtually no one he considered his equal, therefore no one he felt compelled to respect unless his father insisted he at least make the effort. Those occasions arose but were rare, at least amongst the local citizenry. Other exceptions were statesmen, men of industry, finance and others of influence, usually from Chicago or Springfield, sometimes Washington.

Even as a child Clifton had rarely displayed much other than a prodigious bullying nature. It was that trait which had caused much of the animosity between him and Pete. The confrontations that had occurred during those early years were what Sackett remembered, times when Pete had intervened on behalf of any number of Clifton's victims. Clifton had always been a large boy; large and soft. Manual labor of any kind had never been required of him and it showed. The two came to blows three times while growing up, and each time it was Clifton who went home bloodied.

How Buford Janeway would howl! He would castigate his boy severely, but only because Clifton had lost the fight. The reasons for the confrontations meant nothing to the man. He would bring down the thunder when eventually confronting Benjamin McCabe, but Buford was powerless in those particular cases. Benjamin was a self-made man and owned his farm outright, so despite Buford's threats there was nothing more he could do but jaw about it.

At the urging of Hezekiah O'Darcy, no letters from home to Sackett were to mention the only physical confrontation in the spring of 1861 that had occurred between Pete and Clifton once they had reached adulthood. His wife and daughters appreciated, and more importantly understood Hezekiah's concern. Although Sackett was a responsible and mature young man, there was little doubt he would have been on the first train home from Washington if the news of what Clifton had done had ever reached him.

It had taken several very stern admonitions from Hezekiah to keep his youngest son, James, from seeking out Clifton Janeway, even though prior to the incident the youth had always complied unflinchingly with his father's wishes. Besides, Pete had already defended Delicia's honor on that fateful spring night.

***

IT WAS called the Swallowtail Spring Ball, the biggest social event of the year for the young people of Naperville and the surrounding area. It was held in the impressive barn on Swallowtail Hill, on the first Saturday in May. Nearly all the young people anticipated its arrival with a great deal of excitement.

Though a frugal man by nature, it was one of the special times each year Hezekiah relented and allowed his oldest daughters, accompanied by their parents, to take a trip to Chicago to pick out their gowns and other accessories for the ball. The younger girls were allowed to go on the trip as well, but it was understood they would have to be content with hand-me-downs until they reached the age of sixteen.

Although some of the young people, those engaged or close to it went as couples, many of the attendees did not. Pete was to accompany Delicia, but recent rainy weather had created problems on the farm that kept Pete from fulfilling his promise. He had sent his younger brothers Billy and Jackie to deliver the bad news. Delicia was very disappointed but understood. The news was tempered with further tidings that if at all possible Pete would meet her at the ball later that evening.

The weather had created problems on the O'Darcy farm as well, but since Delicia was such a responsible young woman Hezekiah had agreed to allow her to take his best and most reliable carriage. She was adept with such things, and since the carriage would be pulled by their two best horses, there was little reason for concern.

The only problem was the number of passengers. Although the youngest daughters were old enough to attend their first ball, there was no room for them or Mother Annice to come along as a chaperone. It was finally determined they would take two carriages, with Mother Annice taking the youngest two girls, Beth and Joyce. Besides, they could get an earlier start that way and get the youngsters home at a respectable hour. It also gave the older three sisters the opportunity to arrive fashionably late.

Threatening clouds had moved in again, but Mother Annice, Beth and Joyce had no problem getting to the ball ahead of the rain. By the time the other girls were ready to depart it had still only amounted to a slight drizzle. Halfway there however, Delicia and her sisters Ginny and Linda Marie were more than a little grateful their carriage was equipped with a bellows top and side panels. They also had a buffalo robe and a knee boot to ward off incoming rain.

The rain gained urgency and grew to a storm, but not until they were in sight of the barn on Swallowtail Hill. Even in the steady downpour the numerous lanterns, gaily lit as they were against the elements, issued a warm welcome.

It was apparent the large number of earlier arrivals had made the single lane leading to the front of the barn inaccessible, having parked their carriages and wagons upon it. That left but one route that would at least put the girls close to the rear of the structure, although thanks to the unforgiving rain of the last few days as well as the current downpour the steep, southern slope appeared to be a treacherous, uphill approach to say the least. Those on horseback could traverse it, but a carriage filled with finely dressed young ladies was another story.

"I don't see a single carriage up there Delicia," Ginny said, "and the grade offers no relief if we were to slide too far to the south side."

"It's that, or we can stop here and walk through a hundred yards of rain and mud," Delicia replied.

"To be sure!" Linda Marie, the youngest of the three, added. "And won't we be a sight if we decide to walk from here! Conner and Joe Boy can make that grade if any two stallions have it in them to do so." Agreeing with Linda Marie, Delicia urged the two horses up the narrow wagon trace at a determined gait.

True to their reputations, both horses had made it halfway up without so much as a single falter. As they approached the angle that would prove to be the most difficult section of road four horsemen, oblivious to anyone's situation but their own and that just barely, raced up from behind. Two of them thundered by on the left of the carriage, mud flying up from the pounding hoof beats, as the other two attempted to pass on the right. It was all bedlam from there.

The horse of one of the men who had attempted to race by on the right of the carriage lost its footing and nearly tumbled to the ground. By itself that wasn't enough to spook either stallion, but when the rider pitched his near empty whiskey bottle into the side of Joe Boy's head, the otherwise reliable horse lost its footing as well. At that moment the rider, a drunken Clifton Janeway, unleashed a string of obscenities as he righted his mount and rode it partially into the side of the carriage. Due to the side panels he couldn't identify the girls at that point, not that it mattered to him. The shrieking girls, with the exception of Delicia who was fighting the reins with all her might, exacerbated the situation as well.

Soon both of the stallions were off the road, and if it hadn't been for Delicia's determined maneuvers they would have continued to bolt as the carriage bounced precariously about on its leaf springs to such a degree it was seconds from ending up on its side if not all the way down the hill itself. Delicia's steady hand and stern words to her sisters to quiet themselves was all that prevented a likely disaster.

When she had finally managed to bring the stallions to a halt they almost bolted again when Clifton came charging back and started in with a continued stream of loud obscenities. Due to the poor light and steady downpour plus his drunken condition, he still wasn't aware of the girls' identities, but he knew his vindictive utterances were being directed towards a carriage full of females which bolstered his resolve.

"You stupid God damned whores! You could've killed me! I should slap some sense into to you God damn it, you idiotic little bitches!" At that point he had made his way closer to the front of the carriage and finally saw to whom his wrath had been directed. The other riders approached as well, but backed off the instant they recognized the three O'Darcy sisters. Not Clifton Janeway. He simply laughed as he spoke.

"Well, had I known it was you three lovely creatures, I wouldn't have been so harsh. Not to say a sound spanking might not be in order!" He looked around to accept the laughter he assumed his comrades would offer for his wit, but all he saw was the three of them riding back down the rain-soaked road.

"Go on then, you shit-heeled cowards! I'm man enough to handle these three myself!"

Despite the steady rain and attending mud Delicia was out of the carriage, whip in hand as Clifton watched her with drunken amusement. She stopped first to further calm the stallions, Conner on the left then around to Joe Boy on the right. Clifton was ten feet away weaving unsteadily astride his horse, the light from the carriage's side lanterns osculating in the gusting wind and pouring rain.

"I see the rain must feel cold to you, Delicia, judging by the chill on your breasts, ample as they are!" The rain had indeed soaked her thin gown completely, especially the front, leaving little to the imagination even in the dim light. "Perhaps we should find shelter where you can remove that sorry gown. I'm certain my shy friends will join us if your sisters would care to tag along!" Clifton again laughed at his words, in a mocking, drunken tone as he leered at the two shaken girls huddled together in the carriage. "Just how big are *your* tits, ladies? I'm a fair judge of -"

He hadn't even seen it coming, not the first lash anyway. Delicia had delivered the blow with such force it had knocked Clifton's wide brimmed slouch hat from his head before ripping across the right side of his face. Before she could deliver the second blow, blood had already begun to appear. Shocked half sober, Clifton almost managed to grab the snaking whip when the second blow arrived but only managed to deflect it. Still, it stung his left ear to the extent he wasn't positive it was still completely attached. With that, he was off his horse like a shot. Delicia attempted a third lashing but Clifton was on her before it could be delivered.

"You deranged bitch!" He said, spitting broken raindrops as he yelled. Delicia fought furiously, but the much larger Clifton held her fast against himself with one arm while he attempted to wrestle her whip away with the other.

Although Ginny and Linda Marie were screaming again, their cries couldn't be heard through the downpour, especially since the barn was over fifty yards away and above the road. Music could be heard coming from the barn, further drowning out their urgent screams.

Clifton managed to drag Delicia a good twenty feet from the front of the carriage, groping her breasts as he dragged her along.

"Damn these are beauties!" He said in a husky voice as Delicia tried in vain to avoid his hot, whiskey-stained breath. "I should lay this whip across your bare ass, but these are reward enough," he said as he continued his groping, squeezing one breast then the other.

His attempt to reach inside the top of her soaking wet gown renewed her rage, and when his preoccupation with her breasts caused him to loosen his grip Delicia reacted quickly with an elbow to his exposed windpipe. She caught him flush, allowing her to move several feet away as Clifton reacted to the blow by staggering about as he clutched at his throat.

The screaming sisters couldn't be heard inside the barn, but the same couldn't be said for the approaching rider. When Pete homed in on the source of the cries, he spurred Black Hat into a dead run through the mud and rain. Coming up rapidly on the right he immediately recognized the carriage if not its occupants. Linda Marie was still screaming hysterically as Ginny tried to control the panicked stallions. Pete did, however, recognize Delicia, barely illuminated in the dim, swaying lantern light as she frantically searched for her whip. Then he recognized the large man who was still choking not ten feet from her.

"You *animal!*" Delicia screamed after finding the whip.

Clifton saw her coming, arm raised, at the same time he spotted Pete who had dismounted and was closing fast. Clifton, his breathing having returned almost to normal, held an arm above his head to ward off Delicia's impending blow while holding the other straight out to warn Pete he had come close enough, all the while chastising himself for not having brought along his new Philadelphia Derringer.

"You've come close enough, McCabe, not another step mind you, or else -" The whip descended upon Clifton's raised arm, partially catching the top of his head before he could finish his sentence.

For Pete, no words were necessary. His fist caught the side of Clifton's head, but it was just a glancing blow. Both men had initially lost their footing on the wet ground, especially Pete, but he recovered in time to deliver a second, more effective strike that sent Clifton tumbling to the ground. He started to get up but thought better of it. His nose was broken in two places and even in all the rain he was aware of his own blood.

Pete went immediately to Delicia. "Are you all right? What happened here?" When she threw her arms around him Clifton made his move, one that kept his sorry reputation intact. Before Pete could react, the bleeding man surprised no one by stumbling to his horse.

"Let him go," Delicia said, holding onto Pete with all her strength. He wanted to drag Clifton from his mount, thrash him further then sort things out later, but in an instant his chance was heading down the muddy road along with Clifton.

"There's gonna be hell to pay for this, McCabe!" He yelled over his shoulder when it appeared unlikely he'd be pursued, still angry with himself for not having his derringer.

Delicia never did tell Pete the extent of Clifton's assault, nor anyone else. Her sisters attested to her having been dragged away after the whipping, but in the dim light amidst all the confusion and rain they hadn't actually seen the groping. That had come as a relief to Delicia; she knew Pete. Nothing nearly as vile had ever happened to her before, but as much as she wanted Clifton Janeway punished she didn't want Pete to be his possible murderer. Even without him having known the extent of Clifton's assault, it had been all she had been able to do to keep Pete from running him down to finish what he had started.

***

"IS YOUR mind back home Pete, or are you contemplating the immediate future?" Sackett said with a grin when his friend's stoic demeanor remained unchanged for the better part of a mile.

"A little of both I suppose," Pete said as he slowly replaced the veil upon his thoughts of that disturbing night. "How much farther?"

"See the smoke beyond the rise?" Sackett said as he pointed to the southeast. "Those are campfires."

"Lord, there must be over a hundred of them." Pete said before the encampment itself came into view, marveling at the sight of all the smoke.

"That times five more like it. It appears, however, the camp has sent out a welcoming committee." Sackett added after noticing the approach of a small group of army personnel from the camp. He wasn't able to make out their identities as they rode towards the column, but Pete recognized one of the soldiers as if by instinct if not by the unique way he had always carried himself in the saddle.

"I can't say how welcome we will be to the three who are trailing, but it's doubtful the lead rider will be glad to see us." Pete said when the riders were still over a hundred yards away.

"Do you know him?"

"So will you, Sackett. If not by the bend of his body then by the gaudiness of his uniform. How many of your fellow officers dress so dandily?"

"By my stars, Pete, is that who I think it is?" But Sackett's question was rhetorical. He could indeed recognize the peculiarities of the officer in the lead. "Must be him indeed," Sackett observed with narrowed eyes. "Who else could affix so much gold upon a captain's uniform but Clifton Janeway?"

III

Pete hadn't been gone a week, yet Delicia had managed to complete five letters and was finishing up a sixth. She included a tintype of herself and her sisters, a photograph that had been made during happier times. She had already given Pete one of just herself the evening before his departure, but sending along another helped connect her to him somehow, as if a wisp of home, of *promise*, could remain with Pete regardless wherever fate, amoral happenstance or, in her mind, the whim of God took him.

She almost mentioned the recent visit of Buford Janeway to the O'Darcy farm and the subsequent meeting between him and her father but thought better of it. Rekindling the memories of that night and the weeks that followed and then passing them along to Pete by insinuation or otherwise felt selfish to her somehow. His impending ordeals offered enough for him to worry about. She would spare Pete any further agitation even though the meeting's outcome had, at the very least, produced a surprising outcome.

***

FOR ONCE it had appeared Buford Janeway felt something besides his usual fractiousness after he tipped his hat to Hezekiah O'Darcy. Hezekiah had stepped onto Pinecraig's porte-cochere and was waiting under it atop the steps, arms crossed, after he had seen Janeway riding up the lane on that overcast day. Since Janeway had been displaying a repentant demeanor Hezekiah decided to hear the man out. At least the old scoundrel had attempted to kick one of their frolicking, barking golden retrievers after he had dismounted, indicating he was at least somewhat recognizable, therefore whatever it was that had caused such an apparent change left something to which Hezekiah could relate.

"Good afternoon, O'Darcy," Janeway said as he approached the steps of the porte-cochere, silently resenting the two story home, the second largest residence in Naperville. Only Janeway's imposing house was bigger, but not by enough to quell Buford's resentment, tinged as it was with a fair dose of irrational envy. "I have come to offer an apology." He almost held out his hand but hesitated, sensing correctly the gesture would have been at least premature.

"An apology from Buford Janeway. Now that's something I would never have wagered upon."

"I can appreciate your sentiment, sir, but ask that you hear me out."

Rather than reply, Hezekiah instead held his visitor with a steady gaze, arms still crossed. Taking that as consent, guarded though it was, Janeway continued.

"Last spring my son acted abominably. Strong drink is no excuse, but its contribution to his actions cannot be wholly dismissed."

"That's a big story," Hezekiah said, his contempt mounting, "and not the same one you told Sheriff Murray if my memory hasn't failed me."

"I'll not deny as a father I felt compelled to defend my son, but simply to avoid any legal action that would have only served to bring even more notoriety to all of us, including the McCabe family."

"Defend? Or help your boy avoid the consequences of his deplorable actions? My oldest son is still unaware of what occurred, to the best of my knowledge. Perhaps time enough has passed for a more thoughtful response on Sackett's part, but had he been made aware at the time I fear even my intervention may not have been enough. Had he been there or found out about it last spring, perhaps both of us would be mourning the loss of a son. Yours perhaps beaten to death and mine hung or in prison."

"Pete McCabe was there, and the sound thrashing he gave my boy appeared to satisfy him," Janeway said.

"Not sound enough, by my estimation. My daughters could have been killed, Janeway, and that boy of yours manhandled my eldest daughter! Pete is a fine young man as evidenced by his restraint, all things considered, and as much as I admire my boy Sackett, there is more of a warrior in him that at times cannot be controlled. Your boy was lucky."

Janeway felt his own anger rising but held it in check. He knew his confrontation with Hezekiah had not promised to be easy. "In a roundabout way that is why I have come with my apology. All our boys are in the thick of it now, or soon will be. Isn't it time we set aside the past and focus on what will no doubt prove to be of more dire consequence than a misguided, youthful prank?"

Those were the first words spoken by Janeway that gave Hezekiah pause. Truth told, they had been the first words ever spoken by Janeway that gave Hezekiah pause other than to keep his temper in check.

"These are perilous times, Buford, on that we agree. It's well known you have aided our boys from hereabouts who are in the 1st Naperville, and I'll resist the temptation to question your motives as things now stand. As for accepting an apology, I will have to insist such a request come from Clifton before I give it further consideration."

"Fair enough, Hezekiah. Let us at least, however, not part as enemies, but as fathers praying for the safe return of all our young men." With that Buford Janeway finally offered his hand, and Hezekiah O'Darcy took it.

As Janeway rode away he had already begun to draft a letter in his mind, the one he would soon be sending to Clifton:

Son,

I feel guardedly confident I have managed to smooth things over a bit with your immediate superior's father. The pompous wretch wasn't even aware that you would be serving under his son, if I read him correctly. Further, it appears that whelp Sackett most likely is unaware of that silly matter regarding his sisters. Use that to your advantage while I go to work on Sackett's superior. That old mooncalf Smithington's not cheap, but I can afford him. Until then don't do anything foolish.
Father.

***

ON OCCASION Delicia used every pretext at her disposal to take the small carriage over to the McCabe farm. Mother Annice and Father Hezekiah found continual amusement in the creativity of their daughter's entreaties, if for no other reason none were necessary. They understood. Sister Ginny was always eager to accompany her older sister, since her feelings for Pete's younger brother Robert were as strong as Delicia's for Pete.

The purpose of their latest visit needed no excuse at all, since it had been suggested by Mother Annice. She had asked the girls if they would be so kind to deliver an invitation to the remaining McCabe family members to share Thanksgiving with them. It was only natural, with all the McCabe boys off to war save one, and was in keeping with Mother Annice's heart that was as free from affectation as anyone's this side of heaven, or so most folks said.

"How frightened and lonely poor Grace and Benjamin must be feeling, bless their hearts." She was fond of saying. "The approaching holidays will only fuel their despair, so we must do our best to ease their burden."

***

THE LATE fall air was crisp the afternoon the girls set out. It was a cloudless day, and the sun's brilliance exaggerated the array of colors still on the trees and bushes with an ease that belied its grandeur. Some fields danced golden in the shifting breeze, while others, as if a sense of decorum were in order, displayed a soft brown or modest beige hue. By contrast, a few of the fields had even remained a resplendent green, giving fair warning to the approaching winter its impending grip could be denied after all, at least for a while longer.

"How lovely everything appears, Delicia." Ginny remarked as the two young women traveled down the road in the small carriage that was being pulled by Conner as if the stallion had no weight behind him at all. "Times such as these make it seem so improbable we are a nation at war."

"I wish times such as these, or anything for that matter, could make war impossible." Delicia said.

"If wishes were horses then beggars might ride," Ginny responded with a smile, teasing up an old joke they had been trading back and forth for years.

"You sound like Mother," Delicia countered with a smile of her own as she held up her end of the ribbing.

They traveled on in silence, taking in the beautiful day while hoping in vain its promise might put their hearts at ease, if just for a short while. As they approached the last crossroad before arriving at the McCabe farm however, any such promise was quickly dispelled. Delicia eased Conner to a halt, and there the young women sat until the blue clad column of soldiers heading south had passed. They recognized many of the men, even if more than a few of them were men in name only.

"Look, Delicia," Ginny said as she waved, "it's the Carver boys. Good heavens, they aren't much older than young Billy McCabe." Both boys, not yet eighteen, smiled and returned the ladies' overtures, taking great pride in themselves dressed as they were in new Yankee blues. They envisaged themselves as resplendent examples of military manhood as they marched along with shoulders back and chests out, but their baggy uniforms did little other than parade the truth of their years. Before the first buds leafed out the following spring, one would be dead and the other legless from above the knees.

The sisters rode on in silence after the soldiers passed and the dust had drifted away. Soon they were turning into the McCabe farmstead, grateful to be somewhere that, for the most part, conjured up happier times. Several months had passed since the two families had held one of their picnics, and although those were indeed warm memories, it seemed as if the young ladies sensed the presence of ghosts. It always seemed to feel that way now that most of the McCabe boys were gone. Their melancholy was broken by the sight of Mother Grace, smiling as she approached.

"Benjamin, Billy, we have guests!" She called, hoping one or both of them were within earshot.

Billy was the first to arrive, the brightness in his light blue eyes confirming the warm smile on his attractive face, partially covered by a shock of undisciplined, corn-silk hair.

"By my stars, Delicia," Ginny said, her gloved hand covering her smiling mouth, "I fear for the hearts of the younger girls about, especially Linda Marie." Delicia acknowledged her sister's remark with a knowing smile of her own.

"Hello girls," Mother Grace said as she reached out to hug them after they had alighted from the carriage. "How very wonderful it is to see you! *Benjamin?*" She called again. "Billy, go fetch your father. He'll not want to miss a moment of such lovely company!"

"Yes Mother." Before he departed, he addressed the two young women. "How is Linda Marie? I wish your sister could have come. Has she asked about me? Please tell her I said hello." The girls smiled and said they most certainly would do just that, and yes, she had mentioned him just the other day. Billy had another question. "Miss Delicia and Miss Ginny, would you like to meet President Davis?"

"Off with you boy, and stop pestering our guests." Mother Grace said, knowing full well the girls found her youngest son anything but a nuisance.

"Such infamous company you keep, Billy." Delicia said, playing along with him. "Is he perchance hanging from a sour apple tree?"

"Oh, that's no way to treat a goat," Billy replied, feigning a solemn tone, "unless he resides in Richmond."

"Off with you I said!" Mother Grace scolded, but not with her eyes. "The O'Darcy girls have heard enough about your President Davis!"

***

THE TIME spent with the McCabe family, what was left of it, flew by. It had been marked with lively conversation and gaiety, as much as possible. Still, looking about the spacious home had caused its share of somber reflections, what with all the memories that were revealed to both girls with every turn of their heads. Moreover, it was not uncommon for any given conversation to find itself burdened by an uncomfortable silence, precipitated by a reluctance to continue along a vein that had, on occasion, done little more than remind everyone how lonely things were now that Tin Pan Alley was so empty, and how frightening it was to contemplate where the missing young men were now residing. When it was time to leave, however, Billy changed all that after having excused himself to the barn. He wasn't there long.

Father Benjamin, Mother Grace and the O'Darcy sisters were offering their final goodbyes while standing on the long front porch when Billy reappeared.

"Hurrah, hurrah, to Southern states hurrah, hurrah for the bonny blue flag that bears the single star!" Billy was singing full-throated in his clear tenor voice, leading his goat on a short rope, but then added immediately, "Enough of that seditious blather, you four-legged secessionist! Miss Delicia, have you a decent length of sturdy hemp handy? Or you, Miss Ginny?" Between Billy's theatrics and the timely bleating of

President Davis at the mention of a rope, it was all the O'Darcy girls could do to keep from laughing themselves into tears, which they did anyway. All the emotions of the day had focused upon the moment, and even Father Benjamin and Mother Grace had fallen victim to their youngest son's antics.

"Remove that bleating traitor from our sight!" Father Benjamin said through his laughter, all the while dabbing his eyes with his handkerchief after removing his spectacles. "Better yet, tie him to the butternut tree and assist these helpless damsels into their carriage!" Again, like a welcomed medicine, the laughter flowed.

Later that night, Mother Grace cried herself to sleep.

IV

His eyesight wasn't keen and without a pair of spectacles his vanity could never abide, it had again failed Clifton Janeway. He and his small entourage were inside forty yards from the head of the troop column being led by Major O'Darcy and Corporal McCabe before Clifton was certain of their identities.

"I hadn't been informed your impending arrival would be so soon, O'Darcy," Clifton remarked upon his approach as if he were held in such high regard his lack of being informed must have been an oversight.

"That's Major O'Darcy, Captain, and you are being informed of your lapse for the first and final time."

"My apologies, *Major* O'Darcy," he responded, ignoring Pete completely. "I can assure you a second reminder will not prove necessary." Sackett eyed him coolly, allowing an awkward silence to ensue if only for a moment.

"Don't you recognize the man next to me, Captain?" Sackett finally said, as if it were a challenge.

"As I live and breathe, if it isn't Pete McCabe," he answered, feigning a contrived astonishment that fooled no one. "I hardly recognize you out of your humble farmer's garb and in uniform. I hope now that we are comrades-in-arms our past differences can be set aside so we can attend to the task at hand, which I'm sure you will agree takes precedent over any childhood differences."

"*Child*hood differences, I'll grant you that Captain Janeway." Pete replied. "I fear the task you brought up is gonna be handful enough."

"No need for fear, McCabe, we commanding officers will be here for you," Clifton replied, his condescending tone being his true response. It was Sackett who spoke next.

"What is your purpose here, Captain?"

"Orders, Major. Brigadier General Trailmen was under the impression you and the 1st weren't due in camp for another week, but when the scouts reported a column of cavalry in the vicinity he sent me to investigate, and guide you in."

"My thanks to the general, but my maps have proved accurate thus far. You are dismissed."

"But the general said -"

"I know the way, Captain."

"The 1st Naperville Cavalry is but one of his many concerns, Major. Regardless, as second in command of our hometown outfit, I would think it prudent if I were to lead you in, with your permission of course."

"Then ride down the column and greet the men first, Captain. You can join me after your hellos," Sackett said. "And mind the dust. I'd hate to see your impressive uniform soiled." Clifton saluted, but his eyes remained stone cold as he wheeled his mount and rode off.

"I hope things improve from this sorry beginning." Sackett said to Pete as he motioned the column forward.

"Sackett, this just doesn't make sense. Buford Janeway may have influence, but his boy a captain?"

"Clifton had local involvement with the military before the war," Sackett responded, "as I'm sure you know. That's how his father managed to introduce himself and his money to General Smithington, among others. Besides, being in the Western Theater, Illinois doesn't figure to be that crucial in the scheme of things, though I doubt that school of thought will remain intact for the duration."

"*Playing* soldier fits Clifton to the ground, that much is true." Pete said. "He never had much else to occupy his time other than mischief. Lord knows an honest day's work was never required of him. It was my understanding the military exercises he supposedly conducted were nothing but excuses to camp, fish and drink, sometimes in the company of certain "ladies" brought in from Chicago."

"That was quite a mouthful, Corporal. I don't recall my old friend Pete ever having so much to say if opinions and gossip regarding another's shortcomings were the subjects. Do I detect a measure of envy, or are you simply demonstrating distain for a superior officer?" Fortunately, Sackett was smiling as he spoke, although Pete was perceptive enough to see past it.

"I won't mention it again, Major O'Darcy. I want to be a positive addition to the 1st Naperville. I'll respect the rank, if not the man."

"Spoken like a true politician, old friend. And if you're positive no one is within earshot, calling me Sackett will do. Truth is, hearing it once in a while connects me with home and happier times. For old time sake, Pete, I'll race you to camp. Order the others to follow once Janeway is farther back. In the commotion our illustrious second in command will play hell getting back up here in time. Besides," Sackett called out as he spurred his mount, "I want the 1st Naperville Cavalry to make a resounding first impression!"

***

THE MEN, led by Major O'Darcy, indeed made a resounding impression when they thundered by the encampment then dismounted just to the south of it. Sackett had also been correct in his prediction that Captain Janeway would play hell making his way back to the front of the column. By the time Clifton entered the encampment Major O'Darcy had already made his way into Brigadier General Trailmen's headquarters.

"Greetings, Major O'Darcy," the general said when Sackett entered the large tent. "You and your new cavalry put on quite a show. I'm sure the infantry boys were heartened by your timely arrival, even if they'd be loath to admit it."

"Thank you, sir. I've known many of my men since childhood, and most of them are at least fair horsemen."

"That is indeed unusual for Northern farm boys, Major, but I'll take your word for it. My other concern is their proficiency with those new Spencer rifles they were fortunate enough to acquire. How many of them have fired upon an enemy position while under a full charge? None I'd wager, let alone on horseback as rare as that may likely be. God help them if before they are properly trained they come across an enemy cavalry force, those Southern horse soldiers have been riding since childhood. Shooting from horseback comes natural to them."

"It's true, sir, my men haven't experience along those lines, but my plan is to make such training my first priority."

"You have less than a week, Major. General Grant is on his way to Columbus as we speak. Bishop Polk and his Rebels are already there or soon will be, and if I know Grant he has every intention of making things hot for those Johnnies and then some. That would explain my orders to join him post haste, at any rate."

Sackett was in shock, but tried to not let it show. He had known they were going to see action sooner rather than later, but had assumed even a worst case scenario would have allowed him three weeks to properly train his men, perhaps four or even five.

"The enemy, General, will be green as well. I'm sure my men will make a good accounting of themselves."

"Make no mistake, Major. Polk's men, a good portion of them anyway, are not as green as we would prefer. They have tasted battle and are the better for it. There are a few hours of daylight left. That first priority of yours begins now, Major O'Darcy. You are dismissed."

V

Beaux Hollow, Georgia, was one of those places whose exact location remained a mystery to most strangers until at least two other towns of slightly more significance were offered as points of reference:

"I'm from Beaux Hollow, twelve miles east of Sharpson Grove." A local might offer, but that limited information rarely helped. "Sharpson Grove is twenty miles south from Briarsmit, that is maybe fifty miles from Dallas if you head –"

"Texas?" A stranger might ask, as if something must have been missed.

"No, Dallas *Georgia!*" And on it went for another town or two until the stranger's eyes brightened with recognition or pretended to, or in exasperation the stranger lost interest in the conversation altogether.

Some strangers were quick to respond they had, however, heard of Whisper Manor, a plantation of impressive size in the heart of the Beaux Hollow countryside. Whisper Manor was home to the Ransom family and had been since the 1700's. It was also home to well over five hundred slaves, most all of whom could trace their families back at least that far and beyond, thanks to stories of Africa that had been handed down over the decades.

There was always an abundance of white help to keep order, and although the Ransom family had always treated their slaves in what they believed was a humane manner, any serious infractions or displays of brazen disobedience were dealt with severely. Any slave who demonstrated such behavior wasn't usually long for Whisper Manor. It was common knowledge that after being whipped, if the infraction so warranted, they would end up being sold off somewhere very far away where the work load never ceased. It was also understood it was highly unlikely they would ever see any members of their families again.

Over the decades the Ransom family had bred their human chattel from four original African families of the highest quality stock, they liked to boast, and had taken great care to ensure there was no inbreeding amongst family members themselves unless they were far enough removed. Moreover, and highly unusual for such a large antebellum plantation, there was not a drop of white blood in hardly any of the Ransom slaves. Indeed, with very few exceptions there wasn't a mulatto, let alone a quadroon, to be found.

On the infrequent occasion when a mulatto was borne, the infant was sold as soon as possible. Though rare, sometimes worst fates had occurred. Over the years, once the father's identity had been discovered, it meant disinheritance if the culprit was a Ransom, but over the decades that had happened but twice. Several overseers or their white help had at least found themselves wanting for a job if they were the culprits, but that too was a relatively small number, all things considered. The newborn's mother, however, as one family patriarch after another maintained over the years, never suffered: "You cain't blame a nigger wench for wantin' to be covered by a white man. Long as they identify the offender, no harm will come to 'em."

That many of the mothers pleaded for their child not to be sold meant nothing to their masters: "They'll fret and carry on some, just like a child, but are soon over it. God blessed niggers with that peculiar ability, least ways the good ones." One Ransom patriarch after another had steadfastly insisted.

Over the decades, the Ransom patriarchs also "weeded out" as they were apt to put it, any child who didn't, in their practiced eyes, meet their strict qualifications. The mental capacity and physical prowess of their slaves who did meet their exacting standards were a great source of pride to them, as well as an envious source of profit.

That alone put Whisper Manor on the map, if not Beaux Hollow. Slave traders were keen on its whereabouts, of that there was no doubt. If they were in the market for superior quality, so much so that price was secondary, Whisper Manor was always high on their lists. "Black as pitch on a new moon midnight, but some of the finest nigger stock anywheres in the South!" Was an entreaty, or a variation thereof, commonly used by more than a few slavers.

***

ON THE surface Whisper Manor was a beautiful place. Its spacious grounds were immaculate, from the well tended lawns and abundant flower beds to the shrubbery and fruit orchards. Even the sloping meadows and wooded areas on the two thousand acre estate were cared for with exceptional diligence. Imported crushed rock, white as snow, made up the quarter mile, magnolia-lined road that circled around the front of the mansion, with nary a wisp of dust made by horse or carriage despite any dry spells which occurred. During such times, a dozen or more slaves could be seen from sunrise to sunset carrying their large sprinkler cans, ensuring just the right amount of water was applied to thwart any invasion of the powdered sugar-like granules. During social events at the mansion, the watering would go on all night if need be. All the lanes and walkways within shouting distance of the mansion were tended in similar fashion.

The nearly ten thousand square foot mansion was three stories of perfection, inside and out. It was constructed of special kilned, deep red brick, also imported at great expense, and it never failed to impress the most seasoned traveler or guest. Even the four massive columns in front were made of the unique brick, those having been rounded and laid so perfectly the most discerning eye could not detect the slightest deviance.

There were a few obligatory cotton fields, but it was the quality fruit groves and massive vegetable gardens, pecan groves and tobacco fields that were Whisper Manor's pride, next to its slaves. Any given slave's status was measured by which of those entities he or she tended. The cotton fields, as odd as it seemed for that part of Georgia, were lowest on the list. If a slave happened to be assigned to work them it was generally due to an infraction of one kind or another. If their assignment was permanent, it usually meant it was the last one issued before being sold. That was the rub - even those poor souls were of such comparatively high quality stock, nary a slaver thought anything of it unless he was on a truly expensive mission for one of his clients. Cotton had made a number of the Ransom family's neighbors rich, but it was the price people from as far away as Texas were willing to pay for Whisper Manor slaves that cemented the foundation of the Ransom fortune.

The descendants of each of the four original families worked almost exclusively on one of the plantation's enterprises, depending on the season. The Jetty family held sway over the peach orchards and vegetable gardens, the Sable family over the tobacco fields, the Onyx family the pecan groves and apple orchards and the Sooty family the livestock and grounds. The house servants were gleaned from all four families, and were without fail the most intelligent and trustworthy slaves of all, and the competition to be assigned to Grand House was fierce.

Unlike many slaves from elsewhere in the South, all of the Ransom slaves carried both Christian and surnames. Not only was that practical for obvious reasons, it also served as a source of pride. "Ain't met me a nigger in six counties whats kin boast more'n one name," was a common refrain amongst some of the Ransom slaves who were allowed to tend to business off the plantation from time to time.

One slave, Cusman Sable, was allowed even more independence or at least more responsibilities. If the current patriarch, Trenton Ransom, had a business trip planned and wanted his brightest and most responsible slave to accompany him, it was a given it would be Cusman.

It was against the law in Georgia and elsewhere in the South to teach slaves to read. Master Trenton Ransom, like his ancestors, was law-biding enough if the laws fit his purpose. If a law proved to be bothersome, especially if it interfered with his extensive business dealings, exceptions were made. After all, he was Trenton Ransom, and woe to any local authority that failed to keep that in mind. Besides, he had always maintained most slaves should indeed be kept innocent, for their own good. He was convinced the overwhelming majority of them were too simple, too emotional not to be unduly influenced by abolitionist propaganda. If they were to get their hands on such insidious blather, he maintained, no telling where it might lead. Still, if a slave of uncommon abilities proved useful to Trenton, a slave of special character who could be trusted, relatively speaking of course, he or she would be educated in any way the owner of Whisper Manor deemed prudent. Cusman Sable was more than qualified using such criteria, and had been taught to do more than simply read. Once, when Cusman had come down with an illness, Master Ransom delayed an important business trip to Atlanta for over a week until Cusman's illness was completely in check.

Small wonder; Cusman's attributes were such that in the entire history of Whisper Manor no one could recall a slave of superior quality, except by Ransom elders whose opinions were tainted by wistful reminisces of long ago days lost to them forever. None of them, however, could point to a slave from their past, or the past of their ancestors who unequivocally eclipsed Cusman Sable. Even the most sentimental musings fell short in that regard. When such debates did occur, usually after some sour mash or cognac had been consumed, the pontificator defending a long ago slave of exceptional skills finally conceded Cusman was at least their equal, or "so damned close to it I'd hate to try'n draw a breath between the difference".

Cusman was only in his early twenties but had always displayed a thoughtful maturity well beyond his years. He was a huge young man. Six foot nine, two hundred and ninety pounds and so well defined his owner often said, "I swear, Michelangelo his own damned self must've rose from the grave to chisel that boy's features!" Trenton Ransom usually went on to insist, "Why, his waist ain't never been over thirty-four inches, I swear it ain't."

Although Trenton enjoyed crediting Michelangelo's ghost, it was Cusman who was responsible for his extraordinary physicality. Hardly a day went by when the young man didn't put himself through at least a two hour series of strenuous exercises. With his master's blessing regardless of Cusman's other responsibilities, it was common to see the young man start his mornings with a three, sometimes five mile run followed by log and boulder lifting as well as a complex series of calisthenics.

He was sometimes joined by other young slaves who wanted to demonstrate their own physical prowess, but no one had ever been able to keep up with the determined young man. If on occasion someone did keep up, Cusman would head over to the steepest hill on the estate and begin his wind sprints all the way to the top, one after another. He enjoyed the competition, especially when his rival eventually collapsed. It was not uncommon for some of them to lose their breakfast if they had been foolish enough to eat first. Cusman usually helped them afterwards if needed, and rarely failed to compliment their efforts coupled with some good natured teasing.

At first blush Cusman's face did not show him to be a particularly handsome young man, but that was quickly lost once his other qualities were revealed. Indeed, once those shone through, which happened almost immediately, his facial features had a way of redefining attractiveness as most folks knew it.

He was so trustworthy Trenton Ransom hadn't so much as a twinge of a qualm when it came to Cusman learning to shoot, even if there had always been very strict rules regarding slaves and firearms at Whisper Manor. It was a rare hunting trip indeed where Trenton, along with his two sons, didn't bring Cusman along. In tune with his other attributes it came as no surprise when Cusman's proficiency with firearms also proved to be remarkable.

***

ONE DAY a few years before the war, a slave trader of some renown from Memphis, a Mr. Nathan Bedford Forrest, a man who would go on to gain infamy or hero status depending upon where one's sympathies fell during and after the Civil War, offered Trenton Ransom a sum so impressive it actually gave the Ransom patriarch some pause - but not for long.

"That is a goodly sum, sir," Trenton Ransom had replied, "and I am honored by your offer, coming from a man of your stature and obvious knowledge of quality stock. Truth is, my conscience would not leave me alone for any amount. I am mighty fond of that nigger boy."

"As well you should be, sir," Forrest had replied. "Niggers of that caliber are rare indeed, even if he is black as a moonless midnight. Might Ah implore you ta sleep on mah offer, if Ah was ta double it provided you throw in that quadroon beauty who announced mah arrival at your front door?"

"Oh, my dear wife would see to it my conscience would suffer double if I was to consider that generous offer, sir. I pray you understand my dilemma. As fond as I am of Cusman, you can fold that over six times and it won't stack up to her feelings for that sweet child. Why, Missy Nell is her pride. Mrs. Ransom grew up with her mama, and there would indeed be hell to pay hereabouts if I so much as broached the subject with her. But again, sir, I thank you and appeal to your sympathies. I again pray you understand."

Nathan Bedford Forrest understood, but had no respect for a man who allowed a woman to cower him, or allowed his sentiments to sway his better judgment, especially when it pertained to honest business dealings as Forrest understood them to be. He pulled his lean, muscular frame to its full height and locked his dark, piercing eyes on Ransom. His glare was made all the more intimidating by his chiseled face adorned as it was with a thick, perfectly trimmed beard and mustache, both of which were as dark as his demeanor at that moment.

"If that is your final word, sir, Ah will leave you with your self-imposed dilemmas. Good day ta you." With that Forrest immediately mounted his impressive horse and spurred it forward, taking pains to share his glare with Cusman and Missy Nell who were standing together on the massive front gallery. He also took pains to avoid the snow-white crushed rock, opting instead to gallop across the front lawn, manicured, as always, to a fault. At that Trenton Ransom had turned quickly towards the house as if he hadn't noticed the slight. He fooled no one.

"You s'pect Mas'r is dwellin' on what that dark mood of a man had to offer?" Missy Nell asked Cusman after the front door closed behind their owner.

"Oh, he's likely to dwell on it some, though not as much as that snake-eyed slaver's insults." Cusman replied. "Never seen anyone, white or slave, take a horse one step on that lawn what Mas'r didn't have words with 'em. Weren't six months ago he took his ridin' crop to that no-account quadroon from the Jones farm when that very thing happened, though in Mas'r's defense that boy been warned more'n once."

"There ain't no defense for takin' a whip to somebody jus' 'cause they put a hoof mark or two on some grass. You best remember that, Cusman Sable."

Cusman fell silent after Missy Nell's reproach. He agreed with her in principle, but had no use for Carmel, the slave in question. On more than one occasion Carmel had proved to be utterly lacking in character, moral or otherwise. When Carmel wasn't trifling with the young girls about the plantation, flaunting his cream color as if it were a badge, it was a safe bet he was up to something equally nefarious. Cusman knew it had been Carmel who had impregnated little Nealy Jetty when she was barely thirteen, even if the child swore it had been the son of a slaver from South Carolina, their arrival and departure having conveniently coincided with the onset of her condition. If something went missing it was another safe bet Carmel had been by on one of his master's errands. Ever since the riding crop incident Carmel had been banned from Whisper Manor, and in those six months nary a ham from the smokehouse or any of Auntie May's prize capons had gone missing.

Still, upon reflection, Cusman had to admit the whipping for the one thing Carmel had been caught doing was repugnant since it never would have happened to someone white. True enough, a white man known to be a common miscreant might expect such treatment, but what did that say? Fair enough if Carmel had been the only one, but over the years similar punishments had been meted out to otherwise wholesome folks unfortunate enough to have been borne into slavery right on that very plantation. With those thoughts on Cusman's mind, precipitated by Missy Nell's rebuke, he decided to demonstrate his admiration for the young woman he not only respected but loved unconditionally.

"You're right, Missy," he said, taking her hand. "Cain't let my feelin's for that no-account Carmel cloud over such things. Keep my focus I will, promise you that."

***

MISSY NELL was a sight, of that there was no doubt. She had been borne in Grand House itself which was extremely rare for a slave, and there was never any doubt her duties would ever have her residing anywhere else. Even as a small child her qualities and exceptional beauty were evident to the most callous observer. By age five she could sing so beautifully it was a given no social event at the plantation was complete until little Missy Nell had given a performance, and not one of those ever ended without at least two encores.

Everyone agreed she was every bit as talented and beautiful as her mother Missy Diane had been. The pox had taken her away on her twenty-fifth year. If that hadn't been tragedy enough, it occurred on what was believed to be her birthday. Mrs. Jennifer Ransom, Trenton's wife, grieved as much as Missy Nell herself, who had been a child of six when her mother passed. Jennifer had grown up with Missy Diane over on the Butrane plantation, which had been her home until her marriage to Trenton. If the truth was known, she would have sooner endured the passing of her own sister than the death of her dear Missy Diane.

Indeed, Missy Diane and Missy Nell were the only slaves who had ever resided on the Whisper Manor plantation not related to one of the four families. That had been the cause of a great deal of Ransom family tension, at least at first. When she passed, however, the tears flowed freely from both black and white.

Colbert Butrane, Jennifer's widowed father, had been especially heartbroken. He had been profoundly in love with Missy Diane, and although he had always steadfastly denied it, he was Missy Nell's biological father. In order to quell the rumor, he had allowed a pregnant Missy Diane to move to Whisper Manor with Jennifer after her marriage, although it broke his heart. When Missy Diane passed he never forgave himself. Indeed, his grief, fueled by overwhelming self-incrimination, was what eventually killed him – in his heart, mercifully so.

There was no doubt Jennifer Ransom's heart was wrapped every bit as tight around Missy Nell even before the tragedy; more so afterwards, if that possibility existed. She was light skinned, her mother having been a mulatto and Missy Nell a quadroon, which was another direct violation of Whisper Manor policy to say the least, especially given the suspicious circumstances but again an exception had been made.

By the time Missy Nell had reached her mid-teens her childhood beauty and talents had evolved into something truly remarkable, even given the high expectations that had followed her throughout her years. By then Cusman, himself in his mid-teens, had been transferred to Grand House where his attributes as they pertained to mathematics, calligraphy and a variety of other skills helpful in running the large plantation could be put to full use. It had been obvious he was exceptionally intelligent, and had learned all of his more advanced skills in a relatively short time.

He had fallen in love at first blush, and although that may have been the case with Missy Nell she had known better than to play that hand too soon. It was a month before she even acknowledged Cusman's existence, and a good two months before she returned his polite salutations with more than an expeditious nod. Before long a smile had been included. A short while after that a few words of conversation were forthcoming, words she used to evaluate the character of the large boy on the verge of manhood. At no time did Cusman Sable come up wanting, and before too much longer, except as far as Cusman was concerned, they were taking strolls and finding excuses to be together on a frequent basis.

Missy Nell's nearly total lack of a slave accent intrigued Cusman, although she did have a hint of dialect the other slaves shared. Having been raised, for the most part, by Jennifer Ransom who, like her parents before her spoke with no southern accent at all, it had been natural for Missy to adapt her mistress's manner of speaking and figures of speech. Soon after the two of them began speaking to one another Cusman began to imitate, and eventually adopt the same manner of speech as well, although in his case more of his former accent remained. At first Missy Nell found Cusman's attempts a source of amusement, but before long was impressed by how quickly the young man picked up on things, even though it was apparent certain speech patterns were so entrenched it appeared highly unlikely Cusman would ever abandon them entirely.

"I'm hopin' to be free someday," Cusman had told her, "and when that day comes I want folks knowin' I got me a head on my shoulders. S'pect I'll have a leg up if I don't sound like some field hand, 'cept it makes me feel like I'm turnin' my back on them - I mean *those* - I love. Truth is though, better I kin do for myself the better I kin do for them, I git the chance."

The character of both young people was such that hardly a soul at Whisper Manor had any reservations concerning their budding relationship, with the understandable exception of more than a few envious souls who toiled outside Grand House and, truth told, within. Trenton, and more importantly Jennifer Ransom believed it was an ideal match. Given the overall circumstances concerning their approval, what else could have possibly mattered? It would take a civil war to find out.

VI

Sheer hell was looming. Even the swollen morning sun on November 7th, 1861 appeared ominous as it inched its way from the horizon, undulating slightly in the thick, humid air; a smoldering red omen.

Over three thousand Union troops were at the ready nine miles below Cairo, Illinois. They had disembarked from four transport vessels at a steamboat landing situated along the western shore of the Mississippi River, just three miles above Belmont, Missouri. It was there General Grant would strike; an all-out, frontal assault against a Confederate garrison of equal strength bivouacked around the three unimpressive shacks that made up the small hamlet.

It would be the first battle for most of the Union men, including the 1st Naperville Cavalry that was coming off a mere five days training. A skirt of timber had veiled the Union disembarkation from the transports, and skirmishers were already making their way through mud and brush towards Belmont. The rest of the Union infantry soldiers were right behind, marching in long Yankee blue lines once they made their way to a large meadow, guns at the ready.

Major Sackett O'Darcy and his men were riding amidst the trees to the left of the advancing force, their intent being to strike hard and fast at the Confederate right flank located in the south section of the meadow immediately after the Union cannoneers' opening salvos. Major O'Darcy's strategy was to charge in from the nearby woods, blast away with their new Spencer repeating rifles, rush back into the protection of the trees and strike again just to the rear of the same Confederate right flank. If successful, the confusion, fear and desperation created amongst the Confederates would give the main Union body an opportunity to crush the middle of the opposing force, since the Confederates, some of them anyway, would likely rush to defend their besieged right flank.

"Take that feeling in your guts that mimics fear and turn it to your advantage," Major O'Darcy had implored his men just prior to their charge. "We all possess it, make no mistake of that, and we all have it within ourselves to use it as a weapon. Look each other in the eye, men, share your emotions as they will bond us together, then prepare to strike a blow for the Union! Prepare to make those Johnny Rebs howl!"

Within moments after Sackett's address the terrible roar of nearly three thousand Union Springfield rifles coupled with cannon fire shattered the calm. It was answered immediately with an eruption of equal intensity coming from the Confederates.

"Forward, 1st Naperville!" Major O'Darcy yelled, and the thunder of nearly a hundred men on horseback exploded from amidst the trees on a dead run; hearts pounding in the breasts of the men and their horses as well.

Relatively lightweight and accurate within range, the first volley from the new Spencer rifles, accompanied by the incoming Union cannon and musket fire, slammed into the men and boys on the Confederate right flank. Even the deafening roar of gunfire could not drown out the screams of the panic-stricken wounded, who just moments before had emptied their single shot Enfield rifles into the advancing Union force directly in front of them. The survivors were in the process of reloading when the 1st Naperville Cavalry had opened up, while the second and third lines of Confederates took turns firing at both the advancing Yankee infantry as well as the charging 1st Naperville Cavalry.

Soldiers from both sides would come to understand true carnage as the war years passed, each person holding onto their sanity as inner strength, rationalization and conscience would allow, but at that moment in time insanity was the rule as the hail of bullets and canister from the roaring cannons ripped apart woefully frail bodies in an unending variety of ways so grotesque, the horrific impact destroyed forever any notions of the glory of battle for those so inclined or simply involved. Every imaginable body part; hands, feet, fingers, toes, skulls, arms and legs were suddenly displaced, rearranged and otherwise mutilated in a gory spectacle so profound the strongest constitutions within the bloody maelstrom were rendered all but useless or at least somewhat traumatized, some completely so. Abraham Lincoln put it in perspective: *"Military glory – that attractive rainbow that rises in showers of blood, that serpent's eye that charms to destroy."*

Before the surviving lines of Confederates on the right flank could reload and fire, most of Sackett's men, having closed the distance to less than three hundred feet, continued their barrage until all but a few of them had gotten off the seven shots their Spencer rifles held before reloading became necessary.

"Back to the trees, men!" Sackett yelled in full voice. His order was immediately relayed from one cavalryman to another in rapid succession as the men wheeled and spurred their mounts when the order reached them, or when they noticed the others already heading back that way. By then some of the Confederates who had been able to reload in time opened up, but their panic-stricken, hurried response managed to drop but a few of the retreating enemy, with most of those falling because their horses had been hit.

One of those had been Captain Clifton Janeway, even though he had halted his horse behind a thicket of canebrake a good two hundred feet behind and to the left of his comrades. During the mayhem his cowardice had gone undetected, but after he had spurred his mount towards the retreating cavalrymen without having fired a single shot, he had fallen. His gaudy uniform had indeed been noticed, by an over-anxious Confederate sharpshooter. In his haste, the sharpshooter missed his target, but not Clifton's horse.

Pete, following up the rear, spotted him as a terrified Clifton struggled through the marshy grass and mud to the south, wild-eyed with fear. Pete, like the others, was unaware of the circumstances that precipitated Clifton's predicament. Pete did, however, spot the sharpshooter who was now standing as he quickly prepared his long rifle for another shot. Pete wheeled his mount back around with only one cartridge left in his Spencer.

"Hit the ground, Clifton!" He yelled above the din, as he got off a well aimed shot that slammed into the young sharpshooter's head as best Pete could tell from that distance. The head had snapped back anyway, and his rifle had dropped immediately along with the sharpshooter's body. Pete spurred his mount towards Clifton at a dead run, mindful of the Minie balls that whizzed by from the Confederate right flank, fully convinced the next one would find its mark.

Clifton had struggled back to his feet, vomited, then grabbed onto the back of Pete's sweat-soaked blouse and managed to swing himself onto the rear of Pete's mount. The horse, as wild-eyed as his new passenger, took off after the rest of the cavalrymen who had already reached the relative safety of the trees, where they were frantically reloading their Spencer's as they prepared for the second, rear assault.

"Leave me here, Pete!" Clifton hollered when they were also in the trees, "My blood is up and I want to continue the fight, but without a mount I'll have to be content with covering your rear from this precarious spot! Thank God I was able to drop those other three sharpshooters before your timely arrival!"

"Clifton, take my sidearm since your rifle is lost!" Pete hollered amidst the turmoil. "You'll need more than the one you have! I'll be back for you if I can! When I catch up to Major O'Darcy he'll hear of your bravery! God's speed!"

As soon as the last cavalryman was out of sight, a trembling Clifton Janeway clawed his way under several low hanging honeysuckle branches that canopied a slight gully and covered himself with an assortment of leaves and other debris, and once again began to vomit.

***

BY THE time two hours had elapsed the Confederates were in full retreat and the Union forces had control of the Rebel camps in Belmont. The retreat had been made in such haste bacon was still smoking, burnt black in pans over the dying embers of morning campfires. The Union men were joyous, so much so General McClernand mounted one of the captured cannons as if he were an actor upon a stage and gleefully ordered the men to give three resounding cheers for the Union. Their celebrating was as premature as it was ill-advised.

The retreating Confederates, bolstered with fresh regiments sent over from Columbus, attempted to drive a wedge between the Union troops and their boats. It was almost successful, as Grant's regiments made it to the steamers a mere breath ahead of the determined Confederates. Even General Grant, whose original mount had been shot from under him, barely climbed aboard in time.

Because of that debacle, the Union men on the departing steamers had little to cheer about because the Union forces had suffered their own special hell when the Confederate artillerists on the Columbus bluff had opened up on them once their own men were no longer in the way. It was the Union's turn to witness some of their own brothers-in-arms being torn literally into pieces, and hardly a man amongst them could drive those horrible images from their minds any easier than the Confederates had been able to do.

***

IT WAS under that cloud when Sackett and Pete, huddled together near the stern of the last vessel to depart, had a chance to go over the day's traumatic events.

"That was the last I saw of him, Sackett. I'd hoped he'd had a chance to make it to the Belmont camp, but we hadn't made it back with enough time to search."

"We barely made it back with our skins, Pete. I shouldn't have gone that far after them. I thought they were whipped though. The last thing I expected was those reinforcements making it across the river in time."

"You weren't alone, Sackett. Even the generals were taken by surprise. Not the most reassuring God damned thing for a soldier to endure." Sackett looked at his friend, but did not speak. It was the first time he had ever heard Pete take the Lord's name in vain. *It was a perfect fit though,* Sackett concluded.

"I still don't know how Clifton and I managed our way out of that terrible fix. Good thing he got three of those sharpshooters. If just two more had been on that rise I doubt we'd be having this conversation."

"He told you he was pinned down by four sharpshooters all in the same place?"

"That's what I took him to mean, but there wasn't much time for talk. The limited range of Clifton's Spencer would have to mean they couldn't have been too far apart if he indeed hit three of them."

"True enough, Pete, true enough. That's the part that won't leave me alone. Those Rebel commanders are bright fellows. We all learned in our first year at West

Point how to position sharpshooter fire. Confusion in battle is a given, but often times it come about well into the fight. We were the first ones to approach that flank. Why the hell would four sharpshooters be bunched together when the fighting *began*?

"I know I've been away from home awhile, but I seem to recall you and those Gould boys were the ones to beat at those Fourth of July shooting contests. From what little I saw of Clifton Janeway's proficiency with a rifle this past week in camp, it appears he still can't hit his ass with a board, yet he dropped *three* sharpshooters who shouldn't have been bunched together in the first place, and in the heat of his very first battle? His story goes begging, Pete, it sure as hell does."

Pete nodded his head in concurrence, took a deep breath, and stared straight ahead. His jaw was set, and his eyes weren't focused on anything in particular. Sackett sensed his friend had something else on his mind, and asked Pete about it.

"Never killed anyone before, Sackett. I know that sharpshooter was about to kill Clifton, perhaps me, but still. He had a name, probably grew up on a farm, people back home too, just like us. Same with the ones I shot during our initial attack. Never dawned on me I'd feel this sick inside. Feels like I've violated some kind of natural law, gone against something I can't explain. Somethin' tells me I'm gonna have a lot of explaining to do though, not now maybe, not while I'm alive anyway, but some-time, somewhere. Don't have me a whiff of a notion though, can't think of nothin' I can say that would make things right. Worse yet I'm gonna do it again, I get the chance."

Sackett started to say something, but hesitated. He knew his friend, knew he had already gone over all the rationalizations or thought he had, and was fairly amazed Pete had been so forthcoming. He had never been much of a talker before, at least not about such deep personal feelings. War had profound effects upon men, but even so, it was disconcerting coming from Pete. Sackett took a deep breath himself, and joined his friend as both of them stared straight ahead, lost in a silent disquietude that continued to gnaw inside both men.

***

CAPTAIN CLIFTON Janeway, unlike the rest of the men on the first transport, needed to make a conscious effort to control his exuberance. He discovered right off, however, none of the infantrymen were even mildly interested in hearing about his brave exploits - not the five sharpshooters he claimed to have killed with as many shots, nor how he managed to save a frightened corporal who hailed from his own hometown, a naïve farm boy whose courage Clifton had felt obliged to bolster when his own unbending mettle had been needed most.

Clifton was well aware he was the only member of the 1st Naperville Cavalry on that particular transport as his story unfolded, and that not a man besides himself was even from Illinois, much less Naperville. Indeed, none of the men indicated they'd even heard of the place. It was enough for him to know he had not only made his way to the first transport to escape the fighting, but was one of the first Union soldiers to board. It was also enough for the soldiers who listened to his story as well, and he soon found himself alone with his self-bestowed gallantry.

***

IT WAS nearly a month later when Sackett received the news. Captain Clifton Janeway was to be awarded a citation for bravery as a result of his dauntless acts of courage during the Belmont campaign. Since there wasn't an official United States military award for conspicuous gallantry available in 1861, Clifton's award would have normally been issued by his local commander. His exploits, however, had been reported to General Smithington in the form of a letter from Buford Janeway, which also included a wartime contribution of five thousand dollars General Smithington was to use for "any purposes you deem appropriate". If the good general felt young Clifton's exploits deserved whatever military recognition might be available, all the better. Lieutenant General Smithington wasted no time ordering Brigadier General Trailmen to issue the citation. Buford had also arranged for local newspapers to report his son's glorious actions, and to reserve space on their front pages where the heroic account no doubt belonged, he had insisted. They were happy to oblige.

***

"I HAVE my orders, Major O'Darcy, and you have yours. Just award the damned citation and be done with it." Brigadier General Trailmen announced as if their conversation was over.

"Sir, we have not one eyewitness to verify Captain Janeway's big story. Unless I have been laboring under a false impression since West Point, isn't that a requirement for such an honor?"

"General Smithington is of a mind Corporal McCabe's account of that day's events is sufficient. Lord knows what all the general's report contained, and I am not about to press him further."

"Sir, even if Captain Janeway had shot a few sharpshooters, how could that translate into a citation for bravery?"

"Good God man, Smithington insisted Captain Janeway's actions included a damn sight more than killing some sharpshooters, that much I do know. He is insisting your troop's entire left flank was saved by Janeway's actions during your initial attack, then your right flank when you headed south, and I am not about to argue the points. Smithington's even insisting Janeway saved Corporal McCabe's life, at great risk to his own. It isn't the first, and won't be the last time a citation has or will be awarded under dubious circumstances.

"I recommend you concentrate on the task of helping win this war and let this matter alone. One more thing. You are to refrain from any more talk about this subject, verbal or otherwise. I had better not find out any word from you, whether here or in the form of a letter home, creates a controversy that somehow reaches General Smithington's ears. That, Major, is a direct order. You are dismissed."

***

"GENERAL SMITHINGTON indeed," Sackett said to Pete when they were alone in the major's tent discussing the matter. "That narcoleptic old fool has again demonstrated why too many of our superior officers are a laughingstock."

"General Trailmen ordered you not to send a letter home but he didn't order me." Pete thought out loud.

"Best leave it alone old friend. The general will conclude either you or I had a hand in it, perhaps both of us. It's probably a good thing we haven't said anything to the rest of our troop. I sense there is more to this than meets the eye, and superiors, especially guileful ones like Smithington, are capable of making us pay a heavy price if we interfere with their nefarious little schemes. Besides, if I know that pimple Clifton Janeway he'll eventually find a way to show his true colors in a manner no one can dispute.

"I don't fault General Trailmen. I'm certain he's seen this and worse over the years, and he is correct about one thing. We have a war to help win, so we had best make that our priority. Even so, don't be surprised if I lose my breakfast when I present that sullied citation. What a disgraceful way to treat such an honorable commendation."

VII

Mother Grace, like mothers and fathers most everywhere during the war, lived for the letters from her soldier sons. On the morning of December 23, 1861 she received the greatest Christmas gift of all that year, all things taken into account, after Father Benjamin had picked up letters at the post office from each of their sons save one. Later that day, even though an impending snowstorm fulfilled its promise more generously than the postal worker and his horse would have preferred, he nonetheless made an unprecedented trip to Tin Pan Alley with yet another letter, that one from Pete. All the McCabe boys were accounted for and all of them, as far as their parents knew at that moment in time, were alive and well.

Their oldest son, Don, was stationed on a gunboat somewhere on the Mississippi. He told of a harrowing experience. An enemy shell had ripped a hole in the port side of his vessel. Along with other frantic Union sailors he had patched the gaping hole while under intense fire. Although there had been a number of casualties, Don had not been one of them even though he had been near the very spot where the shell had struck. Miraculously it hadn't exploded, but after it had stopped ricocheting about, killing a few sailors in the process, it had come to rest less than ten feet from Don and had continued to hiss. Mother Grace took great comfort in his surviving the attack, convinced her constant prayers were not only being heard but answered.

Their fourth son, Lieutenant Benjamin McCabe Jr., had been in the thick of it as well. As countless enemy Minie balls had whizzed through the air, he had held his company intact while completing a pontoon bridge. The hastily built bridge had allowed hundreds of Union soldiers to scramble to the safety of the ramparts on the other side of a wide stream that led into the Potomac River near Leesburg, at a place called Ball's Bluff. His local commander issued a citation for bravery to Ben for his imperturbable leadership while under heavy fire.

Their son Robert, the third oldest, had also been at Ball's Bluff. His infantry regiment had been camped in a clearing surrounded by a large stand of woods one night when a surprise cavalry attack occurred. He had, along with a few other musicians, been entertaining a group of soldiers. Apparently several sentries had also been enjoying the music as well, more than they should have as it turned out, because those were the last tunes any of them were to hear this side of Providence, Robert wrote.

Robert was a gifted musician, so much so the divisional commander often times allowed him use of the commander's personal harpsichord Brigadier General Charles P. Stone felt obliged to take everywhere regardless of the inconvenience.

Musical ability wasn't Robert's only talent if bravery counted as such. Although he hadn't mentioned it in his letter, he had been amongst the first Union soldiers to muster a counterattack upon the charging Confederate cavalrymen, and had managed to wrestle a sword-wielding captain from his mount and pin him to the ground. Although he could have easily killed the captain, using the officer's own sword no less, Robert wasn't by nature a vicious man. He had held his struggling captive face first in the mud until help arrived. Afterwards, because the Confederate captain was such a talkative fellow when a double cocked Colt Dragoon was pointed at his skull, General Stone made a gift of the harpsichord to Robert. He had even offered to have his orderly care for it as he had done for the general.

Brother Jackie, the youngest McCabe brother save Billy, had experienced a harrowing event of his own. While stationed near Jefferson City, Missouri, a band of raiders sympathetic to the Southern Cause had descended upon the farmstead of an active Union supporter and set it ablaze. By the time Jackie and his patrol reached the place the raiders had done their worst, or not far from it. The farmer had been beaten, stabbed and left for dead. The barn had been set ablaze and was all but gone with the house soon to follow. Jackie had been amongst the first to hear the screams coming from a second story window, and had been the first to barge through the front door amidst the smoke and flames. After having bounded up the stairs in a sprint, he had burst into the room where the cries had originated, and had discovered two young girls under the age of ten screaming hysterically as they tried to revive their unconscious mother.

With the help of two brave soldiers, Jackie had managed to carry the woman and her daughters to safety. Moreover, because of his recent training as a medic, the same field his younger brother Billy was hoping to enter, he had also managed to save the farmer. Jackie's recently acquired knowledge of proper tourniquet application had kept the man from bleeding to death from a knife wound to an artery in his leg. Like his brothers, his letter home left out a few of the more alarming details or attributed them to others.

Pete's letter had contained certain particulars of the Belmont campaign, but he had followed Sackett's advice as it pertained to Clifton Janeway's actions. His assumption was that Father Benjamin was already skeptical of any newspaper accounts, and further doubt would be cast upon the affair since it was conspicuous by its absence from Pete's letter. He was right on both counts.

***

AFTER ALL the letters had been read numerous times by both parents and Billy, Mother Grace took them upstairs and placed them in the family Bible she kept on her bed stand. There, in the darkness of her room with the blizzard howling outside, she eased down upon her knees by one of the windows, the one with a southeastern exposure and began to pray. The house was well built, but drafts would still come through that particular window if the winds were high. Like many upstairs rooms in winter it was gripped by cold, but kneeling next to the window gave her a sense of closeness to her boys as she gazed southward. She also felt an uninhibited sense of closeness to her God which had thus far answered her prayers, she believed, amongst the thousands offered up on a continuous basis from both sides of the terrible conflict.

The colder she became, the more it steeled her resolve. She kept her slender hands clasped tightly and allowed her tears to flow unchecked, tears that first left her blue eyes warm, but cooled as they made their way down her face. By the time they were past her cheeks they felt cold as ice water, but to her it was a welcomed sensation as she gazed upwards. Her lips formed partial words she knew her God would interpret with ease.

It wasn't until Father Benjamin arrived with an extra shawl before she arose, and then reluctantly. He took her in his arms and held her close, silently offering a prayer of his own. He wasn't much on religion as others defined it, but he had to believe if there was a God, He was probably paying attention since it was Grace Rickert McCabe he held in his arms.

***

IT PROVED more difficult for Pete to refrain from spilling the sordid affair involving Janeway all over his letter to Delicia, but he persevered and barely mentioned the man. He had faith in her strength, but given the times he could not justify any further test of her constitution, nor justify any selfish need on his part to relieve his own frustrations. He instead wrote of happier times and all his plans for their future. He mentioned the praiseworthy job her brother Sackett was doing regarding the training of his men, and how due to his West Point education and general bearing there was an overall sense of confidence that could not be denied. If any cavalry troop could do their duty while suffering the least amount of damage as possible, it was the 1st Naperville Cavalry, Pete had maintained. He did say Clifton Janeway had a way of stepping in dog dung only to have the soles of his boots come up summer roses.

Delicia smiled as she read the letter. She was well aware of Pete's intentions, and his obvious attempt to set her mind at ease warmed her; he never could veer from or omit the truth convincingly. If, however, it meant sparing someone's feelings he nonetheless tried.

She wasn't just pining away the lonely, frightening days, far from it. Delicia and her sisters had formed a soldier's aid society to help out with food, clothing, the making of bandages, the scraping of lint and other activities. They produced barrels of sliced potatoes packed in salt, bushels of fried doughnuts, along with the knitting and sewing of needed garments of every description.

Delicia's most ambitious project was the Naperville Sanitary Commission she had helped form, one of many that were precursors to the American Red Cross. Wounded soldiers had started coming home first in a trickle, but with each bloody engagement the numbers swelled accordingly throughout DuPage County. With the guidance and perseverance of Doc Wygant, a hospital and sanatorium had been established. It was there Delicia spent much of her time.

Young Billy McCabe also assisted when he could take time from his chores and other duties on the farm. Thanks to $180,000 paid out from the DuPage County Treasury, he, along with others manning the home front, took advantage of the opportunity to volunteer more of his time. Half the money went to the military volunteers themselves, with the other half appropriated for their families to live on during their absence. The three McCabe family members at home had been offered an amount higher than most the other families because they had five sons fighting for the Union, but Father Benjamin and Mother Grace declined the extra money.

"Whether it's one son or five away from home, the inconveniences remain relative. I suppose five sons could share a greater work load, but is the load placed upon the souls of parents with fewer sons in harm's way any less of a burden than ours?" Father Benjamin had told the county treasurer.

***

DOC WYGANT was growing more impressed with Billy's progress with each passing week. By the time March of 1862 was upon them, it was not uncommon for his young protégé to undertake medical procedures usually reserved for full fledged doctors. On the rare occasions when Dr. Gilbert Van Craig from Wheaton appeared at the hospital, rarer still if he happened to be sober, more often than not Doc Wygant called upon Billy when skills with a scalpel were needed. One day when the hospital was especially crowded with activity, Van Craig, drunk as usual, created quite a scene when he was again told to relinquish a patient in favor of young Billy. Doc Wygant would have none of it:

"Listen to me, you thick-headed Dutchman! I have seen that young fellow accomplish things beyond your expertise even before your bottle of pop skull has been emptied! Now go lance a boil, or better yet just go! I am tired, Van Craig, of having to remedy your mistakes. God knows these brave men will be better off if left unattended altogether by the likes of you!"

"I am highly skilled," Van Craig said, staring down at Doc Wygant as if condescension were a virtue, "vis-à-vis the most qualified physician in this so-called hospital. The only one, I might add, that has a medical degree, vis-à-vis I am obviously –"

"One more God damned 'vis-à-vis' out of you or any other word except goodbye and I will personally toss your pompous posterior halfway back to Wheaton! Now get out!" Doc Wygant said, eyes blazing, leaving no one in the room with the impression he didn't fully intend to carry out his threat.

Even though Van Craig was nearly two hands taller than his tormenter all he did was stand and glare, mouth agape, until it occurred to the suddenly speechless, blonde-headed man he had, at the very least, pressing business elsewhere.

**

LATER THAT night while Delicia was finishing up with the washing and hanging of bed spreads, Buford Janeway stopped by the hospital. He asked Doc Wygant where Delicia might be found, but his only answer came in the form of a snort and a thumb jerked impatiently towards the laundry room.

"Good evening, Miss O'Darcy," Janeway said as he approached her standing where the clothes lines were located, "or may I call you Delicia?" She glanced at him, and removed the last clothing pin from her mouth.

"How you address me, sir, I'll leave to your own sense of decorum. Miss O'Darcy, however, since I am no longer a child, would seem more appropriate, especially given the circumstances."

"By circumstances am I to understand you mean that we are alone, or has the bad blood between you and my son put a stain on his father as well?"

"We are hardly alone, sir, if that answers your first question. May I inquire as to the purpose of your visit? I have a great deal of work to finish and the hour is growing late."

"I have a letter from Clifton, addressed to you, and he requested I bring it to you personally."

"Sir, I cannot imagine there is anything your son has to say to me, whether written or otherwise, that would accomplish anything other than ignite memories I do not wish to revisit. You'll notice a fireplace in the parlor when you depart, just off the foyer. I suggest you deliver the letter there."

"Come come child, my boy has grown to condemn his youthful misbehavior. The rebellion has made a man of him, replete with a Christian conscience to go along with his acts of valor of which you are no doubt aware. His sins against you and your lovely sisters gnaw at him constantly. His only wish is that you at least read his heartfelt apology, in case Providence dictates he not survive to deliver it in person."

"Sir, even if I were to read his letter, there is little hope of my accepting his transformation much less his apology. No amount of valor upon the battlefield can erase what has been done, and I fear no amount of contrition, Christian or otherwise, would be enough to sway Clifton Janeway. I will offer you an apology for my bluntness, but understand I meant every word."

"People can change, Miss O'Darcy. I have to believe an intelligent young woman such as yourself will come around to that conclusion. Allow me to leave the letter upon the mantel of the fireplace you mentioned, and if you decide to deliver it to the embers, well, I'll leave that between you and the Almighty."

Delicia busied herself with renewed effort after Buford Janeway departed, but no amount of work could drive away her ambivalence. Although his last words had been patronizing, there was some truth to what he had said. Her abiding faith dictated she at least consider the possibility there had been a conversion, but then the memories of that horrible night would invade her thoughts and she was right back where she had started.

"Read the God damned letter." Doc Wygant said when he entered the laundry room. "I'll be switched if that no-account Clifton Janeway has changed his stripes, yellow as they are, but then war can have peculiar effects upon a man, even one like him. Wouldn't bet on it though."

"And sometimes long hours in a hospital can affect the manners of good men," Delicia countered, a smile on her face as she poked Doc Wygant's thin chest with a forefinger. "You heard the whole thing, you blaspheming old scoundrel!"

"Heard enough to conclude you should read the God damned letter, then burn it for all I care. If the story is true, a dubious possibility at best I'll grant you, he saved your Pete. That possibility would merit a reading, I would imagine. Something feels funny about that whole business though, I'll grant you that, too."

It was close to midnight when Delicia finished her work. Her father had been waiting for her outside in his carriage a fair length of time, so she was hastening her steps as she made her way into the foyer. She reached for the doorknob, hesitated, and glanced into the parlor. She saw an envelope resting atop the mantel. With a heavy sigh, she went in and opened it.

Dear Miss O'Darcy,

 Many's the night I have been alone in my tent, regretting my unforgivable actions of which we are both sadly aware. Although strong drink would be a cowardly excuse, I want you to know I have touched nary a drop since riding off to defend our beloved Union. It is with sober reflection I appeal to you to reconsider your justifiable hatred of me, and come to understand I have found God amidst the most harrowing of circumstances. Without

Him, and my acknowledgement of Jesus Christ as my personal Savior, I do not know how I could survive during these trying times.

The regimental chaplain was quick to inform me that one of the tenets of my conversion demands I apologize to any and all I have offended by my past actions, but I had long since come to that conclusion as it pertains to you. If you cannot accept my apology I will understand, but please accept the Devine Spirit within my born again soul that compels me to beg your forgiveness.

Tomorrow I will be riding out yet again, this time to thwart the enemy, or die trying, somewhere near or past Memphis. General Grant will be in command, so we feel confident God will see fit that we carry the day.

I have come to admire your brother, and all of us consider ourselves blessed to have such an able man as Major O'Darcy to lead us into battle. Pete McCabe has also been a blessing, but I have not as yet offered my apologies to him. I wanted to plead my case with you first, and to promise you I will do all in my power to assist both those fine men, as well as my other brothers-in-arms, in whatever way God deems appropriate. If I am to be sacrificed while performing my duties, I will do so knowing I have fulfilled my promise to our Lord God, and fulfilled the promise I made to myself to offer you my heartfelt and humble apology. May the love of God be with you and yours forever Miss O'Darcy, and may He guide this army to victory and find a way to deliver both Sackett and Pete safely back to you. As for myself, I would consider it an honor to once again come to their aid, even if I am the only one not to survive.

Yours most humbly in the service of our Lord Jesus Christ,
Clifton Janeway

Delicia did not read the letter twice, but she did not feed it to the dying embers either. During the journey home she asked her father what he knew about the Memphis area, and points just beyond. Hezekiah had been there on two occasions conducting business in the mid 1850's, and knew the area at least that well.

"Well, my dear, it is a beautiful part of the country or was when I visited last. There are a number of quaint but charming smaller hamlets and farmsteads about as well. I seem to recall a particularly fetching place that was located on some high ground close to the Tennessee River, a ways east of Memphis, in Hardin County. Shiloh, I believe it was called."

VIII

Cusman Sable did not want to believe what he was hearing. Although it wasn't his nature to eavesdrop on his master, for the most part anyway, the first words from Trenton Ransom to his wife Jennifer that afternoon in the south parlor had left Cusman riveted just outside the doorway.

"I too have deep reservations, and many regrets of my own, my dear. My deepest concern, however, is for the welfare of our family. I am not at all convinced the early victories by our brave men-in-arms offers irrefutable evidence their triumphs are the precursors of things to come, far from it! I have spent time in the North, as you well know. Didn't I always tell you of their industrial superiority? Why, in New York City alone there are more factories and other industrial enterprises than can be found in the entire South! Northern population dwarfs ours by the millions, and -"

"Yes, Trenton, you have told me those things and more, but wasn't that also the case when our nation was borne? I seem to recall the British were even mightier when their leaders saw fit to sail home in defeat. Those initial victories of ours you mentioned were a luxury our founding fathers did not enjoy, but still they persevered! You must have faith, Trenton. The second American Revolution has begun, and with much more initial success than the first one. You know that is true, and so do the Yankees."

"Oh, they know it to be sure," Trenton said, "but I fear all that has accomplished is to further steel their resolve. I don't know of any agricultural society in the history of the world that has ever been able to defeat one with significant industrial superiority. Once the North begins to pour their all into this war, and I fear they will, the South as we know it will be finished. Say what you will about that treacherous bastard Lincoln, but I have little reason to doubt his resolve or that of his henchmen. No, my dear, the prudent path we must follow needs to take us, and all we can take with us, as far from the South as possible. Now is the time to sell Whisper Manor, slaves and all, while there are still men of means willing to pay a fair price, delusional souls that they are."

Cusman was in shock. His master had not uttered one word about keeping any of his slaves, but then why would he? Since his plan included getting as far away from the South as possible, didn't that have to mean a place where slavery was outlawed? Perhaps, Cusman, rationalized, he meant to take his most prized slaves which would naturally include Cusman and Missy Nell. *Why, Mas'r gonna need assistance for any new venture, so maybe his plan includes freein' his ablest slaves and payin' them a fair wage. Better to hire those he knows and trusts than to gamble on strangers,* Cusman told himself and wanted desperately to believe. It wasn't lost on him that once he and Missy Nell were indeed free, the decision to stay with the Ransoms would no longer rest with their former owners; freedom meant just that, and Cusman knew staying with the Ransoms wasn't something he or Missy Nell would eventually want. The conversation in the parlor, however, continued to darken:

"Where exactly, Trenton, do you expect to find anyone in such trying times willing to buy both Whisper Manor and most of our slaves? Given the circumstances, you should just free them anyway. If not, I am giving you the benefit of the doubt you do not mean that I would be expected to part with Missy Nell, nor you Cusman I would imagine, and let us not fail to include Auntie May. Free them of course, but hire them nonetheless."

"Trying times indeed, my dear, so much so I am forced to accept any serious buyer would be familiar with our place, and its most valuable assets. He may not want all our niggers, but it's unlikely he will not want the cream of the crop. Your sentimental desire to see all of them freed is of course out of the question. The rest will have to go anywhere there is still a market for them. Yes, trying times indeed, with terrible sacrifices to be made, but not as terrible as allowing wishful thinking to cloud our better judgment! If we wait, the future will see our family as penniless as the slaves you wish to free, and they will end up lost to us anyway."

"Then at least free Missy Nell and Cusman now, Trenton, and we will hire them as our servants and bring them with us if things are as dire as you predict."

"Damn it woman, you are not understandin' me!" Trenton yelled. He rarely used that tone with her, and when he did his usual habit of imitating his wife's virtual lack of a southern accent was always abandoned. "Do you presume Ah am not torn apart bah all this?" He continued, his rage surging. "Mah great grandfather started this place, and now Ah am forced ta sell or we will perish! Mah family is buried here, mah whole bein' is at one with all'a this, and it is me that will have ta answer ta them in the Hereafter! Ah won't go ta mah grave without doin' what Ah must do ta protect mah family, just as mah great grandfather was forced ta do when the Protestants forced him from Ireland!

"It is lost, Jennifer, our way is lost forever even if the majority of our countrymen are too blinded bah their hopeless cause and ridiculous self-delusions ta see it! We will survive only if Ah act now, and no amount'a wishful thinkin' comin' from you or anyone else will alter that fact! If Ah could spare Missy Nell and Cusman Ah would, Auntie May too, but they are simply too valuable, too much a part'a this place. Why, the two most likely men Ah have been in touch with regardin' an all-out sale have both mentioned the two'a them, and one'a them mentioned Auntie May as well! Do you believe Ah did not try ta save our most beloved niggers? Ah was turned down flat in that regard, and that is the long and short of it!"

There were more emotional outbursts, but Cusman had heard enough. His master rarely won arguments with his wife, but there had never been any of that magnitude Cusman could recall, or even recall having heard about from others. Affairs of the plantation as it pertained to hard business considerations had never been even discussed between Mas'r and Missis before, as far as Cusman knew. That was Master Ransom's domain, and his mind was clearly made up, as was Cusman's.

***

LATER THAT evening, after they had gone behind the smokehouse, Cusman told Missy Nell everything.

"Unless we act, Missy, it ain't likely you and me will be together much longer. Mas'r himself knows as much, knows once he's rid of this place there's no tellin' what's to become of all us coloreds except hard times. He rightly knows his business, and it's tellin' him to get as far away from all this as he can, as fast as he can. I s'pect we best do the same."

Missy Nell had no argument. She started to say Missis Jennifer would never allow anyone to sell her, but she knew Cusman would say she was at least one daydream away from reality. She also realized what could easily be her fate if the worst did happen. Even if a new master kept her and Cusman, it would only be temporary if Mas'r Ransom was right about the direction of the war. A new master would soon be in dire straits himself. He would sell off anything and anyone he could, and in a greater panic than Mas'r Ransom was currently facing. A girl with her beauty would be the first to go, and she shuddered when the probable reason why entered her mind.

It was just as obvious she and Cusman would probably be separated, no doubt forever, even if she wasn't sold off right away. She shuddered when the thought of losing him forever suddenly felt like a hovering reality.

She again grappled with the thought of what a new master or another male in his family would likely want from her, perhaps more than one of them. There were no good choices for her and Cusman, certainly no safe ones, but at least a choice did exist. There was no need to discuss what it was, just how she and Cusman planned to implement their escape.

***

SLAVES OF lesser value were hunted with a tenacious sense of purpose by those who viewed them as nothing more than commodities. No doubt the slave catchers would be even more motivated when it came to Cusman and Missy Nell. Trenton

Ransom was very wealthy, therefore the reward would likely rival the highest price ever offered anywhere in the South, or close to it. Payment for the capture of Cusman and Missy Nell would no doubt equal or surpass the normal amount offered for half a dozen or so ordinary slaves. Not only would the monetary reward be substantial, but the captor would also attain an elevated status amongst his peers that would likely allow him to increase his fees for future expeditions.

There had never been much of a shortage of such men. Although logic appeared to demand the outbreak of the Civil War should have depleted their ranks, and in many cases had, other realities arose to refute that claim. Home Guard units had already been formed in some states, and all eleven Southern states would have them by 1863. Although their primary responsibilities did not include tracking down runaway slaves it wasn't a totally uncommon practice, depending upon the unit, when their other duties didn't interfere. It usually helped if a substantial bounty was involved.

Even in areas where a shortage of slave catchers did exist, often times the ones who were available tended to be adept at their trade. Those men and others would travel virtually anywhere if the promise of impressive bounties had been offered. Once Cusman and Missy Nell were at large it was a given they would be tracked by experts. The professionals knew all the ploys, especially the ones that had proved successful. If Cusman and Missy Nell were to succeed, their plan would have to be unique with a full measure of luck to go with it. In that regard both of them were at a loss, and their desperate frustration had begun to radicalize their thinking.

"Mas'r been plannin' a trip to Atlanta," Cusman told Missy Nell a few months after their initial meeting behind the smokehouse. "He plans on meetin' up with two men that are fixin' to likely buy this place." Missy Nell looked around before responding even though they were alone in the basement wine cellar.

"Isn't he gonna bring you along?"

"S'pect he would most times, but I'm hopin' the nature of his business is somethin' he don't want me gettin' wind of. That don't mean he cain't meet up with them men with me not around. Sure enough happened before when he weren't needin' me about. I'm thinkin' I kin always make like I'm sick again, that oughta do it."

"How long he fixin' to be gone?"

"A week anyway. Maybe longer. Fact is, he kin still be reached by telegraph once we light out. Even if my plan works, such as it is, we won't get more'n a few days head start before them slave catchers get wind of it."

Forging the documents granting their freedom would pose no problem for Cusman. Most of Trenton Ransom's written correspondence over the proceeding few years had been handled by Cusman anyway, since his abilities as a calligrapher had gone from above average to remarkable. Even so, no documents in the hands of so-called former slaves would necessarily calm suspicions regarding any person of color traveling in the South, let alone two coloreds as eye-catching as Cusman and Missy Nell. Cusman hoped the documents would prove useful if they could make their way into the North, but he wasn't sure. He was unaware things had changed for the better in that regard.

Now that war had broken out Southern slave owners could no longer expect official help enforcing the Fugitive Slave Act once escapees made it to northern soil. If the law applied at all it was only in theory. Some Northern states had passed laws in defiance of the Act even before the outbreak of hostilities. The United States military paid it little heed if at all. Union General Benjamin Butler went so far as to insist the military was justified in refusing to return slaves. Indeed, since the South had broken away, many insisted the federal law no longer applied to the Confederacy, although if the price was right there were northerners willing to turn runaways over anyway.

The loathing of Negroes was common in the North even if it was the abolitionists who seemed to garner most of the attention. How many times had Cusman overheard Master Ransom and his friends insist Yankees were at best hypocrites in that regard? They wanted slavery abolished, but knew next to nothing about coloreds since unlike many southerners, Yankees didn't live anywhere near them, while Master Ransom and his peers had lived with them their whole lives, even in the same house! No wonder so many Yankees felt such contempt for Negroes; who doesn't fear, distrust, some even despise what they don't understand?

"After Mas'r leaves, I'll perk up soon enough so Missis won't have to fret about me makin' a trip to Beaux Hollow. I'll ask her for some extra money, maybe to have a load of oats delivered or some such thing where I won't be needin' no wagon. I'll hide my good clothes in the buggy. No need for you to collect your nice things 'til the night we leave. Missis might notice they're gone otherwise. I won't be goin' to no Beaux Hollow though. Not even more'n part way. You sneak out soon as Missis is asleep an' I'll meet you south of the hilltop pecan grove. Few miles walk an' we'll get to where I'll have the buggy hid. Missis likely won't know you're gone until mornin'. Even then, she's gonna look all around the place before she gets wind. Should give us twelve hours, maybe more before she begins to add it all up. More time'n that gonna pass before she gets word to Mas'r. We'll be over twenty miles away by then, maybe thirty. Might have to hide the buggy though, have to wait an' see. We'll likely be settin' out on foot, stickin' close to woods an' such 'til we get to a train station."

Obvious pitfalls accompanied Cusman's plan, not the least of which was making it even ten miles the first night, let alone thirty, without someone spotting them in a fancy buggy. Everyone within that range would assume two attractive coloreds would most likely have to be from the Ransom plantation, with most folks being able to recognize them outright. Although Cusman and Missy Nell were counting on folks being asleep later on, no explanation would convince the most profound dullard those two had any business being that far away from home in the earliest hours of the morning if by some happenstance they were spotted. It was a chance, one amongst many they would simply have to take.

***

AT FIRST everything seemed to fall in place. Trenton Ransom hadn't even asked Cusman to accompany him, since he was sharing a ride with another plantation owner who also had business in Atlanta. Mrs. Ransom not only had no qualms with Cusman going to Beaux Hollow, but had actually approached him to do so after Auntie May had informed her certain kitchen supplies were running low. All Cusman had to do was busy himself until late in the day so he wouldn't be expected back until well into the night, if not until the next morning. It was not uncommon for him to do so if unforeseen matters in town kept him there longer than anticipated.

Cusman knew the perfect spot to hide the horse and buggy before meeting Missy Nell south of the hilltop pecan grove. He called it Pap's Hollow, because his late father used to take him there when they could get away for a while. Cusman's mother, who had passed away less than a week after her husband died, joined them on occasion, but once Cusman was in his early teens she had insisted it was important for a father and son to share some alone time.

There was a spring-fed pond that always seemed to offer up a mess of catfish, sometimes an occasional largemouth bass. Some of Cusman's fondest memories seemed to come to life once he found himself along the banks of the pond, especially along its north shore where the fishing was best. His father had been a patient man and had thoroughly enjoyed watching his adolescent son fish, particularly when the boy had hooked into a truly large brute. Cusman's wide-eyed squeals of delight had always fixed a smile on the man's face that had been hardwired to the depths of his heart, and it was not uncommon for it to have stayed there long after the fish was on the stringer.

The conversations the two had shared had covered all the subjects a young boy was bound to bring up to his father, and Big Mede Sable had never tired or grown impatient with his son's questions or observations. Alone by the pond, there had been no subjects that had been off limits, even after Cusman had entered his early teen years and the questions had been of a nature best not brought up in front of white folks.

The afternoon and evening of his planned escape found Cusman along that very bank, lounging upon his favorite spot. Although his impending ordeal was foremost on his mind, he found it impossible not to float back to happier times. Looking about from time to time he half expected and fully wished to see Pap stroll by, cane fishing poles in hand along with a bucket of over-ripe chicken livers mixed with Pap's "secret possibles" they had used for bait. A wistful smile appeared on Cusman's face when he recalled the old wooden bucket, how it had been best placed downwind with the leather cover firmly tied just under the top lip. Those rancid livers had sure stirred up the catfish though.

His father didn't show but it felt to Cusman as if he had, so maybe Pap was close by after all. Regardless, Cusman drew strength from his lingering reverie. Given the circumstances he knew his father would be proud of him; worried down to the ground and back again, but proud.

Once Cusman had reached fifteen their conversations by the pond had often had a way of veering towards the notion of freedom. It had always been Cusman who had brought it up, and Big Mede Sable had known his observations that eased into advice had to be well thought out. Many a night he had found himself wide-awake in bed, anticipating the following day's questions his intelligent son would no doubt have waiting for him as they sat by the pond. He had hidden nothing from Cusman as it pertained to slaves on other plantations and farms, whether close by or in other counties and states. Cusman had soon learned, but had not completely accepted his family's envious station in life compared to many others in bondage. To him, bondage had been and still was the evil that rested at the heart of the matter.

Even at such a young age he had been well aware that a sizable number of his fellow slaves weren't obsessed with obtaining freedom. Having been borne into a culture where their parents and other ancestors had grown to accept their station in life made it seem natural, in an unnatural sort of way. Oh, some of them might toy with the notion, even express a desire to be free, but the thought of actually doing something about it seemed to be such a daunting undertaking it remained idle talk, for the most part.

The antebellum South that had existed for decades visited its share of atrocities upon those held in slavery, but it was also common for a sizable number of slave owners to treat their human chattel with kindness and consideration - as long as everyone accepted their station and acted accordingly. Cusman, just like his father had as well, understood what that really entailed. Cusman didn't have any way of knowing what type of life his African ancestors had enjoyed, other than the stories that had been handed down. Cusman and many of his contemporaries had always known their ancestors hadn't been slaves and that those ancestors had possessed beliefs, attitudes and a culture that had been taken away from their descendants; it had indeed been, and still was the systematic alteration of all those things that had most certainly been visited upon their descendants, and that undeniable fact hadn't been lost on Cusman or his father.

There were, in a sense, exceptions of course. Pap had told Cusman about some slaves who literally lorded over white households, upbraiding miscreant white children, teenagers and the like. Some even scolded adults if they felt certain social customs and rules were being violated. There had even been a house slave at Whisper Manor who had seemingly held sway in such a manner, Uncle Simon. He had died when Cusman was ten, but Pap had sure remembered the man. It had not been uncommon for the refined and authoritative man to have dressed down virtually anyone if even a hint of misbehavior or departure from established decorum had occurred, with the exception of, for the most part, Trenton Ransom's parents; and heaven help any slave who had incurred his wrath.

Pap had even told of white owners who fell in love with their slaves, and treated them as if color was no barrier at all. Big Mede Sable had loved to recall one story in particular, and Cusman recalled never having tired of hearing his father tell it: *"Ah swear, there was bein' henpecked, an' there was what Colonel Meyers put up with. One day in Beaux Hollow he was walkin' behind, as usual, his slave gal Miss Sally, jus' as they was leavin' the general store. His arms was full, an' she was'a hollerin' an' carryin' on somethin' awful 'bout his dawdlin' or some fool thing, an' right 'bout then he done dropped a basket of eggs. She lit inta him like he done stepped on a new borne calf, even smacked him upside the head with her umbrella, right in front'a the white folk an' ever'thing. Lord did them white folk howl, most of 'em anyways. Me an' mah friend Pecky was laughin' so hard couldn't see through our tears, Ah swear. Colonel Meyers kept on'a sayin' how sorry he was, tryin' to pick up them broke eggs an' such, gettin' the yokes all over hisself, an' Miss Sally jist kept'a whackin' him wid that umbrella, hollerin' an' carryin' on. Mebbe the law said he owned her, but ever'one knew it was the other way 'round."*

The story had been amusing to Pap and Cusman, but the boy knew it was an aberration. Pap's other stories had carried much more weight for the youth. Perhaps any number of slaves had resigned themselves to their current situation, but not Cusman.

He knew he was smarter, for instance, than both of the Ransom boys. The two brothers had usually treated him and the other slaves well, as long as everyone understood they were a white family's property and behaved accordingly. As a child Cusman used to play with the two Ransom boys, and although they had become fast friends, over time it felt as if he had become more like their pet. By the time the three boys had entered their teen years, when the two sons grew to realize Cusman had surpassed them in both physical and intellectual prowess, he hadn't been regarded with even that much esteem, as if his superiority was temporary or a quirk of nature. Regardless, it was certainly resented.

Cusman considered it no great loss when Trenton Ransom had sent his sons Trenton Jr. and Marcus to Europe in 1858, supposedly to further their educations. Ransom had been fully aware of the impending national catastrophe he had accurately predicted, although he kept his real justifications for their departure to himself. Just prior to, and after war had broken out both young men wrote home incessantly, imploring their father to bring them back immediately. Trenton always responded that their mother and he would be vacationing in Europe soon and they would discuss it then. He also made sure not to send them a penny more than they needed to get by, if that much, just in case they allowed their youthful, misplaced notions to countermand his directives.

Cusman continued to spend the afternoon by the north shore of the pond, contemplating the highlights of his conversations with his father as it pertained to genuine freedom. Pap, as Cusman recollected, had never massaged the truth when conversing with his son. He had steadfastly insisted Cusman was "every bit the equal and a heap more" of any white or colored he had known of, including the few free men and women of color who had managed to obtain their freedom and gone on to make something of themselves:

"If them colored folk kin do it, Lord knows you could if you had the chance." Pap had insisted. *"Ah s'pect you'd pass 'em all up, one way or 'nother. Problem be in gettin' there, an' as problems go, that one stands on top. Ah seen the hides torn off'a the backs'a them runaways what got caught. Bleeded ta death on the ground, sometimes. Mas'r Ransom, he don't have the whip laid on too hard most times, but them others he sell his runaway niggers to sure as heaven done it, still do, jus' like Mas'r all the time be sayin' if'n he spot rabbit in a nigger's eyes. You lissen good, Cusman, it tear your mama's heart out, mine too, you ended up that a way. Worse for Mam, 'cause Ah'd kill the white devil what done you up such, real slow-like, too, Ah git the chance. Be a lucky nigger what just get hung for that mess. Boiled, mebbe skinned alive more like it, least ways so Ah heard. One thing certain. Know'd me enough white men be takin' pleasure in such goin's on. Don't you be forgettin' that Cusman, don't you never be forgettin' that."*

Cusman came back from where his thoughts had taken him. It had been a sizeable swirl twenty feet or so from shore that had done it. A young chipmunk had fallen from a branch that hung low over the water. A huge catfish soon had it, but at least the tiny creature's death had been swift. *Damn,* Cusman realized, *even a tiny thing like that end up better off'n a caught runaway. Catfish have less explainin' to do to the Lord than some white folk hereabouts…*

***

IT WAS a little after ten that moonless night by the time Cusman had made his way on foot to the south end of the hilltop pecan grove. Even in the dark, it remained one of the most enchanting spots in Whisper Manor even if there were no mundane or unattractive ones, from a physical perspective.

An owl, confident its concealment from half-blind, clumsy humans was a given, took its time between hoots but offered them up on a regular enough basis to underscore the creature's obvious sense of superiority within its own environment. When the hooting did echo about, any scurrying of smaller creatures ceased, and when the owl's diminutive prey did start up again their initial movements were usually tentative in nature.

Thoughts of Pap and the pond were behind Cusman, for the most part, as he waited behind a pecan tree. Some residue remained as it pertained to escaping, especially as it related to Missy Nell. Her getting away unnoticed from Grand House and the immediate vicinity was on his mind the most. If she was somehow detected it was unlikely to be assumed she was running away, although suspicions would be aroused since it was wholly out of character for her to venture out that time of night unless she had informed Missis ahead of time, and then only if she had good reason. A thought suddenly occurred to Cusman, and he regretted having asked her to bring along her best clothes and hoped she had reconsidered. How could Missy possibly explain that if the worst happened? How could he have been so stupid? His oversight felt as if it were slapping him, now that things were in motion.

Cusman tried to keep his thoughts from getting carried away, but when his father's admonitions elbowed their way back in it was all he could do not to obsess over what could happen to her.

Missis would never allow a whip anywhere near Missy he told himself, no matter what. The worst that might happen would be a severe scolding, followed by some disciplinary action reserved for a daughter more than a slave. That calmed Cusman until one of his father's observations, one of many forged over a lifetime of observations, set in. Cusman recalled the story behind the observation, a story about a close childhood friend of Pap's when his father had been a teenager. It had involved Trenton Ransom's father, and the man's response when Big Mede Sable's childhood companion from the Jetty family who tended that very pecan grove had been captured after a second futile escape attempt. Pap's friend, Pecky, had attempted both escapes with the girl he loved and hoped to free and marry, Candy.

The story paralleled Cusman and Missy Nell's impending venture, and the similarities sent a chill straight through his soul as he recalled his father's words:

"Sure 'nough not the first time some poor nigger's come up empty after countin' on the pure heart of a white mas'r...or missis. They found them a beast of a man ta pertin' near whup the hide off poor Pecky, then sold 'em off. Sold him off ta that same white devil what whupped him, but not befo' Pecky seen his own gal, Candy, sold off ta another ugly devil what weren't fixin' ta use no whip...wanted ta keep her pretty that blue-eyed devil said, after tearin' off all her clothes right there

*in front'a ever'body, puttin' his hands all over her, used his fingers too, then whooped an' hollered
how she needed her a bath…"*

Cusman heard the rustling of feet through grass before seeing anyone. He was
all concentration as he kept watching the specific area amongst the trees where the
sounds had first been detected, wishing he had the eyes of a cat.

"Cusman, you out there?" Missy Nell implored in an urgent voice. "Cusman, you
hear me?" He stepped from behind the tree and made his way to a slight, tree covered
rise. Looking down, he tried to make out Missy Nell's exact location. A few moments
later she stepped out from behind a large tree herself.

"Oh Cusman baby, you are *not* gonna believe this…"

"Hello Cusman," Mrs. Ransom said when she too stepped from behind the tree.
He could barely make her out but there was no mistaking her voice, or its tone.

"Hello Missis Jennifer," he responded, forgetting himself by using her Christian
name, his heart pounding in his chest. "What you doin' out at this hour?"

"Don't you know, Cusman?"

IX

The stars, prodigious amidst their extravagance were out when the 1st Naperville Cavalry caught sight of the Union encampment after reaching the summit of an impressive, wooded rise. It was a clear night, and from that vantage point the massive encampment to their south, not far away, resembled a powerful city poised for sudden mobility. Campfires, lanterns and their undulating refractions seemed to go on forever, and the sounds of regimental bands too numerous to distinguish one from another blended together as if a giant calliope, influenced by wind and distance, carried its sonorous yet haunting melodies to the horse soldiers as if the distance that separated them from the encampment was a disjointed illusion.

The horse soldiers rode down the south end of the rise, winding their way through the trees, in awe of the spectacular sight until it was temporarily lost from view as they entered the next ravine. Not the blending calliope-like music though, they didn't lose that, nor the sense of guarded assurance it generated as if freedom from uncertainty wasn't a mirage after all. Upon reaching the summit of the next rise, the last hill of any significance before entering the massive encampment, any remaining illusory sensations a few of the men still harbored vanished.

"Woe be to the Rebels or any force on earth foolish enough to insight the ire of this army," a young private, proud in his saddle, announced to no one in particular. His sentiment was echoed in the hearts and minds of his fellow horse soldiers riding near the young private as well. It was echoed amongst virtually all of the men of the 1st Naperville Cavalry and points beyond - including the 45,000 Confederate soldiers under the command of General Albert Sidney Johnston who were much closer than the young private, or any of the men in the 1st Naperville had yet to realize. The Confederates echoed the same sentiment, confident within their pride to be defending the Stars and Bars with their own imposing army.

"Woe be to the Yankees, or any force on earth foolish enough to test the mettle of this army," a young Confederate private, preparing for the Rebel attack upon General Grant's forces the following morning, announced to no one in particular.

***

MAJOR O'DARCY ordered his men to set up camp along the perimeter of the huge throng of Union soldiers. Evening had been edged out by darkness hours before as the night of April 5th 1862 came to a close, so there was no time to lose if they wanted to get some much needed rest. The 1st Naperville had arrived much later than the main Union force, having been ordered to separate themselves from the 40th Illinois for reconnaissance purposes two weeks before that regiment, along with the rest of General William Tecumseh Sherman's Fifth Division had made camp near a small, unexceptional structure called Shiloh Church, or Shiloh Chapel as some called it.

Shiloh. A Hebrew name whose meaning has been interpreted a number of ways, including a place of rest... a *Place of Peace*.

***

AS A clear dawn slowly eased its way across the eastern horizon the following morning of April 6th, advancing Confederate skirmishers, less than two hundred yards ahead of the 3rd Mississippi Infantry from which they had originated, moved as quietly as possible through the thick underbrush and woods. They knew the Yankees, a huge contingency of them, were close by, although they had yet to run into any Union skirmishers.

Well concealed and moving stealth-like, the Rebels hoped to spot the enemy before they themselves were detected. They almost succeeded, until the young Confederate private who the night before had forewarned the Federals if only to his comrades of the Billy Yanks' impending foredoom, tripped over an exposed root. By itself that wasn't so alarming, but when he instinctively reached out to cushion his fall his Enfield discharged. A single shot to be sure, but at just after 5:30 a.m. on such a serene morning it might just as well have been the report from a large bore cannon.

An early morning Union reconnaissance patrol, three companies of the 25th Missouri commanded by Colonel Everett Peabody not only heard the shot, but due to its close proximity realized immediately they had been only moments away from having been first detected themselves.

The Union response was swift and deadly, for both sides. Hundreds of muskets and other rifles opened up, shattering what tranquility still hung in the morning mist as if it had always been a falsehood waiting to explode. For nearly an hour both sides pummeled each other with savage fury as the crescendo roar of their rifles grew; a deafening fusillade of mayhem that eventually caused those Union ranks to fall back when Confederate reinforcements continued to grow in number. The Battle of Shiloh, deadlier than any engagement by American forces which preceded it, emerged under a suddenly seething morning sun.

In virtually no time General Sherman's entire Fifth Division was under attack. Led by General Patrick Cleburne's brigade, the energized Confederates charged, wave after wave. The Union regiments were being constantly outflanked as one after another of them withdrew without warning, terrified not only by the unrelenting enemy fire but the unnerving banshee Rebel Yell that somehow managed to rise above the din as if hell itself was orchestrating the Confederate assault.

Major O'Darcy, along with most of the 1st Naperville Cavalry, had been sleeping soundly after their previous day's long and arduous journey. With any hope of more than five hours slumber having been shattered, Major O'Darcy went about the task of organizing his men as they stumbled from their tents as the bugles sounded and the drums beat. The confidence the huge city-like encampment had generated with such ease just hours before, although not completely destroyed, had most certainly gone missing.

After Major O'Darcy had his men at the ready he immediately sought out General Sherman. The tall, redheaded general was giving orders and instructions to several officers at once when Sackett approached. A clearly agitated Sherman was talking rapidly about several different tactics at the same time. His demeanor was that of an alarmed yet focused commander clearly in his element, even if he had originally underestimated the Confederate threat, or at least the proximity of the enemy. Not anymore.

"Major O'Darcy! Take your men east/southeast and see if you can intercept General Prentiss's left flank. I don't know what may be happening there, but perhaps he has fallen back or is about to and will be in dire need of any assistance you and hopefully other cavalry units can muster. Hit the Rebels' extreme right flank if you can, strike and run, then strike again if possible. Support our men any way you can. It is possible if not probable they intend to cut us off here by crushing our left flank thus forcing us back into the swamps of Owl Creek. Make haste, Major!"

"Captain Janeway! Lieutenant McCabe! Form the men and follow me!" Major O'Darcy hollered as his horse raised on its hind quarters then bolted forward the instant its front quarters touched ground.

Pete had recently been awarded the rank of lieutenant after Sackett's report of Corporal McCabe's heroics at the Battle of Belmont had made its way through channels, although both men suspected it may have been General Smithington's way of offering an implied bribe in return for their silence regarding Clifton Janeway. Regardless, Sackett knew it was richly deserved and was grateful he had a man of Pete's caliber as one of his officers, especially at a time as critical as the one they currently faced.

The 1st Naperville initially galloped east, breaking into a dead run whenever the terrain allowed. Before they were able to head very far southeast they found themselves encumbered by a fair number of Union soldiers who were falling back slowly; others were thoroughly panic-stricken and in full retreat. The horse soldiers finally made it a good distance southeast, not all that far from the west bank of the Tennessee River. After a while they found themselves approaching a sizable number of

Confederates crossing a meadow. Sheltered by a stand of woods, Major O'Darcy ordered his men to dismount, open up with their Spencer's then remount and go to a position farther southeast and repeat their assault in similar fashion.

Though only a hundred or so strong, the 1st Naperville nonetheless created havoc. The Confederate infantrymen in the meadow, though considerably stronger in number, were as yet unaccustomed to the effects of repeating Spencer rifles fired by men who took pride in their marksmanship, and for good reason. After the first Union volley that had smashed into them was followed by several rapidly successive, smoke-filled follies, the surviving Rebels began to retreat south to the safety of a thicket of brambles consisting of a variation of dog rose and blackberry vines that covered the area along the south side of the meadow and points beyond.

A short time earlier those same men had moved with great care through the dense growth, mindful of the innumerable needle-sharp thorns that seemed to be able to penetrate most anything. In their hasty retreat, they flew through the brambles as if hindered by nothing more than a field of daisies.

The Naperville men remounted and moved southward as fast as the trees would allow. Major O'Darcy was assuming the Rebels would be working their way in that direction to protect their initial right flank. Indeed, if the enemy continued to fall back, Major O'Darcy's plan to head due south through the surrounding trees and be waiting for them when the Confederates emerged from the southeast end of the brambles could prove catastrophic for those Rebels.

The expansive thicket was less dense to the west however, and although the original Confederate battle plan had dictated that particular, relatively small battalion of Rebels head north - northeast, it was all their colonel and his officers could do to thwart a full southwest retreat. The Rebel officers continued to holler at their men to form ranks, but failed to keep their men in what remained of the thicket that was now to their left as they ran for their lives, away from Sackett's trap.

Time, as combatants in any furious battle will attest, re-invents itself once the fighting begins in earnest. What in actuality was less than ten minutes felt much longer to Sackett and his men, even if their watches belied their jumbled sense of time. More than a few men of the 1st Naperville kept checking their time pieces, at least those who owned them, including Captain Janeway who had worked his way towards the rear of the Yankee horse soldiers. He pretended to be urging the men to hold fast their courage and to make sure they had reloaded, which, of course, they had already done. He fancied himself anything but a fool, and had no intention of being towards the front of any new assault.

The Rebel infantry never showed, but a contingent of Confederate cavalry eventually did after Major O'Darcy had led his men quite a ways farther south. The Confederate cavalry battalion was well over three times the number of the 1st Naperville.

Worse yet, which Sackett and his men would soon come to realize, they were led by Colonel Nathan Bedford Forrest.

It wasn't Forrest's entire command, but it was nonetheless fearsome. His Tennessee Cavalry Battalion was a battle-tested contingent of horse soldiers who had already distinguished themselves that past February during the Battle of Fort Donelson even though the Confederates had lost that battle. After the current hostilities erupted, a frustrated Colonel Forrest had been given various assignments, none of which, he felt, were proper utilizations of his command, but Forrest being Forrest that didn't last long, to a degree. Once he was aware the various outbreaks of hostilities were well underway, *heard the guns,* he could no longer resist the urge to join the fray any way he could.

Ironically, it was Captain Janeway, atop a heavily wooded rise that first spotted the enemy approach, after having idled behind his comrades while attempting to correct a jam in his new rifle that did not exist. Forrest's advance unit, consisting of thirty or so horse soldiers was what Clifton saw headed towards him in a northwesterly direction not fifty yards away through the trees, but in his mind the fearsome horde might well have been a thousand strong. At first he moved his mount slowly backwards, desperately hoping his presence had gone unnoticed. As soon as the rise he was descending blocked his view of the approaching Confederates he wheeled his horse and galloped straight away, eventually through his own troops situated in a meadow west of the woods. Once he was amongst them he frantically implored men to get out of his way.

"Major!" He said upon his approach with an especially quiet urgency viewed essential to men with his level of courage, "I have just returned from a reconnoitering expedition east through the woods that took me very close to an approaching enemy force. I'm not sure of their number, even though I ventured towards them with little regard for my own safety. I would have proceeded farther, but had I been spotted it may well have put our men at risk, therefore I -"

"How many infantrymen *did* you spot, Captain?" Sackett interrupted, his patience having begun to dissipate the instant he had heard Clifton utter the phrase "reconnoitering expedition".

"Not infantry, Major, *cavalry!* Hundreds, maybe more!" A wide-eyed Clifton exclaimed, looking about as if enemy troops might very well have been approaching from the west as well, when in truth he was looking for a place to hide once the fighting erupted.

Sackett summoned his other officers immediately. After a brief discussion he had his men tether their horses just inside the trees that lined the eastern side of the meadow, southwest of a good-sized rise that was perhaps two hundred feet into the woods. Within a very short time that felt much longer, the men were positioned upon the boulder-strewn rise, mostly treeless and somewhat flat across its top, higher by at least twenty feet in most places from the one where Clifton had first spotted the enemy approach. Better yet, the fairly steep eastern slope and scattered large rocks, especially near the eastern top of the rise, afforded an excellent tactical position.

From their position upon the rise, even if outnumbered, Sackett knew they would be able to inflict serious damage, especially if the approaching enemy horse soldiers were unaware of the 1st Naperville's presence until it was too late. The Confederate advance unit may have been unaware of the presence of a troop of enemy cavalry, but Clifton Janeway had not gone unnoticed.

***

COLONEL NATHAN Bedford Forrest, tall in his saddle, spotted the return of several of his point scouts before anyone else. At six foot two and nearly two hundred pounds of solid muscle he was a large man, but what truly defined him was his innate ability to assess any given situation and more often than not turn it to his advantage. He was as fearless as he was intelligent, by any measure of either army's bravest and brightest soldiers.

"Colonel, we spotted a dandy of a Yankee officer on horseback, fancy uniform and all, yonder over the next rise but one." The young horse soldier first to reach his commander reported. "He skedaddled when he caught sight of us."

"Out on his own? You sure he was by himself, Private?" Forrest replied, looking around.

"Nigh onto certain, sir. He disappeared over the rise what he been settin' on, headin' west 'lessin' he done turned off in the gully."

"Captain Welles," Forrest said as he turned to one of his officers, "ain't likely some Yankee officer's out here on his own, so take your men north then cut around west. Send out scouts mind you, and try ta avoid detection if you spot enemy troops, but keep them in sight as best you can. Ah'll do the same comin' up from the south. Captain Milo, you proceed dead ahead, and engage the enemy when and if you encounter them, but hold off your advance for fifteen, twenty minutes or so unless you hear sustained gunfire, or somethin' close to it. Let's ride, gentlemen! With luck, we got us some God damned Yankee hides ta blister!"

***

THE 1st NAPERVILLE troops were in position with the majority of them facing east. Major O'Darcy had placed a little under two dozen men facing north to cover their less exposed left flank and about the same number facing south, jammed together amongst the boulders that were more numerous on that portion of the rise. The woods below were thickest on the Union left flank, thinning out somewhat dead ahead from that point and thinner still towards the south, although the stunted, bramble-impregnated brush was thicker in that direction. Five minutes passed, then ten.

Under normal circumstances it would have been considered a warm and inviting spring morning, and although it wasn't by any means hot, the Naperville troopers, to a man, were sweating underneath their dark blue woolen blouses. Most of their mouths were so dry their spittle felt like cotton, while the hands of the now gloveless men were knuckled and clammy against the stocks of their rifles they were holding tight.

A bevy of quail erupted from the brush to the south just as the men on the Union left flank first spotted rapid Confederate movement amidst the trees towards the north. Major O'Darcy went immediately to the northern position. The cry to alert everyone had no sooner gone up from the Yankees when Captain Milo's Rebel troops appeared out front; over a hundred and fifty of them interspersed amongst the trees. After hearing the Union cries from atop the rise Captain Milo ordered a charge, ignoring or perhaps misunderstanding Forrest's order to wait for gunfire from the north and south positions.

"Open fire!" Sackett hollered to everyone, and the woods exploded.

The repeating Spencer rifles should have been deadly at that range, and were, to a degree. The trees afforded some protection, especially after most of Captain Milo's men pulled back far enough to tie their horses out of harm's way, for the most part, then moved forward on foot. The massive amount of smoke from the Spencer's had also helped obscure the advancing Confederates, including the ones out front unable to dismount in time.

It wasn't uncommon, especially amongst green recruits, to be intimidated by the sight of such billowing clouds impregnated with pointblank yellow-orange flashes, accompanied as they were by the horrendous eruptions that rained the deadly, heavy caliber bullets upon them. Not Colonel Forrest's horse soldiers though - they appeared, and were, fearless. Still, the 1st Naperville's initial volleys had blasted dozens of Rebels out front from their saddles, and wounded or killed a sizeable number of horses as well.

Captain Milo, leading the frontal assault, fared poorly since nearly a dozen Union men had trained their sights on him the instant they had recognized an officer. He caught four slugs in the chest, while two others found his skull that exploded in a burst of red mist intermingled with brain matter and shards of bone that proceeded to mushroom just behind his body, bespattering those directly to his rear. His body jerked then slumped at an obscene angle in the saddle, first one way then another, until he toppled sideways to the ground. His horse was still moving forward even though it had taken several hits as well, with the dead captain's right foot still in the stirrup. It appeared as if what was left of his skull was painting a red swath along the ground as the wounded, limping mount nonetheless managed to gallop forward.

Exploding volleys from both sides continued, sounding not unlike a Fourth of July fireworks finale turned traitor. And there was no mistaking the whooping Rebel Yell that erupted from the brush to the south - Nathan Bedford Forrest's battle blood was up as was that of his men, all of them convinced no force this side of Providence could stop them.

They came on at a dead run, nearly a hundred strong, their horses smashing through the brush as if it were a field of fresh mowed hay. They were armed with shotguns, sabers and Colt Dragoons, and were all adept in the use of their weapons. Combat conditions seemed to intensify their proficiency.

Within the mayhem it proved impossible for additional Union men to help defend the right flank, due in large part to the boulder-strewn, cramped terrain atop the hill's southern exposure. The men who did have command of that tight area watched in horror as the rapid onslaught charged ever closer. The relatively small number of Yankees fired into them, releasing one volley after another, but Forrest's horse soldiers kept on coming, charging headlong towards the billowing plumes of urgent, white smoke and spitting powder flashes. Some were felled, but it didn't slow the others.

At that moment the Rebels north of the hill came charging and whooping through the trees, themselves nearly a hundred strong. The Confederate troops out front to the east, all of whom were now on foot, advanced on a dead run while raising a fearsome Rebel Yell that started out eerie from a distance then terrifying once it stormed through.

It was pure hell from there, even though hell was already present with a terrible vengeance. The Union right flank was the first to be overrun. Forrest and his horse soldiers dismounted not fifty feet from the boulders and swarmed over them, releasing volley after volley with their shotguns and Colt Dragoons. The effects were devastating, as shotguns at close range can produce so effectively. The Union men situated amongst those rocks were literally blown apart, with blood imbued body parts and clouds of red mist flying about in seemingly every direction.

A wounded Yankee, on his back all but minus his left leg, managed to bring his rifle up and took aim at Forrest, but before he could fire the Confederate colonel brought down his saber, sharp as a razor on both sides, with such force it slashed off the man's left hand and nearly decapitated him.

Over half the Union men defending against the frontal assault reeled around and opened up on the Confederates, not thirty feet away in most cases, dropping a good number of them. Forrest's men kept coming though, but the Spencer's kept the Rebels from continuing their attack towards those men outright. Instead, the Rebels kept moving north along the western top of the hill, firing as they went by, then sought the relative safety of the woods directly to the northwest.

The Union men on the left flank, still commanded by Major O'Darcy, turned to their left and opened up on Forrest's detachment as best they could, although the Confederates from the north were threatening even if their charge had been partially stalled due to the density of the pervading brush and trees, as well as the ferocious rain of bullets coming from the unrelenting Spencer's.

Captain Clifton Janeway was situated there as well, shaking uncontrollably in his soiled trousers. In that regard, he was not alone. He had emptied his Spencer during the initial assault from the north, but his trembling hands had been unable to reload his weapon. The same affliction had kept him from reloading his sidearm as well, after having emptied it in the general direction of the enemy with equal ineffectiveness.

Pete hadn't had time to find and reload his Spencer. He had dropped it after the ammunition ran out due to the Rebels storming in behind from the south. Pete barely had time to pull out his .44 caliber sidearm but did so without a second to spare, dropping three Rebels running by to his rear before they reached the woods below the rise to the northwest.

His last, hurried shot missed Colonel Forrest's head by inches, exploding into a rock formation just ahead of him, sending minute particles of granite flying amidst the screaming ricochet. Forrest turned and hastily fired the last shot from his Colt Dragoon at Pete, barely missing as well. He glared at Pete as the Naperville farmer tried in vain to reload in time, but when Pete finally brought his revolver up Forrest was gone.

"Ghost of a devil *from hell!*" Pete hollered as he holstered his sidearm and reloaded his Spencer after finally locating it from where it had been dropped, using the last tube from his cumbersome Blakeslee cartridge box that was in his haversack.

"1st Naperville, fall back and remount!" Major O'Darcy ordered with all the volume his voice could produce. His order was heard by enough men to repeat his command over and over again, and recognizing a damned good order when one was issued, his remaining men complied immediately. The Rebels out front were still coming on as well, but the steep incline coupled with the withering fire from the Yankees had temporarily inhibited their progress, causing many of them to take cover or attempt to loop around toward both flanks, especially to the north.

Most of the Union men who had been defending the Southern flank were dead or wounded, and quite a few men who had been defending against the frontal assault had also fallen after Forrest's furious rear attack, but over half of the 1st Naperville troopers were able to sprint toward their horses. There were of course wounded amongst them, yet it was a wonderment how quickly all but the most seriously injured could run, especially when Forrest's men, the only ones close by, began to advance and fire from the woods to the northwest.

"Thank God Almighty them woods yonder got such brambles!" A young trooper hollered as he glanced to his right, thankful the ground under him wasn't covered as much with the same impediments. Earlier a bullet had gone straight through his left calf, but no one would have suspected it considering how fast he was still moving. Barely an instant passed before a bullet from a Colt Dragoon slammed into his skull.

The haphazard returning fire the Union men got off as they headed southwest, along with the thick underbrush in the woods to their right, kept many of Forrest's detachment at bay. Enough of them, however, had been able to kill or wound another dozen or so of the Yankee troopers before they reached their horses.

Many of the fleeing Yankee soldiers felt it was Providence indeed that had directed Major O'Darcy to choose the section of woods located southwest from the now blood-soaked hill they had abandoned. Had he chosen to tether their mounts to the northwest, Forrest's carnage would have been all but complete, since that area dipped into a somewhat deep hollow. Any opposing force upon the higher ground to the east would have been able to easily turn that area into a death trap.

Major O'Darcy had spotted that right off. Since Captain Janeway had initially reported enemy movement coming from the northeast, it stood to reason the northwest hollow could have indeed been a death-trap if the worst transpired. The southwest area also sloped down from the hill as well, but not nearly as much. Besides, the southwest area would have been, and was, at least fifty yards farther away from any assault from the north. It too, however, would have been a graveyard had the Rebels commanded the woods above it as opposed to the other side. Providence indeed, many of them believed.

In the mad scramble, over fifty men of the 1st Naperville managed to mount their horses and bolt towards the west. Major O'Darcy decided to take a shortcut across the meadow before entering the safety of the woods beyond, laboring under the mistaken assumption that Forrest and his men hadn't had time to fight their way through the thick bramble that led to the clearing's eastern edge. It was the first major tactical mistake of Sackett's career; had he ridden into the woods to his left there would have been at least some cover, but his concern over not being able to get through that area fast enough had weighed on his mind. Under most circumstances he would have been right about a commanding officer and his detachment not being able to make it through the brambles in time, but "most circumstances" rarely applied to Nathan Bedford Forrest or his men, as Sackett and his horse soldiers soon discovered.

Over half of Forrest's men had made it through with time to spare. If they had been armed with Spencer's or even Enfield's instead of shotguns and Colt Dragoons, the carnage would have been devastating. They fired anyway, and managed to hit an alarming number of the Yankees or shot their horses out from under them. Fortunately for some of those men, a fair number of Union mounts whose former riders were dead or seriously wounded back atop the hill had managed to either un-tether themselves or had been hastily untied and taken off with the rest of the troop, allowing the rider-less soldiers to remount.

Only a few of Forrest's men had rifles with them, including one of their best sharpshooters who happened to be firing away while standing right next to Forrest. Private John Kettle had captured a new, .44 caliber Henry rifle during the Battle of Fort Donelson, along with a plentiful supply of ammunition. Private Kettle had been shooting continuously when Forrest spotted someone he especially wanted to drop. The colonel emptied his Colt Dragoon trying to hit the man, to no avail.

"Private Kettle!" Forrest yelled. "Take careful aim and drop that God damned Yankee lieutenant towards the front, the one on that handsome strawberry roan. That Yank bastard 'bout blew mah head off back on that hill! Aim true, son."

***

MOTHER GRACE shot upright in the chair where she had been resting that day, eyes wide. She screamed, bringing Father Benjamin running into the parlor from the kitchen. "Oh dear God it's Kee, it's *Kee*, Benjamin!"

"Calm yourself Grace, you must have dozed off." Father Benjamin said as he took her in his arms, trying to console her. His heart, however, was beating nearly as hard as his wife's. "I'm sure all our boys are safe," he said with more conviction than he felt, "including Kee…"

***

PRIVATE JOHN Kettle rested the barrel of his Henry on the fork of a small tree, and took careful aim. Nothing would have pleased him more than to fulfill his colonel's request, an officer he would gladly die for several times over if only it were possible. He had the center of Pete's back dead in his sights then squeezed the trigger. Nothing - he was out of ammunition.

"Lucky God damned Yankee!" Forrest bellowed as he shook his raised Colt Dragoon with one hand as he put his other arm around the shoulders of the chagrined private. Before Private Kettle could reload, the remnants of the 1st Naperville had all but disappeared into the woods and points beyond.

***

LESS THAN fifty of the 1st Naperville Cavalry had survived, but some of those were wounded so badly it was doubtful they would be around come nightfall. Miracle though it appeared to be, none of the 1st Naperville's officers had been even wounded, including Captain Janeway. When it came to retreating, Clifton continued to demonstrate a remarkable aptitude.

Still, he had suffered through the worst of it, and no one had really noticed his dismal performance when the fighting had erupted. Everyone had their own devils to contend with at the time, so noticing a trembling hand or dropped cartridges was nothing out of the ordinary. He hadn't turned tail and run, that much could be said. True enough, but when Major O'Darcy had ordered retreat there was no one ahead of Captain Janeway. He would have bolted sooner if he hadn't initially believed they were surrounded.

His being first to bolt, however, had been noticed by Sackett and Pete. Others had witnessed it, but in their own frenzied state thought little of it. Once out of earshot from the other officers after they were safely in the woods to the west and north of the clearing, Captain Janeway admonished some of the privates: "When the major issues an order, it is your responsibility to react immediately! Fortunately, I was there to lead the way, even if there was no way to tell how many bastard Johnnies were lurking about in those woods! I took it upon myself to find out, hoping to draw fire away from the rest of you just in case." That much caused a few of the troopers closest to him to exchange a few glances.

***

MID-MORNING turned to noon as the men made their way north. They were low or out of ammunition, so the men with any at all began to hand what little they could spare to the others, especially the better marksmen.

They were forced to avoid any significant number of Confederates, and there was no short supply of them. On two occasions it had been impossible to avoid the enemy regardless how well the decimated 1st Naperville kept to the woods, but during both of those confrontations they had managed to inflict enough damage to either run the Rebels off or keep them pinned down long enough to escape. Once again, the Spencer rifles had proved invaluable. Due to those engagements over another hour or so had elapsed.

They continued north but their attention was focused southward, although Forrest and his men should have been hard pressed to get back to their horses in time with any hope of catching up to them. Forrest probably had plenty else to keep him occupied. Regardless, most of the Naperville men continued to look over their shoulders anyway.

Farther north and to the west they could hear the roar of cannonade and the constant, muted volleys of what sounded like thousands of rifles going off at once; one rolling crescendo after another. Major O'Darcy recalled what General Sherman had said earlier that morning, so unless the main Union battle formations had changed, those men were in the thick of it; either General Prentiss's division, or General Hurlbut's or perhaps General Nelson's if he had finally made his way across the

Tennessee River - perhaps all of them. Regardless, there was a significant number of Rebels to the west and plenty more behind, so they kept heading north as fast as they could manage.

Finally, still keeping themselves well within the woods to the east of the battle, they spotted the southeast corner of a ten acre peach orchard in full bloom, not far from the west shore of the Tennessee River to the east. The orchard's obvious beauty was obscured by the raging battle primarily to the west of it, as best the men of the 1st Naperville could tell through the trees, although gunfire seemed to be erupting from virtually everywhere in that general direction. They also spotted something else that prompted them to stay hidden in the woods as they headed north - a large contingent of Rebel infantry amassed along the south end of the orchard itself.

Sackett advanced his men farther north, past the peach orchard, then a short ways west where they encountered General Hurlbut's infantry which was situated along the north end of the orchard. Many of the men were just inside the peach trees, facing south. Although the intense look on their faces displayed a variety of emotions, their overall appearance was not unlike cornered, feral cats preparing to bounce. Behind them was supporting Union artillery, and it was apparent Hurlbut's men were anticipating an eminent Rebel attack coming from south of the orchard, directly through the peach trees.

Hunkered down in the general vicinity southwest of the 1st Naperville and Hurlbut's men, were some Union infantry remnants located in a fairly long area that years later would be erroneously dubbed the Sunken Road, even though it was nothing more than a wagon trace that faced a somewhat large, open field to the south, part of which was impregnated with thick brambles. One Confederate advance after another, those having begun hours before, had been repulsed when they had attempted to cross the field and make their way through the thick brambles. It was littered with so many dead and wounded Rebels that some areas appeared as if one could walk on their bodies without ever touching ground.

The men of the 1st Naperville didn't know it at the time, but the Union soldiers they were viewing were what remained of General W.H.L. Wallace's division and Prentiss's men, fighting for their lives in a place that the Confederate infantrymen had named the Hornet's Nest, and for good reason. Every time the Confederates had attempted to cross the field and get through the brambles to overrun the Yankees who were firing from the wagon trace area, barely six inches deep if that, they had been met with an overwhelming number of whizzing Minie balls and cannonade. It indeed sounded as if the Rebels had stumbled upon a massive nest of very angry and deadly hornets each time they had attacked. A dozen or so gallant but costly charges had been made, all without success. The resolve of the Confederates, however, remained in place. They had already paid a very dear price and fully intended to exact their due.

Sackett located one of General Hurlbut's officers north of the orchard and offered what assistance he and his men could offer. He then saw to it his wounded horse soldiers received medical attention and directed what few medics he could find, or what passed for medics, to remove the seriously wounded men from the field. Some of them, however, refused to disengage after re-evaluating the seriousness of their injuries. Sackett ordered most of them back anyway.

"We can use all the help we can get, Major," the officer replied. "The gray backs are still amassed south of the peach trees, and we can't afford to have those rascals flank our left. They damned near succeeded a while ago. I swear, there's no quit in those God damned Johnnies."

***

COMMANDING GENERAL Albert Sidney Johnston had been personally riding amongst his Confederate troops to the south of the peach orchard, offering advice and support. Any number of generals remained content to stay back from the action, but not him. He was a competent and intelligent leader, willing to risk his all despite the danger. Like all sane men he knew fear, but Johnston was fearless. During the time before Shiloh had erupted he had been considered, although with certain exceptions in some quarters, the South's premiere general. General Robert E. Lee was also held in high regard, but had yet to show the true military genius his future accomplishments, on most occasions, were destined to demonstrate.

Johnston had wanted to turn the Yankee left flank all day, but in the heat and confusion of the day's battle the opposite had occurred, his forces having turned the Union's right flank. He had originally planned to personally correct that situation as he rode through his ranks, until he found himself where he believed he was needed most - south of the peach orchard. Since the battle had opened up a Confederate right flank opportunity he was determined to take full advantage of it.

Prior to Johnson's arrival Confederate General Breckinridge's forces had been repulsed in their attempt to roust the Yankees from the orchard, leaving scores of dead and wounded amongst the pink peach blossom pedals that were still descending like soft rain upon the dead and mutilated soldiers as if God's beauty, some of them wanted to believe, could not be completely eradicated regardless of what horrors mankind inflicted. Still, as most of them noticed, on that day mankind had demonstrated an uncanny ability to turn one of God's softer miracles into a portrait of utter inhumanity.

As Johnston helped prepare his men for a frontal assault directly through the peach trees, he rode amongst them and tapped the tips of their bayonets with a tin cup he had liberated from an overrun Union encampment to the west. He informed the men it was their bayonets that would eventually carry them to victory. Sometimes he offered words of encouragement as well, other times he used more forceful words.

Impressive in his saddle, he galloped his horse to the center of the large contingent of Confederate soldiers facing the orchard then moved to the front of them, his tin cup having been replaced by his saber that glistened in the early afternoon sun. A picture of determination, he pointed it towards the northern horizon as if the peach orchard was but their first impediment and spurred his mount. "Men of the South, *charge!*" The Confederates moved into the drifting smoke and cascading pink blossom pedals with a determined urgency, their pounding hearts steeled by their commander's gallant actions.

Not surprisingly, General Hurlbut's Union forces heard the Rebel advance before they got a look at the enemy. Years later, some Union veterans would maintain they had grown used to the Rebel Yell, but not one Yankee situated anywhere near the north end of that peach orchard would be amongst them.

The specific utterances, by themselves, were usually a high-pitched, falsetto howl – "*Woo! Woo! Woo-ah woo!*" Imagining the preceding utterance loses its terror when dulled by history, but when issued by massive numbers of adrenalin-charged, attacking men its effect had been mind-boggling. Colonel Keller Anderson of Kentucky's Orphan Brigade described it thus: *"Then arose that do-or-die expression, that maniacal maelstrom of sound; that penetrating, rasping, shrieking blood-curdling noise that could be heard for miles and whose volume reached the heavens - such an expression as never yet came from the throats of sane men, but from men whom the seething blast of an imaginary hell would not check while the sound lasted."*

Not be to outdone, the Yankees erupted with their own deep-throated "Hurrahs!" as they charged forward, but it was safe to assume the Confederates weren't the only ones who knew they were in for the fight of their lives.

As expected, the fighting was as fierce and bloody as any the combatants had ever witnessed. Along with the withering storm of Minie balls from the long rifles of both sides, roaring cannonade continued to unleash horrific damage. Along with the exploding, concussive shells and their attendant shrapnel came the fearsome cannonade of canister; lead balls, sometimes nails or chunks of hinges and other scrap metal packed within a tin can-like container fired at deadly range. Its massive shotgun effect ripped apart men with ease, as if they were *"grass before a mower"* as some witnesses later recounted. The peach tree branches above them exploded from canister and bullets by the thousands it seemed, creating a rain of urgent pink pedals that initially flew off haphazardly in every direction before alighting upon the dead and wounded, sticking to their wounds. What little remained of nature's beauty had deserted the blossoms and pink pedals entirely, transforming them into bloody funeral shrouds.

The 1st Naperville had left their mounts behind and proceeded on foot with the rest of the Union infantry. They had been most fortunate to have located a supply wagon containing a fair amount of Blakeslee cartridge boxes for their Spencer's, which in turn held ten tubes containing the seven bullets that loaded into the butt stock of their weapons. The time it took to reload their rifles in that manner saved precious moments which proved all the more useful in battles where split seconds often times spelled the difference between life and death.

Canister, cannon shells and rifle fire continued to slam into the charging Confederates and everything around them, but on the Rebels came. Determination was intertwined with bravery, cowardice and every emotion in-between and beyond, and was apparent on both sides within the exploding peach orchard - a screaming, bloody caldron choked with unrelenting smoke and continuous, deafening eruptions that seemed to be exploding everywhere. It felt as if God had indeed abandoned the orchard, but Satan and his minions most certainly had not; no man within the maelstrom that day felt otherwise.

Amidst the erupting chaos, most of the 1st Naperville had been separated from one another. Captain Janeway had suffered the misfortune, in his mind, of being next to Major O'Darcy and Lieutenant McCabe when the Union forces had begun their advance. He had tried several ploys to detach himself from them, but his two fellow officers were well aware of his true intentions and wouldn't allow him, as best they could, out of their sight. Clifton moved behind a peach tree, shaking violently as he grabbed hold of a limb. Sackett grabbed him by the front of his blouse and shook the cringing man.

"You are an officer, so act like one! You will advance and fight, Captain, or God damn it to hell, I will have you shot for cowardice!" Major O'Darcy bellowed over the unrelenting din, his face pure conviction. "Lieutenant McCabe! If this man is the first to turn tail or close to it, you are ordered to shoot to kill! Is that clear?"

"Yes sir!" Pete responded, glaring into Clifton's panicked eyes.

A rain of Minie balls aimed in their direction came from a forward group of Confederates behind a shallow swell fifty yards away and to the left of the three officers. Several other Union men in the immediate vicinity were hit, a fact attested to by the sickening whiz and thud of the heavy lead bullets as they knocked the dying men off their feet.

The conical-cylindrical .58 caliber soft lead projectiles had a way, depending on angle and trajectory, of sometimes ricocheting within a person's body if they had struck and shattered a large enough bone or series of bones, and the effects were devastating. More often the bullet would shatter the bone and exit the body with enough force to repeat the process if it hit someone else. It wasn't uncommon for several or more men to be felled by the same Minie ball.

"Pete!" Sackett hollered. "Secure a vantage point behind that larger tree to the left! Janeway, come with me!"

They had to move fast amidst the exploding confusion that had scattered the few remaining troopers of the 1st Naperville in any number of directions along with the other Union soldiers, before the nearby Rebels could reload their Enfield's and fire. Pete sprinted towards the tree, leaping over more bodies than he could count just as the Minie balls arrived. He managed to dive and take cover as the projectiles slammed into the tree, causing splinters of wood to explode in nearly every direction.

Sackett and an unnerved Clifton Janeway headed the other way, finding protection in a shallow gully containing several boulders - and several dead Union soldiers. Sackett silently cursed himself for having allowed him and two of his officers to have been initially huddled together, even if he had felt compelled to keep Clifton close by. *Didn't I learn a damned thing at West Point? No wonder those advance Rebels had taken special aim towards us*, he thought. Unlucky for the men near them who had been hit, and no small miracle he, Pete and Janeway hadn't - yet. The battle raged on.

From their vantage point, perhaps seventy-five yards west through the battered peach trees from where Pete was pinned down, Sackett continued to fire at the approaching Rebels. Clifton was shaking uncontrollably and would have stayed flat on the ground behind the boulder in front of him, but Sackett would have none of it. Again and again he implored and threatened, the latter being the only thing that made Janeway respond. He could either shoot at the oncoming enemy and take his chances or die right there behind his precious rock, and God help him if he turned tail and ran, although in that regard Clifton would not have been alone.

Pete had managed to make his way a little farther east, after having timed the musket shots the group of Rebels in front of him kept delivering. They were determined to kill the damned Yankee lieutenant one way or another. Using the same strategy as before, during and after his move, Pete had managed to kill or wound six of his assailants with his marksmanship.

That was finally enough for the others. They made a hasty retreat to the center of the orchard, since that would just as likely allow them to kill or capture an officer, or at least some Yankees whose proficiency with firearms didn't match that of the Rebels' previous adversary.

"Damn that Yankee bastard kin shoot that God damned repeatin' rifle," one of them had remarked once they were shed of Pete. "Felt like Ah was hit even when he missed!"

Pete was on a slight rise, somewhat sheltered by an old, fallen peach tree. He watched in horror, his entire body shaking, as the Rebels continued to rout his comrades, but within the mayhem many of the Yankees never did stop pouring deadly fire into the advancing enemy.

Some maintained Spencer rifles, as a rule, didn't jam much, but that's what Pete's did when he encountered an especially troublesome double feed problem. He crouched out of sight behind the fallen tree, furiously trying to correct the situation, all the while keeping an eye out for approaching Rebels, many of whom had already gone past. He was also watching Sackett's position when the heavy smoke cleared enough, although Pete wasn't certain the major and especially Clifton hadn't already headed to the rear.

They hadn't, and once again it appeared as if Providence was shining upon them. There didn't appear to be any Rebels anywhere near them, at least for the moment. It looked to be the perfect time for them to fall back with the other retreating Union men, a luxury Pete didn't have since he was farther away and more to the south, even though it appeared he hadn't been spotted recently. Still, he knew the enemy had to be closer to him than Sackett and Janeway. He was right and wrong.

Four Rebels suddenly appeared out of the blanketing smoke to the south, perhaps fifty feet in front of Sackett and Janeway. Clifton implored his commanding officer to stay down until they passed, affording him and his major the opportunity to shoot them in the back before retreating. Sackett wasn't necessarily opposed to either notion, but since the idea had been Clifton's it felt like a cowardly thing to do and Sackett let him know it. That enraged Clifton, the first emotion he'd felt besides terror all day, and all prior days that had included even the rumor of battle.

He had always despised Sackett, but at that moment it was as if his loathing had reinvented itself. *Putting up with your snide remarks and not-so-veiled contempt on a daily basis is bad enough,* Clifton imagined, *but now, you vainglorious son of a bitch, you are attempting to force me, Clifton Janeway, to commit virtual suicide!* It seemed to Clifton as if Sackett was more than willing to tempt his own fate to an extreme degree just so he could watch his captain prove, once and for all, he was nothing but a craven coward without peer or substance. *You pathetic, vindictive glory hound,* Clifton thought, his rage building. *So making me look like a sniveling reprobate is worth dying for, is it? You sanctimonious, God damned bastard…so you think this is your big chance, do you?*

Oblivious to any emotional change in Clifton, Sackett rose and began firing at the approaching Rebels, killing three and wounding the fourth to such a degree it was unlikely he'd make it another hour. Clifton hadn't even watched the Rebels fall. All he did was glare steel-eyed at Sackett, his lips angled in a silent snarl, sweat pouring down his ruddy face.

Still, the Rebels had managed to get off a few shots of their own. Those missed Sackett - but Clifton Janeway didn't miss. He fired a round from his .44 caliber sidearm that exploded into Sackett just behind his right ear, then instantly removed the entire top left portion of his skull. Clifton was out of there like a shot even before Major Sackett O'Darcy's dead body had hit the ground. He glanced around as he crawled away, and what he saw left him even more panic-stricken; Pete, thanks to a brief, traitorous clearing of the heavy smoke, was glaring right at him. He had seen everything.

Clifton's original intent after the murder was to get as far north as possible, preferably to Naperville, if only that had been possible. Even if it had been, he couldn't leave until McCabe was dead. In his frenzied state it occurred to him that maybe Sackett's death could still be blamed on the Rebels. McCabe hadn't been close by, but he could have easily seen what had happened. Clifton's eyesight wasn't keen, but it was good enough for him to conclude he had been discovered. He hadn't seen the look in McCabe's eyes, seen the *stare*, but it felt as if he had. He crawled away amidst his chaos, never losing sight of Pete's hiding place for long.

At that moment Pete had never wanted to kill anyone more than Janeway, including the enemy. His rifle was still jammed, but he had his sidearm. Before he had a chance to use it though, a large number of approaching Rebels came out of the smoky haze just ahead of him, to his left. He had but a moment to fire at Janeway before Clifton made good his escape, but if Pete did so, he knew he was dead. Before he could rationalize away his own welfare and attempt what would be a very low percentage shot anyway, Clifton was lost amidst the smoke and trees.

The old, fallen tree that sheltered Pete had been there long enough for him to claw and kick away the rotted wood underneath, and after doing so he managed to squeeze himself far enough under to obscure him from the Rebels approaching through the haze. They went right on by, but more were no doubt around so Pete remained hidden. Even if Clifton Janeway managed to save his own skin, Pete vowed, it wouldn't be for long. Janeway was a dead man - if only Pete could survive the next few hours and catch up to him.

***

THE FIRST Confederate assault of the peach orchard by General Breckinridge's brigades earlier that day had been forced back, but not the one led by General Albert Sidney Johnston. The Rebels had succeeded in routing their foe from the peach orchard and points beyond, and were rejoicing amongst the once-again beautiful cascade of peach blossom pedals. They seemed to be floating, soft-hued beings, every bit as alive as the surviving Confederates who were celebrating amongst them.

To be sure, there were mangled bodies and wounded men, some of them screaming, others sobbing and moaning their prayers, apologies and recriminations. Enough of them were being taken from the orchard to give any reasonable person pause, but perspectives change after going through that particular type of hell. Wars and their battles have certain things in common. Amongst those is the ability, over varying degrees of time, to become jaded to the most heinous of atrocities, especially after enduring such an ordeal; to look past the gore and mayhem as if it were an affirmation of a soldier's own survival.

Amidst the revelry in the peach orchard a Confederate private sat upon the trunk of a fallen peach tree that less than an hour before had been knocked down by a shell burst. He was wounded but just slightly. A Yankee Minie ball had creased the side of his head, which over time would leave a scar he would be proud to display. The blood, for the most part, had already caked.

He had just finished rolling a cigarette, the makings of which he had taken off the torn body of a Union infantryman who himself was propped up against the same tree trunk, dead where he had landed. His eyes were open, staring at nothing, but the Confederate private couldn't see them, or any part of the dead man's body above his armpits. His entire upper body had been blown away by a direct hit from a cannon shell that had been fired by a fellow Union comrade. The mutilated soldier's eyes were certainly open, but his head was upon the ground over twenty feet away.

The Confederate private began smoking his cigarette then proceeded to absent-mindedly toss small twigs into the gaping wound. It was nothing personal; his thoughts and actions could not have been more detached. He spotted a few of his comrades, boys from his own hometown. He smiled weakly and waved, then offered them some tobacco they readily accepted. They all sat around and enjoyed a smoke then, talking excitedly, mindful not to put their feet in the coagulating pools of blood, at least where the pools were deepest. The fresh tobacco tasted good to them as they all inhaled deeply then exhaled the smoke as they continued to talk. They glanced at the dead Yankee from time to time and noticed, just barely, the exhaled smoke from their cigarettes seemed to keep some of the flies away…

***

GENERAL ALBERT Sidney Johnston was beside himself, flush with victory. His uniform was torn in places where Minie balls had barely missed him, but his exhilaration was obvious as he rode amongst his men as they celebrated their spectacular triumph as the smoke continued to drift away.

He was accompanied by the Honorable Isham Harris, Governor of Tennessee, who had volunteered to be the general's personal aide. After awhile they made their way towards the center of the peach orchard and continued to discuss the events of the day, especially their recent victory. The general was still shining with excitement and it continued to show. Complete victory was within his grasp, or would be when the Yankees' crumbling left flank collapsed even further. The general's friend Isham was happy for his commander as they sat on their horses looking over the battleground.

Over a hundred yards away, crouched behind an old fallen tree, was a Union soldier. Behind him, unbeknown to him, was another Union soldier, a captain who had just crawled out from a gully where he too had been hiding. The captain carefully made his way to the ridge of the gully, crawling stealth-like, slowly, even though he was not wounded. He spotted the Union soldier who was located a little ahead of him about seventy yards to the captain's left. The captain remained still, not wanting his whereabouts detected.

He noticed the Union soldier was struggling with his rifle in an attempt to correct some apparent malfunction. Momentarily, the soldier stopped struggling and threw his rifle to the ground. He crawled perhaps ten feet away and picked up a discarded Enfield then crept back and aimed the musket as if he was preparing to fire. The captain found that odd since the battle had been lost, even if scattered cracks of rifle fire could be heard from time to time within the peach orchard, many more beyond. He looked south, wondering what, or whom, the soldier could possibly have in his sights. The peach trees partially blocked the captain's view, but he did notice two Confederates over a hundred yards away astride their horses.

"Damned fool." The captain muttered under his breath; then a thought occurred to him: *Even a bully shot would play hell making it through all those trees and give away his location. That could, however, prove fortuitous for me...*

The captain didn't know it, but the soldier had but one chance to hit his target. Although it had been dumb luck the soldier had found a loaded gun, he hadn't any ball and powder with which to reload. The soldier wasn't even certain the Enfield was in fact properly loaded, but at least an unspent percussion cap was in place, indicating it may well have been.

Suddenly the report from the soldier's musket cracked the air. Over a hundred yards away one of the Confederates seemed to jerk in his saddle, as if he had been startled but not hit. He looked around at first, as if he knew he had almost been hit by something that had come close but had indeed missed. He spun his horse around and looked about. He stared towards the peach trees for a while, then reached back and touched the back of his knee. He looked at his hand then slumped across his horse's neck.

Pete McCabe silently cursed himself. General Johnston had been clearly in his sights, and although it eventually became obvious the general had been hit, Pete had missed the center of his back where he had been aiming.

Isham Harris quickly looked about as well, but couldn't determine where the shot had come from. He noticed with alarm Johnston's actions and placed his arm around his commander's shoulders and guided their horses side by side to the relative safety of a shallow ravine. He helped the general to the ground and began hollering for assistance. None came. At first Harris couldn't locate the wound, until he glanced at

Johnston's hand that was again clutching the back of his knee. His initial response was relief; at least his general had only been hit in the leg. Within seconds however, Johnston's hand was all crimson, and blood was spurting from between his fingers as if his heart were plumping mere inches from the wound. Pete McCabe's Minie ball had lacerated General Sidney Johnston's fermoral, more specifically his popliteal, artery.

Hours before, Johnston had ordered his personal physician to attend a group of wounded Yankees they had chanced upon, insisting they were no longer enemies but prisoners. The doctor had attempted to persuade the general to countermand his directive, but to no avail. That fateful decision had re-visited Johnston, accompanied by profound sadness and tragedy. Governor Harris knew nothing about the proper application of tourniquets, makeshift or otherwise, and again he hollered for assistance. Ironically, Johnston had a tourniquet in his coat pocket, but Harris was unaware of that and in his agitated state it wouldn't have mattered anyway.

Blood had filled Johnston's boot and had begun to pool around his leg, with more still pumping from behind his knee. Harris stood and continued to yell frantically with all his might. He looked around, consumed by helpless desperation. A few Confederate soldiers in the distance looked his way, but the events of the day had dulled them to such common occurrences. They were unaware it was their general bleeding upon the ground. Before long Johnston's chief of staff arrived. Both he and Harris knelt down and implored their general to hang on.

If Johnston heard them it wasn't in this life. General Albert Sidney Johnston had bled to death.

***

ALTHOUGH ONLY sporadic gunfire was still occurring in the peach orchard, Pete immediately took shelter beneath the fallen tree after Johnston had been hit. Rebels were still about, and since intermittent rounds were still being fired, it was natural for most men to at least glance briefly in the direction of the report, especially if it wasn't too far away. Several Confederates had done just that, but by the time their eyes had focused upon Pete's specific location he was hidden away.

Clifton had watched the entire episode unfold, and had made his way back to the gully where he had killed Sackett, but from his vantage point behind the rock which he had grown to love unconditionally, he wasn't aware of the event's magnitude - at first. He eventually spotted a somewhat large gathering of Confederates around the shallow ravine where General Johnston's body was located. It was obvious an enemy officer of importance had been hit, as it took more than a common one to draw such a crowd, especially after a battle with that much carnage.

Clifton had also kept glancing to his left and had spotted Pete not only fire, but retreat to his hiding place beneath the log once his bullet had found its victim. It occurred to him that if he had been able to witness McCabe's actions, there was no doubt his own nefarious deed must certainly have been spotted by Pete as well, just as Janeway had strongly suspected.

"Just like that God damned dirt farmer to be watching out for you, *Major* O'Darcy," he said with a sneer, as if he were talking to a powerless ghost. Then the idea struck him.

He again noticed the crowd of soldiers huddled around the ravine in the distance. Looking about, he also observed that the few enemy soldiers still somewhat close by to him were also looking in that direction as well. Janeway reacted swiftly. He crawled from behind his rock and made his way to the four bodies of the Rebels Sackett had shot. One of them was about his size, pudgy belly and all.

"Looks like you must have been able to find extra rations when others could not, Johnny Reb." He was finding it enjoyable talking to dead men he once feared. He heard a soft groan, and looked to his right.

"You're not in hell yet, Reb?" He asked as a nervous, twisted smile appeared on his sweaty face as he glanced about. "Well, that won't do. That won't do at all."

"Mah, mah wife." The mortally wounded Confederate soldier whispered, barely conscious. "Got…got me a letter fer her…her an' the girls…Captain James wrote it fer me, bless his soul…in mah pocket…jacket pocket…"

Looking about again and satisfying himself no one was watching, Janeway reached inside the soldier's jacket after patting the man down on the off-chance he may have possessed something of value. He found the letter, and with it a tintype of a pretty young lady and two tow-headed little girls.

"Well now Reb, that's a handsome woman. Big titties, too. Bet they're a joy to squeeze. I'm partial to big titties, I am that. Ever spank her bare-naked ass? Heard your slut wives can't get enough of that sort of thing. How many cowards back home you figure's buggered her by now, besides her own brothers?"

The soldier tried to move, but it was no use. Half his stomach was gone. Janeway smirked at the man's feeble attempt, then bent the tintype in two and tore up the letter in front of the man's eyes, tossing both away. Then he ripped the strap off a nearby canteen.

"If I come across her," Janeway said, forcing eye contact by grabbing the back of the man's head as he forced his knee upon the wound, "I'll be sure to tell her you died like a squealing pig, right while I'm sodomizing the fat whore." He put the strap around the man's neck and tightened it very slowly, until something in the man's throat, either the pharynx or esophagus imploded, perhaps both. Clifton wasn't sure what the specific organs were called and cared even less, but he found contemplating what it might have been amusing, almost as much as the man's bugged out eyes and the impressive amount of blood that gurgled from his mouth.

Clifton wasted no further time. He removed his uniform and hid it under some fallen branches next to a peach tree, then stripped the portly soldier to his left. After donning the dead man's butternut uniform he arose and moved towards a small group of three Confederates nearly fifty yards south of him who were still looking towards the ravine and the crowd of men who had been around the body of General Johnston. A man on a stretcher was being hauled off, and word had reached the men in front of Janeway their beloved general was dead.

"Hello men," Janeway called out as he approached, effectively using his best southern accent, "Ah sure 'nough could be'a usin' y'alls' assistance."

They turned and looked, noticing the blood on Janeway's stolen uniform that didn't overly concern them. His smile did though. That was not a time for smiling.

"Don't you know?" One of them asked when Janeway stood before them. "That's General Johnston they's a haulin' off. Some damned coward of a Yankee must'a done shot him. Least ways, he's dead."

"Damn it, Melvin," a soldier who had been close to the tragedy said, "I done told you. Them officers said not ta speak on that."

"Hell with 'em," the soldier replied. "Them high and mighty bastards ain't the only ones what's got a right ta know."

Janeway couldn't believe his luck, thus far anyway, but had the presence of mind to display a grim demeanor. He appeared to be the epitome of remorse. He was in his element.

"Boys, y'alls' sad news has done broke mah heart. Ah was fixin' to tell y'all Ah seen where that there shot done come from, seein's how it hit one'a our officers an' such. Didn't know it was the general though, God rest his noble soul. Ah seen who done it too, but we gotta act fast."

That got their attention. In an instant they were following Janeway to the fallen tree where Pete was still hiding, their Enfield's at the ready. Before they'd made it even a quarter of the way Clifton eased behind them, pointing the way, talking constantly. He felt a twinge of pride, having fooled the men with his southern dialect that was bound to sound authentic because he was lying. Everything flowed effortlessly from him when he was lying.

"Now men, y'all take heed, that there no-account Yankee a' hidin' under that there tree trunk yonder kin shoot the nose off a flea. Seen him make that bully shot what kilt our general, but Ah was fresh out'a ball an' powder Ah was."

Pete heard the approaching men and knew they were heading towards him. His ammunition was gone with the exception of two rounds in his sidearm. He crawled carefully to the end of the trunk, peered around, and saw them coming - and Janeway with them. If nothing else, he vowed, he'd kill that pathetic bastard if only Providence would allow. Concerns for his own survival surfaced again then dissipated; no sense embracing such a likely impossibility, thereby losing his last chance for requital.

Pete McCabe wasn't the only marksman upon the field of battle that day, and when the sharp-eyed Confederate private out front saw the revolver rise up in Pete's hand, he fired. Pete had been trying to get a bead on Janeway with the revolver in front of his face, but the others had been blocking a clear shot. The Rebel's bullet would have hit Pete in the face but struck the cylinder instead. The force of the Minie ball knocked the now useless weapon from Pete's instantly bloodied hand. It was down to it then; surrender or run. Pete chose the latter.

"Git 'em!" Janeway yelled, "Kill that Yankee bastard!"

The other two fired. One Minie ball clipped the side of Pete's left shoulder, leaving a slight wound. He instinctively twisted his upper body around to his right, still running. The second ball crashed into the extreme left side of his back, parallel to and just below his shoulder blade. Had the first shot not caused him to twist, the second would have penetrated the rear of his rib cage and likely torn his insides to pieces. As it turned out, his previous movement had caused the Minie ball to hit at such an extreme angle it actually ricocheted away, but not before tearing off a sizeable amount of flesh and breaking two ribs. He was knocked to the ground and they were upon him.

"Shoot 'em, God dammit ta hell!" Janeway hollered at the soldier who had shot Pete's gun away, since he had reloaded immediately after firing. Soon the other two had as well. "What the hell y'all waitin' on, a damned *invite?*" Janeway screamed. "That no-account Yankee done kilt our general!"

Dazed but coherent, Pete rolled slightly and glared at Janeway, his disgust magnified by the uniform Clifton was wearing. "If you men are gonna kill a Union officer don't forget that murdering bastard, sorry excuse of an officer that he is," Pete said, pointing a trembling finger at Janeway. The Confederates looked at the Union lieutenant as if he had lost his mind.

"He sure 'nough is, Yank, and Ah'm Queen Victoria's butler. Cain't say Ah'm proud to make your acquaintances though," the soldier who had fired first said. The other two let out chuckles, their Enfield's pointed at Pete's chest.

"We're a'wastin' time Ah says, here, gimme that there gun!" Janeway said as he reached for one of their rifles.

"You hold on," the soldier who had just spoken said, glaring at Clifton as the Rebel shoved him away. "Wish ta hell we'd done shot 'em dead when he skedaddled, but he's our prisoner now. Us boys gonna git us one'a them there citations bringin' this here bastard in, might even git on the firin' squad, 'lessin' they hang 'em. You! Git up!"

They began to march Pete to the rear, taking a southwesterly route through the orchard. Janeway kept trying to convince the men to just shoot Pete, but the soldiers ignored him, having grown tired of him and his mouth.

***

CANNONADE FROM the Confederates had been blasting into the beleaguered Union forces still defending the wagon trace area in front of the Hornet's Nest, and the carnage was heavy. Some, though not many Yankee soldiers had already begun to abandon the bloody wagon trace area, ten of whom had made their way into the peach orchard that was just a short distance east of the current debacle exploding in and near the Hornet's Nest.

The three Rebels who were escorting Pete, and most of the ten Yankees, saw each other at about the same time. The soldiers from both sides reacted swiftly. It was actually Janeway who had spotted the Yankees first, and he had already flattened himself upon the ground.

Pete went down as well. The searing pain from having landed on his wounded ribs caused him to grow so lightheaded he went into a faint. The Union men opened up, dropping two of the Rebels dead. Only one of those two Rebels had fired, hitting no one. The third one, the marksman, had killed the Yankee he had fired upon. He hollered from his vantage point behind a peach tree where the Rebel had taken cover to reload, directing his words at a trembling, apparently immobilized Janeway.

"Grab that there gun 'fore he comes around, take cover behind a tree an' guard the prisoner!" Except for his violent trembling Clifton didn't budge, wishing he could melt into the ground itself. "God damn you!" The Rebel screamed as he reloaded. "If you ain't no Yankee you sure as hell act like one!" He wheeled from behind the tree and fired before the Union men could reload, sending a Minie ball into the chest of a corporal. He ducked back behind the tree after having first grabbed the unfired musket, and that's when Pete pounced on Janeway's back.

His broken ribs felt as if they were stabbing him, but he clawed at Clifton's face and pounded the back of his head with every ounce of strength he could muster. There was a sudden explosion inside Pete's head as he rolled off a screaming Clifton Janeway. Pete landed prostrate on the ground, unconscious. The soldier, not wanting to shoot his prize catch, had hit Pete with the butt of his rifle, but before he could dart back to the safety of the tree six Minie balls tore into him. He flew backwards like an out of control marionette, arms flapping as he tumbled upon the ground.

The loud reports had alerted a group of twenty Confederates fifty yards south of their recently killed comrades. They made a beeline through the trees, stopped and fired all at once towards the Union men. The Yankees had attempted to duck behind some trees themselves; all but two were hit and killed, or were just a few moments from dying.

In the chaos no one had noticed Janeway crawling frantically away on his belly, again demonstrating his impressive retreating skills. He had wanted to kill Pete, but he hadn't a knife and he feared a shot would draw fire from the Union men even if there had been time to grab the unfired musket. Better to hug the ground and slither away, he felt more than actually articulated in his mind; it came as natural as rain to him.

After a very brief conversation the surviving two Union men took off to the north, mindful to avoid any Confederates in that direction as much as possible. The trees they were running through would offer more protection than the ones where they had first taken cover, especially when Confederate re-enforcements arrived. There were other Rebels off to the east, even farther north from the retreating Yankees, but were too far away to realize what was happening since their view was hampered by the numerous peach trees the retreating Union men used to cover their escape as best they could.

The Confederate men south of them started to give chase. Several of them finally said to hell with it. The Yankees were whipped except for the wagon trace area in front of the Hornet's Nest that would soon be surrounded, and it had already been a very long day. Several hot mugs of liberated Yankee coffee around a campfire sounded more like it, maybe some liberated cigars too.

They were about to head back but decided to rifle through the uniforms of the dead Yankees who had just been killed. Most of the other Union corpses and wounded had already been searched, so if they were going to find anything it would likely be on the fresh corpses. They eventually came upon Pete who had begun to regain consciousness. Rifles at the ready, they told him to stay still.

"You move a finger an' we'll blast your Yankee guts to hell and back, boy!" The one closest to Pete yelled. They almost did anyway until a sergeant took over.

"He's a prisoner now men, a no-account Yankee lieutenant too. Ah reckon command headquarters will have a few questions comin' his way."

Janeway had made it back to where he had hidden his uniform and quickly put it on. Hunched over, he made his way back to the rock where he had hidden earlier, looking all around as he did so. He glanced at Sackett's body and marveled at his bloody handiwork.

"Damn, *Major* O'Darcy *sir*, you appear to be feeling poorly. Can I get you anything? Hot mug of tea? Perhaps a bandage or two? I suspect not. Well, why don't you just rest here and rot. I'll be sure to offer my condolences to your lovely sister and her big fat tits."

He poked his head up and looked around again, then quickly took off to the north, crouching as he moved, mindful of the remaining enemy soldiers out front and to the east. At least they were too far away to notice him, as best he could tell. With a little luck, perhaps he could hook up with those two Union men who had retreated in a northerly direction. He would have to hurry though, and that was foremost on his mind. So much so he had failed to see the two Confederate soldiers who had just stood up after searching a few dead Yankees, not fifty yards to the east of him.

"There goes one!" The first Rebel to spot him yelled. "Looks to be a God damned officer too!" Both men fired.

One Minie ball slammed into a tree just as Janeway was going past it, but the other one caught his left shoulder after Clifton had instinctively cringed away from the exploding splinters and bark. The force of the Minie ball at such close range whirled him around and knocked him to the ground, but he leapt to his feet and tried to continue running before his adversaries had a chance to reload. He made it three steps and tumbled screaming to the ground again, clutching his shoulder. He was badly wounded but it could have been much worse. Instead of ricocheting downward that would have likely torn his insides apart, the Minie ball had traveled straight through his body. Only one bone had been broken, but blood was pouring out at an alarming rate. That would have eventually killed him too unless the Confederates who had fired finished him off first.

Another group of Union soldiers had made their way from the besieged wagon trace area, nearly the last men to escape before the position was surrounded. They hollered at the two Rebels to halt, correctly assuming their numbers would create the opposite effect. They were right. Even if the two had been able to reload in time, which wasn't the case, they were outnumbered four to one. The Union men were much relieved when the two Rebels took off on a dead run heading south through the peach trees. Had the Union men released a volley no telling how many of the nearby enemy would have been alerted. They immediately ran over to Clifton who was lurching about on the ground, his screams choked off by his vomiting.

"Don't you worry Captain, we'll get you outta here!" One of them said. He was true to his word.

***

LATER THAT evening, just after dusk, a group of Confederate cavalry officers along with their men rode into the Rebel encampment where Pete was being held prisoner. He had plenty of company; nearly twenty-two hundred Union men had been taken prisoner from the Hornet's Nest alone, including General Prentiss who had fulfilled his promise made earlier in the day to General Grant. He had sworn to defend his position at all costs, and had remained with his men in the wagon trace area even after it had been surrounded, not that he'd had much choice at that point.

For close to two hours, sixty-two Confederate cannons had attempted to rain canister and concussive shells into the wagon trace area. The unrelenting fire had culminated into a deadly, continuous roar, while virtually everything that had once been earth, trees and brush exploded all around the beleaguered Union men, many of whom had been blown literally to pieces. Prentiss's only options had been surrender or what would have amounted to suicide. He had chosen the former.

Pete had been questioned at length and was being taken back to where the other captured Union officers were being held. He was beyond exhausted, with each step creating so much pain in his left side and back he thought he would faint - again. A Confederate doctor had patched him up but there was no way he would have given the prisoner laudanum or anything else to ease Pete's suffering; there wasn't enough for his own wounded comrades, not even after counting what had been liberated from the dead, wounded and captured Yankees.

A Confederate private noticed Pete pass by and glared at the captive officer. Rather than receiving a look of defeat or fear from the Yankee, although Pete harbored both those emotions, Private Gus Primrose saw nothing but contempt intermingled with a cold assurance the prisoner was more than willing to kill him if given the chance.

"Damn, that there Yankee don't know when he's whupped." Gus said to the men he was with who hadn't been paying much attention to Pete. "Reckon his fightin' days 'bout over though. That cain't be no bad thing. Ah do believe he ain't aware of it though."

***

THE COMMANDING officer of the Confederate cavalrymen who were riding slowly through the encampment was talking to the officer riding next to him, glancing around as he spoke. He looked ahead a ways, a little to his left, and glanced at Pete who was walking stiffly towards the officer as the guards marched him past a series of tents illuminated by lanterns swaying in the dying breeze, angled shafts of burnt-orange light reflecting off things closest, muted to a glowing brown before the surrounding night absorbed all traces of illumination. Pete's blouse was torn open revealing the large, blood-soaked bandage on Pete's left side and another on top of his shoulder. He also had a bloody bandage wrapped around his throbbing head and one on his right hand as well. The officer noticed those first then looked more closely at Pete's face, then his torn lieutenant's blouse, then back at his face again.

It had been a very long day for the cavalry officer too, and it showed on his face nearly as much as it did on Pete's. His colonel's uniform was filthy and torn, but it had the appearance of newly acquired dirt and grime, the kind found on an officer who had suffered through his share of fighting for the day, although for that particular officer not near as much as he would have preferred. Just before the officer rode past Pete he took a final look at the prisoner's face.

"God damn, Lieutenant," Colonel Nathan Bedford Forrest remarked to Pete, who returned the officer's steady glare as the Confederate horse soldier passed by. "Satan musta missed draggin' you ta hell where you belong. Just how many God damned lives *do* you possess?"

X

Cusman stood stark still, all but convinced he'd been surprised by the devil. He wasn't sure how to answer Mrs. Jennifer Ransom. Even though it was nearly impossible to make out her expression in the darkness of the pecan grove, the tone of her voice had filled him with wariness. The essence of his father's words again came back to him: "*Seems like it should make sense, thinkin' honesty saves a whole lotta backtrackin'. Hard to remember your lies, least ways all of 'em. Disrememberin' jus' one same as disrememberin' 'em all, most times anyways. Gots to be careful though. Colored folk ain't got the same hand dealt to 'em as white folk. I swear, lotsa times all white folk gonna lose is a crumb off their dignity. Colored folk git the very same hand dealt, an' there go the skin off their hides, sometimes not that bad, other times worse…*"

"You need to listen to Missis, Cusman." Missy Nell said before he could say anything. Both women moved towards the towering man until they were directly in front of him.

"Your plan won't work, Cusman." Mrs. Ransom said. "Even if you make it fifty miles, a hundred, it would be nearly the same if you had gone five. You can't run faster than a telegraph wire. Even if you make it out of Georgia, you'll have two more states to get through. Three or four if you head northeast. Can you imagine the reward Mr. Ransom will offer? Every scoundrel in the South will be looking for you, plenty in the North as well for that kind of money. Avariciousness knows no boundaries."

"Who said a thing 'bout runnin' Missis? Just wanted some alone time with Missy, that's all, beggin' your pardon."

"It's all right Cusman, just listen!" Missy Nell responded before Mrs. Ransom had a chance to do so, then looked with anticipation towards the woman.

"I am *not* going to allow Missy Nell to undertake such a foolhardy and dangerous journey, young man. Not without me."

Cusman was speechless. Had he misunderstood her? Had she somehow meant to say something else?

"Your plan has several flaws," Mrs. Ransom continued. "The most glaring is obvious. Two coloreds traveling alone, especially the two of you, would draw more attention than you can possibly imagine, or so your current behavior suggests. Forgive me if I sound patronizing, but the two of you are simply too handsome to go unnoticed even by the most casual observer. Professional slavers will be able to easily track you with the most superficial queries."

Cusman drew a deep breath and exhaled, trying to look first at Missy Nell then Mrs. Ransom in the darkness. He knew she was correct, even if his subjective reasoning had seemed valid just moments before. His false hope had been addicting, especially when its antithesis spelled inevitable doom. That was at the heart of their dilemma - wasn't any risk, given the circumstances, worth taking? During his darkest moments Cusman had even considered stealing Mr. Ransom's new .44 caliber Colt Lawman revolvers. He would keep two rounds no matter what, unbeknownst to Missy Nell. If they were caught up in a dilemma that afforded no escape…well, there would certainly be one way of escaping. He hadn't taken the guns, but the ambivalence he felt due to his inaction had never gone away.

"When you said '*not without me*' just what was on your mind, Missis?" Cusman finally asked.

"As you both know, my younger sister Harriet lives in South Carolina with her new husband. I haven't been to visit her yet, although I have several letters from her imploring me to do so. Even Mr. Ransom has asked me if it might not be a good idea for me to go before things get much worse. At least that's how he felt a month ago. If his current trip to Atlanta proves successful he may have a change of mind, at least for an extended visit. A short one however, perhaps two weeks, shouldn't present a problem. Naturally, he would expect me to bring Missy Nell along. I'll also insist you accompany us, Cusman. He may protest at first, saying you are needed here, but he won't deny I will need male assistance. There is no one hereabouts he trusts more than you to undertake such a task. Since my boys are in Europe, I have no white relatives in the vicinity. Other than our boys and his elderly uncles, Trenton has no male kinfolk. Uncle Claudius and Uncle Theo hold off their whiskey drinking until noon on most days, as if a medal should be bestowed honoring their self-control."

The trepidation and uncertainty that had been festering inside Cusman as it had inside Missy Nell until just an hour before had begun to subside. Suddenly, hope contained inspired anticipation. Their forced, illusory scheme had been replaced. Their upcoming trial, despite the wishful thinking they had been previously forced to accept in order to justify their escape had taken on new meaning. He had one major concern.

"Beggin' your pardon Missis, but you know I keep tally of Mas'r's books. He always keeps a close eye on ever'thing. We'll be needin' money to travel in a way fittin' your position and such, 'specially since we'll be headin' a far ways past South Carolina, Lord willin'. Don't see how you kin git enough without him findin' out, I s'pect sooner than later, too."

"Don't you worry about that, Cusman," she answered. "Don't you worry about that at all."

***

UPON REFLECTION Cusman had little reason to question Mrs. Ransom's motives, Missy Nell no reason at all. She had always known the woman loved her as a daughter despite the obvious. When Mrs. Ransom had appeared unexpectedly while Missy Nell had been putting her best clothes in a valise earlier that evening, the young slave had told her everything.

She knew her mistresses' heart to its core, and that knowledge had been the catalyst when having to tell a lie, and not just any lie, to the woman she in turn loved like a mother was the other option. It was a departure from Missy Nell's previous mindset, one that had made sense only in theory. Indeed, once Mrs. Ransom had gazed into Missy Nell's eyes with an expression void of anger, betrayal or requital, sorrow and love were all Missy Nell had seen, tainted as it had been by fear for the girl's safety. Missy Nell had melted at the sight and followed her own heart.

Jennifer Ransom wasn't naïve. She had suspected all along what the two young people had been planning, especially after that day in the parlor when she and her husband had argued. Cusman had thought he hadn't been spotted eavesdropping but that wasn't true. Had he been able to see as well as hear his owners, he would have noticed Mrs. Ransom had moved towards the south window so her husband would be facing her in that direction and not towards the doorway outside of which Cusman had been hiding. She had noticed him pass by out of the corner of her eye, but Cusman hadn't realized she had done so. She had purposely encouraged her husband to lose his temper, to disclose more than he normally would have done. Trenton didn't know it but his wife was fully aware the recent, catastrophic events demanded they leave Whisper Manor. The difference was when and how, and most importantly to her, with whom.

She enjoyed her privileged life and most that came with it, but not enough to forsake her only daughter or the young man her daughter loved. It was a mystery to her, the way so many of her peers could profess love for someone who happened to be a slave then choose, over their professed feelings, the agony of watching them sold or abused in any way. Did mothers love daughters less because they were adopted? If not, was that love inherently conditional if their daughters weren't of the same race?

She knew Trenton could never understand her feelings for her daughter or that Missy Nell even was her daughter. Jennifer wasn't as shocked as she had appeared when he had verified her understanding of his true nature that fateful day in the parlor. No, he could never understand how she felt any more than he would be able to understand why she was willing to forsake him and everything he stood for.

There was no denying she had loved some things about him, all things considered. There were others aspects of his personality that she loathed, however. The slightest gestures made by men he knew found her attractive, which in his mind included virtually all men, could send him into a childish rage. How many times had he questioned her at length over trifling, innocent occurrences over the years? During those times, he hadn't backed off until she had been either in tears or so angry she had stormed away in the middle of his inquisition.

Other than that glaring deficiency he did have certain qualities, but the priority those attributes held in her heart couldn't even be defined as such, not in comparison to her feelings for Missy Nell. Jennifer wasn't the same person she had been years before when she too was capable of certain rationalizations regarding race, before Missy Nell had come into her life.

It was time to leave her husband alone with his irrational jealousies and rigid intolerance; it was time to save her daughter.

***

TRENTON RANSOM arrived home with news. Three men had established a partnership and had made an offer on Whisper Manor. The negotiations were still ongoing, but the last price the men had offered wasn't too far off the one Trenton had set as his absolute lowest amount. His Atlanta attorney and his real estate broker had both pleaded with him to accept it, but Trenton felt guardedly optimistic at least one more increase would be forthcoming, perhaps two. Time was an obvious consideration, but to Trenton a gamble worth taking.

One of the men had once lived in Beaux Hollow where he still owned property. He was familiar with the grounds and of course the high quality of the slave stock. Even if times were at best uncertain, there was no doubt in the man's mind he and the others could recoup the majority of their investment by selling off but half of them. Once the South either won the war outright or at least negotiated a just peace which would of course include the continuation of slave ownership if not the slave trade itself, the remaining slaves would increase in value along with their offspring and the rest of Whisper Manor. Trenton believed it was that man who would convince the other two to increase their offer. It was also the same man who had made specific references regarding Missy Nell.

"Ah have seen me some pretty quadroon gals in mah day," he had remarked over some sour mash and cigars one evening in Atlanta, "but that beauty surpasses 'em all. Ah know of a man in New Orleans that will pay top dollar fer her. He owns the grandest bordello in Louisiana and another one in San Francisco reputed to be even more grandiose. Has another one in Mexico City, where he sends his whores once they been used up. A sordid business to be sure, but the price he'll gladly pay fer that ravishin' nigger gal will indeed be substantial. Wouldn't mind samplin' a taste'a her mah own damn self."

Trenton, of course, refrained from bringing that up once he was home. He felt uneasy about it, but business was business and "a nigger was a nigger" he reminded himself. Did he grieve when a prize mare was sold off for breeding purposes? He found comfort in that, and besides, there was always the chance the new owner might keep Missy Nell around for that very purpose. Why, he would probably keep Cusman too. Those two could easily produce offspring who would no doubt bring the highest price for little pickaninnies at any auction. After realizing the profit of, say, five or six little nigger children, Trenton had reasoned, the new owner could sell off Missy Nell to his bordello-owning acquaintance even if she would only be good for Mexico City after the effects of so many childbirths had taken its toll. A sad end to be sure, but Trenton was convinced the times demanded such sacrifices.

Trenton had indeed kept all that to himself when he discussed the potential sale of Whisper Manor to his wife, but if he believed that would in any way fool Jennifer he was mistaken. When he told her there was a very good chance Missy Nell and Cusman would be kept on, all she did was smile before she spoke.

"Trenton, that is a great relief to hear. Once we're away from here my heart will be at peace knowing those two have been spared a more uncertain fate." Trenton returned her smile, convinced his grateful wife had found comfort in his words, as he had in hers.

Towards the end of that conversation Jennifer mentioned her plans to visit her sister. She also mentioned how she was at a loss, however, to come up with any ideas regarding whom she might bring along, besides Missy Nell of course.

"Well my dear," Trenton responded, "it would naturally have to be kinfolk or a trusted slave. Cusman comes to mind, as long as your stay isn't too extended. He's needed here, you know. Were you planning to be there more than two weeks or so?"

"Oh, I don't suppose so, Trenton. I would imagine my stay at sister Harriet's wouldn't last even that long."

***

AFTER WRITING her sister and receiving a positive response, one filled with anticipation, Jennifer, Missy Nell and Cusman were about to depart. The wagon that was to take them to the Atlanta train station was loaded with trunks, smaller luggage and other containers. There were so many things Trenton Ransom couldn't resist a little ribbing as he stood next to the wagon.

"It never ceases to amaze me just how much a lady deems essential, my dear. I'll count my blessings, however. At least you will have no need to fatten the pockets of those expensive Atlanta dry merchants you're so fond of before catching your train!" Jennifer appeared to share in her husband's mirth, and that warmed him.

"No Trenton, I have already taken so much from you."

"Nonsense, my dear. But I would be appreciative if you would take along a few more things besides the funds I've allotted you, and the money I've allotted to have a man drive the wagon back. Cusman? Come here, boy." Trenton handed him a leather case containing the two Colt Lawman revolvers, along with double holsters and an ample supply of ammunition.

"Just in case," he said in a hushed tone. "Keep them concealed, however. White men that don't know you will be alarmed if you don't. Why, I can only imagine my own response if I saw a strange buck with that much fire power, especially a nigger big as you."

"Thank you, Mas'r suh. I'll keep 'em hid but close at hand if I really needs 'em."

"You're a good boy, Cusman. Best nigger I ever owned." Then Trenton looked again at his wife and Jennifer at him.

"Safe journey my dear."

Jennifer paused before responding, a forced smile upon her face.

"Goodbye, Trenton."

Cusman snapped the reins and they were off. Jennifer couldn't turn around and wave goodbye, not at first. Her eyes were brimming with tears, so she waited until they were far enough away before she turned and waved.

"Lost. All of this lost forever." She uttered softly to no one in particular as she gazed about the spacious grounds of Whisper Manor. The smile on her face faded away as she spoke. She again turned back and looked at Trenton, and reignited the dispirited smile that was filled with emotions that belied the look on her face. With profound regret, reinforced by resolve, she waved what she believed was her final goodbye.

XI

The newspaper accounts of Captain Clifton Janeway's heroics at the Battle of Shiloh were the talk of Naperville and points beyond. Clifton's father had again made sure the local paper had every detail of his son's daring exploits, just as they had been described in Clifton's long letter home he had sent from the hospital where he was recovering. An abbreviated version of Clifton's gallantry even made the Chicago papers.

Buford Janeway saw to it General Smithington had also received a hand-copied duplicate of the letter and a bank draft for five thousand dollars along with Buford's insistence in the form of a request that Clifton receive another citation for his bravery. The general had little else to go on, or worry about more like it, since the surviving men of the 1st Naperville hadn't had much to add. As far as anyone knew only one officer from the outfit, Captain Janeway, had survived the peach orchard.

The letter, for the most part, contained Clifton's account of what had occurred during and after the battle in the peach orchard. All the 1st Naperville men who survived that ordeal hadn't even seen Captain Janeway there except just before the battle had begun. He wasn't seen again by any of them until he was upon a stretcher behind the lines.

The Union soldiers who had retreated from the Hornet's Nest who had carried the wounded captain to safety confirmed what they believed was Clifton's story, as much as they knew of it anyway, stating he had been shot while attempting to hold off the enemy after the Rebels had killed his commander. Once the Rebels had succeeded in doing so, the only prudent course of action the captain could have followed was to make it back to the Union lines. That he had stayed with his commander as long as he had spoke well of him, as well as how he had covered the Yankee retreat with no regard for his own safety. The men insisted that was the case, and if it hadn't been for their own heroic efforts the Union would no doubt have been short one more officer, and a damned courageous one at that.

That was more than enough for General Smithington. Captain Clifton Janeway was again awarded a citation for bravery and promoted to the rank of major. He was also ordered home until he had made a complete recovery. Once Clifton had been fully satisfied that it was indeed a non-rescindable order he protested, and his statement was reported by the local as well as Chicago papers:

My main concern, obviously, is thwarting the Rebellion, but I would be perjuring myself if I did not confess to my more human emotions. I cannot rest until I have avenged the deaths of my fellow officers, especially Major Sackett O'Darcy and Lieutenant Pete McCabe. May God Almighty speed my recovery so that I may again wield His Terrible Swift Sword in order to not only preserve our beloved Union, but to honor the deaths of two men who were not only my comrades in arms, but my very dear friends as well.

Clifton again marveled at his luck. His only reservation was that McCabe may have survived, although he strongly doubted it. There was a chance, he told himself, that at least one of the three Rebels who had been accompanying McCabe to the rear had survived if only long enough to tell his comrades what their prisoner had done to General Johnston. If so, McCabe was surely dead by now. News from the South had reported General Johnston had died in battle, but no mention had been made of any Union soldier being caught and punished for it. No matter, Clifton allowed himself to believe. The Rebels likely felt releasing that information would serve them no purpose. Putting a Union officer in front of a firing squad, or worse yet hanging him for performing his duty could produce dire consequences for their own captured officers. Besides, even if McCabe was alive he was no doubt in a prison camp and obviously hadn't been involved in an exchange. That was another reason to believe the Rebels knew what he had done to General Johnston; no way would they release their premier general's killer. What were the odds of him surviving that ordeal?

What were the odds indeed; that was something he continued to dwell upon regardless of what he wanted to believe. And what were the odds of possibly a few, even just one fellow prisoner in some prison camp surviving, someone who McCabe had confided in? That was one possibility Janeway couldn't dismiss, at least at first. Then a thought struck him.

So what if some former prisoner did show up with McCabe's version of what had happened? That man's account could be dismissed. What difference would the mindless ranting of a man clearly affected by his ordeal make? It was already common knowledge in the North that the conditions in Southern prison camps were more than enough to drive any number of men insane, Clifton surmised, even if the atrocities that would visit prison camps on both sides hadn't as yet wholly materialized. They were certainly bad enough, though. Clifton could only imagine how such a fate would affect him; Clifton always looked at things that way. What good would the word of such a man, or men, be against a major who had twice been awarded a citation for bravery for his exploits, the second one substantiated by at least eight honored Union soldiers besides Clifton himself? Only McCabe's word would likely carry weight - if he had even survived to begin with.

There was no cause for concern, Janeway concluded, no cause at all - as long as Pete McCabe, assuming he was even alive, never got the chance to speak for himself. Money, enough of it anyway, could purchase most anything, including the services of the most highly competent mercenaries, the greedier the better. Chicago was no doubt home to such men. If McCabe was alive he could probably be found. Clifton again discounted the likelihood of that being needed. Even if one of those three Rebs hadn't lived long enough to tell what McCabe had done to their precious General Johnston, there had been other Rebs close by, and with all the gunfire Clifton had witnessed it was highly unlikely McCabe had survived even if his body hadn't been found. Clifton again rationalized things based on how he would have reacted. *Hell, it's a damn sight easier to just shoot someone like that and throw some dirt over him than go to the trouble of keeping him prisoner...*Clifton doubted he had anything to worry about - anything at all — although saying that to himself wasn't capable of extinguishing a pestering disquietude that lingered in his deeper recesses.

***

MAJOR CLIFTON Janeway arrived in Naperville to a joyous crowd. Some of them wanted him to autograph copies of newspaper accounts of his exploits or other things they were carrying. Once others saw that happening they clamored for the same. One attractive young lady even wanted him to autograph the bonnet her infant daughter was wearing.

The crowd wanted him to make a speech although he initially declined, citing his still mending wounds and the weariness he felt from his long, arduous trip. In truth, he had spent the previous two nights in Chicago at the Hotel Sherman with two hopelessly depraved sixteen-year-old prostitutes, and was nursing a colossal hangover. After more urging, which not only came from the crowd but from the town mayor himself, Major Janeway stepped to the podium upon the makeshift stage.

"My fellow Napervillians, your warm welcome is more than I, one of but many servants-in-arms at your disposal, deserves. You have humbled me to my core. My only wish is that someday soon, a day we all know is coming, I will be able to join you in celebrating our inevitable victory over the forces of Southern tyranny. But I have misspoke; I beg your forbearance, for I am weary and not yet at full strength from my wounds. I have another wish, one that will not come to fruition until God Almighty and my personal Savior the Lord Jesus Christ, beckons me home. That wish is to again be reunited in heaven with my brave brothers-in-arms and dear, dear friends, the late Major Sackett O'Darcy and the late Lieutenant Pete McCabe. Many a night while recuperating from my grievous wounds, hovering near death but not fearing it, I found myself dwelling upon the battle that took them from us, and I have often wondered if there could have possibly been anything, any small thing at all, in the heat of that dreadful battle I may have overlooked, something more I could have done to prevent their tragic, though very brave, sacrifices."

"You done all you could, Major!" An emotional man, moved beyond restraint, called out from the crowd.

"I thank you kind sir," Janeway responded with a tearful smile, then continued. "Allow me, my dear friends, to close with a solemn oath: Lord Jesus, with You and our Holy Father and these fine citizens as my witness, I pledge to return to the good fight if it is your will I recover sufficiently from my life threatening wounds in order to fulfill my sacred duty to of course You, dear Jesus, these fine people and all freedom loving, real Americans everywhere, and to the souls of my dear, departed comrades, Major Sackett O'Darcy and Lieutenant Pete McCabe. Thank you my beloved townspeople, and may God in His mercy and wisdom shelter you now, and in the years to come!"

The roar from the crowd was as deafening as it was continuous. Men and women were standing about with tears streaming down their faces, and all but the most inhibited didn't feel a wisp of embarrassment.

"I sincerely hope you have, as usual, some cognac in the carriage, Father." Clifton said as he made his way off the platform. The two of them made their way towards the waiting carriage amidst the uninterrupted ovation, stopping only once when Clifton spotted the young lady who had requested he autograph her baby daughter's bonnet. He said a few words to her, taking in her voluptuous figure when she had looked briefly away, alarmed as she was by the pressing crowd. The two of them were somewhat jostled about in the frenzy. Clifton winced when his left arm was barely touched. It was concealed in a large, white sling that stood in stark contrast to his Yankee blue major's tunic. His right hand, however, wasn't immobilized; far from it.

"Imagine that Father," he said when the two of them had continued on their way, "that round-assed little tart isn't wearing a bustle."

Buford Janeway smiled.

***

LATER THAT evening the two men were in front of a fire in the library. Buford and Clifton were finishing off the remains of a bottle of 1811 *Bisquit Dubouche* cognac Buford had been saving for a special occasion. He poured the last of it into their Nachtmann cut crystal snifters then looked at Clifton with a great deal of pride.

"I have something for you, son," he said, reaching inside his smoking jacket. Buford handed Clifton a savings account passbook.

"What have we here, Father? This is my passbook."

"Haven't seen it in a while, have you son."

"Of course not. It's nice to see it now, though. Let's see how much interest has accumulated on $25,000 these past months." Clifton opened the book and grew light-headed, and not just because of the expensive cognac. "Father, I am at a loss for words. Apparently you have something to tell me."

Back in his chair, all Buford did was light a fresh Havana cigar, take a sip from his snifter and smile. He had been waiting for this moment for what had seemed a long time, ever since he had heard of his son's latest heroics.

"I was going to wait until you reached thirty, but after what you have been through and because it has made me so very proud of you, I thought now was a good time for you to have the means befitting a soldier of your rank, privilege and courage."

Clifton sat there in shock. For once, he truly was speechless. His current balance was $1,025,150 to do with as he pleased.

***

THE PALL that hung over the McCabe farm appeared to have denied the arrival of spring. Even its colors seemed drained of their hues. Instead of soft pastels and the more vibrant colors usually associated with the season's arrival, everything seemed to be cloaked in varying shades of gray on the sunniest of days. The seasonal array of color was certainly present, but no one in the McCabe family really noticed, or cared more like it.

Mother Grace had begun to tend her perennials one morning, but after a short while she simply dropped her wooden box of gardening tools upon the ground and went back inside, moving slowly, in search of her faith. It had never been difficult to locate before, but of late had a way of enshrouding itself with grief and fear, but not absolute uncertainty; far from it. She didn't know the details, but she knew enough.

The only word from the War Department came in the form of a telegram:

WE REGRET TO INFORM YOU THAT YOUR SON,
MCCABE, KEITH A., LT. 1st NAPERVILLE CAVALRY
IS MISSING IN ACTION AND PRESUMED DEAD.

Father Benjamin had been the first to read it. He had always been an avid reader of newspapers and periodicals, and had been following the accounts of Shiloh with special interest because he knew the 1st Naperville had been involved. He had read all about Clifton Janeway's account but hadn't believed a word of it, especially the part about Clifton's new found friendship with his son and Sackett O'Darcy. Then the telegram had arrived.

He had taken the stark telegram with him to the same spot where he always seemed to end up when the effects of a crisis or its antithesis required solitude.

Standing in the High Hayloft, he had struggled with just how he could possibly break the news to his wife. He had known she needed to be informed, but unbeknownst to him, telling her was unnecessary. Mother Grace already knew a tragedy of no small magnitude had occurred and she knew it involved Kee. She didn't need a stone-cold telegram to inform her of anything.

When Father Benjamin found her in their bedroom a little before noon kneeling by the same window she always chose for her special prayers, he left the telegram in his pocket. He stood silently in the doorway as a strange sensation washed over him. She was about to tell him more than he could pretend to tell her; he just knew it.

Some folks swore hair could turn white overnight if the trauma was profound enough, but he never believed it. Still, it appeared as if the auburn highlights of her long chestnut hair had indeed whitened, at least more so than he could recall.

"Kee is not dead Benjamin. In harm's way somewhere very frightening, but not dead. Go tell Billy." She said, not turning away from the window.

Billy was on the front porch slumped in a chair when Father Benjamin came out to him.

"Kee is alive, William. I don't know how Mother knows it, but there it is. *Where* he is goes begging, as does any solid hope he'll be alive tomorrow, but there it is."

***

NO ONE from the McCabe Family had been amongst the crowd to greet Clifton Janeway. Whether anything he had already said held a thimble of truth meant nothing to them. If the truth had ever come out of Clifton's mouth it was mere coincidence; something that conveniently coincided with an ulterior motive; either that, or something impossible for him to deny. Like his father, no moral obligation would ever pry it from him. The McCabe family hadn't been in town when Clifton arrived but Delicia O'Darcy had been, keeping herself away from the crowd.

She hadn't recognized Clifton when he had first stepped unsteadily from the carriage, an exaggerated movement that fooled everyone, including Delicia. He had lost a great deal of weight and although he certainly wasn't a short man, he had appeared taller than she remembered once he had pulled himself up to his full height and waved to the adoring crowd. He had looked handsome in his new major's uniform; even the white sling that cradled his left arm had given him the appearance of an attractive warrior/hero, as did his long, blonde hair that on a man of low rank would have appeared shaggy and unkempt. Not on the returning hero though. She was convinced certain females would take notice of Janeway's appearance, but she held fast to her contempt.

Delicia had told herself she wanted to ask him about Pete and her brother, but the large crowd had been so aroused she never got the chance. She didn't have long to wait.

***

HE APPEARED the following morning at the hospital, supposedly to have his shoulder checked. Doc Wygant wouldn't even talk to Clifton; examining his all but completely healed wound was out of the question. Dr. Gilbert Van Craig offered his services however, jumping at the chance to become the personal physician of a bona fide war hero.

"That man's void of all shame or a blind fool, both I'd wager." Doc Wygant said to Delicia who was wrapping bandages.

"Which one?" She inquired, only half in jest.

"That incompetent old drunkard, that's who!" Doc Wygant replied, not caring who heard. "Not that Janeway's any better, but you would think a man with a shred of dignity would know enough to stay away from here after the things I've said to him, which I suppose explains everything." Doc Wygant glanced over at the two men, and shook his head in disgust as Van Craig continued to fawn all over his new found idol. "That obsequious old fool is about to make me lose my breakfast, damn his eyes. I have half a mind to -"

"Then engage the commonsensical half of your mind, doctor." Delicia replied, smiling. She was one of a very small number of people who could banter with Doc Wygant that way, and regardless of how he responded it was obvious he loved it.

Clifton let out a yelp. "You drunken, reeking imbecile, mind what you're doing!" He finally said.

"Well now, it appears our young Janeway is at least a fair judge of physicians." Doc Wygant announced loud enough for everyone to hear as he left the room.

After unceremoniously dismissing Van Craig who had left sulking, Clifton approached Delicia. It occurred to both of them it was the first time they had ever been even marginally alone. She continued to wrap bandages as if they were needed immediately, not looking at him until he was directly beside her.

Just prior to her glance, Clifton had cast an eye over her figure, especially her breasts. He found it tantalizing to recall how firm they had felt, with just enough young girls' softness to enhance their perfection, he recalled. *And so large*, he said to himself before diverting his gaze just in time. *How on earth can they possibly sit so upright?* After looking into his pale blue eyes that were already back to her face, awash with sincerity, she went back to her bandages.

"Miss O'Darcy, I don't know if you took the opportunity to read the letter I sent you, and will understand if you did not. So much has happened since then, so many,

many things I wish I could undo, as I wish I could undo that terrible night in the rain, for which I can offer no excuse. A letter is a poor substitute for an apology offered in person, so please allow me the opportunity to offer it now, and to tell you how deeply my heart aches for your brother, and of course for you and your bereaved family."

Delicia placed the bandages upon the table in front of her and again looked at him. If all expressions could somehow be sincere, the implied remorse flowing from Clifton was on the verge of sainthood.

"I did read your letter Mr. Janeway. Had it not been for your abominable behavior on the night you mentioned I might have been somewhat moved, but then you would not have had cause to write it, would you?" Her gaze was steady, void of all emotion except simmering contempt. "What happened to Pete and Sackett?"

"I was with Major O'Darcy when those screaming heathens murdered him, trying my best to desperately fight them off, as was he of course. He was such a brave man, more courageous than any ten men I know save your dear Pete, and I'm loath to tell you it was that unswerving bravery and devotion to duty that was your brother's undoing. Six of those murdering Rebels charged our position, foolishly assuming we needed to reload. Major O'Darcy — Sackett, as he eventually preferred I call him - leapt to his feet and opened fire, as did I. We had those new repeating Spencer rifles but the Rebels were not aware of that, or too ignorant to realize what those rifles can do. He dropped four of them, I was fortunate enough to stop two, or so I thought. The last one got off a hip shot as he fell, and the Minie ball found Sackett. A moment doesn't go by when I don't curse myself for not dispatching that murderer with a more accurate shot. Sackett would have done as much for me, but then he was an expert marksman."

"And Pete?" Delicia asked, holding the side of the table as she awaited Janeway's response.

"Dear Pete. I thank God we had at least the opportunity to settle our differences before he died. To be sure, we had become fast friends once I discarded my old ways, accepted Jesus Christ as my personal savoir and heeded Pete's, and Sackett's wise council. I owe a great debt to both of those fine men. If ever -"

"What happened to Pete, Clifton?"

Clifton. That did not pass without notice. He looked upwards, near tears as he gazed out the large window that was across the room. Her eyes had followed his just briefly, and when she looked away he again stole a glance at her breasts that were straining against her thin cotton blouse. She looked back at him again, but he had brought his eyes back just in time (another of his talents) let out a sigh, and continued.

"This will be hard, Delicia, perhaps you should be seated." She didn't protest his using her Christian name, which encouraged as well as titillated him.

"I'll be fine, Clifton. Please continue."

"Pete was to our left, perhaps sixty or seventy yards away among the peach trees. It was imperative he reposition himself, so he took off for the cover of a fallen tree resting on a slight rise. He was attempting to protect Sackett and me by covering our left flank, if you'll forgive my military jargon, and that's when tragedy struck I'm sorry to say. A shell came screaming in from behind, misfired by our own Union comrades in the rear. Sackett and I were so preoccupied with our own predicament we didn't look until we heard the explosion. Everything was so loud upon that field of battle, so deafening, it took an explosion that close to get what little attention we could afford to muster, if that makes any sense at all. When we did glance that way there was a large hole where the fallen tree, and sad to say our dear Pete, had been just moments before. They have reported him missing in action but - are you sure you won't take a seat, Delicia?"

"I'm quite sure Clifton. Please, I must know."

"They have reported him missing in action, but truth be told that is only because they never located his body. It could have been placed in a mass grave after the battle, as the Rebels are fond of filling their fresh dug pits with no regard for rank or anything else. Fonder still to throw our boys into them piled on top one another, and they had command of the orchard and surrounding areas long enough to complete such a grisly task, but I fear that's not the worst of it. Both Sackett and I agreed, just moments before he too was taken from us, there wasn't much left of Pete at all, much less to bury. We have witnessed our fair share of the results from a direct hit from one of those deadly projectiles, and poor Pete was at the very center of one, God rest his brave soul. At least he didn't suffer."

At that Delicia did take a seat, buried her head in her arms that she had placed upon the table and began to weep. Her shoulders heaved as her sobs increased in intensity, and it was at that moment Clifton reached over and gently handed her his silk handkerchief. She sat up and turned towards him to accept it then thanked him, although her words were choked with tears. She placed the handkerchief over her eyes, but before she could turn back to the table Clifton again glanced at her breasts. He shook his head slowly from side to side, a faint smile appearing on his lips.

*It is truly amazing. Just how on **earth** can those beauties sit so upright?*

***

JANEWAY COULDN'T stop thinking about her as he rode home later that morning. Delicia had always been, by Clifton's appraisal, the most attractive girl in town and points beyond even when they were children. He recalled those days, back when all of them had attended school together at the Naper Academy. She had also been the first girl her age to mature, unable to hide her emerging womanhood. He recollected how it must have caught her off guard, and no doubt her parents, at least for a short while during the fall of their sixth grade year in school. For the better part of two weeks she had appeared at school dressed in clothes she had obviously outgrown, and although Clifton hadn't been the only boy to notice, he had been the only one to do something about it.

The O'Darcy property had a secluded pond tucked not far from their house, one where Delicia and her sisters sometimes swam as did their brothers. Clifton had never been invited by Sackett or his younger brother James to go swimming there. Other boys had, on days when the girls wouldn't be present of course. He heard about the swimming parties though, and deeply resented his repeated exclusions.

He had sneaked into the woods adjacent to the pond one afternoon, but not during one of the boys' outings. Well hidden, he had watched as the O'Darcy sisters frolicked about in the water the fall nights had already begun to cool. A thirteen-year-old Delicia had exited the pond, and had gone to get a towel that had been hung on a low limb not twenty feet from where Clifton had been hiding. She had been dressed of course, but not as much as her parents would have deemed prudent. All she had been wearing was a thin, cotton slip which clung to her every emerging curve, its translucency having left little to a young Clifton's imagination.

He never could get that imagine out of his mind, not that he wanted to. It seemed as if every time he came upon any pond in the years that followed, images of Delicia standing there all but naked would return, but in his fantasies she had on nothing at all. The tantalizing image again toyed with him as he rode on that day. If only he could see her that way now, he fantasized.

His thoughts turned to other childhood experiences as he rode along. The constant rejection by his classmates and other children, except the few who were themselves rejects, were foremost amongst his recollections. Even those children had placed him low on the overall pecking order, displaying a puerile cruelty that comes by some children so naturally.

As they entered their teen years his family's wealth helped cement certain relationships with some of his peers, but friendships as defined by the more likeable, usually popular children never lasted nor had they really existed to begin with. Some relationships had started to blossom in that manner, but Clifton had always seemed to find a way to ruin them. He began drinking at an early age, and although he had managed to hold onto a few so-called friends by always paying for their whiskey and beer, he knew what would happen if he ever stopped doing so, and he always despised them for it after he had sobered. Often times while he was still drunk.

He forced those memories from his mind and again contemplated his recent encounter with Delicia. Something wasn't right. He attempted to concentrate within his more characteristic fantasies, ones which kept her an object of at least servility, but something else kept intruding. He again sought shelter in the comfort of his more nefarious images of her, ones where she was performing a variety of perversions upon him and Clifton upon her, but they kept trailing off.

He recalled how she hadn't been blatantly hostile, far from it towards the end of their conversation. She had even used his Christian name and had not protested when he had used hers. She had also thanked him when he had offered her the handkerchief for her tears. There appeared a small flicker then, an intermittent gleam of something besides his usual reaction to arousal, although he had yet to recognize what it may have been. It wavered close to oblivion but was still there and growing, although his depraved fantasies never disappeared for long and soon held sway.

***

THERE WAS a large hole in Billy, regardless of what his father had told him. It was full of denuded emotions he had never been forced to deal with in his entire life. His older brothers, especially Pete, had always been so invincible. Billy wanted to accept his mother's confident appraisal of his brother's fate; his father apparently had, but for once he doubted their previously wise council and especially the conclusion they had apparently reached.

He had also begun to doubt his faith in God; those feelings had been teetering recently which was also something new. They had now steadied themselves and the result had proven to be as frustrating as it was guilt ridden. How could the all loving, all powerful Creator Billy had always adored have allowed such a travesty as the current war to begin in the first place? Worse yet, to have visited such agony upon Billy's loving family? It seemed selfish for him to feel that way, Billy realized, but he couldn't deny its existence.

Alone in the barn, with only his pet goat Jefferson Davis and Black Hat for company, he asked his animal friends the following: "If a wretch like me, a mere mortal, has a loving and understanding enough heart to have prevented such misery if it was within my power to have never allowed it to been borne, how could a divine being whose love and compassion is supposed to dwarf mine failed to have done so when it is easily within His power to do so?"

"Good question, Billy boy." Doc Wygant said, having appeared at the barn door as if he had taken a shortcut from somewhere Doc probably couldn't define either, much less explain. "I confess to having asked myself that very same one on many occasions when my contempt and/or frustration boiled over, but I have yet to apologize for my heresy and I sure as hell haven't come up with an answer. You having any luck?"

Billy whirled around, startled but not completely surprised. He had long ago given up trying to make sense of the old man's uncanny appearances and other peculiarities. His horse and buggy were in all likelihood somewhere close by, but Billy wouldn't have been shocked, at least not completely, if his mentor had simply materialized.

"No sir. Can't even catch a whiff of it."

"You're not alone, son. At least you have the sand to not only ask it, but dismiss convenient answers. Lord knows those damned Baptists have enough of them, although I admit to a certain prejudice when it comes to those holy rollers. Truth is, they don't have a corner on the subjective rationalization market. Hell, *plenty* of nervous folks are just as content with their ability to invent what's needed to help them sleep nights, and don't even get me started on Southern Baptists! Some French fellow named Baudeliare said '*The greatest trick the devil ever played was convincing the world that he did not exist*' or some such thing, but I don't buy that hog swallow. Satan's greatest trick is, and always has been, to get his most devout followers often times to fancy themselves devout holy rollers more like it. Bet that sure frustrates the hell out of God. Does me anyhow."

"What's left then, Doc?"

"Life! Living it! Hell, do you realize how lucky we were just to have been born? Why, there's millions and millions of sperm cells that don't get the egg. If that's not lucky, I don't know what is, unless of course it is not. Some folks would swear to that philosophy anyway, if it can be called such. We should thank God for whatever years we have, most of us anyway, and not get so greedy and selfish pining away for some fanciful God damned eternity!"

"I thought you didn't believe in God, Doc."

"As others define Him I don't, the old scoundrel! He's the one who gave us just enough brains to raise the questions, but not enough to come up with the answers, not enlightened ones anyway. We get to suffer though, He made damned sure of that. He sure as hell knows it too. We're gonna have words when I run into Him. He'll have all the answers probably, but I'm still gonna give Him a piece of my mind. Maybe He just has a peculiar sense of humor. If He can prove that to me where I still don't want to tan His holy hide, well now, *that* would be one hell of an impressive God damned miracle."

"Doc, I fear you're goin' straight to hell."

"Suits me to the ground, if heaven is where all those God damned holy rollers keep endin' up! Had my fill of them here, no disrespect meant to your ma, Billy boy. She's as good as a soul gets. It gets confusing from there, son, not that it wasn't before. My apologies for not having the answers for you. Tell you one thing though. Don't dismiss your mother's enlightenments. God favors that woman, and should be ashamed of Himself for not makin' more like her. Must not be as easy as it appears, even if He obviously knows how to do it. He sure feels compelled to produce the exact opposite in prodigious numbers, assuming it's Him doing it. If it ain't, all that hog swallow about Him being all-powerful goes begging. Anyone says that isn't hog swallow sure must have a powerful urge to hold onto what they know is a load of mule dung. Otherwise, I would imagine they'd do a hell of a lot more singing a merry tune and a damn sight less bawling when they bury a loved one. God damned hypocritical cowards if you ask me. How's the goat?"

"What? Oh, President Davis is fine. Thanks for asking."

XII

Pete, delirious, sick with fever and in agony, had ended up in a boxcar after the Battle of Shiloh. It wasn't near as crowded as the ones for enlisted Union prisoners. Although less crowded, the officers' boxcar wasn't much better. There was straw available, but unlike the others the hay in the officer's boxcar could be used for resting upon; the officers didn't have to shovel out most of it at each stop since it wasn't imbued with excrement, urine and vomit like the other boxcars. The officer's boxcar came with buckets and lids, since there were only twenty soldiers of higher rank in Pete's boxcar to begin with. Over fifty men were in each of the enlisted mens' boxcars.

They were being shipped to the Salisbury prison encampment located in the western third of North Carolina, but none of the prisoners were aware that was their eventual destination. They knew the train was heading east, at least at first; just assumed it later since the train came to many curves and bends, but until their arrival three days later they didn't even know which state they were in.

When they finally arrived the ominous sky had already opened. The cold, relentless rain came in wind-driven sheets, and it was so dark the early afternoon resembled an appalling dusk as foreboding as it was blustery. Pete was ordered into a wagon with ten other wounded men. There was no straw or comforts of any kind, just naked boards, and the crude wagon was without springs or canvas top.

The timeworn wagon had a smell to it, a stench even the drenching rain couldn't wash away. The downpour was prodigious, but only succeeded in mutating the foul odor. Pete and the others didn't know it, but when the wagon wasn't hauling wounded captives it was used for other contaminated tasks, such as transporting bodies to the grave trenches.

Sometimes the bodies, some of them bloated unless the swelling gas had escaped along with oozing, suspicious fluid that seeped into the boards, would remain in the wagon overnight. Those bodies had usually putrefied to an alarming degree, displaying various shades of black and purple upon their swollen faces, hands and most everywhere else, and would still be there well after the hot North Carolina sun had done its worst the following day. The naked planks were indelibly thick with it all.

Pete's broken ribs felt as if they were being kicked every time the wagon hit a rut. The road was more rut than road, so the agony was continuous. His fever had him shaking uncontrollably and his head throbbed with so much pain it made him vomit. Once his stomach was empty, which for the most part it was anyway, dry heaves pulled at his insides. He had a skull fracture, and the lump on the back of his head was the size of an orange. His only respite came when his delirium brought on a surreal semi-unconsciousness, which offered no palpable respite at all.

Others crammed into the jostling wagon were worse off. Some pleaded with the driver for mercy; to pull over and put them on the ground so they could die in relative peace. Their obsession to end the unrelenting agony could not have been more profound. The groans, howls and outright screams never stopped, nor did the sheets of rain, some of which came howling in sideways. Eight grueling miles later they arrived at the Salisbury stockade. The wagon came to a halt by a trench, and three dead soldiers were hauled away by a burying detail. The detail had been waiting in the deluge, assuming correctly they would have work to do.

***

SEVERAL DAYS later a marginally improved Pete and the other officers had demanded they and the other men be allowed to write home, if just to inform their families and other loved ones they were alive. They soon discovered demands made by prisoners were not only ignored in most cases, but often times viewed with contempt.

Dog tags weren't issued by either army during the Civil War, so unless comrades who hadn't been captured could attest otherwise there wasn't much chance of anyone knowing the captives' fate with any degree of accuracy. That was especially true when either side had buried enemy bodies in any type of graves. Often times a truce would be called in order to allow each side the opportunity to gather its own dead and wounded from a battlefield. No such truce had been called immediately after the battle in the peach orchard at Shiloh, since most of the Confederates had advanced in force northward until they had been driven back the following day.

By the time Union burial details were able to make their way back to the peach orchard most of the unburied Union dead had been searched for anything even hinting of value the Confederates could find. It didn't matter much anyway, unless a letter, diary, perhaps the dead soldier's enlistment papers or something else that could offer proof of the dead soldier's identity was found, or someone could identify the corpse. Otherwise, individual identification was all but impossible.

Sackett's body had been recovered, and due to his rank his body had been shipped home after some of the survivors of the 1st Naperville identified it. Since Clifton Janeway had insisted Lieutenant McCabe had been blown to pieces, it came as no surprise when the men on the burying details couldn't find the Lieutenant. He had probably been buried, parts of him anyway. Regardless, they had listed him as missing in action and presumed dead. If something else had occurred, so be it. There was a war to fight.

***

THE JOURNEY to Salisbury had been dreadful, but in relative terms the prison camp wasn't. Developed on sixteen acres that included large oak trees that afforded shade, it wasn't an overly inhospitable place as military prisons went. There were, at least, tents for the prisoners of lower rank and seven structures that served various purposes, including a large four story building that had been the Maxwell Chambers cotton factory during peaceful times.

The prison would become extremely inhospitable years later, horrifically so like prison camps everywhere eventually came to be once prisoner exchange was stopped later in the war. Although Northern camps became abysmal, Southern camps were often times worse. They simply hadn't the provisions to spare, especially after the war dragged on. Ultimately, over 11,700 mostly unidentified Union soldiers, sailors, Union loyalists and suspected spies imprisoned at Salisbury would die from disease, old wounds and malnutrition. They would eventually be buried en masse in the eighteen trenched, mass graves outside the compound.

***

PETE'S WOUNDS finally healed, at least the ones on his body. Inside he was as damaged as ever. As the days wore on, thoughts of home, family and especially Delicia invaded his waking moments on a consistent basis and all his nights were tormented as well. Not a night went by where one nightmare or another didn't descend upon him. Amongst the worst ones, save one particularly gruesome reoccurring dream, were nightmares that almost always put him back in that hellish peach orchard. When those nightmares took over he often times awoke screaming out Sackett's name, or Janeway's. He was lucky when he did awaken at that point. If not, Clifton Janeway was bound to make an appearance, usually howling with glee attired in a bloody Rebel uniform. A satanic Janeway was always armed and appeared more formidable than he could have possibly been in real life. Pete was always powerless to stop him.

A particularly gruesome, reoccurring dream was by far the worst. Pete was home but could never get inside Tin Pan Alley quick enough. He dreaded what awaited him once he did make it in, always through the back door that led to the kitchen. The howls were always there to greet him, as were the mutilated bodies of his family scattered around the large kitchen table, itself having been shattered beyond repair. Sometimes it was all of his brothers and both parents sprawled about in the most grisly of positions. They were still clutching their eating utensils. Blood and gore were everywhere, as well as an appalling stench that mimicked a decaying slaughterhouse, one that might be located in an inescapable, foreboding inner-cityscape cloaked in varying shades of gray; within Pete's delirium the only distinguishable hue of significance was red.

His parents were indeed always butchered, although not on every occasion when he first entered. They always materialized though, hacked to pieces, and the howls coming from somewhere else inside the large house were always present as well. Often times he then heard Delicia's terrified screams intermingled with the unholy howls of Janeway. Sometimes she was pleading for mercy; other times screaming obscenities at Pete for not rescuing her. It was a deep, foreign voice that wasn't recognizable as hers but was Delicia's nonetheless. But the worst screams coming from her didn't resemble screams at all, except the ones he had heard in battle when men had been horribly wounded. In real life those had been hideous enough, but at that point during his nightmare ride Delicia's were beyond any he had ever heard. They were guttural wails that evolved into a kind of blood-choked blubbering, as if she had been disemboweled crotch to sternum and those had been the last sounds to escape Delicia as she watched in horror as her insides spilled upon the floor. The screams and spilling of her insides never ceased though - not the deep-throated blubbering, especially not the endless *spilling*, none of it.

Once he located her, always upstairs in a room with a southern exposure, those things were still happening only with more intensity. Janeway was always standing over her mutilated, naked body or stood close by. Sometimes he was humming a mindless tune and dancing around her, prancing in the gore, waving and kissing her bloody clothing. Others times he simply stood there and laughed hysterically, squeezing torrents of blood and indistinguishable bits of what must have been innards from the same articles of clothing, especially her undergarments.

That was almost always enough to awaken Pete, usually screaming, and regardless of the time of night further sleep was as impossible as it was unwelcome. Prison camp or not he was always grateful to be there, to have escaped the horror, and never failed to acknowledge that hell itself was indeed capable of manifestation whether on a battlefield or within the malignant prison of his nightmares.

Daytime drained Pete and the others as well. Idle within their confinement, there was plenty of time to dwell. The unshakable horror of battle was seared into them all and always would be. Pete wasn't the only one who had lost friends and comrades, but within the cabin he was the only one who had witnessed half his hometown troop killed or seriously wounded. Although his earliest memories were of family, remembrances of those from the 1st Naperville who had been killed were almost as long-lived, many such reminiscences nearly as venerable.

Those childhood memories seemed so alien when juxtaposed beside the scream-ing terror on that bloody hilltop and later within the peach orchard. The horror of that reality defied any attempt on Pete's part to calm his anguish. The memories of the boys with whom he had fished and camped, played the competitive games of youth which at the time they had taken so seriously refused to offer anything except a profound sense of loss that defied reality; it simply couldn't have happened but there he was immersed in it.

Pete recalled the priorities as his friends had defined them during their teenage years - especially the discovery of girls as enchanting beings as opposed to having been merely tolerated just a few years before. Pete had pretended to relate, but De-licia had always meant so much more to him, and in a way he knew many of his friends would have never understood. Later on some of them had certainly under-stood, having fallen in love themselves. Pete wondered if the soul crushing agony created by the death of his friends had abated at all within the hearts of those girl-friends, wives and family members. Was that even possible?

Thoughts of Sackett were always close by, as was the quagmire of hate Pete felt for Clifton Janeway. He believed the likelihood of Janeway having survived the peach orchard was slim, but any thought of the man being dead failed to elicit any mean-ingful solace. Pete wasn't sure what he would feel if he were to someday personally kill Janeway, but he felt certain exacting revenge would allow him a viable direction to follow, if only to lead him away from the entanglements of his present condition. Over and over, day after day, the same thoughts continued to devour him, never abating, always clawing, gripping, squeezing. Then night would come, and the un-welcomed sleep would force itself upon him, hovering, stalking, as if it were waiting for him to be at his most vulnerable before igniting the nightmare rides – over and over, night after night, week after week…

***

APRIL GAVE way to May then June arrived. Prisoner exchanges were still common but not for Pete and the handful of officers who were housed with him. They might have been exchanged if it hadn't been for their failed escape attempt. Only Pete and three others had made the attempt, just four weeks after their arrival. The other of-ficers housed in the rude officers' prison cabin had pleaded with them not to attempt anything of that nature. They had steadfastly maintained it would in all probability not only fail but destroy any chance of them ever being exchanged. As it turned out they were correct on both counts.

Pete had been the ringleader even though there were two captains and a major who outranked him. He had appealed to their honor, stating it was their sworn duty to at least try. All three of the ranking officers were swayed by Pete's argument or at least wouldn't admit otherwise. They too had initially raised the argument of exchange but Pete disagreed:

"Major Miling, you yourself have said the assistant camp commandant has only given you vague assurances, even going so far to admit it could be months before anything might be finalized. If a Rebel says months I suspect years, if we survive that long. What assurances do you have to prove otherwise? We're cut off from all contact from the outside, as all of us know. They won't even let us write home. For all we know exchanges are rare. Doesn't it make sense that if it was yourself in charge of this place you would dangle the same promise of exchange in front of your Union captives, especially the officers? Can you think of a better way to keep men in line and from attempting to escape short of killing them?" Major Miling had no answer, at least not one he wouldn't have felt chagrinned to voice.

Salisbury prison camp was enclosed behind nothing more formidable than a high board fence, so getting through or over it wouldn't be impossible. Getting past the guards was another story, as was making their way to safety once they had managed the other two obstacles.

It had been a rainy, dark night when the four of them went. They had been able to climb atop a storage shed next to the west wall, but the first thing Pete had seen after being the first to make it over the fence was the startling sight of several lanterns, having seemingly appeared out of nowhere. The lanterns had first illuminated the torrent of rain falling directly in front of him. Just twenty feet away however, through the heavy downpour, had been a dozen armed guards standing poised, Enfield's at the ready.

All four officers spent the next seven days in the Hut, a wooden structure smaller than a Conestoga wagon. It had a dirt floor and was barely five feet high. They were given two buckets a day - one filled with rancid food left over from what the other prisoners had been fed that day, or the day before more like it, and another for human waste. They were given just one canteen a day but at least the water was almost fresh, at least in a relative sense, since its suspicious odor was reminiscent of sun-ripened fish. They were given one other thing - the promise they would be placed in front of a firing squad if they dared try it again.

Upon their release from the Hut the assistant camp commandant informed Major Miling that not only were the four of them no longer eligible for exchange, but neither were the rest of the officers housed in their building. Prohibition of contact with the enlisted prisoners in general population was continued and no contact of any kind was allowed with any new captives as well, including officers.

Major Miling had attempted to appeal to the camp commandant, Dr. Braxton Craven, to no avail. Craven had formed the Trinity Home Guard while president of Trinity College that would later become Duke University. Although he and his unit had undertaken quasi-military actions as a Home Guard unit, he had delegated whatever authority he had regarding the matter of the escapees to the conventional Confederate military, more specifically the assistant camp commandant Captain July Evers.

***

THE WAR raged on. The month of July saw numerous battles unfold; the Seven Days Battles near Richmond, the Battle of Murfreesboro and so on. August brought more of the same. When September arrived Union General George B. McClellan, who seemed to prefer training his men rather than sending them into battle, nonetheless caught General Robert E. Lee and his Army of Northern Virginia near the town of Sharpsburg, Maryland. On September 17, 1862 the Battle of Antietam turned that day into the bloodiest of the war, with over 2,000 Union dead and over 9,500 wounded along with 2,700 Confederates killed and over 9,000 wounded. The battle had no clear victor save Death, due primarily to McClellan's reluctance to pursue Lee when it appeared by doing so he would have likely achieved a stunning victory.

Five days later President Lincoln, having desired a victory before doing so and deciding Antietam would have to suffice, issued the Emancipation Proclamation. Many in the South were of course enraged, and few believed the Confederacy would pay much attention to it other than have it boost their resolve to maintain their "peculiar institution" which turned out to be the case.

News of the conflicts reaching the captives in Salisbury was sparse. More Union captives arrived, but Pete and the other quarantined officers received little information except from their guards who occasionally informed them their precious Union and all their damned Yankee invaders were being whipped, and soundly; including Shiloh. The quarantined officers had assumed Shiloh, in all likelihood, had been lost. They had all been captured the first day of that great battle, when the Confederate forces had all but routed the Yankees.

Pete and the rest of the officers felt compelled to scoff at the other reports, given the source, but growing germs of doubt had infected all of them although none would admit to it. At night Pete would find himself pondering the possibilities along with anything else he could think of to avoid sleep. His nightmares hadn't subsided, not even a little. The other officers might have wanted to complain of his late hour screaming, but Pete wasn't the only one haunted in that manner. No one ever said a word.

What if the reports were true? What if the Rebels were in or approaching northern Illinois and his family and Delicia were in harm's way? The other things that plagued him were bad enough, worse than bad, and now he had that to torture him as well. His unrelenting frustration, his *helplessness* was challenging what remained of his sanity. He had to escape.

***

HE DECIDED to go it alone although with few questionable exceptions he had little choice. The assistant camp commandant wasn't an overtly cruel man, but Captain Evers didn't make idle threats either. Asking others to risk certain death if caught wasn't an option for Pete, let alone trying to talk anyone into it.

Pete silently vowed he would never face a firing squad although vowing such a thing, maintaining he would rather die fighting, was easy to do when he was in the relative safety of the officers' cabin. If upon being recaptured he were to surrender that would likely spare him for the moment. His vow could be rationalized away then, as each vow after the proceeding crisis could be until the men assigned to the firing squad squeezed their triggers. Perhaps the bravest souls would realize that fact and acted accordingly; taking as many of the enemy with them as possible the moment they were caught. Pete didn't know if he was that brave; sometimes it felt like he was. Other times, when his depression and feelings of hopelessness had overwhelmed him, the thought of committing virtual suicide horrified him. Most of all he hoped he would never have to find out.

He couldn't tunnel his way out. The cabin where he and the others were kept was too far from the fence. Besides, if it was closer he had nothing to dig with, even if he had been strong enough to do so after all the months of repulsive food and not much of it. There was nowhere to hide the dirt or anything to shore up a tunnel either, nor any way not to implicate the others. Breaking through the board fence was a possibility, but doing so unnoticed would probably be another huge challenge if not an impossible one. Even if that was accomplished he knew he wouldn't likely get very far, especially since a broken section of fence would be noticed much sooner than later. All of the local inhabitants were of course on the lookout for such things, as were the people in the general area as well.

***

ONE OF the outhouses the guards used was fifty feet behind the cabin where Pete was held. On a number of the countless nights while Pete was awake he had noticed one of the sentries who guarded the structure which warehoused the food use the privy, usually between one and two in the morning. The man was prone to spend a fair amount of time in there since his duties weren't considered of much importance. His main job was to keep his fellow guards from helping themselves to the food, as bored men were prone to do even when they weren't all that hungry. The pilfering of food was more of an irritant to the camp commandant than anything, since it was his own men who had engaged in the activity before the sentry had been posted.

Pete didn't know it but the reason the guard usually spent so much time in the outhouse was due to the whiskey he kept hidden under the floor boards. It was something the guard felt he deserved, especially on colder nights, even if the ambiance of his chosen spot left much to be desired. He wasn't responsible for guarding the fence or any of the entrances, not as a primary duty, so the man saw little harm in it. The guard had little to worry about as long as the head cook didn't complain of any food losses, especially the commandant's prized canned peaches. He kept those hidden anyway just in case some rascal made a move while he was enjoying his corn whiskey.

Pete began watching the guard very closely through a space between some wall boards. The windows had been boarded up after the first escape attempt. He began to fashion several lengths of makeshift rope, braiding together lengths of the tattered blanket he had been issued to serve as his bed. He only did so at night after the lanterns were out, having grown adept with his braiding by touch alone. He was concerned about the sturdiness of his ropes. One of them, fortunately, appeared stronger than the others, certainly longer, so his plan was to use that one to hog tie the guard if things went as planned.

He knew the front of the cabin was watched since that was where the only door was located. It was locked from the outside but remained under constant surveillance or close to it anyway. Pete slept against the back wall in the northeast corner. He had managed to remove a few square nails from the lower boards and used them to work others loose as well. He did so as quietly as possible, again late at night by touch alone, and was guardedly optimistic his work had gone unnoticed.

It was early December when he had loosened enough boards to make it possible for him to squeeze his way through. Once outside, he assumed, he was sure he'd be able to replace them so they at least looked as if they hadn't been moved, unless someone inspected them closely.

The night of his attempt Pete was staring through the space between the boards as he had been doing for weeks, waiting for the guard to enter the outhouse. It was a chilly, rainy night which was what he'd been waiting for. The guard would have on a standard issue great coat, so all Pete would need to do is get the man's pants, cap and boots to complete his disguise. He hoped the man's boots would at least be close to Pete's size, since his own had been taken the day of his capture.

The rain started to come down harder, being pushed about by an increasing east wind. The guard, lantern in hand and cowered by the weather, finally appeared and went into the outhouse. Pete took a deep breath, said a silent prayer, and began to gently pull back the three boards closest to the floor. He did it quietly as possible then peered outside. No one was around or watching, as far as he could make out. It was down to it then.

"God's speed, Lieutenant." Major Miling whispered, looking up from his blanket. He then offered a low-keyed, palm out salute even though he knew Pete wouldn't see it in the darkness.

"I'll let your people know you're alive, the others too if I make it," Pete whispered back. He took a deep breath and crawled through the opening. Once outside he looked about and quietly replaced the boards. Then he stole into the night.

***

THE RAIN and brisk wind felt and smelled refreshing, even if they were chilly. Pete made his way quickly to the outhouse then stood by the side of the small structure to collect his composure. He kept looking around, grateful the weather had reduced visibility amidst the muted burnt orange glow of the occasional, waving lanterns hung about, although the outhouse was obscured to a degree by other buildings. He moved in front of the door and rapped upon it.

Pete could see lantern light coming through the wood boards and hoped the guard inside didn't peek through the tiny spaces that suddenly appeared to be anything but too small to accommodate something of that nature. He heard boards being moved about as the guard hid his whiskey. The sound of the movements seemed odd, potentially dangerous. *What was the man doing besides the obvious?* Pete wondered, concerned the man suspected something was amiss.

"Cain't a feller shit in private?" The annoyed guard said in a curiously high pitched voice that contradicted his proportion and apparent demeanor. Pete rapped again, listening for the wooden lock that was attached to the inside of the door to move. The sound of boards being moved stopped. "Ah'm a comin', Ah'm a comin', keep your dern pants on."

Pete heard the block of wood move then looked around once more through the rain. He shoved the door open and saw the man, suddenly wide-eyed, fastening the last few buttons of his pants. Before the guard could react Pete slammed his fist into the man's face then grabbed him by his throat and long hair and drove his head against the side wall of the extremely confined space, again and again. He appeared unconscious, perhaps even dead, although that hadn't been Pete's intention. His plan to gag and tie him up evaporated when the frenzy, the *reality* of the situation erupted, causing Pete's initial strategy to suddenly evolve into a wholly inadequate response, at least for the moment.

He threw the lantern into the privy hole in case anyone glanced that way since the man's feet were hanging part way out the door. He removed the great coat and began pulling the boots after positioning the man atop the boards where the privy hole was located. Before he had the second boot off the man came around, but in the darkness Pete hadn't noticed. The man carefully removed a knife from the sheath on his belt. Pete, unaware of the man's intentions, continued to struggle with the second boot. The man made his move.

He had to thrust the knife at a downward angle. He tried to aim where he thought Pete's head was located, but in the darkness all he caught was Pete's left shoulder and that just barely. Pete reached up with both hands and was fortunate enough to get a hold of the man's knife-hand along with the bottom part of the blade. It slashed Pete just below his left thumb, and although he knew he'd been cut he didn't suffer any loss of movement. He held the hand and knife tightly as he reached for the man's throat with his right hand. Having choked off the man's attempt to finally begin screaming, Pete stood and drove the blade into the man's face. It struck the right cheekbone, slid upwards and into the right eye. Pete pushed with all he had and drove the knife to the hilt into the soft membrane. The man jerked about spasmodically then went limp. Pete tore off a strip of the man's long underwear and wrapped his hand, hoping too much blood wasn't already on him.

The other boot was pulled off and both were on Pete's feet. They were too tight, but at least they were on. The baggy pants were next, which he struggled to put on over the boots, cursing for not having done it the other way around. Pete put on the great coat and fumbled about in the darkness, finally locating the guard's cap. He hoped it wasn't covered with blood as well. At least he hadn't felt anything wet after he'd used his good hand to retrieve and put it on, but that offered little, if any, reassurance.

There was only one place to put the body, along with Pete's own clothes with the exception of his tattered lieutenant's blouse that he shoved into an inside pocket of the great coat. It might prove useful if he made it far enough away. He ripped off the boards that covered the privy hole and shoved it all in. The dead man's body was difficult to maneuver but down it went as well.

The sound it made when it landed in the several foot-deep muck was sickening, and even in Pete's agitated state it made him want to vomit. The knife through the man's eye had been horrible, but the thick splash of a body landing upon that dense pool of excrement had somehow been the most sickening, as was the urgent, stench-ridden blast of air that had been forced upwards in a rush. Pete again shuddered at the thought as well as the smell, the bile rising in his throat. In the most perverse of ways he was glad the man wasn't still alive, and at that moment it had little to do with the fact he was no longer a threat.

In his haste Pete had forgotten to retrieve the knife and cursed himself for it. He would need all the weapons he could lay his hands on, but at least he knew the guard had brought his Enfield rifle in with him. He soon found it after searching about frantically in the dark.

He did his best to replace the boards over the privy hole, but it was no use. It was simply too dark, but it wouldn't have mattered since a few of them had broken when they had been removed. Other guards rarely used that particular privy that time of night so Pete wondered why he had even bothered, not certain whether that was the correct way to look at it either. He struggled to gain his composure. He would need to be in better control if he had any hope of fulfilling his plan, such as it was.

He walked slowly to the small building that warehoused the food, his shoulders hunched against the elements. He stood there for what felt like an eternity in case anyone chanced to glance that way. If they did, nothing would appear out of the ordinary as long as they didn't approach. Ten minutes later that felt like an hour, he began to make his way towards a side gate in the southeast section sometimes used by the guards to come and go. They weren't supposed to; they were all supposed to use the main gate, but it was a shortcut from the outside barn and was commonly used if no superiors were nearby. There most certainly wouldn't be any around that time of night, in the pouring rain no less.

Two sentries were supposed to be posted by the gate at all times but again the weather had played a role. There was only one, and he was too preoccupied with his own bad luck of having been assigned such disagreeable duty. Disgruntled, wet and cold, he at first couldn't have cared less that one of his comrades was approaching, although at least it would break the boredom, if just barely. Maybe he could bum a smoke. If it was sentry Milo Henry, which it probably was since the man was approaching from the general direction of the food storehouse, a taste of whisky might even be forthcoming. His mood brightened; nothing short of a hot stove in a dry cabin compared to several generous chugs of busthead and a good smoke on such nights.

"Hey Milo," the sentry called out as Pete approached with his head lowered against the driving rain. "Ah hope you ain't showin' up empty handed!" Pete, head still bowed, waved with his good hand, keeping the bloody one in his pocket and the rifle cradled in the crook of his elbow.

He made his way to the front of the sentry. Initially the man smiled, and it remained frozen upon his face when he attempted to make out Pete through the semi-darkness and rain. A lone lantern was hanging near the gate, and when its flickering light had finally revealed the man's worst fear it was too late for him. Pete brought the butt of the rifle around and smashed the side of the man's head and sent him sprawling to the ground.

Pete looked around while dragging his unconscious victim to the stockade wall and put him parallel to it, hidden in the darkness where the lantern light did not reach. Pete brought the butt down against the man's skull several times until the sentry was dead. He groped about the body and found a knife, some ammunition and even some money although not much.

After hiding the lantern under his coat Pete went through the wooden door that served as a gate and shut it behind him, grateful for the wind-whipped rain that helped obscure his movements. No one appeared to be around, and if they were they allowed the inclement weather to afford them a pretext to keep their heads bowed against the elements as they manned the top of the fence. Although it seemed logical that such weather would afford a prisoner his best opportunity for escape, it was as if the blowing rain also served as an excuse for the sentries to forego all but the bare minimum of their responsibilities.

Pete glanced towards the top of the fence but didn't see anyone illuminated by the unreliable light of the swaying lanterns, cowered by the weather or otherwise. Perhaps, he thought apprehensively, some guards were in the barn located not far from the south wall. There was no one inside however, just horses in their stalls. That was tempting, except both the front and rear barn doors were visible from the rude guard turrets on each corner of the south wall. He prayed he hadn't been spotted going into the barn but wasn't sure. Regardless, even if the sentries who must have been somewhere in the turrets or on the connected platforms atop the wall had seen him, they must have noticed his standard issue great coat and assumed the obvious. Perhaps they hadn't seen him at all, but a horse and rider weren't likely to go unnoticed. Great coat or not, anyone leaving the barn on horseback that time of night would arouse suspicion unless they had informed the sentries prior to departure, which was standard procedure.

There was only one viable option left and it needed to be initiated the same way he had used to get out of the cabin where he had been housed. Pete hung the lantern that was under his coat on a nail and went to work on the south wall of the barn. The first board was difficult to remove but he succeeded. The others were easier, and he soon created a large enough opening for himself and the best horse he could find. He then disabled the others by damaging their flexor tendons with some well placed kicks. Saddle and tack in place he rode south, the barn concealing his escape into the rainy night until he found cover in the woods beyond, then veered northwest.

It took nearly three hours before the dead sentry by the gate was discovered, and it wasn't until first morning light before a sergeant located Private Milo Henry's body. The sergeant recoiled in horror when the lantern light illuminated the privy hole; recoiled at the sight of a naked foot protruding from the foul mass. Pete was miles away by then. Once they had secured usable mounts however, his pursuers were after him with a particular resolve, especially the sergeant. Private Milo Henry had been his best friend since childhood.

XIII

Cusman was the first to see them coming and alerted the women; three men on horseback heading towards them at a gallop, once they had cleared a rise a few hundred yards ahead. He reached a little ways behind himself and undid the leather case. While the men were still too far away to see his actions, he removed one of the revolvers and placed it next to him on the right side of the seat and put his wide brimmed hat over it. Cusman and the women didn't recognize the strangers once both wagon and riders had stopped, although when Jennifer took a better look she thought the man closest to them looked very familiar.

"Good mornin', ma'am," the one closest to the wagon said. "Nice day, ain't it." He was thick-set, and his dense black beard accentuated his dark, intimidating eyes. There was an angry white scar that ran down from his forehead, cutting an ugly, inch-wide swath into the left side of his beard. His left eye was intact, but the center of the eyebrow was scar tissue as well. He was heavily armed as were the others. Jennifer returned his salutation.

"Not ta be alarmed, ma'am, but bah chance have you seen a light-skinned nigger hereabouts? He run off from the Jones' place a while back. Goes bah the name Carmel. S'pect he ain't usin' it though, lessin' he's dumber than his owner let on. Not the first time some God damned nigger been caught that a ways, if you'll pardon mah swearin'." Jennifer eyed him coolly.

"I most certainly won't pardon your impious malediction, and will inform my husband, Mr. Trenton Ransom of Whisper Manor, of your blasphemous lack of manners." The other two men chuckled but stopped immediately when their apparent leader shot them a scowl.

"Ah apologize, ma'am, we been travelin' a fair piece and Ah fear the company Ah keep has had a poor affect on me." He had heard of Trenton Ransom and Whisper Manor.

"Well sir, we know Carmel but haven't seen him. I would be very surprised if he has run off though. More than likely he's not far away. Check enough slave quarters hereabouts where young girls are housed and you will likely locate him, drunk as a skunk no doubt." Jennifer's comment made Cusman and Missy Nell snicker.

"What are you niggers hee-hawing about? Mind your place!" The words hadn't come from any of the men, but from Jennifer. "I apologize, gentlemen. As you have no doubt noticed I have spoiled these two niggers horribly."

"No apology needed, ma'am." The defaced man said. "Handsome niggers like that is a shame ta scar with a whuppin', but Ah reckon there's a price ta pay for such coddlin'. Have your overseer tie their hands behind their backs and hold their heads underwater a spell, 'til they git some in their lungs. That oughta do it. Least ways works for me. Niggers are sceered nigh on ta death'a takin' on water that'a ways. Ah swear, some of 'em rather git whupped."

"Thank you for your thought provoking advice, sir. Now if you'll excuse me I have a train to catch." The men tipped their hats and rode off.

"That was a mighty handsome woman," Jeeter Kulinan said as the three men headed down the road.

"Handsome or not she's still a nigger. See what ya mean though. Wouldn't mind dallyin' with that wench mah own damn self." Dale Shoots, the man riding next to Kulinan responded. Runyun Stalworthy, the scar faced leader of the group remained silent, lost in thought.

"Not the quadroon," Kulinan replied. "Ah'm talkin' 'bout that high-toned rich lady. She's as upper class as they gits. Always did have me a special hankerin' for them kind'a ladies."

"Yeah, well, you keep on'a hankerin' Jeeter ole boy. Ain't no high-toned Southern lady ever gonna give you nothin' 'ceptin' a rude look or two."

"Don't Ah know it. That's how come Ah got me such a yearnin' for 'em. Anybody kin have them a nigger, whores too'a course, mebbe a low bred cracker bitch. Not them high-toned ladies though. The higher they is, the more Ah wanna bring 'em down a peg or two. That purty lady would be a joy ta see nekked, an' Ah sure 'nough like ta roll her over ass end up an' shove ole Blue where the sun don't shine!"

"Why don't you two shut the hell up and keep your God damned eyes open?" Stalworthy said. "We got us a job ta do."

"Jus' a goin' over it in mah mind, Runyun." Kulinan responded. "Ah kin still *see* good don't ya know, an' that lady's sure 'nough a sight. Jus' wish Ah was'a watchin' her squirmin' under me, that's all. Show that fancy lady a thing or two even if she's gittin' up in years. How old you reckon she be, Dale?"

"Oh, not much over forty Ah s'pect. Fine figured woman though. Purty, too. Did y'all smell that perfume a comin' off'a her? Dang Kulinan, now you got me'a hankerin' for some'a that there sweet meat."

"Ah said shut up an' keep your God damned eyes open!" Stalworthy almost yelled. He had a runaway to catch.

***

"I DEEPLY apologize for my cruel words, you two, but I am certain I recognized that loathsome man. His likeness has appeared in newspaper sketches and the scar he wears is unmistakable. The artists never leave it out. He and those men are indeed slave catchers, and he goes by the name of Runyun Stalworthy. No one is considered more adept at what he does, vile as it is. I do hope, however, I was convincing."

"You were all that, Missis." Cusman said as he put away the revolver. "He was wrong about the water though. Unless he bathed in it first."

Jennifer spotted a stand of sourwoods along a stream up ahead and asked Cusman to pull in. When they were no longer visible from the road she asked both of them to follow her to the back of the wagon.

"Cusman, if you would please, remove all the luggage." Both of the young people exchanged glances then looked at Jennifer, quizzical expressions on their faces. "Please Cusman, it's important." Jennifer said.

Once the luggage and large trunks were on the ground Jennifer asked him to help her as she began to pry at one of the bed boards. He gave it a tug and it came up easily. He stared in awe as did Missy Nell.

"Load it into the leather valise, Cusman, the empty one with the sturdy handles. Keep a close eye on it at all times you two. This gold is our future."

***

"CUSMAN," JENNIFER said after they were on their way. "When it is just the three of us please call me Jennifer from now on. When you are free, God willing, I'm hopeful you will always refer to me that way." He looked straight ahead, but inside he was warmed.

"What about me, Missis?" Missy Nell asked. "Callin' you by your Christian name don't seem proper."

"You, child, would honor me greatly by calling me Mother from now on."

***

THEY HAD a wonderful time in Atlanta. Regardless of what Jennifer had allowed Trenton to believe they made the rounds of some of the city's finest shops. Afterwards they shared a fabulous supper in the suite of a fine hotel, although there had been a disagreeable confrontation with the hotel manager. Jennifer had insisted Missy Nell be allowed to stay the night in the suite but was informed that wasn't possible, not in their hotel, at least not in that particular suite, even if the girl slept on the floor. Jennifer became furious and informed the manager there would be dire consequences if her beautiful slave girl was harmed in any way if forced to share space in the basement with the other slaves.

"This gal is worth at least six thousand dollars, more in New Orleans, and if any harm comes to her, so much as a tiny *scratch*, my husband's lawyers will see to it this hotel, and you personally sir, are held accountable!" Missy Nell was allowed to stay, after Mrs. Ransom assured the uneasy manager the slave girl would indeed sleep on the floor, but Cusman had to be out of the suite by 6:00 p.m.

Jennifer made sure her daughter slept in the master bedroom upon the most luxurious bed in the two bedroom suite. Missy Nell's favorite color wasn't confined to a particular one. She loved all colors with a tint of pastel, and the colors the canopy, matching drapes and carpet issued represented a rainbow of those hues. In the morning Jennifer saw to it her daughter was served breakfast in bed. The elderly dark-skinned woman who served the girl smiled.

***

THE TRAIN ride through Georgia was uneventful except when the conductor told Jennifer her slaves couldn't ride with her. They had to use the rear car with the other slaves, and any free Negroes who happened to be on board. Jennifer again objected, at least as far as Missy Nell was concerned, but to no avail. Either the girl rode in the back car or not at all. Jennifer didn't want to appear too coddling, so when the conductor remained unmoved by the same threat that had worked on the hotel manager she relented. Besides, Missy Nell would be with Cusman, all six foot nine, two hundred and ninety pounds of him, so there was little to worry about. He had kept both leather cases with him; the one weighing over a hundred pounds and the other with the revolvers. Jennifer worried anyway.

***

THEY SPENT a delightful week with Jennifer's sister and Harriet's husband, although their impending undertaking dominated their thoughts and was the true motivation for Cusman and Missy Nell's elation during that time. Over breakfast on the morning of the seventh day of their stay, Jennifer informed her sister and brother-in-law she wanted to take a trip to Charleston.

"That sounds delightful, Sister, Ah haven't been there mah self since our honeymoon. Tredwell kin wire ahead for our accommodations, cain't you dear? Oh! There's a charmin' musical about that Indian gal Pocahontas a few of the ladies hereabouts been swoonin' over, The Gentle Savage or some such thing. Couldn't you wire the theater as well, dear?"

"Certainly, darlin'." Tredwell replied. "Ah'll talk ta mah brother as well. Ah'm sure Nephew Blakeley would be honored ta accompany you dear, and you, Sister, now that he's back from college. He's grown inta such a fine young fellow. It comes as no surprise why mah brother boasts of him so. A man kin be at peace knowin' a son of that caliber will be carryin' on his good name. He'll be off ta the war soon, now that his schoolin's over. Graduated first in his class! Purtin' near anyways."

Jennifer listened politely, smiling and making other complimentary facial expressions at the precise moments they were required. Then she addressed her sister. "How I would love to spend time with you in Charleston, Harriet dear, but if you come with me it will ruin your birthday surprise! I fear I have been forced to compromise your surprise as is, but it would truly be undone if you were to accompany me and my niggers. We'll go together on my next visit. Besides, we won't be staying in Charleston the first night or two. I need to catch a train from there to finalize your surprise."

Harriet expressed disappointment but inside she was filled with anticipation. Her older sister was as thoughtful as she was generous. No telling what she was planning. It would certainly be remarkable, of that there was no doubt. Tredwell sipped his coffee then placed the china cup in its saucer. A warm, fragrant breeze stole over them as they sat on the east terrace, perfumed as it was by the surrounding Cherokee rose and gardenia shrubs.

"At least allow Blakeley ta accompany you, Sister Jennifer," Tredwell implored. "Traveling alone is not prudent, if you'll excuse me sayin' so."

"I won't be alone, Tredwell. As I stated, my niggers will be with me and our boy Cusman is Mr. Ransom's pride. You've heard him carry on about him, especially after Trenton's been imbibing. 'Finest niggah Ah have evah owned, or evah will in all likelihood!'." Jennifer intoned, mimicking her husband's deep southern drawl he refrained from using unless he was in a rage or working on his fourth cognac or so. Most folks insisted he spoke that way because Jennifer spoke without any southern accent, since Trenton certainly had one before he began courting her. Jennifer's impersonation produced chuckles from her two hosts, and after Tredwell reluctantly agreed to the arrangement the matter was settled.

***

THE THREE started out at sunrise the next morning. The weather was delightful as was the entire journey. They came over a rise and saw the impressive church steeples of Charleston.

"This is why they call it the Holy City," Jennifer remarked. Cusman felt differently.

"I 'spect over half them folks down there are slaves. Beggin' your pardon Missis, but that don't sound holy to me."

"Nor to me Cusman, nor to me. And please, call me Jennifer."

***

TRENTON RANSOM was beside himself despite the rationalizations he struggled to believe were true, at least at first. On the very morning his wife and slaves were entering Charleston he had made an alarming discovery.

He considered himself an honorable man but also admitted to a few harmless digressions as he defined them, if only to himself. He enjoyed looking at the gold coins, fondling them really, all fifty thousand dollars worth of the sparkling 1857 twenty dollar Double Eagles. They were all new or at least had never been in circulation. Other currencies could fluctuate but gold was intrinsic, for the most part. Trenton especially distrusted the Confederate dollar even if in 1862 it was still holding its own. He believed, however, it had about as much future as the new republic itself.

Jennifer had received them from her father's estate after his passing. He had no sons and she was his oldest daughter. He had made provisions for Harriet but not any of his prized gold coins; those were for his favorite daughter he had always insisted was most like him. Jennifer kept them in a padlocked strongbox hidden under a false floor in her largest master bedroom closet, but Trenton knew where she hid the key, but it wasn't there. He chuckled, assuming Jennifer was playing a trick on him and had put it elsewhere. It didn't matter; the strongbox had come with two keys, unbeknownst to Jennifer.

His motive that day contained not a touch of suspicion until he had removed the false floor and strained to lift the box. He had wanted to simply play with them, not unlike a child. He enjoyed stacking them into neat, perfect rows or making a pile out of them on the Axminster carpet, picking up handfuls at a time, marveling at their weight as he let them slip through his fingers. He loved the sound they created and would do it over and over. Not that day though; the strongbox had weighed as much as it had on the day of its manufacture. He had unlocked it anyway. Even total hopelessness must be confirmed when the outcome promises to be appalling.

His heart-pounding rationalizations began immediately. Perhaps Jennifer was trying to teach him a lesson, the sly minx. He also considered that perhaps one of the house servants had stolen it and was at that very moment planning an escape. Maybe it was one of the field hands who had somehow found his or her way into Grand House. How would they have known where the key was hidden though, unless someone inside was in collusion with them? Could it possibly have been Missy Nell? That was difficult to imagine but he had to admit it made the most sense, since Missy Nell had access to the room as if it were her own. Could it be at all possible Cusman was in on it too?

Trenton wanted desperately to believe his first scenario, that Jennifer was teaching him a lesson, had to be true. So much so, he forced himself to calm down and assume that was indeed the case, but that was short-lived. He bolted straight down the stairway, not even bothering to put the box away. He flew through the huge front doors and made his way onto the large gallery and looked around.

"Sammy!" He yelled, spotting one of his slaves. "Saddle Blackberry at once and bring him here!" The middle-aged gardener looked at him, waved a smile his master's way with a "Yeow suh, Mas'r suh," and began to amble towards the stables. "Don't dally, damn you nigger! You have Blackberry here in less than ten minutes or Ah will personally tan the hide off your black carcass!"

Sammy went from walking to running. He rarely heard his master say anything like that and never to him, much less in that tone of voice. He began to run even faster, realizing the stallion Blackberry was a very contrary, high-strung animal and might not be receptive to going under tack at that time. He hollered for assistance from a few other slaves who began to run behind him. They had heard their master as well.

Trenton again tried to compose himself while he waited impatiently on the porch. *Jennifer will have some answering to do,* he said to himself. *This is beyond the pale, not in the least bit humorous. Hiding her key was one thing, but this. The nerve of that woman…well, when the gold is back in its rightful place…still, this isn't humorous, not one bit…just what the hell is goin' on?*

Blackberry was the fastest horse on Whisper Manor and most other places around Beaux Hollow. Still, Trenton kept him at a trot until he was on the main road to town, as if by doing so he appeared in complete control, as if nothing much was amiss. As soon as Grand House was no longer in sight he took his riding crop to the stallion's right hindquarter. Less than an hour later he pulled up the lathered horse in front of the general store which was also the telegraph office and hurried inside.

My dear Jennifer,

If this is your idea of a joke, I am not amused. Forgive me, but while doing inventory of our assets I discovered your strongbox was empty. I suspect you are teaching me a lesson, but fear we may have been robbed. My greatest fear, silly though it sounds at first blush, is that Missy Nell is behind it, perhaps Cusman as well, which could mean you are in harm's way. Please respond to this forthwith. You should have it in hand in under three hours. I will remain in town until your reply. I fear for your safety, so respond immediately.

Yours truly, Trenton

Jennifer wasn't there to read the wire, but Tredwell and Harriet were. Tredwell gave the courier a response to wire back as fast as humanly possible. He even insisted the courier read Trenton's message so the man would not be inclined to delay:

Brave Trenton,

I fear time is our enemy. Jennifer and her niggers left this morning and will soon be in Charleston. I am sending a wire to the authorities in the city as fast as the courier can get back to our town. I am also heading to Charleston myself post haste. With God's speed, I shall make it to the train station in time. She mentioned a trip was necessary to finalize whatever she has planned for Harriet's birthday, of which I am assuming you are aware?

As always, Tredwell

***

"ALL ABOARD!" The conductor yelled for what he intended to be the last time before the train pulled away.

Cusman and Missy Nell were already on the train, in the rear car. Jennifer had been conversing with a charming young couple who had just arrived in Charleston for their honeymoon and she mentioned how her sister and brother-in-law, who had so many places to choose from, had chosen Charleston themselves even though they lived close by and could've afforded to have gone most anywhere. After the conductor had called out a third time she excused herself after again complimenting them on their choice.

The train pulled out and was over twenty miles away before the constables arrived, and well over forty miles before Tredwell showed up.

"Ah'm searching for my sister-in-law, Mrs. Trenton Ransom," he said to the man behind the ticket booth. "She has likely purchased tickets recently."

"Ah don't ask their names, mister, just sell the tickets." The gruff, elderly man replied, as if the dandy standing in front of him should have known as much.

"Damn it man, this may be a matter of life or death!" Tredwell said loud enough to get the attention of the station master.

"May Ah be of assistance, sir, and has it ta do with the constables what was here earlier?"

"In all probability, sir. Mrs. Trenton Ransom from Georgia, assuming she's aboard, is travelin' with her two niggers, or was. The girl is light skinned and quite attractive, the boy is very tall and solidly built, black as pitch. Ah don't know which train, much less where she might be bound. What say you?"

"Ah know which train, sir, as Ah told the constables. She's onboard, her fancy niggers too, or least ways they boarded the train at this station that is headed for Richmond."

"*Virginia?*" Tredwell exclaimed. "That's impossible!"

"Impossible or not, that's where she bought the tickets for. Her and both her fancy niggers. She sure 'nough dotes on 'em, especially that big buck."

"Did she appear in anyway distressed? You say the niggers were with her? How would you describe their demeanor?"

"Well, the lady seemed happy as a lark, and a'course her niggers wasn't *with* her, sir, least ways not in the same car. Them niggers acted like niggers, fancy as Sunday, but niggers just the same. One thing though. Your Mrs. Ransom not only hugged the pretty quadroon gal, but that big buck too, nice an' tight, just before them two niggers got in the rear car. Don't know what things is a comin' to when a fine dressed white lady up and hugs a God damned nigger boy that a way, Ah surely do not. That big nigger was likin' it too, spotted it right off Ah did. Didn't let go right away, neither of 'em did, no sir."

Tredwell walked out to the platform in a daze and stared down the empty tracks. What could he possibly tell Trenton Ransom? None of it added up, or did it? As loathsome as it was, perhaps he had an idea what to tell Trenton Ransom after all.

"Oh, there is one other thing sir." The station master said as he joined Tredwell on the platform. "Didn't think it mattered much, but the constables did. Didn't see all'a it mah own self, but one'a mah men told them constables about it. He was loadin' the luggage car and grabbed this here real heavy leather bag that was with your Mrs. Ransom's possibles. That big nigger raised'a awful fuss. To her credit your Ransom lady scolded him good an' proper, then told Kirby it was okay, her nigger would be keepin' it with him. Even tipped old Kirby five dollars, if you kin imagine that. After that's when Ah showed up an' seen her hug that big nigger, a lovey-dovey look in her eyes, real close-like and such, like she was sorry she scolded him. Ah just don't know what things is a comin' to, no sir, Ah surely do not."

Before leaving the train station Tredwell prepared another telegram for Trenton, one that wouldn't be read first by Harriet. She was unrealistically optimistic, Tredwell believed, the one who often times reacted with a naiveté borne from her lack of experience and judgment, especially when it came to certain matters involving the more loathsome patterns of behavior between men and women. Tredwell, on the other hand, was no fool, of that he had no doubt. He was perceptive, wary and very worldly when it came to such things; he had no doubts about that as well. His telegram to Trenton would prove it too. As upsetting as the news would be to the poor man, he simply wouldn't allow Trenton not to have the advantage of Tredwell's vast resource of experience and wisdom:

Brave Trenton,

Brace yourself. My news is dire. It appears your wife is in collusion with your niggers, and I fear in a way decorum prevents me from going into detail about, depraved as it is, in this correspondence. I have an eye for such things, and offer you my sincerest apology for not noticing sooner. Not only has Jennifer run off with them, but eyewitnesses confirm she was much more than friendly with your big nigger Cusman. She was even seen hugging him at great length, and very close to her at that. They also exchanged alluring glances as they embraced that created a great deal of talk as well. Please, as they say, don't shoot the messenger my brave Trenton, but I cannot, in good conscience, hold back the truth from you. I have good reason to fear the very worst, if you understand my meaning. Tredwell

***

JENNIFER GAZED out the window as the train chugged north. They were making good time and for the most part she felt good inside. There were always things to worry about, but it appeared as if her plan was working. Still, she worried; nothing would be even relatively certain until they were away from Southern soil.

Her thoughts kept coming back to Cusman and Missy Nell in the crowded rear car. Cusman could take care of himself but what if something by chance did ensue? What if several men he was riding with made advances towards Missy Nell or began to harass them due to their appearances? Lust and Envy weren't counted among the Seven Deadly Sins for nothing, she believed, and were certainly color blind. Over-powering Cusman would be no simple task but not impossible; he wasn't the only strapping man riding in that car. What if things grew so out of hand Cusman pro-duced the revolvers, much more used them? That would prove to be dreadful. What was a slave doing with such quality weapons, *any* weapons, and upon further investi-gation fifty thousand dollars in gold coins? Jennifer drove those thoughts from her mind, or tried to as she again gazed out at the countryside speeding by so slowly.

***

THERE WAS only one thing left to believe and to Trenton Ransom it was the worst of all possible scenarios. The overwhelming sense of betrayal he felt had ignited an all consuming sense of rage so profound, he would rather they had informed him his wife had been robbed, murdered, perhaps even raped. For all he knew and had come to believe, the hugging and "alluring glances" had most certainly not been platonic. If Jennifer was capable of the other abominations, Trenton concluded, why not sex with a nigger? Tredwell obviously thought so, did he not? Who could tell how long her perverted behavior had been going on? For all Trenton knew she may well be pregnant, even if she was nearly forty-two.

How could I have been so blind, he wondered. *How could such a disingenuous, demented creature have fooled me for so long?* Within his delirium he even suspected his wife's rela-tionship with Missy Nell wasn't any different than the one she was doubtless having with that God damned nigger Cusman, perhaps both at once he imagined. He in-vented everything he could possibly conceive to fuel his delusions, insisting they were true or at least plausible. He had heard of such things, such deranged behavior, but with a few notable exceptions had usually tended to scoff at the extent of their validity. *Not anymore, at least as far as that nigger-loving whore wife of mine is concerned*, he concluded.

The fortification of Trenton's delusional certainties quickly became an addiction. The delusions manifested themselves easily, were extremely intense, and afforded him the opportunity to obliterate any thoughts that didn't accelerate or at least maintain the momentum that continued to grow in his fevered mind. No other thoughts or emotions were allowed to enter except a desperate need for requital that mirrored the intensity of the obsession that had devoured him whole.

It wouldn't have been as bad if Jennifer had done virtually anything else other than what he was suddenly convinced was the truth. Run off with a white man, even if she was carrying his baby wouldn't have come *close* to equaling what she must have done; worse yet, still doing!

He began to play back episodes in his mind, ones that had seemed relatively innocent at the time: *A hand on Cusman's shoulder here, a warm, now obvious smile cast at that black-hearted nigger there, laughing at that God damned nigger's little jokes, those two getting together while I was on one of my unaccompanied business trips, fornicating under my very roof!* It all made perfect sense to Trenton now. *How about the way she watched that huge black buck leave a room, hers eyes no doubt locked on his pronounced buttocks? Of course they had been! They had to have been* **clued** *on that muscular black Judas! The lust she displayed was right in front of me! Those weren't innocent looks, far from it! How in hell could I have been so blind?*

***

"YOUR REPUTATION precedes you sir," Trenton said to Runyun Stalworthy after offering the slave catcher a chair in Grand House's well-appointed study later that afternoon. "I must add, however, your price is the highest by far I have yet to receive." Trenton was willing to pay nearly anything but wanted to better understand the man he was dealing with first. Stalworthy wanted to know the same thing. He already knew Ransom was lying about the other offers; there hadn't been near enough time for that to have occurred.

"That's 'cause Ah'm the best there is. You pay me the five thousand plus expenses, and most anything you want ta happen, *will* happen." Stalworthy's piercing dark eyes never left Trenton's as he spoke, nor did he alter his grim demeanor, enhanced as it was by the hideous scar upon his face. He hoped so anyway; the man he was negotiating with was clearly agitated, possibly unhinged.

"That is good to hear, sir, and I do not doubt you, but we are both aware you have thus far been unable to capture that light-skinned nigger Carmel that has gone missing from the Jones' place how long now? I would suggest some consideration regarding a reduction in your price be afforded me."

"We'll catch that yeller nigger. He's around these parts somewheres. Ah have mah men on it, and would be with 'em mah own damn self if you hadn't been in such a all-fired hurry ta have us chase your niggers down. Since you expect me ta put off Mr. Jones 'til your business is done, Ah reckon Ah should be chargin' you more, not less. Anyways, take it or leave it."

"I'll take it Stalworthy," Trenton replied, suddenly dropping all pretenses. "I want those two God damned niggers brought here alive though, without a mark on 'em, you understand me? Not the white woman though. I… *Ah* want her *dead.*" The cold, seething glare in Trenton's eyes convinced Stalworthy of at least that much. Trenton had abandoned his pretentious dialect, switching to the way he used to sound before Jennifer came into his life. "Ah want it ta be gruesome an' slow, real slow. Don't want what's left'a her found right off though, not 'til you git mah niggers back here, you understand? Folks will believe mah niggers done it, but Ah don't want 'em ta hang fer it, no sir. I have mah own plans fer those two black-hearted niggers."

"You hold on, Ransom. Me and mah men ain't no damned murderers, least ways no Southern white lady. Kilt our fair share'a men an' niggers in self defense though."

"A *lady?* Do ladies run off with nigger bucks they laid with, perhaps carryin' his nigger baby and proud of it?" A red-faced Trenton yelled as he arose quickly from his chair that flew back and crashed to the floor, the veins in his neck throbbing. "Well, *do* they sir?" Runyun Stalworthy glared at the enraged man, in no way intimidated but on guard nonetheless.

"No sir, they sure as hell don't." He answered, leaning forward in his chair. "And Ah think you are warranted if what you say is true, which Ah have no reason ta doubt. But murder is just that, and Ah ain't about ta swing for killin' no white woman, loathsome as she be. S'pect you could kill her though. Ain't a jury what would think you wasn't within your rights."

"Not after what Ah'd do ta that nigger-lovin' whore, they wouldn't! Gonna burn that black bastard Cusman alive, too, Ah swear on it! Take a whip ta that quadroon slut, then sell her off. Ah never should'a had mixed blood 'round here! Won't be much left'a her, promise ya that! But mah wife, well, that's where you come in. You, and fifty thousand in gold plus your fee and expenses."

Runyun Stalworthy was in shock. That would be $55,000 plus expenses. Racing for rationalizations, he recalled what Ransom had said about eventually blaming the captives. That just might work after all, he realized. All he would have to do was leave her body strung up in a tree deep in the woods somewhere, away from scavenging animals as best he could. After that, all he'd have to do was make it back to Whisper Manor with the runaways before any authorities could intercept him.

"Ah'll need half of it up front," he finally said.

"You kin have the five thousand, but not half the fifty thousand in gold. They got that with 'em. If the reports Ah receive conclude that mah whore of a wife's death was brutal, after you're back here with those niggers'a course, you kin even consider the retainer as an extra five thousand bonus. That comes ta, ta, sixty thousand plus expenses. But it damn well better be brutal, an' Ah want her ta know *why* 'fore you do it! Are we in agreement?" Stalworthy added it all up in his head before answering, just to make sure.

"Sixty thousand plus expenses? You're damned right we got us a deal. Ah reckon the report will be brutal enough. Come ta think on it, Ah sure as all hell got me the men for it."

XIV

At least he was out of North Carolina, Pete thought as he watched a small Confederate patrol of three horse soldiers as they advanced down a wagon trace. He was hiding just off of it, perhaps fifty feet inside the woods behind a thick stand of evergreens, petting his horse's muzzle to keep it from making noise. He had been wandering about in the backwoods of eastern Tennessee for nearly a week, after having finally eluded the determined Rebels from Salisbury, and had made it as far as the northeast section of the state. He was weak from starvation, so much so he sometimes found the debility a morbid curiosity if he dwelled on it. He tried not to, but the waves had grown so intense he felt as if he were a rag doll left in the rain. If it hadn't been for a hoary raccoon he had killed with a rock and eaten raw he doubted he'd be standing at all. He still had the Enfield rifle but was loathed to shoot it unless there was an emergency, and building even a small fire was out of the question.

He wasn't far from the Kentucky border but just how far he didn't know. If he could make it across Tennessee there was a reasonable chance he would finally make good his escape. He had no idea how the war was going however, and the uncertainty clouded his hope.

Nearly forty battles of no small consequence were fought on Tennessee soil between 1862 and 1864 alone. Eastern Tennessee was held by the Confederates, and although Memphis and Nashville had been captured by the Union it wouldn't be until after the Battle of Stones River near Murfreesboro that coming January before the Union would have basic control of middle and parts of eastern Tennessee. Subsequently, more than a few Rebel cavalry units continued to occupy the area Pete was traversing. It was bad luck Pete had managed to stumble across some of them, and worse luck he hadn't come across any Union scouting patrols.

Kentucky was a border state but events thus far during the war had solidified its allegiance, for the most part, to the Union. Although there were Rebel sympathizers to be found there, especially close to the Tennessee border even if the eastern part of that state was known to harbor a large number of pro-Union residents, at least there were Union soldiers in Kentucky; Pete had no way of knowing if that pertained to Tennessee as well. How Pete yearned to encounter a company of his own comrades; even a small patrol would be like heaven on earth, he imagined.

He still had his tattered lieutenant's blouse tucked under his saddle. During his captivity he had been able to somewhat mend the torn areas it had suffered after his capture at Shiloh. He had been spotted before and even stopped twice, the last time by some Home Guard rabble that had made a thorough search of his person and saddlebags. He had been worried they were going to steal at least his saddle if not the horse itself, it being such a quality animal. If that had happened and they had found his Yankee blouse he had hoped they were stupid enough to believe it was a souvenir. They had certainly appeared to be dull witted enough to believe most anything.

When Pete had told them he was taking the horse to General Braxton Bragg himself for the general's personal mount, the scruffy men had hesitated. They had likely assumed Pete was lying, but he had on a newer standard issue great coat, even if his attempt at a southern accent had been very suspect or should have been. In that regard he had longed for at least one of Clifton Janeway's dubious attributes. Pete had also shown them a note he insisted confirmed his claim, having guessed correctly none of them could read. It hadn't been much of a gamble on his part, Pete had surmised. If he had ever run into a more dimwitted group of back-country dullards he couldn't recall where or when.

They had finally let him go with all his belongings even though the vote hadn't been unanimous. One of the men, a gaunt, nearly toothless fellow with remarkably bad breath had wanted to just kill him and take the horse. Although outvoted, it had been agreed his suggestion was not wholly without merit. Fortunately for Pete, the thoughtful one of the group had presented the winning argument on his behalf:

"If'n he ain't a lyin', Poteet," the orator had offered in rebuttal to his debating rival, "an' they gits wind'a it some ways or 'nother, it's a danged rope fer us."

***

PETE KNEW the approaching Confederates were cavalry and no doubt more observant. Showing them what had appeared to be a shopping list left in the great coat by its previous owner most likely wouldn't fool them. They rode on by however, appearing more interested in getting back to wherever their camp was located than whatever else they were supposed to be doing.

They hadn't even looked his way, nor had there been any break in their ongoing conversation. Pete continued to stay off the wagon trace and make it towards Kentucky through the woods wherever possible. He went another five miles or so as darkness fell. He was thankful for all the cover the dense woods had to offer. He finally dismounted near the top of a wooded hill and tethered his horse to a tree.

He climbed upon a large outcropping of rock and looked north into the valley below, then upwards. The full moon was bright in the sky, surrounded by countless stars glowing as well. The familiar sight reminded him of home, especially nights when he and Delicia had been alone on a porch or someplace where they could be away from others for awhile. Her knowledge of constellations had always been impressive, but often times he had been lucky to catch one word out of three when she had pointed towards the night sky, especially on nights such as the one he was presently enjoying. On such nights it had been all he could do to take his eyes off her face, bathed in moonbeams as if God Himself had made her the very center of the entire universe, he recalled thinking. She was no doubt the center of his and again his heart swelled in anticipation of their imminent reunion.

It was a crisp night but comfortable enough. He again scanned the valley below and as far beyond as possible. Nothing. Not a single thing appeared as it shouldn't be; no campfires, no sounds other than a night forest at peace with itself. Most importantly, there were no Rebel soldiers moving about out front and down below, as far as the moonlight was able to show. It wasn't daylight to be sure, but there was enough illumination to spot movement if the sounds men made suggested a general direction. As beautiful a sight as it was, and although Pete wanted to hesitate just a few moments longer in hopes of rekindling his images of Delicia, it was time to move on - it was time to go home.

"Stay right where you are, mister." The Confederate standing at the base of the outcropping ordered, his rifle pointed upwards at Pete. "Over here, boys, Ah got 'em! Bet ya thought we didn't see ya a hidin' in them trees back yonder, did ya mister. Now, why you reckon someone inside a gray great coat would be a hidin' from his own kind?"

***

IT WAS over three hours before the Confederate cavalry major had them bring Pete to his tent. The inside was awash in lantern light and the major was sitting behind a small desk. He looked young for his rank, but there he was. He glanced briefly at Pete then went back to his writing for a moment, then put his pen in its holder. There were several other Confederate officers in there and two hefty, heavily armed soldiers close by. Pete's hands were tied behind him and he was wearing his tattered lieutenant's blouse. Fortunately, he had removed the 1st Naperville shoulder insignia prior to his escape.

"From the emaciated look of you Ah'd ascertain you are an escaped prisoner, or perhaps a spy tryin' to make his way back. Either way, those could be hangin' offenses. What name you usin' today, Lieutenant?"

"My name is, and always has been, Robert McEnroe. I'm just lost, Major." Pete replied. "Trying to get home, that's all. Had enough of this damned war."

"And where would home be, Lieutenant 'McEnroe'? Not Kentucky, Ah'm assumin' from your Yankee accent."

"Small place in Iowa. Doubt you've heard of it, Major."

"And care even less. If you are a spy reckon Ah'd sure 'nough have ta string you up."

"I'm no spy Major, take my oath on it. I don't even know enough about these parts to come up with a lie you'd consider, and if I was a spy do you think I'd be wearing a Union blouse?"

"Then you must be a deserter or escaped prisoner, that's mah guess, and it's mah understandin' you had that blouse hid. Spies we caught don't look as poorly as you though. When was the last time you 'et? You're in luck though, relatively speakin' of course. Beats hell outta gettin' hung least ways. Got us a small group'a Yankee captives bein' taken away from here tomorrow mornin', eventually ta Camp Oglethorpe down in Macon if mah men kin git through ta the rail line. That damned rail line is a fair piece from here. That's Macon Georgia, Lieutenant, in case your Yankee upbringin' went beggin' which sure 'nough wouldn't surprise me none."

"I know where Macon is located, Major. Holding on to worthless information has always been an affliction of mine."

"You'll find nothin' ta make jest of once you're there Yank, but Ah reckon you're due your propers fer your quick wit and the pluck ta use it. Get this riffraff outta mah sight. And give 'em somethin' ta eat. He's gonna need it."

***

THE MEN at the rail line responsible for transporting the prisoners to Georgia were told to keep an eye on the new captive. He was most likely a runner and as runners went somewhat ingenious or at least lucky - to a point apparently. It appeared as though he had gone a fair distance although word hadn't reached the Confederates in northeast Tennessee who had captured Pete to be on the lookout for a Salisbury escapee. They put Pete in shackles including leg irons that were chained to a wall and welded to a cannonball. He was in the car where the Confederate guards stayed as well, and was told if he tried anything, anything little thing at all he would be shot.

It took well over a week to get there. Camp Oglethorpe was a rough stockade on nearly twenty acres near the Ocmulgee River, bordered on its other side by railroad tracks. There weren't very many Union prisoners there when Pete arrived due to prisoner exchanges, but he wasn't allowed to mingle with them anyway.

"Heard you got rabbit in ya boy," a Confederate sergeant said to him when Pete was first brought through the main gate after all the other prisoners were well inside.

"Don't know what you're talkin' about, I was just -" The sergeant brought the butt of his rifle up quickly and smashed it into the side of Pete's face, sending him sprawling to the ground.

"You lissen good, bluebelly!" The tall, obese sergeant exclaimed. "Talkin' when you ain't asked to ain't allowed. You best not fergit. Chain 'em in the Shed fer now."

The Shed was used for disciplinary reasons. It was not unlike the structure in Salisbury that served the same purpose, except the one in Oglethorpe had a wood floor and a tin roof. At first that seemed to be an improvement, but it was only December. Once spring and summer arrived, the humid subtropical climate in central Georgia made the Shed unbearable.

The tin roof wasn't in place by accident. When rain had dripped through the roof boards upon the men in the Salisbury detention hut it had been a nuisance, as Pete recalled. Not the one in Oglethorpe. Dripping raindrops would have been a Godsend amidst the stagnant air. There were no windows or even small slats to let in fresh air, and once the merciless Georgia sun focused upon the tin roof the Shed became an oven. More than one prisoner had been put in there during the hottest months only to be found dead or close to it.

Pete was initially left in there a week. On two of the days it had been unseasonably warm for December with temperatures reaching the mid-seventies. They had been cloudless days as well, and Pete thought he would die from thirst if not from the sweltering heat. Back home, even the heat waves of August couldn't compare to the inside of that hell hole. The only saving grace was the lack of rats; even they didn't come in when the sun was up. It didn't affect the lice and other insect vermin however.

When they finally let him out he made the mistake of thanking the guard. Instead of a "you're welcome" Pete received a boot to the groin, and was put back inside for another three days. After locking him up again the guard had a few muffled words that were still audible through the thick wooden door.

"You slow on learnin', ain't ya Yank."

When he was again let out, barely able to stand, they put him in a barn stall, one of a number of stalls used to house especially distrustful or unruly prisoners. The luckier ones were housed in rude huts or tents. Still, the barn was a definite improvement over the Shed.

On his first night in his new surroundings he even received some meat; mostly gristle but at least it didn't stink. There were also a few questionable prunes, a small potato, and water not all that brackish. Pete didn't know why he had been afforded such a luxury. Unbeknownst to him it was Christmas Eve.

XV

Delicia, Billy and Doc Wygant, along with the rest of the hospital staff were hurrying to complete their chores. The Christmas Eve party they had held for the wounded soldiers was over and most of the staff wanted to get home to their own family celebrations.

The party had been a rousing success, thanks to Clifton Janeway's apparent generosity; it had been as much a surprise as it had been magnanimous. Roasted turkeys, chicken pies, a baked spiced ham, six jugged hares in creamed onion sauce and a lamb kidney stew had been delivered all the way from Chicago by express train and wagon courier. Wine and other spirits were in abundance, as were presents for all the wounded men, and of course Delicia. Clifton had spared no expense, which had been accepted by Doc Wygant, reluctantly at first. He wasn't sure why he felt that way besides the obvious, especially since he had such an affinity for jugged hare.

Doc's budget was adequate to run the hospital but there was no way such a feast could have been afforded, let alone all the presents. Each patient who coveted a fine smoke received a dozen Havana cigars and a five pound box of chocolates. For those who didn't smoke, Clifton had seen to it each of them received an enormous jelly lemon cake with a side of coconut pudding from the finest bakery in Chicago. Each patient also received a vintage bottle of Dow's Porto along with a quarter pound of blue Stilton cheese.

When they were finally alone, Clifton handed Delicia her gift. She looked at the small velvet box tentatively, started to protest, but Clifton urged her to at least open it first. Inside was a platinum fine blue sapphire ring with two matching earrings.

"Merry Christmas, dear Delicia."

"I can't accept this Clifton, but thank you, and Merry Christmas to you as well."

"Please reconsider. It's not as if I were so brazen or delusional to offer you a diamond. This is merely a gift of friendship, and they match your beautiful blue eyes perfectly. I pray I am not being too forward with that innocent observation, but you have to admit it is accurate. All the young men hereabouts admire you, as does everyone else except the envious. Am I to be denied the same, simply because I have acknowledged it in a more meaningful manner?"

"I fear in a more substantial manner, Clifton. These must have cost a fortune."

"Well, they are of the highest clarity Tiffany's has to offer, but they still pale in comparison to your eyes. Spoken as hopefully your humble friend, of course. Why not keep them for now. If you decide I have been too optimistic in my hope that we can at least be warm acquaintances, why not donate them to the war effort? If you so decide, I will mask my disappointment by matching your generosity with an equivalent amount in cash. Better yet, I shall double the amount and in your name, if you keep them." Delicia sighed, looking at the impressive jewelry. She hesitated before finally looking at him

"That's very generous, Clifton. Everyone knows you have already donated more than your fair share as is. I'll keep them for now. I must admit they are beautiful," she acknowledged, gazing at them yet again, "but please don't donate anything in my name. It would make me feel deceitful."

"May I be allowed to press my luck and consider us friends?" Delicia frowned, but not with her eyes.

"Let's just say we are no longer enemies, and that I acknowledge the change that has come over you. Everyone should be allowed the opportunity to disavow past digressions, especially those committed when they were young and thoughtless I suppose. This horrible war has destroyed so many young men, but in some cases has allowed others to perhaps find themselves."

"May I sit with you in church this Sunday, Delicia?"

"That wouldn't be appropriate, Clifton. Besides, Father would have a conniption if he found you in our pew. I do hope you understand."

"Then I shall sit directly behind you, and offer prayer that someday you might at least allow me to share the same pew, Father or not." He said with a smile. Delicia returned his smile with one of her own.

"Someday perhaps," was all she said. For Clifton, it was more than he ever thought possible, and much less than he eventually hoped to obtain.

***

DELICIA'S YOUNGER brother was outside that snowy Christmas Eve waiting for her in a carriage. Their father usually insisted upon picking her up after work because he liked being able to talk to his eldest daughter away from others, as well as simply loving her company. Lately he had allowed young James to take over the duties. He would be going off to war soon, despite his mother's pleas coupled with his father's reservations, and appreciated the time alone with his older sister as well.

He didn't appreciate Clifton Janeway however, regardless of what others had begun to say of him. When James saw him leave the hospital he was again filled with contempt. He had his doubts, as did his father, about Janeway's story regarding what had happened to his older brother Sackett or at least how it happened, and suspected the story about Pete McCabe wasn't true either or at least exaggerated. Neither man suspected Clifton of anything as unconscionable as murder, but they certainly couldn't put the words bravery and Janeway in the same sentence either, not in a positive way. When Clifton passed by he waved at James and bid him Merry Christmas, but all the young man did was offer a slight, tight-faced smile and a nearly imperceptible nod.

"Isn't this an enchanting evening, James?" Delicia said as she entered the carriage shortly thereafter. "I declare, we haven't had such a perfectly timed snowfall on Christmas Eve since…well, I don't know when. The flakes are so huge, and not a wisp of wind."

"You seem rather blithe, as did your new friend Clifton Janeway just a moment ago." James remarked as he snapped the reins.

"I wouldn't call him a friend, James, not in the classic sense." She offered, somewhat defensively. "You have to admit, however, he has changed, or is at least making the attempt."

"It will take more than simple attempts to change that man's heart, unless Father and I have missed our guess."

"So suddenly you're taking Father's council to heart again? I don't recall you doing so before enlisting."

"That's an entirely different matter, Sister, but let's not quarrel. As you said, it's an enchanting evening." Regardless, Delicia did not speak to her brother again until they were nearly halfway home.

***

THE APPARENT change in Clifton wasn't limited to his encounters with Delicia; nearly the whole town talked about it. He attended church regularly, helped out at Sunday school, stayed away from the local tavern in the Pre-Emption House and volunteered his services as well as his money for a number of worthwhile causes. Something had obviously come over the young man and most people attributed it to his war experiences. He had even attempted to go back to combat duty, according to the local paper. The townsfolk took notice when the local paper reported General Smithington's response to Clifton's request, thanks to Buford Janeway. He saw to it the letter to his son made its way to the local reporter, just as the elder Janeway had written it:

My dear Major Janeway,

I thank you for your request, although it comes as no surprise coming from a soldier as brave and dedicated as yourself. As much as we could use an officer such as you involved with leading our men into battle, your value to the overall Cause demands that I deny your request.

Among your many attributes are your skills as an orator. The speech you gave on behalf of the Republic's recruitment initiatives in Aurora last month is a prime example. Over fifty young men who had previously failed to join our ranks did so immediately after your speech. Fifteen of them had already paid their $300 to avoid active duty, and not one of those requested a refund. Thanks to you, young men throughout the Chicago area are seeing the errors of their ways, and we have become an even stronger force for freedom our nation so desperately needs in times such as these.

I will go so far as to offer you a permanent appointment to my personal staff, stationed in your fine and loyal community of Naperville. Your glorious combat service alone would merit such a promotion, and your advice regarding overall strategy as it pertains to our upcoming campaigns will no doubt be invaluable.
I remain truly yours,
Lieutenant General Phineas Smithington

The letter was perfect in every way, and Buford Janeway was rather proud of his effort. Smithington and he had abandoned the petty cash bribes that had defined the beginning of their relationship. As long as the general kept a close watch on his son's welfare, Buford would continue to make him a silent partner on a variety of lucrative business ventures. The general's only involvement consisted of collecting his money with the promise of much more to come.

He had already accumulated almost enough to retire but wanted more. He was an obese, lazy man by nature, but he was far from stupid if craftiness and beguilement suggested intelligence. He knew full well what would happen once the war was over and the Janeways' no longer needed his services. With any luck however, the war should go on for at least two more years, perhaps longer. The general hoped so anyway, and if it had been within his power to prolong the bloody conflict it would have been as good as done, but his influence was beyond minuscule in that regard.

High ranking officers assigned to Chicago with no chance of being given more important duties could usually keep their rank if they knew how, but that was the long and short of it. By age sixty-five with decades of experience, General Smithington had become an expert at that game. For years he had longed for the day such tiresome efforts would no longer be necessary, but when it had finally arrived, thanks to Janeway's money and influence, all he wanted was more.

Buford had begun to keep his son in the dark about some of his dealings with the general. Clifton wasn't even aware his father had written the letter that appeared in the paper. Something had come over his boy, and if the elder Janeway hadn't missed his guess it had something to do with Delicia O'Darcy. That was understandable, as long as Clifton kept his wits about him.

Clifton's request for active duty had come as a surprise, but easily remedied. Still, it was wholly out of character for Clifton. Buford assumed it had probably been done for effect to impress the girl, and he also assumed his boy knew it wouldn't be granted. He hadn't, however, consulted Buford prior to his request and that gave the elder Janeway pause. He felt his son had already proven his mettle on the field of battle, already given his father more than enough to feel proud about, so why invite tragedy? No, Clifton belonged at home for the duration, and Buford would make sure that's where his only son stayed.

At least the boy remained more like his old self while at home. If annoyed, he still verbally abused his mother which was acceptable. Hired hands felt his wrath if something went wrong, like a horse not properly groomed or a stall not kept in perfect order, and heaven help the poor maid if the woman failed to have his favorite clothes ready when Clifton wanted them. He still made his trips into Chicago on most weekends. When Buford had been too inquisitive about Clifton's feelings for Delicia his boy mentioned those trips, and supposedly why he made them. Buford felt a sense of pride in that, and would occasionally ask his son about the current quality of the city's most expensive prostitutes, pretending he didn't know.

Clifton told his father about his exploits, mostly fabrications, but not for the reason Buford would have assumed. Clifton had secrets of his own, including the primary reason he had begun to spend so much time in Chicago. It hadn't been easy, but on his last trip he had finally located the perfect man for the job; the perfect man to find and kill Pete McCabe if by some slim chance he was still alive.

***

CLIFTON HAD begun his search in coarse taverns that drew men acquainted with war, or at least the military. Not the taverns active soldiers frequented, for the most part. He looked for ones that catered to the dregs, castoffs and other misfits.

He would show up dressed in a way that wouldn't draw suspicion. He wanted to look like he belonged in such places, and would let his otherwise clean shaven face grow out for a few days as well. He always brought enough cash to buy drinks for those he wanted to engage in conversation but didn't pull out more than a dollar or two at a time. He almost never talked about himself even when pressed to do so, and when he did his responses were vague and of course all lies. He wanted the other men to do the talking and was very good at getting them to do so. He feigned interest in their stories, most often exaggerated exploits if they had occurred at all, but he could see through most of them. *You cannot deceive a masterful liar.* He liked to remind himself with a sense of pride.

He had been searching for weeks and had finally narrowed his search to one man in particular. The man didn't frequent the taverns very much but his reputation was well known; several men had mentioned him over the weeks, insisting he was every-thing from a first rate mercenary to a former slave catcher of some renown. One night Clifton was in one of the better establishments, all things considered, and a man Clifton had been talking to at the bar pointed the fellow out. "Well, speak of the devil hisself. Look who just walked in."

The man was solidly built, not overly large, but had the look of someone who could hold his own; the kind that, win or lose, his opponent would invariably come away knowing the fight could have gone either way. He was perhaps thirty or there-abouts with sandy hair in need of attention, as did his entire appearance.

Clifton waited until the man had found a stool at the bar, then sauntered over and took a seat next to him. He was an easy man to engage in conversation; affable in a simpleminded sort of way, but Clifton had heard enough about his reputation to tolerate his apparent lack of intelligence and personal hygiene. An hour later they were seated at a table, in what Clifton read as an inane and way too lengthy conver-sation.

"Ah reckon Ah kin find dern near any ole body, if'n the money be right." The man said. "Nigger or white man, chink, wetback or stinkin' redskin, don't make no never mind ta me. Shit fire, Ah could track me a fish in the derned oceans!" The man exclaimed with a wide-eyed conviction he was apparently stupid enough to believe was convincing.

Clifton wasn't impressed to say the least, but had allowed the man to carry on due to his reputation, the validity of which had become very much in doubt. "Shit fire, Ah kin dern near sceer fleas off a dog if'n they gits ta thinkin' Ah'm on their trail. Tangles up their common sense, makes 'em zig when they oughta be'a zaggin'! Gotta gits down to their level, if'n you know mah meanin'." With that the man winked at Clifton, then let out a stream of tobacco juice in the general direction of a spittoon, missing it for at least the tenth time. As usual, an amber line of drool stayed on the man's unshaven chin, only half of which, again as usual, he felt compelled to wipe away with the sleeve of his tattered coat.

Clifton had heard and seen enough. The man was an idiot. It was time to aban-don the dolt and renew his search. "Well sir, thank you for your time. Allow me to buy you another round, but I must be on my way."

"Precisely my point," the man said, his eyes going from those of a backwoods dullard to clear and focused. "Often times the best way to find someone is to be certain those you are attempting to glean information from consider you harmless, or at least not nearly as bright as themselves. I'm not dismissing the value of bribery, or the threat or use of violence when the situation calls for it, but people will generally be more forthcoming with information when they don't feel a need to withhold it, when they don't see any harm in so doing.

"That said, the antithesis of same is also not without merit. The key is being able to adapt to a given situation. Take you for instance. You thought I was at best stupid, but have stayed here because you heard I might be your man. That tells me a great deal about you sir, most importantly the level of your desire to find something, or someone. You are very determined, of that I have no doubt. All this time you thought you were evaluating me, but it was the other way around. You're a man of means, although no one here knows the extent of your wealth except the two of us. You want something very badly, so much so you have been in here and other places in search of a man like me for weeks, perhaps longer. I've seen you, although this is the first time you have seen me. That, sir, wasn't by chance. I found you before you even came close to finding me.

"No one around here has any idea who you are, and for that I offer you my compliments. I, however, know exactly who you are. You are Major Clifton Janeway, from Naperville. You are a war hero, or so your two citations for bravery would imply. You come from money, a lot of it. And for some reason you need the professional services I can provide. Do you still want to buy me a drink and depart, or buy me a drink and continue our conversation?"

Clifton was in shock. He couldn't recall ever having been fooled so completely. The man had babbled on like a blithering idiot for over an hour, one inane story after another, and Clifton hadn't suspected anything other than the man was an unkempt buffoon, which had been obvious from the beginning. Yet Clifton had stayed and listened, and the longer he stayed the more convinced the man had become of Clifton's resolve.

"Sir, I am duly impressed." Clifton finally said. "It appears part of your reputation may be well founded after all. Whether I can trust you or not is another issue."

"I didn't build that reputation by failing my clients, or cheating them, Major Janeway. I choose them more carefully than they choose me. I could offer references, but then wouldn't that compromise your position if you were foolish enough to check them out with those far more perceptive than the wretches from whom you have thus far gleaned information, including the man I paid to point me out upon my arrival? You need secrecy, is that not so? Otherwise you would have been more forthright in your search, as opposed to the strategy you have been utilizing. Fortunately, you have succeeded. I can give you an honest appraisal of my abilities and a candid overview of my accomplishments. Then we can talk price, or you can resume your search."

"I'm possibly done searching, sir. Things of this nature come with risks, and I'm inclined to take them if you continue to impress me. Tell me about those accomplishments."

"I have been in the military and still hire myself out to the North or South as a spy if the price is right. I have hunted men throughout the United States, Mexico, Canada and overseas. I rarely fail and haven't in years. I used to go after runaway slaves, and although I might be enticed to do so again I'd just as soon leave it in my past, especially since this war has started. Besides, my brother is very active in that trade, and he's the best I know of except for myself, although he would be loath to admit it. We haven't been in touch for years." That got Clifton's attention.

"Actually, I could use someone with a keen knowledge of the South. He could indeed be of use to me." Clifton said.

"I'm sure he could," the man replied, somewhat impatiently. "But his knowledge of the South is no better than mine. We grew up together in Georgia."

"You certainly don't sound like you're from the South, although you did sound like the epitome of Southern white rabble a moment ago."

"I can convince any local in any part of the country that I grew up next door to him, if my accent is all he has to go on. It comes naturally to me."

"I understand sir, believe me. Please continue." Clifton remarked, smiling to himself.

"You suggested my brother might be useful, so you should hear the rest of it. He's older than me and never allowed me to forget it. We hunted slaves together for over five years, employing a variety of miscreants, talented as they may have been. He was always in charge and never allowed me to forget that either.

"One night down in Mexico things changed, rather abruptly. We were in a small cantina, drunk on mescal. We had just lost the trail of two runaways, and although he was to blame he insisted the fault was mine. The more we drank the more he insisted that was the case. Even the others we were with tried to reason with him but he would have none of it.

"Finally, I knocked him to the floor. It was the first time his kid brother had ever done so and he was furious. He came at me again and the same thing happened. When he got up again, he lunged at me with his bowie knife. I took a jug of mescal and brought it down on his head. It shattered, and a jagged edge made a horrible gash from his forehead down to his jaw.

"We found a local Mexican who insisted he knew how to stitch such wounds, but he was a liar. It became infected and my brother almost died. To this day he carries the scar. He was never handsome, but the last time I saw him the left side of his face was so hideous even whores shunned him, some of them anyway.

"His name is Runyun Stalworthy. Perhaps you have heard of him. If you owned a sizeable number of slaves you would no doubt be familiar with his name. I am Elwood Stalworthy. That said, now it is your turn Janeway. I want to know what you want and what you are willing to pay for it, or this conversation is over."

"His name is Pete McCabe. He was a lieutenant with the 1st Naperville Cavalry, my old outfit. He is almost certainly dead but I have to know for sure."

"So what you need is for me to verify whether or not he is alive?" Stalworthy asked, discarding his large chaw of tobacco in disgust with a perfect toss into the spittoon ten feet away.

"That's part of what I want," Clifton continued. "If he is alive, I want him dead. Now, sir, does that requirement end our conversation?"

"Of course not, but it won't be cheap. Fill me in on the details. I need to know everything." Stalworthy looked around as he spoke. "We'll discuss price in a moment."

"We were at Shiloh together. Ended up in the peach orchard. I assume you have heard of it."

"Of course."

"The Rebels had overrun our position, but a few of us found ourselves trapped, thanks to that glory hound Major O'Darcy. He damn near got me killed, and succeeded in doing so to himself. We were together in a hollow, protected by some rocks when the fool decided to open up on some advancing Rebels. He killed them, but they got him as well, leaving me in a very bad way."

"I read your account in the paper, Janeway. I seem to recall you mentioning this Pete McCabe's fate as well. Obviously, you have a different version for me."

"I do indeed. There was no shell burst, at least nowhere near him. He was to my left, hiding under a log. My position wasn't nearly as secure. I crawled over to the bodies of the Rebels Sackett O'Darcy had killed, and put on one of their uniforms since so many Rebels were lurking about. My plan was to make it back behind our own lines, or what was left of them, if I could get back into my uniform without getting shot after gaining the confidence of those nearby Rebels then eluding them. Before I could do so, I noticed McCabe take aim at some dandy of a Rebel officer, over a hundred yards away. Shot him damn near off his horse. Believe it or not he had managed to hit General Johnston himself, killing him as you are well aware, but not who shot him until now."

"You're telling me this McCabe fellow is the man who killed Johnston? That's a tall story, Janeway."

"High as the sky, but true nonetheless. Saw it with my own eyes. His shot alerted the nearby Rebels, the ones I was hoping to fool. I joined up with them to point out where the Yankee who shot the general was hiding."

"Sounds as if you sure enough wanted him dead."

"Oh, make no mistake about that, sir. At least that was part of it. I also wanted them to leave, assuming they would do so after killing him on the spot. The imbeciles made him their captive after slightly wounding him however, and expected me to accompany them back to their lines."

"Besides the uniform, how did you ever convince them you weren't a Yankee? You sure as hell sound like one to me."

"You, sir, aren't the only one with an ear for accents. Y'all git mah meanin?"

"Not bad, Janeway, but for future reference never use 'y'all' if you are conversing with and referring to only one person. Other than that, not bad."

"Thank you for your advice and the compliment. At any rate, once he had been captured and recognized me standing there in Rebel attire, I loath to call it a uniform as such, he went insane. He tried to tell them I was indeed a Yankee. There he was, caught due to his own absurd sense of duty, and he attempts to expose me for doing nothing but trying to stay alive. They, of course, thought he *was* out of his mind, or perhaps trying to throw them off in a vain attempt to garner some type of advantage. As we were marching him back however, a group of our men retreating from the Hornet's Nest spotted us. They killed the Rebels I was with best I know, but others soon arrived. I don't know if they took McCabe back, or if he even survived the following few moments. He was in a bad way. That's the last I saw of him. I had to do some quick thinking after that, but as you can see I was successful except for the wound I suffered."

"And you think McCabe is probably dead, and are willing to pay dearly to assure that is indeed the case. Yet you painted him a dead hero in the papers, when you could have just as easily made him out to be otherwise. You never mentioned anything about him killing Johnston, which is odd if having him end up a true hero was your motive as your public pronouncements suggest, not to mention that if you had done so in a public forum such as a newspaper it may well have sealed your adversary's fate, on the off chance he has survived. What haven't you told me?"

"I don't see where you need to know my motives, Stalworthy. It's enough for you to know I want him dead or confirmation he already is and I'm willing to pay for it. As for your assumption me mentioning the true story of General Johnston's fate may have served me well, I had to consider it having the opposite effect if McCabe had somehow survived. They may well have executed him, but what if cooler heads prevailed and they traded him for what could well have been a substantial number of their own captured soldiers? Regardless, my motives are, as far as you're concerned, sir, beside the point."

"As I have already told you, Janeway, I need to know *every*thing. Who can tell what might prove useful down the road? It might even be some trifling bit of information that secures our ultimate success. Again, what haven't you told me? Why is his death so important to you, assuming he's alive? You wouldn't be this motivated if all he did is what you have described in the heat of battle when most everyone is not themselves. Unless you are a vindictive fool. You don't strike me as a fool, Major Janeway. You are at least vindictive though, but I suspect more."

"If he is somehow alive and makes his way back it will cost me dearly, both in reputation and as it pertains to a certain personal affair."

"I suppose I can understand the reputation aspect, since you are referring to more than mere embarrassment now that I think about it, but you posing as a Rebel would be your word against his, unless he has solid evidence which is virtually impossible. He would need credible witnesses of your actions, and thus far your reputation is spotless since no one else has been forthcoming I know of. If he is alive, he is likely in a prison of some kind. You saw that happen, or at least you saw him captured, but that's not enough for you - you need him dead. Therefore you are either lying by omission for some reason, possibly a serious love interest which you may have already alluded to even if you didn't come out and say it, and it is apparent he is more than capable of upsetting your plans, correct?"

"You are a very perceptive man, Stalworthy. I am again duly impressed. But that isn't my only motivation. I have despised him since childhood, more so after I was forced to serve with that self-righteous bastard. He humiliated me at every opportunity. What will this cost? I am prepared to pay you five thousand now, and five thousand more when you have convinced me he is dead. No disrespect intended sir, but your word won't do. I will need irrefutable proof he is either dead already or you have done it. Regardless, the evidence has to be solid."

"Such as?"

"You're the professional. You tell me."

"First of all, your offer is absurd. If he is alive and I succeed in finding and killing him and bring back evidence you cannot deny, I will expect fifty thousand in gold. If he is already dead, you will have to be content with my report that will be based, I presume, on an eye-witness report from a Rebel or Rebels who saw it happen. That will cost $25,000. If I cannot supply you with any more than you now know, it will still cost you all my estimated expenses up front, five thousand also up front as a retainer, and an additional five thousand for my trouble when I return. It may likely prove impossible to determine whether or not he was killed, but those are my terms."

"Those are handsome sums," Janeway said, not appearing to be in the least bit fazed. "How do you plan on finding him, and how could you possibly bring me evidence I cannot refute?"

"How I find him is my concern. Be forewarned, however, it will take time. If all goes extremely well, at least three months. Six months more like it, easily longer. As far as the evidence is concerned if the largest fee is owed, well sir, you are familiar with embalming fluids such as formaldehyde, are you not?"

"I've heard of them."

"Then I will bring you his head." Janeway just stared at the man. Stalworthy was dead serious, and had said it as if it was simply one of many things he needed to do, albeit the most important thing if he wanted his money.

"His head." Janeway finally repeated, hoping he had masked his astonishment. His mind didn't stop working though. "And what if it's disfigured, or the chemicals alter the facial properties in a way that still leaves me in doubt?"

"Good points all. Can you recall any unique markings on him? Any deformities, tattoos, anything?"

"Now that you mention it, he is missing a toe. Lost it when he was a boy, farming mishap. The men asked him about it one day when a score of us were bathing in a pond, just before our first engagement with the Rebels down Missouri way."

"Which toe?" Stalworthy asked.

"Which toe indeed, sir. And which foot? Bring me the correct foot missing the correct toe, along with the head of course, and you will have already found your answer and fifty thousand in gold. How much do you need in advance for expenses, did you say five thousand?"

"I said my initial retainer is five thousand, my expenses considerably more I would imagine. Five thousand in gold will suffice, for now, plus an initial $2,500 up front for expenses."

"You are asking a great deal, Stalworthy. Perhaps the upfront money is all you're after. I'm not sure I see why I should trust you, but I will."

"I don't trust you either, or anyone else when it comes to money and damn few when it comes to anything else, and those not completely. If I am all I maintain to be you will pay me the rest. If I can root out someone in the South who might be a prisoner in any one of numerous locations, get to him, bring back his head and foot no less, do you honestly believe I would have any trouble finding a rich man in Naperville or anywhere else he might be? I assume you know what would happen when I found you. It's only important that you maintain a healthy respect for my abilities, and my resolve. We have a deal, do we not?"

"When can you start?" Was Clifton's only reply.

***

THE FOLLOWING day was Sunday and Clifton had arrived early for church services. Delicia arrived shortly thereafter with her family, and said something to her parents after spotting Clifton alone in his family's pew.

"I promised Doctor Wygant I would thank Major Janeway for his generosity at the hospital Christmas party," she told her parents as they headed for their family pew closer to the front, "and I haven't had the opportunity until now. I'll be right back." Hezekiah displayed a frown as he escorted the rest of his family to their pew.

"For someone who promised to sit directly behind me you are quite a distance from our pew, Major Janeway."

"I wasn't sure where, exactly, you personally would alight," he said with a smile. "Your mother is a fine looking woman as are your lovely sisters, but they are not you. Moreover, with my luck I would have ended up choosing the spot directly behind your father. Where's James?"

"He departed Friday," Delicia said, growing somber. "We are all deeply concerned as you can well imagine. Clifton, is there anything you could do to keep him from danger? He is so impetuous, and determined to avenge Sackett's death."

"Such an attitude, though understandable, is enough to get him killed all right. I've seen it countless times. I'll wire General Smithington after today's service since I have business in Aurora anyway. He'll be willing to help. James will be safe, I can assure you."

"Oh, thank you Clifton, I am indebted to you, we all are, but it's best we keep it a secret, especially from James. If he were to ever find out he would be furious with me."

"Our first secret? I am honored, Delicia. But I have a bone to pick with you. Where are your sapphires?" He asked, feigning disappointment.

"At home, where they'll stay for now. They're beautiful Clifton, but I still feel uneasy about accepting them, let alone explaining them to my family."

"I understand, forgive my teasing. But didn't you just say you were indebted to me? Will you lunch with me tomorrow? I can bring something for everyone at the hospital if you like, but I would prefer dining with you away from prying eyes."

"It won't be necessary for you to bring all that food to the hospital, Clifton. It would only cause more talk and besides, Monday is my day off. I would be willing to lunch with you however. Why don't you come by Pinecraig at noon? Father and Mother will be in Aurora tomorrow, along with my youngest sisters. Ginny and Linda Marie will be home, but I think it's time for them to see for themselves the change in you. I know it sounds unpleasant, since they'll certainly be cold at first. They haven't been with you up close since that night at…well, that night. They will want to hear about Sackett I'm sure, so expect tears. On that sad note, will you come?"

"Of course, Delicia. But tell me. If they ask about our dear Pete will my story not cause you further pain? Bringing any grief to you is the last thing I want."

"Oh, I suppose it's time to get that out in the open as well, Clifton. Nothing can bring Pete back, though I wish with all my heart that wasn't so."

"Then it is settled, on one condition," Clifton remarked, trying to lighten things. "You must promise to wear the sapphires."

"We'll see, Clifton. See you at noon tomorrow. I must hurry back. I can feel Father's eyes boring into me." She smiled, her eyes locked on his.

Clifton returned her warm smile and nodded in understanding just before she turned and left. *Father's eyes his boil-covered ass.* Clifton thought as he stared serenely at the statue of Jesus Christ upon the Cross located on the wall left of the pulpit. *Perhaps I have another little job for Stalworthy when he returns…*

***

CLIFTON ARRIVED promptly at noon. He had bouquets for Delicia's sisters and a larger one for her. There were nurseries in Naperville, but Clifton had seen to it the fresh cut flowers had been fetched by a servant all the way from Aurora that morning, since it boasted the finest floral shop outside Chicago.

Delicia had prepared Ginny and Linda Marie for his arrival as best she could, and although the two girls generally adored their older sister and had usually respected her opinions, wise council and common sense, they were still uneasy. Sometimes Delicia could get a little carried away with herself, adopt an air of seemingly innocent condescension as if it were a given her heart was permanently pointed in the right direction or heading that way.

Other times she seemed to be listening when her sisters were making a point, but her eyes indicated otherwise, as if her patience was more a gift than a virtue. Linda Marie especially felt that way, and at times had reminded her oldest sister that Delicia was just that, and not her mother. Linda Marie and Ginny promised to keep an open mind however, and reserve their judgment until Major Janeway was gone and the three of them could discuss things in detail.

Clifton certainly looked the part. He had on his newest major's uniform, custom tailored from silk, and had taken pains to tone it down from the garish captain's uniform he had originally owned, although his new attire still turned heads.

He hadn't gained back any of the weight he had lost. If anything, he looked even better. Once his wound had healed he had begun to exercise regularly, and it showed. He had never been remotely interested in such things before, but then he had never believed Delicia O'Darcy would ever warm to him either. He knew full well how fit Pete McCabe had always been and was determined to follow his example.

The girls thanked Clifton for their fresh cut flowers and proceeded to put them in a variety of vases. They retired to the family parlor until the maid slid the pocket doors open to announce lunch was ready. As soon as they were seated around the dining room table, Clifton, all charm, complimented the center piece, stating he hadn't seen such a beautiful epergne since his family had dined with the governor and his wife at their mansion in Springfield before the war. Believing his flattery had been well received he offered up something considerably more meaningful.

"I have news!" He said, eyes aglow. "Every Monday morning I receive a report from General Smithington's headquarters now that I'm on his staff, and it appears the recent enlistees from Naperville, some of them anyway, have been assigned to Washington or soon will be. Our nation's capital is a wonderful place to serve, especially from a safety perspective. As it turns out, I was able to make sure your brother James was among those chosen. I'm sure that comes as a big relief to all of you as it will your dear parents." The girls were beside themselves.

"Major Janeway!" Linda Marie exclaimed, "That is indeed wonderful news! I can't wait to tell Mother and Father!" Ginny expressed similar emotions, while Delicia simply bowed her head briefly and smiled. *So much for keeping secrets,* she said to herself, but was greatly relieved to hear the news anyway. When she looked up and directly into Clifton's eyes he thought he saw everything he had hoped to find.

"Are you certain James will remain there, Major?" She asked, playing the thoughtful big sister.

"Nothing short of a catastrophe could change that, Miss Delicia. I wouldn't worry about that however. The Rebels have enough on their hands keeping our forces from advancing farther into what they mistakenly believe is their territory. Washington D.C. is the last thing on their minds, unless they are dreaming. James will be fine, I can assure all of you."

It was mostly merriment from there. Delicia's sisters didn't even press him for details about Sackett, let alone Pete, although their names did come up. Clifton was in his element, and the charm, apparent sincerity and grace he displayed had both of Delicia's sisters fawning over him, especially Linda Marie. The only time references were made regarding the other two men was when Clifton announced he had sent a request to General Smithington urging him to consider recommending both Sackett and Pete for posthumous citations for bravery.

"There were three of us holding back the Rebel advance that sad day in the peach orchard, and if it hadn't been for the bravery of Sackett and Pete no telling how many of our brave comrades who had been forced to fall back would have been lost."

"Don't forget your bravery as well, Major." Linda Marie, sixteen and filling out nicely, added.

"I'll never forget the sacrifices our dear Sackett and Pete made," he responded softly, as if his ability to hold back his emotions was about to fail him. "All three of us did everything we could to protect our comrades, but it was the sacrifices made by my two closest friends that deserves to be honored most. I even informed General Smithington my own citations were tucked away in a drawer, and would remain there if those two brave men weren't so honored." Silence fell over the dining room as all three young women dealt with their rekindled sorrows.

The heavy-heartedness was short lived. Clifton, in an impressive display of personal strength despite his mourning, regaled the girls with more lighthearted stories and soon had them feeling relatively cheerful again.

After his departure the two sisters, Linda Marie in particular, had nothing but good things to say about him. His transformation had indeed changed a misguided boy into a fine example of manhood, she insisted. His devotion to God had much to do with it, as did his military experience, but it was obvious his feelings for Delicia could not be discounted either, she teased. Linda Marie's envy consumed her: *If only it were me...*

XVI

Missy Nell was asleep on Cusman's shoulder. The events of the day coupled with the steady movement of the train had lulled her into a sound slumber. Cusman tried his best not to disturb her as beautiful, angelically so he believed, she appeared to him. He had never imagined everything would be so easy, he thought, as the train took them closer to freedom. They still had a ways to go, but if things continued to go half as smoothly they would soon realize a dream that just weeks before seemed so fraught with peril it was as if actually realizing their ultimate goal would likely end up being a miracle or two short of fulfilling its promise.

Cusman fantasized about what their life would be like once they were upon free soil. Jennifer had promised to buy them a house and fund his education, and her word was golden. He considered a variety of fields; a law degree, perhaps a business degree, even running their own farm crossed his mind. His main requirement was to be his own man. When he considered all the possibilities, why not a combination of those things? He was after anything that afforded them the most freedom possible. He would pay Jennifer back every cent for the house and his education too, even though she steadfastly maintained Cusman and Missy Nell had paid a high enough price, all things considered. If he would agree to help her with a few business ventures of her own however, she would be willing to work with him as equal partners on any of those undertakings, which would be payment enough.

He understood the significance of her generous offer, since he was keenly aware that working for any of the vast majority of white people would diminish his freedom, even after the three of them were safely in the North. He suffered few delusions in that regard. The South wasn't the only place where racism existed, far from it. Treating a person of color as if their overall worth was obviously inferior to all but the most reprehensible whites was a reality in the North as well, at least that's what he'd heard from sources he deemed reliable. He recalled what his father had told him: *"More'n a few Northern white folk be sayin' a nigger's just that, an' always will be nothin' but low down, shiftless trash. Plenty'a white folk down this way agree, but least ways they lotsa times don't include coloreds what's loyal an' obedient long as they stay that way. Even so Cusman, toein' that slippery trail cain't promise peace'a mind, an' it sure as heaven sap your manhood."* Cusman directed his thoughts towards more positive things, at least for a while.

They would have children, lots of them. Missy Nell loved to talk about that and how glorious it would be to raise such a family without fear. How many times over the years had the agony of witnessing a child being taken from its parents been endured, including members of Cusman's own extended family? How often had he observed Mas'r Ransom chortling with his peers over cognac in Grand House because he had realized a handsome profit by selling off a mother's child or all her children, sometimes her husband too, while the devastated woman wailed inconsolably in her suddenly empty cabin? Not for long though. She had her duties, and if she carried on too long the overseer or one of his minions would see to it she was back at work after an acceptable length of time had been allotted to accommodate her foolishness.

Trenton Ransom believed he was generous in that regard - he usually allowed the field hands to carry on in such a manner for the rest of that day. *They get over it. After all, they're just niggers…God blessed niggers with that peculiar ability, least ways the good ones*…with that firmly imbedded in his mind, he slept as guilt free as an angel. *I'm firm but fair with my niggers, and deep down the good ones all know it…*

Niggers. Cusman swore if he ever heard any of his children addressed by that designation or any like it there would be hell to pay, and a heap more. He vowed his children would never know bondage, nor would he allow anyone to drape upon them even a hint of what it represented. He would, however, fully expect his children to earn their respect. Until they had the chance to do so he would demand it from anyone who attempted to deny it, egregiously or implied.

He glanced out the window and watched the rolling countryside fly by, grateful Missy Nell and he were finally in a car that afforded them such a luxury. It hadn't been due to any benevolence from the railroad. At the last minute there hadn't been a boxcar available like the one they had taken from Atlanta, so the railroad company had been forced to use a passenger car for "the niggers". The current car was still attached to the back of the train save the caboose, and when some of the white passengers had expressed their disapproval at even that modest arrangement they were assured the car carrying the slaves and the few free Negroes on board would be hosed down and scrubbed thoroughly before being put back in use for white passengers. It hadn't escaped Cusman that the few white passengers who had complained the loudest weren't slave owners themselves, just low bred crackers intent upon exerting their self-importance. "S'pect they gotta be better than somebody," he had said to Missy Nell, "since they ain't."

***

AFTER A while the train began to slow down as it approached the next town. Cusman needed to use an outhouse and hoped there would be one for coloreds. Missy Nell smiled at Cusman as the train eased towards the station, and gave him a small hug. When the train stopped he asked her if she needed to use the facilities as well. She did, so they disembarked and looked around, Cusman carrying the leather satchel and the case with the guns. All they found was one outhouse behind the station marked "whites only". Even the sign was whitewashed for those who couldn't read. They made their way back to the platform and Cusman asked a busy railroad employee where the colored outhouse was located.

"Ain't got none for no niggers," he replied. "You an' your nigger wench kin use that ditch over yonder, but make sure you bury your droppins'. There's a shovel handy, make sure you use it. You understandin' me, boy?" Cusman didn't answer as he led Missy Nell away from the man.

They couldn't decide whether or not their urges were stronger than the humiliation they certainly did not want to suffer since the shallow ditch afforded little privacy. They hadn't gone very far, not far enough to indicate their possible intentions in that regard, when they first spotted the men; six heavily armed riders were coming down the road which led from the small town to the north, their galloping horses stirring up a sizeable amount of dust.

After they had dismounted and arrived at the platform, the one wearing a sheriff's badge began to give instructions as he pointed to the various cars, especially the last one, as the men stood amidst the passengers who were coming and going. Both Cusman and Missy Nell saw Jennifer stroll by the men then stop within earshot of them, as if she were looking for something in her purse. She looked around almost immediately and appeared quite relieved to see Cusman and Missy Nell moving behind some cotton bales, out of sight from the men. She wasted no time getting to them.

"Something is very wrong," she said, her face pure trepidation. "Let's go this way." She led them around the south side of the station and told them what she had heard. "The sheriff received a telegram. They're looking for a white woman accompanied by two armed runaways. Something about a great deal of gold as well. I fear we have been discovered."

"Not yet we ain't," Cusman replied. "Let's go 'round back."

The men had tethered their horses to a hitching post north of the station, just past the rear of it, off its northeast corner beneath the shade of a massive tulip poplar. Cusman, Missy Nell and Jennifer made their way close to the area, staying behind the rear of the building.

There was but one thing to do, and after Cusman had taken the necessary risk of going over to the horses while keeping a close watch as best he could on the activity close to the train, he motioned for the women to quickly join him.

He helped them up on two horses and placed the satchel with the gold in front of Missy Nell, securing its handle over the saddle horn. "Hold tight as you can Missy, if we get the chance I'll figure somethin' else out."

He kept the case with the guns, untied the remaining horses and mounted the largest one while keeping hold of the reins of the other horses. They made their way back behind the station and headed east across a meadow as fast as possible. Jennifer got a hold of the reins of two of the rider-less mounts to assist Cusman as all three of them kept looking back towards the station.

The perilous turn of events was far from over but it loosened its hold on them for the time being. They had disappeared undetected over a rise several hundred yards away, and another fifteen minutes passed before the disappearance of the horses was even noticed.

By then Cusman had both revolvers strapped on and had relieved Missy Nell of the gold and disabled the other horses. Some of the deputies had left their rifles in their saddle scabbards, having assumed their revolvers would suffice while searching the train. There was even an ample supply of ammunition in two of the saddlebags.

The furious small-town sheriff was at a loss. He was so unhinged even more time was wasted just trying to calm him down. If such a dire situation was inevitable the three escapees couldn't have chosen a better town for it to have happened. Not only were the men without their horses, but there weren't any around that could be of use to them either. The only other mounts available were draft horses used only for menial in-town work; even the livery didn't have any suitable horses to offer. The closest horses that would have been suitable for an extended pursuit were over at the Clemson place, twelve miles north of town. Small comfort, since old man Clemson would charge an absurd price to rent them and demand payment in advance.

The sheriff again proved why he shouldn't have been elected in the first place. He had ordered all his men to go after the runaways on foot, and not come back until they had found at least some of the stolen horses. They found them all right, but Cusman had done such a thorough job of incapacitating them they wouldn't be useful for weeks.

Worse yet, it hadn't occurred to the sheriff to send out wires to the neighboring towns until later that night, after a local bartender had asked him if their top lawman, Aluisis Lazhorn, had received any responses from having done so. He said he had not and cursed the other communities for their incompetence. After gulping his drink he said he'd check again, just in case. The bartender just shook his head and sighed as Aluisis strode through the double doors, as if on a mission.

Less than half an hour later he was back in the bar. The telegraph office was not only closed which was expected, but Randolph Scruggs, the only man in town that knew Morse Code, was nowhere to be found. Even the widow Lindstrom didn't know where he'd gone off to, but she knew it was no doubt in the company of Randolph's best friend, Old Jake Beam. He never strayed far from his Old Tub whiskey companion, especially after hours, or most other times if his jug wasn't empty.

***

THE WOMEN wanted to head north, but not Cusman. Not yet. They were greatly relieved no one appeared to be following but they knew that wouldn't last. They had stayed on an easterly course for over twenty miles, finally resting in a lush valley with an abundance of pin oaks and a stream running through it. A chilly night was upon them but they didn't dare light a fire.

"The best way to get to the North is to *head* north, Cusman." Jennifer said as the three of them huddled together by a tree next to the stream.

"If it was your job to catch us, would you look north or south of that train station Missis Jennifer?" He asked.

"I understand that Cusman, but look at us. We'll be easy to spot no matter which way we go. I fear wires have been sent in all directions, why not get as close as possible to the one place where we will be safe?"

"Safe is a long way off no matter which way we choose, Missis. Not distance wise if we head north, I'll grant you that, but that's where they'll be lookin' the hardest, too. If we could somehow get us more common clothes, maybe disguise us in other ways, we might not *look* like what they be lookin' *for*, not as much anyway. Lay low south of here a while, then make our move."

"Well Cusman, that sounds logical, but it's too bad we can't make you two white for a week or so," Jennifer remarked in jest, hoping to ease the tension.

"No offense Missis, but that would be a lowdown tragedy even for a day," was Cusman's only response.

***

THEY CONSIDERED traveling at night but Cusman dismissed that option, insisting their unfamiliarity with the local terrain made such a move unwise. Not only would two coloreds traveling in the dead of night with a white woman look suspicious if some farmer or Home Guard unit happened to spot them, but their ignorance of the area could easily cause them to go from being lost to being really lost. Besides, no one had followed them that they knew of, which appeared as odd as it was fortuitous.

The small valley they were in afforded some degree of protection, and since it was one of many in that particular area it wasn't as if any pursuers would be drawn to it first unless they had dogs or were adept at tracking. They decided to stay put until morning. Sleep was all but impossible so they talked well into the night.

"Trenton is no doubt aware something is wrong," Jennifer said. "When that obese sheriff mentioned the gold I knew there was no way Trenton wasn't behind this. He always has been an old snoop, but I had hoped with all he has on his mind there was a good chance he wouldn't have looked at the gold this time, at least not right away. I can only imagine what his reaction was when it wasn't there."

"He might think I took it, Mother, since I know your room so well includin' under your closet floor." Missy Nell offered.

"You knew it was there?" Jennifer asked. "Who else knew?"

"Lord, all the house coloreds knew it was upstairs somewhere. I s'pect most the field hands too. Lots of talkin' goes on and that story's a favorite. Some said you and Mas'r had at least a hundred thousand hid up there."

"My, we wouldn't have been able to carry that much with any degree of stealth, but it would have been tempting to try. What I don't know is what Trenton is prepared to do. If he had it in his mind you two alone were responsible, that notion must have vanished once he found out it was I who brought you two along when we left Harriet's place then boarded that last train together, for Richmond no less, assuming he somehow obtained that information. Regardless, he has to know by now what I'm up to, and I fear all sorts of things are going through his head, and none of them bode well for us."

***

GIVEN ENOUGH time, Runyun Stalworthy and his men could usually track down anyone virtually anywhere, with only a wisp of information to begin their search. The information they had as they started out for their current prey made their task simple. A wire had finally arrived from the small town, so they even knew where the three runaways had escaped from the train. As the three runaways huddled in the darkness that first night Stalworthy and his men were already riding to the train station in Charleston.

Jennifer's sister had been beside herself when Stalworthy had questioned both her and her husband, refusing to accept what was obviously the truth about her sister. Even if it was true she felt obliged to defend Jennifer. Not Tredwell. Having fostered it he held the same opinion as his brother-in-law, and pitied the poor man.

"Sister or not, there is no justification for such abominable behavior. Don't you feel the least bit betrayed, Harriet? She and her niggers accepted our hospitality for a week, and look at what a fool she made of you. She even played with your feelins', promisin' a special present for your birthday. Well, you have received your present it's safe ta say. Ah wouldn't blame Trenton if he up an' took a bull whip to her, stripped down for all his niggers ta see, right out in the open."

"Tredwell!" Harriet screamed. "Misguided behavior or not, how dare you utter such a loathsome thing!" With that she had fled weeping from the parlor and ran upstairs, locking the bedroom door behind her.

***

STALWORTHY AND his men were on the midnight train out of Charleston, their horses in a special cattle car he had rented for no small amount. Ransom had told him to spare no expense and Stalworthy knew why. It wasn't just because Ransom was so wealthy. In all his years he had never seen a man so unhinged, so obsessed with requital.

Stalworthy was a crude man who nonetheless possessed an innate opportunism that suggested intelligence. He calculated that by padding the expenses he stood to realize perhaps another few thousand on top of the unbelievable sum already promised. He would have to make sure Mrs. Ransom was dealt with in accordance with his employer's demands, but as he had claimed he certainly had the men for that job; including himself.

***

IT WAS close to 2:00 a.m. when the small town sheriff was finally aroused from his drunken stupor and had made his way to the front door of his dilapidated house. He had nothing to offer Stalworthy but the direction the runaways had gone and how they had made their escape, offering up a few lies in the process.

It didn't matter. Two females, both of whom weren't used to hardship of any kind, and a house slave who himself wasn't accustomed to hard riding would be easy to find. Cusman was well armed but no matter. Simply being aware of that fact was enough for Stalworthy, even if the house slave was a fair shot which he suspected wasn't true regardless of what Ransom had told him. Worst case, he assumed Cusman was perhaps half as good as touted. Besides, any proficiency with firearms would almost certainly be compromised under the stress of armed fighting. He knew it was more than unlikely the women could shoot regardless of circumstance.

The key was finding them before anyone else did. It was also imperative to find them somewhere isolated. Witnesses would be necessary only after they had completed the gruesome task of murdering the white woman and were long gone. That would be difficult enough but Ransom had demanded much more, at least when Stalworthy last spoke to him. If the distraught man had experienced a change of heart however, it was too late now. Besides, Stalworthy couldn't imagine Trenton Ransom had changed his mind about anything.

***

CUSMAN AND the women were on their way by first light. They did their best to stay in what cover they could find but sometimes avoiding farms proved very difficult, even though they managed to stay as far away as possible from any farm buildings or homes. They had agreed to follow Cusman's advice and were heading in a southeasterly direction.

Stalworthy and his men had located their trail with little effort. They had followed the easily identifiable tracks to the small valley and had just as easily picked up the current trail. The men had traveled through the darkness for much of the previous night, and even though they were used to traveling by lantern light they had used it as sparingly as possible. They had lost the original tracks a few times but never for long. They had finally made a cold camp later that night themselves, in case they were so close even brief lantern light and especially a campfire might alert their prey. Those three weren't going anywhere that couldn't be tracked come daybreak.

***

AFTER GOING over ten miles that morning Cusman and the women took a short break. They had come upon a thick stand of woods with a small clearing in its center. A large white oak was in the middle of the clearing. The forest stretched for miles north to south and afforded good cover, with a huge expanse of meadow and farmland to the east of it. The women were so sore from all the riding they simply had to dismount for a while. Their buttocks and legs had been especially affected, and it hurt to even walk.

"We can't rest long," Cusman said. "Even if there's been no sign of anyone."

"Why do you suppose those men from the train station haven't showed, Cusman?" Missy Nell asked.

"Not sure, but takin' their horses most likely got somethin' to do with it. Either that or they just figured it was easier to wire ahead somewheres. I gotta believe they are riled over losin' their guns and saddles though, let alone these horses. Even so, maybe they just figure on lettin' other folks catch up with us farther north."

"I doubt we're that fortunate, Cusman," Jennifer said. "They received the first wire and Trenton no doubt followed it up with another about a reward, assuming that wasn't in the first one. We can only pray that had the opposite effect, and that sheriff and his deputies have kept such information to themselves, although others in different towns may have been offered the same thing. We obviously have a good head start, at least from that sheriff and his men."

"Haven't seen 'em, not yet anyway, that's true enough," Cusman observed, looking around at the trees. "But we gotta keep movin'. Even if they did give up they just might'a gone ahead and wired every town they could hereabouts, like you said."

Cusman went over and mounted his horse. "I'm gonna look around 'fore we head out. You best stay here 'til I get back. Won't be but ten minutes or so."

He rode off, leaving the same way they had used to find the clearing. After he approached the edge of the woods he dismounted and made his way on foot for a better look. Nothing. The coast was clear all across the sweep of meadows to the north, east and south. There was a farm on the southeastern horizon, but if they stayed in the woods they could duck farther inside before anyone from there would likely spot them.

Cusman had made his way halfway back to the women, moving cautiously through the underbrush and woods as he approached. Suddenly, he pulled up. The alarm in the female voices was unmistakable, and there was the rough voice of a man. Cusman tied his horse to a tree and removed the Henry rifle from its saddle scabbard. *Least ways them men back at the station fancied modern firearms,* Cusman thought. He quickly checked the revolvers, cocking them before putting them back in their holsters. It was down to it now. Moving stealthily, Cusman went just far enough to see what was happening, staying in the thick underbrush and woods.

"Ah said where's the buck, you God damned nigger bitch! He got the gold too, Ah reckon!" With that Stalworthy delivered a powerful back hand to the side of Missy Nell's head, sending her sprawling to the ground. "Git a hold'a her, God damn it!" He yelled at Jeeter Kulinan. "Dale, you follow them tracks yonder through them trees, and remember that nigger's heeled!"

Jennifer began to struggle, but Stalworthy had her by the back of her neck with his left hand. "Settle down you, or Ah'll snap it sure!"

Cusman knew he could shoot the one heading in his general direction but not the other two; there were too many trees in the way and they would be alerted. The women were too close to the men and he was too far away to assure accuracy. If he didn't kill the men holding the women outright, or incapacitate them enough, there was a good chance Missy Nell or Jennifer might get shot, maybe both, either by accident or on purpose although he doubted the latter.

Cusman didn't have the luxury of time to think things through so he headed back to his horse before being spotted. The men surely wouldn't harm the women if they didn't have to, he assumed, so if he could get far enough away there was a chance, perhaps a good one, he could deal with the situation on his own terms. When the men lit out with the women he might be able to set up an ambush over the next several hours or perhaps after nightfall. His could cover ground faster than three men with two women in tow, so any number of the hills and other wooded areas in the vicinity would make a good vantage point to watch their movements once he determined the general direction they were headed. He was on his horse and gone before the man coming from the clearing even knew it. *They'll spot my damned tracks though,* Cusman realized as he rode off.

Dale Shoots returned and told Stalworthy there was no sign of Cusman except the fresh tracks leading into the clearing from the east. Three horses had come in, and one had rode out then halfway back again, then out once more across the expanse of fields as best Shoots could tell.

"That coward of a nigger won't git far," Stalworthy said. "This here's a good a place as any ta deal with this nigger lovin' bitch. Tie her ta that oak yonder, Kulinan."

"Kin Ah rip her clothes off first, Runyun?" Kulinan asked, quivering with anticipation.

"Might jist as well, easier ta do now than after she's tied."

"The nigger too? Sure 'nough like ta have at her." Shoots said, equally aroused.

"Hell no you horny bastard! Ah swear if you ain't the dumbest bastard in six counties." Stalworthy said. "She cain't be spoiled that a way, Ransom would shit a load. What you fixin' ta do, blame it on that other nigger? Jist tie her up and don't make no marks or Ah'll whup the tar outta you!"

In order to silence Missy Nell's screams after she was bound, Shoots forced a filthy, crusted rag in her mouth before tying his bandana around her head to hold the rag in place. By then Jennifer was tied naked with her back to the oak tree while Kulinan proceeded to grope and probe all over her body. Jennifer was shaking uncontrollably, but didn't cry or break down during the ordeal; just glared at the unwashed man with all the disgust she could muster. At one point he spat out the large wad of tobacco he had been chewing with what remained of his yellow teeth and tried to kiss her. Jennifer spat in his face and cursed him. He leered, not even wiping away the spittle, and again tried to kiss her. Stalworthy acted as if it were business as usual as he made a fire. When he had it roaring he got a pan from where they kept their camp gear.

"She won't be the strong, silent type once these coals are on her feet so we best gag her too," Stalworthy said as he approached the oak tree with the pan filled with red hot embers, switching it from one hand to the other. Before having Kulinan place the coals on her bare feet Stalworthy had him put the gag on her. He glared into her eyes, his face inches from hers.

"After mah man Kulinan here is done roastin' your feet he'll start in on your more private parts, ma'am, beggin' your pardon. Seems that's somethin' along the lines'a what your husband expects. Least ways, that's what he hired me for, an' he wanted you ta know it. We kin start with them purty blue eyes if you want, so you don't gotta watch the rest. How's that sound, Miss *Nigger* Lover?"

"Now hold on, Runyun," Kulinan said, "you said Ah could have me some sugar first! You done promised, damn it. Give ya a hunnert dollars'a mah share if'n you let me, if'n Ah kin untie her first an' turn her 'round."

Stalworthy looked with tired disgust at the animated man. It was one thing to mutilate her with coals before killing her, that was just business, but sodomizing her first was unprofessional, perhaps even contrary to moral principles, although he considered that debatable given her preference of sleeping partners. Unless, Stalworthy thought, the perversion was somehow discovered later and blamed on the nigger buck runaway. Stalworthy looked at Kulinan again and just shrugged his shoulders. "Well, go ahead but hurry up. Gonna cost ya two hunnert though."

Kulinan's eyes lit up. "Got somethin' special-like in mind for this high-toned lady!" He said as he untied and forced Jennifer around, slapping her viciously when she struggled. He shoved her face-first against the tree and pulled her arms around it and tied her wrists together. "Hey Dale, you want som'a this here sugar 'fore Ah commence to burnin' off her hide after Ah'm done with her?"

"Ah reckon." Shoots replied as he finished adjusting the ropes that bound Missy Nell, still pouting because Stalworthy wouldn't let him rape her.

"Well now, Miss Hoyty Toyty," Kulinan said as he undid his trousers and let them fall to his ankles, his eyes fixed upon Jennifer's naked buttocks. "Ah'm a guessin' you ain't never had it this'a way…that there purty round ass is a sight to behold, it is that…" he put his face to the side of Jennifer's, his bristled whiskers scratching; his foul breath permeating the air around her. "Yes Ma'am, yes indeedy, gonna shove Ole Blue where the sun don't shine…"

A rifle shot echoed through the woods. Stalworthy and Shoots flew to the ground instantly, reaching for their sidearms. Kulinan landed on the ground as well, having dropped slower than the other two, vacant eyed, a bullet through the left side of his skull. He twitched a few times then remained still. Shoots made a dash for the safety of the oak tree, barely escaping a bullet that whizzed by his head, but Stalworthy was already up and behind it himself, pressed against Jennifer.

"Git the hell over by that rock!" He hollered at the frantic man, shoving him violently in the other direction. The rock wasn't ten yards from the tree but Shoots didn't make it even halfway. The first round caught him in the neck, the second in his side, going through his left lung and piercing his heart.

Stalworthy, breathing heavily, had crushed Jennifer against the tree by then, his hot, foul breath every bit as nauseating as Kulinan's.

"You got five seconds ta throw down your gun an' march on out here nigger, or Ah'll blow her head off, your nigger whore yonder too!" Nothing. No sound, no movement. "You deaf or somethin' nigger? Ah'll do it, Ah swear!"

Cusman felt he was bluffing. The slave catcher's only chance was keeping at least one of them alive, he reasoned. Missy Nell had crawled into a shallow hollow so shooting her wasn't an option unless the man ran over to her, exposing himself. That left Jennifer, but shooting her would mean the man had only the tree left. He couldn't stay there forever, and he knew what would happen if he tried to make a run for it without dragging her with him. As good a shot as Cusman had proven to be now that he was much closer than before, that option wasn't very promising even if Stalworthy did manage to cut the ropes and drag her along. He was much larger than Jennifer, and too much of him would be exposed regardless of how he positioned her as a shield. It wouldn't be easy though, and Cusman was again concerned Stalworthy's gun would go off while pointed at Jennifer no matter where Cusman's bullet hit.

"You untie the lady, let her go, leave all your guns, and you kin ride off."

"You expect me ta believe that, nigger?" Stalworthy yelled, trying to get a fix on the whereabouts of Cusman's voice. If he had any chance at all, he realized, it would be by diving to the ground and firing in that direction before Cusman had a chance to reposition. Stalworthy needed to act fast, before his adversary could figure that out. "Well, do ya buck?"

"Reckon I don't," Cusman hollered back, "but that's all you got."

Stalworthy flew to the ground next to the tree and fired. He got off three shots from his .44 caliber Colt, and true to his reputation two of them nearly hit Cusman. The woods again filled with the report of Cusman's rifle, but he only needed to fire once. The bullet had slammed into the top of Runyun Stalworthy's skull.

Cusman hurried to the oak tree, making sure to stay behind it as he cut the rope binding Jennifer's wrists. He didn't want her to suffer the further humiliation of him seeing her naked, not up close anyway.

Without looking at her, he grabbed what was left of her torn clothing and handed them to her as Jennifer tore off her gag. He stepped over Stalworthy's body and rushed to Missy Nell. He took off the bandana and pulled the filthy rag from her mouth then cut the ropes. She lunged into his arms, sobbing uncontrollably.

Jennifer had managed to get dressed but her clothing was so torn she had to keep her hands over most of it as best she could. She too was sobbing, her entire body shaking. Cusman placed his jacket around her. She all but disappeared inside of it.

"Gotta get goin' fast as we can," he said. "Them shots might'a been heard, and I still gotta shoot off three more." He went over to the women's horses and grabbed both rifles and handed them to the women. "No tellin' if these men were alone. Might be more close by. Duck into the trees and shoot anyone that shows up. I gotta find their horses. Cain't be far."

Cusman headed into the woods west of the clearing. Three shots rang out. They sounded so loud it seemed as if they could be heard for miles. Moments later Cusman returned. "Hate to shoot such fine animals but cain't have 'em wanderin' off or commence to whinnyin'. Let's move."

They stayed just inside the tree line as they headed south. It was slow going, but they couldn't risk being seen by someone from the distant farm that might show up after having heard the gun shots. There was also the distinct possibility other trackers were indeed closing in, and all three of them looked around continuously. To their relief no one appeared - at first.

***

THE FARMER had heard the shots, and along with his teenage son had gone out to investigate. So many shots were highly unusual for that isolated area. Occasionally a hunter might fire one or two but that rarely occurred. Locals had their own lands to hunt, although once in a great while someone might venture into the general area of the Kirby place. Joshua Kirby and his son Issachar had never heard more than two or three gun shots, let alone the nine or ten that had been fired during the ordeal that had occurred fairly close by.

The two were standing in a sparse grove of redbud trees that partially surrounded a small, spring fed pond in the middle of a field, not far from the main stand of woods the three runaways were moving through to the west. Although the trio thought they were concealed the farmer and his boy spotted them easily.

"Hallo!" Joshua called out, stepping from the redbuds and waving. "You been hunting?" The three pulled up immediately and turned their heads quickly towards the voice. "Hallo!" Joshua called out again, still waving.

"He's not armed," Cusman said. Then he spotted the boy, equally defenseless.

All young Issachar was holding was a stick. He was using it to wave against the horsetail by the shore of the small pond, as if he were casually looking about for small game or anything else that might be hiding there as boys are prone to do. He looked up and waved as well, a smile on his face. He hadn't experienced this much atypical activity since he didn't know when, and appreciated the break from his chores.

"What should we do?" Missy Nell asked, echoing the question all of them were contemplating.

"Well, no sense tryin' to hide," Cusman said. "Looks like we made a mess'a that."

"I'll ride out and greet them," Jennifer said. "If trouble ensues, well, I suppose the only thing to do is for you to come out as well, Cusman. If I wave with my right hand that will mean I haven't endangered us, at least yet. If you see my left hand come up, ride to me as fast as possible. And Cusman, make sure your rifle is seen."

Jennifer moved out of the woods before there could be further discussion. She waved at the two farmers as she approached, not sure what she would say. She realized how odd looking she must have appeared. She was draped in a jacket so large it appeared as if a child were approaching, a female one at that, on a large horse with a man's saddle underneath her. She was hoping to simply tell the truth or at least close to it, depending on what was said to her.

"Good morning, gentlemen. As you can see we are lost."

Joshua and Issachar stood there in shock. What had been a curiosity had suddenly become quite a peculiarity.

"So it would appear, ma'am," Joshua said. "Issachar, remove your hat!" The suddenly red-faced boy complied immediately, dropping his stick. "What brings you to our humble neck of the woods, I pray those gun shots aren't involved. You don't look like a hunter. Who travels with you?" He asked, an expression of concern upon his face.

Jennifer sensed the two were harmless but remained wary. "Are we close to any towns, sir?" She asked, ignoring his question. "Have you or the boy seen any other strangers lately?"

"Meersville is but fifteen miles or thereabouts from here, due east. And no, you are the only strangers we have seen. It is seldom we even encounter folks we're familiar with out this way, let alone strangers. If my question was forward I apologize, ma'am, but those gun shots and your curious attire compelled me to inquire. Are you in a bad way, other than being lost?"

Jennifer still felt wary but given the circumstance she decided to be forthcoming, for the most part. If things went sour she could always raise her left hand. "I fear we are, sir. I was bringing my slaves and an adequate amount of money with me to my sister's home. She lives in the town in that direction," Jennifer said as she pointed northwest, "where the train station is located. She wasn't there to greet us so I decided to try and locate her farm. As you can see I lost my way, and unbeknownst to me some very vile men must have followed us here. I fear they were slave catchers hired by my former husband, and when they came upon us the shots you heard ensued." Jennifer lowered her head as if acutely ashamed. "I hesitate to tell you, in front of the boy, what transpired prior to the gun shots. It's enough for you to know my torn clothing had much to do with it. They were vile men indeed, sir, and if it hadn't been for the bravery of my nigger boy, I fear the outcome would have been much worse."

Joshua winced at her words, leaving Jennifer to assume even the hint of rape was inappropriate for the young lad's ears.

"I most certainly offer you my sympathy, ma'am, and any assistance we can offer, but I must protest you using such words in front of my son as well as myself. We don't condone using such degrading terms to describe our Negro brethren, and owning any children of God is an abomination, if I understand you correctly. Your words don't match up, and I must admit I am perplexed. I do hope you can respect the value we place upon our convictions however, even if you do not agree with them."

Jennifer raised her right hand.

XVII

Elwood Stalworthy had wasted no time; he never did. Before a month had gone by from the day he had departed Chicago towards the middle of January 1863, he had already made his way to Mississippi and located some of the Confederate brigades which had battled at Shiloh, and had managed to join one that had participated in the fighting that had occurred in the peach orchard. Most of the soldiers he came in contact with liked him immediately.

He told everyone his name was Elwood Green and had grown up in Georgia, but when the war broke out he had been in California searching for gold. He hadn't struck it rich but had come close enough. No one doubted him since he had arrived with two pack horses loaded down with all sorts of things he was willing to share.

He had brought coffee, Havana cigars and other forms of tobacco, a good supply of canned goods and a fair amount of quality Beam whiskey. He also had a few dozen honest-to-God ambrotypes of what he claimed were some of the highest priced prostitutes in San Francisco, and the images left nothing to the imagination. Most of the men had never seen such a thing, and the ones who claimed they had were liars.

He told his new comrades how he had heard of their bravery at Shiloh, and how proud he was to be with the men who had whipped the Yankees so soundly at the peach orchard. He usually waited until he was around a campfire with several of the more talkative ones, preferably after they had sampled some of the whiskey he often times passed around.

"So'd y'all take many Yankee prisoners?" He asked one night after a few of the men had brought up the subject.

"Fair amount Ah s'pose," one of them responded. "Our boys what done took that damned Hornet's Nest got a sight more'n us, but we got our share Ah reckon."

"Hope ta hell you captured some'a them no-account Yankee officers." Elwood said as he looked around as if to ensure none of their own officers were listening. "Much as our own kin be a sight full'a themselves from time ta time, ain't nothin' compares ta them Yankee dandies. More spit 'n polish than sand, least ways so Ah heard tell. Some'a them like ta be a hollerin' 'Charge!' while they's skedaddlin' hell bent for the rear!" That produced a round of chuckles. "So, you boys capture any'a them Yankee officers that day in that peach orchard?"

The men thought about it a while as Elwood passed the whisky bottle around again. One of them finally spoke up after taking his turn at the bottle. "Weren't that a Yankee officer Sergeant Comstock brought in, you know, before evenin'?"

"Ah do believe it was Gus," one of the others responded. "Just a damned lieutenant though as Ah recall. Them boys west'a us what took the Nest got 'em a real live general." Elwood began to listen intently even though he had been anyway. He knew it was more than a long shot, but asked anyway. "Did he have him a name? Bet it was a fancy one."

"'Course he had a name, Elwood." Private Gus Primrose responded as he took two healthy chugs from the bottle, belching slightly when he was done. "Never heard what it was though." Gus's timing and delivery had been perfect and all the men laughed. Even Elwood thought it was funny and didn't have to pretend to be laughing along with the rest them. After things calmed down he tried a different approach.

"What the Yankee lieutenant look like?" Elwood asked. "Never seen me one'a them dandies up close."

"You know," Gus responded, "Whupped." He got another round of chuckles but not near as much as before. Slightly chagrined, he tried to make up for it by demonstrating his powers of perception which were actually rather keen. "Kinda tall he was, dark haired, no beard, had on a cavalry blouse Ah think it was, some kind'a patch on it got me ta thinkin' it was least ways. Wait! Ah remember! Said Nappertown, or Napperville or some such thing. Always thought Ah should'a been in the cavalry…" That got Gus a few chortles which he pretended to ignore.

"Hell Gus," one of them joked, "Ah didn't know you could even read much less ride a horse!" Gus chuckled along with the rest of them but he didn't think it was funny.

"A whupped cavalry officer, eh Gus?" Elwood said. "Sceered half ta death Ah s'pose."

"Well now, Ah ain't so sure 'bout that, Elwood." Gus replied, attempting to regain his former status. "He looked tired all right. Hell, we all was, but Ah swear he still had fight in 'em, whupped or not. Anyways, looked like he'd sure 'nough fight back if'n he had the chance. He was still walkin' but wounded all ta hell and looked tired, but his eyes didn't, no sir. You stared at him, he stared right back. Weren't no coward behind them eyes, tell ya that." Elwood tossed a bag of chewing tobacco close to the other men and told them to help themselves.

"What you s'pose happened ta him?" Elwood asked no one in particular.

"The ones we catched, they all went to Salisbury," one of the other men said. "Heard the captain say so."

The following morning Elwood Green was gone.

***

STALWORTHY WAS wearing a crisp Confederate lieutenant's uniform when he arrived at Salisbury mounted on a very impressive palomino horse. He claimed to have come from Richmond and had the documentation to prove it. He was on a fact finding mission for one of President Davis' top aides, who wanted to know how many Union officers Salisbury still held in captivity in order to help facilitate more exchanges. There were rumors the Yankees might be abandoning the Dix-Hill Cartel Exchange, and it was imperative the Confederacy get back as many of their officers as possible before that indeed came to fruition.

"Well now, Lieutenant Remington," the assistant camp commandant, Captain July Evers said as he sat behind his desk and lit a cigar without offering one to Stalworthy, "ain't it just like those politicians in Richmond to send someone all the way here when Ah have routinely been supplyin' them with that very information? A few exceptions have been made for disciplinary reasons, but that's all."

"Beggin' your pardon sir," Stalworthy replied, "as much as Ah agree with you, they have asked me ta personally count all the ones you have. Ah hope that don't inconvenience you sir."

"Don't inconvenience me at all, Lieutenant. All the way from Richmond? You appear to be the one that's inconvenienced."

"Do Ah have your permission then, sir?"

"Why not? Sergeant! Show the lieutenant ta all them officer's quarters. Utter nonsense if you ask me…" The captain muttered to no one in particular as Stalworthy and the sergeant departed.

***

TWO ARMED guards accompanied Elwood and the sergeant as they entered the officer's cabin where Pete's former comrades were housed. The prisoners looked at Stalworthy with tired contempt, not moving from where they were sitting or lounging about. Elwood had a tintype of Pete that Clifton had managed to obtain from Delicia, but Elwood had never risked showing it to anyone.

He looked at all the men closely but none of them appeared to be his prey, even if the tintype was a few years old and not very clear. Janeway had told him it wasn't a very good likeness either, but it was all he had been able to come up with, or the only one Delicia would part with more like it. Clifton had been surprised she had been willing to part with it at all, but when he had told her how much he missed his late friend she had consented.

Elwood began counting then asked the men their names. Major Miling asked why, and when Elwood told him what he had told Captain Evers the men almost tripped over themselves in a rush to comply.

"Captain Evers has ordered us confined to this place, Lieutenant," Major Miling said after giving his name and former outfit as well as where he was from. "He also insists none of us are eligible for exchange ever since a failed escape attempt last fall, even though just a few of us tried."

"Ah wasn't aware of that, Major, and Ah kin assure you Richmond is not aware of any such order." Elwood replied. "It would seem ta me he would want ta be rid of y'all."

"You don't know the captain, Lieutenant." Major Miling said, unconcerned that the guards or the sergeant overheard. He knew they weren't fond of the pompous man either.

"No, Ah don't. But Ah do know he has overestimated his authority if he believes Richmond has nothin' ta say about it. Tell me, are there any other officers about?"

"There were, Lieutenant," Major Miling responded, "but they arrived well after our failed attempt and have already been exchanged best I know. We were never allowed to fraternize with them. The captain wouldn't even allow us to give them our names so at least our families knew we were alive."

"Shoulda hung you all," the sergeant mumbled a little too loud. The other guards shuffled about, nodding with varying degrees of concurrence.

"How else have you been treated? Have any officers died?" Elwood asked, ignoring the sergeant.

"No, Lieutenant. Although one of us finally escaped. Don't know what became of him but there was hell to pay for the rest of us. He killed two guards during his attempt and stole the captain's horse." The sergeant and the other two guards just glared at the Yankee major.

"Ah should be aware of that man's identity," Elwood said. "Mah travels will be takin' me ta more prison camps, and since he may have been re-captured that is information Ah should have."

"Why, so you can hang him?" Major Miling said. "You'll get nothing from us!"

"Ah simply want his name and physical description so Ah kin identify him, Major. Especially the latter. Ah doubt he would use his real name, but who knows. Mah intent would be ta use him as a bargainin' chip so ta speak. Ah would imagine your precious Union would appreciate an officer with his mettle back among their ranks, and we would surely like ta get some of our officers returned as well. That man could fetch us more'n a ordinary lieutenant, Ah would imagine. If he is by chance discovered before Ah was ta locate him, he'll be hanged sure."

"That's a big story!" Major Miling almost yelled. "You'd hang him anyway and only a fool would think otherwise!"

"His name was McCabe. Pete McCabe." The sergeant said. "That murderin' Yankee kilt my best friend and stuffed his body down the outhouse back yonder. If you won't hang 'em, sir, Ah would be happy ta oblige. Know where Ah'd like ta bury 'em, too."

"Ah offer you my sympathies, Sergeant." Elwood said, turning to the man. "What you describe transcends the bounds of decency to an obscene degree. What kin you tell me about the escape besides the hideous act of that despicable man? Let's step outside, gentlemen," he said to the three guards. "The air is foul in here an' not just from the smell."

Once outside the sergeant told him everything he knew about Pete. After his murder spree McCabe took off, but since it took too long to discover the bodies and who was responsible and why, he had managed to get far enough away to elude them.

It had been a foul night and although they had tried to track him come morning, the rain had made that all but impossible. Folks along the way hadn't heard or seen a thing, huddled in their homes as they were. A search party that had included the sergeant kept after him though, and later the following day they had picked up his trail again, thanks to some dumb luck and finally an eyewitness report. Unfortunately, he had a very good horse under him and they had lost him again.

"Which way was he headed when his trail went cold, Sergeant?" Elwood asked.

"West, sir, maybe northwest, best we could tell. On his way ta Kentucky we figured, lessin' he found sympathizers in Eastern Tennessee which wouldn't surprise me none. Sent a few wires off but nothin' came'a them. Don't know no more'n that."

Stalworthy returned to Captain Ever's office before departing and offered his condolences to the man regarding his dead guards. He also handed him six Havana cigars.

"Ah know you appreciate a good smoke, Captain Evers, and Ah would like you ta have these here as a gift for all your cooperation."

"Well, thank you Lieutenant." The captain meant it too; he couldn't recall the last time anyone had given him anything.

"Ah have somethin' else Ah'd like ta offer you sir." Elwood said, turning more serious. "Your good sergeant here told me what that despicable Yankee Lieutenant done durin' his escape, and Ah would like ta offer you my possible assistance. Ah will be visitin' a fair number of our prison camps, and since that cowardly murderer might have been recaptured perhaps Ah could find him and bring him back here."

"That, Lieutenant," The captain said as he lit one of the Havana's, "would be a magnificent thing if you was ta somehow succeed. That damned Yankee stole my best horse!" He puffed on his new cigar and made an approving facial gesture. "These are indeed fine cigars, Lieutenant, again Ah thank you. Oh, and my guards, he will hang for that as well as horse stealin'. Escapin' too. Wish Ah could hang 'em four times. That cur sure as hell deserves it. Ah doubt however, you will be successful Ah'm sorry ta say."

"Perhaps not, sir, but the sergeant has given me an accurate description of the scoundrel. Ah doubt he would be foolish enough ta give his real name but Ah have that too. What Ah don't have, sir, is a letter written on your stationary and in your hand requestin' he be brought back here. If Ah do find him that would go a long way in convincin' the commandant of wherever he may be ta allow me ta remove that so-called lieutenant from his custody."

"Done! Ah will write it immediately."

"Also, sir, in case any further verification is needed, you might be receivin' a wire requestin' same. Ah'm certain you would respond forthwith, and Ah would like your permission ta tell the other commandant so."

"Again, Lieutenant, you kin count on mah full and immediate attention concernin' any matter that brings that Yankee bastard back here. It is a long shot to be sure, but if you do succeed Ah would be eternally grateful ta you. Ah'm goin' ta mention my horse as well, just in case, and Ah want you ta keep your eyes open for a handsome black stallion. Please give me your word you will make inquiries. His name is Beau Black. He knows his name too. Damn, Ah miss that horse."

"Ah promise, Captain Evers," Stalworthy said, as solemn as Death. "Ah deeply regret your loss."

***

STALWORTHY ARRIVED in northeast Tennessee a few days later in civilian garb, ready to dress as either a Union or Confederate lieutenant at a moment's notice. He knew his chances of finding Pete were slim, but over the years he had made a practice of tracking his prey wherever they had last been reported to have headed unless other information became available. The trail would usually grow warmer.

None of the men in the Union camps he came upon had anything to offer, but a few of them had recently captured a few Rebels who hadn't been sent off yet. That too proved fruitless. None of them had anything useful to tell him. After a few weeks he was no further along with his search than when he arrived. One evening that changed dramatically.

The Rebel captive wasn't even sixteen, from the look of him. He was scared, homesick and talkative. He had been in a cavalry outfit but didn't have any information regarding a Union officer having been captured by the men with whom he had been riding. He knew one thing though, or thought he did. The few Union captives his unit had ended up with later on had been handed over to another outfit. That outfit had a captured officer with them, a lieutenant who fit McCabe's description and strongly resembled the tintype. Those men had been sent to Georgia. He didn't recall the name of the prison camp but he was fairly certain it was somewhere near Macon. Stalworthy gave the boy a can of apricots and told him he'd put a word in to the Yankee commander on the boy's behalf. Stalworthy's promise was as empty as the can of apricots after a Yankee guard took it from the lad as soon as Elwood departed.

Macon was a far ways off, but with nothing else to go on it was all Stalworthy had at his disposal. Besides, sometimes a long journey afforded the opportunity to glean more information along the way. He sent Janeway a coded wire with a vague update:

Dear cousin,

Thank you for inquiring about our welfare. Father is getting along, and we did find out Winston is alive, or was after his last encounter with the enemy. We believe he is stationed farther south, but haven't heard from him since. May God watch over him and the brave Union soldiers he is with until I can locate him. If we hear anything we will be in touch. Father says he doesn't know how our crop of winter hay will do, but he remains guardedly optimistic things will work out to our advantage.

Clifton read the wire twice. The second reading was just as maddening as the first. He looked around the telegraph office in Aurora and threw it away. He had been making the ten mile trip to the town every week since Stalworthy's departure, but the latest wire was only the second one he had received. His intense desire for Pete to be dead had overshadowed a more objective appraisal of events that day in the peach orchard, and that realization had hit him full force. *If only those God damned Rebels had shot that bastard when they had the chance, or been better shots when he had tried to run*, Clifton said to himself. Now his entire future was in the hands of a mercenary.

Given Clifton's recent status his word against another man's would probably be sufficient if such a man were to make it back, but McCabe wasn't merely another man. He had always had a stellar reputation with the Naperville citizenry despite some boyhood shenanigans. He had been honest, hardworking and generally helpful to others. All of the surviving men from the 1st Naperville Cavalry spoke highly of him as well. His good looks hadn't hurt him either, but Clifton was prone to overestimate that sort of thing. If McCabe said he had witnessed Clifton murder Major O'Darcy, especially given Clifton's prior reputation, plenty of people would believe he was guilty, perhaps enough to get him executed regardless of his father's influence. Even General Smithington would likely run for cover once the men from the 1st Naperville responded to McCabe's charges, especially since Clifton's eye-witness account of seeing McCabe blown to pieces would be exposed as a bald-faced lie. *And Delicia - oh Christ, Delicia.*

Their relationship was heading in the direction he had fantasized about ever since he had been capable of doing so. Indeed, before he had reached puberty. Delicia's allurement had been impossible to ignore even then, before the barest trace of what he would eventually want to obtain, to *possess* as miserly as the cruelest despot was capable of formulating. It had formulated now, and nothing was capable of diminishing Clifton's compulsive preoccupation, his mania to dominate Delicia in ways unencumbered by any standard of decency as others might define the concept, and that motivation kept him focused on the situation as if nothing else had ever mattered to him: *She's convinced herself Pete is dead regardless of what Billy McCabe keeps telling her,* Clifton recalled. *The little bastard isn't convinced his brother is alive, but his stupid mother's nonsensical insistence her precious son isn't dead has created doubt in the boy's mind.*

It doesn't help that Wygant, the meddlesome old fool, keeps telling Billy as well as Delicia that Billy's hag of a mother shouldn't be so easily dismissed. Still, Delicia has thus far refused to accept any of that prattle, thank God.

Not a single soldier who had been anywhere near the peach orchard had come forth and disputed Clifton's account. If anything, they maintained the likelihood of what Major Janeway insisted he had witnessed having happened to Major O'Darcy and Lieutenant McCabe was probably true. The Union soldiers who had brought him back wounded apparently thought so, and when it had all come down they had been closer to it than anyone from the 1st Naperville who survived, as best anyone knew.

Delicia had been so anguished over the news and Clifton's eyewitness account she had come to accept it. Hope was a luxury that would only serve to put off her agony, so she had decided to deal with her mourning in the here and now. It would never go away but the intensity had to be dealt with before it drove her insane. In her mind, the only way she could ever hope to diminish it was to accept Pete's death.

It was their business if others felt compelled to deal with their sorrow in different ways, although Delicia mourned deeply for them as well. She believed their pain would be at least twofold once they came to accept the truth, once the war was over and no word of, or from Pete materialized. He was dead. He had been killed at Shiloh. It was beyond horrible but it was true. Soldiers die, and that, sadly, was the end of it. It was time to move on as best she could, and she had begun to accept a transformed Clifton Janeway as her possible partner to accompany her down that path.

***

LINDA MARIE had always been the impetuous one. Her family and most folks in town acknowledged she did it in a way that fell somewhere between endearing and frustrating if not downright annoying, depending on who was doing the evaluating, and why. Everyone in the O'Darcy family believed she would settle down once she was out of her teen years, but at sixteen it appeared as if she had a long way to go. She was impulsive, often times careless, and seemed to seldom weigh the consequences of her actions with any consistency. And she was as beautiful as Delicia had been at her age, some thought more so. For the boys and young men about, it was like trying to choose between their two favorite flavors of anything delicious.

Thus far most of her transgressions had been minor. Some had ended up being the main topic of conversation at a few teas and luncheons, but nothing serious given her age. Still, her lack of demonstrating the maturity that might be expected of even a sixteen-year-old was evident to those who felt compelled to judge or worry about her.

Major Clifton Janeway had certainly caught her eye. She thought he was handsome, dashing, suave and of course very rich. So what if he had been a terror in his youth? Not only did Linda Marie pretend to relate to that she found it attractive, so *there*.

She had openly taken special notice of bad boys during her short years, as long as it flustered her parents and others who thought she was rebellious and immature. Her attraction to Billy McCabe didn't fit that description. He could be mischievous, but no one had ever known him to act so with any degree of inconsideration much less maliciousness. Although he had certainly turned her head, her recent infatuation for Major Clifton Janeway was something she believed only a mature woman could appreciate.

Delicia obviously found Clifton attractive, and Linda Marie was convinced only a dimwit couldn't help but notice. She loved Delicia but felt inferior to her as well. If she could get the likes of Major Janeway to notice her instead, well now, wouldn't *that* be something. Besides, she liked to intone if only to herself, all's fair in love and war. That had to be true; Linda Marie had even read it in books, the ones her parents didn't know she had read.

She had no idea how to approach him; in her fantasies she always skipped over those bothersome details. She was always simply alone with him somehow. It was that scenario she concentrated upon and what would happen once it occurred. In her daydreams he always found her irresistible, never failing to acknowledge her extraordinary beauty in the most romantic of ways. He was always impressed by her maturity as well, her obvious transformation into womanhood and all it entailed. He always wanted to kiss her, but in her fantasies she spurned his advances but only at first. His breath was always sweet, his lips and mouth warm and tender, and his embrace was that of a very strong man aware of his strength. Still, it remained gentle in an impassioned sort of way. She used to drift back to the kissing when her thoughts went too far, when she could almost feel her breasts pressed against him, but lately her daydreams had been allowed to go further - after all, they were in love within her rainbow fantasies, were they not? Of course they were; she always came to that conclusion.

***

CLIFTON HAD begun to show up at Pinecraig on days when Delicia was home, away from her duties at the hospital. Hezekiah was generally polite but at the first opportunity made himself scarce. The purpose of Clifton's visits appeared obvious, so even Delicia's sisters gave them some privacy, within reason of course. Clifton and Delicia were never really alone. Maintaining all proprieties was something Delicia would have insisted upon if the need arose but didn't dwell upon the concept, assuming conformity to prevailing rules and conventions was a given. In that regard Clifton was an unerring gentleman, or so it appeared.

Sometimes however, Clifton would amuse himself with fanciful illusions. How very shocked all the prim and proper people, especially Hezekiah, would be if they could read Clifton's thoughts and see what he would really like to be doing to Delicia. *I can just picture the look on that old gas bag's face if he were to find his lovely daughter in the most compromising of positions, with me directly behind her naked, sweaty body while she screams like a teenaged slut, begging for more of my riding crop, for more of* **me**...He especially liked to conjure up such fantasies while shaking Hezekiah's hand upon greeting him or conversing with both of Delicia's parents. It amused him to envisage how their reserved expressions would transform into utter mortification if his sordid images were actually occurring. *You old sots, it appears your conformity to decorum has left you a tad unhinged. Care to take a turn, Hezekiah? My my, dear Annice, you don't look well at all...are you pining for the sting of my riding crop across your gelatinous, naked ass?*

Clifton and Delicia usually sat in the company parlor, but never right next to each other and always with the pocket doors wide open. Linda Marie usually invented an excuse to enter though, and although it often times amused both Clifton and Delicia, it could grow tiresome.

***

CLIFTON HAD stayed away for two weeks after receiving the wire from Stalworthy. His mood was more than dark and he didn't want the always perceptive Delicia to notice the slightest thing wrong. He had claimed he had business in Galesburg and Moline but hadn't gone farther than Morris, Illinois. He spent the first week exorbitantly drunk and most of the second to heal.

It was a Monday when he made it to Naperville and therefore Delicia's day off, so he knew she would likely be home and wanted to surprise her. She wasn't there. The entire family was gone, having left for Chicago on the morning train out of Wheaton. The only one who hadn't gone along was Linda Marie, who was supposed to have been attending a friend's birthday party for the day. She had been, but had grown bored with the party and feigned woman problems. Her friend's brother had brought her home in a carriage, stealing glances at every opportunity.

She noticed Clifton's horse right away but her friend's brother hadn't, or possibly didn't know whose it was and pretended not to care. She offered a hurried thank you and went into the house. Clifton wasn't inside so she began looking out windows. He finally came out of the carriage house where he had been searching for the O'Darcy family's largest carriage.

"Hello Major Janeway!" Linda Marie called, standing on the southwest porch, grateful she had on make-up and one of her nicer dresses. "Are you lost, sir?" She called out in jest, her voice filled with flirtatiousness.

"Well hello to you, Linda Marie," he called back as he approached, smiling. "Have you hidden everyone away or does the missing carriage have something to do with the mystery?"

When he made his way onto the porch she invited him inside, talking about her family's whereabouts the whole time. She made sure to emphasize the time of their likely return several times as well.

"What a lovely dress," he said after she invited him into the company parlor, the same one her sister and he always utilized. "Is it new?"

"Oh, it isn't old, but I fear I have already outgrown it." She moved closer to him as she spoke. "Don't you agree, Major Janeway?"

"I see no imperfections at all. You have truly blossomed into a striking young lady." *My goodness,* she thought, *this is just as I have envisioned it would be!*

"How kind of you to have noticed, Major Janeway." She said, moving closer still.

"Please call me Clifton, dear girl."

"Oh, thank you *Clifton.*" She said, her eyes masking nothing. "Are you sure you don't mind?"

He had begun to realize her possible intentions and wasn't surprised. Her childish attempts at acting as a flirtatious yet mature young woman were nothing new to him, but her antics had always occurred with others around. This was different and potentially dangerous. In the past he would have pressed his advantage, as lovely and so obviously fine figured as she was, but this was Delicia's *sister.* Regardless of the young girl's striking appearance he simply wouldn't allow anything to jeopardize his growing relationship with the only woman he had ever loved, if his total obsession with Delicia could be described as such.

"I certainly don't mind at all my dear, and thank you for your warm hospitality but I must be going. Please tell Delicia I stopped by." With that he started to leave, and was in the vestibule when a somewhat panic-stricken Linda Marie came after him; this wasn't how the fantasy was supposed to end, far from it. *All's fair in love and war...*

"Cilfton," she said as she entered the vestibule, "are you certain you must leave? No one will be home for hours and I need a gentleman's opinion about something. Can't you please wait just a teeny weeny moment?"

That wasn't good and he knew it, but some habits were hard to break. Still, he told himself he would leave immediately after her latest little charade was over.

"Well, just a few moments my dear. I have to finish a report for General Smithington, and..."

She hurried up the main staircase saying she'd be right back. He considered leaving at that point but told himself that would be rude. Besides, if he offended the little tart no telling what she might invent to even the score. He felt somewhat trapped but some of his old feelings were toying with him as well.

She returned, but not down the main staircase. She was at the bottom of the rear stairs when she called to him. "Clifton darling, could you help me please?" *At least the little vixen didn't call from her upstairs bedroom,* he thought, somewhat relieved, or disappointed; he wasn't sure which emotion held sway.

When he arrived she was at the bottom of the rear stairs, her back to him, struggling with the buttons on the back of the new dress she had put on. "Be a dear and help me with these, won't you Clifton?" She was very nervous, and the intensity of her apprehension had her shaking slightly, but this was her chance.

When he walked over and reached for the buttons she turned around, took a deep breath, and slowly lowered the top of her dress. Her perfect, naked breasts were directly in front of him. He had known they were large but what he was staring at astonished him anyway.

"You may touch them if you want, my love of loves..." He inwardly cringed at her last few words, believing them utterly puerile. They even caused him to hesitate, but not for long.

***

ELWOOD STALWORTHY was in a saloon in Macon Georgia after his long, arduous journey, sharing a drink with the bartender early one afternoon in the all but empty establishment. He was back to being a Confederate lieutenant.

"It's a blight, Lieutenant," the bartender said, repeating himself for the third time. "It's usually crowded enough as is, and if the wind's just so nobody but a damned liar wants ta be anywheres near the damned place. Heard some talk they'll be emptyin' it out though, if what Ah heard tell is true. Somethin' about a new one they're plannin' ta build down Andersonville way. Only about twenty folks live thereabouts, so Ah reckon their complainin' won't amount ta much. Sure as hell hope they build it, 'ceptin' business been good what with all you army fellers a comin' and a goin'. Trade that for gittin' rid of that there smell though, most folks in town feels likewise."

"Any word when that might take place, constructing the new facility in Andersonville?" Elwood asked, directing the man to pour another round for both of them.

"Nah. Some captain was in here a while back, Winder was his name Ah think. Said he'd be a headin' down that way come next fall sometime or 'nother, but that don't mean much Ah reckon."

"Well, Ah'm sorry it won't be sooner for you and all these good people, sir. They're not thinkin'a movin' the Yankees at Oglethorpe anywhere else first, are they?"

"Ain't heard me nothin' like that, Lieutenant. Wish they would though."

***

STALWORTHY USED the same approach when he arrived at the Oglethorpe stockade that had worked for him at Salisbury, with one modification. He was not only on a fact finding mission but was looking for someone specific as well. He explained the reason why and asked permission to see all the Yankee officers as well as the other prisoners in case his man was attempting that ruse.

"Hell, Lieutenant," the commandant of Oglethorpe, Captain Edward Bownell, said. "We have over a thousand prisoners here 'bouts, least ways for now. We're exchangin' most these Yankees at a good pace, and gonna be movin' the rest of 'em out right quick, maybe less than two weeks. You plannin' on lookin' at all'a them?"

"If Ah have to. Ah gave mah word to the assistant commandant at Salisbury, Captain July Evers. He is understandably distraught over the matter. Bah the way, you wouldn't happen ta know if any of your officer prisoners had a handsome black stallion when they were captured, would you sir?"

"A damned horse? Christ Almighty Lieutenant, how the hell would Ah know? This is a prison camp for *men*. What kind'a fool question is that?"

"Foolish describes it down ta the groun', sir, but Captain Evers was mighty partial ta the horse that murderin' Yankee stole. Even put it in that letter Ah gave you. Promised him Ah'd at least ask no matter where Ah ended up, beggin' your pardon, sir. "

***

STALWORTHY BEGAN searching immediately. He had a corporal with him and several armed guards. Looking over a thousand men would be daunting, and given their overall condition his prey could prove difficult to recognize. And the *smell* - Stalworthy had a strong constitution but being in that place was almost more than he could stand. So many unwashed men huddled close together was nothing new to him, but what he confronted within the stockade, especially given the extremely poor sanitary conditions, redefined the concept.

They began their search in earnest by checking the huts where most of the im-prisoned officers were housed. Nothing. Stalworthy pretended to take notes as he counted the prisoners, most of whom regarded him warily, some hopefully. Others acted as if he wasn't even there.

"Ah believe the commandant mentioned some stalls," Stalworthy said to the cor-poral. "How many more officers are there?"

"Oh, Ah reckon jist a small number, sir, but more jist'a keeps on a'comin'. Cain't exchange 'em fast enough, 'specially not the enlisted Yankees. That's mostly what's in the barn. Cain't wait til this place empties out in a few weeks."

"Ah'm hopeful Ah kin help with that, Corporal. Lead the way." They made their way across the dusty compound. The ground had been trampled by countless foot-steps. When it rained it became a quagmire. Most of the vegetation had long since disappeared, although some tough, near-dead weeds still hung on stubbornly as if no amount of abuse could finish them off. It was getting hot, and the windless, humid day did nothing to blow away the invasive stench. When the five men entered the large barn where the stalls were located it was all but unbearable.

"Ah heard you a'tellin' the captain you was a lookin' fer a runaway, sir," the cor-poral said, seemingly oblivious to the foul odor, as they stood inside the front barn door. "Come ta think on it, there's one Yankee officer what got here 'round yuletide. Thems what brung 'em here said he was a runner. Keep 'em chained up away from the others least ways."

"Let's start with him, Corporal," Stalworthy said, holding a handkerchief over his mouth and nose even if it made him look somewhat effete if not downright ef-feminate.

When they arrived at Pete's stall he was sprawled across some discolored straw. It was changed every other week or so, if he was lucky. He was supposed to have use of a bucket for his waste but there weren't near enough to go around. Sometimes a slave, one of a few used to handle the more odious tasks would come by with one, but it always seemed to be already filled with feces or nearly so, sometimes inter-spersed with what in all likelihood was vomit. If the prisoners in the stalls couldn't wait or had to urinate, well, there was the straw.

"Hey, Yank!" The corporal yelled. "Look this way."

Pete didn't move at first but his shoulders heaved slightly. He knew enough not to dally too long however. He turned his face towards the voice and stared at the corporal with vacant eyes. Pete had a scraggly, full beard and had lost over twenty pounds from his already emaciated frame, but Stalworthy thought he looked enough like the tintype to warrant a better look. He turned away from Pete and took the tintype from the pocket of his blouse. *Hard to tell for sure*, he thought. *But just maybe...*

"Corporal, have this man washed and shaved. Ah'll be in the commandant's office. Bring him there." Stalworthy couldn't get out of the barn fast enough.

Half an hour later Pete was led into the office not far from the stockade walls, located upward from the prevailing wind that had come up from the west. The windows were open, inviting the cooperating breeze. It was the first relatively fresh air Pete had inhaled in weeks. Even though he had scrubbed down with a bucket of water and had even been allowed to use some lye soap, he still reeked. His tattered clothes hadn't been washed and the smell filled the small room. His face was red from the hurried shave and bleeding from several areas.

"This your man?" Captain Bownell asked as he lit a cigar, in a hurry to get the prisoner and his stench out of his office.

Stalworthy had again studied the tintype while making his way to the commandant's office but he didn't have to look at it again. He had told Janeway three months minimum, and there was his prey standing right in front of him inside that time frame.

"What's your name, sir?" Pete hadn't been called "sir" since his recapture in Tennessee. He looked more closely at the Confederate lieutenant, wondering who he could possibly be and why all the sudden interest, fearing the worst.

"Lieutenant Robert McEnroe. Why am I here?" Pete asked, even if doing so under normal circumstances was considered an offense. This, he correctly assumed, wasn't a normal circumstance.

"Quiet, you!" Captain Bownell bellowed anyway.

"It's all right, Captain." Stalworthy said, raising his hand slightly. "With your permission allow me to answer the prisoner." The commandant gave an impatient wave of his own hand, indicating Stalworthy could continue.

"You are here, Lieutenant Pete McCabe, formerly of the 1st Naperville Cavalry, because Ah have found you. And, sir," Stalworthy continued to say with a suddenly raised hand in order to halt any response from Pete, "because you are going back with me. By the way, whatever happened ta Captain July Evers' horse?"

Pete was already weakened by his long ordeal, barely able to stand, so when the words hit him he nearly fainted. He took a deep breath and his lightheadedness abated, but just barely.

"My name is McEnroe. You, sir, have the wrong man."

"Do Ah?" Stalworthy replied, a condescending expression on his face. "Perhaps, but Ah seriously doubt it Lieutenant McCabe. Regardless, with the captain's permission of course, you are comin' with me. Once we reach Salisbury we'll see if Ah'm indeed mistaken. You earned quite a reputation there. Captain?" Stalworthy asked, turning to the commandant.

"By all means, Lieutenant," he replied. "The sooner the better. If he had committed his atrocities here Ah most certainly would want ta deal with him mah own damn self. Ah'll wire Captain Evers and let him know of your success and your imminent return with the prisoner."

"Thank you sir, Captain Evers will greatly appreciate hearin' the news, especially comin' from one of his fellow commandants. Corporal, if you would, please find this loathsome cur some clean clothes if there's any around. We will be leavin' immediately."

Stalworthy addressed the commandant when all the others had left. "Sir, could you also send another brief wire? Among mah many duties, Ah am responsible for keepin' in touch with some'a our spies up North. Ah'd like ta write a coded telegram and don't know when Ah'll be able ta send another wire. Would you be so kind?" Captain Bownell agreed. With that Stalworthy wrote down his message to Janeway and prepared to leave but the commandant stopped him.

"Lieutenant, Ah presume you will of course want some'a mah more able men ta accompany you." That caught Stalworthy off guard. For once something had occurred he hadn't foreseen.

"Ah thank you again, Captain, but that won't be necessary. Along with mah other duties Ah have occasionally dealt with such rabble. But Ah appreciate your offer and your concern."

"Mah concern ain't simply for your welfare, Lieutenant." Captain Bownell responded, not to be put off. "That man is a runner and apparently a damned vicious one at that. Cunning as well, though he don't look it. Ah cain't afford ta chance him makin' good another escape. How would Ah explain mah lapse of judgment if you was ta end up dead and that there Yankee murderer was on the loose again? No sir, Ah'm not goin' ta allow that. You will be accompanied bah three of mah men all the way ta Salisbury. That, Lieutenant, is final."

There was nothing Stalworthy could do, at least for the moment. *This is going to be more difficult,* he thought, *but not insurmountable.*

XVIII

Cusman and Missy Nell rode up to where Jennifer and the two farmers were still talking, Cusman's rifle back in its saddle scabbard. He had his revolvers accessible though, cocked and ready.

"Good day young man, and to you, miss," Joshua said, reaching up to shake their hands. Issachar did the same. "My name is Joshua Kirby. This is my son, Issachar. It appears you are in a bad way."

"It's all'a that, sir." Cusman replied, sensing a quality about the man.

"Please call me Joshua, young man. How may we assist you?"

"We need to get out'a the open, for starters." Cusman answered. "Does your temperament allow us to hole up in your barn a spell?"

"Yes, it does. But we can do better than that, young man. Please, come with us."

***

AFTER SECURING their horses in the barn south of the house, the five of them headed towards the Kirby's white clapboard two story home. Cusman and the women expected to see more family members about, especially the man's wife, but even after entering the small farmhouse no one else appeared to be around.

"Is your wife not at home, sir?" Jennifer asked.

"My dear Clara is buried beneath the chestnut tree out back, ma'am. We lost her a year from last August."

"I am grieved to hear so, Mr. Kirby. My deepest sympathies to you and the rest of your family." Cusman and Missy Nell offered similar condolences.

"Thank you," Joshua said. "As you can imagine, it has been very hard for Issachar and me. We lost his older sister to cholera just two years prior to that."

Again all three of them offered condolences to both Joshua and Issachar. Looking around, Jennifer and Missy Nell noticed the place didn't appear to be lacking a woman's partialities but refrained from mentioning it.

"I'll make us some coffee," Joshua said, as if their prior conversation had thankfully run its course. "Please, have a seat at our table. You must be worn out. Issachar, please get some bread and preserves. Fetch the butter too, son. You three must be starved."

Joshua waited until the three had eaten before speaking, having insisted they finish the loaf and be more liberal with the excellent strawberry preserves and butter Issachar had placed on the table, along with a pitcher of buttermilk.

Jennifer decided to tell the hosts everything, and she didn't get any objections or even a sideways glance from Cusman or Missy Nell. It appeared highly unlikely either of their hosts wouldn't be in sympathy with their plight. Still, Joshua Kirby was distressed.

"There are the bodies of three men still in the woods. I have no reason to doubt their viciousness was all you said, but even the vilest of men need to be given Christian burials."

"Their horses deserve it a damn sight more than those three," Cusman said, not mincing anything.

"Doesn't denying those men Christian burials bring us all down?" Joshua responded. His soft gaze and charitable demeanor struck Cusman as condescending or at least leaning in that direction. "I sympathize with your plight, young man, and I don't doubt your actions were warranted, but that doesn't excuse you, or any of us from doing our Christian duty."

"And if I shot the devil himself would you want the same for him? 'Cause that's near enough what I done."

"Yes I would," Joshua said. "Satan would be in need of it more than any being, and as a Christian I would feel compelled to show my love for even my most feared enemy as the Bible instructs."

"Well sir, I ain't never read in any Bible I ever picked up I was expected to bury the devil and say words over him, but I respect your devotion." Cusman said. "Least ways I agree they should get buried, the sooner the better since we might be here a spell. The horses, too."

Jennifer had remained silent while the men had words, not wanting to offend either of them. She was proud of the way Cusman had spoken to a white man even if Joshua was most certainly not representative of the great majority of his race, regardless of where they lived or which side owned their sympathies. Cusman had yet to reach freedom but not in his mind. Right or wrong, he was expressing his opinions with no regard for the color of a man's skin, Jennifer noted. He was right about the men and horses; that was also true.

"Joshua," she finally said, "why don't you bring your Bible. I would be honored to read some passages with you. There is plenty of daylight left, and since we have a great deal of digging to do perhaps we should get started."

***

DUSK WAS perhaps an hour away before the dead men had been buried and their somewhat shallow graves had been covered with brush. Cusman, Joshua and Issachar then finished digging the three large holes for the horses, just deep enough to allow barely two feet of dirt to cover them. Even though they were used to hard labor, the men, except Cusman, felt as if their arms could no longer lift so much as half a bale of hay.

The holes had been dug as close to the dead horses as possible, but the hard labor, especially digging into and cutting through and pulling out the indefinite number of obstinate roots, had indeed left the farmers so drained they had to all but fall into the switchgrass for a much needed rest.

"If you can give us but a moment, Cusman, we will help you drag them in," Joshua said through his labored breathing.

"You just rest a spell, Mr. Kirby. This won't take me but a minute or two." Cusman grabbed both of the rear hoofs of the first horse in his massive hand then did the same with the front hoofs. He stepped backwards into the hole, stepped out the other side and dragged the dead beast in as if it were a medium sized dog.

Cusman then grabbed an axe and chopped the legs off due to rigor mortis and repeated the process until all three horses were thus disposed. Joshua rose stiffly and grabbed a shovel, instructing Issachar to do the same.

"Sit back down you two," Cusman said. "I'll handle it." They both helped throw dirt on the graves anyway; one shovelful for each of them to four of Cusman's.

Joshua and Jennifer took turns reading from the man's Bible. Although his head was bowed every prayer Cusman said to himself was indeed for the dead horses, and he assured God he was stone cold serious, and was just as assured He would understand.

All of them were looking forward to bathing in the pond and the hot supper Joshua had promised, and Cusman and the women joked about sleeping for a week.

***

ISSACHAR WAS the first to hear the sound coming from the darkening meadow, just before they brought their horses out of the woods with the youth in the lead.

"Listen." He whispered as loud as one can, moving forward for a better view. "Did you hear that horse whinny?" Everyone froze. "It's horses all right," the youth said as he sharpened his focus. "There they are, coming from the north."

Five men on horseback were heading south across the expanse of meadows. At first the adults hadn't made anyone out in the less than dim light, but the youngest eyes had. At least the riders weren't close to the edge of the woods, which was a minor relief. It appeared as if they would remain a little less than hundred yards away if they didn't alter their course.

"Everyone move back a ways. Take my horse too, Missy." Cusman said. "I'll stay here and keep watch. Stay with me, Issachar. Keep them sharp eyes peeled. Wait Missy, give me my rifle."

***

SHERIFF ALUISIS Lazhorn and his temporary deputies knew where they were, but not really. They knew Meersville was ten, maybe fifteen miles away, but if it turned out to be twenty none of the weary men would've been surprised. They knew that's where they'd find the closest tavern even if it turned out to be closer to twenty-five miles east, or southeast, maybe even northeast. They only had one bottle of whiskey left and Sheriff Lazhorn wasn't about to share that with anyone. Hell, he'd brought only four.

"Ah say we camp in them woods, Aluisis." One of them suggested. "We ain't gonna find us nobody come night."

"Ah'll be a sayin' *when* and *where* we stop!" Sheriff Lazhorn declared, as if far too much of his time had already been wasted reminding everyone who was in charge. "Ah was about ta say them woods over yonder oughta be a good 'nough spot, Ah was about ta say that very thing." The man sighed and looked away from the sheriff. He was used to Aluisis Lazhorn; they all were. Before long they were headed directly for Cusman, moving slowly through the dying dusk.

"Cusman," Joshua said, coming up from behind. "Perhaps Issachar and I should greet them. They can't see the farm from here, not in this waning light, and are probably looking for a place to spend the night. I can offer them shelter and probably lead them away." Cusman agreed, then went back and located the women. The three of them had led their horses deeper into the woods south of the clearing before Cusman had crept back, staying out of sight.

"Good evening, gentlemen," Joshua said when the men were perhaps fifty feet away. It startled all of them. None of the men had even noticed Joshua or Issachar, even though they had been standing just outside the tree line.

"Halt! Who goes there!" Sheriff Lazhorn called out, sounding ridiculous. He had been in a local militia once, and had usually found himself alone on guard duty even though it had been ten years before the war, or anything else other than peacetime.

"I'm Joshua Kirby. This is my son, Issachar. You are on my land, sir. What is your business here and how may I assist you?"

"This here your land?" Sheriff Lazhorn asked.

"I believe I just told you that, sir. May I ask your name and why you are here?"

"Ah am Sheriff Aluisis Lazhorn," he announced, as if that revelation carried a great deal of importance. He had already forgotten the second question.

"How may we assist you, sheriff?" Joshua repeated.

"You seen two fancy niggers and a white woman?"

"No, I have seen no one except you gentlemen. I must protest your degrading terminology, however. This is indeed my land, and it would be appreciated if you would refrain from using such unseemly, declarative utterances." Sheriff Lazhorn had no idea what the stout man was talking about, but suspected he had just been insulted.

"Ah already *knows* this is your land, farmer." The nonplused sheriff declared. "What Ah *don't* know is has you done seen two gussied up niggers and a white woman." Joshua was growing impatient as well as wary.

"Sheriff, I just told you, we have seen no one except your group. Now, may I be of any further assistance?"

"If this here's your land, where's your homestead?" Sheriff Lazhorn asked with narrowed eyes, impressed with his shrewd ability to interrogate.

"Over there, sheriff," Joshua said, pointing to the southeast. "Are you planning on spending the night hereabouts or will you be moving on?"

"You got whiskey?" One of the other men asked.

"Shut up, Conrad!" Sheriff Lazhorn ordered. "Ah'm a doin' the talkin' here! Can you put us up fer the night?" He inquired, looking at Joshua again. "Who's the boy?"

"He is still my son, sheriff. I can lend you the use of my barn for the night, but we haven't any food to spare."

"You seen two niggers and a white woman, boy?" Sheriff Lazhorn asked, glaring at Issachar, still feeling every bit the consummate interrogator. The youth looked at his father then answered.

"I haven't seen two Negros or anyone else, 'cept the five of you, sir."

"How 'bout some other men? They was somewheres hereabouts most likely. Least ways we found us some tracks a ways back. Trail went cold though." Issachar simply shrugged his shoulders as if he had nothing further to offer.

"Sheriff," Joshua interjected. "Night is nearly here and we must be heading back. Do you and your men wish to stay in our barn or not, or will you be moving on?"

"You got whiskey?"

"No, sheriff."

"Well, lead the way then. We ain't got all night."

***

AROUND ELEVEN that night Issachar returned to the woods with blankets and food. Cusman and Jennifer thanked him profusely, and Missy Nell gave him a warm hug. The youth's face reddened immediately, and that was evident although in the moonlit darkness the color on Issachar's face wasn't visible.

"Those men will be in the barn the rest of the night. They only come out to pee." Issachar told Cusman, even more embarrassed since his language had been heard by the women. His demeanor caused them to giggle in spite of themselves.

"I was hidin' not too far off when them men rode up," Cusman said. "Heard most of what was said. Did they say later when they'd be movin' on?"

"No, but it might not be 'til later in the mornin' drunk as they were."

"I thought your daddy said he didn't have any whiskey," Cusman said.

"He doesn't. But he keeps a few jugs of mulled wine around. Makes it every Christmas, but never drinks much of it. Keeps makin' it though. I don't know why. Anyway, he gave it to those men. Said it'll make 'em sleep sound. Guess it works. Got the mule outta the barn and not a one of 'em stirred. Sure was loud before though. Never heard men holler and carry on with each other the way they did. They don't like each other much."

***

CUSMAN AND the women were awake before sunrise on what promised to be a warm, sunny day. They had even made their way to a spot in the woods that was directly west of the field where they had first met their new friends. The farmhouse and other buildings farther east were perhaps three hundred yards away, made visible by the first inklings of dawn. The three of them were just inside the tree line so they could keep close watch on the barn. Issachar may have thought the men would be late risers, but often times those used to strong drink and lots of it couldn't stay asleep if they wanted to.

True to their addictions, all five men were up and about before 7:00 a.m. One of them was apparently having breakfast; he was drinking from a jug anyway, and it looked as if two of the others were awaiting their turn. The sheriff appeared and had words with them, his arms flailing about. Before long all their horses were saddled.

Joshua had been at his chores in a smaller structure next to the barn and emerged as the men mounted their horses. He kept pointing due east as he spoke, and it appeared he was growing frustrated if his body language was any indication.

"I can assure you, sheriff, Meersville is due east, fifteen miles." Joshua repeated. "If you travel southeast, or northeast, you will miss it entirely. It is a small town."

"Ah knows how the hell *small* it is, farmer. Ah ain't *stupid* ya know." Joshua glanced at the other men. They all looked away as if the commonplace fields were suddenly worth a second look.

"Well, suit yourself sheriff. I have work to do." With that Joshua walked away, shaking his head.

A half hour after the men had ridden out of sight, heading northeast arguing the whole way, Cusman and the women rode to the barn and tethered their horses to a railing along the barn's north side, close to its front. Joshua led the three into the house north of the barn and started to make a hearty breakfast.

"Please, Joshua," Jennifer said, "let Missy Nell and me take over. You have done more than enough for us."

"You stay right where you are, ma'am. I have become a fair cook and want to bask in your compliments," Joshua replied, smiling. "Issachar, please fetch some more eggs."

The ham steaks fried in butter and servings of eggs were delicious, as were the hot, fresh baked biscuits, butter and strawberry preserves. The women were full but it was obvious Cusman could eat more. Suddenly Issachar flew through the kitchen door, his basket almost empty. A number of broken eggs were scattered about on the ground outside, from the henhouse to the back porch.

"They're back!"

***

WHEN SHERIFF Aluisis Lazhorn and his men spotted the horses tethered outside the barn they broke into a gallop; when they saw that the ones tethered were *their horses* they spurred their rented mounts into a dead run. When they arrived, guns drawn, Joshua came out and walked towards them, his stride deliberate and his expression grim.

"What now, sheriff?" He said, heading towards the front of the barn as he spoke. The sheriff and his men followed, urging their winded horses with their spurs.

"You know what *now*, farmer!" The red-faced man bellowed, his ample gut protruding as he attempted to keep his horse from moving about. The other men were looking around, no longer intrigued by the fields. "Who brought them horses and where they hidin'?" He cocked his revolver and leveled it at an unarmed Joshua. "*Well,* farmer?"

Cusman had made his way from around the back of the house and through the back door of the barn. When he suddenly came out the front barn door he leveled the shotgun Issachar had given him directly at the sheriff before pointing it quickly back and forth at the others, bringing it back in a blur to the sheriff's face. Both of Cusman's .44 caliber Colt Lawman's were in their holsters, hammers cocked.

"Y'all put yo' guns on da groun', or Ah swears Ah's a'gonna blow yo' sheriff's God damned head *clean* off, Ah is!" Cusman yelled, looking and sounding basically insane.

Sheriff Lazhorn complied immediately, his bladder failing him miserably. Cusman was a very large man anyway, but with a full choke 12 gauge in his hands he looked gigantic. Two of the other men also complied, finally a third. The last one hesitated until he saw the shotgun barrel pointed his way, held by an enraged runaway slave twice his size, clearly out of his mind. The terrified man dropped his gun, eyes wide, as he trembled in his saddle.

"You!" Cusman hollered, pointing the shotgun at Joshua. "Git yo' no-account cracker ass on da groun', or you's gonna be da second ta die! Done run me a knife inta dat peckerwood boy'a yourns, gutted 'em good Ah did! You gonna be next if'n you don't do as Ah says!"

Joshua complied immediately. A disgusting retching sound came from Sheriff Lazhorn, as whatever sour whiskey and mulled wine still in him splattered to the ground.

"Don't shoot, boy!" Joshua pleaded. "I'm down!"

"Who da hell you callin' *boy*, cracker? Hear dat agin, an' yo' white ass be splattered dead!" Cusman brought the shotgun back to the others, holding it in just one of his huge hands with a revolver in the other. Sheriff Lazhorn began vomiting again; Cusman looked *planetary* to him. "Missy!" Cusman boomed towards the house, "Drag dat cracker bitch on out here!"

Moments later Missy Nell, holding Jennifer in a headlock and pulling her roughly along, appeared. Missy Nell looked just as hostile as Cusman, and Jennifer was pleading for her life.

"Quit yo' squawkin' you rasty ole crone!" Missy Nell yelled. "Let's jus' kill 'em all, Cusman!" She yelled as she dragged Jennifer along. "Start with dat fat-assed sheriff!"

"Oh Lord no!" Sheriff Lazhorn pleaded as he started to blubber and cry. "Ah ain't got no truck with y'all! Always been partial ta nig - ta darkies, tell 'em boys!"

"Shut up an' git down off'a dat horse, you fat-assed peckerwood!" Cusman yelled. Sheriff Lazhorn basically fell off and stayed on his hands and knees. His vomiting had become dry heaves but no less disgusting. He managed to look up at Cusman who appeared to be ten feet tall. Spittle and vomit clung to his scraggly beard, and he was shaking so violently he could barely keep from collapsing altogether.

"N - Now boy…"

"*BOY*? Did you say *boy*? Ah's Mas'r Sable ta you, you peckerwood bastard! Lemme hear you say it!"

"Uh, Master Sable…"

"Dat be *Mas'r* Sable!"

"Mas'r Sable, sir, please don't kill me! Them others whats hate colored folk! This here weren't mah doin'!" The others looked at him in shock, as if they would be glad to shoot him if Cusman didn't.

"All y'all! Git down off dem horses!" Cusman yelled, even louder than before. Some of the men were praying.

Half an hour later all five of them were hog-tied in the barn. Cusman told them if they moved an inch in the next three hours he would set the place on fire.

"You two!" Cusman hollered at Jennifer and Joshua, "Git in da house!" He handed his revolver to Missy Nell and told her to take them away. When they were gone he addressed the men again. "Ah might jist carve y'all up, like Ah done da boy. Ain't decided right yet. Sure enough got me yo' horses, so mebbe Ah jist bring 'em along if Ah light out, carve 'em up jus' for fun. Drag dat dead boy wid me too so's Ah kin watch 'em bleed. Ah *loves* ta watch peckerwoods bleed! Don't fergit, y'all move nigh on an *inch* and you gonna burn! *Hey!*" Cusman yelled at Sheriff Lazhorn, "Did Ah jist see you twitch?"

"N - No Mas'r Sable, Ah didn't move a damned muscle! Please don't burn me!"

"Well den, you bes' remember what Ah been a sayin' ta y'all! Now bury yo' faces in dat dere straw! Go on, now!" They couldn't have rolled over faster if they had fallen off a cliff. "We's likely headin' west few hours from now, mebbe longer, but Ah sees you peckerwoods agin, gonna blow dem knees right off'a y'all, den set ever' damn one'a you peckerwoods on fire! Might anyways, any y'all move an' inch!"

***

"RASTY OLE *crone?*" Jennifer said to Missy Nell when they were all in the house except Cusman.

"I'm so sorry Mother. Just wanted to sound convincin'."

"I'm teasing you dear. It's not the right time for it though, I apologize."

"What now?" Joshua asked, placing his arm around Issachar's shoulders. "I guess we'd better go with you."

Cusman came through the kitchen door and heard Joshua's last sentence. "I hate to trouble y'all so much Mr. Kirby, but for now that's the only way. I s'pect them men won't be movin' much for a while. Hid all their guns, and their horses won't be walkin' spry-like for a week or there 'bouts, least ways with men on 'em. You kin tell 'em you and Missus Jennifer escaped on foot, but she lit out. They're stupid enough to believe it. Just tell 'em the niggers got drunk and passed out. I know they'll believe that, but I s'pect they're done chasin' after us anyway."

"You'd better steer clear of Meersville, Cusman." Joshua said. "Most folks there aren't as bad as those five but it would be unwise nonetheless. You're not that far from the coast. If you can make it to Cape Romain perhaps you could take a passenger ship if they're still running, or perhaps a train if no one there is looking for you. I'm sorry I can't offer you more."

"You've already done enough, Joshua," Jennifer said, an endearing smile on her face. "Let's getting going," she said to Cusman and Missy Nell, "we can make up our minds later."

TEN MILES away, after saying their goodbyes to the Kirby's, the three continued to head east. Missy Nell had again hugged Issachar and that time there wasn't any darkness to hide his suddenly crimson face. He couldn't erase his bashful smile, either.

Jennifer had borrowed some of the late Mrs. Kirby's clothes but they were too small for Missy Nell's statuesque frame. Joshua even supplied Jennifer with his late wife's saddle and refused to take a penny for anything. There weren't two lady's saddles, and they decided it would look more natural if a white lady was using the one Mrs Kirby had owned.

Previously, when the five of them had gone a little over five miles from the farm, Joshua had taken them to a pond nestled within a fair amount of brush. The women had bathed first and it had felt wonderful. Cusman had gone next and had been glad Jennifer had demonstrated the foresight to borrow soap from Joshua. While bathing he had scrubbed his clothes as had Missy Nell. They had put them on wrung out and damp, but it felt good to be clean.

After they had gone far enough so that Meersville would soon be on the eastern horizon, Jennifer reached a conclusion.

"If enough wires have been sent out it likely won't matter where we try to obtain useful information about transportation," she figured. "I'd rather take our chances with a small town first. Even if they have been alerted we might be able to get away somehow. Better odds than we'll get in a larger town with a Home Guard force, and perhaps if they haven't been alerted in Meersville, not all the others have either. Even Trenton won't send wires everywhere I would imagine. Besides, as far as he knows we may have already been caught. He'll believe it if I can get a wire off to him. We should have a few more days anyway."

Jennifer had been correct on all counts. Not only had the people of Meersville apparently heard nothing, but the man at the telegraph office even told Jennifer where the nearest train station was located. An obviously refined white lady traveling with her slaves didn't appear out of the ordinary. Before leaving, Jennifer sent a telegram to Trenton. She used the name R. Stalworthy so as to not raise any suspicion with the telegraph operator who had no reason to believe her name wasn't Rebecca, the one she had used upon meeting the man.

Mr. Ransom. I have succeeded. I expect to be in Beaux Hollow as my travels allow - R. Stalworthy

***

THE REST of their journey proved to be as successful as its beginning. Even when it was almost time to enter the North nothing went wrong. Cusman had the proper papers proving they were free Negroes, and with a white lady there to verify the claim not a wisp of suspicion was forthcoming. They managed to rent a horse and buggy that took them to another train station from where they could depart and finally reach free soil, if they could just make it a little farther.

They disembarked in Pennsylvania and strolled over to a small park across the street from the train station. When they were alone in the shade of a large hardwood maple, on free soil, Missy Nell wept. It was all Cusman could do to control the same emotions as Jennifer watched the two former slaves, her own tears flowing.

Moments later however, with Missy Nell sobbing in his arms, Cusman's tears flowed every bit as much as hers. He held her tight then stepped back a short distance, tears still streaming down his face, his massive hands holding her gently by the shoulders as he gazed into her reddened eyes.

"Great God in heaven Missy, we have fought and won us a life all our own." They came together again, so very much in love, sobs of joy spilling from them. *They were free.*

***

WELL OVER a month later Jennifer received a letter in response to the one she had mailed to Joshua and Issachar. She couldn't wait to get over to Mr. and Mrs. Cusman Sable's new house in Amherst, Massachusetts, the town the three of them had decided to call home. Cusman was going to start classes at Amherst College that coming fall, and although he had seemed moody lately he appeared to be looking forward to it. Over coffee Jennifer asked if she could read the letter aloud; it was too amusing not to, she insisted. After standing up she proceeded:

Dearest Jennifer, Missy Nell & Cusman,

Issachar and I were beside ourselves with joy when we received your wonderful letter. President Lincoln may have issued his proclamation months ago, but we all know how much weight that carries here. Your successful exodus brought us to tears. In answer to your question, we won't consider accepting a penny from you as we have previously indicated, but thank you. Now to the rest - when I made my way back to the barn all I heard was nothing. At first I assumed they must have freed themselves and left, but no. When I began to push open the barn door, the first thing I did hear was our dear sheriff's voice - 'Please don't burn me!' His grateful tears wouldn't stop when I told him he was safe. My story about my escape was received just as Cusman predicted, and then some. Have you ever been embraced by a man as pathetic as Sheriff Lazhorn? I pray you never will. I too bathed immediately after they left, but I am getting ahead of myself. Once the others were untied, it appeared as though the good sheriff's days had come

to an end. If I hadn't interceded, the beating they gave him would likely have been fatal. They demanded I at least keep him at the farm until they were well on their way, and I complied with their wishes. Cusman did a capital job on their horses, poor beasts, but the shaken men were able to bring them along even though they had to head out on foot. Sheriff Lazhorn spent the night, but he didn't get any sleep I'm aware of. He has found God, of that there is no doubt, as he spent most the night praying, repenting and sobbing. He is convinced Cusman is an agent from hell, if not Old Scratch himself. Regardless, his days as a man of the law are behind him, or so he maintained. He left at first light on foot, made it several miles, then remembered he had forgotten his horse. He returned, was off again, and I wondered how long it would be before he remembered he had forgotten his saddle. Apparently he never did, or simply couldn't bring himself to return once more. At no time did he even ask about poor Issachar, who had to sleep outside all night, away from the farm of course. That is the last we have seen of our dear sheriff, and I pray it remains that way. Do stay in touch dear people, and may God continue to bless you.
Yours truly,
Joshua & Issachar Kirby

Jennifer finished reading. Her two hosts just sat there, mouths agape. Then the laughter erupted, but subsided when they began to relive that morning. When Sheriff Aluisis Lazhorn's name came up the laughter started all over again.

After a while their conversation turned to more topical subjects, not the least of which was Cusman's upcoming education. Things took a different turn when he took a deep breath and finally mentioned what had been on his mind of late.

"There are free colored men enlistin' in the Union army every day," he began. "I'm a free colored man, and we all know freedom comes with a price. I'm goin' to attend college, but maybe not this fall, or any time before this war is won once and for all. I'm enlistin' tomorrow. My mind is made up."

XIX

A disconcerted Clifton Janeway glanced at the note again and sighed, then looked out the window of his office once more. It was located on the first floor of the spacious white mansion his father had built the year Clifton was born. It was the only genuine mansion in Naperville, located perhaps a mile west from the O'Darcy home on the north side of the road that led to Aurora. Some folks insisted Pinecraig was also a mansion but Hezekiah never referred to his large, Victorian home as such. The Janeway mansion even had huge white pillars out front, reminiscent of the ones more likely to be found on large plantations in the South.

Spring had begun to fulfill its promise in and around Naperville, but Clifton didn't care or even notice all that much; he never did, unless the weather was an inconvenience. The weather wasn't even an afterthought that day, however. The note had arrived in the morning mail. It was short and to the point:

My beloved,

How I yearn for thee! I know how difficult it is for us to be alone, as things now stand, but I must see you, my love of loves! Please meet me this Tuesday afternoon, if just for a few moments. I will be at Wilkins dry goods, in the back where the shelves are high - and private!!!
XOXOXO

The wave of revulsion Clifton had felt the first time he read it returned, as he again reacted to the note: *Thee? My love of loves? - XOXOXO? - What childish drivel. That little vixen may have the body of a woman, a remarkably curvaceous woman at that, but otherwise she displays all the maturity of an adolescent who thinks she has discovered not only true love, but its eternal significance.* "Jesus H *Christ.*" Clifton muttered as he continued to look out the window. "Now *I'm* doing it."

He felt increasingly uneasy, even angry with himself. How many times after entering his teen years had his father admonished him with one of his favorite little maxims, which in Clifton's mind had always been a worn-out, silly phrase that made reference to "which head to listen to" when aroused by a girl. It didn't apply to prostitutes of course, or girls from places far from Naperville, ones he had lied to as far as his real name and place of origin were concerned, and everything else for that matter. *Who cares about those trollops? If something happened, their fathers, husbands or brothers*

would be searching for some miscreant named Ed House or Bill Kowalsky from Galesburg or wher-
ever, if they bother to look at all. Damn, I had to succumb to some young tart from here, Delicia's
sister *for Christ sake.*

To him, Linda Marie had been amazing in bed. She had been inexperienced to be sure, but the word "no" was never uttered, not really, or at least not for long. Granted, she had been reluctant to participate in several of his more depraved requests, but had finally relented. He had insisted upon a few of them, forced her really, but eventually the most unnatural acts Clifton had pressured her into were met with what he defined as enthusiasm. *She pretended to be unwilling, not to enjoy them, but the little tramp obviously enjoyed what I made her do. All women do, eventually.*

He was convinced women only acted otherwise in order to give the appearance of propriety. After awhile, the things he had made Linda Marie do only seemed repulsive to her at first; he was convinced of that as well. They had merely been acts she would come to realize were acquired tastes, and would be met with more enthusiasm if she were indeed a real woman and gave them half a chance.

"*That's how mature women react,*" he had told her. "*Not little school girls, those too young to appreciate what adults found satisfying - is that what I have fallen in love with?*" He had asked her that question after she had balked at one of his more abhorrent demands, and the effect it had generated still amused him in spite of himself. "*Is that all you are after all, a little girl pretending to be a woman?*" He recalled asking as well, the memory causing a simpering smile to emerge. "*Perhaps you aren't ready, perhaps you are still years away from being a* **mature** *woman. Perhaps I need to keep looking for my true love of loves.*" The phrase, as always, made him recoil. *Rather effective though,* he thought, his smirk continuing to grow.

***

LINDA MARIE had her own recollections of that afternoon, and afterwards she looked back on it with bewilderment and shame. She forced herself to fight against those feelings, insisting Clifton had simply wanted her to appreciate adult lovemaking. She had no points of reference, no one she could talk to about what had happened, but she concluded that made perfect sense. What lady would admit to allowing such things, much less enjoy them? Isn't that what Clifton had promised would eventually happen though? Such things were between mature women and their lovers, but she didn't know any women who talked about those things at all, let alone in detail for goodness sake. Her doubts persisted, fueled by the revulsion she still couldn't dismiss. She simply couldn't understand how anyone could even conceive such things, much less act upon them - *enjoy* them.

Her fantasies had always run a much different course. He would take her in his arms with a gentle urgency, totally aroused with kissing and exploring her in the most loving and respectful of ways, in tune with her feelings. He would know what touched her heart, what ignited her passion. Instead, he had made her do vile things, as unnatural as they had been degrading, some even painful. Perhaps she had a lot to learn after all, but there was no way she would allow Clifton to know how she had felt - still felt. If those acts were what grown-ups did then it was her fault if she couldn't appreciate them. She vowed to keep trying, to trust the wisdom and maturity of her *love of loves*.

***

CLIFTON HAD been avoiding Linda Marie as much as possible, and his absence from the O'Darcy household had grown apparent. He had begun to spend more time with Delicia at the hospital whenever possible, despite her suggestions he instead stop by Pinecraig more often. He couldn't continue to make excuses, of that there was no doubt, not if he expected to continue making a favorable impression upon her parents. What kind of suitor avoided a young lady's kin?

He decided to meet with Linda Marie in the vain hope of dissuading her, and perhaps the even more unlikely chance of keeping her from not falling completely apart. Another of his father's bothersome sayings came calling, a quote from some long dead English playwright Clifton seemed to recall, either Shakespeare or Congreve. He wasn't sure which, but it gave him pause. *Heaven has no rage like love to hatred, nor hell a fury like a woman scorned.* He had always believed his father's tired adages were utter nonsense, or at best dubious attempts at whimsy. As Clifton rode towards town for his encounter with Linda Marie, he wondered in what other ways he had underestimated his father.

***

LINDA MARIE was right where she said she'd be. Fortunately the store was all but empty when he arrived, a few minutes late. Clifton acted as if he were shopping; he even picked up several articles of clothing before making his way to the back of the store. When he saw her he placed the clothing on a shelf. He immediately wished he had kept his arms full.

"My love of loves, how I have dreamed of thee and this moment!" The impulsive girl gushed, falling into his arms.

At first Clifton was repulsed, then the scent of her perfume entered his consciousness as did the sensation of her breasts pressing against him.

*Son of a **bitch**,* he felt more than said to himself.

"Linda Marie -"

"Call me darling, my love of loves," she said, eyes wide, filled with adoration.

"Uh, darling, we must talk." She opened her mouth way too wide and tried to kiss him. "Please, Linda Marie, not here. Honestly, we have to talk." She was confused but reluctantly backed away. Wasn't that what he wanted?

"How can mere words express our desire, my love of loves?" She announced, and before he could speak added: "Very well, though. If you insist, I'll listen. But first don't you want just one little kiss?" *Of course he does,* she insisted to herself. She would be exactly what he wanted her to be.

She was quickly in his arms again and that time her tongue was where she thought he wanted it to be; until later, when he would want much more. He would certainly want those other things and she was determined to drive her childish revulsion at the mere thought of them from her mind. After a few seconds that felt much longer to Clifton, he pushed her away again. She didn't know why, but then she had so much to learn, to *understand.*

"You are an adorable creature, all the boys think so as do I, but what happened was a mistake." He watched her closely but reading her wasn't difficult, if the narrowed look that had revealed her extinguished enthusiasm was any indication. "As you know, your sister and I have been seeing a great deal of each other, and it simply won't do for us to ignore that fact. You are a very sweet and desirable child, but there you have it." Clifton held his breath.

"You *know* I'm not a child Clifton, and all's fair in love and war," she said in all seriousness, as if the well worn, laconic aphorism had not only just occurred to her, but she was its original author. "Besides, I have wonderful news!"

Before she could continue the sound of the bell attached to the front door fluttered throughout the store, then the voice of the proprietor was heard.

"Good afternoon, Reverend Galloway, how nice to see you!"

Clifton left the articles of clothing where he had placed them and made his way out the back door. Linda Marie was disappointed, but even in her hopeless state she understood. She stuck her head out the door and called after him.

"We do indeed need to talk, my love of loves. I'll send you another note!"

***

LINDA MARIE was a ravishing young lady who was entering womanhood, she just knew it, even if the intensity of her feelings rushed beyond her ability to understand, to deal with them in a way that wasn't mortifyingly juvenile to her. That had to change. How many had, years later, looked back at their behavior with embarrassment, chagrined by their childish inability to appreciate what grown-up love was really about? She asked herself that question as if she knew the answer. She kept asking it though. The lucky ones were able to read their decades-old diaries or love letters and smile, simply shake their heads in astonishment as they recalled the level of their naive immaturity. Linda Marie was convinced she was following her heart as all women eventually had to do, and would act in spite of her childish feelings, not lose everything because of them.

***

IF THE first note had been upsetting, the second was a catastrophe. Linda Marie hadn't come right out and said it, but Clifton was fairly certain he knew what the troublesome child was implying. This time she wanted to meet him by the old swimming pond on the O'Darcy property. Her parents and sisters would be in Aurora, except Delicia who would be at the hospital. Linda Marie would be near the pond at noon that coming Friday, and had insisted in the short note her "love of loves" not be the least "teeny weeny" bit late.

"Christ on a God damned crutch." He muttered. "This will have to be dealt with." He had enough on his mind. He hadn't heard a thing from Stalworthy, the bastard, but on a more positive note Clifton's recent reluctance to come to Delicia's house and his change of mood in general had not been lost on her. His aloofness had apparently created the opposite effect - Delicia had become somewhat more interested in him; he was convinced of it. *This other issue most certainly has to be dealt with,* he concluded.

***

CLIFTON WASN'T wearing his uniform. He had even taken one of the new horses his father had purchased as opposed to his usual mount. He had nothing specific in mind, but regardless of the outcome he wanted as many options available as possible. When he approached the designated spot by the pond where they were to meet, he noticed Linda Marie had somehow ridden there on her father's recently acquired and most spirited horse, assuming she hadn't walked it there. Grayman was a large stallion and only accomplished horsemen had any business riding him. He was broken in, but the young stallion was prone to ignore that from time to time.

It came as no surprise Linda Marie had chosen that particular mount, or had reason to bring a horse at all - the pond wasn't a quarter mile from the house. She had her reasons though, as obvious as they were immature he concluded. She no doubt felt compelled to impress her "love of loves" with something that was in truth inane, and the notion made Clifton cringe. *What a childish thing to do,* he thought as he approached, *and so very much like her…*

She has seen me coming, he noticed, *but rather than stand there watching my obvious approach and perhaps give a slight wave like a more mature young lady might be inclined to do, someone like Delicia, the foolish child has slipped behind a tree. Oh now look, I'm less than twenty feet away, and all she feels compelled to do is gaze dramatically at the pond as if she hasn't noticed me, hasn't noticed me* **twenty feet away** *on horseback,* he observed, cringing with disgust. *She's continuing to gaze across the water, in her mind the horizon no doubt, striking a pose that is supposed to indicate she is deep in thought, consumed by contemplations of the vagaries of life as only the most provocatively thoughtful and worldly of womankind could possibly understand...* Clifton felt as if he could have vomited at what he correctly perceived as her childish behavior.

"Linda Marie?" He finally brought himself to ask, after his horse had whinnied loud enough to be heard on the other side of the pond. Clifton sighed, staring at her. *Oh Christ, just look at her now, she's continuing her deep contemplations for a moment, and will continue to stare out across the water, if not the entire God damned universe for who knows how long. Just **look** at her. She thinks she knows how sophisticated, how complex she must appear. What utter nonsense!*

"Oh, Clifton, is that you?" She asked. *She still has yet to turn around!*

"You had something you wanted to tell me," he asked impatiently. "I haven't a great deal of time, so could you please turn around?" He continued to say as he dismounted and tethered his horse to a stunted tree.

"Oh," she responded coyly when she finally did turn, "you won't be in such a hurry when you hear my glorious news, my love of -"

"What *glorious* news, Linda Marie?"

"You won't have to concern yourself about Delicia anymore, I would imagine." An affectedly coy smile appeared on her face, one she barely felt as she approached, one that masked her conflicting feelings for her older sister and most everything else. "I'm going to tell Mother tomorrow, she'll have so much planning to do! I'll let her break the news to my sister, however." She was almost certain all worldly ladies would understand what she was being forced to do - eventually, even Delicia. *All's fair in love and war...* floated about inside her.

"What news?" Clifton's heart was beginning to pound.

"That thee and I are getting married, my love of loves!" Her face broke out in an explosion of apparent joy. She couldn't wait for Clifton to sweep her in his manly arms and kiss her passionately. He stood there dumbfounded and stared at her as if she were insane. It was one of those rare moments when Clifton Janeway was truly speechless. When she flew into his arms he recoiled and pushed her back abruptly. He found his voice.

"Like hell we are!" She stood stark still, stunned, and stared at him.

"Like hell we are *indeed* Major, I am pregnant!" He had suspected the worst but it came as a horrible shock to him anyway. She was making it up, assuming she would be pregnant before long anyway, but within his panic that possibility didn't register with any degree of reliability. *This can't be happening...*

"Then I suggest you try to snare one of the other men, or *boys* you have been fornicating with!" Clifton un-tethered his horse and mounted it immediately. "I will deny everything, do you hear me? I will say I spurned your childish advances from the beginning and this is my reward! Are you listening, you brazen little *strumpet?* I have the means to hire any number of fellows to vow they have had you, two at a time no less! Mind you, there are those hereabouts who won't be surprised!"

Linda Marie's temples were pounding as she spoke. "No, Clifton darling, *no!* You're the only one I have ever…you're merely upset, that's all, I understand! Please, darling, *please!*" Linda Marie flew towards him and grabbed onto his leg and tried to pry his boot from its stirrup.

"Linda Marie! Stop this nonsense!" Instead, the distraught girl began to pull at him even more aggressively. "I said *stop it!*" He shoved her violently, and her lithe body flew backwards onto the ground. He heard a sickening thud.

When he dismounted and went to her he saw what had happened. Her head had struck a dark rock hidden in a patch of bluestem grass. The rock was actually much larger than it appeared but most of it was imbedded underground, as if it had been held for ages in the hard dirt and clay. He put his hand behind her head and lifted it gently. There was blood, but not very much. She moaned softly, but hadn't opened her eyes. Finally, her eyes still closed, she moaned slightly, "Clifton?"

"I'm right here, Linda Marie." She heard his voice, and smiled weakly. It was the last sound to ever reach her. After again striking her skull into the rock, just enough to further daze the girl, he placed his hands over her mouth and nose and kept them there, looking around. After some minutes when he was convinced she was dead, he went over and untied Grayman. He knew the horse would make its way back to the barn, saddled and unable to get in. Grayman would certainly do that, and would likely be at that very spot or close to it when Mr. and Mrs. O'Darcy, as well as Ginny and her younger sisters, returned home later that afternoon.

Clifton went about covering the tracks his own horse had made upon his arrival then led the animal into the pond a few feet. After covering the tracks to the water, he mounted and spurred the animal into the deeper water and it swam effortlessly to the other side. He repeated the process near the opposite shore until he was satisfied with his results, then made his way through a large stand of yellow-poplar and sumac. No one would look for tracks there; no one would even be suspicious enough to look. Extra tracks by or near the body were one thing, any others belonged where they were because they were too far away to begin with, but again he doubted anyone would notice. He was right.

***

WHEN CLIFTON made it home he quickly donned his major's uniform and went immediately into town. He needed a drink desperately but the Pre-Emption House right in the middle of town certainly wasn't the place to have one. He made his way down Washington Street, waving and smiling at the people he passed on the way, making sure to stop several of them and engage them in idle chatter. He made pains to enter several shops and engaged owners and customers in conversation as well. After establishing himself firmly in town he rode the ten miles to Aurora and repeated the process, finally stopping by the post office.

"Well look at this," he said to the man behind the counter, after reading the first of two sealed wires that had been waiting for Clifton. "General Smithington needs to see me right away. Clyde, I'd better get to the train station post haste."

The man waved a short goodbye, and Clifton was out the door. He indeed had a wire from General Smithington, asking where a report he was supposed to have received a week ago might be, not that it really mattered to the general. As Clifton walked to where his horse was tethered he glanced at the other wire. "Well now, what have we here," he said softly as he stopped walking, looking around. "What news does Mr. Stalworthy have for me today?"

XX

Pete appeared to be without substance or expectation as they rode down the red dirt and clay wagon trace that meandered through the heavily wooded countryside, but he missed little if anything at all. His shoulders were hunched, eyes vacant, staring straight ahead for the most part - everything about his appearance implied he had forsaken all resistance. His hands were tied so tightly to the saddle horn his swollen fingers appeared as unresponsive as they were purple. His ankles were tied as well, with the rope connecting them beneath the horse's belly.

Even his worn shoes had been removed on the off chance something unforeseen occurred. The forested terrain wouldn't be impossible to traverse but a barefoot man would find it more difficult, even one who was especially motivated. Cut and bleeding feet would eventually slow anyone down, and Pete's feet had become soft and vulnerable during his months of idle captivity. Stalworthy had another reason to remove the shoes as well, and after having done so his curiosity regarding which foot was missing which toe had been satisfied.

Stalworthy kept a close watch on him despite the precautions, but Pete wasn't his only concern. He had hidden the essential items he needed to perform his job effectively; extra uniforms and other clothes, tools, certain weapons and ammunition, even a satchel containing accessories an actor might use to create a character for the stage. Stalworthy could transform into anything from a backwoods ruffian to a collared pastor if the need arose. He also had the large jars of formaldehyde hidden, as if he didn't have enough things inside the two big canvas bags that would prove difficult to explain to the three soldiers. There were also the two pack horses near a brook that ran through a small meadow where they were tethered.

He had to retrieve all those things and he couldn't do it without raising suspicion. Worse yet, his extra supplies weren't even five miles from Oglethorpe. *The three Confederates shouldn't be dealt with so close to the stockade, but they will have to be anyway,* Stalworthy thought, glancing about. Burying four men had definitely not been part of his plan. He had anticipated having to deal with just one body, minus its head and a foot of course, but four bodies would prove to be at least bothersome. When they were less than a half mile from his cache a solution to his problem appeared as if predestined.

He wouldn't have discovered it if one of the soldiers hadn't needed to relieve himself. Once the soldier had walked a short distance from the wagon trace they were on, the others decided it was a good time to relieve themselves as well. Stalworthy tethered his horse and joined them. He took special care tying Pete's horse to a tree, and told him to go in his pants if the need arose.

There was a small brook in the woods that ran along an outcropping of rocks, and when Stalworthy inspected the forested area more closely he noticed a cave on the other side of the winding brook. It was small, barely visible, and probably wouldn't have been noticed by most people who weren't looking for such a place. It might not even be large enough to hide four corpses, Stalworthy calculated, unless he was forced to chop up the bodies. He figured that would be a hell of a lot easier than trying to dig a big enough hole through all the roots and hard red clay and earth, not to mention effectively covering his efforts.

Two of the men were standing as they relieved themselves by the brook, with a third one squatting nearby, behind a bush. Stalworthy would deal with him last. He was proficient with a bowie knife, but he would have to act fast.

The first soldier was easy to dispatch. The rapid slash across his throat with the razor-sharp blade opened a wound so deep his head fell to its side as if it were a puppet's whose operator had let go of a string. The man let out a gurgling sound and began to slump to the ground. Before his body had even landed Stalworthy drove the knife into the side of the other man's neck at an upward angle, the tip of its blade sticking into the inside top of the man's skull. Stalworthy yanked out the blade and dashed towards the bush, which was what alerted the man. Had Stalworthy simply strode over he would have accomplished the element of surprise, but by rushing over the soldier had determined the other noises, the ones which had sounded slightly out of place but not enough to interrupt his business, were something after all.

"What the *hell*?" He yelled as he tried desperately to pull up his trousers. Stalworthy lunged at him with the knife, but the man saw it coming in time and quickly dove to his side and crawled deeper into the thick bramble. Stalworthy couldn't effectively get to him from where he was located, so he attempted to make his way around and attack him from the other side.

The soldier was a large man, but agile and not unaccustomed to hand-to-hand combat. He found a sizable piece of hickory, and rather than wait to be attacked he took the fight to Stalworthy. The soldier feigned a move that caught his adversary by surprise then jabbed his makeshift weapon into Stalworthy's upper chest, just missing his throat. Stalworthy flew backwards and landed in a bush. If he hadn't been able to get one of his revolvers out of its holster so quickly the fight would have been over. He fired once and the fight was indeed over. The bullet had struck the large man in the forehead, and after he fell to the ground part of his body disappeared into the brush.

Stalworthy sat there panting for a few moments and looked around unsuccessfully for his bowie knife, trying to come to grips with what had just occurred. He regained his composure, realizing he had one more man to kill. He rushed out of the brush and surrounding trees and headed towards the wagon trace where the horses were tethered, his revolver still in hand. He looked around frantically; Pete was gone along with Stalworthy's prized palomino.

Although he had to deal with the bodies, that could be delayed. Besides, he could always say McCabe did it if by chance someone discovered the bodies before Stalworthy hunted him down. He mounted the best of the four remaining horses and took off after his prey, cursing Pete for having the presence of mind to take Stalworthy's horse, the best mount of all. Worse yet, Stalworthy realized, like the other soldiers he had not felt compelled to remove his rifle from its saddle scabbard when he had followed those men to the brook. Now all the rifles were gone.

If McCabe was smart, which Stalworthy already knew was true, he would be setting an ambush. If it hadn't been for an overhanging branch barely large enough to accomplish what suddenly occurred, that would have been Stalworthy's last thought. The bullet clipped the branch just enough to throw it a little off course, barely missing his head. Stalworthy cursed his initial lapse of judgment and flew off his horse, keeping the skittish animal between him and the direction of the shot as he made his way into the relative safety of the trees south of the wagon trace. He made it there in time but the horse didn't; the next shot struck its skull. Stalworthy had only his two .44 caliber Colt Walker revolvers. Worse yet, the bullets for his revolvers were in a saddlebag on his horse, and he had but eleven rounds left.

Pete hadn't found the ideal spot for an ambush, but he had found the first available. He figured the lieutenant and the others might get too careless in their zeal to come after him, and that had almost been the case. Pete wondered where the others were and what all the commotion had been, especially the gun shot, as he rubbed his skinned and bloody wrists before repositioning himself.

He had spotted a sharp piece of stone while Stalworthy and the others had been preparing to depart back at the stockade. He had slipped it into his hand after he had bent down and pretended to adjust one of his shoes before Stalworthy had told him to take them off. He had almost dropped the stone when Stalworthy had bound him to the saddle, but had managed to keep it secured between his thumb and palm. He had cut through a good portion of the hemp just before they had stopped, and once the men had gone into the trees and brush he cut through the rest. He had already begun to walk Stalworthy's horse away after having hidden the soldiers' rifles in some switchgrass across the wagon trace, but when he heard commotion and then the shot he had been on the palomino and gone in an instant.

Pete heard movement in the brush just as he finished repositioning himself closer to where Stalworthy had gone into the trees south of the wagon trace. He fired twice towards the sound, then bounded south across the wagon trace and hid behind a large hickory. No shots were returned and he wondered if he had indeed been very lucky. He peered carefully around the tree, and part of its bark exploded in his face. He reached instinctively for his eyes, heard more rapid movement in the brush, then fell to the ground amidst the fairly tall grass while pointing his rifle in that direction. Nothing. No sound at all. Pete very carefully raised his head just enough for a quick look around, still at a loss as far as the whereabouts of the others was concerned. Another shot rang out and missed, hitting the ground just to his right. Pete rolled back behind the tree, and that was when he spotted the wagon.

The creaking wagon could be heard coming as well. Stalworthy could also hear it. After having fired his latest shot however, he had gone too far south of the wagon trace to use the wagon for cover to flank his adversary since it was heading past Stalworthy first. Two older civilian men were in it, looking around as if the shots were at least cause for some alarm, since a dead army horse was back just off the wagon trace. The stockade was in the general vicinity, but the war had yet to reach anywhere near that part of Georgia. Still, something was definitely amiss.

"Who's shootin' out there?" One of them hollered. "Well watch your damned selves! You got travelers a headin' down the road! Them's your horses back yonder? Well, you musta kilt one'a them! You huntin' mebbe? Hallo? Haalloo!" When they passed directly across from where Pete was hiding, about where they thought the latest shots had come from, he made his move. Pete ran across the wagon trace again, and before disappearing into the trees north of it he hollered at them.

"You men best turn back! There's an escapee up ahead and he'll shoot you sure just like he did that horse yonder!" They attempted to comply, but from where they were situated the wagon trace was too narrow for them to turn around. The man driving tried to at least get his old draft horses to go backwards, with limited success.

Pete, moving stealth-like but with much deliberation, made his way east through the woods north of the wagon trace. A short while later he stopped, peering at the spot where he'd made good his escape, hoping to ambush the others. There was still no sign of them, but their horses were there. He fired three shots, killing two of them and seriously wounding the third.

Now it was a race back to the horse he had taken, assuming his adversary as well as the other soldiers had figured out what was happening. If Stalworthy had crossed to the north side of the wagon trace up ahead, Pete would be right back where he had started from, only now he could easily be the one getting ambushed and perhaps have the soldiers as well as the two men in the wagon to deal with even if he did survive Stalworthy.

By the time Stalworthy had heard the latest shots and realized what had likely occurred, he was too far away. Due to the terrain, he had been forced to go deeper into the woods on a southeast angle from the wagon and crude road, hoping to make his way to the horses himself and to find the rifles and ammunition as well, but hadn't been nearly close enough to do either when Pete's shots rang out. Now he was sprinting back west, fighting his way through the brush and trees south of the wagon trace, but by the time he reached the area where the men in the wagon were still struggling with their horses it was too late. Pete was on the palomino and riding west before Stalworthy emerged, and although he managed to get off two shots there was no chance of hitting rider or horse since Pete had made it to a bend in the wagon trace just as the shots had been fired.

"You two!" Stalworthy yelled at the men, "Get down here and unhitch these horses! Ah'm a Confederate officer, and that man is an escapee! Bring the fastest one back where Ah'm headin'! Ah'll meet y'all momentarily!" The men complied immediately.

Stalworthy sprinted back to retrieve a saddle and tack and again look for the rifles, to no avail. He met the men halfway and quickly saddled the horse they had brought, and rode off. The man who had been driving called after him.

"You might be a danged officer, but we need ta git paid fer that horse, even if neither these old nags cain't run a lick!"

The man knew his horses. By the time Stalworthy was on his way, prodding the reluctant draft horse along, Pete was miles away. Stalworthy had to keep going however; once those men had made their way back to the stockade to demand some compensation, it would be only a matter of time before the dead horses and soldiers were discovered. All hell would break out then, even if he convinced the soldiers from Oglethorpe it was McCabe who was responsible. *Hell, I should've just shot those God damned muleskinners,* he fumed.

McCabe would be lucky if the soldiers from the stockade didn't shoot him on sight, and even if they didn't they'd bring him back to be hung, although they'd probably shoot him anyway once they discovered the bodies of their comrades. It occurred to Stalworthy that perhaps he could somehow get the head and foot after that, but he couldn't imagine how since they would likely take McCabe back to the stockade whether they shot him or not, assuming they ever caught up to him. Not only would he have to dig him up, but worse yet McCabe would no doubt be buried just outside the walls in plain view of the guards who patrolled the top of it. Even the darkness of a moonless night wouldn't be much help; there were lanterns lit and hanging everywhere come nightfall. Perhaps the best thing to do was find some sorry fool who resembled McCabe, mutilate his face, take his left foot...*to hell with it,* Stalworthy realized, *Janeway's not that stupid. He'll see the fresh wound where the pinky toe's been cut off. He'll figure I hadn't found that guileful son of a bitch to begin with, then made a couple lucky guesses with a different corpse...I gotta catch that son of a bitch...*

He had to stop in order to retrieve his cache from where it was hidden, wasting more time. Worse yet his pack horses were gone, probably stolen, and therefore he couldn't bring everything else he'd hidden with him. "I'm gettin' out of this damned business after this shit is over," he grumbled as he loaded up the old draft horse that didn't need more encumbrances to slow it down.

XXI

Billy was devastated, barely recognizable. He had found out Linda Marie O'Darcy was dead. He had always liked her, and by the time he was twelve he thought what he was feeling probably meant he had fallen in love with her. By the time he was thirteen, he knew he had.

Falling in love hadn't hit him like a thunderbolt on that beautiful summer day a couple years back, but it had been close enough. His family had attended a picnic at the O'Darcy place. Linda Marie had been her usual happy and outgoing self, joking and laughing with everyone, but on that day she seemed different somehow. She had always been attractive, but it was obvious she had experienced a transformation in ways more enchanting than young Billy had dreamed possible. She hadn't been a tomboy, not altogether, although she had been able to keep up athletically with the boys her age until a year or so prior to that fateful day. Even though Mother Annice had discouraged her from participating in sports and other roughhouse activities with the boys, there had rarely been any stopping the precocious girl.

It had been a simple act; all she had done was bring a platter full of fried chicken to the large picnic table under a tree where Billy had been sitting next to his brother Jackie. She had leaned over to place it down, directly between the two, then turned and smiled at Billy. Her face had been so close to his he had sworn he could feel its warmth. Her dark violet eyes had held onto his light blue ones as if they could cast the spell of an angel, he had imagined. The sensation that he was falling in love that had been flowing inside him for nearly a year had begun to surge unimpeded. A whiff or two of perfume later he was profoundly in love, no doubt about it. He hadn't even noticed Jackie as he filled his plate with the choicest pieces (Jackie had always possessed an insatiable appetite) and for once Billy wouldn't have cared even if he had noticed; food had suddenly become the last thing on his mind.

Later on Billy and Linda Marie had taken a walk down by the swimming pond. She had always been easy to talk to, but as they sat upon a blanket atop the thick bluestem near the north shore he suddenly found that his words kept getting jumbled, as if some perplexing contrivance inside the youth felt compelled to trip him up at every opportunity. The more it happened, the more his exasperation had intensified. Billy, all crimson, had finally stopped talking altogether after making what he had believed was the most ridiculous observation of his life: "Hot as the sun is, it doesn't seem to have much effect on the wetness of the water. Um, what I meant was…"

Linda Marie had smiled at him then, her head cocked to one side. A look of enchantment had been on her lovely face as she had reached over and had gently brushed back a disarray of corn-silk hair that had been hanging below his forehead.

"There Billy, that's better," she had said, looking directly into him, deep inside, as if there had been nothing she couldn't see. "Can't have those sky-blue eyes of yours hidden away, not even for a second."

Later that night Billy had felt little but Linda Marie's soft touch, and could conjure it up most other nights as well.

***

THAT SPELLBINDING afternoon flooded back as he wandered through the hospital. Delicia was still in the upstairs laundry room, sobbing convulsively in her father's arms. Hezekiah was of course devastated, and once he had arrived with the horrible news and saw his oldest daughter, he had been unable to stop his own tears before a word had left his mouth. Delicia had known whatever he had to say would prove to be horrendous, but nothing could have prepared her for such a tragedy.

Billy had been in the laundry room when Mr. O'Darcy had entered, and found it impossible to accept what he had overheard. He left immediately, and just as quickly found himself looking rapidly about at all the familiar things he had passed countless times. He found it eerily simple to concentrate upon those familiar things as he hurried along - the side table in the hallway, the crystal vase upon the table with its fresh-cut purple irises, the smell of Murphy's Oil Soap wafting from the hardwood floors, the framed pictures that adorned the walls; they were all the same as he remembered…hadn't changed, hadn't changed…then it hit him full force. Reeling inside, he fought for air. The thunderbolt had arrived after all.

***

ONCE OUTSIDE he made his way to a large oak and slumped down against it, away from intrusive eyes. It all rushed out then, a flood of emotion even more intense than when word of Pete had reached him - at least in Pete's case there was still a faint hope, if his mother was to be taken seriously. Not this though. Linda Marie was dead, and the wailing he heard coming from the open upstairs windows not a hundred feet away confirmed that in a way so horrible Billy wanted to scream.

Amidst his agony he wondered what had been the cause of her death, but it didn't matter, not really. Then it occurred to him that perhaps it had been something horrific, not that the end result wasn't bad enough. He prayed it hadn't been fire, or something else that would have caused his beautiful Linda Marie to suffer greatly. He suddenly wanted to know but couldn't bring himself to even move, let alone go back inside. He didn't have to; a few moments later Doc Wygant had appeared right next to him as the old man was prone to do from time to time, as if by magic.

"It was a fall off a horse, Billy boy," the old man said, as if telling Billy anything else would have been pointless, as if Doc *knew*. "She didn't suffer, Billy. Her head hit a rock. She didn't feel a thing." Billy kept one hand over his brow, head bowed, elbows resting on his bent knees, and raised the other hand as if to say thank you. He simply couldn't look at the old man, or anything else except the ground blurred by his tears.

"I'll be inside, son. Please come see me when you feel able." Doc made his way slowly back to the hospital, shoulders hunched, head lowered. Something besides the obvious was very wrong, Doc just knew it, but he didn't know what - or why he could hear Linda Marie sobbing right behind him. He fought an urge to look around for her. He knew he wouldn't see anything. He looked anyway. He always did.

***

THE FUNERAL was the largest Naperville had ever seen. The Methodist church was overflowing, and scores of other mourners were just outside. The flag-draped coffins of dead soldiers seemed to be returning by the week throughout DuPage County, with more dead men and boys never making it home from the battlefields. Even so, nothing had captured the hearts of Napervillians as much as the loss of a young girl who had been on the threshold; a beautiful young lady who had been so filled with an essence for living it had been contagious to most, and at least noticed by others.

Even in death Linda Marie appeared beautiful. Amidst his crushing grief Billy felt compelled to pass by her coffin as it sat upon the altar. She looked so serene, he observed, as if she were asleep. He had heard adults make the same observation a number of times, always finding the words peculiar - not anymore. He felt like kissing her cheek. Stinging tears welled up then, but he was oblivious to any embarrassment they had insisted accompany them in the past. He paused for a moment then moved on. He didn't want their only kiss to be upon a cold face that wouldn't have been able to feel his love anyway. He made it a few steps then stopped, sensing a presence, and returned. He bent over, kissed her lips gently, and whispered in her ear. "I love you. I have always loved you, Linda Marie. I always will."

***

CLIFTON JANEWAY was in attendance. His reddened eyes were filled with tears, and he made certain to blink, as if on cue, so they would run down his cheeks and fall onto his custom tailored uniform. He had a silk handkerchief, embroidered with his initials of course, but left it in his pocket. He had made sure to sit on an aisle seat, and when a sobbing Delicia passed by after the service he stood and discreetly reached out his hand and gently touched her forearm. She looked up, and upon seeing his tear-stained sorrow she fell apart further still, but the sorrow in her eyes wasn't alone; he saw gratefulness there as well, perhaps a loving gratefulness. She gave him a small embrace and moved on. The rest of her family passed by, and he made sure to utter the same sentence to each of them. "God bless you, and keep your dear Linda Marie."

Directly behind Clifton and his parents sat Doc Wygant. He was seething inside. As usual he didn't know what inner source ignited his intense feelings, he never did, but something unrelated to his present surroundings, in a sense, was profoundly amiss. He didn't know where it originated from or how, but he knew who had ignited his contempt. A fleeting image of a pond came and went, then returned; a surreal, whispering pond that issued hovering, disjointed entreaties the old man couldn't decipher. A powerful, complex feeling of sorrow and frustration coming from an image entombed amongst some tall grass along the pond's north shore had created the muffled pleas, and had been directed at the wavering image of a blonde-haired man retreating on horseback as he made his way through the water. Doc Wygant didn't recognize the man, not within the vacillating image, but the old man's heart pounded in his chest as he sat in his pew and glared at the back of Clifton Janeway's head.

***

CLIFTON APPROACHED Delicia and her family well after the graveside service at the cemetery had ended, and for once Hezekiah appeared to genuinely appreciate Clifton or at least the seemingly heartfelt compassion he had to offer. After shaking Hezekiah's hand and sharing brief embraces with Mrs. O'Darcy, the other sisters and Delicia, Clifton excused himself and walked over to the fresh mound of soil that itself was buried under a small mountain of flowers. He bowed his head as if in prayer, wiped what must have surely been tears from his eyes, and went over to his horse. As he rode away, Hezekiah turned to Delicia.

"My dear, that young man's transformation must have come from our Savior Himself. Clifton Janeway is welcome in our home anytime, bless his soul."

***

AS CLIFTON rode home to his family's mansion he contemplated the recent events. Spring was in full force on that sunny day with summer waiting impatiently for its annual debut, and it seemed as if everything had blossomed that could, and most everything else displayed every shade of green imaginable with a generally modest pride. It might as well have been muted to nothing more vibrant than gray as far as

Clifton was concerned. It wasn't that he was depressed or even somewhat melancholy; he simply never felt, as usual, any desire to pay attention to such things. Even the warm, fragrant breezes that stole by went unnoticed or at least ignored. The smell of a damp cave or the amazing freshness of a spring breeze held the same emptiness for him; as did a rectangular mound of fresh turned dirt under a small mountain of flowers.

He did dwell upon Linda Marie for a while. In hindsight he wished none of it had happened. He even wondered what he might have done differently if he had somehow known the outcome in advance, if by changing things with sorcery or some such nonsense it could have been avoided. Clifton wasn't prone to whimsy but that afternoon was an exception. Well, he most certainly wouldn't have gone to the O'Darcy home to begin with that first fateful day. If his imaginary revelation had struck after exiting the carriage house, he would have simply waved at the silly girl and departed. If it had occurred while they were in the company parlor he would have followed through with his departure, and would have done the same even when she called to him while she was supposedly struggling with her dress at the bottom of the rear stairway.

After that, things grew uncertain for him. When he envisioned her standing before him, her slightly chilled breasts in full view, his resolve began to waiver. No, he would simply put that from his mind for now. No reason to dwell upon such nonsense. He did anyway, knowing what he would have done. He also realized he would still be riding away from the young girl's grave - from the small mountain of fresh cut flowers.

Perhaps he would change later, Clifton contemplated, when the last few obstacles were cleared from the path that led him to Delicia; who could tell how much he might soften then, within reason of course. The most difficult obstacles had been overcome, save one. Clifton was the front runner for her heart; there wasn't anyone even in the race besides himself, and he believed he was almost there. No one except McCabe, a rival he would stand no chance of defeating if fair play or enough luck were involved. *What had that little minx said?* Clifton asked himself. *Oh yes. All's fair in love and war. How utterly puerile of her, and how utterly true.*

He dismissed those thoughts with a casual smirk, feeling a warm glow as he reached into his inner tunic pocket and took out Stalworthy's telegram again. He loved how it felt in his hand, loved reading it. It was in code, but to Clifton it was as if it were being sung to him as he read it once more. McCabe had been located and was in custody. Where, under what circumstances and what had transpired next Stalworthy hadn't been able to say without possibly raising suspicion, but the hunter of men sounded very optimistic in his wire. It was down to it now; just a matter of time.

Clifton continued west on High Street and passed by the O'Darcy home upon the pine studded rise to his left, not bothering to give it more than a dismissive glance. Before long, around the bend, the white mansion came in view on his right. A few snifters of Courvoisier XO and a fine cigar were in order, to say the least.

Clifton let out a sigh, feeling as if he deserved at least that much. He had endured, he concluded with a slight yawn, a very trying day.

***

TWO WEEKS later Billy was outside working in his mother's favorite flower garden located not far from the northwest corner of Tin Pan Alley, but far enough to afford it adequate sun. Mother Grace and Father Benjamin had taken the carriage into town. Between visiting relatives as well as attending to various things that had been put off for too long, they weren't expected home until dusk.

Billy was working tirelessly. Mother Grace still hadn't touched the perennial garden and he wanted to surprise her. No one had asked him to, but he had mentioned his plan to Father Benjamin in order to avoid an early arrival home by them. Father Benjamin had thought it was a wonderful idea, and wasn't at all surprised Billy had come up with it.

It was a beautiful middle of May afternoon, and although the sun was warm for that time of year Billy didn't mind the sweat pouring off him. Even so, he had grown thirsty and had made his way to the pump located in the west yard. Its water tasted sweetest, although that may have been just an illusion since he usually drank from it when he had been working outside. The sweet water may have been an illusion, but what was coming down the road wasn't. The soldier was limping and had a cane, but Billy recognized him immediately.

"Ben!" Billy hollered, and took off running. It was all pandemonium from there.

They embraced in the middle of the road, whooping and hollering. Finally, one of the brothers had returned, and Billy immediately asked his older brother if he would be staying long.

"I'm home for good, Billy. Where's Mother and Father?" Ben asked, looking around as if he had found heaven itself.

"They're in town, should be back before it gets dark." The excited youth replied as he took a closer look at his brother's left leg. "What happened, Ben?"

"What happened is I made it home alive, Billy boy! The rest is just some minor collateral damage. Didn't need the bottom part of my leg anyway as it turned out. At least my knee is intact."

Billy looked again. It appeared as if his brother's leg was there even if his Yankee army pants were covering it, and besides, he was wearing a boot on what looked like his left foot. Regardless, Billy had tended enough wounded men at the hospital to know when a leg was missing and just being covered up, or so he thought.

"It's not real, Billy, and least the foot isn't. Only lost about three inches from above the ankle. I was one of the lucky ones, believe it or not."

"You made it all this way on one foot, Ben?"

"Well, I spent most my time on a train. Old man Ogden gave me a lift part way from town. I didn't know the man who gave me a ride in his buckboard from the Wheaton station. Some jocular fella named Dave Saunders. Damned nice of him I'll be bound. He offered to bring me here but I wanted to look around in town for a while. I don't know who said there's no place like home Billy boy, but those words are true as sunlight. Lord it's good to see you!" Ben was as happy as he had ever been, inhaling the familiar fresh air as if it were too good to be true.

"Ma and Pa are gonna jump for joy Ben! Wouldn't it have been somethin' if you had run into them in town? Here, let me help you to the house."

"Thanks, Billy, I can manage. What's to eat?"

***

BILLY'S PREDICTION proved to be true; at least half of it. When Father Benjamin walked into the kitchen and saw his fourth oldest son sitting in his familiar spot at the long butternut table, he actually did jump for joy before running over to Ben. Mother Grace might have offered a slight leap as well, but it was all she could do to keep from collapsing in a chair. She stood there at first just staring in knowing wonderment before embracing her boy when he rushed to her. Both parents noticed the limp, but Ben was alive and looked hale and hearty. Details could wait. Mother Grace's tears had become a torrent, the first ones borne from joy in a very long time.

They all talked well into the night. Ben explained how a blast of canister had come in low and mangled his foot beyond repair. If it hadn't been, ironically, for a new doctor, one who was tending to his first wounded soldiers, his leg would have been amputated above the knee since a fair amount of shrapnel had hit him there as well. The more experienced doctors tended to not take chances, opting instead to increase the odds of avoiding future complications by taking more, not less. Thanks to the new doctor's so-called inexperience, Ben not only still had his knee but partial use of his calf muscle as well.

He had kept the news from his parents the whole time he had been recuperating, even insisting in a letter home he was fine after Mother Grace had written, convinced something dreadful had happened to him. He had not only wanted to spare them the obvious worry but extinguish it completely. He decided the best way to accomplish that was to walk through the front door of Tin Pan Alley, a smile on his face and in his heart. How he had dreamed of that moment, and although it hadn't gone exactly as planned the result had been just as glorious.

At one point he asked about his brothers, but before his parents told him what news they had, Mother Grace mentioned the recent tragedy at the O'Darcy home. Billy excused himself immediately, before having to suffer hearing Linda Marie's name mentioned. He had to check on the livestock, he maintained, and was out the back door in an instant.

"I'm afraid your younger brother had feelings for the poor girl that went beyond friendship," Father Benjamin said after the door closed.

"I fear way beyond, Benjamin," Mother Grace added. "It was foolish of me to bring it up just now."

"He will have to learn to accept tragedy, Mother." Ben said in a dark tone that was alien to both parents. Ben had always been the one who had lightened moods with quick-witted or endearing comments designed to defuse more somber feelings a given situation had created. War in general changed most people, horrifying battles and their aftermath even more so. "Tell me about my brothers," Ben said, his voice growing graver still. "Tell me about Pete."

XXII

"What the *hell* do you mean, Corporal?" Captain Bownell all but exploded as he leapt to his feet from behind his desk. "How could some emaciated Yankee overpower four men and make good his escape? Hell, he was even tied up!"

"We don't know, sir. Like Ah said, Malachi, Zack and Kyd is all dead. Cain't ask them. Accordin' ta them muleskinners outside, that Lieutenant Remington feller lit out after that Yankee, but on a horse slower'n molasses, seeins' it was his palomino what got took." The commandant dropped back heavily into his chair and just stared at the soldier.

"You would have me believe that God damned Yankee got himself untied, slit the throats of two of my ablest men, shot a third, then made off with Lieutenant Remington's *horse?* Where the hell was Remington when all that happened, and how come he ain't dead? You sure them muleskinners know what the hell they're talkin' about?" Captain Bownell may as well have asked his questions in French.

"Like Ah said, we just don't know, sir. Found a bloody bowie knife though. Don't recall our boys ownin' one, but that Lieutenant Remington sure 'nough did as Ah recall." Captain Bownell just stared at the soldier a moment before speaking.

"That no-account Yankee bastard musta got his hands on it somehow, a gun too, and surprised 'em. But how'd he do that, and how come that damned Remington didn't git a scratch?"

"We don't know that fer certain, sir, he mighta got a scratch or two."

"That's not what Ah meant, you thick-skulled mooncalf! Git them muleskinners in here!"

They had little to add. Shots were fired, some sort of running gun battle, the escapee had lit out on a palomino, the muleskinners' horse was gone and they wanted their money. The Confederacy could keep the horse, and the two civilians tried to insist the army buy the other one as well, or let them trade up for better animals.

Captain Bownell strode outside and confronted the rest of the men who had returned from the scene of the crimes. The two mysteries that defied logic remained after all the men had spoken. How could three experienced soldiers have been overtaken in such a manner, and how the hell did Lieutenant Remington lose a knife that was on his belt and not end up dead, or seriously wounded? He should have been the first to get killed, especially since the Yankee must have also gotten his hands on a gun, or did he?

"There's a nigger in the wood pile," Captain Bownell finally said, "and Ah'm not convinced there's just one." The commandant made his way to where the camp telegraph was located. He sent a wire to Richmond, more specifically to military headquarters. Just who the hell was this Lieutenant Remington?

***

PETE KNEW he had a good head start. Even if the lieutenant and the others had made their way back to the stockade in a timely manner, any pursuers still had to be at least twenty miles behind him, probably much farther. Perhaps, however, the lieutenant didn't go back; something had occurred that Pete didn't understand. He never did see any of the other Rebels after the commotion and gunshot, a shot that had come from the same gun that had fired at him as best Pete could tell from the reports. Pete didn't understand what had happened, but he realized that Remington fellow may well have reason to stay clear of the stockade.

Pete had made his way off the wagon trace after having gone ten miles or so, then had crossed a series of meadows, swampy areas and stands of woods and forests; anything to make finding him as difficult as possible. He crossed numerous brooks, streams and a few rivers once he found a decent place to ford, although for all he knew it may have been the same rivers that simply curved back and forth across the countryside. He stayed in a few of the streams, sometimes a mile or so if they were basically set upon the landscape in a north / northwesterly direction. He stayed off roads for the most part, although he occasionally went down a few of them if they didn't appear to be main roads of which there were few. He had to avoid human contact as much as possible, and in that regard he had been successful as far as he knew. Strangers like him were always suspect, especially a barefoot stranger on an impressive mount.

If nothing else, Pete observed, the lieutenant knew his horses. The large stallion Pete had commandeered was not only fast but tireless. Even when Pete had stopped by a creek to give it some water and rest, it hadn't been because the magnificent palomino had showed a desire to slow down much. It hadn't been reluctant to get underway again either. He didn't know the stalwart palomino was used to such travel, that it had been owned by a man who specialized in tracking people. Stalworthy knew how to chose horses all right, and the one Pete had taken was the best horse Stalworthy had ever owned.

"You need a name, boy," Pete said to the handsome stallion as the animal was drinking from the creek. Pete had dismounted and stroked its off-cream mane as he spoke, marveling at the overall size, strength and beauty of the horse. "How about

Yankee? Fast as you got us away from there, I have to believe you don't want any more to do with the Johnnies than I do. Yankee it is," Pete said.

The animal looked at him then, as if the sound and smell of the primate next to him met with the beautiful horse's approval. Yankee went back to drinking, leaving the impression he wanted to get it over with and be on their way.

Pete continued in a north / northwesterly direction for several days, and did his best to avoid the small towns and plantations he came upon. Most towns were so small he didn't concern himself with the possibility of wires having been received, but he avoided them anyway. He had only come across a few telegraph poles since leaving the stockade until he was near Atlanta, and most likely wouldn't see any in the general area he was presently traversing as long as he steered clear of the city and any of the other towns. He made a wide circle west of Atlanta then continued north.

At least the clothes he had been given wouldn't give him away, although he sure wished he had some boots. He wondered why the lieutenant or the commandant hadn't insisted he wear something that would have indicated he was a prisoner. Upon reflection, however, he didn't recall ever having seen such garb. It wasn't even a low priority, and therefore not worth the trouble or expense. Still, Pete thought his captors, under unusual circumstances like transporting a single prisoner, would have come up with something. He didn't realize Elwood Stalworthy hadn't planned on Pete being alive long enough for it to matter, with nothing left of him above the ground except his head and foot.

***

PETE WAS starved, and had been especially so once the adrenalin had subsided. He had grown accustomed to the feeling while imprisoned, but the mental and physical strain of his ongoing ordeal had taken so much out of him he was ready to pass out. He felt so weak it was all he could do to stay on Yankee. He had found a few edible roots and other plants as the days went by, especially along the sides of creeks and river banks, but it was too early in the year for berries or other fruits. He couldn't risk shooting at the game he came across, nor did he want to stop to set up a few snares. He wasn't adept at that sort of thing anyway, and it would have been too time consuming. He had managed to grab a few guppies, crawdads and snails, all of which he ate raw, but was considerably more interested in moving along. For the most part he just kept going, day after day.

***

IT WAS almost dark one evening when he spotted it from the wagon trace he had been following; a shack tucked away in a clearing. Behind it was a limestone cliff, perhaps thirty feet high, its top covered with trees. Running next to the bottom of the cliff was a small creek that frolicked along as if it had been doing so forever. A meager waterfall danced from a crevice atop the cliff and the pure water landed in a pool no bigger than an averaged sized room, creating a comforting sound every bit as eternal as the timeworn stone it had been married to for eons. The pool was perhaps fifty feet from the back of the shack, the first structure of any kind he had seen since morning. There were a few rundown out-buildings that had never seen a coat of paint, and the overall condition of the rest of the place wasn't much better. He didn't see anyone, but there was lazy smoke curling from a chimney along the north side of the shack. Random breezes moved it about when they had a mind, but the escaping smoke was mostly left to its own devices on what had been an otherwise windless day.

Pete rode to about fifty feet from the front door and sat slumped over Yankee, resting his head on the horse's mane. He was barely hanging on, and was afraid if he did try to dismount he'd tumble to the ground. He hoped any people inside were just ordinary folk, as detached from the war as he wished he could be. He knew he had to have appeared harmless, save the rifle in its saddle scabbard which he didn't appear strong enough to grab anyway, which may or may not have been a good thing. The people inside were poor, apparently beyond poor, and if nothing else his horse, saddle and new 1862 Henry repeating rifle, a .44 caliber rim fire, were things that would sell for a handsome amount. His eyes were also growing weary as he barely clung onto the saddle horn. Just when he thought he could no longer hold on, the door opened.

The young woman was holding a shotgun. She eyed the horse and rider suspiciously then called out. "Who are you, and what do you want?"

Pete looked up, but when he tried to rise and call out he slipped from his saddle and fell to the ground.

When he came to the young woman was kneeling beside him with a tin cup of water, urging him to drink. Standing next to her was a towheaded boy maybe seven or eight years old, and a little wide-eyed girl with hair blonder still, perhaps four years younger than the boy.

"Here, drink this." The woman said. Pete took a few sips and looked at her. She was plain, but not unattractive. Her long, blonde hair brushed against the side of Pete's face as she again brought the cup to his lips.

"Ma'am, could you spare some food?" He asked in a husky, weak voice. "I can't pay for it, but I could do some work around here." She looked at him and smiled. *She has a nice smile*, Pete thought. It was as if a touch of humanity had found its way into his lonesomeness and fear, had entered the surrounding wilderness to search him out. It was a boundless wilderness fraught with at least imperilment, a bewildering place that seemed to go on forever both in and outside of him.

"Mister, you'd be doin' good if you could just stand. S'pect Ah kin spare a little food if you don't eat much." She helped him to his feet and guided him into the one room shack with ease. Even in his worn-out state Pete noticed her strength; uncommon, he concluded, considering her slender frame. She was still carrying the shotgun in her free hand. The children followed, and when Pete was slumped in a chair at the rude table the boy asked him if he was a robber.

"No, young fella. Just down on my luck."

"How come you talk so funny?" The boy asked. The woman was by a small stove fixing a plate of what may have been hash, but she was listening.

"Well, I'm not from around here. What's your name?"

"Ely." The boy answered. He didn't ask Pete his name, but he had another question. "Where you from?" The woman came over and put the plate in front of Pete. Without answering the boy he began to devour the food. She went over and cut him a thick slice of bread, then returned.

"This is all Ah kin spare, mister. You'd best eat slow." Pete thought he had been, and offered his apologies. He immediately resumed wolfing down the concoction that resembled hash, as fast as before. It was by far the best tasting food he had eaten in months. When his plate was empty he had to fight an urge to stare at the iron kettle atop the small stove that held the hash, looking at the boy instead. He decided not to lie. He was sick of lying.

"I'm from Illinois. You ever heard of it?"

"You a Yankee?" The boy asked, as if he were suddenly talking to someone just about as mysterious as a person could get.

"I'm just a man, son, like most others." The woman walked around the table and sat across from him.

"What's a man from Illinois doin' way down here?" She asked. "Guess you know there's a war goin' on. That got somethin' to do with it?"

"It does, but I'm not fighting it. I just want to get home, ma'am."

"You don't look like you kin make it out'a this *county*," she said. Pete noticed her smile again. She was rather pretty after all. Straight teeth, soft green eyes; her eyes were alert, too.

"Probably not, ma'am, but I have to try."

"Mah name is Desiree. Desiree Fairchild. Callin' me ma'am adds a few years Ah ain't lived yet, and Ah sure as goodness hope Ah don't look like Ah have." She was smiling again. Upon further observation, Pete doubted she was much over twenty.

"My apologies again, Miss Fairchild. Or it's probably Mrs. isn't it."

"It's Mrs., but callin' me Desiree suits me. You got a name?"

"Pete."

"Your momma an' daddy give you a last name, Pete?" Again, the smile.

"McCabe. Can't believe I just told you that, though."

"Long as you don't mean no harm, it don't matter none ta me. Don't look like you do. Don't sound like it neither. Lord, Pete, when was the last time you 'et? You ain't nothin' but bones restin' in sunburnt skin." The little girl came over and tried to climb on her mother's lap. Desiree helped her up, brushed the child's hair back and kissed her cheek.

"That's a beautiful little girl, ma'am - Desiree. And you're a handsome young fella, Ely. What's your sister's name?" Before the boy could answer, the little girl called out.

"Ah'm Desiree too!"

"Well, hello Desiree Too. Glad to meet you."

"Just Desiree! Like Ma!" The adults chuckled.

Pete found out Desiree's husband had left for the war over a year ago and hadn't been heard from since. Rumor had it the men from around there had been at Shiloh, but Pete didn't mention he had as well. Her husband didn't know how to read or write, which the young woman used as the reason she hadn't heard from him. Besides, she couldn't read or write either. Pete knew plenty of soldiers, although not from his hometown, who weren't literate, but it wasn't difficult to get someone to write for them. He suspected Desiree may have been aware of that, but let it go.

Her husband hadn't been much of a provider before the war, but she said he had a kind heart. He had no business fighting anyone, she maintained, let alone in any derned war, civil or otherwise. He wouldn't have gone off at all but all the young men from around there had left, even quite a few older ones, so he had also felt obliged, as well as not really having a choice. Pete understood completely.

Beardsley, her husband, had gone to Mexico once, with his widower father the year she and Beardsley had married. His uncle had some kind of business opportunity someplace outside Mexico City, but it didn't work out. They were back within a year, and about the only thing they brought home with them was an affinity for marijuana. They had brought some back, along with a large bag of seeds.

His father had insisted they were from then on in the hemp business, but he seemed to spend a great deal more time producing plants with resin coated buds and flowers than he did with those better suited for more conventional hemp products. He ended up with a few loyal customers, but moonshine was still the overwhelming drug of choice throughout the area. Realizing the wisdom of diversification, the father owned a still as well.

Neither his father nor Beardsley could bear to see quality *mota* go to waste, and since they had never been mistaken for motivated salesmen there was never a short supply. There still wasn't a shortage; even though both men had gone off to war, the hardy weed flourished both at the father's place and in a field of volunteer plants Pete must have passed not far from the shack. They had spread into ditches and other areas as well.

"Beardsley never was one for work," Desiree said, "but after he took ta smokin' that stuff he took bein' lazy like it was a little tune, then up and turned it into a symphony or some fool thing. Most he ever did was go huntin' or fishin'. Kept us fed, though. Been hard times since he left."

"Looks like a lonely place, Desiree." Pete said. He glanced at the kettle upon the stove, despite himself.

"Peaceful more like it," she responded, getting up to fill his plate. "Now this really *is* all we kin spare. Looks like you need it more'n us though."

"When I get my strength back, I'll get in some hunting before I head out. Seen a few deer today, some wild pigs too. Any folks around?"

"Fresh meat would truly be a blessin'," Desiree said as she put the plate in front of him and sat back down. "Ah cain't shoot worth a lick and all Ah got is that there shotgun. Only six shells left, too. Beardsley took the rifle. Ain't nary a soul within ten miles. Maybe you kin tell me why you asked, besides bein' a Yankee, if easin' mah mind is somethin' you kin afford. "

After devouring the second plate of hash Pete told her he had to lie down or fall asleep at the table. He offered to bed down in one of the two dilapidated structures but Desiree thought better of it.

"No tellin' what might gnaw at you in one'a them hovels come nightfall. Don't even like goin' in 'em come daylight, an' my youngin's ain't allowed in 'em at all. You kin bed down over in the corner. Ah'm trustin' you, Pete McCabe."

"Thank you, Desiree. I'll tend to my horse and get my bedroll." Pete stopped at the door and turned. "I haven't done anything wrong, Desiree. Just tryin' to get home. Good chance there's some fellas tryin' to stop me." She smiled in appreciation, shadowed as it was by a disquieted apprehension.

***

ELWOOD STALWORTHY was a tenacious man on his slothful days. His determination usually bordered on obsession. As he rode over the countryside it was as if everything another person would need to continue were needless things he could do without. Food, rest, let alone sleep, were things he most times didn't even consider as an afterthought. When he did stop during his pursuit of Pete it was only because the second horse he had purchased after getting rid of the first nag needed to rest so damned often.

He had bought the second horse, his current mount if it could be called such, near the small town of Dallas, located in Paulding County in the northwest section of Georgia. Stalworthy had already grown frustrated with the animal all right, just like he knew he would. *God damn, I miss that palomino,* he thought on a regular basis.

The widow in Dallas who had sold the second horse to him demanded at least twice what it was worth during its best days, all of which were behind it. She had also insisted his current horse had to be part of the bargain. The shrewd lady not only wouldn't take a dime off to take the animal, but had insisted he pay extra for the feed it would eat until she could sell it off, which she maintained would take no less than three months. At least she had thrown in a knife, but Stalworthy had to almost beg for it. It wasn't a bowie knife, but good-sized and sharp.

She had been an attractive woman, not much over forty. She was a good five foot nine inches tall, long brunette hair and pale blue eyes, but any attempt to appeal to her vanity had somehow backfired. He didn't know how she had done it, but there was no question she had turned Stalworthy's attempts to her advantage which riled him further still; he had always considered himself a lady's man, and for good reason if his past exploits counted for anything. He could have sworn she had fallen victim to his charms as well, what with all her infectious laughter and flirtatiousness, not to mention those pale blue eyes that sparkled when she smiled, but his lightened pocketbook told a different story. *Contrary, intelligent women,* he mused, *are the bane of mankind, especially when their beguiling ways are fortified by whatever beauty they are convinced they possess.*

McCabe had proven he was a difficult man to track. He was obviously a shrewd and determined fellow himself. Stalworthy had correctly calculated the general direction his prey had taken however, by always asking himself what he would do if he was the one on the run. Although Pete hadn't been aware of it, he had been spotted by several talkative people as well as a number of slaves when he had veered too close to one plantation or another. Strangers always drew attention in isolated areas, and on the rare occasions when one did appear, their arrival, even if just passing through, became a much needed topic of conversation. Stalworthy seldom found it a problem to get such people to open up when it came to strangers; the antitheses of what usually happened if his inquires had to do with local inhabitants.

One of his biggest concerns was the horse McCabe had stolen. *That damned palomino can go on forever,* he recalled with frustration. Even if Stalworthy thought he could eventually catch up, which he did believe, who could tell what might happen to McCabe in the meantime? There were always local miscreants to worry about, men and even women who would think nothing of murdering a stranger for such a fine animal, not to mention the new Henry rifle McCabe had also stolen. Every day that passed meant McCabe could stumble upon some Confederate soldiers or Home Guard units as well.

Captain Bownell had no doubt sent out telegrams, perhaps a lot of them. McCabe's escape was bad enough, but the murders of Bownell's own men coupled with how Stalworthy could possibly explain what had happened must have been weighing on the captain's mind. Bownell was a tad gullible but not a stupid man, and by now he must have concluded Stalworthy was at least culpable. If it had been discovered he was a charlatan, a likely possibility, McCabe wasn't the only one in trouble.

Stalworthy had his array of clothing, and had fortunately kept all his cash with him as well - almost. Besides what he had with him, he even had $2,400 hidden cleverly away but always within reach, until recently. McCabe didn't know it, or so Stalworthy hoped, but that damned Yankee had the rest.

Stalworthy didn't have a quality horse, but had his abilities all those years of experience had taught him. The weeks wore on, with Stalworthy following one dead end after another. Pete had been sighted, or at least a man on a handsome palomino supposedly had been, enough times to send Stalworthy over much of northwest Georgia. It was arduous and time consuming work, the kind that would discourage less motivated or inexperienced trackers. Most of those types would assume Pete must have surely made good his escape, given the time that had elapsed. That wasn't lost on Stalworthy either, but then someone he came across while following a lead would recall a palomino and a barefoot rider they had spotted. When those reports stopped coming from locals farther north, he would turn back south, and again those sightings would occasionally be reported. Even so, Stalworthy was about ready to abandon Georgia and continue his search as far north as Chattanooga.

He had finally backtracked south all the way just north of Cedar Town, Georgia. The following morning he made up his mind; McCabe, in all likelihood, must have made it to Chattanooga, his most logical destination. If it hadn't been for a very lucky encounter with a local boy less than a day's ride from Cedar Town, Chattanooga was most likely where Stalworthy would have ended up.

"Ah seen that feller all right," the boy said. "Fancy palomino too. Thought he musta been dead, the way he jist laid there on the ground next to Lanny's Brook. Looked like Death eatin' soda crackers, nothin' but skin an' bones. Ain't fer certain, but Ah cain't feature he could'a gone ten more miles, likely not that far."

"How long ago?" Stalworthy asked, handing the boy a quarter.

"Goodly number'a weeks, maybe not that long. He finally headed half dead up that road yonder. Cain't feature he got far, though. Thanks fer the quarter, mister!"

***

PETE FELT relatively confident he had found about the best place possible to rest up for awhile, all things considered. Desiree's husband had left a worn out pair of boots behind and they almost fit. He had also left behind an old, chipped straight-edged razor, so at least Pete could shave. His strength was returning, thanks to the game he had shot and Desiree's cooking abilities once she had something with which to work. Plentiful fresh meat improved everyone's mood, especially those who hadn't had very much of it for so long. Pete could now eat his fill, and as the weeks went by his body had again grown accustomed to large quantities of food.

He had told Desiree everything. She had a trusting way about her and it helped to unload his mind. She told him he was welcome to stay, more than welcome, and Pete hoped he had misunderstood at least part of the reason why. Lying didn't come natural to her though, whether spoken or implied by no more than a glance.

He had started to fix up the place but soon realized that was a stupid thing to do. No one ever showed up, none since his arrival anyway, but if a local did happen by and saw substantial improvements or perhaps any at all it would likely garner un-wanted attention.

Desiree had begun to keep the inside of the small shack cleaner and more tidied up. The same could be said of herself, even though she had generally paid attention to personal hygiene, same with the children. She had no make-up of course, and her clothing was all worn, but washing it on a more regular basis had become a priority. She always made sure her long blonde hair was washed weekly or at least brushed, having abandoned her usual practice of keeping it tied back. When she did tie it back it was usually down before Pete returned from hunting, something he spent a great deal of time doing.

He had noticed her efforts and staying away seemed to be the wise thing to do. He sometimes had to make a conscious effort to drive her from his thoughts when alone in the woods or late at night. His best ploy was to conjure up images of Delicia, and that always seemed to calm any lingering feelings that intruded despite his overall sense of propriety. There was never room for anyone else once images of Delicia came calling.

He had wanted to write her and his parents, but Desiree had no pen and paper. Even if he could have written, the closest town was over twenty miles away. Desiree maintained the small hamlet didn't even have a post office even if he was to write and foolish enough to go there to do it. She didn't mention the postal worker who rode through the town every few weeks, at least before the war. If lying by omission was indeed lying, she paid it little mind.

Local folks knew she couldn't read and write so even if she made the journey to get writing supplies and returned with a letter Pete had written, which local would she say wrote it for her? Everyone thereabouts knew everyone else, especially those who were literate. If a passing stranger had written the letters, addressed to Illinois no less, wouldn't that create even more suspicion? Besides, Pete had to assume it was highly unlikely any reliable mail service existed between the warring states.

No one was aware he was around or even in the vicinity as far as Desiree or Pete knew, but the two of them didn't know that for sure so there was always the chance someone from the town or points beyond may have spotted him passing by in the countryside prior to his arrival at Desiree's place. As the weeks passed and his strength slowly returned, that threat diminished. He would certainly be spotted if he went to town, though. What if the locals had been alerted about a murdering Yankee escapee from Oglethorpe, especially if there was a reward?

He was forced to hold off writing until the day he was able to eventually make his way far enough north. Still, it haunted him. He could only imagine what his family and Delicia must have concluded, and the thought of causing so much agony to those he loved so dearly ate away at him. As much as he wanted to alleviate their suffering, he had to wait at least a little longer until the devastating effects of his captivity had subsided. God, how he hated the war and all the anguish it draped upon so many good people as if it would cling to them forever.

***

ONE DAY in the early afternoon Pete had been fortunate to shoot a small razorback within his first hour of hunting. He field dressed it and was bringing it back, several hours before he usually returned from hunting. He had almost emerged from the woods north of the shack when he heard squeals of delight coming from the children. There was splashing going on too, and when he looked at the pool with the waterfall cascading into it his first instinct was to turn away. The children were there of course, but so was their mother. Like the children, Desiree was naked, and if there had been any questions as to how well she was proportioned they had certainly been answered. Realizing he hadn't been spotted, and besides the guilt which had momentarily kept him from looking again, Pete glanced back anyway.

They were splashing each other and Desiree took pleasure in submerging herself under the clear, sand-bottomed pool then popping up and saying "Boo!" to the animated delight of the youngsters. She bounced about as she did so, and since the pool was so shallow, she could get down on her hands and knees and crawl after them as well. From that position the water came almost halfway up her thighs, but that was all. When she was facing away from the woods where Pete was standing the sight was more than a little disconcerting, and since that wasn't all Pete felt he finally headed back into the woods. Way back.

It took an hour to get over the sight, and another to get it completely out of his mind or at least tamed. Thoughts concerning Delicia, as always, helped; they helped a great deal even if it felt as if she were a million miles away. He went over all their plans again, including the picnic fantasy he held so dear when - or if, more like it - the day of his homecoming ever became a reality. He desperately hoped it would anyway. He even thought about the names he had come up with for their children, wondering if she would approve. Before long he was convinced he was back to normal, but spent another two hours in the woods anyway.

He finally made his way back to where he had seen everyone in the water. He knew they would likely be close by, probably in the shack, and felt a mixture of relief as well as a few bothersome things that lingered. He glanced briefly at the waterfall, then the small pond that welcomed its cascading flow. The pond was deserted, except for the obstinate vision of a naked Desiree that refused to stay in its place. He would force it to, and that was the long and short of it. That's what he told himself. He felt confident he could do it, if confidence didn't mind sharing a little space with loitering disquietude. He heard it then, heard the whinny come from a place where it didn't belong - it didn't belong there at all.

***

IF STALWORTHY had hidden his horse in a gully or ravine far enough back in the woods south of the shack Pete probably wouldn't have been alerted. As it was, Stalworthy had chosen the north woods, not far off, and when Pete heard the impatient whinny he turned to look, but still couldn't see the horse through the trees and brush to his right. He didn't have to. Yankee was where Pete usually left him in the one shed he had cleaned and fixed up, even if half the boards were missing. The sound sure as hell hadn't come from there, he realized.

He heard a scream cut short when he was less than fifty feet north of the shack, having made his way along a ridge that afforded him cover; a good thing, because Stalworthy had been keeping a close watch out all the windows on a regular basis, and had just missed spotting Pete after he had made his way from the shelter of the trees to the relative safety of the ridge. Stalworthy had even glanced in Pete's direction right after the scream, but the savvy horse soldier had maintained a low enough profile behind the ridge. Stalworthy hadn't heard his mount's whinnying, or it hadn't registered since it was a complaining mare. Either way, the scream made him look again.

"You let out one more of those and I'll gut you sure, your kids too, you hear me?" Stalworthy said to Desiree in a way that left no doubt about anything. "All I want is him, and if those little brats mean more to you than some God damned Yankee you best keep yourself and them quiet!"

A trembling Desiree nodded her head, clutching both of her terrified children close to her naked body. Stalworthy had come upon them while they had still been in the pool and hadn't allowed them to dress, after having first surveyed the immediate area and checking inside the shack. He had discovered his palomino in the rude shelter as well as the saddle, its rifle scabbard empty, so he knew an armed McCabe would no doubt be returning.

"Don't harm my babies mister, they ain't done nothin'." Tears were streaming down Desiree's face as she spoke, and her trembling had increased, intermingled with that of her terrified children.

"Listen you stupid whore, I don't give a hot damn who I kill. You best remember that. If guttin' them or you is what I need to do, all three of you are gonna rot in here! And that's just what I *will* do if you don't keep 'em quiet! Hell, might just do it anyway, so you best not rile me God damn it! You're only alive now 'cause it might serve me later. I can lose that an' still get what I need, most likely. Don't need your murders pestering me, doubt they would anyway, but it's enough for you to know I'll sure as hell do it if I have to!" He again looked out the windows. Nothing.

Pete had made his way to the north side of the shack, again very close to being spotted. *Now what,* he wondered, his heart pounding in his chest. If he rushed through the door there would be gunfire. In such a small place no telling how many would get hit, maybe everybody. He was almost certain he could shoot the man inside who was no doubt after him, but what if there was more than one? For all he knew other horses could be hidden somewhere around as well. Regardless, he had to do something. He heard more talk, but only from one man. He waited a little longer, but that was the only voice except for some wailing of the children that erupted.

"That's enough!" Stalworthy yelled. Then he said something that chilled Pete to his core. "I warned you *bitch,* God damn it!"

It hadn't been what the man had said; well it had, but it was how he had said it that was so terrifying. It had been the tone of someone done making threats.

"I'm out here you *son of a bitch!*" Pete hollered. He made his way quickly to the front corner of the shack and peered around, his rifle ready, but Stalworthy wasn't that foolish. He knew what his Henry could do in the hands of someone accustomed to killing. He also knew he held the advantage, thanks to his human shields. If McCabe didn't give a damn about them he would have already begun blasting away into the shack. Rude boards were no defense against a Henry at close range. Stalworthy drew one of his revolvers, the knife still in his other hand.

"And I'm in here, McCabe! You got five seconds to drop that God damned rifle I know you're carryin' and stand out where I can see you, or I'm gonna gut the little girl! The boy too, then their ma!" More screams came from all three of the captives; Desiree's was the loudest. There were sounds of urgent movement and guttural wailing. Time had run out.

Pete came barging through the front door and fired, the deafening roar filling the small room. Why the man had his back to him made no sense at all, but Pete's shot had struck Stalworthy square between the shoulder blades. For some reason his revolvers were holstered, including the one he had been holding just moments before. Stalworthy's upper body lurched forward, chasing an explosion of red mist intermingled with minute particles as it flew forward, then Stalworthy tumbled sideways and ended up on his back. A pool of blood began to swell, oozing from underneath him. It grew slow at first, then insistent. The handle of a knife was protruding from the front of his body, just below his sternum. None of the blade was visible. Desiree's right palm was bleeding, so were her fingers. Pete just stared at her, dumbfounded, but she wasn't. After glancing at the dead body she looked back at Pete. She was still trembling but her face was all grim determination, as if she were still driving the blade into the man.

"Pete, would you please drag him outta here? Me and the children would like ta get dressed."

XXIII

Missy Nell had finally resigned herself to the inevitable. She had tried everything to convince Cusman to wait at least a few weeks or so. The last resort would have been to threaten to leave him, but that would have been as impossible to do as trying to convince him it was even a remote possibility. He was a free man now, and for the first time in his life he had a country. It was in trouble, serious trouble, and he believed if he didn't do all he could to defend it then he might as well not have a country at all, and certainly didn't deserve one.

"I never been a nigger, and I'm not about to give them that's been stewin' in their contempt, overlookin' most ever'thing that don't suit their cold hearts, reason to call me one now."

***

THE 54th MASSACHUSETTS Volunteer Infantry, one of the first official Negro units in the United States armed forces, had been authorized in March of 1863 by Governor John A. Andrew. They had been training near Boston at Camp Meigs since then, and rumor had it they would be heading out near the end of May. So many men had tried to enlist that the military had been forced to turn a sizeable number away, but Cusman wasn't deterred.

They had put in place a rigid physical exam, but when Cusman arrived at Camp Meigs there had been no doubt he would pass it. One look at him was all the doctor had needed. He examined him anyway, which included certain exercises. The doctor marveled at the young man's strength, especially when he asked Cusman to do some chin-ups. He went over to the bar and adjusted it higher, grabbed a hold and started. Thus far the three minute record had been seventy-five, and although Cusman was a huge man he easily surpassed that mark. Cusman made it to eighty-five just as the three minutes elapsed. The doctor congratulated him. Cusman paused, still holding onto the bar.

"I kin give you another fifteen, twenty if it will guarantee me gettin' in," Cusman said, hanging there as if the test were meant for children. The doctor told him that wouldn't be necessary. The rest of the exam, he stated, wouldn't be necessary either.

Although Cusman didn't get much of a chance to train, his superior marksmanship was noted right off as well as his other physical and mental abilities. Colonel

Robert Gould Shaw himself commented upon the gigantic man's attributes. Colonel Shaw commanded the 54th, having been selected by the governor to do so. He was a young man, raised in Boston by abolitionist parents.

Shaw had even wanted to have Private Cusman Sable promoted to second lieutenant, but since Secretary of War Edwin Stanton had decreed only whites could be officers, Shaw had to settle for issuing Cusman the rank of sergeant. That too was unusual for most black soldiers.

On May 28th the 54th Massachusetts would be departing Boston. Cusman had only been with the unit a little over a week. When he requested a three day furlough from Lieutenant Colonel Norwood Howell, second in command, it was refused. Cusman desperately wanted to spend some time with Missy Nell before departing though, so he went over Howell's head. Colonel Shaw had been reluctant to countermand his lieutenant colonel, but when Cusman explained the recent ordeal he and his new bride had been through, the fair minded colonel relented.

Cusman and Missy Nell had already gone over all the admonitions, denials, warnings and other things couples discuss prior to a soldier marching off to war, so their short time together was spent more like a honeymoon. They both had longed for more time, but with Boston about ninety miles away by train that just wasn't possible. Jennifer had stopped by briefly and insisted Cusman take some money with him, but at first he refused.

"The other men, most of 'em anyway, have to get by on what little pay we're gettin', especially compared to the white soldiers. S'pect I'll do the same. But thank you, Jennifer."

She tried to come up with reasons why he should take at least a little cash, but again he refused. "You already been helpin' support Missy and me, and I got quality weapons. What else would I need?" Jennifer thought about that for a moment.

"Well, you'll need more ammunition I would imagine," she finally offered. "Who knows where you'll find some later on, especially for the quality weapons you possess. Might as well stock up in Boston before you leave. Please Cusman, do at least that much for Missy Nell, and me. It could make all the difference." He finally relented and accepted the money. He already had ammunition of course, but upon reflection he realized Jennifer was correct; who could tell where the 54th would end up or what would happen when they arrived?

***

MORALE WAS very high the day they shipped off from Boston Harbor. Men of color would finally be given the opportunity to prove once and for all they were soldiers indeed. There were brave white soldiers on both sides of the terrible conflict, but that had been a given to most people. Even sympathetic newspaper editorials always seemed to qualify their praise of the black recruits: "Even though they are colored boys" or "Despite being Negros" were not uncommon observations. Such attitudes would be changed, some of the more optimistic insisted, but Cusman and the majority of his black comrades remained skeptical as it pertained to the attitudes of most white people.

Except for any future children and despite his previous stance, Cusman concluded he wasn't going off to prove anything to anyone besides himself. Others could think as they pleased, white or otherwise, but he would demand the respect he had every intention of earning. He had a new country, one that made him free, or relatively so. He would be fighting to preserve that freedom and expand upon it as much as possible.

The Union's enemy had been so only after they had fired on Fort Sumter - Cusman's since the day of his birth - his parents and their parents as well, ever since his ancestors had arrived from Africa. Cusman didn't want accolades, he wanted requital; and especially the assurance no one would ever again be able to buy and sell him or his loved ones, or anyone else. He knew he couldn't undo all the obscenities that had been visited upon so many of his brethren, but he could help exact a reckoning; he could do his part to bleed the evil right out of those so imbued.

They had given him a pick and shovel instead. They had given most of the black soldiers picks and shovels. Others had been issued rakes, brooms, or any variety of other implements needed to do manual labor when they hadn't been training. That went on, when they weren't indeed training, until the day before they left Boston Harbor for Hilton Head, South Carolina.

Before long they were in Georgia. Cusman had assumed he would end up fighting somewhere in the South, perhaps even Georgia if the rumors were to be believed, but when they had actually arrived in the very state he had escaped he couldn't shake the unsettling feeling *being back* created. He refused to think of it as his former home. The South was one big prison to him, and Georgia had been his cellblock, and now he was back inside.

He was part of a formidable group of heavily armed Union infantry and artillery men, and that was indeed comforting. Still, he was *back*. Ever since the ordeal he and the women had endured came to an end, dark dreams had haunted him. It was always the same type of nightmare that invaded - he was back in Georgia, although the specifics changed from night to night. He was always a slave again, that never changed, and it was that soul-crushing realization he found so disturbing. He had experienced similar dreams during their harrowing ordeal, but had assumed they would subside once, more so if, he ever made it safely out of the South. Formidable force of soldiers or not, he couldn't completely shake the disturbing sensation even when he was awake. Simply viewing the countryside and smelling the air made him uneasy, even if the coastal area of Georgia wasn't all that similar to where he had grown up. Still, it was close enough.

On June 10th the 54th Massachusetts finally arrived outside the town of Darien, in the southeast portion of Georgia. It occurred to Cusman he was actually farther south than Beaux Hollow, more specifically Whisper Manor. He thought about all his extended family members, old friends and acquaintances, and how he would have felt if the 54th had ended up there instead. He could just feature the face of Trenton Ransom. He even fantasized about what the outcome would be if his former master, clearly enraged, spotted his onetime slave and attacked, or some other fool thing. An unlikely scenario, but Cusman teased it up from time to time. He saw himself grabbing the soft, white man by his neck and swinging him around as if he were killing a chicken for the pot. It occurred to Cusman he would not only be well within his rights, but it would have been expected of him to defend himself in any manner necessary. Cusman slowly shook his head at the thought. *Who's your favorite nigger now, Mas'r?* He envisaged saying just before snapping Ransom's neck.

***

JAMES MONTGOMERY, a Union colonel in command of the 2nd South Carolina Volunteers, had brought his Negro troops over from St. Simons Island. He was from Kansas and an avid Jayhawker. He despised everything Southern and at times wasn't prone to distinguish civilians from combatants. If they were Southern, people didn't have to be wearing a Rebel uniform in order for him to despise them, or look the other way while his undisciplined troops did their worst, or close to it.

Even though Darien wasn't a strategic location, in Colonel Montgomery's mind it was close enough. Besides, it was there. Although the 54th Massachusetts was also involved with the assault upon the defenseless town, it was the men of the 2nd South Carolina Volunteers who were responsible for most of the destruction. They beat nearly everyone they could lay their hands on, although most of the citizens had abandoned the beautiful little town when the shelling had begun. The 2nd South Carolina men burned or otherwise destroyed nearly everything in sight. Colonel Montgomery not only failed to curb his unruly men, he encouraged them. They even went after what few blacks they could find, and burned most of their homes and slave quarters as well.

As disgusted as Colonel Shaw was with all the senseless mayhem and destruction, there was nothing he could do short of ordering his men to actually engage the forces of the 2nd South Carolina. He believed that wasn't an appropriate response to say the least, especially since he had ordered his own men to confiscate any goods useful in camp. Maybe he couldn't or wasn't willing to stop the destruction and abuses to the few remaining townsfolk, but Cusman and six other men weren't so inclined, at least as far as one family was concerned.

***

THEY HAD come across the home of a white woman and her two teenage daughters who thus far hadn't been touched. The woman and her daughters had foolishly stayed inside laboring under the naïve hope their presence would discourage the destruction and looting of their house. There was a slave woman also living there and she too had a daughter; a very attractive thirteen-year-old. All the females were of course terrified, but Cusman told them he and his men weren't there to cause harm but to escort them to safety. They weren't there to cause harm, but close to a dozen soldiers from the 2nd South Carolina who soon arrived had different plans.

Once they realized the house apparently hadn't even been ransacked and looted, let alone burned, they proceeded to the front door and started to kick it down. That proved unnecessary, because after the first blow Cusman opened it. The soldiers closest to the door stopped cold and stared. Cusman not only towered over them, but both his Colt Lawman revolvers were pointed directly at their heads. Holding them at chest level, Cusman didn't even have to adjust the barrels upwards in order to do so. The men behind the soldiers in the front could see a huge black soldier standing there, his head and shoulders anyway, but most of them couldn't see his guns. They hadn't even realized there was a problem that couldn't be solved by shoving the men in front of them forward, as many as there were.

Cusman was facing black soldiers wearing Union uniforms. He knew what they had already done, and what they were intent upon doing. Still, given the circumstances, he couldn't justify squeezing the triggers. It didn't stop him from pistol whipping several of their heads, however. Three of them fell immediately and some of the others tripped over them in the bedlam. The other men with Cusman began to strike the men with the butts of their rifles, and before long only two remained standing on the front porch. They took a good look at Cusman and a better one at the revolvers he was holding. They were gone in an instant.

Cusman ordered his men to guard the front porch while he headed inside to find the women. They were huddled in the kitchen, crying and trembling with fear. He told them it would be best if they came with him and his men, since they wouldn't be able to fend off a larger group once they had been alerted. The females seemed to calm down, but suddenly started to scream. A soldier had burst through the back door and leveled his Springfield at Cusman.

"What's wrong wid you, nigger?" The black soldier said, looking nervously around. "Now you get yo' big ass the hell outta here, an' order them other niggers off too! You don't, I'll shoot you where you stand." The soldier glared at the women then, his eyes stopping when he saw the pretty young black girl.

"You gonna be mine, little lady. Fix you good for takin' up with these here white devils! Fix you up good an' proper, me an' my men, mebbe them little white gals too! Git goin' nigger," he said to Cusman, glaring at him. "Go on, git!"

The young slave girl screamed and clutched her mother. The soldier glanced briefly at her again, and that's all it took. Cusman drew one of his revolvers and shot him twice, the first a head shot and the other into the man's chest. The man's rifle went off, but the Minie ball did nothing but spray ceiling plaster about.

Cusman quickly led the women and girls to the front porch, stepping over the still semi-unconscious men lying or groping about. He ordered his men still on the porch to come with him.

"And this time," Cusman added, "we shoot *any*one that tries to stop us!"

***

IT HAD been a small victory, all things considered, but Colonel Shaw thanked Cusman and his men anyway. He made sure the women and girls were cared for, but with the exception of a few other unscathed locals who had determined at least this Yankee colonel wasn't a savage, many of their neighbors weren't as fortunate. Numerous civilians had lost their homes and businesses to fire, or might as well have. The town was in ruins. In his report, Colonel Shaw described the actions of Colonel Montgomery and his men as a "Satanic Action". Later on, Shaw told Cusman he almost wished it had been Montgomery he had shot, and had no intention of informing the colonel or anyone else it had been Cusman who had shot Montgomery's man.

"You're carryin' a sidearm too, Colonel." Cusman replied, looking directly at Shaw as he spoke.

The colonel looked away before he replied. He was young and inexperienced, but at that moment he realized he wasn't as inexperienced regarding the brutality of war and the men who reveled in it as he had been just that very morning. He turned and looked at Cusman.

"Yes Sergeant, I am," he said with a trace of malice in his voice that was no reflection on Cusman. "And thank you. I will remember that in the future. You are dismissed."

Later that night Cusman couldn't sleep. He couldn't get the insane irony out of his mind. It was swirling about in his head, some thoughts disjointed, others rushing together in a torrent. He had escaped slavery, joined the Union army, ended up all the way back to the very slave state where he had been raised in bondage to fight those who bore responsibility for all he had suffered, and where many of his people still suffered much more than he had ever experienced. And the very first soldier he'd killed had also been a slave. And he had killed him to defend, among others, a white slave owner and her daughters; something he would not hesitate to repeat if he had it to do again.

He had experienced his first taste of war, or what it could mutate into, and wondered if that day's events were simply precursors, if most of his previous notions of why he was fighting had been a lie, if only by omission - if he had, at the very least, been nothing more than hopelessly naïve. Cusman wasn't accustomed to such uncertainties, but had to accept them.

Over in his tent another soldier had also found sleep impossible. Colonel Robert Shaw had not only experienced his first taste of the vagaries of war, but had remained inert, done nothing when innocent people had needed him most. He had been shocked and irresolute during the entire debacle, and had buried everything he had always believed in, and told himself that because of his refusal to do the honorable thing, to make the tough decisions commanders who were worthy of their commissions had the responsibly to do regardless of personal consequence, civilians had been at least beaten and had experienced the tragedy of their entire life's work and homes destroyed before their eyes. He had been tested, and in his mind had failed miserably. His own naivety had been shattered that day, but rather than act upon it all he had done was virtually nothing, except order many of his own men to loot, even if they had also been ordered not to burn and destroy civilian homes and businesses, and certainly not beat anyone who hadn't precipitated a violent confrontation.

Sergeant Sable had been right, and at least Shaw's faith in a person's character regardless of color had been confirmed. Now if he could only find the wisdom and courage to follow that person's example. Colonel Shaw didn't know it that night as he finally did drift off to sleep, but he had already found that and more.

XXIV

Although Billy had given his word to Doc Wygant, he was determined to abandon their agreement if only he could find the courage to finally do so. He'd be sixteen next year anyway, the same age his brother Jackie had been when he left for war, so what difference did a few months make? There was already a new system in place, established by a man named Jonathan Letterman, the medical director of the Department of West Virginia. General George B. McClellan himself had issued Letterman a charter to do whatever was necessary to improve the system. Billy was more than qualified, and he knew it.

Doc Wygant knew it too, even if the cagey old man held their agreement over Billy as if it were carved upon a stone tablet, with Doc holding it high over his head while standing on Mount Sinai. Billy didn't believe he painted Doc Wygant as a hypocrite when the youth conjured that up, although in his frustration that retort did come to mind. The irony certainly wasn't lost on the boy. Maybe Doc would appreciate at least that much.

Billy had been going through the darkest mood of his life. He no longer believed his brother Pete was alive even if his mother continued to insist otherwise. He didn't share his feelings with her but he did with his brother Ben. Upon hearing the whole story, or what many of the locals thought it to be, Ben also doubted Pete was alive even if Janeway's story wasn't true.

There had been plenty of prisoner exchanges, especially officers around the time his brother had gone missing, including officers who had been captured at Shiloh. If Pete had also been captured, why hadn't he been amongst those men? And upon their release, why hadn't any of their official reports mentioned having seen Pete alive? No letters or wires home either, so if he hadn't been captured at Shiloh why hadn't there been? All of the men he had served with in the 1st Naperville who had been questioned eventually supported the probability of Major Janeway's account. Even those who still had little use for the man had come around to accept that conclusion, or at least not deny it outright. None of them believed Lieutenant McCabe had survived, regardless of how he had died. No, Ben told Billy, it was best to accept the grievous fact Pete was gone. Ben, like Billy, never said much of anything to either parent about it, even when Father Benjamin had asked him. "I suppose anything's possible in war," had been Ben's only response.

Billy's guilt found new life. He had one brother already dead, another missing a foot and who knew how brothers Don, Robert and Jackie would make out? And there was Billy, with all his medical training, tucked away safely at home. That was no longer acceptable; there would be no more excuses. He was going off to war.

***

THE FATES of his brothers and his guilt over staying home weren't the only things that had made up his mind. There was Linda Marie, or at least the memory of her. Not yet sixteen and Billy had already experienced the strange sensation of being profoundly in love with a dead girl. She was gone, but when he visited her grave, recalled how beautiful she had appeared even in her coffin, it tore at him that she was but six feet beneath his feet. Oh, there was her soul to consider, but that was something else Billy had grown to distrust. Even so, he didn't want his memory of her tainted by what he perceived would amount to cowardice if he chose to stay behind any longer.

His faith in God was all but gone, or at least shattered so much it seemed beyond repair. The singular event that had cemented his recent departure from his once unwavering faith had occurred after spring had evolved into summer.

He had gone to the cemetery with some flowers to place on Linda Marie's grave. He hadn't been there since the funeral, and when he approached her large tombstone he was grateful no one was around to see the tears he couldn't control. It had started out a sunny day, but by the time he had arrived thunderclouds had developed. The large ones were majestically stalwart, barely moving. The lowest ones raced beneath them, as if in their urgency they needed to get wherever they were going as fast as the wind would allow. Billy envied them.

He had placed the flowers upon her grave then took a step back. He kept telling himself he no longer believed her spirit could hear him, or that anyone even had one at all. Once he was standing next to her grave however, he spoke to her anyway. He told her summer had arrived, and spring hadn't been the same without her. That struck him as a childish thing to say; he didn't know why since he had meant every word. He stared directly at the ground, at the place where she was but six feet from him and said how much he loved her, and how much he always would. The last few words were choked off by his sobbing; his red, tear-stained face contorted into a portrait of utter anguish.

The clouds erupted. He sensed they were speaking to him in a voice filled with contempt and confrontation, as if it were a challenge. The distant lightning had arrived, along with a deluge that soaked him to the skin. He just stood there and cried, teeth clenched, eyes jammed shut. When he finally did open them he noticed the delicate flowers he had brought Linda Marie. The downpour had all but flattened the deep purple pansies and snow white petunias. There wasn't much grass on her grave, mostly weeds that meant no harm. The rest had just been dirt, waiting for the grass seeds to complete their germination and compete with the weeds, as if they were waiting for the mood to hit them. The dirt had been instantly transformed into mud, and the flowers Billy had brought for his Linda Marie had been driven into it, choked by water, dying helplessly. Billy's profound sorrow turned into rage.

"You unholy coward!" He yelled, looking directly towards where he once believed God and heaven must be, the rain pummeling his face. "Damn you to *hell!* You evil son of a *bitch!* You cold hearted *bastard!* You're so God damned fearsome, come on! Kill me you craven *beast!* You can kill a girl, you can kill her, you God damned *murderer!* I'm not backing down from you and *all the hell you can bring!* Come on! Come..." then Billy collapsed within himself, consumed by his agony in a way he wished would kill him so he could be face-to-face with whatever adversary he was raging against.

He headed home, in no hurry to get there, feeling abandoned but eerily serene. Lightning was shooting everywhere, instant flashes of seething, electric branches perhaps in search of him, but he didn't care. If there was a God He was too much of a coward to hit him, to *face* him. Billy just knew it. God killed defenseless young girls, the more beautiful the better. He killed people who were afraid of Him. Billy wasn't afraid of God, not anymore. He hated Him too much, which remained the youth's only justification to not entirely deny God's existence.

***

DOC MAY have been impressed by the irony of Billy's Moses-inspired observation, but he lost his temper anyway. Delicia cried and hugged the youth as she begged him to reconsider. Mother Grace was inconsolable. Father Benjamin threatened to inform the military authorities of Billy's age after his more subdued entreaties had failed. Brother Ben also ended up begging him to reconsider, after threatening to tan the holy hide off his youngest brother. A few days later Billy was on a train out of Chicago heading east. God could try and kill all the men and young girls he wanted; Billy was going save as many as he could or die trying - he *wanted* what he perceived as the Ultimate Confrontation.

***

BILLY KNEW his father. He had never been prone to making idle pronouncements, whether he was referring to anything from a promise to attend a Sunday picnic or using deadly force if a situation called for it. He had never heard his father threaten to do the latter, or even heard of him ever having done so, but if the need were to someday arise Billy knew Father Benjamin would follow through if he had so promised. Therefore, Billy assumed his father had already contacted the military authorities, and he was right. It wouldn't make any difference though. Billy hadn't attempted to enlist in Chicago like he had said he was going to do.

He was on his way to Washington D.C., but only had a ticket to take him as far as Pittsburgh. He didn't want his final destination to somehow get discovered, but he was already out of money unless the twelve cents he still had counted for anything. Twelve cents certainly would count for something, two nickels of it anyway; it was about to usher in something that would change him forever.

He was starved, and after disembarking in the strange city and walking a few blocks he spotted a tavern that advertised a free lunch if a nickel beer was purchased to wash it down. Billy didn't drink but he sure could eat, almost as much as his brother Jackie unless it was a contest. The best part was he could go back for seconds. He had made himself another thick sandwich, filled the rest of his plate with baked beans and made his way back to the small table where he had been sitting.

"You plannin' on drinkin' that beer, lad?" The young man who spoke sat down right across from Billy, dressed in a Union uniform that was tattered and worn.

"Sure I am," Billy responded, as if it were a foolish question. "I always drink after I eat, that's all."

"Sorry to hear that. Tis a waste." The young man said. "Me own self, I hate to eat on an empty stomach. Ain't got me so much as a nickel though, and I sure am thirsty, that I am. Went an' blew the last of me pay on a quality bottle of the Creature and an even higher quality whore. Had me a grand ole time though. Sure was pretty she was, unless it was the Jameson." The man sighed, and gazed longingly at Billy's untouched mug.

"Well here then," Billy offered, sliding the mug over to the young man, glad to be rid of it. The young man's eyes lit up, and he emptied the mug before putting it back down.

"Little hair'a the dog, don't ya know." Billy had no idea what he was talking about, although the rush of beer appeared to soothe the fellow or at least point him in that direction.

"What outfit you in?" Billy asked, as if he were well versed in such jargon.

"It's the outfit I'm gonna be in that matters," the fellow replied. "Gonna join up with the Fightin' 69th. *Faugh a ballagh!*" The young man hollered as he threw his fist in the air. "That's their war cry lad, means clear the way, in case your Gaelic is a touch rusty. They're headin' up this way with Meade's whole damned army, found out yesterday. Name's Shawnessy O'Keefe, glad to make your acquaintance." He held out his hand and Billy took it, nearly dropping his overstuffed sandwich. Some of the insides spilled out anyway.

"Bill McCabe, glad to meet you too, sir." That got a laugh.

"Hell, I ain't no sir. You can call me Shawn."

There was more conversation. Billy liked the large, red-haired Irishman immediately. He even spent his last nickel to buy him another beer. When Billy mentioned he had only two cents left, Shawn laughed again.

"Saints be praised Bill, at least you're richer'n me by two sad cents!"

Billy asked him about the army, and although his questions suggested he didn't have much knowledge about the military other than what he had picked up in the hospital, Shawn answered them in a way that wasn't condescending. It turned out the Fighting 69th was an Irish brigade of some renown, and their previous commander, Brigadier General Thomas Meagher, had resigned his command in protest over the army's refusal to allow him to return to New York to recruit more men after all the casualties they had suffered at Chancellorsville. Colonel Patrick Kelly was now in charge and was rumored to be looking for volunteers, preferably Irishmen.

"Well, that's me all over and back again, Bill, and with the last name of McCabe you'd be welcome as well I'd be suspectin'." That grabbed Billy's attention.

"What do I need to do to join up?" He asked.

"Just show up, Bill. The problem is gettin' there. Heard they might be headin' this way, but it ain't for certain. Best thing to do is get to them. If we could get ourselves close, I'd find 'em. Hard to miss an army that big, but since between us we only have two lonely cents I don't see how a train ride is in our immediate future, and we sure as hell can't afford horses."

"We could jump a freight," Billy suggested. "But wouldn't you be a deserter?"

"Now that's an idea, lad. Why didn't I come to think of it? You sure it's but two cents you have? Still a might thirsty I am. Still, why didn't I think of that grand idea?"

Perhaps it was because he was still drunk from the night before if Shawn's breath was any indication, as well as the odor which seemed to emanate from him in alcohol-laden waves, but Billy kept that to himself.

"And I'm no damned deserter I'll have you know." Billy thought he had possibly insulted the man. He had, but Shawn dismissed it as an innocent mistake. "Captain said I was free to go. Even gave me the necessary papers. I'm suspectin' he was weary of me always askin' for a pay advance or worse yet a loan. I'm no damned good with money."

Before the afternoon had made its way to dusk they were both in a freight car, heading east.

***

THEY JUMPED off the freight train sometime after daybreak. They had lost track of the hours unless early morning counted. Billy had, of course, no idea where they were. Shawn didn't either; he wasn't even certain they were still in Pennsylvania, but swore he could smell an army fifty miles away. It turned out he was either right, or very lucky. When they came upon General George G. Meade's main body a few days later at a place along the south side of a creek near Taneytown, Shawn was all pride over his accomplishment. Both of them were starved, but that didn't last long. Before another day passed both he and Billy were in new uniforms.

***

IT WAS a huge encampment with tens of thousands of Union soldiers all about. Billy had heard of such armies of course, but its massiveness still astonished him. It was as if a temporary city of substantial size had suddenly appeared out of nowhere. All types of men were present, from all walks of life. Many were young farmers, but men who had never been out of New York City and other large cities until the war had erupted were there as well. Horses, mules, wagons and armaments of every description were in great abundance, and the sheer volume of it all made Billy wonder how any force on earth could keep it from doing as it pleased. It was as if, once on the move, it would be impossible to stop or even alter in any way. When Billy considered an opposing force of similar size it gave him pause; he couldn't pretend to imagine what the outcome would be if they collided. He was surprised to hear there were even more Union troops, thousands of them, easily within a day's march or close to it.

***

"YOU SAY you have medical training," Captain Terry Donovan, M.D., said to the young private standing before him. "May I ask where you received it?" Billy wasn't used to lying, but found it was easy enough to do if the situation called for it.

"Worked in a hospital in Chicago, sir. Raised in an orphanage, on the South Side. Doctor at the hospital said I showed promise. Just turned eighteen, so I figured it was time, sir."

"You're eighteen? Don't look it. Which hospital?"

"Cook County Hospital, sir. Treated a lot of wounded men there. I'm not afraid, sir. I would like to volunteer as a battlefield medic. I read where General McClellan issued some charter, sir."

"One 'sir' or thereabouts is usually sufficient, Private. But you can call me Doctor Donovan, or just Doctor D. We can use you though. Not too often men volunteer for such hazardous duty. You got here just in time. General Meade is looking to pick a fight with Lee's army, and it appears he will soon find it."

The next day a courier arrived with an urgent message for General Meade from General John F. Reynolds. He had engaged the enemy in force near a small town west of Meade's forces, and was in dire need of assistance. The town was called Gettysburg.

***

BILLY WAS issued a first-aid kit and two armbands that were supposed to identify him as a medic. The other men he would be serving with told him it was a good idea to wear them, although in the heat of battle it was likely at least some of the Rebs would shoot at him anyway. As he sat around his first campfire as a genuine Union soldier he had plenty of questions, but the other field medics understood and were patient with him. None of them believed he was eighteen, but that didn't matter. All of them had seen boys younger than Billy shot to pieces, and worse.

"It's that damned canister that tears a man up," a lanky private twice Billy's age said as he stirred the coals with a stick. "God damned canister. It can do more damage than anything. Seen me piles of meat that you would hardly know were men if torn up uniforms weren't mixed up in it. Hope you got a strong stomach, Bill. Anyways, after while you'll get used to it if you live long enough."

"Make sure you got that laudanum they was supposed to issue you when the fightin' starts." Another medic said. "You got some, right?"

"Two bottles," Billy answered.

"Won't be enough. Get yourself three more, at least. That won't be enough either, so don't let 'em have too much no matter how much they scream. And Bill, you are gonna hear some kind'a screamin'. Ain't as loud as constant cannon and rifle fire, but it will sure as hell seem like it is."

***

ON THE evening of July 1st a large portion of the Army of the Potomac was on the move, converging from a variety of areas in the general vicinity heading towards Gettysburg. Billy had hooked up with Shawn again as they marched along with the rest of their new comrades, a number of whom had been members of the Fighting 69th at Chancellorsville, some before that bloody conflict. They were a rugged bunch of Irishmen, men who had been through hell and back and were willing to go there again. They knew, or thought they did, what was waiting up ahead. Although false bravado was virtually non-existent amongst them the same wasn't true for everyone, especially some of the new recruits. Billy sensed their fear, felt it himself, so he and Shawn spent their time amongst the experienced men as much as possible.

"Keep a close watch on these lads, Bill." Shawn told him. "When things erupt, it can be the little things that save you. They're still standin' because they've seen what those are."

"You mean that's all it takes?" Billy asked.

"Oh, that and not bein' where a bullet has a mind to go. Minie balls can be insistent that way, downright stubborn I'll be bound. Never heard of one yet that lost an argument it had a mind to win. You're a brave lad to put on those armbands, but they won't impress hot lead. Where might your rifle be, lad?"

"Don't want one," Billy replied. "I'm not here to shoot anyone. This kit is my weapon." Shawn glanced at his young friend, one eyebrow raised. *Perhaps the lad ain't just talkin' to the wind,* he surmised.

"I hope that's not the last thought you end up havin' in this world, Bill. I truly do."

***

GENERAL ROBERT E. Lee's battle blood was up, along with his confidence. His Army of Northern Virginia had won at Chancellorsville that past May, and if the first day's fighting at Gettysburg on July 1st of 1863 was any indication, his 72,000 man force would again be successful. They were up against the nearly 94,000 man force of General Meade's Army of the Potomac, but Lee's army had faced and defeated superior numbers before. If they could do it again Washington D.C. itself, only ninety miles away, could end up in Confederate hands, perhaps easily so. First, however, Lee had work to do, and he had every intention of making the Yankees bleed a river.

The morning of July 2nd promised to be another sweltering day as well as a bloody one. Temperatures would climb well into the nineties accompanied by an abundance of stifling humidity. Six of the seven corps of the Army of the Potomac was present on the battlefield, including II Corps, the one that included Billy and the Fighting 69th. They had actually arrived the previous night, and along with the XII and the III Corps had joined up with I [First] Corps and XI Corps that had fought so hard on the first day.

***

ON THAT morning along with the rest of II Corps, Billy found himself positioned near the southern half of a place called Cemetery Ridge, just west of Taneytown Road that led into Gettysburg following a north/south direction. A mile west, running parallel along Seminary Ridge, the Confederates were facing them, having established a line of their own. They weren't the only Rebel troops around, though.

The heat and humidity were all-consuming. It felt as if the sun had somehow managed to move closer, much closer, or at least focus itself over the battlefield as if it were the only place left on earth. It would have felt miserably hot in the shade, dressed in a light shirt. Billy and his comrades were huddled under the scorching sun, hour after hour, dressed in dark woolen Yankee blue that reeked of sweat. The only thing that remained dry was the inside of their mouths. Troop movement and battles were in progress as the afternoon wore on, approaching four o'clock. It was indeed locked in the nineties, growing hotter, and most of the red faced men had long since emptied their canteens. Thirst gnawed at them all, and the God awful heat and torrid sun were impossible to ignore. Fear increased the sweating, remarkably so. It would take something unimaginable to get their minds off the thirst and unrelenting heat that arose in waves. Within a few minutes, thirst and heat weren't even vague considerations.

***

THE SOUNDS of battle had been exploding everywhere it seemed, and Billy was finally in the midst of it. Confederate General James Longstreet's divisions had slammed into the Union III Corps led by Major General Daniel F. Sickles. His actively engaged force of approximately 10,000 men was in front of Billy and to his left. Sickles had ignored, or at least taken it upon himself to interpret General Meade's arguably vague order to hold a defensive position upon the ridge, and had led his men west towards higher ground that would gain blood-soaked infamy called the Peach Orchard (the significance of which wasn't lost on Billy) and a rocky wasteland southeast of the Peach Orchard aptly named Devil's Den.

Sickles foolhardy move would eventually cost him roughly a third of his men as well as his right leg when a cannon ball all but blew it off. Worse yet, his action had created a vulnerable salient west, north and south, leaving the entire section of the battlefield well south of Billy subject to Longstreet's fearsome attack, and the youth made his way there as fast as he could. He wasn't aware of Union or Confederate battlefield strategies as everything exploded around him, but he hadn't lost sight of why he was there even if he was terrified beyond reason.

Despite being warned to at least initially hold back, Billy ran into the withering fire, as if his terror was a motivating factor as opposed to the effect it had on other men who would have been inclined to stay put or run for their lives and hide. He proceeded to staunch the bleeding of as many wounded men as he could, mindless of where he was heading. His very existence was suddenly imperiled in every direction it seemed, so any one part of hell was as dangerous as the next. When he did the best he could for one man he was on to the next. It didn't matter to him where the Fighting 69th was located; if a soldier could be reached, and even when it looked like he couldn't, Billy was there or on his way.

His apparent courage was contagious, even if he didn't feel courageous, or recognized it as anything he had previously believed defined the concept. Many of his fellow medics had viewed it as such, and had gone into the heart of the bloody fray themselves. One of them had just arrived not twenty feet from Billy when a Minie ball slammed into his chest. Billy ran to him, but there was nothing the youth could do. Billy was already low on bandages and other supplies so he grabbed those the dead medic had been carrying and proceeded on.

The heaving, seething nightmare was exploding all around, and the only way he could deal with the insanity was to keep moving, keep going from one wounded man to another, and a mind-boggling number of dead ones. It was as if the entire universe had, and continued to explode all around him; a powerful Beast of extraordinary proportions doing its best to devour the youth and everything around him.

If he had believed he had at least a general idea of what a major battle would entail he had been woefully naïve. No matter how descriptive others had been about the horrors of war, and despite his best efforts to steel himself for such gory mayhem, he would have been traumatized had he stopped even an instant to contemplate the bloody carnage that continued to wail all around him. He kept on running from man to man, even when others had fallen back.

One terrified medic, almost as green as Billy, actually tossed him his kit as he sprinted by. The young man had tried to administer aid to a fallen soldier, but his hands, his whole body, had been shaking so violently he hadn't been able to even open his kit. He wasn't a hundred feet away from Billy when a concussive shell exploded directly in front of the young man, as if it had been searching for him alone. Billy saw the explosion but didn't see the medic afterwards. Nothing remained of the young man much larger than the kit he had tossed towards Billy.

Billy heard screaming coming from a crater that had been made by another shell burst. It was up ahead and to his right, and although Rebels were advancing towards that position Billy lit out for it anyway. Several Minie balls whizzed by him as soon as he had started to run, and by the time he reached the hole it seemed as though a cloud filled with Minie balls had burst directly in front of the youth. It was as if he were running through a sideways torrent of rain, although it sounded more like an enraged nest of demonic wasps moving at incredible speed. As insanely loud as the battlefield was, the bullets came so close he could easily hear them whizz by, seemingly infuriated they had missed their target.

He dove to the ground just as he reached the hole and rolled in, frantically searching for the bullet holes he knew had to be in him somewhere, even if he hadn't felt any pain. A few of his comrades had told him it wasn't uncommon not to feel much of anything when first hit, other than the sensation of having been punched. He hadn't felt anything like that, nor did he see anything that indicated he'd been wounded. He didn't see that, but he saw the red-haired man who had been, and still was, screaming. When Shawn recognized his friend, he finally stopped wailing.

"Bill, lad." He hollered. "Save yourself if you can, you're lookin' at a dead man."

Billy ripped open Shawn's woolen blouse and shirt, fully expecting to see the body wounds that would mean his friend was indeed lost. Blood was everywhere, but not a single bullet had hit Shawn's torso. As bloody as he was, even his leg and arm wounds didn't indicate any major arteries had been hit. He had been hit by four Minie balls, one having left a bloody crease across his skull, but not a single one of them had ricocheted through his body or obliterated any bones.

"You're not dead yet, you lucky God damned Mick!" Billy yelled over the tumultuous din as he quickly staunched the more serious wounds. "Looks like you won quite a few arguments with those damned Minie balls after all! Here, drink this." Billy held the back of Shawn's head and helped him drink from his last bottle of laudanum. "This stuff's got a lot more kick than that Creature you're always moonin' over. Here, drink some more." Billy's hands were shaking so much it was all he could do not to spill the narcotic, getting most of it in Shawn's mouth.

The intensity of the constant, roaring cannons and the rolling thunder of thousands of muskets and other rifles continuously going off were so loud, Billy and Shawn could shout their words yet just barely understand one another. Even so, both of them heard the unearthly, shrieking *Woo! Woo! Woo-ah woo!* Rebel Yell as it pierced through the shifting smoke and permeating haze. Billy looked up and saw what appeared to be a howling sea of humanity coming towards them. After struggling to do so, Shawn saw them coming as well. Most of the charging enemy suddenly broke off to the right, but a group of about a half dozen Confederates were heading straight for the crater, bayonets fixed, their eyes wild as they bore down on their prey.

"Been nice knowin' ya, lad." Shawn hollered as he slumped back into the hole. "Let's go out like true Sons of Erin. Take me rifle, get that big bastard out front." Billy just looked at Shawn, speechless. "Well go on lad, I know it's not your way, but given half a chance that wild-eyed son of an Orange slut is goin' to kill more than just us I'll have ya know!"

Billy picked up the rifle, aimed at the advancing Confederates and fired over their heads. He was actually an excellent marksman, if target shooting counted. Shawn had propped himself up again and saw what the boy had done, looked at the youth, then slumped back down. The screaming men were seventy then instantly sixty feet away, closing fast. They had seen Billy too.

"Perhaps I should of invested me last thirty dollars on that Colt revolver I'd been eyein' back in Pittsburgh instead of that whore. She sure was a sight though lad, and most accommodatin' I'll have ya know. Loved her work, that one. Of course it was most likely me charm and good looks." Shawn smiled weakly at Billy, as if to say goodbye, and offered him his bloody, quivering hand.

The two huge explosions couldn't have been louder if the projectiles had landed right next to them. Another thirty feet and they would have, and if Billy and Shawn hadn't been in the crater it wouldn't have mattered anyway. It had mattered to the group of charging Confederates though. Only one of them was still alive, and if there was a merciful God in heaven he'd be dead within the hour, preferably much sooner.

Billy grabbed a hold of Shawn and started to drag him out of the hole. It felt as though the big man had cement for innards, but Billy hardly noticed. He couldn't get Shawn over his shoulders though, and dropped him after going ten feet while attempting to carry him like a groom might carry his bride over a threshold. The rain of Minie balls started up again, not that they had ever stopped, but Billy kept dragging his friend along. One bullet took off Billy's cap as if it had been snatched by a gale, and others nicked angrily at his uniform as well as Shawn's. Billy pulled even faster, and after making it back over fifty miraculous yards they tumbled behind a long trench occupied by hundreds of Union infantrymen who were firing at a line of approaching Rebels who soon realized they were definitely heading in the wrong direction.

Two other medics arrived and put Shawn on a stretcher. Billy felt compelled to head out again; he didn't know why other than he had to, but a lieutenant, having witnessed the entire spectacle and describing it an honest to God miracle, ordered Billy to the rear.

"I don't know why God watches over you, son, but take your gift and keep with that man you brought in. He's one brave Mick and may still need your Devine Guidance!"

After Shawn was safely in a large hospital tent Billy again tried to get back, but Dr. Donovan stopped him. "I need you here, Private. There's plenty of men in this tent who are going to die, but you can save just as many here as you can out there." Outside the tent the battle raged on.

***

"WELL, IF it isn't Saint William of Naperville himself," Shawn said weakly late that night when Billy made his way to the Irishman's cot. "Any chance you might be willin' to perform another miracle and change that pitcher of water into Jameson for a grateful friend?"

"Sorry Shawn." Billy said with a smile, watching his friend carefully. "Dr. Donovan has a bottle of Bushmills in his haversack though. Want some of that?"

"*Bushmills?* Jesus Mary and Joseph lad, that's a Protestant drink. Rather have the damned water, unless you have a touch of that other elixir on you. Almost worth gettin' shot over, it tis."

"That stuff is addicting, Shawn. Better go easy on it." Shawn looked at him as if the youth were insane. Billy continued to speak. "Anyway, looks like you're on your way to a hospital in Washington if Lee doesn't get there first. Doesn't look like it though. We held 'em good, Shawn. There's talk some colonel and his men from Maine held off the Johnnies trying to get around our left flank, Chamberlain I think his name was. Anyway, I heard some of the officers say that might've meant the Rebs would've had a good chance of gettin' to Washington even. Don't know about that for certain, but it looks like tomorrow's gonna be more of the same. You might be halfway to Washington by then, Shawn, except with all that's happened there's just a slim chance, if any. Too many wounded, and no way of movin' them, but a few are gettin' moved out. I'll check with Dr. Donovan."

"Wish you were goin' with me Saint William, not that I'm too worried about what's goin' to happen to you here." Shawn offered a weak smile as he looked at his friend more closely. "Just why is it God and his most precious angels favor you so?"

"I have no idea, Shawn. None at all."

XXV

By the time Billy's first letter arrived at Tin Pan Alley those who loved him had resigned themselves to what he had done. They were all praying another letter would be forthcoming. The one they had received had been written the day before he had marched off to Gettysburg, and between the newspaper accounts of that tremendous battle and their years of knowing Billy's temperament as well as the limitations of his physical abilities, at least as they pertained to fighting, there was cause for much concern.

"I warned him not to go," Ben told Doc Wygant one day at Tin Pan Alley while the old doctor was checking Ben's leg. "I've seen what enraged men can do when they're out of their minds. Billy wouldn't stand a chance. Hell, some of those men look to kill medics almost as much as officers and flag bearers. Found one of our medics strung up by his heels, naked. Had so many knife and bayonet wounds in him only his own brother recognized him, and that was because he spotted some damned mole. Can't say some of our boys aren't just as bad, though. Hell, I've seen men aim at some of those low types even if they were one of us, and put a slug in 'em during a battle. Can't say I faulted 'em, either. There's plenty of ugliness on both sides, that's for sure."

Doc Wygant listened to Ben without comment. He knew the young man well. He knew all the McCabe boys well; he had delivered all of them except the second youngest, Jackie. He would have delivered him too if the infant hadn't been in such an all-fired hurry to get into the world.

Doc liked all the McCabe boys, which was something coming from a man who generally had a low tolerance when it came to people in general and most of those he knew personally. He patched them up all right, and tended to them with the utmost care when they were ill, but most folks had a way of disappointing him if they talked too long. For some folks it only took a sentence or two. Not the McCabe family though. Even so, the change that had come over young Ben disturbed the old man.

It wasn't the loss of his foot either. That no doubt wasn't a good thing, but the young man had adjusted to it better than most, if not all the local men and boys home from the war minus a piece or two. It was the other things Ben had gone through that had changed him, the things only men who had tasted the horror of war could truly understand. Doc had always thought he could understand those things too, but suspected that was no longer the case. Someone with the strength of character Ben possessed that had changed so much made the old man re-evaluate his notions, and he wondered how Billy would turn out once, more importantly if, he made it home.

"Must have been hell, son," Doc Wygant finally said. Ben just looked at him. The look in his eyes conveyed a tome of sorrow so profound the old man felt shamed by his own inadequate observation. Doc Wygant rarely felt foolish, but he did that day.

It lingered well into the night, and was waiting for him once he had wiped the sleep from his eyes the following morning. He gazed at himself as he lathered his face in front of the mirror, finding it impossible not to feel contempt towards the image that gazed back at him. "God damned-able war," he muttered as he slapped his straight-edged razor against the strop with more urgency than usual.

***

DELICIA AND her sister Ginny came by to visit more often now that Ben was home. That usually cheered him up, and his old self would sometimes emerge once they got to talking about all the good times before the war. His old sense of humor would come back for a brief while, and soon all of them would be laughing about the things that had occurred in what now seemed like the old days. Delicia would appear to warm up then, but more often she felt like an actress upon a stage, merely feigning merriment.

Mother Grace and Father Benjamin hadn't been aware of most of the accounts brought up, nor had they even suspected. The young people assumed since the episodes had occurred so long ago, when they were mere children or close to it, it was now okay to reveal their shenanigans from bygone years. The older folks went along with that, but inside their recesses the events seemed like yesterday was closer to it. Still, the much needed respites were cherished by everyone.

***

EARLY ONE evening Delicia was alone with Ben on the front porch, enjoying the fresh summer breezes before the impending darkness reigned them in. Since no one else was in earshot they talked about Pete, but it was the rumors Ben had heard in town about Clifton Janeway he really wanted to discuss.

"With Pete gone it stands to reason you have to get on with your life Delicia, and perhaps it's just my memories of Janeway when we were younger that troubles me, for the most part anyway, but why him?"

"It doesn't make sense, I'm aware of that Ben, but you don't know him now. You yourself have commented on how much the war has changed some people, formerly good people who can no longer lay claim to virtues that once defined them. Isn't it possible for the opposite to be true?"

"Yes, it is. Witnessed it myself. There were two brothers from Michigan in my outfit who were so incorrigible some judge told them it was prison or the army. They proved their mettle at Antietam, and after that as well. One of them didn't make it, but the other has become a chaplain." Delicia let out a slight giggle, in spite of herself.

"Well, I doubt Clifton will follow that path, but he *is* teaching Sunday school."

"Janeway a Sunday school teacher? Things *have* changed during my absence. How does your father feel about him, and what opinion does James hold? I seem to recall they weren't overly fond of Clifton or his father."

"Father has grown to like him, and if it hadn't been for Clifton who knows how James would have fared. Got him assigned to Washington, but don't you breathe a word of it. None of us want James to know a thing until the war is over, if then."

"Are you in love with him, Delicia?" Ben's question hadn't caught her off guard, but it might as well have. She had been trying to accomplish that very thing, to feel what she did - or had - no *did* for Pete, but regardless of what she had been trying to convince herself was indeed a possibility, she was still in love with Ben's brother even though it felt as if she were in love with a ghost.

"Oh, not in the classic sense I suppose, as I have come to know it, but many women grow into such feelings. He's certainly in love with me."

"Who isn't?" Ben joked, lightening things somewhat.

"Not you I hope!" She joked back.

"Me? Granted, it was a few years back, but after serious contemplation I came to realize you were the only one for me. I was all of three." They shared a laugh, and talked of happier times.

***

CLIFTON WAS again beside himself, and growing weary of the feeling. He had asked Delicia to marry him, and she hadn't said no. She was a ways from yes, but he had reason to believe she was heading in that direction. His latest turmoil had to do with Elwood Stalworthy. He hadn't heard from him in months, and the last time he had things were supposedly well under control. Clifton had expected at least a wire by now, possibly the man in person with a couple jars of body parts. Clifton had no way of reaching him of course, and the suspense was driving him mad.

He had a large safe in his study at home. It contained over half of his personal fortune in cash, if a sudden departure ever became necessary. It was paper currency for the most part, with the exception of $75,000 in gold coins. When Stalworthy produced the evidence he could have all the gold if he was shrewd enough to ask. Clifton assumed he would be, and also knew he would gladly pay three times that amount, even more. Perhaps not *gladly* once he was convinced McCabe was dead, but that wasn't the point. Besides, Clifton would have a few conditions regarding the extra money. He hadn't made up his mind, but General Smithington and Hezekiah O'Darcy were still in his thoughts. Perhaps time would decide their fates, or perhaps Clifton would; extra money would at least secure the services of the right man for the job. But what the hell was Stalworthy up to, and where the hell was he?

***

PETE HAD buried Stalworthy in a small clearing deep in the woods. A large boxelder had fallen across the middle of it, and with the aid of horses and ropes he had moved it over and dug the grave. Once he had finished it was just a matter of putting the tree back. After a few days and especially after some rain the grass in the clearing wouldn't show Pete and the two horses had even been there.

He was excited as he made his way back to Desiree's shack, anticipating what her response would be when he handed his surprising find over to her. Just before he had rolled Stalworthy's body into the grave he had pulled off the dead man's boots, since they had appeared to be close to Pete's size and well made. They had felt unusually heavy even for quality boots, and that's when he found the Double Eagle gold coins. They had been slipped between the lining and outside counter, up and down the boot tops. Twenty coins in each side of each boot, eighty coins in all; sixteen hundred dollars worth.

A thought had occurred to Pete while throwing dirt over the body. The only other leather the man had of any consequence were his saddles, including the one Pete had been sitting on for weeks. It had always seemed heavier than normal, something Pete had attributed to its quality.

Pete had brought the body through the woods taking both horses with him, with Stalworthy's body on the same animal he had been riding when he arrived. Pete had been on Yankee. He took out the knife that had killed Stalworthy and had almost begun to cut the saddle. When he had turned it over however, he noticed a crease along an outside edge. He hadn't had any reason to pay attention to it before, but when he put in the tip of the blade it slid in a little ways. He then used his fingers and pulled. There they had been, resting in an ingeniously made space between the rawhide cover tree and the seat leather - another $2,400 in gold coins. A fortune to be sure, but for Desiree and her children it would be a king's ransom. It was unlikely Desiree had ever seen a twenty dollar gold coin, much less two hundred of them.

Pete was going to keep five of them when he finally departed, something he kept telling himself he had to do sooner rather than later. Not immediately though. He told himself Desiree was naturally traumatized over what had occurred even if it didn't show, and Pete insisted to himself it was his fault. If he had just rode by that first day she would still be dirt poor, but at least her life and that of her children wouldn't have come so close to ending so horribly. Yes, he concluded, it was his fault all right.

Pete still marveled at how she had done it, how she had managed to stab a man who had clearly been much stronger than herself and well armed. She had told Pete that's what did the man in. He hadn't considered her much of a threat when he holstered his .44, unsheathed his knife with his right hand and grabbed for Little Desiree to use as a shield, but he hadn't taken into consideration what a mother was capable of accomplishing during that type of situation, or wasn't aware such things were possible. When he had reached for the child with his left hand Desiree had grabbed both the bottom of the blade and his right wrist, and with one continuous motion fueled by everything inside her she had quickly turned the knife, and shoved it into him while at the same time having had positioned her right foot against the back wall for leverage. Then Pete had burst through the door and fired.

***

WHEN HE emerged from the woods, walking the two horses behind him, he glanced at the small pond beneath the waterfall. She wasn't there, but the memory of her in the water came back to him. Pete forced the vexatious image from his mind, wishing it would just die out and stay that way. Ely was in front of the shack and came running when he spotted Pete.

"Where's the wild pig? You ain't kilt no razorback, no deer or nothin'?"

"Not today, Ely. Where's your ma?" Desiree emerged from the shack and waved to him, carrying her daughter. The little girl's arms were around her mother's neck.

Pete walked over and tied the horses to the hitching rail. His excitement peaked because of what he was about to show her. He took his time though, savoring the moment. There she stood, happy to see him and even happier she and her children were safe, and the evil man who had tried to kill them was a long way off and under the ground. Otherwise she was poor as ever, or so she assumed. Perhaps it was a good thing he had stopped by her place after all, he concluded.

"What would you do if you were rich?" Pete asked. She looked at him the way someone might when confronted with a question they hadn't expected.

"If Ah was rich? Well, let me feature that a spell. Don't rightly know, 'ceptin' Ah'd git me and these youngins' away from here." She looked at Pete, assuming for some reason they were engaging in whimsical conversation. She decided to play along. "What would you do, Yankee?" She asked with a smile. The children had gone over to raid an anthill, Ely in the lead, stick in hand. Little Desiree was looking for a stick too, pleading with her brother to give her his. Ely always found the best sticks.

"How about if I gave some fortune I might've found to you?" Pete replied. Desiree looked closer at him. There was a sparkle in his narrowed eyes that caused a tingling sensation to grow in the pit of her stomach.

"You playin' with me, Yank?" Her own eyes narrowed as a look of curious anticipation stole over her face. Pete smiled and went over to the saddlebags on Yankee. He brought them back slung over his shoulder, and sat on the front step.

"Have a seat," he said, patting his hand upon a spot next to him. She sat down, not taking her eyes off him. Still smiling he opened the saddlebags. "Look inside."

"My sweet Jesus," Desiree said as she stared at the gold. She started to ask him where he got it but she had already figured most of that out. "How much is it, Pete?"

"Four thousand Yankee dollars."

"Four *thousand?* There ain't that much money in the whole of Georgia!" She said, still staring inside the saddlebags.

"There was and still is," Pete said, his grin growing larger. "And it's yours." He couldn't bring himself to mention the hundred of it he had planned on keeping. As it turned out he didn't have to.

"Half maybe." She said, her mind spinning. "Don't know what Ah'd do with that much even."

"Get away from here, remember? And I'm not taking half. A hundred will do me." That got her attention. She finally stopped looking at the gold.

"Do you for what? You goin' somewheres?"

"After a little while. Can't stay here. No telling when the next one will arrive, maybe more than one."

"It's settled then." Desiree said. "We're all headin' out tomorrow."

Pete hadn't considered her leaving until she mentioned it, therefore the thought of a well-heeled Desiree and her children actually going through the motions of pulling up stakes and moving, the practical application of actually doing it, hadn't crossed his mind either. Coming with him had been even further from his thoughts. Still, it made sense, if only for her protection. Most anyone, especially a young woman and two small children traveling alone during those times would be taking a risk. Besides, if the authorities were after him they were looking for just one man, a scrawny Yankee at that, not some well-fed husband traveling with his family. All of them would be better off.

"Tomorrow it is," Pete replied, "first light."

***

"I HEARD back from General Smithington, Delicia." Clifton told her after they made their way into the company parlor and sat on the loveseat. "As I feared, there's nothing he can do."

"He can't even get Billy reassigned? His folks, all of us, are worried sick. He's in the thick of it, Clifton, and he's just a boy."

"One among many, my dear. He's too far off for the general to help," Clifton lied. He hadn't, of course, even communicated with Smithington regarding Billy McCabe. "Like he said, the military is in dire need of medical personnel regardless of their age, within reason of course. Any young man who worked in a hospital tending wounded soldiers is of great value to the Union, even if he's only sixteen."

"Fifteen, Clifton. And Billy is years away from being a *young man*. I don't know what this country has come to if it needs to rely upon children to do its fighting!" Delicia paused, and corrected herself. "That was unfair of me, wasn't it. I apologize."

"No reason to, darling." Clifton said as he took her hand. "These trying times have all of us distraught. I pray nightly for young Billy, as we all do. I have also prayed that if God blesses you and me with a son of our own he will be half the emerging man young Billy McCabe has become."

"Clifton, please. Everything has me so upset. I don't mean to toy with your affections, but at least for now could you please continue to be patient and understanding?"

"Of course I will, Delicia darling. But may I at least show you something? It's not an offering as such, but a promise for sometime in the future when you are less troubled." He reached in his pocket and pulled out a small velvet box. She didn't make a move to take it so Clifton opened it himself.

It didn't surprise her coming from Clifton, but the size of the five carat diamond did. It sparkled brilliantly, in a garish sort of way, as if it were not only capable of displaying vanity but entitled to do so. Delicia just looked at it and sighed. Clifton, not surprisingly, misread her response.

"It does take one's breath away," he said as he marveled at it, recalling how much it had cost. "I'm praying that someday you will wear it proudly."

"It makes quite an impression," was Delicia's only reply.

Clifton put it away, convinced she had been at least impressed. They talked of other things. Clifton asked how her parents were holding up, taking the opportunity to make his eyes brim with tears after he mentioned Linda Marie's name. Delicia didn't want to discuss the subject of their engagement so he figured he might as well show her his sensitive side, or rather his impressive ability to invent one.

"Father appears strong, but it's only for Mother's sake, and my sisters'."

"Not yours, my dear?"

"Oh yes, and I have been doing the same for him and Mother. I'm worried about Ginny though. She just received a letter from Robert McCabe. He has always sent nothing but cheerful letters in the past, but his latest one insinuated a darker side that no doubt can be blamed on the war. No mention of his music which was odd, he loves it so or did, but he did mention he'd refused a commendation for bravery in action. Said the military was hypocritical to make such a fuss over him, since so many brave soldiers had died doing so much more than himself, yet didn't receive proper recognition for their gallantry."

"I'm not surprised another McCabe has proven to be brave, as well as unselfish. Not unlike our dear Pete, God rest his soul." *That had better be the case, damn his arrogant eyes.* Clifton said to himself, reaching for his handkerchief.

***

THEY NEEDED to purchase a wagon, and as soon as Pete and Desiree came upon a farm or small town that's what he planned to do. He had several gold coins in his pocket, with the rest hidden the same way Stalworthy had done. Whatever else that alleged Rebel lieutenant had been he hadn't been foolish, until it had mattered most. At least he had known how to hide his money, Pete concluded.

Pete was still puzzled by the contents of the two duffle bags he had found on Stalworthy's mare after he had been killed; the two jars filled with some strange liquid, the Union and Confederate uniforms and all the rest raised more questions than they answered. It was another perplexing reason to get away from enemy territory, away from everything and everyone still infected with the disease of war and what clung to it.

Desiree had left virtually everything she owned back at the shack. She had only taken along food, clothes, the shotgun, some cooking utensils and a few sentimental pieces of jewelry her late mother had passed on to her, if the knickknacks could be called such. They weren't worth anything to anyone else, if they had to reach in their pockets. The pieces were all she owned that she could touch to remind her of her mother who had died after a life that would have been completely filled with bitterness if it hadn't been for her wonderful daughter. The only good thing that had happened to the poor woman besides that was when Desiree's father had been hung.

Desiree had dismissed Pete's questions about her own husband's possible return. Beardsley was probably dead and in most respects he already was, at least to her. He had a good heart if it was still beating, but not only had he been lacking when it came to providing for her and the children, she knew what would happen to the money if he ever got his hands on it. Even a huge sum of nearly four thousand dollars wouldn't last long. After awhile luxuries would become necessities to him, and Beardsley would end up unable to support whatever lifestyle he eventually stumbled upon.

Better to start a new life for her and the children. Little Desiree didn't even remember her father, and Ely had stopped asking about him now that "Mr. Pete" had come into his life. Pete had certainly come into Desiree's life as well, although she thought he wasn't aware of her deeper feelings. He talked about that Yankee gal, Delicia, in a way that told her to be careful. Still, if given enough time...

The children were a handful though, especially Little Desiree, what with having to keep them on the horses as they rode along. Ely was perched proudly behind Pete on Yankee, and insisted he wanted nothing to do with "no derned wagon" the adults kept talking about buying. If he couldn't stay with Mr. Pete, whom he was supposed to now be calling Pa which intrigued him, then he wanted a horse of his own; a white one, white as a cloud, not a speck of any other color anywhere on him. He had to be a boy horse too - *that* was non-negotiable.

***

THE GENERAL terrain of northwest Georgia they were traversing was an assortment of hills, valleys, meadows and miles of unending forest. As the travelers headed north they encountered the southern Appalachians, a mountainous area with long, deeper valleys and thicker woods. A wagon, for the most part, meant they would have to stay on established roads that often times were nothing more than wagon traces, if that.

Staying in the open didn't appear to be as risky now that Pete was a family man. He was far enough away from where he'd escaped that any of the few locals they might happen upon wouldn't likely have any knowledge of him anyway. A military patrol or Home Guard unit might possess such knowledge, but he no longer resembled an emaciated escapee. He was still somewhat underweight but improving, and had a healthy glow about him.

The important thing he had to keep in mind was his northern accent. He tried to imitate Desiree and the children, but he was woefully lacking when it came to mimicking another region's dialect. Folks would know he wasn't from, and certainly didn't belong there, and even if they weren't about to get involved personally, they could spread word some Yankee was traveling through their midst. If he wasn't an escaped prisoner or a spy he sure was lost, and beyond unwelcome; especially if some Home Guard unit stumbled upon him. An idea came to Desiree.

"Why don't you try and sound like you're from Europe someplace." She offered on their second day of travel. "You know, Italy or some such place."

"Never heard anybody from Italy talk. Knew some Germans back home though. A few Swedish folks too, over Geneva way along the Fox River."

"Well try an' talk like them folks then."

"I doubt I'd be any good imitating those folks either, Desiree."

"So what's that gotta do with the price'a cotton? Lord, Pete, ain't likely anybody in these parts ever heard them folks speak a word. Least ways you sure ain't gonna fool nobody tryin' ta talk regular, like us. We're country, not stupid."

She had a point. From then on, Pete had grown up in Berlin unless he discovered Stockholm was a better fit. He hoped any locals, however, and especially any Home Guard unit they ran into happened to be a little feeble-minded, or prone to disregard all but obvious threats.

***

IT WAS a farm, but to Pete it didn't look like much of one. It was small, and the farmer who had cleared the land over the years looked as if the backbreaking labor had at least crippled him. Clearing the thick woods must have been bad enough, but dealing with all the stumps, roots and vast number of rocks, both large and larger, must have been a monumental task. *That* had sure aged him.

At least the farmer was glad to get rid of a nearly used up wagon hiding in a stand of shortbread plumegrass, but the horses were a different matter. The crusty, middle-aged man who looked much older had but three, and was only willing to part with one; the worst of an aging, worn out lot. Pete told him, with motions more than words, he had only forty dollars, but at least it was in the form of two genuine Double Eagles. The gnarled man was impressed by the gold but not Pete's manner of speech.

"Where you hale from, mister?" He asked, as if he were addressing some damned foreigner with a speech impediment. Actually, he was.

"I comepth frem Beerleen, in Dercherland." Desiree had to cover her mouth and look away. Ely glared at him as if his new father had lost *all* his marbles. It was hard to tell what the farmer was thinking, although he had apparently never heard of "Dercherland".

"You're a fer piece from home, wherever the hell that be. Got yourself a wagon an' horse though." Pete also insisted the farmer throw in some food, but all the man's wife would part with was a loaf of bread and some questionable fatback.

They were barely out of earshot when Desiree lost all control. Pete wasn't amused, or so he pretended. *Desiree's laugh is as warm as her eyes,* he thought. Since his inner smile refused to fade, he attempted to pacify the enchantment he felt that had been generated by Desiree's demeanor by concentrating, as best he could, upon his memory of Delicia's entrancing laughter. His effort wasn't wholly in vain, but Desiree's charm lingered as well, as if he were caught up in an enchanting dilemma, the significance of which was so profound he had to deceive himself in order to diminish its intensity.

***

THEY WERE camped one evening in a small clearing just off the winding dirt and weed wagon trace they had been on for several days when about twenty riders approached. They didn't possess an intrinsic look of Confederate cavalrymen, but they were well-armed. After spotting the wagon and noticing the campfire and frying fat-back they had first smelled from nearly a quarter mile away, they pulled up their horses and put away their guns after seeing nothing but a family of civilians.

The lead man, obviously in charge, dismounted and approached. Pete hadn't made a move towards his rifle that was with his saddle which was over a fallen tree, but he had both of Stalworthy's revolvers strapped on.

"I'm Captain Waylen Buckston, you folks seen any riders today?" The captain seemed to ignore how close Pete's hands were to the guns he was wearing.

Pete gestured as if they hadn't seen anyone, shaking his head. "Noo," was all he said, managing to butcher his feeble attempt at an accent with even that short utterance. Desiree stood immediately and moved next to him.

"Wilhelm don't speak much, Captain, him bein' German an' all. We ain't seen nobody though."

"What's a German doin' 'round these parts? Not too many foreigners end up anywheres hereabouts Ah ever heard tell of, least ways not these days."

"Comepth heir to marry frawleen, mien capateen." Pete felt Desiree's elbow, her expression unchanged. For such a slender young thing she sure was strong. He recalled the knife buried to the hilt in Stalworthy.

"He understands English better'n speaks it, Captain." She said, sounding apologetic. "You wouldn't be havin' some coffee, would you sir? Be pleased ta brew it up for you an' your men if you do. We're fresh out."

"Well, if you folks don't mind, Ah reckon we could camp here tonight. Corporal! Bring some canteens and coffee!" Captain Buckston called over. "Be safer for y'all if we stay. We've been chasin' some no-account Yankees that cain't be too fer off. Ain't regular army, least ways they ain't no more. Deserters, Ah s'pect. Murderin' thieves, more like it."

The captain and two of his men sat around the fire and talked, mostly to Desiree. Whatever Pete was, he wasn't much of a conversationalist which was a relief to the captain. Even when that damned German did try to talk, the captain thought, it didn't make much sense. Captain Buckston said they were a partisan warfare brigade, even if there were only twenty of them. They weren't Home Guard though, and he bristled when Desiree had asked if they were.

"Ah used ta ride with Nathan Forrest but we parted company after Shiloh." Pete looked more closely at him then, wondering if he had fought against him that day on the rocky hill. Pete hoped the man didn't have the kind of memory that pesters until it has its answer, the kind with an eye for detail that eventually comes into focus.

"Ah ain't much fer army regulations, orders and such. Forrest is a good horse soldier, but it was like tryin' ta reason with a mule. He never could let a disagreement go 'til it been resolved ta his likin'. What it was didn't matter much. Exact color'a some damned clouds come evenin' or which flank ta strike, he couldn't abide no opinion but his. We both come 'round ta thinkin' it was best we parted. No hard feelins' though."

The next morning the men rode off, after again warning their hosts to keep a sharp eye out. The men they were after hated southerners, and it wasn't likely they'd be too fond of Germans either.

***

IT WAS slow going anyway, but two days later after a drenching rain had completed its handiwork the road was a quagmire. Nearly every time they came upon the bottom of a rise, let alone a steep grade, Pete had to hitch Yankee to the front of the wagon to help the other two horses get it moving through the deep mud that was present in low spots where water had settled. Sometimes both he and Desiree had to push from the rear with Ely astride Yankee, urging on the stallion and other horses. Pete again marveled at Desiree's strength as the adults pushed.

"I have a kid brother back home I know you could whip if you weren't inclined to kiss him first. All the girls like Billy boy." Pete mentioned after a particularly grueling bout with the wagon.

"Even Delicia?" Desiree asked, immediately wishing she hadn't. Pete didn't seem to mind.

"Oh, she's commented about what a heartbreaker he's gonna be in a few years, especially her younger sister's heart, although breaking it is the last thing on that boy's mind. Billy's always had his heart set on her. I s'pect Linda Marie is quite a sight these days. Almost as pretty as Delicia when I left." Desiree definitely wished she hadn't brought her up.

"Well, maybe Ah'll take a shine ta one'a them other brothers you're always talkin' 'bout." That stopped Pete cold.

"Desiree, I was plannin' on gettin' you and the children as far as Chattanooga, figured you'd be safe there. Union might just have control of all Tennessee by now. At least the war shouldn't bother you there if that's true."

"You let me worry about that Pete McCabe, and Ah'll be makin' up mah own mind about where Ah end up, thank you. Ah was only joshin' you. You must be right full'a yourself!" She stalked off and climbed in the wagon, as if it were Little Desiree who needed comforting.

***

THEY WEREN'T sure how far they were from the Tennessee border. Pete had been through wilderness areas before, but northwest Georgia had offered up at least as much as he had ever experienced. It seemed to go on forever, day after day. He had also been born and raised a flatlander. His idea of a mountain was what locals in northwest Georgia referred to as a hill, and not a very impressive one at that by their comparisons. "We'll git a better idea after we git ta the top'a that hill yonder," Desiree might say, and to Pete he might as well been sitting astride Yankee at the foot of the Rocky Mountains. German Alps more like it; he was beginning to feel, albeit delusional, comfortable in his new role or so he let on.

To help pass the long hours it wasn't uncommon for Pete to break into his rendition of a German immigrant. He maintained he needed the practice, but the merriment he elicited from Desiree and Ely was his true motivation. Even Little Desiree would get involved in the laughter, wanting to join in the fun even if she wasn't sure why everyone was so happy.

***

THEY HAD come to the summit of a short plateau when Pete thought he'd seen something move amongst the trees to their right in the valley below. He wasn't sure, but after so many days and miles of virtually nothing but the same basic terrain he had grown accustomed to most of its nuances. He didn't think it had been a deer but it may have been, or perhaps a bear or like-sized animal. He didn't think so, however, as he continued to survey the area and told Desiree to keep her eye on that general area as well.

"There somethin' is," but neither of the adults had spoken. "There's another one, did ya see 'em?" Ely asked. Pete and Desiree looked closer. Nothing.

"Are you sure you saw somethin', darlin'?" Desiree asked the boy as she sat next to him in the wagon. Perhaps he was just saying it because he was still pouting over not being allowed to ride with "Pa" that afternoon and was just looking for some attention.

"Not somethin', some*one*." Ely replied, still watching. "There was two of 'em, two men."

"On horseback, Ely?" Pete asked, knowing that's not what he had seen.

"No, Pa. Just two men. They was watchin' us."

Pete hadn't seen anything else but wasn't so sure Ely hadn't spotted something. He looked around for a place to pull over and hide, but there was nothing but thick forest on either side of them as the wagon trace descended into a valley. He pulled out a revolver and handed it to Desiree, then removed his Henry from its saddle scabbard.

"Get the kids down. Might as well stay here for now. No place to go anyway. Keep your eyes and ears open." Ely protested but got down with his sister, keeping his head just above the side of the wagon, still watching. He hadn't made up a thing.

Whatever may have been out there didn't appear again. They sat still for almost an hour since moving the wagon would have created too much noise, with Pete and Desiree standing by the wagon they kept between themselves and the right side of the wagon trace. He occasionally glanced across the wagon trace in all directions, listening intently, but there was nothing besides thick woods and brush along with the familiar sounds of a few birds and other forest noises. If anyone was nearby, most of those sounds would have altered, decreased, or perhaps stopped altogether. They decided to move on, keeping a close watch the whole time.

They kept going through the moonlit night. The children had grown antsy but the small group kept moving. The children finally fell asleep; first Little Desiree and then Ely, although he had managed to fight it off for quite awhile. He had asked for one of Pete's revolvers then demanded it, but all he ended up with was another reason to conclude life was indeed unfair if you were only eight. He couldn't wait to turn ten.

At morning's first light Pete was fighting to keep his eyes open. He looked over at Desiree. She was sitting up, sort of, but mostly asleep. The two horses pulling the wagon just kept plodding along, even if they resented the unfairness of their plight as much as Ely. Finally their indignation and exhaustion became too much for them. They had come to a rude wooden bridge over a narrow creek, deep for its size, and decided it was time to lodge a protest. Besides, there was a small meadow on the right side of the wagon trace and the thick grass, impregnated with other delectable looking plants, proved irresistible to the hungry animals.

Pete looked around, listening carefully now that the wagon wasn't moving, but nothing seemed out of place. Perhaps, if the earlier sightings had been men at all they were just local hunters or men simply going about their business. It had been at least fifteen hours or so since the encounter, so Pete assumed there was little to worry about, since anyone so inclined would have already made, in all likelihood, their move.

Desiree stirred as did the children. Pete, numbed by the all night journey, had her pull the wagon a little ways into the meadow. She drove it to the side of the woods south of the meadow so no one who may have been following would be able to spot it, at least from the wagon trace, until they had been spotted or at least heard first. Even so, Pete told Desiree to keep an eye on the woods as well. He bedded down in the back of the wagon and fell asleep almost immediately.

Three hours later the children's playing awakened him, and the smell of frying fatback kept him that way. Desiree tended to the cooking as the children continued to play along the shore of the small creek that ran along the north side of the small meadow. Ely was determined to find the source of a croaking bullfrog while trying to keep Little Desiree from walking ahead of him. It was an overcast day and looked to stay that way.

Pete stood up in the wagon, stretched, then decided to head into the woods across the wagon trace. He didn't need to go far to get a little privacy, and proceeded to do his business. Fifteen minutes later he emerged from the woods and walked back across the wagon trace.

He could hear the fatback still crackling in the skillet, and if his sense of smell wasn't fooling with him it smelled like it was burning. He noticed one of the horses was missing; the one Desiree had been riding before they had hitched it to the wagon. He saw the other horse in the middle of the meadow, concerning itself with the delectable grass and plants. Pete's heart began pounding in his chest as he hurried past the wagon. He didn't see Yankee either, or anyone else. It was as if they had all simply disappeared.

Pete had been groggy from just three hours sleep, but the rush of adrenalin had shocked him wide-awake as he pulled a revolver from its holster and immediately followed the tracks into the woods south of the wagon. He went in about twenty feet then stopped and listened - hardly a sound. Even the chirping of morning birds had diminished, and Pete imagined the ones still making their short, high-pitched sounds did so cautiously, as if they were issuing warnings. He couldn't see much, as thick as the forest was throughout the entire area, but the tracks of the two missing horses were visible. He assumed they couldn't have gone far, yet half an hour later he had not only lost sight of any tracks, but hadn't seen anything else of note either.

Panic-stricken and at a loss, he considered the possibility the horses had gone one way and whatever people were involved another, at least some of them. He made his way back to the clearing and inspected the footprints amidst the damp grass. He couldn't tell with any degree of certainty if that had indeed been the case and cursed himself for not having conducted a more thorough search of all the prints before chasing after the initial ones he had spotted.

What the hell has happened? He wondered. There had been no sounds of a struggle which was highly unusual; not even the children had made a sound, nor the missing horses, not even Yankee. Desiree would have certainly called out but all she and the children had done, as well as the two horses, was simply vanish. His Henry rifle was gone along with the saddlebags that contained all his ammunition. He had the six shots in each of his revolvers, but that was all. His saddle was missing too, and with it the $2,400 in gold coins. He chastised himself for even considering the money.

He went over everything in his mind but had nothing to go on except the obvious disappearances. Nothing made sense. Was it possible Desiree had lit out with someone? Had he insulted or hurt her pride when he had said he was planning on leaving her in Chattanooga? Even if that had been the case which he knew was extremely unlikely, how come he hadn't been able to easily catch up with someone encumbered by a woman, two children and two horses? Why hadn't he been able to anyway? And why had the trail of tracks leading out of the meadow disappeared? Nothing made sense at all.

He just stood there and looked around, but not for long. He had to do something, look somewhere. He went over to the wagon to get some food for his journey, but it too was missing - all of it. Only the clothes and utensils Desiree had brought along were still there. He tossed the burnt fatback on the thick grass to cool it off. It was black and smoking. He wolfed it down even though his hunger had abated, then was on his way.

Pete spent the next few hours following what few tracks reappeared. He had decided to follow what may have been a second set but it was no use. He wasn't a skilled tracker to begin with, and in his agitated state he either missed what a proficient tracker would have noticed or misidentified what he had found.

He finally sat down on a log, every bit as confused and puzzled as when he had started - and he was lost. The heavily overcast day meant he could only guess at the sun's location; he wasn't even sure which way would take him back to the small meadow. He heard the movement of something large heading towards him through the forest and brush. Two men were approaching, dressed in remnants of worn-out Yankee uniforms. They hadn't spotted him yet, but just as he reached for his revolvers a voice from behind stopped him cold.

"Touch them guns, you're a dead man."

XXVI

Missy Nell and Jennifer kept themselves busy with remodeling and landscaping projects, although sometimes it felt as if there were too many hours in any given day, time that allowed concerns best kept at bay to intrude. Along with the house Jennifer had purchased for Missy Nell and Cusman, she had also purchased one for herself a few blocks away from the Sable home. It was a small Cape Cod shaded by mature oaks, and the grounds were more flower garden and ground cover than lawn. It wasn't near as large as the Sable two story framed colonial, but it was perfect for a single woman who had no intention of altering her marital status in the foreseeable future, if at all.

She hadn't obtained a divorce or dared try. If the subject arose she was a widow, and if there were further questions of a personal nature she let it go at that, insisting it was too painful to revisit. She was now Jennifer Windsor, assuming Trenton had finally realized she was probably still alive. If he had, which was all but a given, she had to believe he would either stop at nothing, or do nothing at all. She strongly suspected the former.

There was a great deal of excitement being shared by the women; Missy Nell was pregnant and her doctor suspected twins. Missy Nell and Jennifer weren't so sure. The Sable men were notorious for siring very large babies. Cusman had been over nine pounds at birth, almost ten. Regardless, Missy Nell had obviously begun to show.

The impending birth did usher in some pensive reflection, at least for Jennifer. She had always felt a hole inside ever since she had made up her mind to leave Whisper Manor and Trenton, but not necessarily because of those considerations. Her sons were a different matter, and with Missy Nell being pregnant the hole inside Jennifer had grown so deep it was impossible to ignore.

She prayed Trenton Jr. and Marcus were still in Europe, but with all that had happened who could tell what Trenton might have allowed? They were his sons as well, so perhaps he had continued to protect them. After what his response had been when he discovered what she had done, however, there was no telling what he might do to punish her. They had her blood in them, so anything was possible even if Trenton did think she was dead.

He had always been, like his ancestors, a big believer in the pureness of blood lines. How many times had he sold off the children of slaves when he had determined they were in any way tainted? He had even killed one when his rage had overtaken his usual business priorities, drowning the mulatto baby girl himself within hours of her birth. He had already warned the grief-stricken sixteen-year-old mother, on two occasions no less, not to dally with the white help. He had been beside himself with rage even though the grief-stricken girl had insisted her participation hadn't been consensual.

On that occasion, if Trenton had believed there would have been no chance of legal reprisals he would have taken a bullwhip to the father, the overseer's son. On other occasions, rare as they had been, it was a given any child suffering a birth defect was "put down" as Trenton and the previous patriarchs of Whisper Manor, amongst others, described it. Tainted blood was just that, and since on a number of occasions he had demonstrated how he dealt with such things, Jennifer's concern continued to deepen, creating a troublesome place in her heart.

There wasn't anything Jennifer could do, however, at least not for the present. If she somehow learned unequivocally Trenton had died that would be different; she might be able to contact her sons. She didn't know how she could ever find out. Her own sister didn't know what had become of her and there was no way Jennifer would chance writing her, or hire a detective; what if he succumbed to greed once his inquires took him to Whisper Manor, or to her sister's home? No telling how her brother-in-law Tredwell would react, but Jennifer knew it would probably involve alerting Trenton. It was best to leave those things alone, at least for the time being, and concentrate on the present and immediate future.

She finally wrote her sister anyway, mailing the letter from Boston as a precautionary measure after securing a post office box, but had received no response. She had obscured her identity and the letter's content in case Tredwell read it. Jennifer had taken the precaution to such a degree even her sister may not of known its author, since Jennifer had resorted to printing instead of using longhand. Jennifer doubted that was the case, which could mean her sister had disowned her or it had been lost in the mail or worse yet, discovered first by Tredwell; upon more objective appraisal, she came to realize any suspicious letter would likely point to her.

Jennifer had taken a risk, perhaps a big one, and was regretting it. Those concerns had also kept her from writing her sons in Europe, assuming they were still there. She had been sorely tempted to do so, but finally concluded it was best to hold off until she had a clearer understanding of what, if anything, was transpiring back in Georgia.

Missy Nell had received several letters from Cusman and had of course written him. She had believed she might be pregnant and had mentioned it to Cusman prior to his departure, but she wished he could have been with her when it had been confirmed. She had missed a few cycles, but never experienced morning sickness. Now that she knew the truth it pained her she had missed the look in Cusman's eyes when he had found out for sure. She could just feature him reading her letter by lantern light in his tent, or perhaps around a campfire, and could envision him looking north with a smile on his face. Sometimes she felt his smile as well, wishing she could ease the wistfulness she knew it contained.

She was always wondering how things were going for him, and more importantly when he would return. She prayed it would be before she gave birth, but who could tell? The stunning Gettysburg victory and General Grant's coinciding victory at Vicksburg on July 4th had generated a great deal of hope in the North, and many thought the war was won even if it wasn't over, so perhaps it wouldn't last too much longer. Still, Cusman was away, and although his last letter said he was in Georgia of all places, she wasn't sure just where. He wasn't still in Georgia however; he was in South Carolina, not far from Charleston. A place called James Island.

***

ON JULY 10th the men of the 54th Massachusetts were elated after having received word of the Union victories at Gettysburg and Vicksburg. Federal forces camped on Folly Island had overrun the Confederate defenses on three quarters of Morris Island and were stopped only by a large, strategically placed earthwork called Battery [or Fort] Wagner. They had found Southern newspapers in the trenches they had overrun on Morris Island, and if those always biased reports conceded their Sons of the South had been defeated then the victories must have indeed been spectacular.

Colonel Shaw had been beside himself. Union Major General Quincy Gillmore, aiming to attack Charleston, had undertaken operations against Morris Island but had excluded the 54th Massachusetts from his plans. The first phase had gone well for the Union, so the general relented and told Shaw he and his men would see action if the Confederates made a move on Sol Legare and James Islands.

On July 16th that's what had happened. The 54th acquitted itself well in repulsing the Rebel attack near Grimball's Causeway. Their fierce resistance allowed the 10th Connecticut to escape a trap set by Confederate Colonel Carleton Way. Vicious hand-to-hand fighting had ensued, and the Confederates had been forced to grudgingly accept men of color were indeed formidable opponents. Even the understandably biased Charleston Courier reported the fighting abilities of the Yankee Negro troops surpassed that of the other Union forces, although certain white Yankee soldiers insisted the newspaper's objective was to insult them as opposed to reporting the facts. The black Yankees and their white officers knew better.

Afterwards both sides discovered the hungry fiddler crabs didn't care what color the corpses had been as the creatures foraged amongst them. The horrors of war weren't confined to the actions of humans. The crabs had devoured the soft tissue of the dead soldiers with an appalling tenacity. Coming upon a corpse covered with the ravenous creatures, sometimes hundreds of them fighting over the flesh and entrails, left more than a few men traumatized. Their nightmares didn't need more encouragement, but the gruesome sight grew like a tumor inside some of the men. Some awoke screaming, flailing at the hideous creatures that refused to let go as if hell itself held sway over them.

Shaw was informed he and his men had more than proven their mettle. They would be involved with the attack on Fort Wagner. Not only that, they would be given the honor of having the lead position. It may have been an honor, but Colonel Shaw knew the terrain and what they would be up against. During the late afternoon on July 18th he made sure to give a reporter with the New York Daily Tribune who was covering the campaign several letters and other personal papers. Shaw most certainly did realize what they were up against.

***

AS TWILIGHT approached on that day Sergeant Cusman Sable helped form the regiment on the beach, and with the rest of the men awaited Colonel Shaw's arrival. The air was thick with humidity and the smell of the ocean, which during happier times would have been invigorating - would have been *peaceful*.

None of them were long-time veterans of warfare, experienced men who could take a brief look at a given situation and determine what they were up against. Regardless, all of them realized they were about to embark upon a very hazardous mission, if not a suicidal one. Some men prayed out loud as they prepared for battle, others were more subdued but equally reverent, but most of them simply stared ahead, their stoic expressions stone-cold and deliberate if their eyes didn't give them away. Most of them would rather die than shirk from the task at hand, or wanted to appear that way. They were on a beach, at a momentous time in their lives as well as history itself, and soon they would again prove to themselves and everyone else men of color could confront anything others had been compelled to face. Those other men had persevered, or died trying, and so would the men of the 54th. If some of them wanted to turn back, and like any number of soldiers at such a moment that was a natural inclination, it was something practically all of them kept deep within their most private recesses. Turning back may have been a natural inclination for some, but it was no match for the overwhelming sense of resolve possessed by virtually all the men of the 54th Massachusetts.

***

CUSMAN STEPPED away for a moment and walked closer to shore. He gazed out over the water, and found himself feeling envious of the endless waves that lapped upon the sand. Waves could dissipate and reappear but could not be harmed, and even if something could harm them the ocean had countless more at its disposal. How many millenniums worth had already come and gone despite anything civilizations had done, had deemed important, Cusman wondered. How many more centuries would pass before anything could even approach making an impression on such a powerful, seemingly disinterested entity? Or perhaps a wise one, he considered. Men were again on the brink of destroying each other, but even if the eternal, patient waves weren't impressed by another of mankind's countless follies, Cusman knew his cause was justified and its unshakeable morality every bit as eternal as the waves.

He wasn't going to be around for hundreds of thousands of years, but he was in the here and now; and heavily armed men dressed in butternut and gray that were defending everything he despised were waiting just a few hundred yards away. He wondered how they could feel so righteous, so utterly convinced they were following the only moral path that could possibly exist no matter how many eons had, or would pass. How could so many be so wrong, he wondered, so *im*moral? The ocean tossed another wave across the sand, almost reaching, at the very least, Cusman's feet.

He could hear the sounds of an army preparing for battle behind him, sounds that had themselves been made for thousands of years by countless armies, but Cusman still hesitated to turn around and rejoin them. He had a few more minutes, at least he had those, even if the ocean remained unimpressed with his woefully inadequate definition of time.

He thought of Missy and their unborn child. Maybe it would be twins, but he too doubted it since he couldn't recall any who had been borne in his family. Perhaps at some point in time, twins had been borne in Missy's family. If so, it could sure enough happen again. A girl and a boy he hoped, then four or five more. He would come home and finish college and make all of them proud. They would respect him, and not just because he was their father. He would protect all of them, and teach them the value, the *necessity* of protecting themselves. Missy and he would live to be a hundred or so, he could just feature it.

The ocean offered another wave that glistened briefly against the sand in the fading twilight as if it were trying to tell him something, he imagined. *It hopes I can understand, knows I cain't too, not the whole of it, but maybe enough…*

Children, grandchildren, and great grandchildren would grow and thrive in a world so different from the one he, his parents, their parents and so on through the ages had been forced to endure. Another wave came calling then dissipated in what seemed to be patient frustration, but no longer void of all hope. He looked northward, hundreds of yards away, at the distant thirty foot sand and earth wall of the fort they were about to attack across the beach they would soon be rushing across, the beach he would have to get through and back again to make it home. Cusman took a deep breath then turned and went back to his regiment. Colonel Shaw and the rest of his officers had arrived. It was time.

***

THE MEN had expected a short speech, but all they had to do was look at their commander. Words weren't necessary. Everyone knew why. Cusman formed ranks with several of the men he had been with that day in Darien and again during the hand-to-hand carnage near Grimball's Causeway. They had become close in a way only those types of experiences can forge. Two of the six men who had been with him at Darien had been killed on James Island and two more wounded, one grievously, but many others were still on the beach with Cusman - where they had to be.

One friend of Cusman's had been wounded in the left arm and leg but he could still shoot. His thigh was very sore from a Minie ball that had removed a piece of it, but for some reason it hurt more to walk than run. Once they were ordered to charge he would barely notice it at all.

The Union bombardment of Fort Wagner from both land and sea ended. Colonel Shaw faced his men and drew his sword, the blade zinging as it escaped its scabbard.

"Men of the 54th, *forward!*" A deep-throated hurrah arose from the depths of the marching men of the 54th Massachusetts and the Union brigades directly behind them, a total of nearly 5,000 strong.

No one heard the ocean sigh. No one ever did.

***

THE UNION soldiers broke into a full scale charge when the Confederate artillery began to explode amongst them. The Rebels atop the thirty foot walls of the fort opened up with their rifles, raining Minie balls into the charging blue mass. As the Yankees drew closer the fire intensified, or so it seemed. There was less than a sixty-yard-wide approach of beach to the fort with salt marshes to the west. An alarming amount of sand was soon covered with the blood of the dead and wounded, some maimed beyond recognition, ripped apart by the concussive shell bursts. The men kept charging.

Two friends of Cusman's on either side of him went down, one with a Minie ball that had shattered his skull and the other with one that had torn through his chest. The taller of the two had barely made it to Cusman's chin; how the Rebel marksmen had missed such a huge man as Cusman remained a wonderment.

If the previous Union bombardment of the fort had done damage it hadn't been appreciable. Confederates were all over the top of the wall firing from positions so secure it seemed as if the returning shots from the charging Yankees only added to the pandemonium. Occasionally a Rebel was hit or appeared to be, but he would no sooner fall before another took his place. Any Union soldier on the beach that evening who knew he would come through unscathed was either delusional or insanely so. Men were dropping everywhere, the screams of the wounded all but smothered by the roar of cannonade, rifle fire and the constant hollering of the charging men. A concussive shell would land in the mass of men and an explosion of body parts, blood and sand would fly into those nearby and points beyond. The sand would blind most of those closest, and in all the mayhem it was sometimes difficult to tell if the blood that covered them was theirs.

They kept charging, finally taking cover where it could be found outside the fort. They remained pinned down for what seemed an eternity. Most of the men who exposed themselves long enough in order to fire became targets immediately. They all knew their current position was untenable, and much of their former zeal had been replaced by terrifying uncertainty. Colonel Shaw finally concluded any fate, save capitulation, would be an improvement over the inevitable slaughter, so when dusk finally surrendered to darkness he did the opposite; hollering an order over the unrelenting din for a full scale attack. Most of his men complied without hesitation.

There was a somewhat shallow ditch in front of the walls, but it offered little cover. It was filled with five feet of water and was surrounded by sharpened palmetto spikes and buried land mines. Cusman leapt in and began firing. He had his repeating rifle and emptied it into the Confederates he could see atop the wall, dropping at least two of them best he could tell.

Minie balls whizzed by him as he stood waist deep in the water, firing and reloading. Time passed, losing all significance. A Minie ball suddenly tore into his right side. He dropped his rifle, lurched forward and fell upon the side of the ditch and ripped frantically at his blouse and shirt to assess the damage. The bullet had delivered just a flesh wound, but the blood still flowed.

He drew both of his Colt Lawman revolvers and fired as the enemy bullets kicked sand up around him. He reloaded his revolvers and along with a sizeable number of other men charged the walls. From that moment on any fighting would be at close range, a bloody hand-to-hand confrontation whose intensity would be equaled only by its savagery.

Another Minie ball struck and passed through Cusman's left forearm, just missing the bone. He looked at it in horror then glanced upwards. He saw Colonel Shaw, who had made it through the ditch and climbed on top of the parapet with a number of other men. Shaw fired his sidearm into the Rebels until it was empty then used it to motion the rest of the men in the ditch and at the base of the wall to continue following him and the others who were already with him. Cusman lurched forward, and looked with horrifying astonishment as Colonel Shaw took a Minie ball through his chest. His revolver fell from his hand as several other bullets slammed into him as well.

Cusman's horror was replaced with rage, and a moment later he was on the parapet. He fired both revolvers into as many Rebels as he could, then holstered them and grabbed a rifle someone had dropped. It had its bayonet in place, and a bleeding Cusman, along with dozens of other members of the 54th, engaged in the fierce hand-to-hand combat. The huge man would drive his bayonet so violently into a man even the barrel of the rifle would disappear. He lifted his victims in the air and flung their bodies onto others who were attacking, and attempted to kill them as well.

The mayhem was so intense most of the Rebels didn't have time to reload their muskets, at least the ones attempting to thwart the black Yankees who were amongst them. Very few of them attempted to engage Cusman in a man-to-man fight, choosing smaller men instead. They had plenty to choose from, but Cusman, growing light-headed from his wounds and the relentless rush of adrenalin, found the Rebels anyway.

A wounded Confederate who had been felled right next to Cusman by a bayonet to his stomach took out his knife and drove it into the huge man's calf, it being all the higher the dying man could reach. He slashed downward, opening an ugly wound almost to the ankle. Cusman let out a howl and brought his other foot down on the man's skull. It burst apart as if a ripe melon had been smashed against a stone floor.

Everything flashed white to black after an explosion of urgent, minute stars shot through Cusman's skull. He stumbled backwards and fell from the parapet, rolling onto the sand below. He momentarily regained a modicum of semi-consciousness as the din of battle blasted into his head, then felt a body roll on top of him, then another. The battle raged on.

"Sergeant Sable! Can you hear me?" The young private yelled, hunched over his fallen comrade as he frantically tied off Cusman's arm and leg wounds. Dead men were everywhere, and more were dying all around. "Sergeant! Can you hear me?" The private began to slap the large man, and Cusman's eyes opened. His head was covered with blood from the blow he had taken, and his other wounds had been bleeding profusely as well until they'd been tied off. "Can you make it to the marsh?" Minie balls kept spitting into the sand all around them.

Cusman tried to move, and with the help of the private half crawled and half limped towards the relative safety of the salt marshes west of the fort. Everything was still chaotic with men running, some tripping over bodies, going in all directions. A few of them had even made it deeper into the fort. Some went into the ocean, so panic-stricken they hadn't realized the direction they had been heading towards, or were beyond caring. The most seriously wounded drowned; others were shot then disappeared under the timeless, sighing waves.

***

OVER 1,500 UNION soldiers were dead or wounded, including over forty percent of the 54th Massachusetts. Almost all of their officers were dead as well. The Confederates has suffered less than two hundred casualties, and Cusman had been responsible for at least ten of them. Now it was all he could do to survive, if he didn't bleed to death first.

The Confederates were whooping and hollering at the retreating enemy, firing as fast as they could reload. They targeted anyone they could, especially as many black Yankees as possible, and killed many of the ones they could spot who had been wounded. They concentrated their fire, for the most part, on the sandy beach and any movement they saw in or near the ditch. If the young private hadn't finally arrived, Cusman would already be dead.

The two men crawled through the marsh, heading into it as far as they could while still crawling south. Nearly half an hour later they emerged, but when Cusman tried to remain standing after limping a ways he collapsed upon the beach close to shore. A wave eased around him and retreated towards the sea, taking some of Cusman with it. A damp, dark swath spread across the thirsty sand, its red hue darkened amidst the burnt orange glow of the nearby lantern light. The hue was most concentrated beneath and next to Cusman, losing its intensity as it disappeared under the departing waves when they reached the ocean. The next methodical wave, and the next, diluted the trail of blood further still. After several men finally carried Cusman away, any trace of his presence was eventually reclaimed by the yawing sea.

***

"I STILL don't know why you didn't bleed to death, Sergeant." The middle-aged doctor said. "Must be your size, near as I can tell. If infection doesn't set in, you just might make it." Cusman, dulled by laudanum and fatigue, looked at the doctor.

"How bad?" Was all he said.

"Gonna lose your left leg, Sergeant. Least ways half of it. Maybe part of your left arm, too."

"No I ain't," Cusman said, glaring at the man. "You or anyone else come near me with a saw, *I'll bust you to pieces.*"

"Then you'll die," the doctor replied, used to hearing such talk. "Your other wounds might not kill you but that leg wound's a different story. At least we can do something about that. Maybe infection won't set in, but if it doesn't it would be a miracle. Best to take it off now before it's too late." Cusman wouldn't budge.

"If it gets infected, I know how to take care of it." The doctor let out a sigh, then left.

"You forgot this bottle." Cusman called after him as he picked up the laudanum off the small stand next to his cot. The doctor kept going. Cusman dropped it on the ground of the hospital tent.

***

TWO NIGHTS later he was torched with fever and consumed by a shivering coldness more severe than he had ever felt, or thought possible. He looked around then forced himself out of his cot. He almost collapsed from the pain, or was it the fever? He couldn't tell. All he had on was a makeshift gown, but what was left of his pants was on the ground next to his cot. He bent over to retrieve them and then he did faint. When he came to it appeared as if no one had noticed, so he put them on. The left pant leg had been cut away. He took off the gown and put on his blouse, the pain almost causing him to faint again. He couldn't find his boots.

He could barely walk, but didn't have far to go. There was a fairly large hole several feet deep less than twenty feet behind the hospital tent. It was dark outside, but all he had to do was follow the stench. It was indeed dark, but he could hear the buzzing of thousands of flies, the intensity of their frenzied sound growing louder as he approached. He looked around and lit the lantern he had brought with him, the wounds to his body screaming at him.

He gazed into the mass of rotting legs, arms, feet and hands just below from where he stood. Some looked as if they had been put in the hole recently, others had obviously been there for days, putrefied and blackened by time and the unrelenting heat and humidity. He looked about until he spotted the movement he was looking for. He put the lantern on the ground along with the small leather bag he had also taken from the tent.

The off-white, slithering mass looked as if it were being balanced by someone holding a large cooking sheet and moving it around, trying not to spill its contents. The undulating mass moved with somewhat more urgency when Cusman reached down and began to scoop up handfuls of the maggots, trying to avoid the near jelly-like rot they were feasting upon. The insane buzzing of the flies intensified, seemingly frustrated since that was all they could do to protest his intrusion.

After having removed the bandages, Cusman began to place handfuls of maggots on his leg wound. He would have discovered it reeked almost as much as what was cooking in the hole, but it was impossible to distinguish from the two sources. Most of the maggots appeared to glissade off, others simply fell. Still others seemed content with their new food source; one rotting leg was as good as another. When he had as many on as he could keep in place, he wrapped his leg with fresh bandages from the small leather bag. He tied it loosely, but thoroughly enough to keep the maggots in place. Less than thirty-six hours later all the rotting flesh was gone; only healthy, pink tissue remained that was healing rapidly.

"It worked good enough for my pa," Cusman told the doctor when the bandages were removed. "Seems like you should know that instead'a just reachin' for your damned saw all the damned time."

"Time? Who the hell's got time, soldier?" The doctor said as he walked away.

XXVII

Pete stood stark still. He had no reason to believe the man standing behind him in the small clearing wouldn't shoot, and was somewhat surprised he hadn't already. Why was the man bothering to take a chance with some stranger who had just made a move towards two .44 caliber Colts strapped to his sides?

"Over here, Mitchell!" The man called out. The two men on horseback Pete had spotted earlier in the trees turned then headed towards the small clearing. Before long, three other riders emerged from the woods as well.

"Where's that no-account pa of yours, and your inbred brothers?" The man named Mitchell demanded, leveling his rifle at Pete. He was broad-shouldered, about Pete's age, dark hair and eyes, and had an air of authority about him exaggerated by his full beard.

"I'm not from around here, Captain." Pete answered, noticing the man's Union blouse.

"You sure as hell don't sound like it, I'll grant you that. And I'm no damned captain. Got this from the son of a bitch that wouldn't let me forget *he* was, though. Just who the hell are you?"

"Pete McCabe. I escaped from a Rebel prison camp. I'm from Illinois." Mitchell looked closer at him.

"You don't look rawboned enough to be no damned escapee. What was your unit?"

"1st Naperville Cavalry. Can I put my hands down?"

"Hand over that gun belt." Mitchell replied. Pete unbuckled it and handed it to the man behind him.

"I heard'a Naperville," the man behind Pete said. He was tall and wiry, with the appearance of someone who welcomed fighting, or was at least used to it. "Never been through it though. Ain't no damned train what stops there I know of."

"Where *is* Naperville?" Mitchell asked Pete. "And don't tell me Illinois, reckon I know that much."

"About thirty miles west of Chicago," Pete replied, "as the crow flies."

"That right, Dirch?"

"S'pect so, or thereabouts." The man replied, himself from DeKalb.

"All right then, looks like we don't have to kill ya, least ways not yet." Mitchell said, after letting out a stream of tobacco juice. "What prison camp?"

"Oglethorpe, down Macon way. Been travelin' awhile."

"S'pect you have, if you ain't lyin'. You seen any men?"

"We came across some Rebs a ways back. You're probably the men they were lookin' for."

"When? And whadda ya mean 'we' and how come they didn't just hang you?"

"I've been travelin' with a Southern gal and her kids I met up with a good ways south of here. They disappeared just a little while ago. I was lookin' for 'em when you showed up. Those Rebs thought I was her husband."

"I asked you *when*."

"Night before last. They took off south." Mitchell looked around and digested the news.

"Reckon I know what happened to that gal and her kids. Same damned hillbillies what's lookin' for us."

***

THE BRANCHES, thick underbrush and thorns had left cuts and scrapes all over Desiree and the children. All three of them were gagged. Their hands were tied behind them, even Little Desiree, and along with the gags had been since their abduction.

Two of the four men had watched Pete when he had emerged from the woods earlier that day. It was obvious he was unfamiliar with his surroundings and would be fooled by the false trail the men had left for him. They hadn't shot him because they also knew the others they were after were somewhere nearby. No sense in alerting them, but the two men had decided not to simply gut Pete with their knives; there probably wouldn't have been anything simple about it. The stranger had two revolvers, and besides, he had initially taken off in the wrong direction and had done so again after foolishly pausing first to eat. He'd probably be lost before long, they had reasoned. If someone didn't know those woods, valleys and mountains, it was sure enough an easy thing to do.

The ragged looking, odorous men had been aware of Pete and his small group's presence in the area for miles. Ely had spotted two of them after Pete had noticed something the day before. The mountain men had been looking for the Yankee deserters, but had instead investigated the trail left by the Confederate partisan brigade which had come across Pete, Desiree and the children, suspecting that trail had been made by their prey before the mountain men realized that wasn't the case; when they had noticed Desiree in the area, coupled with the fact they needed to backtrack anyway, they decided to follow her. Besides, those Yankees were looking for them too so they probably weren't going to vanish from the general area, not if they wanted their captured man back. The mountain men didn't know that was only one of the Yankees' objectives, and that getting Mitchell's kid brother back wasn't the reason they were still in the area.

Mitchell and his gang had raided a small homestead nearby and murdered the family. That had been bad enough, but the woman they had raped before torturing and killing her had been the youngest sister of Janny Beal. He was not only the patriarch of the family of men who had abducted Desiree and the children, but leader of the entire clan of mountain people who lived in the area. He was past sixty, but stood tall and straight. His peppered beard was a good ten inches below his chin and his fierce eyes didn't indicate the advancing years had inconvenienced him much. He had been a man to be reckoned with in his youth, even more so in later years after his deeds had cemented his legend. There wasn't a man alive who had ever bested him in a fight of any kind, but a fair number of dead and maimed ones had tried.

Most of the Beal clan families were third generation, their ancestors having arrived in the area decades before when it had been part of the Cherokee Nation, although other tribes had disputed that claim from time to time. The clan had all been skilled hunters and trappers, and the Cherokees had, for the most part, tolerated their presence. The Native Americans didn't need any help when it came to hunting and trapping, but over the years the clan had displayed a willingness to keep other whites out of that particular area so their presence had been deemed useful. Besides, they hadn't claimed the area as their own, with the exception of the small enclave nestled in the Low Cloud Valley area. That was where the men were taking Desiree and the children

There were close to seventy people living there, and although women made up over half the inhabitants, none of them were as fine looking as Desiree and already had husbands; most of them since they were thirteen or so. Although the opportunity seldom arose, abducting women such as Desiree had been going on for as long as the clan had been in existence. Any men who had been with the hapless women had almost always been murdered, and sometimes the children too. That's what Janny Beal's youngest son, Tray, had wanted to do with Ely and Little Desiree.

"Jist gonna slow us up, Pa." He had said when they were tying their captives. "How 'bout Ah jist slit their throats, then gut 'em."

"Reckon you could at that, son, but Widow Porticia done lost them fool boys'a hers last fall you might recollect, an' she might be a willin' to trade that big sow for the little gal. You kin gut the boy, if'n you have a mind." Desiree had shoved the man who had been trying to tie her up and had knocked him to the ground before she had run over and taken Ely in her arms.

"Please, mister, Ely won't be no bother. Ah'll do whatever you say!"

"Damn, you're a feisty one ain't ya," Janny had said, smiling at her. He had only indicated his son could kill the boy to see Desiree's reaction, having had no intention of actually allowing the murder of Ely to happen. "Reckon Ah could spare the boy if'n you give your word ta marry up with Cleavon an' don't make no fuss. He ain't much ta look at, but he needs him a wife."

None of them were much to look at, but when Desiree had glanced at the man his father had pointed to she had seen why he was still unattached. Cleavon's filthy, foot long blonde beard was light enough to exaggerate what was left of his brown teeth, and the only time he came close to bathing was if he happened to get caught in the rain. He was a huge man, over six feet, and the only obese one amongst them. If he weighed less than three hundred pounds it wasn't by much.

Cleavon knew the woods and the ways of his people, but his rheumy eyes remained dull and unresponsive unless he was staring at Desiree's breasts. Something was wrong with his ears, especially the right one. There was a thick vein of wax that had oozed out and hardened over time, with a more recent discharge glistening over half of it. For some reason that condition seemed to become exaggerated when he became agitated or aroused, and there was a permanent, copper stain on his neck where he had wiped some of it away. He seemed to enjoy looking at the discharge from time to time while he rubbed it between his fingers, sometimes tasting it. The smell intrigued him too.

"You leave mah Ely alone, Ah'll marry up with him." Desiree had said, knowing she would probably have to kill him as soon as the opportunity presented itself.

"That's settled then," Janny had announced. "Tray, if'n that young Yankee soldier feller don't git ta talkin' a sight more'n he already has when we git back, y'all knows what's in store for 'em. Let you cut the rope, boy." Tray had smiled, his teeth almost as brown as his brother's.

***

PETE HAD managed to convince Mitchell that even if he wasn't one of them he sympathized with what they were doing and would be glad to join them. Pete was obviously a Northerner, and regardless whether or not his story was true he was no longer in the army. It was just as obvious he had been; he knew enough about army life although Pete had left out the part about being a lieutenant. Mitchell and most of his men had made it obvious they hated officers almost as much as they did southerners.

"I don't know how they could've made off with the woman and her kids, even my two best horses, without me catching up to them." Pete said as he strapped on the revolvers Mitchell had given back to him. Mitchell just snorted.

"Them filthy bastards can do more'n that. My brother was just takin' a shit when they made off with him. We didn't hear nary a sound neither, and he weren't but thirty, forty foot away."

"How come they did that?" Pete asked.

"None'a your damn business. Not sure no how. We took a spread back yonder, kilt some Reb sympathizers. Reckon that had somethin' to do with it."

"How come they didn't just shoot you?"

"You sure are a nosy son of a bitch, McCabe. How the hell I s'pose to know? It's enough for you to know we're goin' after 'em. Heard they got gold. S'pect you might be useful if you know how to use them hog legs you're carryin'."

"Rather have my Henry, they took that too."

"You mean to tell me them hillbillies got themselves a Henry? How much ammunition?"

"Three full boxes and another over half full."

"Aw *shit*. That sure as hell ain't good. You boys hear that?" Mitchell called over to the men who were unsaddling their horses. "What the hell you men doin'? We gotta get a move on! A God damned Henry. *Shit...*"

***

PETE HAD no idea where they were, but Mitchell did. He even knew where the mountain men lived. The people back at the homestead had tried to save themselves by telling him he was making a terrible mistake. They had said they were kin to the leader of the Beal Clan, as if everyone would know what that entailed.

Mitchell had pretended their information impressed him and it had, once the terrified husband had said the clan possessed a sizeable amount of gold. Mitchell said he would check their story out if they told him where the clan lived. Mitchell had told them he had modern firearms to sell, and had been looking for people who had the money to buy them.

After the trembling husband had told them the location of the clan, over his young wife's frantic protests, Mitchell had dragged him outside and stabbed him to death. The woman had wanted to lead Mitchell and his men to the enclave, but her husband had foolishly divulged the whereabouts, giving away their only bargaining chip. Mitchell had then re-entered the shack after murdering the husband and butchered her two children right in front of the screaming woman, then told his men they could do what they wanted with her.

Several days later Janny Beal found out about it. He and his sons had covered the rugged ten miles from their home to the farmstead in record time, and when he found his sister's nude and mutilated body and those of her husband and children, they went after the murderers with a vengeful obsession. After their murder spree

Mitchell and his men had made themselves scarce for a few days, but were presently back in the area; Mitchell wanted that gold.

Janny wanted to know, specifically, the identities of those who had raped, tortured and killed his sister. They were all going to die anyway except perhaps one of them, but he wanted to make sure those who had committed the atrocity against his immediate kin paid a special price. If it had been all of them so be it; if not, he wanted one left alive to spread the word about what happened to anyone who came into his woods with that type of evil in their souls, especially Yankees.

Mitchell's younger brother, Wendall, became the obvious choice. He wasn't out of his teens, and would be the likeliest to tell the truth when even the threat of shoving a red hot tip of a knife under his toenails was made, or so Janny had maintained. Just the sight of the knife had indeed done the trick. Wendall had demonstrated the presence of mind to buy some time by insisting he hadn't killed or raped anyone and wanted to personally identify the murdering rapists, just as Janny had predicted. He felt confident he and his boys could kidnap the rest of the men too, most of them anyway, unless he had to kill them on the spot. Regardless, it would again show the clan he was not only in charge, but decisively so.

Some of the younger clansmen had been displaying hints of disrespect lately, and needed to be reminded who their leader was and always would be, and one of his sons after he was gone. What he was undertaking no one else would consider doing, not to that extent. Janny and his sons would again have everyone fearing them, especially the younger men in the clan. Their deference had better be utterly respectful in nature as well, and at all times.

Desiree's capture would only add to his family's lore. Not only were the Beal men on a hazardous mission against well-armed Yankee raiders, but right in the middle of it the Beal men were bringing in the best looking woman anyone had seen in years.

***

LATER THAT afternoon Janny, his sons and their captives arrived at the enclave in Low Cloud Valley. It hadn't changed much over the years, nor did its inhabitants see any reason why it should. When it rained the walkways and crude roads became a quagmire, thoroughfares that were used by animals and people alike. There was always a smell to the place, but after it rained and the sun came out the hog, cattle and dog feces seemed to be especially offensive to those not used to it.

That's how it affected Desiree and the children when they were paraded down what passed for the main road through the small settlement. Everyone stopped what they were doing to gawk at the new arrivals. One of the mongrels came up behind Little Desiree and all but buried its nose between her buttocks before Desiree kicked it so hard the cur ran away squealing more like a pig than a dog. Everyone howled at the sight.

Cleavon grabbed Desiree by the back of her neck and began to drag her towards his hovel, maintaining it was time to "wed up" with her. When he reached around and grabbed one of her breasts Janny came up and slapped his son across the face.

"You ain't doin' nothin'a the kind, boy, til Ah wed you up proper!" Cleavon bowed his head, and reluctantly removed his large hand from the struggling woman's breast and readjusted the front of his trousers. "We got us work ta do!" Janny announced loud enough for most everyone to hear. "Carley! You take this here woman an' lock her up in the smokehouse, her boy too. Tell Widow Porticia Ah done fetched her a daughter if'n she'll trade fer her prize sow. Lonnie! Git over here boy, an' tend to these here horses. Take right good care'a this 'un, he's mine." A filthy, towheaded lad ran over and took the reins of a skittish Yankee. "Git the other one too, ya damned halfwit, or Ah'll tan your hide sure!"

Janny and his sons took off again, Cleavon pouting like a child, and soon disappeared into the forest. It would be easier to accomplish their task in the cover of darkness. Janny had the Henry rifle and marveled at the modern weapon, constantly caressing it as he figured out the mechanics of the impressive firearm.

***

PETE WAS able to ride since Wendall's mount was available. They were heading southeast through the woods, with Dirch and another man spread out up ahead a hundred yards or so into the woods, guns at the ready. As darkness began to invade the already faintly lighted forest Mitchell ordered his men to stop and make a cold camp. He had chosen a spot with a sheer cliff to its rear and two deep ravines on two other sides. The only approach could be easily guarded, and Mitchell had two men in place for that purpose. Before long Dirch came in, but the other man, Connie Spriggs, wasn't with him.

"Where the hell's Connie?" Mitchell asked before Dirch had even dismounted.

"He was off to my right last I seen 'em. Said he was headin' back near half hour ago."

"Well he ain't here God dammit, you ain't seen nobody else I take it." Mitchell surveyed the area as he spoke, but all he could see was nearly total darkness and the barely silhouetted trees.

"Course not. I'da fired if I had," Dirch responded as he dismounted, looking around like everyone else. "Like Connie was supposed to do."

"Everybody take up positions. Nobody sleeps tonight." Mitchell looked at Pete. "Don't you go noddin' off on me now. These hillbillies are guileful sons of bitches."

***

"THIS HERE one'a them?" Janny asked Wendall as the boy sat tied up in a stall, the floor beneath him covered with considerably more horse dung than what passed for straw. The lantern cast a cold light upon Connie Spriggs' terrified face and in the immediate vicinity of the small barn. Wendall looked at his companion helplessly, every bit as unnerved. "Ah done asked you a question, boy. You best shame the devil by bein' truthful. Ah'll know if'n you stray."

Wendall had generally liked Connie, but in his terrorized state of mind he couldn't find the courage to defend him. Besides, he believed the angular old man was mysterious enough to tell if he *was* lying.

"Yeah, he done it. But it weren't just him!" Wendell added, realizing immediately that had been a foolish thing to say, even if in his agitated state it had been meant as some kind of justification.

"Bring the boy along too, an' a good rope!" Janny said to his sons Cleavon and Tray.

The two captives were led to a tree that had a thick branch which hung over a hog pen close to the barn. Over a dozen lanterns issued an ominous glow, announcing what was about to transpire. By the time Tray had climbed up and draped one end of the rope around the branch, half the people in the settlement had congregated around the hog pen. The hogs knew something was about to happen; as filthy as they were it had no effect upon their memories. They began to squeal and fight amongst themselves, flinging mud and feces seemingly everywhere.

The lights and commotion had alerted everyone else, and soon people were shoving and pushing almost as much as the fifteen full grown hogs. There was only so much room with a good vantage point around the pen, and the spectacle was something virtually no one wanted to miss. Connie's hands were still tied behind his back, and he was blubbering through his tears for mercy. Janny went over to Wendall, towering over the shaking teenager.

"This here's what's in store fer you if'n Ah catch you'a lyin' ta me boy. You best never fergit it neither. Reckon you won't." Janny climbed on the pen's bottom fence rail and addressed the crowd.

"This here no-account Yankee raped and kilt mah sister, put hot coals on her too! This here's what happens ta thems what go agin' me an' mine!"

Janny strode over and put the noose around Connie's neck, and told Tray to hoist him up. The young mountain man gave it all he had, and Connie's feet came about three feet off the ground, his legs kicking against the outside rails of the pen. Janny grabbed him by the back of his long hair and his belt, and picked the good-sized man up over his head, momentarily creating slack in the rope. "Give it a pull, Tray!"

After his son complied, Janny threw his victim over the top rail. Connie began to kick wildly as he swung back and forth just above the squealing hogs directly beneath him. Janny didn't want him to hang to death, just swing there until his windpipe was crushed or close to it. When Connie began to make choking sounds so horrifying Wendall almost fainted, Janny hollered for Tray to cut the rope. The young mountain man's eyes filled with excitement as he slashed away, and filled with even more anticipation when Connie fell into the mud amongst the frenzied hogs.

He hadn't been unconscious when he landed, but was unable to emit anything but the most guttural of sounds as the hogs began to rip him apart. Once one of them had a decent sized chunk of flesh the hog ran off to devour it, fighting off any hogs that followed. Most remained with the noiselessly screaming but no less terrified man, tearing off anything they could. The crowd cheered at the spectacle, all of them remaining until nothing was left but glistening bones and blood-soaked, shredded clothing that was last to be devoured. The hogs even lapped up any blood-imbued mud and feces as well. One of them, the largest, was rooting out what it could find inside the skull.

"Strung up an' hog 'et!" Janny declared as he again climbed upon the bottom rail. "Mah sentence done been carried out!" Then he turned to Wendall as he gave an order to Cleavon. "Git him back in the stall. Best keep in mind what Ah tolt you, boy."

***

THE FIRST light of morning filtered through the forest, and Mitchell's group was on the move. Mitchell was still grumbling about the Henry rifle he maintained Pete had been foolish enough to lose, and it had grown tiresome. Pete enjoyed conversation as well as good natured bantering, but when he grew silent those who knew him also knew there was probably a good reason. None of his brothers, if asked, would have been able to recall an incident where Pete had spent any time at all threatening anyone with what he was *going* to do. Even as a boy Pete hadn't been inclined to engage in frivolous threats other youths employed to mask their uncertainties and fear. Pete had always reduced any such incident to one of two responses; react or ignore it completely. Mitchell Hayes was about to find out which one was waiting for him.

"How some God damned fool could wander off to take a damned shit an' leave behind a gun like that in this country is -" He didn't get any further. He had been riding just to the left of Pete during his latest diatribe, and if he saw the back of Pete's hand coming it hadn't been in time. The blow had knocked him back with such force only his stirrups had kept him from flying off the back of his saddle. By the time he had righted himself, his lower lip bleeding profusely, Pete already had a revolver in his left hand. The others were nearly as shocked as Mitchell but no one made a move. Silently, the others had enjoyed the spectacle.

The next move was up to Mitchell. Like any number of bullies who had been called out in such a manner, all he did was make an attempt to defuse the situation before it escalated, as if it were a given he certainly had the sand to stand up to his adversary as soon as the time was right. Mitchell spat blood and tobacco juice then wiped his mouth, glaring at Pete, and at the gun pointed at him.

"We'll settle this later, like men." He declared, spitting red and brown again. "You picked the wrong man to sucker punch." Pete kept his gun drawn as he urged his mount a few steps behind the bleeding man. A short while later Mitchell invented a reason to ride up and yell at one of the others, and Pete put his gun back in its holster, still cocked.

***

THE MOUNTAIN men knew the terrain, borne to it, and although the heavily armed men they were hunting weren't strangers to such places and circumstances themselves, Mitchell's disquietude was obvious despite his fleeting attempts at bravado. Two of his men had already been kidnapped and their adversaries had also made off with the woman and children without so much as a trace, let alone a sound. It was obvious to Mitchell the Beal men knew as much as any Indian when it came to ambushes, and since the woods were so dense and there were so many gorges, valleys and other spots perfect for setting such traps, Mitchell had the six of them stay within sight of each other as they moved along. When those hillbillies made their next move at least Mitchell and his gang would be able to finally put up a fight, he kept declaring, as if that would mask his nervous eyes that never stopped darting about. In that regard he wasn't alone.

He considered setting a trap of his own but decided against such a strategy. The best thing to do was make an attempt to be where they would least be expected to go or impossible to track while still making their way to the settlement. His plan came into focus when they came upon a stream that was larger than the other creeks and brooks they had encountered, one that flowed in an east-west direction.

"We'll go east through this," he declared, "unless it bends off up north a ways. Not likely with the slant of them hills up yonder. If we're lucky, we might just lose them hillbillies long enough to cut back from the southeast. By the time they find these here tracks we might just be close enough to attack their homestead. Don't reckon the folks there will be much of a match for our rifles if we can catch 'em off guard. You good with a Spencer, McCabe?"

"Better'n most," Pete replied.

"Oh that's right, you're a *cavalry*man, so you say anyways. Here, take this one."

***

DESIREE AND Ely had been in the smokehouse nearly twenty-four hours. Ely had developed a persistent cough, and his throat and nasal passages felt as if sandstone were rubbing against them and had been for quite a while. Desiree felt much the same and was proud of the way Ely hadn't been complaining; the way he kept trying to comport himself so stoically now that the ordeal of their forced march was over. She was proud, and frightened beyond reason. She had no idea where her daughter might be, except with some loathsome old widow named Porticia. How anyone could live amidst such squalor filled her with shuddering contempt, and she feared for her little girl's health as well as her overall safety.

Desiree had been poor, but at least she had kept herself and the children clean. They had always bathed in the pool beneath the waterfall at least once a week, more often when the hot Georgia weather was unrelenting. After Pete's arrival she made sure to bath every other day. These people were so disgusting they could easily be smelled twenty feet downwind, farther if the breeze was up. It wasn't the odor of men after a long day's labor in the fields either. That would have been an immense improvement. The stench that had been emitted by Janny and his sons when Desiree had been brought there was a mixture of odious filth so reprehensible she had gagged several times; the mere thought of it brought her close to the nauseating sensation.

Once she and the children had arrived in the settlement all the reeking, confluent odors had bombarded them as if the pungent smells were competing with one another for the contents of the captives' stomachs. Except for the always hungry mongrels foraging about, their vomit wouldn't have been even noticed, or at best a source of amusement.

Although Desiree's hands and feet had been bound, she managed to crawl over to a rancid piece of hog fat that had fallen onto the ground next to a butcher block. She used it to grease her hands and wrist, and although she had finally managed to free herself, both wrists were raw and bleeding. She untied Ely and pondered her next move.

She had no idea if Pete was searching for them, or if he was even alive after what she had overheard. When two of Janny's sons, Tray and Buddy, had caught up with their father and Cleavon, they had mentioned they had been forced to leave Pete unharmed. No matter, Janny had said, he would be easy to find once the captives had been secured back at the settlement. Even if he lit out he wouldn't get far, not on the broken down horse they had left in the meadow. "No sense in killin' a horse what acts like it's a deader anyways," Janny had said. His son's had chuckled dutifully. "If'n he do light out," the patriarch had continued to say, "it be one less thing ta trouble us. Least ways, he'll be gone."

Whether Pete was dead or alive, looking for them or not, Desiree had to do something. She had been born and raised in northwest Georgia, but was totally unfamiliar with her current surroundings. Unless she could somehow get very far away very quickly there was little chance of eluding her pursuers, especially with two small children in tow.

One thing was certain; she had to get Ely out of that smokehouse. His cough had grown worse, and even in the dim light which came through a few of the boards of the rude structure she could see the pallor on his face. His normally bright green eyes were dulled and his listless expression had become more noticeable.

She remembered something Beardsley had once told her, one of the few things he had ever come up with that showed the slightest glimpse of an original thought on his part. Upon reflection she wondered where he had heard it. *If you're somewheres you ain't supposed ta be, carry on like you own it.* Perhaps her husband had left them something worthwhile after all.

Desiree began pounding on the inside of the locked door then proceeded to slam it with the flat of her foot. By itself that wouldn't have been enough to elicit much concern, except the rude structure wasn't very well constructed and after all, it was the only smokehouse. If the door was broken it was one of the few someone would have to repair immediately. A rotund woman finally waddled up and began to yell. Judging from her girth, her concern for the integrity of the smokehouse was obvious.

"Quit that there bangin'! You addled or sumpin'? Like ta break it down!"

"Ah'm s'pose ta meet up with Widow Porticia! Janny done said so! You git me over ta her else there be hell ta pay!"

"Janny ain't here, his boys neither," the woman replied.

"Ah know that! You git me over ta the widow else Ah'm'a tellin' Janny on you! Gonna tell Cleavon too!" The woman lifted the thick board from their catches on either side of the door and told Desiree to come out.

"She's in that there shack yonder, past the hog pen. Ya best be truthin' me gal. Ain't nowheres ta go if'n ya ain't! You hear me?"

Desiree had Ely by the hand, walking with a determined stride. She rapped on the door when she arrived, fully expecting the ugliest of old crones to answer. When the door opened Desiree looked inside, past the woman, and saw Little Desiree sitting at a table. She had a plate in front of her but came running when she spotted them. The child threw her arms around her mother, and that's when Desiree looked closer at the woman.

"Ah s'pect that sweet child knows her ma all right," the old woman said, her expression a mixture of compassion and longing. "You an' yer boy come on in. Ah got somethin' fer that cough. Honey, molasses, butter an' salt. Never know'd me a child yet what don't cotton to it. Got some poultice fer your wrists, too, darlin'."

***

THE STREAM had indeed gone in a southeasterly direction. It had been somewhat deep at times, but the water hadn't made it past the bellies of the horses. Mitchell and the others had made it a good five miles, perhaps six, when they rode out of it after spotting a rocky shore comprised mostly of gravel that would help cover their tracks. They made their way into a valley that headed due south. After a few miles they had cut west into Low Cloud Valley. They pulled up when they spotted the settlement in the distance, and hid their horses in a thick stand of loblollies. There was some concern they may have already been spotted as they crept a ways farther through some tall fescue, since the valley was more meadow than forest.

"Check all your guns," Mitchell said.

They all had Spencer or Sharps rifles, Colt revolvers and three shotguns between them. Mitchell's was a sawed-off double barreled twelve gauge. What it could do to a person's skull at close range never failed to fascinate him, and as he fondled the weapon he wondered out loud if he could break his own record. "Thirty-six feet, that's how far one chunk went. I swear, if that little Rebel gal hadn't been standin' at the bottom of a rise I'da got me another ten foot easy. Had a little head though, that gal. She weren't but six or seven," he said with a smile, "bigger head might'a throwed off more chunks." Pete looked away, wavering between bewilderment and disgust. He couldn't wait to be rid of Mitchell Hayes, if he could somehow find Desiree and make good their escape.

"Damn, Mitchell," Dirch said, apparently ignoring the man's repulsive nature, "lookit all them. Must be nigh on to twenty come an' gone so far. Only a few of them men was heeled though."

"S'pect the rest will be soon enough if we just charge on in there. Prob'ly all good shots, too." Mitchell replied. "Reckon there's more'n twenty though. We commence to firin', the ones we can't see might shoot us before we know it. Still, I reckon we can take 'em. Sure wish I knew where that gold's hid. Need to find out which'a them shacks the men that's after us lives in. If it ain't in there, somebody might be that knows where it's at."

Pete was initially at a loss regarding his own situation, but as he surveyed the area an idea began to formulate. Desiree could be in any of the shacks, if she was there at all. The best thing to do was get into the barn and see if Yankee was there. If someone was inside of it or showed up later, there was a chance he could find out where Desiree and the children were being kept. With two, maybe three horses they could continue west through the valley if they were very careful and at least somewhat lucky.

"You stay here," Pete suggested. "I'll sneak around back and try to get in that barn. If I can overpower someone maybe we'll at least find out where the gold's hidden." Mitchell pondered the idea.

"Take Dirch with ya." He finally said. "And don't get no notions about that woman in case she's there, you hear me McCabe? Dirch, see if you can find out where Wendell is, if he's alive which I doubt. Connie neither most likely. Sure could use the extra gun hands though. Git back here soon as you can. In a hour or thereabouts we'll come ridin' in whether you make it back first or not, shootin' everything that moves. If you have to start shootin' before that we'll come right away. Damn, there's lotsa people there. Keep your wits about you, boys. This one ain't gonna be easy."

***

PORTICIA FED them the first real food they'd had in a day and a half except for a few johnnycakes Janny's son Buddy had given them during their forced march. Desiree and Ely had been ravenous, but at least the old woman had seen to it Little Desiree had been fed. The inside of Porticia's shack had been an unexpected surprise. It was actually clean, and even though the woman herself could use a bath, Porticia wasn't near as filthy as everyone else Desiree had encountered. The old woman carried a fair amount of weight on her body which seemed to compliment her grandmotherly comportment, and her faded blue eyes, dulled by all her years, were soft and kind. Her thick hair was yellowish white and well past her shoulders. Desiree thought it odd it appeared so clean.

"How come you stay here, ma'am?" Desiree asked once she was full. Ely was still eating.

"Oh, Ah know this here place ain't much ta look at, but it's home," Porticia said as she took a seat at the table. "Cuthbert, that was mah husband, done brought me here when Ah was maybe twelve. Ah was growed-up lookin' fer mah age, though. Had me two boys, but they's with their pa, bless his soul, bless theirs too Lord willin'. Cuddy, that's what Ah called mah man, was a good soul. Him an' Janny was friens'. Ole Janny was right upset when mah boys up an' got kilt. Only ones hereabouts what took off ta that derned war. Janny done warned 'em, but they took off anyways."

"He's an evil man, that Janny." Desiree said. "Kidnapped us, an' almost let one'a his boys gut my Ely. Wanted ta kill Little Desiree too, that one did."

"Oh, Janny's sure 'nough got hisself a mean streak. Don't much cotton ta strangers 'lessin' they's purty like you. Got him a good side though, even if that noaccount Tray don't. Ah s'pect he's the one what wanted ta gut your children."

"That other one, he ain't no better," Desiree said. "That Janny thinks Ah'm gonna marry up with that ugly heap'a fat." Porticia laughed at the notion.

"Oh, ole Janny says things now an' agin what don't amount ta much. Don't you fret on it gal, if Janny gits ya married up it likely be ta his boy Buddy. He ain't a bad sort, that one. Won't be the first time Cleavon been turned away, reckon it won't be the last neither."

"Ah got me a man, if he ain't been kilt. That Janny kin go straight ta Hades if he thinks Ah'm gonna marry any'a his boys."

"No call fer that kind'a language in front'a the youngins, child. Ah know you been through a lot, but Ah don't abide raisin' up evil spirits in mah home. Satan don't need much promptin' as is, Ah reckon."

"Ah apologize, ma'am. Won't happen again." Desiree lowered her head and sighed. "Ah'm just scared for my little ones. S'pect Ah should be prayin', not cursin'."

"Well, Ah'll talk ta Janny, child. He gives me his ear now and then. Like Ah was a sayin', Cuddy an' him was friens'. Best ta hold off a while though. He ain't hisself on account'a what happened to his sister, Lord keep her sweet soul. That feller last night found out what's what, an' Ah reckon them others will too soon enough. Mind if'n Ah set your little girl on mah lap?" Desiree smiled, indicating her approval. Little Desiree climbed on the old woman's lap willingly.

"What was all that commotion last night?" Desiree asked.

"Satan got holt'a Janny agin. Young feller was strung up an' hog 'et. Ah s'pect Ah was the only one what didn't watch it, 'ceptin' Janny's wife Biddy. Hangin' is one thing. He deserved that. But lettin' them hogs at 'em, well, Ah'm feared ole Janny's a gonna end up in Gehenna his own self. Maybe we best go talk ta Biddy, that's Janny's wife. Did Ah say that already? She'll be a needin' some Christian company after last night. You love Jesus, she'll take up fer you and your youngins sure."

***

PETE AND Dirch had made their way crawling through the relatively high big bluestem and Indiangrass or on foot when the few trees could afford enough cover. They had to stop several times and stay hidden due to the day-to-day activities of the locals. The two men were within a thick stand of sumac, waiting for some children to move farther away when Dirch offered Pete a bite of chaw.

"Thanks anyway Dirch," Pete said, waving off the plug. "You been with Mitchell long?"

"Near six months. Seems longer. Sure as hell wish I was back home."

"Why aren't you? If you deserted, you sure as hell headed in the wrong direction."

"Don't I know it. Had me a row with that same captain Mitchell killed. He was a loathsome cur. I found out too late Mitchell was even worse. By then I was a few hundred miles south of that other direction. Been stuck with them others ever since. Wouldn't of lit out to begin with 'cept I would'a been accused of murderin' that captain sure as thunder. Can't say I was all that sorry he got his head blowed off, but I sure enough would'a been a hell of a lot sorrier if I'd stuck around.

"What Mitchell and them others did to them poor folks back a ways was the last straw. I would'a shot the son of a bitch 'cept me and Wendell was a few miles off when it all happened. Spose I should'a shot him anyway, but I didn't. Doubt I could'a killed all of 'em anyway. They ain't much better, 'cept Wendell, but me killin' his brother might'a turned him against me too. Brothers an' such can get peculiar that way. When this is over I'm leavin' if I ain't dead. Damn well could use some'a that gold. Sure you don't want a chaw? Ease your nerves some." Pete shook his head, looked around, and the two of them moved forward.

***

THEY FINALLY reached the back of the barn after exiting a gully which ran parallel to it, not fifty feet away. They only had their revolvers since rifles would have impeded their movements through the tall grass. Pete slid the rear door open a few inches and looked inside. He saw Yankee's head above the stall he was in, but other than two more horses and a few milk cows that weren't out to pasture it appeared empty. Both men crept inside. Pete turned back and looked outside before closing the door behind them as Dirch moved farther into the barn.

Jubal had been milking a cow in one of the stalls when he had heard the barn door open. He couldn't see the rear of the barn without exposing himself, which bode ill for him regardless. The mountain man wasn't supposed to be helping himself to the milk without permission, since the milk cows were Janny's property. He could hear Dirch's rapid footfalls upon the planked floor, and eased himself to the side of the stall hoping to avoid detection. His eyes widened when Dirch passed by. The stranger with the strapped on revolvers had to be one of the Yankees, and Jubal realized he could go from thief to hero status with one powerful jab from the pitch-fork leaning upon the wall next to him.

Dirch was ahead and hadn't seen the man coming from behind, but Pete did the instant he turned back around. A barefoot Jubal had moved quietly from his hiding place with the pitchfork, concentrating on his prey, closing in on his toes towards Dirch's back. Pete had time to draw one of his revolvers as he rushed forward as silently as possible, but pulled out his knife instead. He knew it would be close. Everything happened at once. Jubal tried to dispatch Dirch before he could respond to the footfalls he had suddenly heard coming from behind, but Pete was on Jubal just as the pitchfork's sharp tines were about to strike Dirch full force in the kidneys. Pete yanked Jubal back by his collar and drove the blade into Jubal's upper back, severing the spinal cord. Dirch had turned by then and saw both the pitchfork and the man fall to the ground.

"Sweet *Jesus*," Dirch said, his heart pounding in his chest. "Looks like I owe ya one there, McCabe. Lord that was close."

"Who's there?" Someone very frightened called out. Both men froze, but Dirch recognized the voice.

"Wendell? It's me, Dirch."

"Over here!"

"Where's Connie?" Dirch asked after he and Pete made it to Wendell's stall. The boy glared at Pete, suspicion and fear in his eyes. "He's with us, boy. Where the hell's Connie?"

"Dead. Nothin' left of 'em neither. We gotta git outta here, Dirch. These folks are plum crazy!"

"Well, I s'pect most of 'em are gonna be dead after Mitchell comes chargin' in. Him and the boys are waitin' in some trees just east'a here. What happened to Connie?"

"They hung 'em last night then fed 'em to the hogs. God it was awful. We gotta get the hell *outta* here!"

"Mitchell wants the damn gold. Hell, we all do. You got any idea where it is?" Dirch said, looking around.

"Gold? In this hell hole? That's a big story. Untie my damned hands. We're gettin' the hell outta here. How'd you get in?" Dirch and Pete cut the ropes, their boots sliding about in the reeking manure which was past their ankles. They both ignored Wendell's question.

"Mitchell said we was supposed to get back to him unless we had to start shootin' folks, but he's gonna wanna know about that gold," Dirch said, as he and Pete helped Wendell to his feet.

"Where's the girl?" Pete asked. "They likely brought her in yesterday, with her two kids unless they just murdered them."

"Don't know nothin' 'bout no girl. I been here 'cept for the hangin' last night. God that was awful. I ain't slept a wink."

Pete went over to Yankee that was more than glad to see him. The saddle and other tack were on the floor outside the stall, so he started to put it on the stallion. Dirch could see Pete and the palomino were glad to see each other, and marveled at the beauty of Pete's horse. Then he realized what Pete was up to.

"You can't just go ridin' outta here, McCabe," Dirch said when he and Wendell approached, the boy covered with filth. "Unless you're plannin' on doin' a whole lot a shootin' with nothin' but them hog legs. Let's get back to Mitchell and the men then decide our next move. Hell, once we get the gold I'm for all of us gettin' outta here too, like Wendell says."

"I'm just gettin' him ready, that's all. And I'm not goin' anywhere til I find the girl, if she's here. Go ahead if you want. Tell Mitchell I'll cover him from here. Lord knows he's gonna need it if he's fool enough to come bargin' in here."

Pete went over and looked out the front door, barely opening it. The barn was located at the west end of the settlement, and he didn't see anyone in the immediate vicinity. When he looked north he spotted her; Desiree was walking with some old woman and both children, on their way to see Janny's wife Biddy.

"Desiree!" He called out, just loud enough for his voice to travel to her, or so he hoped. She stopped and turned. He motioned for her to come over, but before she moved she said something to the old woman. Whatever she said, the old woman didn't appear to like it. She didn't call out though, looking around instead.

"Get in here, quick!" Pete said when Desiree and the children made it to the door. "I'll saddle another horse. You seen my Henry?"

"Some old man named Janny had it last Ah knew. Lord it's good to see you!" She said, throwing her arms around him.

"You gonna kill these folks too?" Ely asked, excited and scared all at the same time.

"Hope I don't have to, Ely. Can you ride a horse real fast?"

"Sure! Is there a white one?" Pete smiled and shook his head.

"I'll saddle the other two then," Pete said. "Come on Desiree, you can help."

"You hold on, McCabe," Dirch said. "You're with us, least ways for now. Just leave her here an' you can come back later. Hell, you're gonna more'n likely need a rifle if you try an' get away from this place. Better chance if you and Wendell come back with me an' get one. Michell's gonna want that gold before them other men get back anyways, assumin' they're gone. Best we try'n get it before that happens."

"Mitchell can go to hell if he thinks I'm gonna help him!" Wendell said. "I'd rather go with these folks, head west on outta here through the valley."

"An' leave your own brother?" Dirch responded. "Hell, he come here takin' up for ya, didn't he? That an' the gold, grant ya that."

"He come for nothin' *but* the damned gold what ain't even here if ya ask me!" Wendell said. "You got any sense Dirch, you'll come with us right now. You didn't see them hogs eat Connie! You don't *ever* wanna see nothin' like that!"

"Well dammit Wendell, at least stay here til I talk ta Mitchell. Like McCabe said, you can cover us if we commence to shootin'. We all stand a better chance with seven of us."

"Go ahead then Dirch." Wendell said. "Just gimme one'a your pistols. 'Nother cylinder of ammunition too."

Dirch handed over one of his Colts and an extra loaded cylinder and made his way out the back of the barn. Wendell just shook his head and looked at Pete. "Mind if I go with you, mister? You ain't stickin' around, right? I ain't like them others, honest I ain't. Didn't rape that woman, Dirch will tell ya. He didn't neither. Just here on account'a my brother. Truth is, I been wantin' to get away from him and the rest'a them ever since I don't know when. Killin' Rebs is one thing, but that weren't right, what they done to that woman an' them kids, and these folks mean business."

"Help saddle the horses, boy." Was all Pete said as he went to do the same.

XXVIII

Dr. Terry Donovan hated to lose his brave and competent young medic, but when Billy received the wire from home the doctor knew there was only one thing the youth could do. Father Benjamin had also sent a wire to none other than General Meade himself, and although one of his subordinates had dealt with the matter the result had been the same. Mother Grace was ill, grievously so, and the fifteen-year-old lad was needed at home. His age alone would have been enough to get him discharged, but Father Benjamin had left that part out of the wire Billy received. Father Benjamin had made sure General Meade knew about it though, or at least someone on his staff. All the boy knew was his mother might well be dying, and she had been begging for his return before it was too late.

A second lieutenant from Meade's staff had delivered the order for Billy to return home the evening of July 14th, after the rear-guard action at Falling Waters had ended near the Potomac River. General Meade had been pursuing Lee's army after Gettysburg but his chase had been half-spirited at best. President Lincoln was beyond being merely frustrated with his general, stating that *"Our army held the war in the hollow of their hand and they would not close it!"* Lincoln went on to say, *"We had gone through all the labor of tilling and planting an enormous crop and when it was ripe we did not harvest it."*

Lee had made it across the rain swollen Potomac, and although his retreating army had lost its aura of invincibility they were still a fearsome army. Meade's army had swollen to over 105,000 men after he too was across the Potomac, compared to Lee's decimated 50,000 man force. Regardless, Meade still exhibited more caution than anything. Once Lee fell back beyond the Rapidan by August 4th, the final chapter of Gettysburg came to a close. The war would rage on; all the killing, maiming and destruction wouldn't continue for just a few more months, but for nearly two years.

***

TO BILLY, it seemed as if Naperville had barely rolled over in its sleep. He had walked the eight miles from the train station in Wheaton to his hometown, and when he had made his way to Washington Street which ran through the heart of Naperville he slowed his pace. He allowed his boyhood memories nearly each block revealed so effortlessly to wash over him as he walked along in the summer sunshine, still in uniform.

He wasn't wearing it to impress anyone, at least not in the way others might have done. He *was* making a statement, however. Technically he was no longer in the army, but if a technicality ever took on human characteristics it was walking down Washington Street that afternoon in the form of Billy McCabe. Once things at home had been resolved, for better or worse, he would be off again. He planned on getting his father to sign the consent form necessary to re-enlist. Failing that, he would simply take off again and lie about his age.

Still, it was good to be home. He recalled the day he had spotted his brother Ben walking, limping really, down the dirt road in front of Tin Pan Alley. *Tin Pan Alley.* Just like his father to name such an impressive house with so unpretentious a title. Billy wondered who would be the first to see him, perhaps even Mother Grace if she happened to glance out her bedroom window. He hoped she would be the first, and hoped even more she was capable of doing so. He hadn't prayed for it though, nor anything else. That, he decided, he would keep to himself; especially in front of his mother. It would do nothing but create more harm if she knew that if her youngest boy *did* believe Jesus Christ existed in the form of a caring entity, He despised His own Father.

He had heard countless men during the Battle of Gettysburg pray out loud, some at the top of their lungs, for God's mercy. Later on while tending the wounded he witnessed more of the same. He had kept his contempt to himself in the hospital tents, but not when he had been on the battlefield. He had hollered it then, with all he'd had in him. He had heard others say there was no such thing as an atheist in a foxhole when the fighting was intense or almost underway, but Billy knew that wasn't true, even if he only pretended to embrace atheism in order to spite a God he no longer knew. During some of his most harrowing moments upon or near Cemetery Ridge, with shells exploding, bullets whizzing by and men being torn apart by canister right before his eyes, all he had done was tell God to go back to hell where he belonged. Hell was, he believed, as much of a fairy tale as an all-loving God, at least for the dead. Not for the living though, especially the wounded and permanently maimed. For them, hell was anything but an illusion; Billy was convinced at least that much was true.

He forced all that from his mind as he picked up his pace while passing the cemetery, struggling with ambivalence as it pertained to visiting Linda Marie's grave. He wanted to go in and he didn't want to; another bothersome dilemma amongst a host of nagging vagaries. He finally turned west off Washington Street south of town onto the familiar road that would soon have him standing in front of Tin Pan Alley, in front of *home*.

Uncertainty masquerading as contempt may have infected the here and now for him, and his future was no doubt in for it as well, but not if he could help it even for just a little while, perhaps longer. There was good in the world, for those willing to fight for it - for those who weren't afraid to tell God to go to hell. *Damn*, Billy said to himself, *just bury it for now. God and all His mayhem can wait. Let Him stew a while in the mess He's made.*

***

AS JOYFUL as Ben's return had been there was something special about the return of the youngest McCabe son. It had begun just as Billy had hoped; he heard his mother's joyful scream coming from the open window of her upstairs bedroom all the way out on the road. Father Benjamin had been in the barn and hadn't heard his wife, but he sure heard Ben holler out the back door. Ben had then shot through the house and out the front door as if his left foot was still attached to him, and embraced his kid brother after Billy had bounded up the front porch stairs.

"Mother's upstairs," Ben exclaimed, holding his brother at arm's length, happier than he'd been in quite some time.

"I heard her," Billy said, beaming with an excited smile as he took off into the house and ran up the front stairway. He rushed down the hallway and stopped outside her open bedroom door.

"Hello Mother, how you feelin'?" He said when he made it into her bedroom. She had already made it out of her bed and collapsed in his arms as soon as she reached him.

"Thank You dear God!" She said through her tears. Billy held her close, as if he were protecting her from that very entity.

Father Benjamin agreed to sign the consent form after supper that evening, but put it off. Mother Grace, as she had for the past few weeks when she could eat, had her supper upstairs, and her husband and sons had eaten theirs in her bedroom as well. Whatever ailed her seemed to be on the run, just like all of them had hoped Billy's arrival might accomplish. With the grace of God, all but one of them silently prayed, it would stay on the run too. Billy's feelings were every bit as desirous as theirs, but he was content to hold his mother's hand and allow the emotions inside him to take responsibility for her healing.

***

BILLY CHANGED into his civilian clothes after carefully hanging his uniform in the free standing cedar wardrobe closet he shared with his brothers. He had noticed Pete's favorite shirt; a red, green and black wool plaid made by some English fellow named Thomas Kay. Billy smiled when he recalled how Pete would always wear it when he was about to call on Delicia, and how Pete's brothers would tease him about it so; that, and the bay rum he always applied too liberally. Father Benjamin had just about thrown a full blown conniption when he discovered what Pete had paid for the shirt, and the memory caused Billy's smile to grow and warm him further still. After a few moments he grew somber when thoughts of Pete had taken their usual place inside him, edging out the happier memories.

Billy took Pete's shirt off its hanger and tried it on. He had been growing but it was still too big for him, especially in the shoulders. If Pete and the rest of his brothers had been home he thought how humorous it would have been if he happened to come downstairs wearing it, drenched in bay rum, especially if Delicia was there. Pete would have looked at him in a way that said his kid brother had perhaps ten seconds to get back upstairs, and the shirt had better be right where Pete had left it. Billy smiled again, then took off the shirt and hung it back up; just like Pete would have wanted.

Over supper all of them had discussed the latest news regarding the rest of the McCabe boys. Once word had reached her sons of Mother Grace's illness, their letters home increased although all of them had been good about staying in touch as their personal situations allowed. They had all stopped asking about Pete, even though Mother Grace seldom failed to mention him in her letters. She still insisted he was alive even if there was nothing to support her claim, especially now that so much time had passed. Everyone indulged her but only Doc Wygant still took her insistences to heart. Even Father Benjamin, if only to himself and to Ben on occasion, had begun to accept the worst.

***

DOC WYGANT and Delicia were every bit as glad to see Billy as his family had been. Even Clifton Janeway, who was also at the hospital the following morning, acted as if he were glad to see the boy, even after Delicia threw her arms around Billy. It was when she wouldn't let go that irritated Clifton the most. Neither Billy nor Delicia noticed any change in Clifton's demeanor, because as usual he displayed only what he wanted others to see. Clifton felt comfortable in his ruse until he glanced at Doc Wygant. The old man was looking at him as if Clifton were loading a gun. Clifton allowed his smile to grow as he folded his arms across his chest, shaking his head as if a more joyous occasion would be impossible to imagine, much less duplicate.

He glanced again at Doc Wygant, when he knew the other two weren't looking. The old man looked as if he wanted to kill him. *Spooky old bastard*, Clifton thought as he smiled and told Billy, who was still in Delicia's embrace, how hale and hearty he looked. *Wish I **was** loading that gun*, Clifton said to himself, wondering why on earth he was suddenly completing a train of thought that had not been on his mind to begin with.

XXIX

Missy Nell's mood went from anguish to joy in a matter of seconds. When the two army officers had shown up at her front door she had of course feared the worst. When the junior officer of the two had begun by telling her Cusman had been grievously wounded during the assault on Battery Wagner, the ferociousness of which had been widely reported, she had broken down completely.

The senior officer glared at his subordinate as if the young man were a simpleton of the first order, then the major took over. What really galled the senior officer was he had just told the young officer, less than an hour before their arrival, a little joke he shared with all the men he was training to visit civilians with unfortunate and all too often devastating news:

"…Then the captain told the green second lieutenant to be especially careful in his choice of words, to always bear in mind the significance his bad tidings represented. The second lieutenant knocked upon the door, and when the dead soldier's wife answered he asked if he was addressing the Widow Jones. 'Why no, sir, you are not', the woman said. 'The hell I ain't!' The second lieutenant replied."

The subordinate had heehawed like a mule at his superior's joke, albeit a tad too heartily the major suspected, but apparently the moral of the facetious little story had been lost on the dullard. *No wonder he's being kept as far away as possible from anything that requires more brains than telling people their loved ones are dead or wounded,* the major thought, *and the mooncalf can't even get **that** right.*

"Your brave husband is fine and mending well, Mrs. Sable," The senior officer said, still glaring at the chagrinned lieutenant as if he wanted to wring his neck. "As a matter of fact, he will be arriving home within the month, perhaps sooner." Missy Nell's tears continued, having suddenly transformed into tears of joy.

***

CUSMAN MISSED Colonel Shaw. The new commander of the 54th Massachusetts, Colonel E. N. Hallowell, had informed him he would no longer be serving with the regiment, at least temporarily. Although most of Cusman's wounds had healed the damage to his forearm hadn't responded at the same pace, and besides, a man of his caliber was needed back in Boston to help train new Negro recruits, at least until such time he had full use of both arms.

Cusman's initial response had been to insist he could still fight with one good arm, and had even dropped to the ground and did over fifty perfectly executed single-armed push-ups. The colonel, along with his staff, couldn't help snickering and told the huge man to stop. Cusman despised being viewed as a laughingstock, especially if he was being portrayed as a stereotypically foolish "darky" even if the colonel nor the others hadn't come out and said anything along those lines. That would have been redundant; Cusman knew how the minds of too many white people worked.

In hindsight he realized he had not only been hasty with his demonstration, but also when he had slammed his right fist down on the colonel's table that day in the commander's tent. Cusman had been fortunate his meritorious actions in battle had been taken into consideration, since the solid oak table had ended up in two pieces.

***

WHAT REMAINED of Cusman's resentment dissolved when the ship finally docked in Boston Harbor and he saw his pregnant wife waving so enthusiastically after spotting him as he stood by the railing. Missy Nell looked so beautiful it was all he could do not to shove men aside as he hurried down the gangplank. He did anyway.

Jennifer had accompanied her daughter to the dock, and upon seeing Cusman her eyes filled with tears. She recalled the afternoon she had stopped by to check on Missy Nell after the story had broken about the devastating battle at Battery Wagner. She had brought along a copy of the Boston Herald, but when she arrived her daughter already had her own copy. Jennifer had done what she could to bolster the pregnant girl's morale, even though her own was faltering. 272 casualties had been reported for the 54th Massachusetts alone, a shocking forty-five plus percent, with 116 killed outright including Colonel Shaw. Jennifer insisted Cusman was a survivor and always had been, but even so Missy Nell hadn't been alone with her fears.

"I just don't know why they can't say what happened to him, Mother." Missy Nell had said through her tears that day. "He has always been so willin' to head right into the middle of things, you know that. Big as he is, those Rebels must'a took special aim at him. He sure enough was easy to spot."

Cusman's name had appeared on the casualty list, but no mention had been made whether he had been killed or wounded. If he had just been wounded, how bad? It was over a week later when the officers had arrived at Missy Nell's home with the news. She had not only been given her life back but perhaps that of her unborn child. She hadn't been able to eat hardly anything, and sleep had been all but impossible. After consuming more food than she had in nearly five days, Missy Nell had slept ten hours straight.

***

CUSMAN NEVER did report to Camp Meigs in Readville to train new recruits. He had gone straight to Amherst, insisting if his left arm wasn't good enough for Colonel Hallowell then he couldn't have the rest of him in any capacity either. A few letters arrived inquiring about the progress of his healing, but no one followed up with a personal visit, or anything else that indicated a continued interest in their wounded sergeant.

Missy Nell was elated, and although Cusman was glad to be home it was apparent he was struggling with a variety of emotions, especially guilt. Many of his former comrades were still with the 54th, including quite a few who had also been wounded. It was true they had use of all their limbs, but Cusman's left forearm was slowly improving. It was also true his huge presence, both physically but especially as it pertained to his overall bearing made him the ideal person to encourage such qualities in new recruits. How many men would be able to use what he could teach to better enable them to deal with the vagaries of war, to keep them alive while effectively defeating the enemy? Those questions haunted him and they weren't alone: *As much as so many others want those devils defeated, can anyone want it more than me?*

Eventually, that's what helped him make up his mind. How to break it to Missy Nell with the baby coming so soon was a different matter. He convinced himself he owed it to his unborn child and the others which would follow, as well as his wife and all people of color which had been, and still were in bondage that it was his responsibly to continue fighting. If the 54th Massachusetts no longer wanted him for that purpose there were other colored outfits that surely would. They were being formed in a number of areas, in large part because of what the 54th had done. He kept all that from Missy Nell and had even enrolled in school, but one day while at the library at Amherst College his intentions came into focus.

***

CUSMAN WAS walking by the college church one morning on his way to the library when he first encountered Sedman August. The young man appeared to be about the same age as him, every bit as black as Cusman but barely half his size if that big. If he was much over five foot four it was because of the heels on his polished shoes, and he couldn't have weighed appreciably more than one of Cusman's legs. He was dressed in a fine suit of clothes and it was apparent he took additional pride in his appearance if his adherence to personal hygiene was also taken into consideration. He was carrying several books that day, and had been in a hurry as he made his way from the church and onto the sidewalk; too much of a hurry as it turned out.

Sedman was thumbing through one of his books as he hurried along, as if he had been borne to do several things at once. He didn't see the group of young men approaching, or more likely misjudged how close he was to them when he was about to pass by on the sidewalk. They had seen his approach though, and none of them demonstrated the slightest willingness to move, let alone step aside. The largest young man amongst them, a red haired fellow who had the look and demeanor of an athlete, not only didn't move but made sure his shoulder caught the advancing small man squarely. Sedman was jolted sideways and nearly lost his footing.

"Excuse me then!" Sedman said, his articulate voice edged with sarcasm.

"You speaking to me, you little capuchin monkey?" The red haired young man asked, causing his companions to snicker and make several demeaning remarks of their own.

"Your sense of humor is as pathetic as your mind. Good day, sir." With that Sedman continued on his way, or tried to.

"Big words for such a little monkey," the young man replied, urging his companions to share in his derisive laughter. Sedman kept walking. "I'm talking to you, *nigger*. Get your nigger monkey ass back here."

"S'pect if he's a nigger I am too," Cusman announced as he came up behind the group of four young men still facing Sedman. They all turned around and glared at Cusman, but their initial line of vision had to be adjusted upward. Moreover, the huge man standing before them easily took up the whole sidewalk, eclipsing the morning sun in the process. They decided, without another word, they had pressing business on the other side of the street and points beyond.

"That's a good way to land both of us in jail." Sedman told the mountain who was looking down at him. Cusman smiled as he approached.

"You a student here?" Cusman asked.

"I'm not one of the janitors. Are you surprised?"

Cusman held his hands up in mock defense, still smiling. "Never seen a janitor dressed like a dandy before, no offense intended," he said.

Sedman eyed the huge black man suspiciously. "Well now, if I'm not mistaken at least several of your words contained more than one syllable. Probably more than can be said of those louts."

"Really?" Cusman said. "And I was always of a mind 'nigger' had two of 'em, 'monkey' too. My name is Cusman Sable." He held out his hand, all fifty pounds of it or so it appeared to Sedman, and he took it, his own disappearing inside of what he instantly concluded was not only the largest hand he had ever seen, but had ever heard of.

"You could palm a fall pumpkin with that thing. I'm Sedman August. Are you a student here?"

"I'm not one'a the janitors." Cusman said, looking down at the refined young man. A grin appeared on Sedman's face.

As it turned out they were both on their way to the library. Cusman immediately found it easy to talk to the young man, revealing things about himself most of his living and dead friends from the 54th hadn't ever heard about, at least not in such detail. He was also intrigued by Sedman's history. Cusman had come to know quite a few young black men who had been borne free, young men whose parents had managed to escape, buy or had their freedom left to them in their former owner's will. Stedman was the first man of African descent Cusman had ever met who not only had never been a slave, but none of his ancestors had either. His great-great grandfather, along with a sizable group of his fellow citizens had come to America decades before from West Africa. Sedman had descended from a distinguished family which had been held in high regard in the Kingdom of Dahomey, until his great-great grandfather spoke out against the slave trade many of his contemporaries had embraced.

"The rest, if you'll forgive the cliché, is history," Sedman told Cusman as they sat at a table inside the library. "Fortunately, my ancestors brought a fortune with them, and despite our skin pigment money talked, and still talks, louder than words. There I go again. You must think I haven't an original thought in my head."

"Some'a the men I served with talked about Africa, others I knew back on the plantation did too." Cusman said, ignoring his new friend's last comment. "Mostly just stories that had been handed down, but I couldn't tell how much was true."

"Stories do have a tendency to inherit the storyteller's whimsies, but it's been my experience many of the tales are based upon the truth as I've come to know it. I would imagine all the slaves residing at your former home have tales of their own?"

"Well, a lotta 'em did, since Mas'r - I mean Trenton Ransom - didn't sell most of us that descended from the original four families. Neither did his pa, and so on down the line, not that it didn't happen too damned often since that's how they made a pile'a their money. White folk back there didn't like such talk though, about Africa and such. Maybe it made us seem almost human to 'em somehow, or made us feel human more like it. Least ways, there still weren't any way'a tellin' how much'a it was true."

"It doesn't surprise me your former owner and too many of his kind would demonstrate such an attitude," Sedman said. "Logic certainly isn't one of their strong suits. It brings to mind a quote from President Lincoln: *'The shepherd drives the wolf from the sheep's throat, for which the sheep thanks the shepherd as a liberator, while the wolf denounces him for the same act as the destroyer of liberty, especially as the sheep was a black one. Plainly the sheep and the wolf are not agreed upon the definition of the word liberty; and precisely the same difference prevails today among us human creatures...'"*

"Cain't argue with that, Sedman." Cusman said. "'Cept that ain't all President Lincoln said. I recollect him sayin' somethin' about not freein' any slaves long as he could preserve the Union. That sure enough ain't in keepin' with my view'a things."

"Actually," Sedman replied, "he said: *My paramount object in this struggle is to save the Union, and is not either to save or destroy slavery. If I could save the Union without freeing any slave, I would do it; and if I could do it by freeing all the slaves, I would do it; and if I could save it by freeing some and leaving others alone, I would also do that'.*

"Them words give it a different color, but it's the same damned portrait he's paintin' far as I can tell," Cusman said. "If he seen his own brother get whupped or his mama sold off, maybe his kids too, I s'pect he'd be seein' one color an' one color only." Sedman looked at Cusman more closely, as if his initial appraisal of him, though positive, needed to be at least re-appraised.

"That's a good point, Cusman, but consider this: how much support would Lincoln have with the general Northern population if he were to speak what is truly in his heart? I dare say the Copperheads and Northern Democrats would have a field day if he were to do so, and use it to their advantage. Opposition to the war would increase, alarmingly so I would maintain, and recruiting efforts would suffer greatly as well. I doubt the overwhelming majority of white men would be willing to risk their all to free anyone of color, as Lincoln well knows. He is also aware they *are* willing to do so to preserve the Union." It was Cusman's turn to do some re-evaluating, although he wasn't convinced all of Sedman's assumptions concerning Lincoln were undeniably true and told him so.

Not surprisingly, as Cusman would come to realize about his new friend, Sedman's arsenal of quotes was far from depleted. "Consider this, my skeptical friend. It's my favorite Lincoln saying: *'This is a world of compensations; and he who be no slave must consent to have no slave. Those who deny freedom to others deserve it not for themselves; and, under a just God, cannot long retain it.'* Does that sound ambiguous to you, Cusman? Or how about another Lincoln quote? Consider this as well: *'The world has never had a good definition of the word liberty, and the American people, just now, are much in want of one. We all declare for liberty; but in using the same* word *we do not all mean the same* thing. *With some the word liberty may mean for each man to do as he pleases with himself, and the product of his labor; while with others the same word may mean for some men to do as they please with other men, and the product of other men's labor. Here are two, not only different, but incompatible things, called by the same name, liberty. And it follows that each of the things is, by the respective parties, called by two different and incompatible names — liberty and tyranny.'*

Or this, Cusman: *'Slavery is founded in the selfishness of man's nature — opposition to it in his love of justice.'* And lastly my new friend, for now anyway: *'As I would not be a* slave, *so I would not be a* master. *This expresses my idea of democracy. Whatever differs from this, to the extent of the difference is no democracy.'* Cusman just smiled and slowly shook his head.

Their conversation continued. Sedman was especially intrigued by Cusman's account of his experience in the 54th, and what had occurred during and after Sedman's new friend's final battle. Sedman had tried to enlist in the 54th himself but had been turned away. Due to his diminutive size he hadn't even been allowed to attempt any of the tests to prove one's physical prowess. When he had appeared before the very first doctor, he had been dismissed without so much as a physical exam.

"I've heard the commanders of the colored outfits in the Western Theater don't care about that sort of thing as long as you're willing to fight." Sedman mentioned. "My parents are dead-set against it, but I've been giving serious consideration to venturing out to perhaps Tennessee, now that the Union controls most, if not all of it. Perhaps Kentucky. Have you ever heard about the colored artillery battalions being formed out there?"

"Heard tell of 'em, but that don't mean nothin'. Been thinkin' 'bout findin' me a new outfit though. Good a place as any I reckon."

"Doesn't." Sedman said, looking directly at Cusman.

"What?'

"You said 'don't'. You should have said 'that doesn't mean nothing', although you should have also said 'anything'." Cusman glared at him, but his attempt at intimidation didn't come close to fooling Sedman, who wasn't quite done with his new friend: "Any man of color who knows the word 'nigger' has two syllables, if you feel obliged to dignify that loathsome epithet by calling it a word, ought not to speak in a manner which would allow others to question his intellect."

"Capuchin got three syllables, don't it?" Cusman responded. Both men just looked at one another, each refusing to blink. Then they both started laughing.

***

CUSMAN DIDN'T want to bring up the decision he'd made at the wrong time, even if there wasn't a right time as far as Missy Nell was concerned. One thing was certain; he wouldn't say a word until after she gave birth. One other thing was certain as well; Missy Nell was indeed going to birth twins.

"That is splendid news!" Sedman exclaimed when Cusman had told him about it. Sedman had come to know Missy Nell and Jennifer, and was thrilled by the news as was Jennifer the evening the two of them had been invited to supper.

"I'll be the proudest grandmother in all of Massachusetts, the entire world I'll be bound!" Jennifer proclaimed. "I have every intention of spoiling them rotten, and I won't hear a contrary word about it!"

"May I humbly request your permission to have them refer to me as Uncle Sedman? It has a considerably more endearing ring to it than Mr. August."

"Of course, *Uncle* Sedman," Missy Nell replied, smiling at him. She thought he was simply "adorable" as she had told Jennifer a few days prior to the supper party. Jennifer had liked Sedman immediately and she too thought he was special - and yes, adorable.

"Tell me, Sedman," she asked, "What was your family's name before your ancestors migrated to America?"

"Osho," he replied, "but it appears they thought it prudent to change it to a name that would diminish the appearance of being excessively foreign, although I have no idea how they, given their appearance and rudimentary grasp of English, had ever hoped to accomplish anything of the kind."

"I think Osho is a beautiful name." Jennifer replied. "It brings to mind a placid sunrise over the Atlantic on a day whose promise of a benign tranquility cannot be disputed, but for the life of me I don't know why it affects me so."

Perhaps it's because it sounds vaguely similar to "ocean", but then only one of us thinks she has the counterpoise of a bard... Sedman thought, immediately scolding himself for being such a snob. Besides, he found Jennifer more than a little attractive. *Just how enlightened and tolerant is she?* He wondered.

***

LATER THAT night Cusman and Sedman were alone on the front porch with their cigars and brandy. It was a warm August night even for that time of year, but a delightful breeze kept both of them comfortable. Missy Nell was fast asleep. Jennifer had returned home over an hour before the men had retired to the porch.

Sedman was excited with the news he had been waiting to tell his friend, although his emotions had been tempered by the reality of Cusman's situation. He swirled the cognac in his snifter after pouring some from a bottle of Courvoisier XO he had brought along, and addressed Cusman after inhaling the intense bouquet and taking a small sip.

"I received a letter regarding the colored artillery battalions I've mentioned that are being formed that proves the newspaper reports are accurate. Regardless, they are anxious to have us join up with them. Not very many of the colored troops out there can even read. According to the letter, two educated colored men from the East would make a fine addition. They were wondering when we might be able to arrive in the West." Sedman took another sip of cognac and looked more closely at his friend.

"How soon they want us there?" Cusman asked.

"The sooner the better, although they didn't make a direct reference as it pertained to when, exactly. It's obvious you can't go now, but how much time will you need after the babies arrive?"

"Haven't said a word to Missy about it but she knows somethin's on my mind. S'pect I'll wait until she's back on her feet after the birthin'. There's somethin' else been on my mind, Sedman. Now don't you get all uppity when -"

"*Uppity?* Why, no suh, massa suh, I sho' 'nough ain't'a gonna gits ta bein' uppity! Sedman a good little nigger he is, yeow suh massa suh!" Cusman just shook his head and sighed, a barely perceptible smile upon his face.

"What I mean is, there was a good reason why they didn't take you into the 54th. Most them doctors are officers too, and knew what you'd of been up against in battle. Go ahead on, get all mad at me, but I know what I'm talkin' 'bout." Sedman took a breath, seemingly in control of his emotions before he spoke.

"I know you do, and don't think I haven't considered it myself. I can only imagine how I would fare in hand-to-hand combat as things now stand, but these are artillery units. I can help fire a cannon as well as any man."

"I know that, Sedman. But just because you're standin' behind some damned cannon don't mean your position won't be overrun. Stoppin' cannon fire is a priority, and them Rebs will be makin' a real big effort to do just that."

"I understand that Cusman. I've studied military tactics, I'm aware of the risks. All of us will be in harm's way. Are you inferring men my size don't go into battle?"

"No, and some of 'em kin fight like hell. Dynamite sure 'nough comes in small packages, seen it myself. But you ain't used to fightin', far as I know. That's a death sentence for a fella like you if some screamin' Rebs come chargin' in. Seen that, too. If nothin' else, at least let me show you a few things."

"That, I had assumed, was a given, and thank you, but I have something else in mind. Besides, I am also an excellent marksman, and plan on bringing my own guns. You're not the only one who owns Colt revolvers. But we're getting ahead of ourselves. It appears as if you have quite a dilemma of your own to deal with. Is it imperative you have to wait until the babies are born before informing Missy Nell of your intentions? Seems to me she would be even more upset to receive the news then. At least if you tell her now she'll have the opportunity to digest it all. Perhaps the war will end soon, and we'll both be back in the relatively near future."

"I'm not goin' anywhere until after the birthin', but I s'pect, Sedman, you're right about holdin' off tellin' her. I'll do it tomorrow. This war don't leave heartache alone much, does it."

"No, it *don't.*" Sedman replied, in all sincerity.

XXX

The horses were saddled and Pete had made his way to the front barn door to take another look around. A number of people were going about their usual business, or so it appeared. Dirch probably hadn't made his way back to Mitchell and the others yet, or if he had they hadn't made up their minds.

"What happened ta *him?*" Ely asked, after having approached the dead mountain man upon the planked floor where Pete had left him. The young boy had approached tentatively at first, having stopped after noticing the blood that had pooled around the dead man. Desiree went over to the boy and led him back to where they had all been standing, keeping herself between the boy and the corpse. Pete sighed, and reproached himself for having left the body in plain sight.

"He was trying to hurt the man I was with, Ely." Pete said, looking down at the boy. "I had to stop him before he did."

"How come he's bleedin' so bad?" Ely asked, looking up at Pete. He didn't want to lie to the boy, but he didn't want to answer the question either. Pete bent down and put his hand on the boy's shoulder, looking directly into Ely's eyes.

"I had to stab him, Ely. I didn't want to, I just want to get us out of here, and that man tried to stop me and my friend with a pitchfork. I'm gonna need you to be brave. I know you are, and I know you're gonna help your ma and me by doing what we say. You stay with her now Ely, your sister too. I'm countin' on you to do what I say." The boy glanced back at the body then looked at Pete again.

"Yes Pa," he said. "Ah don't wanna stay here neither."

***

"THAT WOMAN you were with is headin' over here." Pete called over his shoulder to Desiree. She had gone over to adjust a cinch while Little Desiree and Ely stood next to her, the little girl holding onto her mother's skirt. Desiree looked over, then picked up her daughter and walked over to Pete. Ely was right next to her. By the time she arrived Porticia was at the front barn door.

"Let me in, mister." She said to Pete as if his doing so was a foregone conclusion. He stepped aside as Porticia eyed him carefully. "This here must be your man."

"It's him," Desiree said, somewhat abashed to say so in front of Pete. "We're goin' with him too. You won't warn nobody, will you Porticia?"

"No child, Ah won't, but Janny ain't far off Ah reckon. Ain't likely this feller made it here without Janny an' his boys not a knowin' he was a headin' this way, an' he'll be here shortly if'n Ah know him. Y'all kin count on that."

"Ma'am, I don't know you, but I guess Desiree does. Don't wanna see you hurt. I came in with five others, they're waitin' just east of here. They're heavily armed and they think there's gold hereabouts. I'm pretty sure there's gonna be trouble. You best hide somewhere."

"Well Ah'll be jiggered. You're a Yankee too. Reckon you an' that young feller best skedaddle if'n you have a mind 'fore it's too late. But you child, if'n you go an' Janny catches up with you, your purty face ain't gonna save you or them youngins. You best stay here." Porticia glanced over and spotted the body. "Oh dear Lord, what happened to Jubal?"

"He was about to back stab one of us with a pitchfork." Pete said. "I didn't have a choice."

"What choice you think you got now, Yank?" Porticia asked, still staring at the body.

"Gettin' the hell outta here comes to mind." Pete said, looking out the barn door again. "I'm sorry about that fella over there ma'am, I truly am, but this wasn't my doing."

***

"MCCABE SAID he'd cover us from the barn, Wendell too. I gave him one'a my Colts." Dirch told Mitchell after he'd made his way back to the stand of trees. "Wendell said there ain't no gold, though."

"How the hell would he know? That gal's husband said there was, he'd know before that fool brother'a mine would." Mitchell replied. "Anyone down there suspect anything?"

"Don't think so," Dirch said. "Wendell said we should all just get the hell outta here. They strung up Connie last night an' fed 'em to the hogs."

"Damn. Could'a used his gun. That boy could shoot. You seen if them hillbillies got back yet?"

"Didn't see nobody come in from the woods. Don't know what they look like no how. Most'a them others walkin' 'round ain't heeled yet neither. Seemed like mostly women and children. Can't say for sure, but I didn't see more'n fifteen men once I got down there. Don't know where them others we saw down there earlier is."

"We can kill that many easy enough if we move fast," Mitchell replied. "Put a gun in some little kid's mouth, them folks probably tell us soon enough where the gold's hid. Let's ride!"

"Mitchell?" Dirch asked before they rode off. "Ain't you glad to hear Wendell's alive?" Mitchell just spurred his mount as he let out a contemptuous snort, just as Dirch thought he would.

***

DESIREE THANKED Porticia for her concern and everything else she had done, but she was going to take her chances with Pete. They were leading the horses past the stalls, towards the back of the barn when they heard the initial roar of gunfire followed immediately by a considerable amount of screaming and hollering. Pete looked out the back way, hoping to make a run for it.

"Oh hell!" He said. "There's gotta be ten men out there comin' on fast! Someone must've spotted Dirch!"

That had indeed been the case, but the mountain men weren't interested in the barn. They ran east of it, and took up a position in order to fire upon the men charging on horseback when they rode by. Mitchell and the others didn't even make it that far, and had been forced to dismount. Musket fire from a few of the shacks had killed two of them outright. Mitchell, Dirch and Cager were the only ones who had not been hit. They took cover in a shack after a shotgun blast from Mitchell removed most of a man's head. The man had fired from the window of the rude structure, and had been busy reloading when Mitchell arrived.

"Follow me!" Mitchell hollered as he ran out the back of the shack. He had discarded his shotgun and had both his Colts drawn, wishing he had his Spencer that was still with his horse. Dirch and Cager had theirs, however. They went around the rear of the shack then positioned themselves off its northwest corner. They were all excellent marksmen, and with their superior weapons had soon killed or wounded half a dozen people. They took off for the rear of a shack west of the one they had first entered. As soon as Mitchell peered around its northwest corner, half of the ten men waiting east of the barn fired, hitting no one. The three of them rushed out and began firing at the men before they could reload their muskets. The withering fire coming at the mountain men was so accurate five of them were hit immediately. The ones who had initially held their fire opened up, yet only managed to hit Cager, but he only suffered a flesh wound to the outside of his left shoulder.

The three Yankee raiders were accustomed to battle, but the men who lived in Low Cloud Valley weren't. They were all good marksmen, but that proved only marginally useful given the situation. The ones who had survived the gunfire made a hasty retreat and managed to join up with fifteen other men, taking the opportunity to reload. If Mitchell and the others tried an all-out assault on their adversaries' new position behind several cords of wood, Mitchell's bunch would be cut to pieces. They couldn't get back to their horses either, since three of them had been shot and the other two were nowhere to be seen.

"Where the hell's McCabe and Wendell?" Mitchell hollered. He soon found out.

Just as Pete started to lead Yankee out the back of the barn a bullet slammed into the door right next to him. Tray Beal cursed himself for missing, and quickly reloaded.

"The back's covered, don't know how many." Pete said as he rushed to slide the door closed. "Stay with the horses Desiree, you too Ely. Wendell, come with me!" They ran to the front of the barn. Pete slid the door part way open and peered out. Sporadic gunfire was going off to the east, not far away. Suddenly another bullet came at Pete, and although it missed him it hadn't missed Wendell. The boy stumbled back a few steps, staring at his stomach.

"Oh *sweet Jesus*," he cried as he slumped to the floor of the barn. He wasn't dead yet, but he might as well have been. Pete had recognized the sound of the gunshot; it had been fired from a Henry rifle.

More fire erupted, but it hadn't been directed at the barn. Cager had been only wounded the first time he'd been hit, but when the bullet from the Henry rifle struck his skull he died instantly. Mitchell and Dirch turned and flew to the ground. They took cover behind a log as they returned fire towards the trees to the northwest of them. They hadn't hit Janny Beal or his sons Cleavon and Buddy, but they had come close.

"We sure as hell can't stay here!" Mitchell hollered as both men quickly reloaded. "That barn's our best chance, come on!"

Porticia was on her knees, trying to comfort Wendell. She had ripped open the boy's shirt, and although she tried to encourage him it was obvious the wound was fatal. Pete had Desiree hide in the stall nearest the rear of the barn with the children, then slid open the back door again. He had kept out of sight as he did so, but another bullet slammed into the door anyway. More gunfire erupted out front as Mitchell and Dirch came rushing through the front door. Pete had both his Colts pointed at them after having ducked into another stall, and called over so they wouldn't start shooting.

"Why the *hell* didn't you cover us?" An enraged Mitchell bellowed. Dirch went over to Wendell then looked at Mitchell.

"Don't look good," was all he said. Mitchell glanced at his brother then looked at Porticia.

"Who the hell is she?" He said as he approached the old woman, his revolver pointed at her.

"You leave her be!" Desiree yelled. She had made her way over to Pete, who still had his guns pointed in Mitchell's general direction.

"Guess I know who you are," Mitchell responded.

"You in the barn!" A voice from outside yelled. "Got y'all surrounded! Gonna burn the barn y'all don't come out!"

"They ain't gonna burn nothin'," Mitchell said. "Some'a their horses are here, an' their damned milk cows. This old woman, too."

"Janny and them others kin git more cows an' horses," Porticia told him. "Build another barn, too. He's riled. Don't give a hang 'bout me neither. You best do as he says, mister."

"I heard what they done to Connie! Ain't nothin' left'a him 'cept a pile'a pig shit!" Mitchell erupted, his gun still pointed at her.

"Best thing for us is to ride out back," Dirch said. "There's a gully 'bout fifty feet away. Might be able to head west if there ain't too many back there." Mitchell glared at him, then back at Porticia.

"Who the hell are you?"

"Ain't nobody, mister," she replied, then went back to tending Wendell.

"What's your God damned name, crone?" Mitchell came towards her, double cocking the hammer on his Colt.

"Her name's Porticia, you leave her be!" Desiree yelled. "Pete, do somethin'!"

"You out there!" Mitchell hollered after going over to the front door and barely sliding it open, dragging Porticia with him. "Got Porticia here! We're ridin' out after you give us the gold, you shoot an' I'll blow her damned head off! Get them horses over here, McCabe!"

Outside Janny's son Buddy spoke to his father. "Pa, they gonna kill her sure no matter what if'n we let 'em ride off. Cain't let 'em kill Auntie Porticia. Let me make a deal with 'em." Janny thought his son was probably right about Porticia, and even if he didn't know what Buddy could do to save the old woman he also knew the young mountain man was his only son with any intelligence. Janny figured the Yankees could perhaps get away with enough horses and luck, and suggested they just shoot them when they came out, but Buddy was insistent.

"All that shootin' prob'ly kill her, Pa. Mebbe Ah kin reason with 'em."

"Go 'head'n talk to 'em boy, but them Yankees likely kill her anyways, you too if'n you ain't careful. Take this here Henry." Buddy shook his head.

"You men! 'nough folks shot already!" Buddy hollered. "Mebbe we kin make some kinda deal! Ah'm a comin' in, no gun, so don't y'all shoot!"

An unarmed Buddy came out from the trees north of the barn, his arms stretched out from his sides. When he was standing in front of the barn door Mitchell opened it a small ways and glared at him.

"The deal is me an' my men are ridin' out with the gold, an' this old hag is comin' with us."

"Best let me in, Yankee. An' there ain't no gold." Buddy replied. "You let her go, an' Ah'll go with y'all." Buddy offered as soon as he was inside and Mitchell had closed the door. Buddy held up his hands, then carefully reached over and slid the door part way open. "Them outside gotta hear if'n Ah need ta talk to 'em. Ah'm Buddy, Janny's boy." He added, as if that was all they needed to know about his worth as a hostage. "Y'all gotta let me have one'a them pistols though. Y'all kin keep me covered. If'n y'all gits a notion ta kill me, reckon Ah kin take some'a y'all with me that'a way. If dyin' don't suit ya Yankee, this here's your chance."

"Unless you open up on us soon as we ride out this barn!" Mitchell replied.

"So any y'all got a better idea'r? Yankee, y'all gonna die sure lessin' you do what Ah says."

"There's not enough horses," Pete said. Everyone looked at him. "Only got three. That's enough for me, Desiree and the children. Dirch too, if he's of a mind to ride with us."

"That bitch an' her kids ain't goin, McCabe, I am!" Mitchell yelled, pointing his Colt at Pete, holding Porticia in front of him as a shield. "Don't see no reason why you should neither! You ain't fired so much as a shot, *cavalry*man! Now holster them guns, or I'll shoot you and that gal'a yours before you can get me, and if I don't get your woman Dirch sure as hell will! Them damned kids too, by thunder! Dirch ain't wantin' to go with ya no how!" Pete put his cocked revolvers back in their holsters. His hands were shaking, his whole body, as he watched Mitchell and Dirch closely.

No one noticed the rear door of the barn slide open half a foot or so; almost no one. Tray took careful aim, his rifle pointed directly at Pete's back. An explosion roared through the barn and everyone ducked immediately before looking towards Wendell who was propped up on his left elbow. The boy looked at Pete, smiled faintly, then dropped his smoking revolver and passed out. He wasn't dead but would never regain consciousness. Outside, Tray stumbled backwards then fell to the ground, a bullet through his skull. The back of his head was gone.

"What the hell was that?" Janny yelled from out front. "Buddy, you all right boy?"

"Ah'm all right Pa! Some derned fool tried sneakin' in from the rear, near Ah kin tell! Tell 'em ta stay on back!"

Mitchell glanced again at his brother, then at Dirch. "Get the horses Dirch." Then Mitchell addressed Buddy. "You got a deal, hillbilly, but no gun, and don't move til I say so, you understand?" Buddy nodded, watching Mitchell's gun hand carefully.

Dirch stood holding his Spencer, but didn't move. He just looked towards Pete, then back at Mitchell who still had a hold of Porticia.

"Well go on, Dirch! Hell, just shoot him if ya have to or I will!"

Dirch lowered his Spencer, but just slightly. "I ain't gonna shoot 'em, Mitchell. He took up for me'n Wendell."

"You!" Mitchell yelled at Desiree. "Get over here else I'll blow this old crone ta hell!" Desiree looked at Pete. He nodded then spoke to her in a low tone, still shaking. "Go slow, stay off to my left."

Mitchell glared at Dirch, then at Pete. The look in his eyes told Pete all he needed to know. He drew and both he and Mitchell fired. Pete felt a bullet tear into the left side of his chest. His shot had struck Mitchell in the mouth, shattering his teeth then tore open his right cheek. He let go of Porticia and both men fired again, but Mitchell's shot came in low, hitting Pete in his right thigh as he collapsed to the floor. Mitchell fell as well, even though Pete's second shot had missed. Pete had missed, but Dirch hadn't, hitting Mitchell just below the Adam's apple and through his neck, pulverizing his spinal cord.

"Pete!" Desiree screamed as she ran to him. Ely finally came out from the stall as well, having watched the horror unfold from between the slats. Little Desiree was right behind him, screaming hysterically.

"Don't look good, ma'am," Dirch said after he and Porticia rushed over. Pete was still conscious, but just barely. "Looks like your time, McCabe. I am truly sorry." Dirch knelt down as he spoke, while Desiree buried her face in her hands. "You! Stay where you are!" Dirch leveled his Spencer as he hollered at Buddy.

"What's goin' on in there? You all right Buddy?" Janny yelled from outside.

"Jist hold on Pa! Two more'a these here Yankees is dead, done shot each other! 'Nother one still got a gun on me!"

"McCabe, can you hear me?" Dirch asked. Pete barely opened his eyes and nodded. Dirch let out a nervous sigh. "I'm gonna make a run for it, out back. Gonna take that palomino of yours."

"Ah ain't a goin' with ya mister," Buddy said. "Auntie Porticia neither. It's jist you now. Ah'll holler out back fer them out that a way ta let you ride off, if'n you promise not ta shoot us first. Cain't promise they won't commence ta firin' though."

"Well go on then," Dirch said. "You'd just slow me up anyway." He looked at Pete again. "Ridin' fast an' hard 'bout the only chance I got, s'pect that horse of yours can do it if any can from the look of him. If I get to that gully might just make it." Pete looked up at him.

"If you make it home, promise you'll go to Naperville, you do that Dirch? My folks will be easy to find. Tell them I...well, you know. There's a girl, too. Delicia, Delicia O'Darcy...tell her I never stopped...never stopped lovin'..."

"I'll do it McCabe, Lord willin'... *McCabe?*" Pete's eyes had closed. Desiree lost all control.

After Buddy had hollered out the back he slid open the door the rest of the way. Dirch was on Yankee, but before riding out he looked again at both Wendell's body and Pete. He sighed as he spurred Yankee out of the barn. Musket fire erupted as the palomino bolted towards the gully.

***

WHEN PETE first opened his eyes he wasn't certain he was still alive, except for the pain. He certainly didn't know where he was. Perhaps a bizarre parcel of heaven, since he doubted hell smelled of fresh baked bread. "Git your ma!" Porticia called over to Ely, who was stirring coals in the fireplace with a stick. "Go on now boy, skedaddle!"

"Look who come back from the dead," Porticia said to Pete as she leaned over him on the bed, his head on a pillow damp with sweat. She had a smile on her face. Porticia was the closest thing the clan had to a doctor, although for any serious cases all she could usually do was marginally ease her patients' suffering before they died. "You're the luckiest feller Ah'd ever know'd, Yankee, lessin' you up an' die on me anyways. That bullet missed your lung by mebbe'a inch or two Ah reckon. You liked ta bled ta death too 'fore Ah seen that puddle'a blood under yer leg. Other bullet might'a nicked up one'a them arteries. Lucky Janny let me pour some shine on it, other wounds too. Hated ta waste good corn on a blankety-blank Yankee he said, but he gives me his ear now an' then."

Desiree came bursting through the front door and ran over to Pete. "Praise the Lord!" She exclaimed. "You too, Porticia! He gonna be all right?"

"Praisin' the Lord an' me in the same breath is right nice'a you child, but Ah ain't fer certain God in heaven won't be'a lookin' sideways at you. Your man's fever done broke, if that ain't no sign from heaven don't s'pose Ah know'd what one is."

"Pete?" Desiree said, hope brimming. "How you feelin'?"

"Could use a taste of that corn liquor if that Janny fella don't mind," he barely whispered.

"Guess you is feelin' a might better," Porticia commented as she went to the cupboard. "Don't be a worryin' none about Janny. Buddy tolt him you saved mah life an' his, too. Even tolt him it was that other Yankee what kilt Jubal. Ole Janny done fed that no-account Yankee your friend kilt ta them hogs, though. Them other Yankees too. Hung 'em all first even though they was dead, even the boy." Desiree shuttered at the thought.

"Somebody oughta shoot them hogs," she said. "Take 'em out yonder an' burn 'em, too. No Christian would eat their meat, Ah'll be bound."

"Ain't too many real Christians 'round here, child," Porticia said when she returned with the whiskey jug, pouring some into a tin cup. "Take this real slow, Yankee. You ain't near yourself yet. Reckon you know that much."

"What about Dirch?" Pete whispered, unable to lift his head to take a drink without help. The pain in his chest felt like a knife was being twisted deep inside him. His right leg throbbed as well. "They feed him to the hogs too?" He coughed then, just slightly, but the pain it created was so intense he almost fainted.

"Nother lucky derned Yankee," Porticia said as she shook her head and smiled. "That horse'a yourns ran like lightnin'. Ah s'pect he got that derned Yankee halfway home by now. None'a the men caught up with 'em. Not even close. Said that horse could dern near fly, an' didn't slow up a lick. Said bullets must'a bounced off it too." Pete smiled weakly then took another drink. *Good for Yankee,* he thought, *and good for Dirch.*

"Where's my boots?" He asked, barely audible, too damaged to sit up and look around.

"Under the bed," Porticia answered, "but you ain't goin' nowheres for quite a spell, Yankee."

"How long I been here?" He asked as he looked at Desiree, trying his best not to cough.

"Been three days now, Pete." She said, stroking his hair. Her hand felt good against his damp scalp. "Janny said you an' me could stay at his sister's place when it's safe to move you, my babies too."

"Ah ain't no baby!" Ely said. Desiree smiled and placed her hand on the boy's tow head. He continued to feign indignity, but softened at his mother's touch.

"*My* ain't no baby neither!" Little Desiree pouted until her mother touched her head as well. Desiree looked back at Pete.

"Some'a these folks wanted ta hang you and - well, you know, them hogs an' all, but Janny kept sayin' no. Even give Porticia her sow back." That made the old woman chortle.

"Janny would'a anyways. He gives me his ear now an' then."

XXXI

Missy Nell's crying had eased into sobs then ceased altogether. Dabbing her eyes, she wandered over to the bedroom window and looked absently at the raindrops that were competing to make it to the bottom of the sill. A low rumble of thunder finally arrived through the threatening afternoon sky, although the previous flash of lightning had left the assumption it should have arrived sooner. She took a deep breath and exhaled slowly as she again dabbed her eyes with the damp handkerchief clutched in her hand.

"Cusman," she said, without turning around. "What's it goin' to take before your mind's at ease?" The large man shifted his frame slightly from where he was sitting on the bed, weighing his thoughts carefully before he spoke.

"Ain't never gonna be at ease, long as those that would do us harm still tryin' so hard to do just that."

"I read the papers too, Cusman." Missy Nell said as she turned and faced him. "Gettysburg, Vicksburg. General Grant hot on their tails, other Yankee generals too. The South is back on its heels, Cusman. Just a matter of time, even if they don't know it yet, and I s'pect more'a them do than admit to it. The Union army's gettin' bigger, and accordin' to the paper more Southern men desertin' than joinin' up these days."

"They ain't whupped yet." Cusman replied as he searched in vain for some concurring understanding in Missy Nell's reddened eyes. "Been how long now since President Lincoln freed the slaves down South, nigh on a year? How many our people still under the whip? How many women down there gettin' ready to have *their* babies that might get sold off, or whatever else their mas'r wants done with 'em?"

"You think that's fair, Cusman, bringin' that up now? How am I supposed to answer that? Just look at me!" She said, placing both hands on her swollen stomach. "Anyway, you already spilled your blood for them, an' spilled plenty'a Rebel blood too. You done your part for the Union, Cusman. More'n your part, now's the time for you to stay here an' do your part for your family!" Cusman looked down and sighed.

"Missy, it ain't *over* gal. Jus' 'cause you bloody a man up in a fight don't mean he's done fightin', let alone whupped. And I *am* doin' my part for our family. How you reckon I'm gonna answer our children when they're old enough to ask me what all I done? I kin tell 'em I fought with the 54th, got all shot up, stabbed even, and I s'pect they'll think I done all I could, but I'll know better and so will you. I wanna stay *here*,

Missy. That's what I want, but what choice I got when there's whole armies still tryin' to do what they can to make me an' mine slaves agin? Ain't enough to just bloody 'em up. Gotta destroy their way'a life, kill that an' them too. Least ways enough'a them, so they cain't never own us, or sell us, our children, or anybody else or their children *ever* again, an' that's the Lord's truth."

Missy Nell took a breath and stood a little taller, her hands still on her stomach. "You go on then Cusman, you go on, and don't come back til you know you won't *ever* leave us again." She turned back to the window as she dabbed her eyes. There was another flash of far off lightning, but that time the thunder wasted no time finding them.

***

EVERYONE WAS worried about Sedman. He had always been sickly growing up, and his recent bout with pleurisy had left him bedridden for nearly three weeks. It was another two weeks before he was really on his feet again, but even then he could attend only half his classes. After Cusman had mustered the courage to inform Missy Nell of his intentions, he changed his mind about waiting until the babies were born before departing.

Missy Nell felt tinges of guilt whenever Cusman reported on their friend's condition, at least when her husband would inform her Sedman was still doing too poorly to head off to Tennessee. She felt guiltier still when she insisted Cusman couldn't just leave his friend and join up without him, like he kept hinting he might do. Perhaps the Union would have the Rebels whipped before Cusman and Sedman could go, she prayed to herself, but only mentioned to Jennifer. One word of that to Cusman and he just *might* head off without Sedman.

It was already October, and the twins were less than two months away from their estimated date of arrival. If Cusman was still around for that, at least one of her prayers would be answered. When word reached Missy Nell that Sedman had suffered a relapse and infection had set in she prayed night and day for his recovery, but asked her Lord to take special care in order to make sure He got it right this time. Sedman continued to improve, but it was slow in coming.

Every night while in bed next to her husband she always lifted up the same silent prayer: *You're doin' a good job, Lord, so don't get to frettin' Sedman is comin' along too slow. You don't need to hurry things along, the miracle You're workin' on is doin' just fine, just as right as it kin be. Just want You to see to it my babies born first, that's all, unless You kin find a way to end this war. Amen.* Six weeks later she was again calling upon her God for His Divine Intervention - screaming for it, actually.

***

JENNIFER HAD been spending a great deal of time at the Sable household as her daughter's due date approached. She and Cusman were sharing coffee in the kitchen when they heard Missy Nell call from the downstairs bedroom one morning. It was the tone of her voice that spurred the two of them into action. Just one word: *"Mother!"*

Cusman glanced into the bedroom then rushed to the small barn out back, and was soon riding off to fetch the doctor. Eight hours later the twins arrived, first a boy, then his sister. Missy Jennifer Diane weighed in at eight pounds, her brother Mede, eight pounds eight ounces.

The doctor said both babies appeared to be in excellent health, and said the same about Missy Nell. Later that evening Sedman stopped by. He had fully recovered, but that evening over supper both men refrained from bringing up Tennessee or anything else that had to do with the war, at least in front of the women. Jennifer had served Missy Nell her supper in bed, and when she returned to the kitchen it was obvious the men had been talking about something not meant for her ears.

"I hope you two weren't discussing any specific plans, on this of all days." She said as she took a seat at the table. Neither man responded, as if their supper had suddenly become the only thing they had on their minds. "Missy Nell is going to need time, Cusman, and I don't just mean until she's on her feet again. One baby is handful enough. I'll help of course, but those babies are going to need their father." Cusman placed his flatware on his plate and looked at her.

"I was hopin' you might stay here permanent-like, least ways after I leave." He said, adding: "Sooner we get goin' the sooner we get back."

"So you and Sedman are planning on ending the war all by yourselves, then? Even Trenton knew the South was doomed from the start, and now that it appears he was right you two are still hell bent upon risking your lives unnecessarily. Why not wait until spring? If the war takes a turn for the worse you can join up then." It was Sedman who replied.

"If enough men were to heed such advice who knows how things might turn out? I dare say the Confederacy would welcome that fortuitous turn of events, and would no doubt encourage other Federal wives and mothers to make the same argument. I can't speak for Cusman, and I would agree he has already done his part and is indeed needed here, but thus far all I have done is offer words in support of my country. I'm leaving in two weeks."

"And I'm goin' with him," Cusman said to Jennifer. "None of you kin say what I done is enough, that's for me to decide. Rebels ain't done fightin' so I ain't either."

"The least you two could do is compromise," Jennifer said. "Christmas is less than a month away. If you will wait until mid-January, I'll move in here tomorrow and support your decision, Cusman. I pray you will at least think it over."

***

LATER THAT night Cusman was sitting in a rocking chair next to one of the tall, narrow windows in the downstairs bedroom. There was a full moon, and the hushed, silver light momentarily illuminated Missy Nell as she slept on her back in bed, turning steel blue as it reflected off the purple down comforter that covered her almost to her chin. The faint light revealed her beautiful face as if it were a portrait the moonbeams had been especially waiting to evince, an affirmation that all things could be endured and a quiet calm would ultimately lend itself to all those who persevered.

Her breathing was steady, and as much as Cusman wanted to be next to her he wanted the perfect image to remain undisturbed for at least a little while longer. The babies would soon stir, so the precious moments he was enjoying would end soon enough. The babies. He glanced over at the two bassinets. They were in the corner, away from the moonbeams that were no doubt searching for them as the patient, silver light inched closer to the infants by the minute.

Some fathers, he imagined, might need a while to bond with their babies, to fully appreciate the miracle that had occurred. It had taken Cusman all of two seconds once they had begun to squirm in his arms; one instantaneous flash of time for each child. Even though he was sitting across the room he could sense their warmth and recalled the way they had struggled in his arms as if they were impatient to discover what magic awaited them. Perhaps their little souls had been elsewhere, and had suddenly found a haven so safe they could finally explore what had been just outside their grasp for who knew how long. *Perhaps,* Cusman thought. There was no question in Cusman's mind about him being a safe haven.

All the rationalizations he had been employing to convince everyone, especially himself that he had to leave for war, suddenly appeared to have been chiseled in ice exposed to a warming rain. He could sense his babies' contented souls all right, and the effect was obvious. Before along his rationalizations had taken a different course. Missy Nell's angelic face was no longer aglow in the soft shower of moonbeams, and he watched as the silver-blue luminosity began to caress the bottom portions of the white linen bunting around the bassinets. The moonlight would soon find what it was searching for, as would Cusman.

It would have been so easy to give in, he reflected, to allow his recent musings to take root and flourish. He thought about his mother and father, and how they had no doubt looked upon him in his rude crib nearly a quarter century ago. He had grown to realize their love for him had been every bit as strong as what he was feeling at that moment for his babies. What safe haven could his parents have promised him? What if, back then, Trenton Ransom's father had gone over his books and decided some extra cash flow would have been helpful or some such thing?

Cusman turned his head and looked out the tall, narrow window. A slow moving cloud, the only one he could see on that otherwise clear night, had eased over and absorbed all of the moonbeams. By the time the cloud had moved on so had Cusman. He would tell Missy in the morning when she awoke; Sedman later that day, just before the class they shared at Amherst College. He owed it to his parents, and he owed it to his babies and their babies. Missy would come to understand he owed it to her, and himself, as well. On January 15th of 1864 he was leaving for Memphis, Tennessee.

XXXII

Billy hadn't been to Linda Marie's grave since before he had left for the war, the day of the thunderstorm. So much had happened since then, so many things had changed, but when he cleared the rise and looked down towards her granite headstone, the largest one along with Sackett's in the immediate vicinity, it was as if nothing had changed at all.

He had brought a Christmas wreath with him, and although the brisk December gusts again reminded him he should have worn his heaviest coat, he stood erect upon the unsheltered rise anyway, not moving. The O'Darcy family had already attached a wreath of laurels to her tombstone and that of her brother, both much larger than the one he had made from the branches of a blue spruce, but he hadn't planned on hanging it anyway. He made his way to the grave and placed it on the ground where he imagined her breast might be. It would be closer to her that way, and perhaps the love that had gone into making it would somehow find its way to her.

Small snowflakes were scurrying about, snow pellets more like it, but it didn't appear as if they would amount to much. He hoped they would, however. He wanted the wreath to be hidden so only he would know how close he had placed it to her heart, to all of Linda Marie's soul. He was done hating God, if simmering contempt wasn't hate, but he certainly didn't trust Him. In truth, he had to admit he didn't know God at all, not the one he used to know anyway. He began to struggle with all those eternal controversies again, but dismissed those musings. He was tired of the relentless battling. Besides, Billy concluded, he was there to be with Linda Marie, not quarrel with some treacherous old ghost who fancied himself a god.

"I'll be sixteen in a few months, Linda Marie," Billy said as he looked towards the ground beneath his wreath. "Same age as you. Had me a time at Gettysburg, that's a town in Pennsylvania. Terrible battle took place, but we whipped the Johnnies good." He stopped talking and looked around, then wiped some snow from his face. He was grateful they weren't tears as he steeled his dubious resolve against them, and just as grateful the cemetery was deserted. "War's still goin' on though. S'pect you know that. Had me a fight with God, but if He's really there I s'pect you know that too. Shawn, he's a friend of mine from the army, said God protected me'n him at Gettysburg, but after what I said last time I was here and plenty times since that doesn't seem likely. Nothin' does, when it comes to Him - meanin' God of course.

Can't help but wonder if Pete is with you. Hope so anyway. Wish you could answer me Linda Marie, tell me what's what. I sure don't know, confusin' as everything is. Looks like Delicia's gonna marry Clifton Janeway. She's wearin' the biggest diamond ring I ever seen, once in a while anyway. Well, I best be gettin' back to the hospital. More men arrivin' every week it seems. I...I love you Linda Marie. Hope you heard that." He again wiped away some of the pellet-like snow from his eyes, and that time the tiny specks weren't alone.

***

DELICIA HADN'T accepted Clifton's proposal to marry, but she had agreed to an engagement of sorts. She had promised to make her final decision one way or the other, perhaps before June, but no later than that month. It was either that, or she would not keep the ring. Most men would have considered such an arrangement pure folly, and although Clifton realized that, he also knew he had made it further along than he would have ever dreamed possible. Besides, he knew why she was delaying, or thought he did.

He was mired in a quandary regarding Pete McCabe's fate. Just because something had perhaps happened to Stalworthy, that didn't have to mean McCabe had fared any better. Clifton was no longer convinced Stalworthy had even located Pete to begin with, regardless of what the last telegram had said. For all Clifton knew the task had proved impossible or at least too difficult, and Stalworthy had simply disappeared with the money he had already been given, although he might show up to try and collect the rest per their arrangement. Maybe Stalworthy was still looking, in search of something worth reporting. Clifton wished the last telegram had contained more information though, assuming it was accurate and not just based on some rumor Stalworthy had come across only to discover it wasn't true. That would explain why he hadn't heard from him again, and most important of all it could easily mean McCabe had been long dead even if Stalworthy couldn't prove it yet. McCabe had been missing since Shiloh, two years ago come spring, and not a word from him to anyone. He must be dead, Clifton all but concluded. Still, his doubts refused to dissipate.

Clifton had finally headed back to Chicago in search of another man similar to Stalworthy. Now that he had until June it couldn't hurt to at least try, or so he had first assumed. A few weeks after Christmas he had located a man who had known Stalworthy. He hadn't been nearly as impressive, but had a southern accent he had come by honestly and would try to verify whether or not McCabe was a prisoner or had perhaps escaped. If he was lucky, maybe he'd find out and be able to prove McCabe was dead. The man had refused to do more than that, other than try to locate

Stalworthy as well, but since he said he'd do at least that much for a thousand dollars and only two-fifty up front, Clifton had agreed.

Clifton also considered continuing his search for other men who might be useful, but feared giving any of those the information they would need was too reckless, which also raised an alarm. *McCabe has to be dead, God damn it,* he kept telling himself. A few days later Clifton began to worry more about the man he'd hired than the possibility of McCabe being alive, but that proved to be an easy fix. He was to meet him at the man's rundown apartment in Chicago with the $250. Clifton didn't bring the two-fifty, but he brought along his knife. Problem solved.

***

THE NEW walking bridge over the DuPage River was almost completed. The men assigned to the task didn't concern themselves with the cold temperatures December and now January always brought forth, but the recent snows and accompanying ice had halted construction. Billy was looking forward to its completion. Not only would it allow him to take a short cut home from the hospital by being able to cross the river south of Eagle Street, but it would also afford him the opportunity to pass largely unnoticed by the western side of the cemetery by cutting through the O'Darcy property.

The east side of the cemetery was abutted by Washington Street, and although that wasn't much of a time and distance factor as far as access to the cemetery was concerned, at least no one would likely see him enter and leave from the other direction. Leaving was his biggest concern. He had yet to do so without tears in his eyes and all that encompassed, which was something he wanted to keep between himself and Linda Marie; he hoped so anyway. He had often passed by the cemetery before and after work, hesitating to go in for that very reason. Soon it would be easier to visit Linda Marie's grave on a more regular basis; there was so much he wanted to discuss with her, but the two of them being alone together was just as much a priority.

Both Delicia and especially her father were looking forward to the bridge's completion as well. After picking up his daughter at the hospital each evening Hezekiah would be able to cross the bridge and catch the angle where High Street met with Oswego Road. A quick right and they would be home, since Pinecraig was set back about a hundred yards on their property just past the angle on the south side of Oswego Road. They would no longer have to go all the way to the Main Street Bridge then cut back west. In the milder months that was barely an inconvenience, but during winter the time saved would be greatly appreciated.

The citizens of Naperville were impressed by the scope of the project. Not only was it being constructed by the most able carpenters and bridge builders in all of DuPage County if not the entire Chicagoland area, but the materials being used were of the highest quality even though the country was in the midst of a great war. Although it was being touted as a walking bridge, it was wide enough to accommodate carriages; even wagons, if they weren't too wide, could traverse the bridge regardless of the weight of their loads. Limestone from the nearby quarries could now be hauled much easier and relieve the stress and traffic, if it could be called such, on both the Washington and Main Street bridges that were themselves in need of at least repair if not replacement.

At first it was going to be a covered bridge, but those plans were discarded or at least placed on hold. Getting it completed was the primary goal, and if the weather cooperated it appeared as though that would happen no later than March. Although it would add to its aesthetics to include the cover it was still going to be pleasing to the eye. Local residents loved their small community, but even the most subjective amongst them knew other towns like Aurora and Wheaton, towns with train stations, had made more progress. The new bridge by itself wouldn't correct that, but it was a step in the right direction.

A reporter from a New York newspaper had been in town recently covering a trial, and his comments had been less than complimentary. There was no train service, no telegraph office and most of the structures were single story homes and buildings whose owners were apparently unaware paint came in colors other than white. His comments were offensive to the good people of Naperville, but no less accurate. That, most of the locals concluded, needed to be addressed. The new bridge was a good start.

Doc Wygant of late had been in good spirits as well. His efforts at the hospital had been recognized by none other than President Lincoln himself in the form of a Certificate of Merit. By itself that wouldn't have made much of an impression on the old man, but when the doctor found out Illinois' native son Abraham had also managed to secure a five thousand dollar grant for an additional wing, he was elated. The two story brick structure that once served as a home was also in need of repair, and if the new wing was modest enough in size, overall improvements, as well as new medical and hospital equipment would also be possible.

Work had begun even before the money arrived. Doc Wygant loved to head north on Eagle Street and view the work in progress as he approached. He sometimes approached from the east using Franklin Street where the hospital was located, depending on where his house call had taken him. The northwest part of the L intersection where Eagle and Franklin Streets met was where the hospital was located, and the new wing would come out almost to the lowest branches of the huge oak to the west.

There had been talk of a railroad station being built in town, and if it did happen Doc Wygant insisted it would be just northeast of the hospital. He had sent a letter off to his new friend President Lincoln asking if he might consider using his influence to speed things up, but hadn't received a reply. "A might busy with the war I suppose," Doc Wygant explained to anyone who pestered him about it, "but don't be surprised if the new station winds up no more'n a few blocks northeast of here."

***

MOTHER GRACE and Father Benjamin continued to receive letters from their sons still off to war, with of course one notable exception. Mother Grace never referred to Pete in the past tense and bristled if anyone else did in her presence. She had fully recovered from her illness, but Father Benjamin was concerned about her overall health anyway. He had replaced all the windows in their bedroom, taking special care to insulate with newspaper the one she always chose to kneel by when offering up her prayers, until recently. She had always preferred the one in the southeast corner, and when she had begun using the one located in the southwest corner Father Benjamin asked why.

"It's a bit closer to Kee," was her only reply.

It hadn't been easy for Father Benjamin to finally sign the consent form, but Billy had experienced a change of heart once it had been done and agreed to stay as Doc Wygant's assistant. The real reason he stayed had to do with Mother Grace. Once she got wind of Billy's possible intent she took sick again, and in a way that left no doubt she wasn't faking her illness, not that she would have anyway. It was Doc Wygant that sealed things for the youth.

"You go ahead on, Billy boy, you just go off to war again. Wounded men right here in the hospital will die with just me lookin' out for them, many as there are. Hell, I'm an old man, only got so much stamina left in me I'll be bound. You can save lives here or off in some damnable battle I suppose, but there's one you'll save here that means more to you than any soldier. I'm tellin' you the truth, son. You leave, your mother is going to die. It's a feelin' I have, and it hasn't got a damned thing to do with my profession. That doesn't bode well for your mother if you light out."

Billy stayed.

XXXIII

Pete had initially appeared to be mending as well as could be expected, but his progress, months in the making, kept getting interrupted by setbacks. Fever had set in again, and for over two weeks it looked as if he wasn't going to make it after all. He again rallied, but was still in no condition to be moved. A week after that he had another relapse so severe Janny had told his son Cleavon to go dig a grave in the woods. The obese, odorous man chose a spot behind the pig pen instead, hoping to avoid the roots he would have been forced to contend with if he had dug where his father had requested.

It was Buddy who first spotted Cleavon digging, so he grabbed the shovel, found a pick and axe then marched into the woods and dug the grave himself. He refused to allow the body of the man Desiree obviously loved to be treated with such disrespect. Cleavon had argued, even if he did hate to dig graves or anything else, and used his younger brother's affront as an excuse to challenge him. He was still smarting over Desiree being taken from him, something Buddy, amongst others, had insisted upon. Cleavon couldn't argue with Auntie Porticia, much less his father, but Buddy was a different story. Buddy obviously had eyes for Desiree, and coupled with the rest of the things he had been up to recently Cleavon wanted to kill him, brother or not.

Buddy had shaved off his beard, just like the Yankee, and was even taking regular baths in the creek; sometimes as often as once a week. Kept his clothes relatively clean too, washing them *himself,* almost as often as his body. With his long beard gone he was a fairly handsome young man, nearly six feet tall, narrow of hip and broad at the shoulders. His sharp blue eyes signaled his intelligence, and his dark brown hair had some curl to it once it had been cut and washed more often. The haircut had been the final insult for Cleavon, until the grave digging incident. Not only had that been the latest final insult, but it was the one that prompted him to demand Buddy meet him behind the barn, and to bring his knife. "Gonna settle your hash once an' fer all," Cleavon had said.

Buddy accepted the challenge, but when Janny got wind of it both brothers were ordered into the barn. Buddy already had a shovel, and Janny made sure Cleavon did as well. It took them the rest of the day to load the wheelbarrows with manure and dump it in the ravine out back. It hadn't helped Cleavon's mood any that as soon as they were finished his kid brother had gone directly to the creek and taken another bath; the second one in as many days. Things only grew worse. Three days later that damned Yankee's fever broke again, and it didn't look good; he just might make it after all. Both brothers felt that way, but for Buddy there was some guilt involved.

***

CHRISTMAS HAD come and gone, although not very many people in Low Cloud Valley paid it much mind. Desiree had hoped Pete would have been well enough to move into the shack in the woods before then, but as much as they both wanted out of the settlement there was no way he could have made such an arduous journey. The shack was only about ten miles away, but it was a very rugged ten miles, for the most part. Perhaps by February Pete would be able to make it if he continued to improve.

Desiree and Ely had been to the shack in the woods several times with Buddy, leaving Little Desiree with Porticia. Buddy had been a big help fixing and mending things, especially the roof until it could shed the heaviest downpours. On their first visit he had told Desiree it would be best if she and Ely stayed outside and took a scythe to the weeds and grasses around the shack. After an hour had passed she had gone inside. Buddy had been working on the floor boards. The ones that had been stained with blood the worst had been ripped out, turned over and nailed back in place. The others had responded to the chunk of sandstone he had used to scrape off even a hint of old bloodstains.

"Don't reckon the little ones will be a botherin' you with no sad questions what ain't got nothin' but sadder answers right behind." He had said.

"Thank you Buddy," Desiree had replied, "that's right thoughtful of you."

"You sure 'nough welcome, Miss Desiree. Ah'll go on an' tend ta that fallin' down wreck of a barn. Ah swear, that brother-in-law'a mine sure did hate ta put a peg ta wood, Lord rest his soul."

***

"YOU DONE tolt me that there gal was mine, Pa. That there's what you done tolt me." Cleavon said to his father for what seemed like the hundredth time as they were dressing a deer they had killed deep in the woods. "An' now that there brother'a mine's fixin' ta wed up with her sure. Ain't fair, Pa, jist ain't fair." Janny glared at his least favorite son, and answered him for what also seemed like the hundredth time.

"She ain't fer none'a y'all, how many times I gotta tell ya? She's that Yankee's woman, long as he's alive, an' it looks like he ain't got no quit in 'em near's I kin tell. Porticia got her say in it too, God dammit, an' she don't want none'a y'all gittin' any fool notions in yer fool heads 'lessin' that there gal is willin', which she ain't. That clear 'nough fer ya, boy?"

"Yeah Pa. Ceptin' Ah don't reckon Buddy's payin' that no never mind. He's fixin' on weddin' her sure."

"He kin think what he likes, don't change nothin'. Stop frettin' on it Cleavon. There be other women what comes along, or mebbe one'a our local gals. Hell, a few'a them's damned near thirteen. Now hand me that there scraper an' shut the hell up."

**

PETE WAS on his feet before February was over, and by early March made the journey to the shack although by then it looked more like a home. Janny had even loaned them a milk cow although it had been Porticia who had insisted upon it. He gave Pete his Henry rifle back for hunting, but not until the Yankee promised to be on his way later that spring and take his woman with him. Janny also made him promise not to breathe a word of their agreement to Porticia. She had grown very fond of Desiree and the children, and hoped they would eventually grow to love their place in the woods enough to make it their home.

Buddy stopped by occasionally, although at first he was concerned the Yankee wouldn't want him around. Pete not only didn't mind, he encouraged the young mountain man to stop by whenever he was in the area. The children loved having him around, especially Ely. He had even come to call him Uncle Buddy, and looked forward to their forays into the woods where Buddy allowed him to shoot a real gun. One morning Desiree and Pete came running when they heard the boy's screams. They had made it halfway to the woods when Ely came running out, flush with excitement and pride.

"Shot me a razorback! Clean through the head! Uncle Buddy's dressin' it, come on, Ah'll show y'all!" That evening they had a veritable feast, and Ely was allowed to sit at the head of the table. Desiree had even baked the sweet potatoes Porticia had given her; blackstrap molasses, salted butter and all.

"Buddy," Pete said when the two men had stepped outside after Desiree and the children were down for the night, "I'm feelin' like myself again. Thinkin' about headin' out." Buddy didn't answer right away as he looked closer at Pete.

"Reckon Desiree and the youngins goin' too, ain't they?" He asked

"Haven't told her yet. But I'm tellin' you if she wants to stay that's fine by me, as long as you promise to watch over her and the children."

"What *ain't* you a tellin' me, Yank? How come you're willin' ta leave her an' them youngins behind? Ah ain't of a mind she'll be'a wantin' ta stay no ways."

"Doubt she will, I just want you to know it's fine by me if she does. Your pa expects me to take her along, so I guess you and Porticia will have to deal with that if she decides to stay. My gal is back in Illinois. If she's still waiting, I'm gonna marry her. Desiree knows that, Buddy. Thought you should too."

"Figured that out in the barn that day," Buddy said. "Thought you might'a had a change'a heart, though."

"I haven't. Don't think my gal back home has either, except she probably thinks I'm dead. Lord knows what that could mean. I'm goin' home anyway though. Don't plan on bringin' anyone with me."

"Won't be easy, Yank. Last Ah heard there's been a powerful lotta fightin' goin' on north'a here, up Chattanooga way. That ain't but eighty or so miles away, seventy as the crow flies. Don't know what come of it, 'ceptin' you Yankees got whupped but fer some reason our boys lit outta there. Could be they's scattered all through them woods north'a here. Don't s'pect you'd be a wantin' ta run inta them."

It was the first news Pete had heard about the war in months. So much time had passed it was as if it had almost ceased to exist for him. Apparently a peddler had passed through the area when Pete had been bedridden, and had informed the folks in Low Cloud Valley all hell had broken loose all the way from Pigeon Mountain to the Tennessee River and points north. The Federals and Confederates had been going back and forth for control of Chattanooga and the vital railroad and water routes in the area. Last the peddler had heard, the Confederates were mostly out of Tennessee and the Yankees were in control.

"I'll be damned," Pete muttered. "If I can only get to Chattanooga…Buddy, I have a proposition for you."

Buddy liked the sound of it from the beginning. If he would agree to accompany Pete and the rest of them to Chattanooga, Pete would head out by himself and leave Desiree with Buddy. If she wanted to settle in the town herself, Buddy could then decide what he wanted to do. With the Federals in control, if that was the case, she just might want to stay, maybe go back with him or stay in one of the other towns nearby. Either way, Pete would be gone and Buddy would be the only one left she could rely upon. He left out the part about the nearly sixteen hundred dollars in gold he still had tucked in his boots. Buddy didn't need to know about that until they'd reached their destination, if then. Pete would let Desiree decide how that would play out.

"If the wagon is still in that meadow," Pete said, "and you can get your pa to let us borrow three horses, we could be on our way in a day or two." Buddy walked away from the front of the shack, pulled up a long blade of grass and put the moist, white end in his mouth. Dusk had almost finished turning into night but there was enough light for Pete to see Buddy's face.

"Reckon you could use mah help gettin' away from here, an' Ah know the area we all'd be a headin' into. Ah don't talk like no damned Yankee neither. That's likely ta help some. Maybe a lot. Ah'll go tell Pa. You kin tell Desiree."

***

JANNY WARMED to the idea, especially when Pete reluctantly agreed to give him the Henry rifle in exchange for borrowing the horses. Pete had tried to get the mountain man to let him keep the Henry since the horses would be returned and one of them had been Pete's horse to begin with. Had Pete haggled harder Janny would have probably relented, since getting rid of the Yankee and his woman was his top priority. Pete tried to talk Janny out of one of the Spencer's or Sharps rifles taken from Mitchell's gang, but Janny used the excuse those had already been claimed by others who had lost kin during Mitchell's raid.

Buddy had left out the part about Desiree's possible return. Janny knew her continued presence would cause nothing but trouble between Buddy and Cleavon, and with Tray dead that left only two sons, and one of those was at best feeble-minded. Janny couldn't feature Cleavon ever being in charge of things someday, and even though a clash between him and Buddy over that was no doubt inevitable, it could be dealt with when the time came.

Cleavon was a dolt but ruthless in a simple-minded sort of way. Janny could see him doing something stupid again like when he had challenged his brother to a knife fight over some girl. Buddy had been forced to accept the challenge of course, and although he probably would have come out on top it was cause for concern anyway. Getting Desiree away from there was the best solution, and Janny vowed the next woman who suffered the misfortune of getting caught would have to suffer even more when she found out who her new husband was going to be. Cleavon would calm down then, having his own woman and all. At least he'd probably quit pestering the livestock, which had caused more than a little embarrassment for the family over the years.

Desiree didn't warm to the idea. The longer she and Pete stayed at the small homestead the better the chances were he might eventually come around to accept her as his wife. After that, they could head off to wherever he might like to take them. He never stopped talking about his girl back in Illinois though. Getting home was all he ever seemed to really care about. If she insisted upon staying it would no doubt be the last she would see of him. She had no good choices in that regard, so the only thing left for her was to agree with the plan. Perhaps he would have a change of heart along the way, or when the time came for them to part, but she doubted it. She would miss Porticia and Buddy but leaving the Low Cloud Valley area, at least the others who lived there, would be best for her and especially the children if Pete wasn't there with them.

Three days later they were almost ready to leave. Desiree, however, had kept insisting she wanted to say goodbye to Porticia. Pete wanted to thank her again himself, but making the arduous twenty mile round trip held scant appeal for him, especially since he wanted so desperately to finally initiate what he hoped was the beginning of the end of his perilous odyssey. He finally decided to just get it over with. Upon arrival, he had tried to give five of his twenty dollar gold pieces to Porticia but she just smiled and shook her head.

"Reckon that Yankee you shot in the barn was right about one thing," she had said. "The gold he was hankerin' fer's right under the floor, down there." She pointed to the bed Pete had spent so much time recuperating upon. "S'pect you ain't the only one what hides gold," she had continued to say, still smiling. "Them boots'a yourns seemed a might heavy. Lucky fer you Ah was the only one what picked 'em up. You take good care of that sweet child an' her youngins, hear?"

***

PETE HAD previously handed over his Henry to Janny and all the remaining ammunition, but it still bothered him. He knew it had been a poor trade, potentially a dangerous one, but they had to have horses.

It was a long trek back through the woods early the following morning. It was a clear day, warm for that time of year or would have been if Pete was home. Ely wasn't any trouble, but Little Desiree had to be carried most of the way and getting the three horses through the woods proved difficult at times as well.

After hitching two of the horses up to the wagon they were finally ready to leave. Pete looked around and contemplated the vagaries of life as the small group began moving. He was astride the smallest horse, having asked Buddy to drive the wagon. He wanted him to stay close to Desiree, and Buddy certainly had no objections. Perhaps their time together would heighten her feelings for the young man. Unless Pete had missed his guess she was already at least somewhat attracted to him. Maybe she didn't know it yet, but when Pete was gone anything might transpire. Pete hoped so anyway.

They came to a rise in the wagon trace about three hundred yards north of the small meadow where the wagon had been, and Pete glanced back. Vagaries of life were indeed on his mind. What would have happened if he had just kept going that fateful morning? Janny and his sons had obviously been tracking them, but perhaps Mitchell and his gang would have come in contact with the mountain men before they could have sprung a trap. Pete figured he would probably have been home by now if he hadn't been killed or captured again. Well, he was heading home now by

God, and if he could only make it to Chattanooga there was a good chance he'd get there this time.

The very thought of home got him thinking about Delicia, longing for her really, although the rest of his family was on his mind as well. Just eighty or so miles and he would be able to catch a train behind Union lines, a place he had feared on more occasions than he cared to remember he would never set foot on again. Just what was everyone back home thinking?

The first thing he'd do upon reaching Chattanooga was get a telegram off to Tin Pan Alley then another to Delicia, realizing he would probably do it the other way around. Everyone had to believe he was dead by now, or at best held captive in some Rebel prison camp, good as dead; and what had become of his brothers? It was unlikely they were all still alive, but not impossible. Casualty rates were usually high, twenty-five percent and higher being not uncommon for many battles, but that still left the majority of soldiers unscathed. Still, the more battles one was in the more likely their luck would eventually run out. *Sweet Jesus,* Pete thought, *what if I'm the only one left save Billy? At least he's still too young to go off to war, if Ma and Pa have anything to say about it.*

He could only imagine the joy Mother Grace and Father Benjamin would feel when his wire arrived. His only reservation was it might indeed be tempered by the death of some of his brothers, perhaps most of them, but he drove that from his mind, or tried to. If he could survive so could they. Perhaps a few of them were even home by now, but he doubted it. He'd have a better understanding of that after reporting to the commander of the Union forces in Chattanooga, or one of his subordinates more like it. They would likely be able to get off priority wires of one kind or another, and with luck he'd get priority responses.

What a story Pete would have for them and all the people back home! Especially Delicia – oh God, Delicia. Hadn't they loved each other since childhood? He knew if their situations had been reversed he would have waited for her, but what if it had been her who had been killed almost two years ago? He glanced at Desiree then, but didn't have to. He already knew. If Delicia was involved with someone else he couldn't blame her; the fates maybe, but not her. Lord knows she no doubt had all kinds of fellows competing for her affections, he imagined. What would be her reaction if that was the case and she was married or at least betrothed, and then his telegram arrived? He didn't want to think about that but he did anyway. It was as if the nearest telegraph office was suddenly a million miles off and somehow the distance was growing farther away the closer he got to Chattanooga.

Delicia was stubborn though, borne with a generally unrestrained perseverance, itself borne from an optimism Pete couldn't recall having faltered much over the years. It wouldn't surprise him if she was waiting for the war to end before giving any serious consideration to some other man. After all, it was possible he had indeed been in a prison camp all this time and somehow survived, he kept reminding himself. If so he sure wouldn't have been the only one, both North and South. It wasn't like either side went out of their way to inform the home folk about anything, even if the soldier was an officer, unless a high ranking one, as best Pete knew. *Lord*, he thought, *my back pay should amount to quite a sum, maybe enough for a down payment on our own farm...a house in town anyway, for starters. Delicia must be waiting*, he concluded, and with that stuck firmly in his mind he rode ahead of the wagon. He wanted to be alone with Delicia for awhile, and their plans.

***

AFTER GOING several miles Pete decided to pull up and wait for the wagon. He had entered a deep valley, and although the often uneven wagon trace was dry, his help might be needed for the others to make it up the particularly steep grade in front of him after they had cleared the rise and caught up to where he was waiting. He couldn't keep his excitement down nor did he care to try. He wasn't used to riding and his left side was bothering him, but that would most likely pass. If it didn't, so be it. He had too much to feel good about, ecstatic about really, and it felt wonderful to let the rapture wash over him; it had been a long time coming, or at least felt that way.

He looked about, taking in the beautiful spring morning, and marveled at how quickly everything had begun to bloom. The leaves were already out or pretty much so, at least a good month ahead of what was probably happening back home. He couldn't wait to tell his kinfolk about it, especially Mother Grace. He could just picture her smiling as he told her, knowing full well she wouldn't trade her little corner of the world for all the early springs in the universe.

He turned and looked for the wagon. That was odd, he thought. It should have already cleared the rise. He wondered what had broken down now, but before his horse had made three steps back in that direction his soldier instincts had already alerted him to other possibilities.

He tied his horse a little ways into the woods east of the wagon trace and made his way south through the trees, a revolver in each hand. He again regretted having traded away his Henry without at least demanding one of the Spencer's, but it was too late now if his worst fears were confirmed. It wasn't his worst fears he spotted, but it was close enough.

"She's a comin back with me, Buddy, ain't no two ways 'bout it!" Cleavon said to his brother, his musket pointed at Buddy's chest. "You kin jist keep on'a headin' north, an' take them kids too." Cleavon half turned his head, not moving his rifle away while he kept Buddy in his peripheral vision. "Ah knows you is in them woods,

Yankee!" He hollered over his shoulder. "You try back shootin' me Ah'll shoot Buddy sure, mebbe one'a them youngins 'fore Ah die, swear Ah will! Come on out here!" Pete came out, keeping both Colts trained on Cleavon.

Pete knew he could shoot him, but the closer he got the more likely he would be able to get off a head shot so he kept moving forward. That damned large bore musket though; Cleavon would probably be able to pull the trigger and it would tear a huge hole through whatever it hit at that close range.

"I'm right here, Cleavon." Pete said in an even tone. "No sense anyone gettin' hurt. Why don't you lower that thing and we'll talk."

"Done mah talkin'! That thar gal's'a comin' with me. We gonna wed up! Rest'a y'all kin jist keep'a headin north! Now put them hog legs down Yank or Ah'll blast Buddy sure! Mebbe one'a them thar youngins, swear Ah will!"

Pete realized Cleavon was stupid enough to do something foolish. The mountain man had only one shot, but Pete feared the extent of the man's addled condition was such he could very well shoot someone besides the one pointing two revolvers at him. That was Cleavon's best chance other than just walking away, but that didn't mean his child-like mind could comprehend the significance those chances represented. Pete put one of his revolvers on the ground.

"There! I've met you halfway, Cleavon," Pete said as he stood up again. Cleavon cocked his head towards Pete, trying to grasp what had just occurred. Then he trained his musket on Pete - on what he didn't understand.

"You leave Pa alone!" Ely screamed at Cleavon as the boy jumped from the wagon and ran towards Pete, startling the confused and desperate man.

A wide-eyed Cleavon was standing not far from the wagon on the driver's side, and leveled his musket at the boy. If intelligent people did most everything for effect, stupid ones did most everything to unintentionally announce their objective, especially under the type of circumstance that had ensnared Cleavon. That's all it took for Buddy.

He moved so quickly Pete didn't have time to shoot. Buddy flew from where he was sitting and landed on top of his much larger brother before Cleavon could bring his musket around in time. Pete hurried over and tried to get a bead on the large man, but the two brothers were struggling so much he couldn't get a clear line of fire. Then it was over. Buddy had slashed his brother's throat with so much force Cleavon barely had time to pull the trigger, and when he did the barrel had been pointed towards the ground as the gunshot echoed through the woods. Everyone was frozen in place, watching Cleavon twitch on the ground as blood spurted from the severed artery in his neck, and the white smoke from his musket drifted across the wagon trace, disappearing into the forest beyond. A few moments later he was dead.

Desiree jumped from the wagon, ran over and took Ely in her arms. Then she looked at Buddy who was standing next to his dead brother. He dropped the knife and just looked at her.

"You saved Ely, Buddy. You saved his life." Desiree said as she stood there trembling, tears welling up in her green eyes.

"Cain't just leave it like this Ah reckon," Buddy finally said. "It's gotta be me what tells Pa. S'pect he know'd would come down to this someday. Ain't fer certain how he's gonna take to it though."

***

"BETTER IT was him an' not you, boy." Was Janny's response when Buddy arrived at the settlement with the body across the back of a horse. "Ah knew it would happen someday."

Pete had accompanied Buddy to the settlement while Desiree had stayed with the children. Pete asked Buddy if he wanted to hold off leaving until after his brother was buried, but he said no. He didn't even want to spend what remained of the day anywhere near the area, insisting they travel through the night to get away from there as far as possible.

"When you git back, we'll talk on it boy," Janny said as he shook his son's hand before he departed with Pete. "Don't you git ta frettin' 'bout Cleavon. Best fer all'a us he's dead, him too Ah reckon. Some folks better off not bein' borned. Cain't say it don't leave a hole in me though, even if Cleavon was addled. Sometimes he weren't poor company, but what's done is done. Ya best go see yer ma 'fore headin' out agin. First your sister then Tray, an' now Cleavon. Least ways we still got you. That'll ease her mind."

They traveled through the night, rested some the following day, but for the most part just kept moving. Pete stayed close to the wagon, and just before sun-up on their last day of travel he glanced over at his companions bathed in moonlight. Desiree was asleep on Buddy's shoulder, her arm intertwined with his. Pete smiled wearily and Buddy smiled back, mostly with his eyes.

***

THE VIEW of Chattanooga was magnificent from only halfway up Lookout Mountain, but Pete wanted to see it from closer towards the top. He wanted the most panoramic view possible of his recovered freedom. It was as if his entire life had been given back to him against odds so incredible he had to pause long enough to fully appreciate it was really happening. It was a clear morning, and the valley below wasn't obscured by inverted fog which wasn't an uncommon occurrence. The warm breezes below had lent themselves to cooler ones the higher he went. The sun shined upon him as he climbed atop a large boulder and gazed northeast at the city, a combination of well-used dirt and gravel roads, framed houses, two story brick buildings and hundreds of tents in perfect rows that seemed to go on forever - Union tents, so white within their brilliance, their *promise*, they almost shined.

He didn't stay very long. In a short while he would be amongst it all, hurrying to report to the military authorities and most importantly get the telegrams off to his loved ones. Still, he took a few moments to take it all in. The dream that had kept him going was no longer an irremediable fantasy or an elusive aspiration beyond his grasp. He had a strangle hold on it and wanted to savor the moment he knew would remain a vivid memory throughout his life. In a few days everyone back home would know he had survived, perhaps sooner. Whatever battles that had been fought in the area were over, so it stood to reason his wires would go out immediately; he hoped so anyway.

He could just imagine the look on the faces back home when the telegrams were being read. Delicia's tears would flow like steady rain. She would hug loved ones as quickly as she could pull them into her arms. Mother Grace would clutch the telegram to her breast and offer heartfelt thanks to God, tears also flowing; Pete could just picture it. Father Benjamin would head off to the High Hayloft; a safe bet if there ever was one. Billy would whoop and holler and go off running. He wouldn't have any particular destination in mind, at least at first, and would care even less. He'd stay away from the High Hayloft though, another safe bet. He'd probably end up in the barn though. He would want to tell the draft horses and especially Black Hat that his older brother had somehow survived and by doing so had performed a miracle; perhaps quite an impressive number of them at that. He'd say it in a voice loud enough to let Father Benjamin know his youngest son was just below, in hopes of getting his father to come down and join the celebration. Pete took a deep breath, inhaling the wonderful mountaintop air and let out a sigh he'd been holding in for a very long time.

***

HE SPOTTED the two Union soldiers talking to Buddy and Desiree after coming around a series of trees and scattered boulders about fifty yards from the wagon. It didn't appear anything was amiss, but he called out anyway and waved at the men dressed in Yankee blue; *beautiful* Yankee blue. They waved back enthusiastically, which was a good sign.

"These folks said you escaped from a Reb prison," the soldier wearing sergeant stripes said when Pete was in earshot. Pete smiled and kept coming towards them.

"I'm Lieutenant Pete McCabe of the 1st Naperville Cavalry," he replied, his words sounding as gratifying as they had felt to say. "I was taken prisoner at Shiloh, escaped some months back." Both men looked at him in astonished disbelief, but there was no denying his accent.

"Well don't that beat all," the sergeant remarked, a large grin on his face. The soldier next to him, a young private, was beaming as well. "I got scant reason to doubt you sir," the sergeant went on to say, "but I'll have to ask you to hand me your gun belt. You can have them Colts back after we reach headquarters and your story's checked out."

"You can have my knife as well, Sergeant," Pete replied with a grin. "I'll want that back too, however." He handed his weapons over, looked at Desiree, then back at the sergeant. "Give us a few minutes, Sergeant." It felt good to give an order again. Both soldiers complied immediately, moving about twenty feet away.

"We'll all head into town. I'm sure we can find lodgings, then a more permanent place for you to stay, if that's what you want." Pete looked at Desiree sitting next to Buddy in the wagon as he spoke. She let out a nearly imperceptible sigh while glancing at Buddy as Little Desiree climbed from the back of the wagon onto her mother's lap. Ely just stood on the wagon bed, mesmerized by the two real live soldiers; *Yankee* soldiers no less, with guns and everything.

"Ah s'pect we could do that Pete. What do you think, Buddy? That sound all right by you?"

"Well, Ah ain't got no money. Them there Yankees - uh, soldiers, they gonna put us up, Pete?" It was the first time Buddy had ever referred to him as anything other than Yank or Yankee. Pete stifled a grin in spite of himself.

"Oh, I suppose we can do better than that, Buddy. I've got a little money, and I sure enough owe you." Pete sat on the ground and removed his boots, and with the soldiers and Buddy looking on in amazement, removed the nearly sixteen hundred in gold coins.

"This is Desiree's, Buddy. But I guess she'll let me use a little of it."

***

AS THEY headed through Chattanooga Buddy was every bit as disquieted as Pete was ecstatic. Ely, of course, had never seen such a sight and couldn't stop pointing and asking more questions than all three adults combined could hope to answer. There were hundreds of Union soldiers everywhere, thousands really, and the only sight that could possibly be more welcomed was the one Pete would see when he arrived home in Naperville. *Good God, just a week or so by train.* He imagined. *Maybe sooner.*

After getting Desiree, Buddy and the children set up in the best rooms the hotel had to offer, Pete and the soldiers made their way to command headquarters. He was told to wait in the hallway with the private, but wasn't kept waiting long.

"Sure is busy around here, sir." Pete remarked after being led into the office of Major Kenneth Rice, an officer on General William Tecumseh Sherman's staff. He was a handsome man, with curly, sandy-colored hair and light blue eyes that missed nothing.

"It ought to be," Major Rice replied. "Chattanooga is the supply and logistics base of operations for our upcoming Atlanta campaign, and then some. Uncle Billy keeps insisting he's going make those Rebels howl, and I have no reason to doubt him. If there's a finer general in this army than William Tecumseh Sherman I'm not aware of him." Major Rice shuffled a few documents about until he found a blank sheet of paper. He reached for his pen, its nub a glistening gold, and continued. "So I am to conclude you are a lieutenant who has escaped from the Oglethorpe prison camp in Macon? You certainly look well fed for a prisoner."

"That was a while back, Major Rice. I've been trying to make my way north since last fall." Pete went on to tell him the rest of his ordeal.

"You understand, of course, we'll have to verify your story." Major Rice said after Pete had finished. "I'll get a wire off to headquarters in Chicago. Should have an answer in a few days. By the way, what can you tell me about Chicago, and the town of Naperville where you're from? Born and raised in Waukegan myself. Family owns a nursery there. Largest number of greenhouses in the entire state of Illinois I'll be bound, Wisconsin too. Made a few deliveries to Naperville myself."

Pete knew why the major was asking, and they spent the next hour talking about what they had in common with the general area of northeastern Illinois. If Pete was indeed a Reb spy, the major surmised, he was either a damned well informed one or a Northern-raised Copperhead turned traitor. He suspected none of those possibilities were likely.

"I was hoping, Major, to get off a few wires of my own. My family and friends don't even know I was captured far as I know, and likely believe I'm dead."

"I'd be happy to oblige you, Lieutenant. Just write your messages and supply me with the recipients' names and so forth and the wires will go out within the next few hours. I'll see to it your messages are given the highest priority, straight through to military headquarters in Chicago."

Major Rice had concluded Pete's story was true. He even told the sergeant to give Pete back his weapons and allowed him to return to the hotel unescorted. The major did, however, order Pete to report back to his office the next day between two and three in the afternoon and to be in uniform. He could stop at a supply depot on his way back to the hotel and get one issued there, and Major Rice wrote a note authorizing his directive. The major would be in meetings all the next morning and needed to discuss Pete's current status with his superiors - and yes, he would be given all his back pay and perhaps a bonus, especially if he could supply any vital information since he had just traversed part of the area General Sherman would be marching through on his way to Atlanta on his upcoming campaign.

It felt as if he were immersed in a cloud of elation all the way to the hotel. The hot bath, shave and Pete's new uniform felt good, wonderful even, and it felt better still to return the palm out salutes from the multitude of soldiers he passed along the way. He hoped the major would make good on another promise he had made, to at the very least obtain a one month furlough for Pete if not an outright honorable discharge itself. Major Rice had said it was at least a probability, and even if Pete was required to stay in the army he could likely expect to be stationed close to home, no farther away than Chicago. Pete wanted to believe him but remembered enough about the realities of military life, especially during wartime, to give him pause. He forced that from his mind; so many terrible things had happened, surely he was due a healthy dose of their antithesis.

When Pete reached the hotel he decided to stop at the front desk and check the train schedules. More good news; if he made all his connections he would be home in three days after Major Rice had his confirmation, four at the most. He thanked the clerk and started for the room he was sharing with Buddy, having put Desiree up with the children in the adjoining room of the suite.

"Excuse me sir," the clerk said before Pete had made it five feet. "I didn't recognize you in that uniform, my apologizes. The people you arrived with have checked out, and the young lady had my assistant write a message addressed to you. If you could wait just a moment, please." He returned momentarily and handed a folded piece of paper to Pete.

Dear Pete,

I hope to see you again someday, but I don't believe that's what the Lord has in mind for either of us. Thank you for the money, although I wish you would have kept more for yourself. Bet you are walking with steps so light you can't even feel the ground! Buddy ain't going back to the valley, least ways not for a while. Promised to help me get settled first. Remember that pretty little town we passed through a ways back, LaFayette? It had that handsome brick school. Thanks to you, I got the money to get me a small house there and the school would be perfect for Ely and later on Little Desiree when she ain't so little no more! Ely wanted to say good-bye, and so did I, but it's better this way. I love you Pete, you know that, just like I know you love that gal Delicia. Buddy is a good man, the kids love him, and maybe I can too. Goodbye and God bless and keep you, Pete McCabe.
All my love,
Desiree Fairchild

Pete read it twice, then folded it carefully and placed it in the inside pocket of his new lieutenant's blouse. He knew he would keep it, even show it to Delicia. Maybe someday, years after the war was over they could take a trip back to the area, perhaps with their own children. In some ways best kept deep inside, he missed Desiree already.

***

GENERAL SMITHINGTON had all three telegrams in front of him, resting on his desk. Only the telegraph operator knew about them, at least up North in the Chicago headquarters, and he had been sworn to secrecy. The telegraph operator was used to that however, and knew full well the penalty for violating the most cardinal rule of all as far as military telegraph operators were concerned.

The general, being a shrewd man, had a strong feeling Major Clifton Janeway would be very interested in the contents of all three telegrams. Major Janeway had not only steadfastly maintained he had witnessed Lieutenant McCabe's death at Shiloh, but according to Buford Janeway his son was engaged to McCabe's former girlfriend. Buford had even bragged about it, and on more than one occasion. Major Janeway would no doubt appreciate their business relationship a great deal more than he and his father already did, which was substantial.

Unless the general had missed his guess, the information he now had was extremely valuable all right, and the general's undying loyalty, his *discretion*, more valuable still. Rather than have the operator send a wire, the general decided to have his personal courier hand deliver a note to Major Janeway that very afternoon.

He would be instructed to meet with the general the next day for lunch in Chicago. There was an urgent military matter the general wanted to discuss with him the note stated - a very urgent matter.

XXXIV

Sedman was so excited he simply wouldn't stop talking. He was seldom at a loss for words, but as the train he and Cusman were on headed west it was as if he barely took time to breathe. Cusman humored his friend by letting him ramble on as they sat next to each other, barely interrupting him even when his musings bordered on being alarmingly naïve. Sedman's latest soliloquy proved to be too much, however.

"Have you ever heard of *jujitsu,* Cusman? It's a form of Japanese martial arts, been around for centuries. The *Samurai* warriors developed it in feudal Japan. It's called the "art of softness" but don't let that mislead you. By incorporating a complex series of pins, locks and throws, one can use his attacker's energy against him rather than directly opposing said force. It's an ideal method of combat for a man of my stature and physique, and I have been taking lessons at the college. I wanted to surprise you with it, and I dare say I have become rather proficient with said application of same. Why, I now have the ability to take a man of your size, no less, and put him on the ground in a manner that will render him defenseless in a matter of seconds!" Cusman looked down at his diminutive friend sitting next to him and sighed.

"You gonna put me on the ground without usin' a weapon when I know it's comin'?" Cusman asked.

"That's the beauty of it, Cusman! You wouldn't *know* it's coming! One moment we would be, theoretically of course, facing one another, preparing for mortal combat, and the next you will be flat on your back and I will have crushed your windpipe with a well-timed kick as lethal as it would be unexpected!"

"You best stick to cannons and them Colt Dragoons you brought along. The only kickin' you need worry 'bout is kickin' your little black ass in the other direction if them whoopin' Rebs come chargin' in." Sedman glared at his friend, falling silent long enough to quell his rising vexation. He took a deep breath then continued.

"I would put a dozen well trained *Samurai* against three dozen men your size."

"You ain't no damned *Samurai,* Sedman. You best remember that. I read a little bit about them fellas too. Knew you was takin' them lessons, Jennifer mentioned it." Again Sedman glared.

"She *what?* She promised not to breathe a word!"

"She didn't breathe it, she flat out said it. Scared her near to death you did, all that talk 'bout you flippin' Rebels all over the damned battlefield and such, kickin' their peckerwood asses halfway back to Georgia, crushin' their windpipes. Shit, you crazy or somethin'? Don't you know that fine lady has eyes for you? What made you think she'd be cozyin' up to you with all that *Samurai* talk? That ain't what she sees in you." Sedman's rising vexation was extinguished immediately.

"What did she say to you?" He asked, no longer the least bit interested in *jujitsu* or anything else that had to do with fighting.

"Cain't say. Promised I wouldn't 'breathe a word' or some fool thing."

"Apparently, keeping secrets is a low priority within our little group." Sedman responded. "I would tell *you* if the shoe were on the other foot, my friend." That made Cusman smile.

"It's what she told Missy, not me, over two weeks ago," Cusman said, relishing what he was about to reveal. "Now that Jennifer's in Amherst, she kin go with how she feels, not what others think she should feel, though seems to me she usually did anyway. She said Eastern college towns are more tolerant'a such things, but I ain't so sure 'bout that. Grant her one thing though, back in Georgia she'd be lucky if all they did was tar and feather her pretty self over such a thing, so I s'pect up here she kin at least -"

"Would you stop beating around the bush and tell me what she said?" Sedman had grabbed Cusman by his upper arm and squeezed with all his might. Cusman took a casual glance down at his friend's hand and sighed again. *Gonna take more'n some damned* **jujitsu** *if that's all you got…*he thought.

"She said her feelins' for you went beyond friendship or some such thing. Said if she was twenty years younger wouldn't mind havin' your baby." Sedman's hand dropped slowly as a grin appeared on his face. It reminded Cusman of a wide-eyed slave child being handed a peppermint stick on Christmas morning. He did his best to stifle his laughter, failing miserably. Sedman, however, misinterpreted his friend's merriment.

"That's not humorous, Cusman." Sedman went from feeling giddy to being bitterly disappointed in less than a second with what he had perceived as his friend's insensitive joking. Cusman caught the misunderstanding immediately.

"Ain't funny if it ain't true, so that means the look on your face is funnier'n hell. If I'm lyin' I'm dyin' Sedman. That's what Jennifer said. Swear on the souls of my babies." They both broke out with large grins then.

"Yes!" Sedman finally hollered as he threw his head back in ecstasy, pumping both fists.

***

LATER THAT night Cusman found himself alone with his thoughts as he stared out the window into the darkness as the train rumbled through the countryside. Sedman had retired to the sleeping car for coloreds, having insisted he pay for both of them to go first class as long as the railroad company would allow them to travel with the white passengers even if they weren't allowed to share the same sleeping car. Once they were out of the East that would no doubt change, but for now they enjoyed the relative luxury of not having to ride in some boxcar towards the rear of the train.

Their departure had been delayed by another bout of Sedman's pleurisy, but he had made a complete recovery or so he maintained. Regardless, nearly six more weeks had gone by from their original departure date of mid-January. Both men had appeared anxious to depart, but for Cusman his feelings had been, and still were, filled with ambiguity.

Leaving Missy Nell and the babies had proven to be harder than he had imagined, and he had always imagined it would be difficult. It had been the act of actually doing it that had torn at him the most, the precise moment when he had handed the babies to Missy and walked down the front porch steps and climbed into the carriage where Sedman had been waiting so patiently. Duty, honor, responsibility and the courage to uphold his values, his fundamental principles, had all been tested once again during that tentative, that *awful* moment. All the rationalizations that insisted he reconsider had surged through him once more, but he had managed to keep them from taking over.

He had taken one last look at his family standing on the porch as the carriage had pulled away, and had waved a solemn goodbye that he had prayed wouldn't be his final one just before he had told Sedman to hurry up. Cusman had kept his eyes focused on the road ahead. They were still focused as he stared out the window of the train. Except for certainty, the dark, oblivious landscape hid nothing as it rushed by.

***

BY THE time the train was approaching Memphis a few days later they were in the last boxcar with close to twenty other black men whose sense of duty mirrored their own. All of the men were former slaves, and since Sedman wasn't he was an oddity, for that and other reasons. He told a number of them he was a college student from the East. Judging from his use of language which bore no resemblance to their dialect, no one doubted him even though he was the first man of color they had ever met who had made such a claim. Cusman had been the second, but he had found it easy to lapse into their dialect so they didn't view him with as much curiosity other than his size. Besides, the big man himself had been a slave, but the little fellow didn't even have any *ancestors* which fit that description; unique indeed, at least for the men in that boxcar.

"You some kinda prince then?" A tall, sinewy man named Obediah asked Sedman. "Your great grandpap bein' a king an' all, reckon you must be somethin' like that."

"He was my great-*great* grandfather," Sedman replied, "and not a king or even close to it in the classic, European sense for instance, although he did hold a prestigious rank within the hierarchy of the Kingdom of Dohomey."

"He done what?" Obediah asked.

"He was a man with a great deal of power and influence, but obviously not enough." Sedman replied.

"Reckon not," Obediah said, "else you wouldn't be ridin' in this here car with the rest'a us niggers." That produced laughter amongst the others. Even Cusman had to chuckle, despite the glare Sedman had waiting for him when he looked his way.

"Wish our pappy been a king," a large man but still noticeably smaller than Cusman said, "then me an' my brothers mebbe could have us one'a them harems an' such." That produced another round of laughter, and that time Sedman was able to join in.

"My name is Hiley," the large man said, offering to shake both Sedman and Cusman's hands. "Them two scrawny little niggers sittin' yonder is my brothers, Kiah an' Kit. Don't look like much, but they kin git ornery as a hive'a bees you rile 'em 'nough. Git over here you two, say hello ta a couple'a high-toned colored gentlemen." The two teenagers, identical twins, were on their feet immediately. They appeared to be perhaps sixteen, and considerably more prone towards shyness than their older brother. They too offered their hands, smiling with little eye contact.

"Where y'all from?" Cusman asked.

"Alabama," Hiley answered, even though Cusman had been addressing the twins. "Run off to join up wid the Yankees after our no-account mas'r sold off Mam an' our little sisters. Took a whip ta me an' Pap. Kilt Pap too it did."

Kiah spoke up at that, finally finding his voice: "Losin' Mam, Dolly, Cattie an' Cassie what kilt Pap, Hiley, that an' the whuppin'."

Kit, also finding his voice, agreed with his twin brother: "That's the Lord's truth. We shoulda kilt Mas'r 'fore we lit out, took a whip ta that white devil, tear *his* ugly white hide off'a him like he had that blue-eyed devil overseer do ta Pap. Said it then, say it now. Shoulda kilt both them white devils! Stripped our little sis's naked them other devils did, stripped Mam too, then them peckerwoods had at our woman-folk in the barn 'fore they took 'em off. Our little twin sis's weren't but twelve, Dolly maybe fourteen or there'bouts. Screamed somethin' awful they was, 'specially little Cattie an' Cassie." Sedman just stared at the youth, his shoulders slumping as he let out a sigh. Inside he was all fury.

"I simply don't have the words," he said, keeping a steady tone. "I can't empathize, but I can certainly sympathize with you." The three brothers knew Sedman was being sincere, even if they didn't know what, exactly, he had just said.

"Sedman's right sorry," Cusman added. "I am too. Them Rebs got a heap'a payback comin', an' this is our chance to pay 'em back good and proper. Keep carryin' on 'bout havin' their own country, state's rights an' such, like that's what this is all about. S'pect I know what they'd be fightin' over if their daddy been murdered by some damned whip, their mama an' sisters raped, sold off to the stone cold bastards that done it."

A pall descended over all the men in the boxcar as each of them descended into their own dark memories. Most of them were sitting. Some were looking at the floor between their legs, jaws set, others glancing sideways or straight ahead. No one was making eye contact, and if they did just briefly. There were a few scattered coughs, some shifting of legs against the floor as a number of men found it necessary to clear their throats and sniff in with their noses. The constant clickity-clack of the train continued as if its forward motion was taking them away from their individual sufferings and transporting them to some destination where they prayed a measure of requital was no longer an elusive concept.

Hiley looked at his twin brothers for a moment then turned away, lost in dark thought that was on the verge of growing darker. Perhaps Kiah had been right; maybe it was the loss of his father's womenfolk that finally killed him. Perhaps, but then Kiah hadn't seen all of what that drunken overseer had done with his whip, although he had seen enough. *Lord that evil man was good with that damned snake*, Hiley recalled as he stared off at nothing, jaw set.

Both of the twins had run off to the barn that awful day, trying to stop what was going to happen to their mother and sisters…*lucky they didn't get the whip fo' what they done,* Hiley recalled. He recalled all of it, all of what happened that day, and knew he always would as if he had been branded by it. It always felt that way when he couldn't keep himself from going there, as if he had *just* been branded by it. He stepped back in time, pulled back more like it, as the horrific incident engulfed him again:

***

ARCHIBALD LAWSON loved his honey. The bees that made Lawson Palace Plantation in Alabama their home made sure the family patriarch had plenty of it too, and not just any honey. Wherever it was those secretive bees went to cover their legs and fill their pollen baskets was a mystery, but they always returned with pollen that made nectar so delectable no one had ever sampled it and not come away with anything but the highest praise.

Archie Lawson had been addicted to it since childhood and it showed on his squat, obese body, but as an adult he loved it best when he added six ounces of bourbon, using six ounces of the wonderful honey to complete his favorite drink. It had to be exactly six ounces of each, and God help the house slave who veered from their master's recipe or hadn't stirred it properly - ten swirls with a long twist of cinnamon, no more, no less, and mind the tempo. Even a first offense was dealt with severely, and any subsequent transgression usually meant the slave would be banished from the house to work in the cotton fields. When it came to Archie Lawson's honey and bourbons there was no room for error, and no quarter for the inept or careless.

If Devine Intervention was needed to protect such a bungler that was doubly the case if any slave was caught stealing the famous nectar. Pebble, Hiley's father, had always had a special affinity for the honey. In his youth he named it Sticky Heaven, or Sticky Hell when he had been caught stealing it over the years. The punishments had always been as severe as promised, attested to by the scars on his back, buttocks and legs; even one across his face. He had been caught no less than five times by the time he was sixteen and the last whipping had almost killed him.

He was so scarred his owner knew he would never bring much at auction or anywhere else, so Archie Lawson had to resign himself to keeping Pebble. Besides, he was a good worker. His scars didn't get in the way of that once he had healed, and for that Archie Lawson was grateful.

After Pebble's near fatal whipping close to his sixteenth birthday as best anyone had known, Archie had made sure to murmur up a special prayer the following Sunday in church: *"Dear Lord, we both know that thievin' nigger had it comin', but please don't send 'em to nigger hell jus' yet, please don't do that Lord, You know Ah got that south fifty what needs a pickin', and that nigger kin fill a bag like all git out. Thank you Sweet Jesus fer temperin' mah han' 'fore Ah kilt that nigger, you know how Ah kin git, and may your Sweet Father in heaven bless and keep you. Amen."*

Pebble's love of the honey had been passed on to his children. Hiley had gone under the lash when he was ten, and again when he was fourteen. He hadn't stolen any honey the second time but his younger sister Dolly had. She had been only eight, but Hiley had known what awaited her. She had done a poor job of it, even damaged a few combs. There was honey all over her hands and clothing when the overseer had found her, and things had looked grim for the child until Hiley had stepped in. He had told the overseer he had done it, and had given a piece of the broken comb to Dolly.

That was it aw'ight, Hiley recalled as the Requital Train rumbled along. *Jus' like Pap done that last time when he took up fer Kit and Kiah like Ah done fer Dolly...wish Ah'd a been there 'stead'a in that damned cotton field when it all started that sorry day...*

That day, years later, it had been Kiah. Along with his twin brother, he had become adept at sneaking off with just enough honey so it wouldn't be noticed, but on that day he thought he heard someone coming. A horse whinnied anyway. He tried to replace the comb, bees buzzing about, a few stinging him, but in his haste he broke it. The bees really went after him then, but he knew it was nothing compared to what would happen if they were caught.

His father had been splitting logs not far off in the woods when he heard all the commotion. By then both his twin sons were frantically trying to correct what Kiah had done but only succeeded in making things worse. They were frantic, and their unintentionally loud voices were sure to alert someone. Pebble sprinted out of the woods and told his boys to run back into the safety of the trees and wash up in the creek, wash the Sticky Hell from their hands and arms. After they were out of sight Pebble tried to repair the damage himself. His efforts weren't in time. Rye McKee, the overseer, spotted him. Pebble was thankful his sons had gotten away, but he knew what awaited him.

By two o'clock that afternoon all the slaves had been gathered around, thankful to be given a respite from the hard labor they had been doing in the hot Alabama sun. They suspected what was about to happen, but tried to remain optimistic until their worst fears were confirmed.

Pebble had been tied naked to the whipping post in front of the west corral, not far from the barn. It wasn't just a post, not a single one anyway. It was a cross made from four-by-fours with a shorter block of wood situated halfway up, perpendicular to the center four-by-four, which kept the mid-section of the victim away from the cross a good twelve inches. The strange looking torture device was painted white. Archie Lawson insisted that was what God and Jesus wanted. He had never been able to articulate why that was so, other than it had to have been God's favorite color. Beyond that declaration his explanations always took detours, going this way and that, until he would usually storm off as if the person or persons he had been explaining himself to were too addled to understand, or didn't possess his uncommon sense of piety.

Archie had already consumed three of his favorite concoctions and had a fresh one in his hand when Rye McKee had entered the house and went to the study. When Rye told his employer it was Pebble tied to the whipping post Archie was shocked but not surprised, if that was possible. Pebble hadn't been caught stealing honey since before he had been paired with his woman over twenty years ago, *a handsome nigger wench if there ever was one*, as all of Archie's family proudly declared. Even the birth of all her children hadn't done much to diminish her. "Lively nigger too." Archie sometimes told certain male companions over honey and bourbons. "Does ever'thing Ah tells her ta do *when*

Ah tells her. Ah swear, them nigger gals kin sure git ta carryin' on when a white man is a coverin' 'em. Acts like she don't like it, but you know that's a lie."

Rye McKee asked if he could have a drink himself, since what he was about to do needed fortification if he was to do it right. His employer told him to hold nothing back, and Archie meant *nothing*. He let his overseer have two of the honey and bourbons, and told the man to take his time drinking them.

"Let that God damned nigger bake a spell, think on what he done, rest'a them niggers too. Do 'em good." Rye McKee thought that was an excellent suggestion.

The large, bearded man had his whip with him, as always. He liked to feel it, sometimes with authority, other times with a fondling touch, as if he were stroking a tranquil diamondback with both eyes barely open. Rye especially liked how its wide-reaching influence over others made him feel. It had been custom-made for him in Australia from the finest kangaroo skin, dyed black as pitch. Its thong alone was twenty-two feet, and the handle was just under fourteen inches; a big bullwhip for a big man.

There wasn't a whip expert in the county more adept with his weapon, or anywhere else Rye McKee would admit to. Most local folks agreed. He could stand in a field of daisies and pick the blossom clean off any daisy stalk he or someone else had pointed out, and almost never missed.

He had once killed a two hundred pound cougar with Black Jack, the name Rye had given his fearsome weapon, the largest cat anyone except liars could recall even having heard about in Alabama, much less seen. The cougar's scarred hide was hanging over the fireplace mantel in his cabin, and if the occasional visitor didn't comment about it which almost never happened, Rye would feel insulted and immediately reevaluate his opinion of the person.

***

THERE WERE over seventy slaves gathered around the corral area when Rye and Archie arrived, including Pebble's family with the exception of his oldest son Hiley, who had yet to arrive from the most distant cotton field. The instant Rye unfurled Black Jack with his signature flourish a hush fell over the crowd as the whip cut through the air. All was dead quiet except for the noisy summertime insects and Pebble's wife Dosey. She pleaded for Mas'r Lawson to reconsider, telling him how much Pebble was needed for the cotton that was ready and had just started to have been picked, but her owner was beyond caring.

Randolph and Spoon, two hired hands who sometimes worked at the plantation were present and armed with shotguns, and although Archie didn't need any encouragement, they offered it up anyway.

"Have 'em tear the hide off'a that there nigger, Mr. Lawson!" Randolph hollered, clearly excited over what was about to occur. He was a heavy-set man with a full red beard, partially stained with tobacco juice. He usually preferred swallowing the brown spittle, especially when he was drinking.

"Let ole Rye give that black nigger bastard what fer, Mr. Lawson!" Spoon chimed in. His rail-thin body was quivering with anticipation, and although he was the skinniest man present he was sweating more than anyone. He always did; it was a peculiarity. Why Spoon was even working there would have been a mystery to anyone who didn't know him personally, but was aware of his financial situation. He didn't need the money since his father owned several of the stores in the nearby town of Green Neck, as well as the only bank in town, and sizable land holdings. Spoon followed his friend Randolph everywhere though, even if it entailed work. Good friends can be hard to come by; for Spoon it had always been all but impossible.

"All you niggers hear me good!" Archie Lawson called out. "Pebble done been warned more times than Ah kin shake a damned stick at! Thought he'd done changed his thievin' nigger ways Ah did, an' now y'all gonna see what happens if'n mah *dee-crees* ain't abided upon! Let 'er rip, Rye!"

Rye McKee whirled Black Jack over his head in a huge circle, incorporating his signature flourish, and in a blur brought it around with a lightning snap of his wrist. The crowd remained dead silent except for the crying of Pebble's wife and daughters as the cracker cut the heavy air with a sustained hiss, then exploded like a gunshot after finding its mark. The cracker had snaked around and struck Pebble's right nipple that was suddenly hanging by just a few shreds of flesh. The blood began to pour out of the wound as Pebble gritted his teeth, not wanting to give his tormentors the satisfaction of hearing the scream that had been so close to escaping.

Pebble's wife Dosey and their daughters screamed though; their wailing could be heard a quarter mile away, farther still down wind. So could the explosive crack of the whip. McKee brought Black Jack back, whirled it above his head minus the flourish and struck again. The second blow sent the cracker across the bridge of Pebble's nose, exactly where McKee had wanted it to land. It hadn't removed Pebble's left eye, but he would never see out of it again. The next blow half scalped the bleeding man, lifting the front of his close-cropped hair a good three inches straight up before flopping back upon his skull at an angle. Within seconds Pebble's face, nearly his entire head, was covered with blood.

"Hee hee!" Spoon squealed. "Looks like a damned jig-a-boo woodpecker that nigger do! Hee hee hee!"

McKee stood motionless for a moment, to allow more blood to flow. He was very proud of his last shot. He brought Black Jack around again, aiming at a spot a few inches below Pebble's buttocks. That time, Pebble could not stifle his screams. If he were to survive, he would never be able to sire children again.

"Lookee! Lookee there!" An animated Randolph hollered as he pointed at the gaping wound. "That damned nigger gonna be a singin' sopranee from now on!" Spoon was beside himself with hysterics; his friend always seemed to come up with the most hilarious observations.

Archie Lawson glared at the men with a stone face of self-importance, arms crossed but inwardly amused, then nodded again at McKee. Before his overseer could bring the whip around again, Archie ordered one of his house slaves to bring him two more honey and bourbons. The elderly house servant was grateful to get away from the horrific spectacle, but knew better than to take his time. Mas'r Lawson was not a patient man, especially when it came to his honey and bourbons.

Again Black Jack snaked, its serpentine hiss competing with the cicadas in the thick summer air. The ravenous horseflies that had been feeding on their banquet buzzed quickly away as the bloodied cracker tore apart the skin below Pebble's shoulder blades with an ear-splitting ***crack*** that reverberated amidst the wails of Pebble's family.

The sound Pebble made was a groaning wail, but it was difficult to believe it was coming from a human being. It was as if a hellish creature inside of Pebble had unleashed the unearthly sound which caused most of the already traumatized children to scream in terror. Some of them, the ones who could, ran away. Archie Lawson ordered McKee to hold up, and yelled at the parents to chase down their offspring.

"Y'all git them little pickannies back on over here!" He yelled. "Else Ah'll put y'all under the whip! Where in blue blazes mah drinks? Man could die'a thirst waitin' on that dawdlin' ole nigger!"

The elderly house servant was making his way onto the large front porch, mindful not to spill either of the tall drinks he was carrying as he backed the door open with his hips. Mas'r's blood was up, and if the elderly man lost so much as a drop no telling what might happen. Archie saw the elderly man and motioned impatiently for him to hurry. When he finally had the drinks he called Rye over. Archie chugged half of the sweet concoction before handing the glass to Rye, then took a sip from the one remaining. At that point Hiley showed up with several others slaves who had been picking cotton in the field farthest away.

"You! Hiley!" Archie hollered over to the young man who was trying in vain to comfort his mother. Hiley glanced at his father, the sight leaving him traumatized, although not enough to quell his rising fury. "Where in hell you been, nigger? Go an' fetch a pail'a water!" Hiley finally glared at his owner, still holding onto his wailing mother. "*Now*, nigger!" Hiley continued to glare. If he did let go, he swore it would be to attack. "Randolph! Spoon! Tie that no-account nigger to the corral! If'n he fights use a knife on 'em!" Archie pulled out his LeMat sidearm and pointed it towards Hiley and his mother. Everyone nearby took a few steps back, fearing the worst. No telling what Mas'r Lawson might do drunk as he was; he was bad enough sober.

Randolph and Spoon, with the help of Rye, dragged the struggling young man to the fence railing and tied him to it while Archie kept his revolver pointed at Dosey.

"You keep puttin' up a fuss, boy, an' Ah'll shoot yer mammy sure!" The red-faced man bellowed as he took another swill from his glass then hollered for another.

When Hiley was secured Randolph fetched the pail of water. Archie had him pour it over Pebble, trying to revive him. It worked, but just barely. He looked over at his oldest son with his good eye, blinking back the bloody water best he could. The horseflies, countless in number, were feasting again; even amidst the delirium of Pebble's agony he could feel the greedy, sucking bites of the ravenous insects; it felt as if coal oil had been poured over his wounds and set ablaze as the corpulent, buzzing insects fought with a tenacious frenzy for their meal. He gritted his teeth, his entire body shaking, and watched as Hiley was stripped of his shirt and trousers. Pebble began to weep. Then he made an attempt to call over to his owner.

"Ah'll take his whuppin', Mas'r. Ain't no need ta lay no whip on him…"

"Ah'll be'a decidin' that, nigger!" Archie again bellowed, waving his revolver haphazardly, honey and bourbon-imbued spittle flying about. "Lay it on both'a them uppity niggers, Rye!" With that Archie went over to his overseer and placed his hand on Rye's forearm before he could bring his whip around. "Keep it low on Hiley, don't want no unusual-like scars on 'em, nothin' what damages him too much anyways. Be'a wantin' to sell him off 'fore long, rest'a that family too Ah reckon. Ain't nothin' but trouble, whole damned bunch'a them is."

Spoon overheard the drunken man, and approached. "If'n you gonna sell off them gals, Ah just might be interested in takin' 'em off your hands, Mr. Lawson."

"Your daddy gonna be all right with that, Spoon?" Archie asked. "Gonna want me a purty penny fer them handsome gals. You gotta take their mammy too." Spoon grew very excited.

"Yes suh, Mr. Lawson! He sure 'nough will! Gonna want me a taste'a them purty niggers first, me an' Randolph both don't ya know, their mammy too. How 'bout we drag 'em off to the barn?" Archie considered the request then named his price.

"Done!" Spoon exclaimed. With Randolph's help he went and grabbed the girls, along with the help of several slaves ordered by Archie to lend a hand.

Kiah and Kit's profound guilt was intermingled with a helpless rage so all-consuming they didn't know what to do. If they tried to intervene on behalf of their brother and father they too would get whipped or perhaps even shot. They decided to go after their sisters and mother, although they had no idea what they were going to do when they made it into the barn. They soon found out there was nothing they could do. The three slaves who had been ordered to help drag the females into the barn stopped the youths just as the boys entered.

"You two git on outta here," one of the slaves said. "Mas'r gonna whup us all you don't behave, might be'a whuppin' y'all anyways. Go on, git!"

The twin boys heard the wailing then, accompanied by the shredding of clothing. Their twelve-year-old twin sisters were screaming the loudest, or at least with more terror or so it seemed to the boys, but Dolly and their mother were equally traumatized. Spoon called two of the slaves over to help hold the women. The instant they were secured Spoon and Randolph raped them all, starting with the twins.

Outside the whippings had continued, with the most brutal of it visited upon Pebble. When he was totally unconscious Archie ordered him cut down and dragged away to his rude shack. Hiley's lower back and thighs were bleeding profusely, but nothing that approached what had happened to his father.

Before Pebble regained consciousness two days later his wife and daughters had been marched the ten miles to Green Neck. Dosey had been bloodied just on her face. A traumatized Dolly, Cattie and Cassie had bled as well, and for them walking had been especially painful.

Spoon's father was enraged his son had struck such an expensive deal, let alone without consulting him first, and a month later the females were sold off to a slaver passing through town. Not long after that, they were sold off separately at auction in New Orleans. They would never see each other again. Less than a week after their departure from the Lawson plantation Pebble had died from his injuries. All the white people and most of the slaves were surprised he had held on that long.

A few weeks after burying their father, Hiley, Kiah and Kit had made a successful run for it. They had stopped long enough to destroy the honey bee nesting boxes, smashing them to pieces. Kiah and Kit had wanted to steal into the main house and kill Archie along with all other whites thereabouts, steal guns and find McKee and his whip, but Hiley had overruled them - just barely. They had taken a big enough risk destroying the nesting boxes before escaping, he had insisted.

***

HILEY WAS still traumatized from where his recollection had taken him when the train began to slow. Even though he was physically in the present, inside Hiley was still stuck in the past as if Black Jack were wrapped around his legs - squeezing, *pulling*.

The train slowed further then stopped. They were in Memphis, even if the essence of Lawson Palace Plantation hovered around him like a merciless fog. It never cleared for long, and never completely.

***

IT WAS March 11th, 1864 and there was a great deal of excitement amongst the men, especially when they arrived at Fort Pickering located south of Memphis. The fort was a flurry of activity, and the number of colored units being drilled was a welcomed sight to all the new arrivals.

Cusman and Sedman's timing couldn't have been better; they were assigned to the newly formed 1st Battalion, 6th U.S. Heavy Artillery, comprised of Companies A, B, C and D under the command of Major Lionel F. Booth. They were told to report to the major himself when Sedman informed the officer in charge of processing new arrivals it had been he and Cusman who had written all those letters. The major was impressed with Cusman's earlier military experience as well.

"You were with the 54th Massachusetts at Fort Wagner?" Major Booth inquired. "How did such a large target manage not to get killed?"

"They tried hard enough, Major. Got the scars to prove it."

"I have no doubt you do. What was your rank?"

"I was a sergeant, sir. S'pect I'll start out a private here, but that's fine by me. S'pect I'll be gettin' the chance to earn my stripes back soon enough."

"And I 's'pect' you won't be waiting that long, Sergeant Sable. I'll have the papers drawn up immediately. Do you have any experience with artillery weapons?"

"Only when they tried to blow me to pieces, sir, 'cept for some trainin' I had at Camp Meigs. Always been a fast learner though, I kin promise you that."

"You'd better be, Sergeant." Major Booth replied. He looked at Sedman. "Now, what is your story, Private August?"

***

AFTER SEDMAN had finished his lengthy dissertation, or tried to before Major Booth had cut him off, he remained a private. Both he and Cusman would be serving together though. They were assigned cannoneer duty and were to receive their instruction with a crew of other cannoneer trainees, a total of nine men including Cusman and Sedman.

The crew was one of three under the overall command of Captain Alan Munn. Lieutenant Charles Wright was one of the officers in charge of the actual utilization of the six Howitzers that made up the battery, responsible for two of them including the one the new arrivals had been assigned to help operate.

There were both 12 and 24 pound Howitzers in the battery. Cusman and Sedman were assigned to a smoothbore Napoleon 12 pounder that would be used primarily for canister when the conditions were right.

"The effective overall range of this 12 pounder is somewhere around 1,000 yards when firing nine pound solid shot or shell," Lieutenant Wright explained during the new volunteers' first day of training, "but canister is most effective from 250 to 600 yards. It's still deadly, of course, within 250 yards, but has a more effective spread if it travels a little farther, depending on the load." He stopped speaking and looked at Sedman, who had taken a pad and pencil from his blouse pocket and was jotting down notes. "Private, just what the hell are you doing?"

"Taking notes, sir." Sedman replied, as if that should have been obvious, then added: "By all means, please continue. I would like to know all there is about these guns, sir, especially the uttermost limit of their effectiveness from a maximum distance perspective. You haven't as yet supplied that information unless you meant to say, or would have us believe, 600 yards is the unsurpassable range for inflicting appreciable carnage." Lieutenant Wright thought he had seen and heard just about everything during his years of service, but then he'd never met the likes of Sedman August.

"Put away the pencil and pad, Private," he ordered, "and listen carefully. All of you listen carefully. The weaponry in front of you isn't intended for a Saturday morning turkey shoot. Have you ever heard of General Alpheus Williams?"

"As a matter of fact I have, sir." Sedman interjected. *"Brigadier* General Alpheus S. Williams, to be exact. He has been involved in a number of major campaigns, including Gettysburg, where he heroically defended a left flank assault from the Confederate Stonewall Division, having previously convinced General Meade of the strategic importance of Little Round Top. He hasn't received due recognition for his efforts I might add, due primarily, I would maintain, because having never attended West Point he is looked down upon by those officers who not only attended that venerable institution but graduated from it as well. Furthermore, I am of the opinion _"

"That will be all, Private." Lieutenant Wright said. "For our purposes here, I am going to quote the *brigadier* general, and none of you need write it down." Lieutenant Wright glared at Sedman, eyeing him coolly until Sedman reluctantly put away his pad and pencil. Then Lieutenant Wright continued. "Here's what Williams said: *'The Rebels followed with a yell but three or four of our batteries being in position they received a tornado of canister. Each canister contains several hundred balls. They fell in the very front of the line…stirring up dust like a thick cloud. When the dust blew away no regiment and not a living man was to be seen…'* Are there any questions?" Lieutenant Wright hadn't stopped staring at Sedman. "Well, Private?"

"How far away was the enemy when the cannons opened fire, sir? Within the 250 yard range? Just beyond? If closer in, how could so many have been neutralized if they weren't situated at the optimum range you previously described, sir? How many cannons did indeed actually fire? Regardless, could it be possible entire regiments were indeed killed? Not a single enemy soldier merely wounded? Doesn't that seem unlikely? Were they firing up hill? Down? What was the overall topography in the immediate vicinity, or in general for that matter? Did weather conditions play a part? And lastly, sir, since our 12 pound Napoleon fires canister rounds containing but 27 balls on average, what type of weapon was the general referring to that contained canister rounds that held hundreds of balls? Is that even possible?"

Lieutenant Wright, mouth half open, eyed Sedman suspiciously. Cusman simply rolled his eyes and sighed.

"Is it possible you have missed the point, Private?" The lieutenant finally asked, then spoke again before Sedman could respond. "Just man the left of the breech, Private." Sedman appeared uncertain where to go, although in truth he wasn't positive the lieutenant had spoken to him. He wasn't the only private in attendance and had again reached for his note pad and hadn't been looking at Lieutenant Wright. "That's the *back* of the cannon, Private August. You will be manning the number four position, priming then firing the cannon, if you don't talk the enemy to death first."

Cusman, being a sergeant, was the detachment's Chief of the Gun and in overall charge of the cannon's operation, or would be once he had been properly trained which didn't take long. His main duty was to ensure all the men did their jobs correctly and as rapidly as possible, then ordered the cannon to be fired after the gunner, usually a corporal, mounted the sight and aimed the gun. Most of the men assigned numbered positions were responsible for preparing the gun until it was time for Sedman to pull the lanyard, which actually fired the weapon after he had inserted the primer into the vent, which was attached to the lanyard just before he stepped back, waited for the command to fire and then pulled.

The number one man, Hiley, would then swab the bore with a damp sponge attached to a wood pole to put out any burning embers so the next round wouldn't explode prematurely. Next he would ram the load. The number two man, Obediah, first inserted the charge then the projectile into the muzzle, the number three man tended the vent, then Sedman, the number four man, primed the piece and waited for Sergeant Sable's command to fire after the gunner was satisfied with the range and trajectory. The number five and number seven men carried the ordinance, and the number six man was in charge of the limber. Other men had their duties as well, but it was the numbered men, gunner and sergeant who had the most important duties and took special pride in their assignments.

Sedman was pleasantly surprised he had been assigned such important duty, until Lieutenant Wright informed him he didn't look strong enough for most of the other tasks. He added Sedman thought too much to ever be a gunner or Chief of the Gun regardless of whatever rank he managed to attain. Still, he would be the one firing the cannon, and even though he pretended he hadn't felt chagrinned by the lieutenant's words, Cusman knew better. Later on that evening he took Sedman aside.

"You'll be performin' an important duty," Cusman told him, "so don't let some damned officer get under your skin. If he didn't have confidence in you then you'd be back with the horses and other equipment, with Kit an' Kiah. He just wanted to knock you down a peg or two in front of the others, an' he'll do it again you don't quit flappin' your gums so damned much."

"That's a fine state of affairs when an enlisted man can't question his superiors, and I use that term loosely." Sedman responded.

"Use it any way you want, just not in front of him or them other officers. Captain Munn already knows you got a brain, Lieutenant Wright too, just make sure you don't show them attitude to go along with it, you understand?" Sedman nodded, but Cusman had a feeling his friend still had a lot to learn about the realities of military life.

***

AFTER NEARLY three weeks of training, their crew had become as efficient as any in the entire battalion. Some of the men made note of their accomplishment, Sedman literally, bragging about it as well, but not Cusman. He knew the difference between training exercises and the real thing. Soon they all would. It was Captain Munn who approached the men one afternoon while they were packing up after training that day.

"Atten*tion!*" Lieutenant Wright hollered.

"At ease, men." Captain Munn said after he was in front of them. "I want to congratulate you on your progress. You have all the makings of an effective detachment, and now your first real test is at hand. I have just been informed by Major Booth we will be moving out in the morning. If you haven't written home recently I suggest you do so this evening, and if any of you haven't prepared your wills do so post haste. If you can't read and write, Private August and Sergeant Sable will help you. We might be going up against a formidable opponent if our reports are accurate. Perhaps some of you have heard of General Nathan Bedford Forrest. We may possibly be engaging his forces soon or other enemy forces, defending the earthworks at Fort Pillow."

***

KIAH AND Kit weren't literate, and they had no one to write home to, but they were both eager to learn as much as Sedman could teach them. They didn't leave his side as Sedman wrote down what the other soldiers had dictated to him, asking so many questions that Cusman, sitting at a desk next to Sedman's in the large tent, wondered if perhaps his friend was getting annoyed with the teenaged twins. He wasn't; far from it. He even gave the twins pencil and paper, and made room for them at the desk where he was sitting.

He was impressed not only by their enthusiasm, but their intelligence. They were both quick studies, and displayed remarkable penmanship for beginners. They stayed at the desk well into the night, until the last man had left. Even then they had wanted to stay, reading to Sedman and each other or comparing what they had written as best they could.

Sedman was truly in his element, Cusman observed. His usual tendency to grow impatient had vanished as if it hadn't existed to begin with, causing Cusman to feel yet another reason to be impressed by his friend. As long as the boys had questions and wanted to incorporate Sedman's answers and council, he apparently wasn't going anywhere. It wasn't until Kit had fallen asleep at the desk, with Kiah not far from joining his brother before Sedman told them to go get some sleep.

"Those two boys are remarkable," Sedman said to Cusman after they retired to the tent they shared. "Not only can they read and write almost enough to get by, but their respective appetite to learn is insatiable. Thank God they fell asleep before continuing to insist I teach them math." Sedman tried to sound as if he were grateful the boys had nodded off, but Cusman wasn't fooled.

"I s'pect so, Sedman. Wait! You hear that? I think it's them boys comin' this way." Sedman caught himself in an instant, but not soon enough to hide the look of enthusiastic surprise that had spread across his face before he realized Cusman was just being Cusman.

"Blow out the lantern, you lummox," Sedman said. "It's been a long day, and would have been considerably longer if it had been you trying to learn as much as those two did tonight. Why, do you realize, Cusman, that those two -" but the large man had already rolled over in his cot, a moment or two away from his first snore.

XXXV

General Smithington waited until the nattily attired waiter in the posh restaurant had placed their meals in front of them and departed before getting to the real reason he had summoned Major Janeway to Chicago. The general had been talking about the war and its effects on the home front, especially how it related to their overall business dealings, but an impatient Clifton, knowing that wasn't the real reason he had been invited to lunch, had begun to fidget.

"As you know, Major," the general finally said when he noticed Clifton's vexation and was satisfied no one was within earshot, "I have taken a great deal of interest in your military career and fully appreciate everything your father and you have done for me as well. I'll be retiring as soon as the war is over, perhaps sooner, and hope our business dealings will continue to prosper well into the future." That peaked Clifton's interest, since neither he nor his father would have any use for the general once Clifton was out of the military.

"I plan on leaving the military myself, General, as soon as the war is over. I was hoping you would be staying in yourself at least that long. You have been very helpful, and I would hate to think you would no longer be in a position to, well, lend your assistance regardless of when hostilities end. I am quite comfortable with my current assignment, and would hate to be at the mercy of a different commander. I'm certain you understand." The glint in the general's eyes was nearly imperceptible, but Clifton noticed it immediately.

"Oh, I suppose I could indeed be here for you until such time my services are no longer needed, Major, from a military point of view. I was hoping, however, our business relationship, and more importantly the friendship we have forged, will continue. It's been my experience friendships can prove to be extremely valuable to all parties concerned, especially when friends can be counted on to supply valuable information and demonstrate the tactfulness necessary to keep such information confidential; to guard it so to speak. If one cannot trust his friends, whom can one trust?" The rotund general smiled at his last comment, and placed a cloth napkin upon his lap.

"I couldn't agree more, General. Am I to assume you have some news about the war or some other information you would like to share that requires my confidentiality?" Clifton took a sip of wine, eyeing the general carefully.

"Confidentiality is very important, Major. I'm sure we both understand and appreciate the value of it. As friends, especially close friends such as us, it stands to reason we can both profit greatly from sharing certain things others would want to know, things we alone can profit from that leaves our mutual rivals out in the cold as it were. Wouldn't you agree?" The general balanced a large forkful of braised salmon glazed with honey mustard, dipped it in dill sauce then put it in his mouth.

"Of course, General. But what is it I need to guard so carefully?" General Smithington smiled, somewhat condescendingly Clifton thought, as he swallowed his food before answering.

"Oh, it is I who will be guarding the information, Major. I suspect it will be you who will want to act upon it, with my assistance. I received three telegrams yesterday. All the way from Chattanooga. It appears one of our heroes from Shiloh has reappeared." Clifton was in the process of taking another sip of wine when the words hit him. He put down his glass immediately.

"And the name of this hero?"

"An old friend of yours, Major. Lieutenant Keith Allen "Pete" McCabe." Clifton tried to maintain his composure, but wouldn't have been surprised if the general could see his heart pounding through the blouse of his uniform.

"McCabe is *alive?*"

"Alive and well, according to a Major Kenneth Rice who is on General Sherman's staff. McCabe is the author of two of the telegrams himself, including one to your fiancée." Clifton was shocked so thoroughly he thought for a moment his pounding heart must surely have been heard as well as seen.

"He, he sent a telegram to Miss O'Darcy?"

"And his parents as well, but you have nothing to worry about, at least not yet, likely never I'd wager. They came across my desk, and no one is aware of their existence except my telegraph operator and of course Major Rice and Lieutenant McCabe. Oh. And perhaps General Sherman, but I'm getting ahead of myself. You look pale, Major, have some more Chablis." Clifton gulped what remained as the general held the decanter then refilled Clifton's glass.

"What is his current status? What are his plans?" Clifton asked, clearly unhinged.

"Well, Major, at first those appeared to be problems, but I took the liberty to react on your behalf. As far as McCabe and this Major Rice fellow know, McCabe's telegrams have gone through. I also took the liberty to wire General Sherman, informing him he had a very able cavalry officer on his hands and should give serious consideration to engage his services in his upcoming campaign. I received a response from his headquarters just this morning, from Major Rice again. Apparently Sherman already has his officers in place for his Atlanta campaign, but men are needed throughout the Western Theater, including the western side of Tennessee, near

Memphis. I don't know if McCabe is aware of it yet, but that is where he is headed." Clifton took a deep breath as he looked around before addressing the general.

"Allow me to be blunt, General. I can, and will, see to it you will have more money than you have ever dreamed possible. My father is planning something that, quite frankly, does not include you. If you can prove your friendship to me, beyond any doubt, I can guarantee not only your participation, but a full share without you having to invest a dime. You will realize at least $250,000, and if you are willing to ensure that McCabe never makes it out of Tennessee alive you can have my share, which will be another $250,000."

The general raised one eyebrow and stared at the young major. The brash young man was not only interested in the news, he was offering ten times what the general had been hoping for, even if he was asking for something that didn't come without risk, possibly a great deal of risk although the general doubted that would be the case. It appeared as if his dream of retiring in Europe and spending his remaining years in luxury had been realized after all.

"Trust is the foundation of our relationship, our *friendship* Major. That said, it will take some doing on my part to ensure my end of our arrangement is carried out to your satisfaction. That will give you the time you need to draw up the necessary contracts and other documents to ensure your end of the bargain will be held up as well. Agreed?"

"Agreed, General. I assume you already have a plan in mind?"

"Oh yes, Major. I most certainly do. I haven't been in this man's army over four decades without forging other trusting friendships as well. You can rest assured McCabe will never set foot in Illinois again."

"What if he sends off other telegrams or letters when he doesn't hear back from anyone?" Clifton asked.

"Oh, it's highly unlikely you have to worry about that, Major. What makes you think he won't receive answers, moreover that he already hasn't? Anyone can send wires, myself included obviously. I simply took liberties with my identities. He thinks he received wires, or will soon think he did, from Benjamin McCabe and Miss O'Darcy. He'll be riding to Memphis content in the knowledge his loved ones are indeed waiting for him. They, on the other hand, have no reason to believe anything has changed at all, nor will they. War is indeed hell, Major, for those foolish enough to fight in one. No offense intended."

"Memphis, eh?" Clifton remarked. "And what's happening down there?"

"I have certain intelligence reports that indicate quite a bit is happening down there, or soon will be. You are no doubt familiar with General Nathan Bedford Forrest? Of course you are. Actually he is a major general now, and the rascal is stirring things up in that area although his movements are, as usual, unpredictable. Regardless, there is at least a fair chance he may end up in the same place where McCabe is going. Have you ever heard of Fort Pillow?"

***

PETE COULDN'T remember the last time he had slept so soundly, or awakened so abruptly once he experienced his first glimpse of consciousness and realized where he would be going that day. He was up and dressed in no time, and could barely contain himself until it was time to report to Major Rice's office again. There had been some delays since his first meeting with the major, but after attending to a few details he would be on a very special train in less than twelve hours. He was going *home*, and that realization ignited feelings so intense not even the sum of all his ordeals could compete with them. It was an unrelenting surge of elation so overwhelming it felt incapable of dissipation.

There was no way he could stand being in his hotel room very long so he decided to head out, maybe do some shopping of all things and pick up some gifts for the folks back in Naperville. *Naperville*. Even saying it to himself in that particular context sent shivers through him. He hurried out of his room and made his way to the lobby.

"Lieutenant?" The desk clerk said when he spotted Pete rushing by. "There's some wires here for you. Just came over from army headquarters not an hour ago."

Pete thanked the clerk then took a seat on the circular velvet couch in the middle of the lobby. He opened the first telegram:

Dear Keith,
Thank God you are alive. I'm sure you can imagine how the joyous news was received here at home. Your Mother and I are anxiously awaiting your return, but will understand if your sense of duty and other circumstances requires you to see things through to the end. Your loving father.
Benjamin

Pete sighed as he put what he thought was his father's wire aside and opened the second one. As much as the first telegram meant to him, it was the second one he was interested in the most. A slight twinge of guilt accompanied that realization, but there it was.

My dearest Keith,
How I have prayed for this moment. I can scarcely believe it has arrived. I will continue to pray for the day you will be coming home to me. I understand your duties to end this horrible war must come first, and want you to know I understand. My love always,
Delicia

Something wasn't right, more than one thing actually, but Pete told himself he mustn't allow imagination to cloud his better judgment. Still, it seemed odd his father had referred to him as Keith instead of Kee, and Pete couldn't recall Delicia ever having referred to him as Keith unless she had been feigning a shocked demeanor or scolding him. Not a single word, either, about other loved ones had even been alluded to in passing. That seemed odd as well, but there was a war going on and perhaps both his father and Delicia felt any news could wait, or perhaps putting it in the confines of a telegram wasn't appropriate. And perhaps they had called him Keith in order to assure the telegrams were indeed delivered to him; but why did both of them do that, without knowing the other had as well? He concluded he was being overly analytical, perhaps foolishly so. Besides, he also concluded, no news was good news as far as other family members were concerned. If an adage ever held merit, that one certainly did given the overall circumstances.

He took a deep breath, exhaled and rose to his feet. In just a few more days he would be able to catch up on all the news in person. At least Delicia hadn't indicated he had any reason to doubt things had changed between them, quite the opposite. He headed outside and decided there was one gift in particular he would try to find. He had kept just eighty dollars but that would probably be enough. Perhaps he could get his back pay later that afternoon, or at least some of it. He wasn't sure what an engagement ring cost, but an acceptable one had to be at least eighty dollars.

***

"GIVEN YOUR situation, Lieutenant," Major Rice told Pete that afternoon in the major's office, "I too was astonished. I thought you would at least be given a furlough." Pete just sat there staring at the major. He wasn't incapable of understanding what he was being told, but what he had already heard left him temporarily dumbstruck.

"Not even two weeks?" He finally asked, already knowing the answer. "I realize the war isn't over, but from what I'm hearing its outcome is no longer in doubt. Seems to me our side has done a pretty fair job in my absence."

"I wish I had better news for you Lieutenant. As far as the war is concerned, I don't unequivocally agree with those who maintain its outcome is no longer in doubt. The Rebels certainly don't think so, too damned many of them anyway. As far as Memphis is concerned, your experience as a cavalry officer is still needed at this time. I think I might have some good news however." Pete looked at the major, but remained skeptical.

"I could use a dose of that, Major."

"The cavalry troop you will be joining has been assigned to accompany the 6th Heavy Artillery under the command of Major Lionel Booth. They are currently in

Memphis where your troop will meet up with them. Once there, your troop will be used to escort the 6th that is going a ways north to a place called Fort Pillow, arriving before the end of this month. Once they are in place your troop will be heading back to Memphis. Perhaps you will be able to procure a furlough then, maybe even get an assignment closer to home."

"So the cavalry won't be participating in any planned offensives? How about reconnaissance?" Pete asked.

"Perhaps some recon on the way to Memphis, but planned offensives? None I'm aware of, but since Nathan Forrest has been reported to be in the general area who can tell? I know you have been away for some time, but I assume you know of him."

"Nathan Bedford Forrest? Yes, Major, I know of him. Sorry to hear he's still alive."

"That resourceful scalawag apparently has as many lives as you, Lieutenant. Almost lost all of them at Shiloh. He was involved with some rear guard action when the Rebels lit out, at a place called Fallen Timbers. He charged right into two infantry brigades accompanied by the 4th Illinois Cavalry, but apparently he didn't give a hot damn. He emptied his Colts into our brave boys then went after them with that damned saber of his. Heard he keeps it razor-sharp on both sides. Took a Minie ball in his hip, that rascal did. Damned near knocked him off his horse if the stories are true. Got away though, obviously. Some say he was the last man wounded at Shiloh, and there were a hell of a lot killed and wounded on both sides before we won that battle."

"We won at Shiloh?" Pete said. "Well I'll be damned. Sure wish *I'd* been the one that had a bead on Forrest with that musket at Fallen Timbers, sir. Sure enough would have liked a second chance at that devil."

"You, Lieutenant?" Major Rice asked with arched eyebrows.

"Guess you're right, since I haven't explained what I mean. Had my chance at that ghost from hell at Shiloh my own damn self. Yep, sure wish I had been aimin' that Springfield at Fallen Timbers, I do that."

"You might get another chance, Lieutenant, possibly in short order."

"Perhaps, Major. Guess I'd best write a few letters home. How's mail delivery these days?"

"Slow, at least two weeks, but much better than in the areas still under Rebel control I would imagine."

"Well then, I'll write the letters this evening."

Pete wrote his letters to Delicia and his parents and posted them the following morning. True to his word, however, General Smithington had indeed been in the military long enough to forge certain alliances. He already had a man in place to handle everything, which included keeping careful watch at the military post office. Pete's letters had been easy for Captain Calvin Baileen to intercept. The savvy, middle-aged army officer had no reason to believe the rest of what General Smithington wanted would be very hard to accomplish either. He had certainly offered Captain Baileen enough money for it.

***

PETE HAD already inspected the horses in two army corrals, but hadn't found one that suited him. Perhaps he didn't want to, or was holding out in a vain attempt to locate a horse which at least looked to be as good as Yankee had been, since a good number of the mounts he rejected had appeared to have been decent enough animals. After the second week of March arrived, however, he knew he would have to choose something. Major Booth himself had been to Chattanooga on a short visit, and told Pete and the other cavalry officers he wanted to arrive at Fort Pillow from Memphis no later than March 28th.

Pete had been impressed by the young man. The dark-haired major couldn't have been over twenty-five, even if he did sport a beard in what Pete assumed was an attempt to appear at least somewhat older. In Pete's mind the major's demeanor accomplished that more than his beard; he appeared to be an intelligent young man whose bearing was enhanced by a steadiness Pete thought would prove its worth if hostilities broke out.

Pete made his way to the third corral and glanced at the fifty or so horses that were milling about. Suddenly his eyes stopped on a stallion, and he couldn't believe what he saw. The stallion was half a head taller than the rest of the horses, but it was the muscular physique and beautifully light, chestnut color and off-cream mane that made it stand out; but then Yankee always had stood out.

"I'll take that tall palomino, Sergeant," Pete said to the soldier in charge of the corrals.

"Sorry, Lieutenant," the portly sergeant said, "but that there horse is spoke for."

"He isn't anymore, by God." Pete responded as he entered the corral. The other horses moved off as he made his way through them, but not Yankee. At first the stallion just stood and stared at the approaching soldier. Yankee finally threw back its head, whinnied, and trotted over to him.

"As I live and breathe!" The soldier who had approached the corral hollered out to Pete. "Guess I best find me another horse!" Pete turned around and looked at the man.

"Dirch!" Pete hollered back, a broad smile on his face as he stroked Yankee's mane. "How come you're not dead?"

"*Me?* If I didn't know better," Dirch replied, himself smiling, "and I ain't for certain I do, I'd swear I'm talkin' to a ghost!"

***

THE LONG ride to Memphis was uneventful as was the forty mile trip north to Fort Pillow, for the most part. Some of the men in Pete's troop had grumbled about having to escort Negro soldiers, but Pete paid them no heed. Soldiers always complained about something, and if it hadn't been for the Negro artillerymen of the 1st Battalion of the 6th Heavy Artillery it would have been the weather, nettlesome insects or anything else the men could come up with, real or imagined.

Pete, like most people from Naperville, didn't know any Negroes, at least not personally. There were no Negroes living in Naperville, and very few in DuPage County as far as he knew. His parents had always insisted their sons treat everyone with respect until such time a given individual proved they no longer deserved such treatment, and by the time the McCabe boys had matured that had become second nature to all of them.

Pete recalled how Father Benjamin had once chastised him when, as a boy, Pete had used the word "nigger". He hadn't been fifteen, and had been explaining how a family of coloreds had been traveling through Naperville earlier that day. A local merchant had refused to allow them to enter his grocery store. Pete had been quoting the store owner, but even so it hadn't been acceptable to his father that evening around the supper table.

"How would you feel if we were in a strange town and your mother and I were turned away for no other reason than the color of our skin, and a store owner used such a word to describe your parents, making sure you and your brothers could hear? You think about that, Kee, and don't fail to ask yourself how repeating such a word makes you any different than Mr. Richardson, except you said it behind their backs. To my mind, and I'm sure to yours once you've thought about it, that takes a special kind of cowardice and is no less reprehensible."

Pete recalled how his father's words had stung, and how the silence that had ensued over the supper table that evening had settled over all his brothers as well. None of them had been unblemished if they looked back upon their own behavior honestly enough, as innocent as they had all wanted to believe it had been, but all of them had concluded they would be more careful from that moment on. Although none of them had considered themselves racist, they all had to admit they had made casual remarks over the years that in hindsight had been anything but simply innocent, offhanded remarks or jokes that hadn't amounted to much - or so they had believed. They had, however, been able to imagine themselves in front of that grocery store witnessing their own parents' humiliation.

***

PETE WAS riding next to Dirch before the contingency of soldiers was supposed to bivouac for lunch when they were about halfway between Memphis and Fort Pillow. They had been recounting the experience of that day in the barn, and although they had been over the subject a number of times something would come to one of them and they'd be talking about it again. Although Dirch had mentioned it before, he felt compelled to bring up one of the episodes again - felt compelled to air his guilt.

"I'd made it about five miles," Dirch said, "'fore I thought'a anything other than gettin' the hell away. I knew that horse of yours weren't gonna let anything come close to catchin' me by then, an' that's when I started wonderin' if you was dead yet. Figured you was, or soon would be. Then I recollected other fellas shot up real bad after battles that somehow pulled through, and what a tough *hombre* I figured you prob'ly was. 'Bout then I give some thought to headin' back when I recollected them hogs, but figured we'd both end up in that God damned hog pen if I did. Anyway, I kept goin'."

"I would'a too, Dirch," Pete said. "Not much you can do for a dead man, and I'm sure glad you saved yourself and Yankee. Even missed ridin' on this saddle, too."

"You missed the *saddle*? Why the hell would anybody miss a saddle, even if it was broke in? One's 'bout good as another, ain't it? Besides, that one's a tad heavy."

"Maybe so, but it's good to have it back anyway." Pete said with a chuckle before adding one more thing, still smiling: "Maybe it's lined with gold or somethin'." Dirch looked at Pete and chuckled at his friend's apparent whimsy. Another thing was on his mind as well, and it extinguished his mirth.

"And I was gonna get to Naperville, Pete, honest I was. Let your kinfolk know what happened, that gal of yours too. Needed some money though, and figured I'd re-enlist, earn some and light out again. It's a good feelin' knowin' I won't have to."

***

"GIT YOUR little darky ass off that log, boy!" The private said after Sedman had sat upon a fallen tree with his plate of food. "Let a white man sit there. Go on boy, move!"

"I prefer to stay," Sedman said, glaring at the bearded soldier who appeared to be twice his size.

"And I prefer to sit on that damned log!" The soldier replied, "and not next to some God damned nigger!"

"How you feel 'bout bein' stretched out bleedin' on the ground?" The large soldier turned towards the sound of the voice, but had to look up.

"I can take care of myself, Cusman." Sedman said as he went about eating his lunch, or at least moving the food about with his fork. "But there's some room next to me if you'd care to take a seat." Cusman glared at the soldier, and at the four others that had just approached.

"Well now," the soldier said with a nervous sneer, "looks like this here log's spoke for by more'n just one'a us." The other four men crowded around, as did several black soldiers who had been near the confrontation.

"What's the problem here, Private?" All the men turned and looked at the lieutenant who was approaching.

"This little nigger's sittin' in my place, Lieutenant." Pete looked around at all the assembled men then focused on the talkative soldier.

"I don't like your choice of words much, Private," Pete said. Then he glanced at Cusman Sable. "From the look on this soldier's face, he doesn't either. I suggest you find another place to eat your lunch before this fellow takes it from you. Now move! That means all of you, white or otherwise!" The men began to disperse, but Cusman took a seat next to Sedman.

"I just gave you an order, Sergeant." Pete said to Cusman. The large man rose to his full height and looked down at Pete.

"Yes sir, but my friend here asked me to join him before all them other men showed up. With your permission, I'd like to stay." Pete took stock of the huge man, and decided to probe a little further.

"Does your friend require your protection, Sergeant?"

"I require nothing of the sort, sir." Sedman replied as he arose, before Cusman could speak. "I had the situation well in hand prior to his arrival. Sometimes the sergeant feels compelled to offer his assistance when it is as unwelcome as it is unnecessary." Cusman glared at Sedman, but said nothing.

"I admire your sand, Private." Pete said, stifling a grin. Sedman didn't look as though he could hold his own on a grade school playground. "You may need it before long. May I join you two for lunch?" Sedman and Cusman exchanged glances before they nodded.

The three men sat upon the log and introduced themselves, exchanged a few pleasantries, then Pete asked where they were from and what brought them there. Both of their stories fascinated him, especially Cusman's accounts of his escape from slavery and his experience in the 54th Massachusetts. Sedman asked Pete for his story. Pete told them about Shiloh and what came after it, leaving out most of what had occurred in Low Cloud Valley. After that he talked about his desire to get home.

"Lookin' forward to that myself, Lieutenant," Cusman said, "soon as this war is won."

"I haven't been north of Tennessee since before Shiloh," Pete said. "My people thought I was dead until a couple weeks ago. I'd be home now if it wasn't for this expedition. Once you fellows are situated that's where I'm going too, war or no war." Cusman looked hard at the lieutenant.

"All due respect, sir, but don't you wanna see it through to the end? Most of us got kinfolk back home. You ain't the only one." Sedman stiffened at his friend's words, and kept a cautious eye on the lieutenant. Pete remained silent for a moment before speaking.

"My father used to say if someone says something that gives you pause, it's best to do just that instead of talking right away. Looks like both of you have sand. And you, Sergeant, have a point. I'm goin' home anyway, though."

***

"WHAT WAS all that, Sergeant Sable?" Hiley asked Cusman when everyone was preparing to resume marching. Kiah and Kit were with their brother, obviously just as interested in Cusman's answer.

"That lieutenant's good people," Cusman said as the men began to march. "A might fed up with the war, but seeins' what he's been through guess that makes sense, least ways to him. Where the hell you three been? 'Bout had us a regular donnybrook a spell back. That Lieutenant McCabe kept them peckerwoods in line, though part'a me wished he hadn't."

"We was eatin' lunch," Kit answered. "Kiah an' me was goin' over that book Mr. August done give us." Sedman had been walking next to Cusman, but since being next to his friend was the equivalent of being next to an old growth oak he hadn't been noticed by the three brothers.

"We *were* eating lunch," Sedman said, correcting his young protégé, "and you should have said Kiah and *I were* going over the book *given to us* by Mr. August."

"Sorry, Mr. August. I'll be more careful chosen' my words," Kit said.

"Mind you do, you two as well, Kiah and Hiley," Sedman responded. "I don't want the three of you ending up being burdened with Sergeant Sable's grammatical afflictions." Cusman looked down at his friend.

"That's enough outta you, *Private* August," Cusman said. "You two young men doin' jus' fine, you too Hiley. *Private* August told me you been learnin' to read an' write too."

"Not near as good as these two scrawny little niggers," Hiley said with a smile, but it's comin' 'long. I like that there math Mr. August been teachin' me. Says I gots me a head for figures. Don't that beat all?" Sedman started to correct Hiley's grammar as well then thought better of it, trying a different approach.

"You do have a head for math, Hiley. By the time I'm finished with you and your brothers, I dare say the three of you will be able to run your own business. Like I've told you, Boston would be a good place for such an endeavor. I would be glad to help you get started, both financially and mentoring-wise." The three brothers beamed at each other, their eyes all anticipation. It was Hiley who spoke.

"We would sure 'nough be grateful for that, Mr. August, if your words mean what I think they does, and want to thank you agin for all your learnin'." The five cannoneers continued their marching, a spring in all their steps. With what they believed was a little luck, they would arrive at Fort Pillow in less than a day.

***

JUDE "JT" Ternar and Mark Lunge had watched everything unfold while they had been lounging against the side of a boulder eating their lunch. JT was older, perhaps in his early fifties, with somewhat curly, sandy hair. He was at least six feet tall and had beady eyes that narrowed when he bullied someone, which had always amused him. He was a loud, egotistical man, which was somewhat of a curiosity since he had nothing to suggest he had ever been successful, except the ability to excel at lawn games of all things. It was that oddity that had been responsible for bringing him together with Mark Lunge, who also possessed that useless ability. Mark was taller than JT, somewhat thin with dark hair, and considered himself better looking than virtually everyone. His arrogance was so profound most folks considered it amusing. Although they were ne'er-do-wells if anyone had ever fit that description, it had been commented upon it was a wonderment they could both fit in a room together if they attempted to fit their egos in as well.

They had watched everything unfold during lunch that day, but then they never did allow Lieutenant McCabe out of their sight except at night, and even then they knew of his whereabouts. Things had been uneventful up until that little lunchtime confrontation, but they still had time. One thing was for sure; it would take more than a small disagreement before they would likely be able to act. A good situation would be a skirmish of some kind with a few Rebels, although a full scale battle would be ideal. It was easy to kill someone under those conditions, especially someone fighting on the same side that wouldn't be expecting a bullet in the back.

They already had a hundred dollars each. General Smithington's old acquaintance, Captain Baileen, had promised another four hundred for each of them once the deed was done. Neither man had been in the army long. Captain Calvin "Cal" Baileen had approached them back in Chattanooga, where they had been working for the army hauling supplies. It wasn't the first time the captain had hired them for some nefarious deed, but it was the first time he had ever insisted they had to enlist and then kill someone. It was also the first time they had ever been paid more than fifty dollars. Once they had accomplished the deed, they had been promised a great deal more opportunities, as well as the extra four hundred dollars each. With a little luck they would never again have to spend another day doing manual labor of any kind, or at least in the foreseeable future which to them amounted to the same thing.

If nothing presented itself before they reached Fort Pillow, at least the rumors indicated they would likely have a few opportunities once they arrived. Their only concern was the order Captain Baileen had received to return to Memphis once their cavalry troop had escorted the other soldiers from the 1st Battalion of the 6th Heavy Artillery to the fort. Baileen had, however, assured them he could delay things long enough to allow them a chance to kill the lieutenant as long as it didn't take more than a week, two at the most.

If the Rebels were planning an assault, they reasoned, the problem would take care of itself; otherwise JT and Mark agreed it could be "blamed on some niggers". In that regard it hadn't helped that the lieutenant had shown himself to be "a God damned nigger lover," JT had said after having watched Pete share lunch with a couple of them, "sittin' right *next* to 'em even, jus' like they was white," JT had added, but no matter. "Who wouldn't believe a nigger done it 'ceptin' maybe another nigger?" JT went on to say. Mark Lunge agreed JT's plan was, in that regard, flawless.

***

PETE AND Dirch, along with half the other men of their cavalry troop were out front when they saw Fort Pillow on top of the First Chickasaw Bluff north of the small town of Fulton. The Mississippi River, majestic in both size and strength, was visible to their left as it had been, off and on, since they had left Memphis.

"That bluff's so damned high must be halfway to heaven. Looks like a good spot for a fort, wouldn't you say Pete?" Dirch remarked, paying no attention to his superior's rank. Pete didn't care.

"I guess so," Pete replied, "depending on who, and how many, decide to attack it. Heard most those in there are green, know the men in the 6th are too, a lot of 'em anyway. They better hope those reports about Forrest aren't true. If he shows up there's gonna be hell to pay. It might look like a fearsome enough place to attack, high enough anyway, but if I know Forrest that won't slow him down much."

"You know Forrest?" Dirch asked. "How come you never told me that?"

"Fought 'em even, back at Shiloh. No quit in him, I can tell you that."

"Well, he just might meet his match here, *mi amigo*. Look at that place. Would you wanna attack it?"

"Nope, sure wouldn't. But if I had to, I'd be wishin' the tables were turned and Forrest was a Yankee leadin' us in, even if there were a thousand enemy soldiers up there. Heard there's only about six hundred men, or will be once we arrive. Six hundred mostly green men against Forrest and his bunch? Hell Dirch, that place could be twice as high and made of granite instead of those earthworks for all the good it'll do if Forrest has his whole cavalry with him. If he only has half, it would still be one hell of a fight. Don't get me wrong Dirch, but I'd just as soon be back in Memphis if that plucky bastard shows up. He's one jimhickey all right. Give 'em that."

***

THE AREA around Fort Pillow's perimeter was mostly forested wilderness except for some meadows and where the land had been cleared for timber and some crops. The entire area was in sharp contrast to the bustling city of Memphis. There was a ditch about six feet deep and twelve feet high in front of the fort. Over the next two weeks Major Booth had the soldiers build a high earthen wall along the inner fort, planked on the inside. There were six narrow openings for artillery built into the wall, and although it looked formidable, Pete couldn't help but wonder how effective it would be if a full scale charge ensued.

He remembered the furious charge Forrest had led against the 1st Naperville during the Shiloh campaign, and was especially concerned about the location of the black soldiers' barracks. They were very close to the south side, and would be especially vulnerable to an all out charge. Pete was concerned Major Booth had made a mistake in that regard, even after he had directed the men to build a larger inverted "w" shape from the smaller crescent around the smaller fortification.

Pete climbed on top of it and looked around. It was an impressive sight from up there, but when he envisaged a couple thousand or so screaming Rebels rushing forward at full speed, led by General Forrest no less, he just shook his head. He remembered Nathan Bedford Forrest.

***

THE 6th MADE camp inside the small section of earthwork together with the 2nd U.S. Colored Light Artillery. Along with the other new arrivals, Cusman and Sedman pitched their A-frame tents over what floor boards they had scrounged up.

"All things considered," Sedman said, looking around from the top of the parapet, "it appears the enemy will have their hands full if they are foolish enough to attempt an offensive maneuver against this fortress." Cusman looked at his friend as Sedman gazed about, marveling at the view.

"That's what them Rebels thought back at Fort Wagner," Cusman remarked. "We got inside though."

"And then what happened?" Sedman asked, his question as rhetorical as it was condescending. "I seem to recall it was the forces *inside* the fort that easily prevailed."

"That what you recall, Sedman?" Cusman responded, offended by his friend's callous remark. "Damn, an' all this time I thought you was goin' to classes back in

Amherst, wearin' a clean starched shirt, shiny shoes an' such, talkin' too damn much as usual."

"Point being," Sedman continued, "well fortified high ground is the bane of any attacking force. If the rumors turn out to be accurate, I can't wait to rain canister down on any graybacks fatuous enough to attempt an assault."

"If fatuous means what I think it does, that don't mean they won't be shootin' back." Cusman countered. "Lookit that high ground yonder," Cusman said, pointing to an area of hillsides outside the fort. "Them *fatuous* graybacks you been yammerin' 'bout kin get a bead on just about all this parapet. Them boys kin shoot, too, you kin believe that shit. It's one thing to fire off some damned cannon in a field back in Memphis, but the angle here ain't near as good. 'Round here there gonna be bullets comin' at us too, an' a whole mess'a screamin' Rebs assumin' they show up. You best remember that, Sedman."

Cusman stalked off, still agitated. He was used to bantering with his friend, took pleasure in it, but that time had been different. The unsettling feeling Cusman harbored about the overall situation at the fort was bothersome as well. He kept walking, heading down the bluff towards the landing and small town of about eight structures near the river where a number of the civilians were living. He needed some alone time, or at least away from his friend for a while.

***

THE LITTLE girl was standing on a rock near shore, crying. She had dropped her rag doll while attempting to climb upon the rock and it had landed in a small backwash. If she didn't get to it before long, the river would take it away. She was frantic. Her grandmother, who had died a slave the previous winter, had made the doll for her. It was the only thing the five-year-old child owned that was precious to her, the only tangible thing left to remind her of the old woman she had loved and still missed dearly.

"What is it child, why you carryin' on so?" Cusman asked as he approached.

"It's Mary, I dropped Mary," she replied, looking up at the largest man she had ever seen. His size was intimidating, but his words had sounded kind. "Can you save her 'fore she gets drowned up?"

Cusman glanced to where the child was pointing. He took two steps into the swirling water, reached down and retrieved the doll. "Here you go, little one. Mary gonna be fine. Just got a might wet, that's all. What's your name? I'm Cusman."

"Lucy," she replied, her large brown eyes looking at Cusman as if she still hadn't quite made up her mind about him. "Are you a giant?" Cusman's warm grin told her if he was, he was a nice giant.

"Just a tad bigger'n most men, Lucy." She smiled up to him, clutching her doll to her breast. "You know where you got them pretty dimples?" The little girl shook her craned head, eyes wide, big as a fawn's.

"Well now, that's where an angel kissed you darlin', that's what happened. She must'a kissed you extra hard, deep an' pretty as they are. Musta thought you was extra special. I think you are too." Lucy's smile glowed larger.

"Baby what you doin' down by the water? What have Ah done tolt you 'bout that?" The approaching young woman, Lucy's mother, asked. Her tone was reproachful, but loving.

"Hello ma'am," Cusman said, tipping his cap. "Had us a little emergency. Mary fell in, but Lucy pointed her out. Things are fine now."

The young woman looked up at Cusman and smiled. He saw where the little girl got her pronounced dimples and beautiful eyes. She thanked him, and led her little girl away. Cusman tipped his cap again, smiling. It had been a short respite, but therapeutic. He looked towards the fort atop the bluff, and started up the hill, back to the war. He glanced over his shoulder. Lucy was holding her mother's hand, cradling her doll with her other arm. Even from a distance Cusman could see her dimples as the child beamed at him again. He sighed a smile her way, waved, then trudged upward with deliberation.

***

MAJOR BOOTH was young, but he wasn't unobservant. Although he had ordered his men to spend two weeks re-fortifying the place, he still had doubts. He kept asking himself what he would do if he was directing an assault upon the fort, then acted accordingly. Even with that, he wished he had more men and firepower. In the final analysis, one which never really remained final in his mind, he had to accept that virtually all commanders in his position would want more men and guns, especially men experienced in battle which he most certainly did not have, at least not in abundance. His concerns refused to dissipate. A few rationalizations managed to temporarily assuage them, but only one rationale appeared to remain with any degree of consistency – just how likely could it be that General Forrest or any sizable contingent of enemy forces would deem it prudent to attack such a redoubtable fortress?

***

PETE WAS furious with Captain Baileen. The beady-eyed, round little man had not only insisted Pete stay at the fort, but had sent most of the other horse soldiers of Pete's troop back to Memphis over a week ago. When Pete again reminded the captain what his orders had been, all the captain did was accuse Pete of cowardice.

"Major Booth needs soldiers who have tasted battle, Lieutenant," Captain Baileen had said, "and if the reports of your past experiences are accurate, which I'm beginning to doubt, that would include you. Try not to show your trepidation, Lieutenant. This is a well fortified position, and I don't need you cowering about. It's bad for the men who aren't afraid of some traitorous Confederate rabble. One more word from you about what my *orders* may or may not have been, and I'll have you, at the very least, put on report for insubordination."

Pete had wanted to wring the round little man's neck, or at least smash him in the face. Instead, he simply saluted and walked away. With the captain's alleged heart condition which he seemed to want everyone to know about, one blow just might kill him, Pete mused. Court-martial proceedings were one thing, murder charges another. Captain Cal Baileen wasn't worth either.

***

"LORD I hate this rain," Dirch said to Pete after entering the lieutenant's rude cabin later that afternoon, shaking the water off his great coat. All of the officers had structures of some sort while most of the enlisted men, and all of the colored soldiers, had to make do with tents – all too often leaky tents. "There's mud, then there's this shit when the rain won't let up. "You got any more'a them cigars, Pete?"

"I only got six left," Pete said, still in a mood over his confrontation with Captain Baileen.

"Hell, I only want *one*," Dirch responded with a smile, wondering what was bothering his friend besides the obvious. Pete smiled back, chagrined, and gave him three.

"Here, now you have as many as me. Anything goin' on out there besides the rain and mud?"

"Nah. Boring as usual," Dirch said as he puffed a cigar to life from Pete's lantern. "Boring and wet. How the hell did we end up here when all them others got to leave for Memphis?" Dirch asked Pete, as he had a number of times before. This time Pete had more of an answer.

"Just had me a little talk with Baileen. For a man who won't carry his own saddle bags because he's afraid his heart might give out he sure is determined to stick around this place. Said he wanted cavalrymen with experience here with him, too."

"Shoulda kept my damned mouth shut 'bout all I done then." Dirch said as he inhaled a deep drag from his cigar and exhaled a cloud of smoke the cool, moist air exaggerated with ease. "That don't add up though, Pete. Most them other horse soldiers he sent away seen their share'a fightin' even if just half their bullshit was true. Besides us and the captain, only that no-account Ternar and his boyfriend Lunge is still here. I swear, those two never seem to be apart. Don't that seem queer to you?"

"Hell Dirch, I don't know." You're not foolin' me though. I heard you requested to stay. You crazy or somethin'?"

"Damn right I'm crazy. Thought you knew that much anyway. Anyhow, still owe ya for that time in the barn. Those were some mighty sharp lookin' tines on that pitchfork, and me shootin' Mitchell don't count, seeins' how you had already plugged him. Yep, those tines was sharp all right."

"Yeah, they sure were," Pete said, remembering how close Dirch had come to getting the full brunt of them through his back. "If those graybacks show up though, they'll be toutin' more'n a few farm tools. Lord, I hope Forrest is off creatin' mischief elsewhere."

"Think he is?"

"I think he'll be where he isn't supposed to be, unless where he's *supposed* to be is where he thinks *we* think he's supposed to be, in which case he'll be there, because ultimately we won't believe he'll *really* be there, if we think on it too much, which he knows we will."

"Say what? Mind slowin' that down a touch, Lieutenant?"

"We're in for it Dirch, unless we aren't, which means we are – maybe."

"Well, *that* sure as hell clears things up. No wonder they made you an officer. Can't understand a God damned thing you're talkin' 'bout."

"Can't argue with that. But at least me bein' an officer's keepin' us outta the rain, and it got us a couple Spencer's too. Might as well grab your bedroll and bunk in here tonight. Got me a half-dog of whiskey, least we can fight off the dampness for one night anyway. Thought it was 'posed to be warm down this way in April, and here it is the 11th already. Maybe it'll brighten up tomorrow. April 12th in the Sunny South. That sound about right to you, Dirch?"

"I'll get my bedroll, if it ain't been washed halfway back to Memphis."

***

CUSMAN WAS awake, and had been since before daybreak. It was a cloudy and fairly cool morning for that time of year, but at least the rain had stopped, not that it mattered much. Everything was so wet more rain couldn't make it much wetter. Still, it was better than the ebb and tide of downpours that had plagued the men over the past twenty-four hours or so. Cusman had made his way to the top of the parapet and gazed about. It was an impressive sight, especially when he looked to his right at the rain-swollen Mississippi that didn't need more water to be impressive. He had never seen such a massive river before, swollen or otherwise.

He was worried about Sedman. His friend had been coughing again, deep hacks from the depths of his chest, and Cusman feared his friend's pleurisy was making a comeback. If it was, he knew what that would probably mean if Sedman didn't get back to Memphis before long, and maybe if he did.

The post surgeon, Dr. Charles Fitch, had given Sedman a small amount of laudanum, but it hadn't helped much. Sedman had been lucky to get anything. Quality medical care was all but non-existent in a remote area like Fort Pillow. Disease often times killed more men than battles, and if Sedman did have pleurisy it would be a miracle if he survived, at least if the rumors bore out and they remained under siege for any length of time. *Could be something else though,* Cusman rationalized. *Ain't like every cough is a damned death sentence...*

***

CUSMAN TURNED his head quickly when he heard the shots coming from the Fulton Road Gate area. There was only one logical reason why men would be firing rifles down there that early in the morning. Besides, Cusman knew the difference between target practice or perhaps a few shots fired at a deer. He knew the difference between those things all right, and a fusillade of shots fired in...

"Rebels comin'!" Cusman hollered.

XXXVI

They were both quality rifles, but Billy preferred the .22 Remington-Rider. Doc Wygant liked the .22 caliber Henry, mainly because of its fancy engraving. Hezekiah O'Darcy had loaned both rifles to them since neither actually owned a gun. Doc Wygant had it in his head he wanted to go rabbit hunting and had asked Billy to come along, even though all the youth would do, as always, was some target shooting.

It was sunny and rather warm for April as they headed west from Naperville to a pristine wooded area in the countryside that hugged the banks of the west branch of the DuPage River. Doc Wygant knew everyone in the surrounding area of course, including the McDowell family. Farmer McDowell had told him he was welcome on his property anytime, whether to fish, hunt or just stop by for a visit.

"Got me a full blown craving for some of Widow Harvey's rabbit stew, Billy. No one makes it near as good as she does, no offense to your mother, but without the main ingredient my insatiable longing will remain unfulfilled. Besides, we could use a little time away from the hospital."

They hadn't parked Doc's carriage and made it fifty feet before three plump rabbits shot out from under an old, fallen tree, most of it ensconced amidst tall grass and weeds. Doc Wygant shouldered his rifle but before he could fire Billy's gun went off, dropping one of the rabbits. Doc Wygant stared at the youth in disbelief.

"Never thought I'd live to see the day, Billy boy."

"Had me my share of rabbit stew over the years, Doc. High time I helped fill the pot. Let's see if we can find those others." Billy reloaded the single shot rifle, grabbed the dead rabbit then headed in the direction of the two that had made good their escape.

Doc Wygant followed, but he was still having a hard time accepting what had just occurred. He knew Billy had gone through a great deal during his brief stint in the army, but still… If anything, Doc Wygant had assumed Billy's experience would have further steeled the boy against shooting anything that drew a breath. Another rabbit appeared and again Billy dropped it before Doc Wygant could react.

Billy had always been a good shot, thanks to his brother Pete's patient instruction, Doc Wygant recalled. All the McCabe boys were, but Billy had always confined his shooting to target practice and competitions at local fairs as far as Doc knew. Something had obviously changed. As usual Doc Wygant didn't know why, but Billy's actions and demeanor had begun to ignite those odd, familiar feelings in the old man, the ones which insisted he pay attention to things as if he could feel what was going to happen but didn't know what, exactly, it was. The feelings usually pointed him in a particular direction though.

"A couple more and we can head back," Doc Wygant said. "Guess I didn't need to pack us a lunch." Billy had been eyeing the spot where the second rabbit had bolted from, then looked at the old man.

"Sorry Doc. I'll let you take the next few shots. Maybe we could have lunch over by the bend next to McDowell's north forty where we buried that fawn last year, remember? With all that rain last night I'll bet I could find some arrowheads where it's been fresh plowed." That sounded more like the Billy Doc Wygant knew, but his odd feelings persisted.

"How many in your collection now, Billy?" Doc asked in an attempt to forestall his feelings until later. He knew it was no use, but tried anyway.

"Oh, over two hundred I guess." Billy loved talking about his arrowheads, and all they represented. "Last year I found my two favorites over by Messinger's Spring, just above the pond where the water trickles out of the gravel along the east bank. One's not much bigger than a thumbnail, but the detail is downright astonishin'. That was one artistic Meskwaki who carved it, patient fella too. Every little nick is there for a reason, and that Indian didn't put in a one that didn't compliment the others as perfect as you please. The other one must have been for a spear, you should see it, it's huge. I'll bring 'em to work tomorrow."

"I'd like to see those, the others too." When did you start shootin' game, Billy?"

"About ten minutes ago."

***

CLIFTON JANEWAY was impressed as he stood in the telegraph office in Aurora reading the wire. General Smithington had been true to his word, at least thus far. Apparently he had not only found the right man for the job, but it appeared as if no time had been wasted in doing so either. The whole affair was going to cost a damn sight more than Stalworthy had thus far, but it appeared as if the job would finally get done. Besides, what did some money matter if it could keep McCabe from telling his version about Major O'Darcy's death, assuming he hadn't already done so. Clifton assumed that was unlikely since General Smithington would have likely heard something. Regardless, killing McCabe would put an end to it and lead him to the altar with Delicia. Clifton put the telegram away, and allowed his mind to drift towards his favorite fantasy.

Summer wasn't far off, and Delicia had stopped changing the subject when he had brought up wedding plans. She hadn't agreed on a date, or even promised she would, at least not unequivocally. Clifton knew women though, or thought he did. It had even been brought to his attention that Delicia had said a few things to a group of women her mother had invited over for an afternoon tea party, one that Clifton's mother Cortance had been invited to attend. That alone was a first. According to her, Delicia had not only mentioned the possibility of a summer wedding, but had been to Chicago with her mother and all her surviving sisters looking at wedding gowns, accessories and such.

Clifton's mind reeled when he thought about their wedding day; their wedding night more like it. Delicia hadn't even allowed him to kiss her yet, but oh how that would change. In his fantasies Delicia would be every bit as enthusiastic, or at least as willing as her younger sister had been, perhaps more so since she was older and no doubt even more hungry for a man; Clifton could just imagine it. He wondered if such thoughts were on her mind as well and concluded they must be. How could one girl be so willing to do such things and her very own sister behave appreciably otherwise? Delicia was stronger, more mature, but in Clifton's mind it stood to reason even she couldn't contend with what had to be a family trait to at least some degree.

He had been with a fair number of beautiful women, at least if he counted the most expensive prostitutes Chicago had to offer. They had been just that however - prostitutes, whores, *sluts*. The very dregs of womanhood, he believed, even if they were nice to look at, along with their other attributes. Come summer he would not only be with the most beautiful woman he had ever known, but the most virtuous one as well. Linda Marie had of course been beautiful, for a child, but he wasn't at all convinced she had been a virgin. He had to believe Delicia was, and the image of her stretched out naked and oh-so-willing on a large bed in the finest hotel suite Chicago had to offer left him weak-kneed. He might have to use a somewhat different approach, but ultimately a willing Delicia, her true self emerging, would be doing everything Linda Marie had done. The image of Delicia moaning, pleading and even screaming while he was defiling her had aroused Clifton more than in his mind. It was a warm day, but Clifton found it prudent to button his major's tunic all the way past his waist before he exited the telegraph office. He had to take special care to adjust himself as well, looking around first, before he mounted his horse.

Before long his thoughts had drifted back to the business at hand as he rode along, and his impending meeting with General Smithington. The general had a few things to tell him that apparently he hadn't wanted to put in a telegram. The telegram had indicated it was good news, however. Clifton couldn't wait to hear it, and hurried his horse along to the Aurora train station.

***

"I'VE KNOWN Captain Baileen for years, decades actually." General Smithington told Clifton after he had arrived at headquarters in Chicago and the door to the general's office was closed. "Realizing the importance of our plan I wanted to secure the most able man for the job, and we were damned lucky Captain Baileen was still in Chattanooga."

"Obviously you trust him, General, but what are his qualifications?"

"Qualifications? Baileen? He is one of the most opportunistic men I have ever known, clever too. It's not all that easy to put oneself in a position such as his without an exceptionally scheming mind, at least for as long as he has done it without getting caught. He's not a wealthy man by your standards, Major, but he has done quite well for himself. With the fifty thousand I've offered him to ensure the desired result I can assure you he won't fail. Hasn't yet, anyway, and for considerably less money. Fifty thousand will give him exactly what I myself have always sought - a golden retirement. Trust me, Major, we are in very capable hands." Clifton didn't trust anyone, but thus far liked what he was hearing.

"I assume you haven't called me all the way to Chicago just to tell me about this Captain Baileen's worthiness, correct?" Clifton said as he helped himself to a cigar from the humidor on the general's desk. "What news have you that couldn't be put in a telegram?"

"Baileen is in command of the cavalry troop your friend McCabe has been assigned to, and they could very well be in Fort Pillow as we speak. For all I know McCabe might already be dead, if I know Baileen. Regardless, he soon will be.

"I received a wire from another acquaintance of mine, Colonel Micheal Shea on General Hurlbut's staff. He has about as much respect for Hurlbut as anyone else with half a brain, in other words, none. My acquaintance Colonel Shea, an informed individual if ever there was one, insists Fort Pillow is woefully undermanned if the reports about General Forrest's movements and troop strength are accurate, although General Sherman doesn't seem overly concerned which may also bode well for us.

"Baileen may not have to kill anyone, or have it done more like it, and if I'm very lucky might even get killed himself. Under different circumstances I'd hate to lose such a worthy connection, but saving forty thousand dollars at this juncture of my life would be well worth it. Too bad I already had to send off ten thousand, but no matter. We are, Major, in a very envious position.

"The next telegram you receive from me will in all likelihood be the one you have been waiting for, and when it arrives you can begin celebrating. It will also be cryptic and to the point. Look for something like this: *Fort Pillow has been attacked. Some of our fine officers have been killed. Long live the Union.* Once you've read those words, more specifically the second sentence, I would suggest opening the finest champagne at your disposal, and perhaps finalize your wedding plans, Major, if I may be so bold."

XXXVII

Major Booth sent out skirmishers after he had been told what was unfolding. Fires had already broken out in the contraband camp area closer to the river down by the steamboat landing, and higher up a second column of Rebels had begun to attack the fort's middle hill located farther east. A skirmish line of Union soldiers took position at a breastwork on the middle hill in order to repulse them.

Behind the inner fortification farther north, Booth ordered Captain Munn and Lieutenant Wright to have their units prepare two more strategically placed artillery stations, but Cusman's group had time to put together only one. The other stations hadn't been entirely completed, not all of them, so Cusman and the others began to work furiously at getting a makeshift platform built and rolled their cannon into place. In order to improve the angle of fire, Captain Munn had ordered his cannoneers to place the station upon a flat area near the top of the wall. It would expose his men, but he saw no other way to significantly improve the angle of fire towards the advancing enemy troops. He wanted at least one crew in a position to do so regardless of the risk. Judging from the intensity and swiftness of the initial Rebel onslaught, Captain Munn concluded positioning his men there could make the difference between being overrun and being overrun immediately.

"It's down to it now, men!" Lieutenant Wright hollered as Cusman and the others prepared the gun for firing. "Blow them Johnny bastards back to hell!"

The words had no sooner left the lieutenant's mouth when a Minie ball slammed into the center of his back. Captain Munn went over and knelt beside his dying officer even though he knew Lieutenant Wright's wound was fatal. With Minie balls spitting all around, he stood and faced his crew and ordered them to continue preparations for firing. He too was a large man, just several inches or so shorter than Cusman. Due in large part to his rank as well as his size he hadn't gone unnoticed by the Confederate sharpshooters on the hillsides.

The first Minie ball that struck him shattered his left elbow. He lurched sideways, then drew his Remington-Beals .44 caliber sidearm with his good arm and staggered towards the front of the cannon, just to its right side. Shielding his men, he aimed his Army Model Remington, noted for its accuracy, at the last puff of powder smoke he had seen coming from the hillside, and the rifle he thought may have shot him. Before he could fire, another Minie ball caught him in his right thigh, and a third tore off most of his right ear. That would have been enough to drop a normal-sized man, but Captain Alan Munn wasn't normal in physical size. It was his intrepid heart, however, that truly defined the man.

He stood shielding his men, and when he saw what may have been the long rifle that had all but shot off his left arm rise again, he kept squeezing the trigger. One .44 caliber explosion after another erupted from his weapon, and his crew let out a hearty cheer when at least two of the bullets slammed into the Rebel sharpshooter. Even from such a great distance they had seen the soldier's head snap back, and the exploding, red mist that had been the top of the man's skull told them all the needed to know about Captain Alan Munn's extraordinary marksmanship.

Two more Minie balls tore into his torso but he still didn't fall, and although it felt to him as if he had reached over to steady himself against the cannon's barrel with his left arm, it hadn't moved. It couldn't. He squeezed the trigger one last time but his revolver was empty. He slipped to the ground, still clutching his gun as he died.

By then a good number of Union skirmishers on the middle hill opened up on the opposing hillsides, forcing the Rebel sharpshooters to exhibit more caution. The Rebels were still able to get off a number of shots, but since they had exposed their position their element of surprise had been compromised.

Sedman almost tripped over Lieutenant Wright's body as he rushed up, coughing uncontrollably. Cusman wanted to tell his friend to go back, find a hospital tent for the colored soldiers or at least his own since earlier both of them had moved their tents farther inside the fort, but he knew it would do no good even if it was a direct order. There was a post hospital for the white soldiers, but it was too far away, down by the river. Besides, regardless of what was happening, there was no guarantee they would have allowed Sedman to enter, especially since he wasn't even wounded. Cusman watched as his brave friend took his position and placed the primer into the vent and stepped back, waiting for Cusman's command.

"Fire!" Cusman yelled. Sedman pulled the lanyard. Nothing. "God damned fuses!" Cusman hollered. "Get another! Fast!"

The next one was defective as well, but the third wasn't. The explosion was massive compared to the spitting musket fire, and the charging Confederates ducked instinctively. Little actual damage was inflicted since the angle was still too sharp. In no time the Rebels were on their feet again, charging forward.

"Move! Move! Move!" Cusman yelled, and the cannoneers reacted more rapidly than they ever had during training. They got off two more rounds before another defective fuse stopped their progress. By that time the Union skirmishers had abandoned their position on the middle hill and retreated to some rifle pits within the inner fort. It was around 8:00 a.m. but no one was paying attention to time, which had lost all significance.

***

PETE AND Dirch had come running out of the cabin, weapons in hand. They both had Spencer rifles and .44 Colt's but it was the rifles they were preparing to fire as they ran to a low bench behind the fort's earthen wall. The soldiers already in position at that strategic location had only muzzle-loading, single shot Springfield's.

"Don't go pokin' your head up for long, Lieutenant!" A private hollered at Pete. "Them Rebel sons a' bitches will shoot it off!"

Pete rose anyway, aimed and fired. His bullet hit a sharpshooter over two hundred yards away. Just as Pete ducked for cover three Minie balls slammed into the earthwork from where he had just fired. Dirch followed suit, and just as he fired a Minie ball creased his shoulder while several others just missed.

"Think I hit one, Pete!" He hollered. He had, all but removing the sharpshooter's jaw.

"You men count to five on my order then rise and fire!" Pete ordered. "Dirch, come with me!" The two men made their way about twenty feet away and took position. Pete nodded at the other men as both he and Dirch watched the group count to five, moving their upper bodies to indicate they were doing so before they elevated and fired. A number of bullets came back at them just as they ducked, but two of them hadn't gone down quickly enough. As soon as the enemy bullets hit, Pete and Dirch shot up and began rapid firing their Spencer's as fast as they could before the enemy could reload, hitting at least two more Confederates. By then the other Rebels on the high ground had a bead on Pete and Dirch's position, as both men had assumed the Rebels would. "Let's get the hell outta here!" Dirch hollered, and both of them took off in the direction of the river below.

"There he goes," JT Ternar said. "This is a good a time as any." Mark Lunge was shaking so badly all he could do was nod, but all he wanted to do was get to the river and grab a rowboat or anything else he could lay his hands on. He noticed a large group of civilians down by the river scrambling onto a coal barge that was being towed by the Union gunboat *New Era*. It was hugging Flour Island, a fairly large land mass near the mouth of Cold Creek that emptied into the Mississippi west of the fort.

"Ta hell with it JT!" Lunge hollered. "Let's jist git ta that barge somehow an' the hell away from all this!" JT Ternar wasn't any braver than Mark Lunge, but he *wanted* that extra four hundred dollars.

"All we gotta do is kill that bastard! Hell, in all this commotion ain't nobody gonna even notice now he's away from them others! Come on!"

"Where the hell we gonna find Baileen?" Lunge retorted. "You think he's jist gonna mosey on over an' count off our money? I ain't waitin' 'round fer that!"

"We can kill McCabe then skedaddle!" JT insisted, hollering over the din. "Collect our money back in Chattanooga for all I care. Now come on, Marky boy!"

Captain Baileen was hiding behind a dead horse when he saw Major Booth get hit. The major had been walking rapidly, with much deliberation, along the lines urging his men on when he fell. He had collapsed the way men do when they are dead before they hit the ground. Baileen had already ripped part of his own uniform for effect and partially covered himself with the blood from the dead horse so if the need arose he could pretend he was wounded as well. He had also made use of another horse, a live one, or would if the opportunity presented itself. It wasn't likely; the Confederates had the fort surrounded, having taken positions to the north, east and south. The river seemed to offer a western retreat, but there were plenty of Rebels on the hillsides and other strategic points covering that route as well, especially near the shore. Still, the river was his best bet; his only one, he realized.

The Union forces were obviously outnumbered, but Baileen and the other Federals didn't know the extent of the disparity. There were around 1,500 Confederates, perhaps more. If there had been 600 Union men when the battle erupted, there weren't that many anymore. Baileen had hoped for some sort of confrontation that would have made earning his forty thousand easier, but he hadn't bargained for what was unfolding that day.

He was a resourceful man and hadn't given up hope of escaping and collecting the extra money, but if McCabe was going to get killed it was very unlikely he would personally have anything to do with it. The Rebels would probably take care of that anyway, he figured, assuming Ternar and Lunge hadn't already. Regardless, his present location was untenable. He made his way through the frenzy, heading to the steep slope that led to the river, acting as if he were a soldier with a purpose; damn his non-existent wounds. He did his utmost not to expose his panic or himself, the latter being his biggest concern.

***

MAJOR GENERAL Nathan Bedford Forrest had proceeded to conduct reconnaissance over some of the outer areas his forces had surrounded, although he had generally remained at least a quarter mile away from the actual assault. He was, however, oblivious to the mayhem of battle, or at least not afraid of it. Other men might duck and cover when gunfire erupted near them, but Forrest acted as if bullets and even cannon fire were simply minor annoyances, like so many Yankee mosquitoes.

Pete and Dirch had stayed near the bluff after all, away from the river. They had worked their way to the northwest of it, and that's when Pete spotted an officer he strongly suspected was Forrest.

"Wish he was closer," Pete said.

"Who?" Dirch asked as they stayed inside a section of earthwork, peering out from time to time.

"My old friend I'm pretty sure, Forrest. Hell with it. Might as well take a shot." Pete rested his Spencer on top of the earthwork, and took careful aim. It was a difficult shot, well past the rifle's effective range of two hundred yards, but it was the best one Pete figured he would probably get. It was all but impossible, Dirch thought, the way the Confederate general kept moving about let alone the distance involved. Still, he was glad it wasn't himself Pete had in his sights. Pete squeezed the trigger. At first he thought he had actually hit Forrest, the way his horse reacted as they both tumbled to the ground. Pete fired several more times, as did Dirch, but Forrest was up and had limped to safety. His horse didn't move, nor would it again.

"I think ya got 'em, Pete!" Dirch said.

"Maybe, but I doubt it. Think I only got his horse with that first shot. The others didn't have a chance in hell of hittin' 'em. If it was Forrest, I sure as hell wish I'd killed that devil."

Both shots came from behind them, and both had been intended for Pete. Lunge had been shaking so much he had missed Pete entirely, but his poor marksmanship proved deadly for Dirch. The bullet had hit him below his left shoulder blade causing him to jerk upwards then roll over, away from Pete. JT's shot had just missed Pete's head. As JT prepared to fire again, angry with himself for having gambled with a head shot, Pete wheeled around and pulled the trigger of his Spencer, shocked by having been attacked by his own comrades. There was a click, but nothing else. Pete frantically threw down the rifle and reached for his Colt revolver, but JT had him in his sights. The quivering man had to go for a head shot now; a body shot would likely give Pete enough time to fire back. Lunge was struggling with his rifle, shaking so badly he kept fumbling with the lever action. He was so unhinged he was screaming at the mechanism, cursing as if it were conspiring against him.

If Dirch hadn't fired at that instant, JT Ternar's second shot, which had seemed to go off almost simultaneously with Dirch's, would have been more accurate than his first attempt. It turned out it was; his second bullet missed Pete by an even closer margin than the first. Dirch hadn't missed though. JT, a shocked expression on his ruddy face, slumped to the ground with a bullet through his sternum. Pete had his Colt out by then, and both he and Dirch fired at Lunge at the same time just as the trembling man was raising his rifle. The rounds crashed into Lunge, and he went backwards as if doing a short-step death dance. Like Major Booth minus the honor, he too was dead before he hit the ground.

"Aw, shit." Dirch said as Pete tore open his friend's blouse and sighed. "Damn, Pete, at least we're even for that pitchfork... you...you can keep the horse too," Dirch offered, sharing one last joke with his friend.

"You hang on Dirch! You..." Pete knew it was no use. Dirch had a slight smile on his face, staring off vacant-eyed towards a place very far from Fort Pillow, an alluring place that whispered a suggestion of home.

***

BY NOON a few of the Union cannons were still keeping up as steady a barrage as possible, but the Confederates had taken over the barracks just outside the fort and had been able to pick off many of the cannoneers in the southernmost ports with relative ease.

Miraculously, just a few of the men in Cusman's crew were dead or wounded, and although Sedman wanted to at least try and keep firing Cusman ordered the survivors, including Hiley, Kiah and Kit, to abandon their position and told Obediah to put down the ordnance he was carrying to the cannon and join them. Cusman knew maintaining their position was not only suicidal, but pointless since their cannon's angle of fire was woefully ineffective.

Deeper inside the fort, Sedman collapsed in a fit of coughing so intense Cusman had to carry him to his tent. When Sedman, burning with fever, tried to talk, the coughing would start up before he had three or four words out. Cusman caught the gist of it though. "How can a (coughing) man of your size (more coughing) manage not to get (still more hacking) hit?"

"Didn't I tell you? Bullets bounce off'a me. Most of 'em anyways." Cusman said, his face all tragedy. There was still gunfire outside but it wasn't as intense. "Them Rebs prob'ly gonna be demandin' a surrender before long, there bein' so many of 'em and all, an' that could take awhile. I'm gonna try an' scare up some'a that laudanum, though I s'pect there ain't none left or soon won't be. Be back soon as I can, Sedman. Keep them Dragoons handy, just in case. You take special care, hear?"

"Cusman!" Sedman called out just as the tent flap had fallen and blocked his view of the huge man. Cusman reached out and pulled it back, then bent down and looked inside, waiting for his friend to speak. "You take care as well, my friend." Then Sedman collapsed into a fit of uncontrollable hacking.

***

CONFEDERATE FIRE continued to weaken, and by early afternoon it had become relatively sporadic. Their ammunition had run low, but they had such a strategic advantage in both vantage points and men all they had to do was wait to be re-supplied. It turned out to be a fairly long wait, and in the meantime it appeared as if the Union forces might seize the day after all.

Major William Bradford had assumed command after Booth had been killed, but Forrest didn't know it. He knew one thing though; if the smoke coming upriver was being created by transport steamers filled with Yankee reinforcements, his victory wouldn't be as much of a foregone conclusion as he had believed. It could even mean a defeat, or at best a hasty retreat. Neither option was acceptable to him, so he hurried a demand of surrender to Major Booth, under the assumption he was still in charge.

The Union soldiers, along with local civilian supporters trapped with them were elated when they spotted the smoke coming upriver. Major Bradford was also joyous, convinced salvation was at hand. He gloated as if he had known all along it would happen, but his self-satisfaction would be short-lived.

Forrest sent over a flag of truce with a demand for surrender around 2:00 p.m., mindful of the approaching steamboats. He indicated the men garrisoning Fort Pillow would be treated as prisoners of war, and hadn't excluded the black soldiers from his demand. He added, however, *Should my demand be refused, I cannot be responsible for the fate of your command.*

He also sent one of his officers, Major Anderson, along with a detachment of men under his command to the riverbank below the fort in order to ascertain the situation regarding the approaching steamboats. The major unleashed cannonade upon the approaching vessels whose return fire, directed higher up on the bluff, was ineffective due to the steep angle. Even though they were just warning shots coming from the Rebels or at least served as such, they were intimidating enough for the boat captains, especially since their cannons couldn't be elevated enough to inflict appreciable damage upon the Confederates in front of the fort. Two of them kept steaming upriver, and the third one turned about and headed south, taking with it any hope the Fort Pillow Yankees had been entertaining as it pertained to re-enforcements.

There was still some confusion, however, along with conflicting developments. *Olive Branch,* one of the steamers heading north and the larger of the two heading in that direction, also had cannoneers and their guns aboard. How many wasn't known to the Confederates, or more importantly, whether or not there may have been troops in force onboard as well. If *Olive Branch* ran past the fort and hooked up with the *New Era* that was upstream near Flour Island, there could still be cause for at least some concern on the part of the Confederates.

Major Bradford, who didn't indicate the Union response was coming from him but instead from Major Booth, requested an hour to respond to the surrender demand so he could consult with his officers and the captain of *New Era.* Forrest scoffed at the request, and gave him twenty minutes. He would have scoffed anyway, but the horse Pete had shot, one of two that had been shot out from under Forrest earlier, had left more than a few bruises, aches and pains, so he was in a foul mood anyway. "Ah would sure 'nough like to get my hands on the God damned Yankee what shot Dancer." He had said to some subordinates. "That was a fine animal."

Forrest subsequently stuck with his demand. His battle blood was up, and when Major General Nathan Bedford Forrest's blood was up it was never good news for the Yankees or anyone else who wanted to hinder his progress in any way.

Major Bradford refused to surrender and had the unanimous support of all his officers; at least none of them had voiced a different opinion even if that was how they felt. If the several sideways glances that were shared by a few of the junior officers were any indication, that was indeed the case although none of them found it in themselves to raise an objection.

***

LIEUTENANT PETE McCabe had been correct; Fort Pillow was occupied by men woefully inexperienced in battle and its horrific ramifications. Taunting from both sides was a common occurrence during the war, probably all wars when the adversaries had the opportunity to do so, and during the truce at Fort Pillow it was again evident. Union soldiers, black and white, took the opportunity to let the Rebels know what would happen to them if they tried to storm the fortifications that to the green, subjective Yankees still appeared to be all but impregnable regardless of the difference in troop strength or their strategic positions. The front lines of both armies, to a degree, weren't all that far apart so the bantering carried easily, especially to the Rebels that had crept closer even though it was a serious breach of military conduct while a truce was in place.

Most Confederate soldiers had never owned a slave, but a lifetime of growing up in a region where slavery existed had conditioned them to view people of African descent in a way that demanded subservience, or at the very least outward displays of respect if not inferiority, implied and especially otherwise. Taunting from the white Yankees was bad enough, but when the insults came from the black soldiers it was, in the minds of most if not all of the sleep deprived and hungry Confederates, beyond unacceptable to an obscene degree. There would be hell to pay.

The afternoon dragged on. The Union soldiers knew the Rebels weren't very far away, but many of them had grievously underestimated many of the Rebels' overall proximity. At 3:15 or thereabouts, after Forrest finally ordered a second assault, they found out. The blare from the bugles cut off the taunting and replaced it with an explosion of Confederate rifle and cannon fire, and the most hideous howls coming from the charging Rebels the majority of Union soldiers had ever heard in their lives. Well fortified or not, if the Rebel Yell that seemed to carry over the roar of gunfire and cannonade was an indication of what was to follow it was hell itself on the move. In that regard the Yankees were finally correct as they abandoned their subjectivity and offered up return fire that soon proved to be as pointless as it was ineffective.

In no time at all it seemed, the Union line crumbled under the relentless on-slaught of whooping Rebels and their firepower. The green Yankees had never experienced such a horrendous spectacle, but they were during that moment in time. The rout was underway with vengeful authority. The Union soldiers stumbled back as some of the panic-stricken men tried in vain to take shelter behind rocks, stumps and fallen trees; even the dead and wounded bodies of their fallen comrades, in a vain attempt to protect themselves from the withering rain of Minie balls and other projectiles.

Other Union soldiers were tumbling, jumping, and all but flying down the steep bluff as they frantically tried to reach the river. Some of those men attempted leaps of distances no sane person would attempt under almost any other circumstance. It felt as if they were trapped in a nightmare, the kind where they would jump from great heights and be airborne, but unlike such a nightmare ride they didn't wake up at the crucial moment. Trapped within the reality of their predicament many of them came crashing down only to suffer inguinal hernias, broken or sprained ankles and wrenched knees. Any portion of their bodies which slammed into the logs, stumps, rocks and unforgiving ground suffered similar fates. The Confederates held the riverbank to the north and south, guns at the ready. Since the whooping Rebels which were giving chase were closing so fast, the Union soldiers were trapped.

Being the most athletic of the three, Hiley was ahead of his twin brothers. After he had successfully hurdled over a large boulder stuck into the side of the bluff he stopped and turned, in hopes his brothers could catch up to him. Coming on fast was a panic-stricken Kiah, with Kit, equally terrified, right behind him.

"No!" Hiley screamed, but it was too late. Four wild-eyed Rebels, breathing heavily, had caught up to the twins.

"Where be your Yankees now, *nigger boy!*" The largest of the four Rebels yelled as he thrust his bayonet into Kit's stomach even though the horrified lad had raised his hands and screamed surrender. He hadn't been carrying a gun or any other weapon either, having dropped his rifle when he had begun his frantic retreat.

"Yeah, oh *yeah!*" The Rebel hollered as he kept stabbing the boy, using his boot to pull out his bayonet after it had become wedged deep within Kit's eye socket and into the back of the lad's skull.

"We surrender! We -" Those were the last words Kiah ever spoke. Two of the other Rebels had descended upon him, one with a saber and the other with his bayonet. The one with the saber had rammed it into the boy below his belt, and twisted it as a terrified Kiah screamed in agony. The soldier kept twisting the blade, howling with deranged glee as his comrades joined in the slaughter, equally enthralled. One of them forced his bayonet between Kiah's lips and shoved it forward with all his strength. He moved the bayonet up and down with so much force it shattered the lad's teeth. Before the Rebels were done stabbing the lifeless bodies again and again, both teenage boys were virtually unrecognizable.

They were so preoccupied within their insanity they hadn't seen Hiley coming. He too was without a weapon as he lunged at the largest soldier, the one who had first stabbed Kiah. Hiley slammed into him and had the man by the throat, and dug his thumbs in until the man's trachea ruptured. The others were quickly on Hiley, but not quick enough to save their comrade. Before they could stop him, Hiley managed to drive his thumbs deep into his adversary's eye sockets, causing both retinas to burst. The horrified man attempted to scream, but the only sound he was capable of producing was a guttural, high pitched growl so hideous it was as if Hiley had strangled a rabid dog.

The Rebel with the saber brought the blade over Hiley's head and placed it against his neck, grasping the saber with two gloved hands on either end. He made a sawing motion, slicing open Hiley's throat with the sharp blade, while the others began stabbing him with their bayonets. A Confederate officer ran up and fired his revolver at point blank range into Hiley's face, for no apparent reason other than to watch it happen.

"Go on you men!" He yelled, pointing to five Union soldiers kneeling on the ground with their hands in the air - four black privates and a white corporal, overwhelmed with terror as they screamed surrender. "Kill them black-hearted Yankee niggers! Kill 'em all!"

The soldiers unleashed a hasty volley into their victims as they rushed over and began thrusting their weapons into the shrieking men, first into their midsections and groins then into their faces, jamming in their blades over and over as they whooped and hollered.

They left the white corporal alone, save for a rifle butt to the side of his head. A few minutes later he was dead as well. Another group of Confederates had come upon him, and since the black soldiers were already dead they had to settle for the young corporal just as he had regained consciousness and had again attempted to surrender.

The entire bluff was soon covered with the bodies of dead Union soldiers, the majority of them black. Most of them had tried to surrender or had simply been running away. Still others were on their knees pleading for their lives, having discarded their rifles earlier in order to run faster. Some of them had turned and fired – only a small number of panic-stricken men had done so - and if an excuse to continue the slaughter was needed, which apparently wasn't the case if some of the survivors' on both sides stories were true, the sporadic Yankee gunfire was as good an excuse as any.

In their frantic haste to escape, to *survive*, it hadn't occurred to any of the Union soldiers to take down the fort's flag thereby exhibiting their surrender. Afterwards any number of Confederates, including the officers, indicated the Union soldiers' failure to do so was another reason the slaughter had continued.

"Please, suh! Got me a family, same as you! I surrender, suh! I *surrender!"* The nameless black soldier screamed as he was stabbed to death, then had his skull crushed by the heel of a boot that was repeatedly slammed into it, over and over again. The grinning Rebel hollered over the wails and gunfire, spittle flying from his mouth as he continued to yell, stomping the dead soldier's skull into a red, beige and yellow mass as unrecognizable as it was hideous.

If most of the Confederate officers were trying to stop the brutality as was later claimed it hadn't been effective up to that point, and well beyond in some cases. It was total insanity, its brutality and cruelty limited only by the imaginations of the butchers themselves, whose creativeness appeared to be boundless. There were Confederate soldiers revolted by the deranged spectacle, but once insanity sweeps over men under such conditions, it becomes so infectious even those least likely to commit unspeakable atrocities find themselves involved in the mayhem or at least incapable of doing anything about it, which was also reported to have occurred.

One such soldier, a Confederate private who had recently been conscripted into General Forrest's cavalry, discovered how that worked. He had been farther away from the bluff than many of the others, but he saw some of what was happening while standing only twenty feet away from General Forrest. The general had finally ridden into the inner fort from Middle Hill, over a quarter mile ride, to supervise the movement of a Yankee cannon to the bluff's periphery to fire at the *New Era* gunboat. The general was hollering encouragement to his men as well, at least the ones he could see.

The private had reloaded his musket, but when he saw some Yankees throw down their weapons and flee, many screaming surrender but running anyway because there was no let up to the slaughter, he held his fire. He was new to battle, and it hadn't occurred to him that shooting unarmed, retreating soldiers in the back or especially when they were on their knees pleading for mercy was an acceptable thing to even consider, much less do. The private just stood there slack-jawed, his rifle by his side, horrorstruck by the sudden realization that Satan himself had descended upon Fort Pillow.

"What in *hell* you doin', Private?" General Forrest bellowed as he rapidly approached the private who couldn't have been older than eighteen. "Fire, God damn you, *fire!"*

The youth blinked, as if he had been awakened, just barely, from a trance he was convinced had been instilled by the devil himself. He looked to his left and saw the imposing figure of his general standing next to him. The tall, bearded horse soldier towered above the youth by at least a head. "Sir? Oh, it's you, ain't it. What did you say, sir?"

"I said fire, Private! Take up your weapon and *fire!*" General Forrest wasn't Satan, but one look into his eyes convinced the youth his commanding officer might as well have been.

"But, but sir, them there Yankees ain't a firin' at us," he replied, as if that should have been obvious.

"Not *now*, but they was, and will again we give 'em half a chance! Why in hell you reckon they's headin' for them gunboats? Them Yankees lookin' for cannon fire cover, that's what! They git it, you kin bet they'll open up on us sure! Now fire, by thunder, or I will see you end up in front of a God damned firin' squad! Go on Private, *fire!*" The wide-eyed private, secure in the belief he was indeed conversing with the devil or one of his immediate subordinates, put his rifle on his shoulder and pulled the trigger. He didn't know if he hit anyone, Yankee or otherwise. He sure hadn't been aiming at anything other than perhaps the Mississippi River down below.

"Now charge!" Forrest bellowed as he slapped the back of the youth's head before storming off.

***

CUSMAN HAD seen it coming, at least the probability of a rout, but he had not been prepared for the extent of the wanton butchery. He had surveyed the area prior to the battle that morning as he had been doing since their arrival, much like that lieutenant had always done, the one he had shared lunch with that day which seemed an eternity ago. Both men had been through enough to realize the worst time to decide where to go was when it was *almost* too late because that usually meant it *was* too late.

The current debacle at Fort Pillow, however, wasn't like anything either man had ever experienced, although to Cusman it sure reminded him of one place he knew he would never forget. Still, it was as though the longer the war dragged on, the more it brutalized the very souls of some of the men fighting it; honing their callous viciousness to an edge so severe it had been whetted beyond even a wisp of humanity.

Cusman had made his way down to the post hospital area near the river prior to the last Confederate assault. He had been ordered to assist Dr. Finch by carrying some of the wounded men to nearby hospital tents. He had also helped the doctor by placing red flags around the tents, indicating they were indeed hospital tents. He had finally managed to secure some laudanum, but not until after the Confederate bugles had initiated the charge.

In seemingly no time at all the Rebels had swarmed down the very bluff Cusman needed to ascend. Although he was aware he could probably kill a few Rebels, he wouldn't survive to tell about it, nor be able to help Sedman. Looking about at the bloody chaos he doubted he would survive anyway. He couldn't help his comrades win what was clearly a losing battle if there ever was one, but perhaps he could make it back to Sedman's tent in time and somehow escape with him to the east.

Hundreds of Confederates were everywhere, but with so much attention being focused on the retreating Union men who had been running down the bluff there was a chance he might succeed. He had before, and the memory of crawling through the salt marshes at Fort Wagner bolstered his resolve if not his hope of being able to repeat such an undertaking. He was staying out of sight as best he could, using whatever cover he could find. Cusman knew he was losing precious time as he ducked and hid behind, or in, the bushes and brambles just south of the bluff. Still, twinges of guarded optimism held partial sway. Most of the charging enemy soldiers, as best Cusman could tell, had already rushed away from the area where Sedman's tent was located on higher ground. Cusman stayed south of the bluff, moving stealth-like.

He had just exited a thicket of brambles when he saw it; a small group of recently killed civilians in a small clearing. Their corpses were behind a large stand of bushes where they had also attempted to hide. He glanced briefly and froze. Cusman wanted to tear his eyes away from the horrific sight, but couldn't bring himself to do so. The huge man began to shudder. The civilians had been hacked to death by any number of bayonets, swords and knives. It was a bloody, gruesome sight that suddenly became even more tragic. Cusman wouldn't have been able to make out the identity of the little girl, as severely as she had been hacked and trampled into the mud next to her butchered mother. He recognized her rag doll, however; her rag doll Mary. It was still clutched in the little girl's lifeless hand.

He continued to keep out of sight as much as possible, still traumatized by what he had just seen. As much as the overall mayhem affected him, the sight of the little girl and her mother had been especially heart-rending. It was as if the luminosity of humanity that had once flowed from them, their connection with whatever decency the outside world possessed, had been destroyed; obliterated because it *had* been so beautiful. It was as though their inner beauty, their love for one another, had been especially threatening to whatever Beast had descended upon Fort Pillow, making them particularly vulnerable. Cusman felt powerless, unable to quell or even diminish the madness. He kept going but couldn't manage to elude, much less throw off the Beast.

After a while Sedman's tent was only a hundred yards away. With all the Rebels charging about, however, it may as well have been five hundred. Still, Cusman was determined to try. He desperately needed to focus on something that afforded him even a shred of hope, anything to drive away, or otherwise obscure the tragic image of that small hand and blood soaked rag doll.

***

THEY WERE truly unhinged; the three Rebel soldiers didn't even recognize each other, not really, not in a way that even hinted they may have once been sane men. They had already butchered a fair number of black soldiers, and had grown accustomed to the savagery. Still, they wanted - *needed* - more of it, as if brutality was a drug so seductively vicious it would only satiate them if they not only continued to butcher, but do so in the most horrific ways imaginable - in truth *only* in ways they couldn't begin to imagine until they were doing it. They heard the coughing coming from a tent, stopped, and smiled at each other. Their hideous grins were all they needed to convey their intentions.

They went over and lifted the tent flap. Sedman was racked by coughing so pitiful he didn't have time to react, and when he did the first man to reach him, a sweaty, toothless Rebel, had brought his saber down with tremendous force on Sedman's slender forearm before he could double cock and fire his Colt Dragoon. Sedman attempted a scream as his hand and part of his wrist were severed amidst a flow of pumping blood, but his throat constricted so much he couldn't breathe consistently, just gag.

Sedman had to let go of what was left of his right arm in order to grab his other revolver. When he did let go of the gaping wound the blood spurted out, but he went for his gun anyway. One of the others, a barefoot, stench-infested dwarf of a man rushed over and kicked Sedman's left wrist hard enough to make the gun drop, but was disappointed he wasn't strong enough to have seriously injured it.

"God damned little nigger's got hisself hard bones, that's all." The odorous, tiny Rebel pouted to his comrades who had begun howling when their comrade hopped about rubbing his stubbed toes. Sedman was coughing, but managed to speak as he locked his eyes on the diminutive soldier.

"Burn in hell you filth-ridden *scum!*" The howling stopped immediately. Sedman tried to get up, but a rifle butt to his chest stopped him, fracturing his breast bone.

"Mouthy little nigger, ain't he." The toothless Rebel said. "Reckon we kin fix that. Got me an idear…"

He began to rip up the rude floor boards until he had removed half of them. He then placed them on top of the boards next to Sedman's cot, and proceeded to dig out the now accessible nails with the aid of his knife, concentrating on the largest ones. "Put 'em on them boards, an' hold down his feet!"

When the others had pulled Sedman from his cot and done as they had been told, the toothless Rebel removed his heavy pistol from its holster and grabbed it by its barrel to use for a hammer. After yanking off Sedman's boots he proceeded to drive the first nail, one of the two longest, through Sedman's left foot and into the wood underneath. Sedman wasn't capable of screaming; his throat could barely allow in air, but in his fevered brain he was wailing, pleading for death. The Rebels were all laughing, howling really, as the other foot was nailed to the wood. The sound of snapping foot bones could be heard whenever the man missed the nails. Then he moved up to Sedman's left hand while the dwarfish Rebel held tight Sedman's wrist, or tried to. Sedman had managed to break the man's weak grip, and flailed at him. Sedman raked his fingernails across the tiny man's face, flesh building under his nails as the blood began to form on the screaming man's cheek.

The third Rebel grabbed Sedman's wrist, forcing the hand palm side up. The toothless Rebel jabbed the tip of his last square nail into Sedman's palm, and began to hammer away until the top of it was less than an inch from disappearing into the bloody mess. He then hit the nail sideways to bend it over until it did disappear into the gore, catching on a few splintered bones.

Sedman was half unconscious and moaning, or trying to. His guttural sounds kept getting choked off, but he didn't pass out. In his frenzied agony he glanced at the stench-ridden cretin, who was taking apart the lantern Sedman had used to read by a lifetime ago.

"Ain't got us no pig," the cretin announced as he dosed Sedman with the lamp oil, making sure to get over half of it below his belt, "but gonna have us a roast jus' the same!"

"Sure 'nough is!" The toothless Rebel chortled. He dropped a burning match that landed just below Sedman's belt. The small flame dancing on the match head came to life with a *whoosh* as it enveloped Sedman; enveloped him as if it couldn't burn him to death fast enough, as if it didn't *want* Sedman's agony to end.

He couldn't control his screaming, although that's not what it sounded like. Whatever the unholy noise was, it had the desired effect upon the three Rebel soldiers. They had tears in their eyes they were laughing so hard, slapping one another on their respective backs as they exited the tent.

***

CUSMAN KEPT trying to reach his friend's tent, ducking and hiding whenever an object presented itself for him to do so, but had only made it part way when he spotted the three Rebels running off, whooping and hollering with deranged glee. They soon blended into a group of other Confederate soldiers and continued their rampaging. Cusman looked around, then made his way another ten feet or so. He stopped cold, suddenly mindless of whether or not his actions had alerted anyone. "God *No!*" He bellowed when the smoke that had been floating lazily out of Sedman's tent had begun to billow. Before Cusman was able to sprint the rest of the way the tent erupted in flames. Cusman kept running and screaming, and was less than ten yards away when two Minie balls tore into him.

He seemed to be floating then, floating above himself. He felt no pain, none at all. At first he wasn't certain if the image of the huge black man upon the ground was even his, since the image was obscured by the wavering, urgent heat waves caused by the inferno that had engulfed Sedman's tent. Cusman somehow knew it was indeed himself, as if predestination was no longer a vague concept but something timeless, something he had known about all along, forever actually, as familiar as breathing…was he still breathing, he wondered? Perhaps, not that it held any significance, or seemed like something he still needed to do…where was Sedman though? *Shouldn't he be up here too?* Cusman asked himself. *Of course he should…of course…but where is he? Where you at, my brother?* Then darkness and light swirled together in a way he had never experienced before, although the surreal image seemed familiar as well. He just knew that was true as he drifted into the soul of it…into the soul of it all and all…

***

PETE WAS in a thicket of swamp grass not five feet from shore. The Rebel sharpshooters had spotted him on two previous occasions, but amidst all the chaos had assumed the last time they had fired at him their aim had been true. Pete had worked his way behind two of them as they fired into the Union soldiers who were trying to swim away. The desperate Union men and boys were such easy targets they might as well have been hanging by their hands from a tree limb or some such thing, taunting the Rebels to take their best shot. The retreating Yankees, one after another, were being picked off, their bodies rising when they were hit then disappearing beneath the surface, oozing life as they sank.

How a massive river the size of the Mississippi could turn to blood was unimaginable, but there it was, at least twenty feet from shore and growing to a length of nearly two hundred yards. Pete watched the mayhem unfold, horrified beyond any semblance of reason. Even though the blood was caught in the southward flow of the mighty river, it appeared as if the blood were being pumped from an underground spring with a limitless supply the muddy water easily transformed into a maroon, watery grave.

Pete looked with horror at the Union men still heading towards the water, towards the bloody grave; some getting cut down before they made it, others just after they did, still others butchered if they stopped and tried to surrender farther up the bluff. Some of the white Union soldiers still stumbling down the bluff were being shot and hacked to pieces as well, but it was the black Union soldiers, *the nigger Yankees* the Confederates preferred to concentrate upon the most.

***

THE TALL, lanky black soldier knew he couldn't make it; it was a wonderment he had made it that far, just fifty feet from shore and running fast. Pete saw one of the Rebel sharpshooters take aim at him. Pete forced himself to muster what little composure he could and took out his .44. He blasted a hole in the Rebel's lower back, but it was the hole in front, the one Pete couldn't see but knew was there, that was so gruesomely impressive. He could have fit his fist in it if the forward explosion of the man's entrails were any indication; Pete just knew it.

Even though the Rebel had to die, had to be stopped from killing, Pete desperately wanted the same to be true for him, even though he tried to convince himself his actions were justified. Killing was another thing he couldn't stop doing though; halting his own brutality was one more thing he was being denied.

The other Rebel sharpshooter turned towards Pete just in time for another round to explode into the man's face. Pete quickly scrambled back into the mucky, tall grass closest to shore, his entire body shaking as he held on as best he could to what was left of his quavering equanimity.

He was all but certain he was going to die, but no sense rushing it, no sense in asking for it to happen. He reloaded his revolver and stayed hidden as much as possible. That was the worst part, his inactivity, he felt more than thought. The sudden mayhem of previous battles had been just that; an explosion of frenzy so profound all he had ever been able to do under those circumstances was react, constantly react, with no time to reflect. The obscenity of what was occurring at that moment, however, had plenty of time to infect him; it was everywhere, and as he buried himself in the mucky grass the terror swallowed him whole. He was trapped in the middle of it, including the screams, void of all inhibitions coming from men consumed by insanity on both sides. The men on each side had their own reasons to be devoured by the uninterrupted madness. The relentless reports of gunfire were everywhere, as were the unholy wails. He was hopelessly entangled in a howling wave of utter inhumanity.

Pete's pulse was pounding throughout his entire body as he looked at the almost white, bright gray sky, such a familiar sight which was totally out of place, as were all things familiar as he looked about - the smell of the river and rotting plants where he was immersed, the trees, how he envied their invulnerability - and the frog whose two periscope eyes watched him for a moment then disappeared so easily under the green-flecked water of a stagnant pool, escaping it all so effortlessly; how he envied that tiny creature as well. Pete raised his head, convinced he was in hell, and was immediately back inside the Infernal Creature, the *wailing* he hadn't come close to escaping or ever would; he was convinced of that as well.

***

THE LANKY black soldier Pete had briefly saved held up his hands as the two Rebels charged at him as he stood by the shore, but Obediah realized the folly of attempting to surrender. *Keep on comin', you peckerwood devils, jus' keep on comin'...*

"You gonna die, *nigger!*" The enraged Rebel out front screamed as he rushed forward. His musket was empty, but the blood-stained bayonet was poised to strike.

Obediah clasped his hands together over his head, and reached inside the sleeve of his private's blouse. He found the handle of his knife in its sheath, the one he had owned since he was ten. Mas'r had given it to him as a reward for saving a favorite hunting dog from dying in some swamp mud that had almost sucked the hound under. Obediah recalled how ecstatic he had felt when Mas'r had given him the nine inch hunting knife. Less than a month later, after finding out his father had been sold, he swore to his inconsolable mother he was going to use it on Mas'r, but never did. The irony of what the knife had finally come to represent overwhelmed Obediah as the screaming Rebel closed in. Obediah didn't know the word "irony" existed, but he was profoundly aware of its meaning as he clutched the handle of his knife that had once masqueraded as a gift.

"This here's for you, too, Mas'r *suh!*" He hollered as he sidestepped the charging Rebel and quickly buried the blade into the side of the shocked, soon-to-be-dead Rebel. The other Rebel stopped and then advanced more cautiously, obviously every bit as green as the first one since he too hadn't bothered to reload. They weren't two of General Forrest's more experienced men. The more experienced of Forrest's horse soldiers didn't use bayonets since they didn't fit on their short rifles. Moreover, seasoned soldiers would have usually taken time to reload at every opportunity.

The remaining Rebel lunged, but he didn't come close to stabbing the agile black Yankee. Obediah grabbed the barrel of the Rebel's musket and pulled it, bringing the frantic young man with it as Obediah opened the Rebel's throat with a vicious slash and kicked him dead to the ground. Hideous gushes of blood gurgled out of the man's wound, his body spasmodically jerking about, twitching; but not his eyes - they didn't move - fixed on nothingness as if they could see at least that far.

Half a dozen shots spat angrily into the water next to Obediah as he swam, maybe twice that number, but he was too busy swimming for his life to pay them much mind. If there was one thing Obediah had always excelled in it was swimming, and his long, sinewy arms soon had him near the middle of the river. Rather than slow down, even though the current was much stronger than it appeared, he plowed even faster through the murky, lumbering water once he realized he just might make it after all. A sharpshooter had a bead on him and fired. The bullet shot into the water less than a foot in front Obediah's head, *zip!*

"Nice shootin', *peckerwood!*" Obediah hollered over his shoulder, spitting broken water as he plowed on, more determined than ever.

A little while later he was on the west shore of the Mighty Mississippi, heading towards California about sixteen hundred miles away. He made it, too; ended up with an impressive orange grove and twelve grandchildren. He even witnessed the birth of the 20th century. He kept his knife hanging over the mantel of the largest fireplace in his sprawling hacienda, and made sure all his children and grandchildren knew why it was there. His three sons, Hiley, Kit and Kiah, saw to it their father's amazing story never died, as did their children, and their children as well.

***

THE MAYHEM had dissipated into sporadic acts of barbarism. Although fewer numbers of Yankees were being butchered, the horrors they experienced, and the experiences those Union soldiers yet to die would soon suffer, were no less horrific. Others may have felt relieved the brutality had slowed, as if by doing so they could pretend the lessoning of its magnitude somehow gave them cause to believe the worst was over. That may have been convenient for them if it afforded peace of mind or even a shred of it, but not for the victims. For them, hell had not only failed to diminish, it was more intense than ever. Jimmy Jay knew that was true. He would come to realize the viciousness all around him was inescapable even if a dying glint of hope still remained in him, if it was indeed hope hiding deep inside the terrified youth.

The young Yankee soldier was almost sixteen, having lied about his age two months earlier. He had been forced to, he insisted, or else how would he have been able to be part of what he had just known wouldn't wait for him? The war would be over soon he had believed, or over too soon. First, the simultaneous Union victories at Gettysburg and Vicksburg had taken place, and before long General Sherman would be moving in force through the very heart of the Confederacy if the rumors were true.

That's where Jimmy had wanted to be, with his hero General Sherman, but bad luck disguised as fate had placed him at Fort Pillow. The Rebels hadn't butchered him when he had surrendered; he wasn't sure why. They hadn't spared the other four soldiers who had attempted to surrender, and they had been right next to him. Those Union soldiers hadn't been much older than him, but they hadn't been white, either. Jimmy knew he would never forget how they had died, how they had been butchered. He kept forcing it from his mind, or trying to; he knew it would drive him insane if it hadn't already. He wondered how he would know for sure; know he had lost his mind.

He was sitting dazed in the mud, covered with it along with his own feces. He wasn't sure when, exactly, he had soiled himself, let alone how it had ended up all over him. Maybe that meant he was insane. *Only a crazy person would sit in the mud, covered with his own mess and not know how it got there, ain't that so? Gotta be so. Wait* - Jimmy Jay thought with a shudder. He remembered now. He remembered how it got there. The Rebels had done it, or at least made him do it after he had lost control of his bladder and bowels. They had laughed, thought it was funny. How they had smelled it coming from him amidst the pervading stench of his dead comrades who themselves had lost control of their bodily functions the youth didn't know, but the Rebels had noticed all right. He remembered now, that's what saved him, almost anyhow. *It was that other thing, that's what saved me, when they forced me to put some…that's what really saved me 'cause it made 'em laugh so hard.* Jimmy Jay grew rigid then, rigid as Death when he remembered the rest.

The little one, Jimmy Jay remembered, the one whose own unique odor competed successfully with the rest of the permeating stench, had pulled the trousers off one of the dead colored soldiers. …*That little Rebel cussed somethin' awful when he burnt his hand, burnt it on the smolderin' trousers when he grabbed them…that's right, that's what happened.* Jimmy recalled. …*the others laughed, thought it was real funny…thought all they was doin' was real funny…* They had laughed when they had set the wounded colored soldier on fire before he had died, and laughed some more when the odorous little Rebel had burned his hand. …*That's what they did, they laughed at that smelly little one… It didn't stop him though, not him. They was all evil, but him…Then he made me do it, forced me to put some on a piece of hardtack and put it in my…*

The boy went from being rigid to shaking, shaking all over as the convulsions set in. Hit bit his tongue, not once but at least three times. The warm, rust-like taste of his blood burned his throat. …*That must be what burns so God awful, the rust…* The vomiting took over again - dry, painful heaves that aggravated his sore stomach muscles as if they had always been galvanized by pain.

Two Confederate officers had arrived on the scene and told the other three Rebels to leave Jimmy Jay alone and move on. The officers also departed though. As soon as they were gone the tiny Rebel appeared as if out of nowhere. They were all grinning at Jimmy, all three of them, especially the odorous cretin. How Jimmy Jay wished it was yesterday, or especially two months ago when he had been safe on the farm, the one back home just outside Madrid, Iowa. *Most everyone not from there usually says it like it was in Spain or some such place…* Jimmy recalled …*but that ain't it, that ain't true…* a faint smile deep within his recesses told him. …*it's Madrid, like "bad rid" only with an "M", not a "B". Shucks, everybody in Boone County knows that…*The faint smile inside of him flickered again, searching in vain for Jimmy's reclusive hope as it fluttered precariously, then died.

The stench-infested cretin suddenly yelled in a high-pitched voice. He had the toothless Rebel's saber, and drove it into Jimmy's stomach and yanked it back and forth as rapidly as his spindly arms would allow. "Tyree!" The tiny Rebel continued to yell, shaking and grinning as he removed the sword and grabbed a hold of Jimmy Jay. "Help me drag 'em! He's a sight heavier than he looks!" The two Rebel soldiers dragged Jimmy Jay as the terrified Iowa farm boy clutched his stomach in agony. "Wendall!" The smelly cretin said, "kick them coals around, an' throw on more'a them thar boards!"

***

SAMUEL GREEN was about to die, of that he had no doubt. Three of his fellow black soldiers had already been killed, after they had been ordered to their feet while they had been begging for mercy, hands in the air. They had been lined up in a tight bunch. A Rebel soldier had shot the first man in line at point blank range, and the Minie ball had gone through him and the rest of the men. A number of other black soldiers in the immediate area had made it to their feet, as ordered. To do otherwise meant they would have been shot where they had been kneeling. In the mayhem Samuel hadn't stood though; he had remained on his knees, glaring straight ahead as he waited for the gunshot to his head or the saber through his guts.

"On your feet, nigger, an' keep your kinky head bowed!" The Rebel with a course dark beard said, an even tone in his deep voice. Samuel wasn't the only black soldier in the vicinity about to die, but he was closest to the bearded Rebel soldier.

Samuel didn't move, especially not his head as he stared at the man. He was done taking orders from white men. He was a dead man, he knew that, but he wasn't going out that way, not taking one last order from the blue-eyed devil with the dark beard and disgustingly pallid skin even if it was sunburned. He heard the Rebel double cock his revolver, since none of the three soldiers had taken time to reload the musket.

"Sergeant!" A large voice boomed. "Put away your sidearm! Do it *now!*" The bearded Rebel lowered his weapon and looked towards the authoritative voice. When he saw it belonged to General Forrest, he couldn't put his revolver away fast enough.

"Yes sir!" The bearded Rebel replied, standing at attention. Two others holstered their weapons without being told, at least not in words directed at them. Forrest's dark glare had been more than sufficient.

"This here nigger's a God damned prisoner, you men *understand?*" Forrest demanded to know. All three nodded in unison. All three said "yes sir!" more forcefully than ever before in their lives, or would ever again with such apparent conviction.

Samuel didn't know why the imposing Rebel officer had spared him, or why he was attempting to do the same as the general headed off to another group of Confederates under his command. *Took him long enough*, Samuel thought. *Ain't likely he done jus' got here or somethin', and there sure as hell been plenty'a butcherin' already.* General Forrest had stopped it though, finally, at least for Samuel and the others close by. Samuel would attest to that by God, if he survived; he swore he would. During the years that followed Samuel Green kept his promise. He never bowed his head again either, especially not in church.

***

A VICTORIOUS celebration was underway around the time 4:00 p.m. arrived. The Confederates weren't done massacring prisoners, but by then could only do it when their officers weren't around - most of the officers anyway. Looting was of course going on, as well as the desecration of bodies. One Rebel had stripped the body of Major Booth of its uniform, and was parading around in it to the delight of his comrades. The little man, not five feet tall and suffering from an extremely odorous condition as if he carried dead fish in his pockets as a matter of pride, looked ridiculous in the over-sized Union uniform, but he seemed to revel in the attention.

After night set in, down by the river, a Union officer was crawling through the muck and tall grass close to shore. He heard something, and carefully raised his head for a look. Captain Calvin Baileen spotted a Union soldier helping three wounded black soldiers onto a coal barge, also noting there weren't any Rebels close by either. He got up and made a dash for the barge, startling the four men.

"At ease, men," Baileen announced as he quickly approached, covered with muck. "You are in good hands now."

They finished boarding, then the Union soldier who had been helping his wounded comrades finally cut the rope that held the barge tethered to a tree. Soon they were in the current, and the Mississippi took them south. They made it over three miles before getting hopelessly beached inside a small bay on an island.

"These men sure as hell can't swim, Captain." The soldier said. "Reckon the Rebs gonna spot us after while. What should we do?"

"Hide best you can and I'll go for help. I have a bad heart, but only in the physical sense. If I drown in an attempt to save you brave men, I'll go to our Maker knowing I have done my all. Have you any money? I may need to bribe some locals if I survive." The soldier checked his pockets and came up with less than two dollars. Baileen took the paltry sum and a little over three dollars from the others, telling them to swim for it regardless of their condition if he wasn't successful.

"For God and country!" Baileen exclaimed as he waded into the water. He made it to the east shore of the huge river, allegedly bad heart and all, with strength to spare.

He wandered about the countryside for over two hours before he spotted the small farmhouse. He moved toward it with stealth, mindful of any barking dogs that might be around. He hated dogs; always had. None seemed to be in the vicinity, so he proceeded into the barn.

"Well," he remarked, "Aren't you a fine animal for such a decrepit place." A short while later he was on the horse, and less than an hour after that Captain Calvin Baileen discovered a road that led southward, all the way to Memphis.

***

PETE COULD have fired; he could have killed the lad. The young Rebel, even in the darkness, had reminded him of Billy though, the way he moved, and although that wouldn't have normally been enough to stop Pete, it was that night. Sporadic shots could still be heard, but not very many. If the killing had stopped he didn't want to be the one to start it up again. He had considered swimming, but he had never been partial to deep water or able to go very far. His brothers had told him if it was swimming he insisted upon calling it, it was only so by the most dubious of definitions. Besides, he hadn't had a thing to eat all day, since the night before with Dirch.

Dirch. Pete recollected. *Survived the barn, all those mountain men, Lord knows what else, only to get killed by one of his own comrades. Some comrades.* Pete wondered what all that had been about, recalling how Dirch had saved his life a second time, but mostly he just missed his friend. *Dirch made some poor choices over the years. Perhaps that was it.* Pete felt disgusted with himself for even considering that improbability. Too many loathsome men had survived during the war, and too many good ones had died in their stead. Pete knew where Dirch had stood, and would always remain in his memory.

The young Rebel was soon joined by three other Confederate soldiers, not thirty feet away, who had been standing in a clearing near the shore around a campfire they had started. They talked in low voices, their southern drawls sounding familiar since Pete had heard so much of it the past two years or so. They were joking about, but in a subdued sort of way. Pete wondered if their calm demeanors belied their true selves, if they had participated in the massacre the magnitude of which Pete was not yet aware. He had seen enough though, and imagined that was plenty to haunt him for a lifetime or two.

He actually considered surrendering, but not for long. He'd had enough of that, and hoped the soldiers would soon depart so he would no longer have to consider the possibility. General Forrest wouldn't be sticking around anyway, that wasn't his style or purpose. Hit and run, inflict as much damage as possible, take needed supplies, prisoners and horses, destroy the rest; that's what was going to happen. Better to stay hidden a day or two and wait for the Union forces to arrive that were probably on their way. Forrest would likely be long gone by then.

One of the soldiers walked over close to Pete and began to relieve himself. Pete seriously doubted the man could see him hidden in the tall grass. The soldier didn't, but even in the dim light of the campfire he noticed the indentation in the grass where Pete was hiding. From the soldier's vantage point it appeared to have been made by what was probably a body.

"Looks like there might be 'nother dead Yankee a lyin' in the grass," the soldier remarked over his shoulder. "Think he been searched yet? Reckon so prob'ly. Guess Ah'll take me a gander anyways." Pete put his hand on the handle of one of his Colts, but he didn't keep it there. He had no idea how many other Rebels were close by, and even if tall grass could hide him it sure as hell wouldn't stop bullets. Too late to swim or dog-paddle, or whatever it was that got him through the water. To hell with it, he decided. It had been a spontaneous decision, and he may well have made a different one if he hadn't acted upon it immediately, but there it was:

"Don't shoot, Reb. I'm comin' out. Now don't you shoot."

***

THEY LED Pete up the bluff and into Fort Pillow. There were campfires and torches burning everywhere as well as lanterns, casting an eerie pall as if the Underworld had leached from the Depths and devoured what just hours before had been simply another military outpost nestled in the wilderness. Weary burying details were hard at work, Union prisoners for the most part, and it was apparent they had a lot to do.

Pete had seen the aftermath of battles before, and although many of those engagements had produced more casualties, it was clear things had been different at Fort Pillow. Something had eclipsed horror as Pete had come to know it, and he had known it if any person ever had, or so he first imagined. Mutilated bodies weren't new to him, but those had usually been caused by an instant discharge of violence during battles fought by two opposing forces locked in mortal combat with both sides fighting, not one side trying to surrender to the minions of something beyond comprehension - something void of all things common decency might demand - something at the very least unholy, as if some kind of raging entity had held sway over the day's events and was now marveling at the spectacle the Beast had created.

Many of the dead Union soldiers Pete looked upon had been stabbed, gored and shot repeatedly; some with skulls smashed in, others with saber and bayonet wounds to their faces, groins and everywhere else imaginable. Men had been burned, some even nailed to boards and still others disemboweled, with lengths of their entrails scattered about with hoards of flies and other insects competing over them. A few of the Union prisoners were picking up parts of the dead with shovels. Other soldiers attempted to drag the victims, only to have legs and arms come off the corpses.

Most of them had been Negro soldiers, but not all of them. The stench of burnt flesh intensified as Pete walked along. At first, from a distance, it had smelled like a barbecue left unattended, but when Pete and his captors were closer he saw what it was, where the suddenly overpowering stench was coming from. Although his stomach was empty he had to fight down the acrid bile that clawed at his throat as if it needed to escape as well. Some of the bodies were so charred it was as if they had been naked to begin with. A few burnt boots which hadn't been removed and smoldering shreds of Union uniforms indicated otherwise.

One such body, still popping and oozing though just barely, was immersed in the embers of what had once been a sizable fire. It was the body of a diminutive man, a boy really, but Pete wouldn't have been able to recognize Jimmy Jay's burnt corpse even if the lad had been his own brother. The lad's white teeth stood in stark contrast to the charred remains of what had once been his face, as if his last scream would never cease.

They kept walking, and came upon a detail of Confederate soldiers who were burying in a large pit the remains of perhaps a dozen dead Union soldiers, or so it appeared. The Confederates stopped as Pete went by, resting an elbow or forearm on their shovels, glaring at him as they stood bent over their implements. As soon as Pete had gone by they resumed their grisly task.

"No...please no..." the wounded black soldier groaned as he attempted to crawl out of the freshly dug pit where the men were working, lurching unsteadily over the dead bodies of his comrades. "I surrendered, I done surrendered...need me a doctor..."

The Confederate soldiers glanced again at Pete who was now about twenty yards off, moving away. One of them smirked, then filled his shovel with heavy, wet dirt and looked at the struggling man. "You sure 'nough was actin' dead a little while ago, nigger." He threw the dirt on his shovel in the wounded soldier's face, and the other Rebels quickly followed suit.

Union corporal Willie Bryers, eighteen, tried to fight his way out, tried to get away from the cascading mud and dirt that had forced his eyelashes under their lids. Some of the wet soil made its way into his mouth. The Confederates kept piling it on with renewed determination, hooting and hollering. Soon Willie's torso and legs were covered, then finally his bleeding head. The muddy, gravel imbued dirt was getting heavy, weighing him down. His mouth continued to fill with mud and dirt as he tried in vain to spit it out, but it was no use. He tried to cough but only gagged as he struggled for the sweet, stench-filled air that was no longer available to him. His arms and legs could still move, but with every shovel-full of mud and gravel his frantic movements became more difficult, until it only *felt* like he was struggling. Willie was consumed by his frenzied attempts, reeling inside, until the eruption of panic-stricken terror of being buried alive ushered in so thoroughly he lost the last of his sanity. His lungs seemed to implode, sucked inward until the screams he emitted were only in his fevered mind. Finally, thankfully, he floated off then, as the Black Hell pressing in devoured the young man whole.

***

"WE DONE caught us an officer, sir," the young Rebel who Pete had first spotted by the riverbank said to General Forrest. Pete's hands were bound behind his back, and although his ankles had also been tied before being taken to the general he was able to take short steps.

General Forrest looked at Pete by the light of a campfire and the several lanterns hung around his makeshift outdoor headquarters. He studied the prisoner for more than a little while, concentrating on Pete's face.

"Have we met, Lieutenant?" Forrest finally asked. Pete returned the imposing man's glare.

"Not formally. I see you're a general now. You weren't at Shiloh. A colonel I believe." Forrest looked harder.

"Good God Almighty, now I remember you. Damned near took my head off with that shot back at Pittsburg Landing."

"You returned the favor, at *Shiloh,* I seem to remember it bein' called."

"You address the general as *sir,* or *General!* You hear me Yankee?" A Confederate captain hollered, trying to impress his superior. Pete barely gave the officer a glance, and remained silent as he glared at Forrest.

"That will be all, Captain." Forrest finally said. "Seems Ah recall seein' you much as you are tonight, Lieutenant. Captured. How in blazes have you stayed alive?"

"Almost didn't. Looks like your men don't understand surrender when they hear it, most of 'em anyway." Forrest glared at Pete then. It was as if a massive furnace had rumbled to life inside the general.

"Stopped it soon as Ah could. Too many green men, too much confusion. If you God damned Yankees had lowered your flag, just cut the damned halyards, mah men down the bluff would'a seen it. How the hell was they supposed to know y'all surrendered? It's your own damned faults."

"Since when does a man throwing up his arms and hollering surrender no longer count, *General* Forrest? One at a time, or in groups doesn't matter to you Rebels anymore?"

"*You're* alive, ain't you Yank?" Forrest replied, his fierce glare indicating the furnace was being fed, gaining strength.

"For now, with a bunch of your God damned officers standing about! Besides, I'm *white.* Most the men I saw butchered, and what's left of the ones still scattered around sure as hell weren't! Have you *seen* what your *gallant* men have done, *General* Forrest?" Pete was shaking with fear and rage, the two emotions ricocheting, and although Forrest wasn't shaking, he was close to exploding. His short-fused temper was legend, and being provoked by some damned Yankee lieutenant after such an event held the potential of being as good as suicidal on Pete's part.

"*You*, sir, are very fortunate Ah remember you, recall your bravery. Get 'em outta mah sight." With that Forrest turned away, but his eyes were suddenly filled with an uncharacteristic, nervous intensity, as if for the first time in his military career he was consumed with uncertainty, or at least had to acknowledge its presence.

Two soldiers began to pull Pete away, and as they did he hollered over his shoulder. "How many got butchered, *General?* How many surrendering soldiers did your brave men *butcher?* Have you seen it, Forrest? Have you seen what they *done?*"

Forrest ignored the Yankee lieutenant, or appeared to as the conflicted general ran his hands through his hair as he walked in the opposite direction, staring into the darkness beyond the burnt orange lantern light. The obscurity of the night sky was a meager respite. Hell, Forrest realized, it was no respite at all.

***

THE CONFEDERATES suffered a death toll of perhaps twenty men. That's what General Forrest put in his official report anyway, the one he later sent to Colonel Thomas M. Jack, an assistant adjutant-general. Forrest also stated sixty of his men had been wounded, but it was probably over eighty or so. He noted they had captured 164 Federalists, 75 Negro troops and 40 Negro women and children who had also been in the fort. He didn't know how many Union soldiers had been killed, insisting many had drowned trying to escape into the river: *"Many rushed into the river and were drowned, and the actual loss of life will perhaps never be known."* Forrest maintained in his report. He also had no way of knowing how many had received Minie balls in their backs as the Mississippi swept them away; that too would never be known.

It was later verified that between 277 and 295 Union soldiers had been killed, although it was impossible to verify how many had died in battle or were simply massacred while attempting to surrender during and after the battle. The most striking numbers, the ones which infuriated so many people, were the percentages of dead to wounded soldiers coupled with the disparity between black and white soldiers killed.

It was highly unusual for death rates during the Civil War to be over 10% in any given battle. On average less than 7%. Yet at Fort Pillow, the Union soldiers who were killed represented somewhere between 47% and 48%, a number exceeding *seven times* the overall average of those killed in all battles fought during the entire Civil War. In other words, any given combat soldier during the war had, on average, less than a 7% chance of getting killed in any given battle. A Union soldier at Fort Pillow, approximately a 48% chance; even higher for the black soldiers, since about 65% of the Union soldiers killed at Fort Pillow had been black.

Although it had been apparent considerably more white Union soldiers were offered quarter, that hadn't necessarily been the case for white officers in command of black soldiers. Indeed, no less than thirteen of those white officers had been butchered along with their men. If a massacre of obscene proportions hadn't occurred, that was lost on the overall Northern population and many southerners as well after the reports came in, and the letters from some of their soldiers from both sides arrived home.

The day after the battle Federal troops, reporters and others arrived at the fort on steamships, including the *Platte Valley*, and talked to paroled Union soldiers who had witnessed the carnage. They told of bodies burnt beyond recognition, some nailed to boards and other atrocities committed that were so unimaginable in scope it defied the bounds of decency to such a degree it wasn't likely anyone who had witnessed it or saw the aftermath would ever be the same, let alone forget what they had experienced. Even if there had not been so many survivors to attest to the slaughter, and not just Union soldiers, the magnitude of the barbarism would still have been at least partially ascertained by what was found that day and over the next few weeks.

Months, years and decades later eyewitnesses who reported the carnage would die off, one by one. Those men who were there that day would go to their graves believing they knew the truth of what had occurred, and knew, in their frustration, that others would continue to diminish and even flat-out deny what had happened, at least in the manner and magnitude the witnesses maintained was true to their dying day. To those individuals, the indisputable numbers didn't lie - and neither had they.

Even some historians would dismiss much of what the eyewitnesses reported, as if at least some academicians simply could not accept, or were perhaps unwilling to do so publicly, that an otherwise honorable man such as Nathan Bedford Forrest, one of the greatest and bravest officers on either side during the Civil War, could have been culpable regardless of what anyone said they saw happen. Hadn't Union Captain John T. Young reported to a number of reporters he saw Forrest shoot one of his own men who had refused to stop killing? Although that suggests Forrest must have witnessed the massacre, more than a few historians apparently overlooked that possible, if not probable likelihood. Hadn't Dr. Charles Fitch, Fort Pillow's post surgeon, stated the massacre had occurred "without Forrest's knowledge"? Whether Dr. Fitch was in a position to offer an accurate appraisal of Forrest's overall involvement is debatable, since he obviously wasn't with the general during the debacle, but he did make the claim.

There is no evidence to suggest Forrest took precautions to prevent a massacre, but there isn't a single eyewitness account that he ever issued a massacre order either, although some Confederate soldiers insisted that he had, even if they had not personally heard him do it. It has been reported Forrest had always been quick to anger, viciously so in some cases, but generally followed his outbursts with a more compassionate resolution to any given situation. That would add credibility to reports that Forrest did what he could to eventually stop the massacre, but it also helps support eyewitness accounts that it nonetheless occurred, and Forrest saw it; perhaps much if it.

Some historians and others had difficulty accepting a statement approved by The Joint Committee on the Conduct of the War. Some still insist upon dismissing it. The statement includes eyewitness testimony regarding the massacre at Fort Pillow, along with a report on the inhumane treatment of Union prisoners held in Confederate prison camps. The United States Congress went so far as to print and distribute sixty thousand copies of the report, an exceptionally large number during the Civil War. It stated, in part, that individual Union soldiers who had attempted to surrender *fell victim to the malignity and barbarity of Forrest and his followers. No cruelty which the most fiendish malignity could devise was omitted by these murderers.* Mention was also made in the report of how some of the wounded Union soldiers were burned alive as well as other wounded Union soldiers who were buried alive. The Confederates were also charged with murdering some of the civilians who had the misfortune of being present that day.

Perhaps Forrest wasn't culpable, as many people claimed and still claim. Perhaps a man who was known to rule over his men prior to and after the debacle with such authority, a man few dared cross or even disagree with was innocent of all accusations because his men on that fateful day had decided Forrest's authority didn't apply to them any longer. His ironfisted authority had certainly existed prior to Fort Pillow, although it was reported there had been minor breakdowns of absolute discipline. Forrest's authority existed afterwards, but for some reason not then, not there at Fort Pillow?

It was also reported the Confederate soldiers had been deprived of sleep and adequate food prior to the battle. The taunting during the truce served to further enrage many of them, but that could be said of other battles where massacres of that magnitude hadn't occurred. As for the burning of wounded soldiers to death, some nailed to planks, others buried alive and still others shot and literally hacked to pieces while attempting to surrender, the magnitude of the Fort Pillow atrocities, with a few notable exceptions such as the Battle of Poison Spring, stands virtually alone as it pertains to the Civil War.

Perhaps Forrest, a man who had started life in poverty and by 1860 had amassed a fortune of approximately $1,500,000, (over forty million in 2008 dollars using the Consumer Price Index) wasn't guilty of allowing atrocities to be committed against black soldiers, even though at least part of his fortune had been made by buying and selling slaves, their wives or husbands - their children. At the very least Forrest strongly supported the "peculiar institution" that legally supported such practices. Perhaps he hadn't encouraged any of the butchery to happen, or had at least tried to stop it as quickly as possible as he later maintained. He was, however, one of but a few Confederate officers to reportedly have declared unequivocally he was fighting to *maintain* slavery. After the war, he was active in organizing the Ku Klux Klan, and became its first Grand Wizard. It has been reported he later quit the organization because of the odious tactics it came to embrace, and perhaps that is the truth.

On July 5, 1875, two years before his death, Forrest gave a speech in front of the Jubilee of Pole Bearers, an African American society, one of the precursors to the next century's American Civil Rights Movement. His speech was short and concilia-tory, made by a man who apparently no longer held on to strict racist views. He even kissed an African American woman, Miss Lou Lewis, on her cheek after accepting flowers from her.

Perhaps some men, powerful men accustomed to the unwavering subservience of others eventually look back with more clarity. Perhaps those men come to believe their final judgment will be in the hands of an entity they are powerless to cower. Perhaps they eventually determine their justifications and rationalizations will be judged naked, stripped of all pretenses.

It is known that Forrest was a religious man, a Christian to the bone in his later years, as were many of the butchered Union soldiers at Fort Pillow. Perhaps he had known or at least assumed those men were Christians too, and those dead men had already rendered their testimony to an entity that could not be deceived, much less cowered. Perhaps that was the one thing Major General Nathan Bedford Forrest came to realize he had no chance of accomplishing, and never would.

XXXVIII

Captain Baileen was all anxiety. News of Fort Pillow had already made the newspapers with fresh reports and eyewitness accounts coming in daily. He had purchased a fine set of civilian clothes in Memphis and had sent a wire to General Smithington in Chicago. All Baileen could do was wait, and that was not only contributing to his growing disquietude but driving him half crazy.

He spent most of his time in his hotel room, but it wasn't a very luxurious place, far from it. He couldn't take the chance of staying in a better hotel; the risk of being recognized by any number of high ranking military personnel being his biggest concern. He hadn't as yet, far as he knew, been accused of desertion, but when his body didn't turn up odds were he would be since according to the newspapers most, if not all of the captured Union officers had been paroled. He held out hope the men he had abandoned on the island may have been rescued, and reported Captain Baileen may well have drowned. That would certainly be helpful, and even more reason for him to stay out of sight. He pulled out the handwritten copy of the wire he had sent to Smithington, and read it again for about the tenth time.

My dear General Smithington,

How good it was to hear from you after all this time. It seems just like yesterday when I was a young second lieutenant down Mexico way and you were my captain. Regarding our little matter, I am happy to report all went as planned, as the traitor met his just fate, the fate we had been praying for. Saw the body myself. My priorities have me sorely pressed for time as I am sure you can understand. If you would be so kind as to forward me the remainder of what you promised I would be most appreciative. As always, my discretion will remain in place since I have no reason to doubt my admiration and trust in you. A bank draft will do, sent to post office box 330 here in Memphis. I look forward to the time we will be able to quaff a stein or two in celebration of the impending Union victory. Forever your friend and servant, I bid you what I pray is a temporary adieu.
Calvin B.

***

GENERAL SMITHINGTON was beyond elated. Thanks to his old acquaintance he now considered a close friend, and for just the trifling amount of fifty thousand dollars all things considered, the general was more than set for life. His mind was swimming with all he would be able to do with his fortune as he made his way to one of his banks in Chicago. He had already sent his personal courier to Naperville and within hours Clifton Janeway would know his nemesis was finally dead. He would also have the general's second and largest installment of the fortune which was owed sent back with the courier, in cash no less, of that Smithington had no doubt. Why should he doubt a thing, he imagined. Who else knew as much as he regarding Janeway's personal affairs? If ever a man was assured his end of a bargain needed to be upheld it was Clifton Janeway.

Visions of the South of France were caroling in the general's head, as were all the other exotic places he had heard others brag about over the years, places he had never been able to afford. He would soon taste all of it, and everything, every little thing, would be first class all the way. He could only imagine what a few hundred dollars would buy for a weekend in Paris. He had, of course, seen some very beautiful women in his day, women he had never been able to woo much less afford if that had been the case. The kind of money he already possessed would no doubt buy him girls so amazingly gorgeous and refined, five or six at a time no less, it was enough to make him giddy with anticipation. And the food and wine, the veritable palaces he would be living in with their stunning views, all of it; all of it *his*.

***

CLIFTON BEGAN to tremble as he read the note the courier had delivered in the sealed envelope. He had waited until he had retired to his office to read it. He told his father it was just some military matter of no special importance after Buford Janeway had inquired about the arrival of the courier, who was still waiting for Clifton on the front porch. He didn't have long to wait. Clifton soon emerged and handed the courier a locked, leather case containing the rest of Smithington's money. Clifton even smiled at the young soldier, something he had never done before. Indeed, it was the first time the major had ever made eye contact with him, or acknowledged the fellow's presence with anything other than a dismissive wave of a hand.

Clifton had never known such relief, such unbridled joy. Within a few months Delicia would be Mrs. Clifton Janeway, as impossible as that dream had been just months before, not to mention years. None of his old schoolmates at the Naper Academy would ever have believed such a thing could have happened in a million lifetimes. Well, they would believe it now by God, Clifton all but sang out loud.

The wedding would be the largest one Napervillians had seen, or ever would see, but it wouldn't be in Naperville. The finest accommodations Chicago had to offer would be secured, including a night in the city's finest hotel for the invited guests and all that entailed. Why, he would even ask General Smithington to be his best man. *It's the least I can do for the old gasbag,* he concluded.

The general had finally received all his money or would when the courier made it back to Chicago, although Clifton had entertained another option. *But no, those days are behind me.* He had reminded himself. *Besides, why risk murdering the rotund sot over a few dollars? Still, if the old cough dropped over dead from a heart seizure or something wouldn't that be convenient?* The general did know way too much, Clifton realized once he had really thought about it, rekindling his prior consideration. *No, damn it, it simply isn't worth the risk; things are perfect now, going along smoothly, but still…it could be blamed on Southern antagonists…no, no, no.* Clifton knew he was contemplating an absurd notion. *If anyone can keep a secret it's that conniving old wolf's head, at least if he wants more money in the future. Besides, it isn't as though he isn't implicated. He might decide what's been paid isn't near enough, however…to hell with it,* Clifton concluded. That could be addressed later if at all. He had more pressing matters to attend to, all of them wonderful, all of them involving Delicia O'Darcy.

If a lingering disquietude was still lurking inside Clifton it did not register as a conscious concept. Recent events had been able to obliterate his usual skepticism, or at least bury it so deep it simply couldn't - or at least wouldn't - develop in Clifton's mind. He *needed* to believe the recent developments were true. He wasn't dealing with a mercenary this time, a total stranger, but two individuals of high military rank that considered each other longtime friends that had been successful with their schemes, mutual and otherwise, for decades. The Fort Pillow incident was being widely reported on a national basis; even the early reports indicated an unusually high number of Union fatalities. No, Clifton had nothing worry about at all; he just knew it – he knew it simply *had* to be true.

***

CAPTAIN BAILEEN recalled how he had heard mention of an illusory place called Cloud Nine, but until he actually had the forty thousand in his possession he had never really experienced riding upon it or its equivalent. He was experiencing it now he imagined, in the form of a gripsack containing the forty thousand in magnificent Yankee cash. All he needed to do was get back to Chattanooga, grab the rest of his money and disappear.

He'd heard about some interesting opportunities in South America, diamond and gold mines to name a few, especially in Brazil. That sounded like a good choice, now that the Confederates' dream of winning the war and eventually extending their empire to include Central and South America was all but dead. If by some miracle the South were to win decisively, a man with means would still be able to do quite well, since an even greater fortune could likely be made by investing in the profitable slave trade that would no doubt flourish. *Oh well*, he thought, *there is still money to be made. Women do love their diamonds...*

Less than three months later, former Captain Calvin Baileen had indeed deserted and was the owner of an impressive hacienda in Rio de Janeiro with breathtaking views of Ipanema Beach and the seascape beyond. The view from the western veranda was "pulchritudinous" as he loved to intone, especially when the sun was setting and he had a chilled bottle of the 1811 comet vintage of *Veuve Clicquot* resting close by. Years later he developed a preference for *Cristal*, but his love of the beautiful sunsets never wavered.

Although he wasn't able to deal in the defunct slave trade, he did remarkably well in both the diamond and gold industries. He married a charming Argentine girl whose strength of character was so profound she actually succeeded, along with the help which years of reflection and maturity can sometimes produce, in changing his priorities if not Baileen's heart itself.

He became a devoted husband and father, and was eventually regarded as a kind and generous man by those who thought they knew him best. At no time did he ever elude to his true past, not even to his adoring wife, and died loved and respected in 1899 - his heart beating strongly until his kidneys shut down. On his deathbed he asked his God to forgive his past transgressions since he had been unable to do so. He passed quietly, uncertain, but with a faint glow upon his face that suggested a lingering hope.

***

PETE KNEW the Confederate forces wouldn't tarry long. Of more importance, for him and perhaps the rest of the prisoners anyway, neither would General Forrest as far as making up his mind about his captives was concerned. Even if the general determined it would slow him or his subordinate General James R. Chalmers down to take most of the prisoners with him, there was little doubt in Pete's mind that at least some of the captured officers would be kept, even if a number of them had already been paroled. He knew he sure as hell hadn't been. Maybe Pete would get paroled or maybe not, he certainly hadn't before, and was well aware of the pitfalls such things invited. There was only one thing for him to do, if at all possible to begin with, and perhaps little time to do it.

It wasn't all chaotic revelry in and around the fort that night, but it was close enough. Pete was being held, along with a number of other prisoners, at a campsite a little east of the fort. Although Forrest's veteran troops knew what they were doing when it came to guarding prisoners, there was no doubt in Pete's mind his experience gave him the advantage. He was used to studying men who guarded other men, familiar with what they looked for, and what they eventually assigned to a lower status on their lists of priorities; things that eventually proved to be important to them only in hindsight.

None of the Rebels wanted to be there, standing or sitting around a group of enemy prisoners. They wanted to be with their other comrades, the ones who didn't have to keep watch, the ones who were free from such responsibilities, especially after a battle had been won if Fort Pillow could be called such. Swilling liberated whiskey and beer, searching for what valuables were available, joking, bragging, playing cards or simply wandering about, that's what the soldiers guarding Pete and the others wanted to be doing.

Most of their comrades had specific duties, but at least they could duck away from the officers from time to time or make up excuses which freed them from responsibility for a while, but not the men who had pulled guard duty. They had to stay alert, remain focused. It only took a few of them to resent their plight to the extent they lost their focus, even if only for a short while; that's what Pete was looking for. He knew how quickly an opportunity could be lost, how easy it was for defeated men to exaggerate their predicament and allow what could be their one chance to suddenly slip away from them, to forever vanish without taking advantage of it. He knew, because he had done that very thing, but he had also done the opposite and succeeded.

The ones Pete watched closest were the youngest guards. Like so many young men their age, they especially resented the fact their friends were off having a high time, and would no doubt have stories to tell of what they had found, the exciting things they had experienced. The more those young men on guard duty thought about it, the more they imagined what they were missing intensified. Whiskey, beer, an attractive colored girl, loot; those things and more were just beyond their grasp, beyond what some poor sap stuck on guard duty would ever be able to realize.

Pete noticed three likely candidates milling about over by a rude stable, a little south from the front of it, about two hundred feet away northwest from where Pete was being held. They were rolling and smoking cigarettes from the makings they had confiscated, looking around as they did so. Pete noticed they weren't looking so much at the prisoners, but for officers who would berate them for not being closer to the prisoners.

Compared to what their comrades were enjoying elsewhere the smokes were a mean respite, but even that would be viewed as at least somewhat of a dereliction of duty. How unfair was that? Others were lining their pockets with Yankee cash, watches, rings, reading love letters taken from dead and wounded soldiers, enjoying liquor, perhaps young colored girls all the more alluring because for the young men on guard duty they were unobtainable. The lucky ones were enjoying all sorts of those things, but not them. A smoke was low on that list, not even on it, and it was as if Pete could read that even from a couple hundred feet away.

He made his way slowly towards them, stopping frequently, acting defeated and displaying a dejected demeanor void of all hope. He finally made his way to a heavyset Rebel along the perimeter of where the prisoners were being held, perhaps a hundred feet from the stable.

"Need to relieve myself, soldier." Pete said after he sauntered up to the man.

"Piss on the ground, Yank." The soldier replied, after spitting a stream of tobacco juice that had splattered close to Pete, some of it landing on his feet.

"I'd have'ta squat, can't I just go over behind them bushes?" Pete said, pointing to a spot about thirty feet closer to the stable. "Stinks enough 'round here as is." The soldier looked at Pete as if his point was well taken, or at least not wholly without merit. Besides, the Yankee wouldn't get far even if he was foolish enough to attempt anything.

"Go on then, but dig a hole with your hands an' bury your mess. Don't take all night, neither." Pete moved away utilizing short, stiff steps even though his ankles were no longer bound. His boots had of course been taken.

He had a pained expression on his face bordering on comical, as if he hoped he'd make it to the bushes in time. The guard watched him leave, half amused at the Yankee's plight, then turned back towards the other prisoners when Pete was behind the bushes. The soldier glanced over there a few times, but wasn't overly concerned.

The three young Rebels were rolling up another batch of cigarettes, taking their time as if in protest to their unenviable situation. Pete glanced through the bushes, looking back at the first soldier he had encountered. Pete finally approached the other three, keeping the bushes between himself and the first guard as best he could.

"Evenin' men," he said as he approached, feigning a severe limp, a smile on his face and defeat in his eyes. "That guard yonder told me I could take me a shit in the stable. Said there was enough stink back yonder." The young Rebels looked briefly at one another then motioned Pete to go in. They were right there, right by the only exit and well-armed, although that wasn't necessarily a conscious thought on any of their parts. Why would it be? If something extremely unusual were to happen, like a crazed, limping Yankee making a run for it and thereby inviting certain death, wouldn't that at least be something marginally exciting? Nothing exciting would happen for them otherwise; that was reserved for the lucky bastards not on guard duty.

For those willing to take chances, things can sometimes appear too good to be true. That's how Pete felt when he saw him, when he saw Yankee in one of the stalls. He would have been grateful to find virtually any horse as long as it could run, but Yankee? Although it was the same small stable Pete and his fellow officers had used, there was no way he would have allowed himself to believe Yankee would still be in there. He sighed a heartfelt thank you, dashed over and opened the stall gate. He grabbed a saddle and tack, his own saddle no less, with the $2,400 in gold still in it judging by its heft. Moments later he was leading the surprised and happy animal out of the stall, even if Pete didn't know what good that would do. If he tried to use the stable door he knew what would likely happen and probably before he made it fifty feet. Then it struck him: *It worked in North Carolina, and by Jesus it just might work here.*

He went back into the stall and began pulling at the boards in the back of it. He pulled the first one in and looked outside to the north, not seeing anyone close by, and none of the Rebels he did spot were guards. The woods were close though, if a hundred and fifty feet or so wasn't considered far. With Yankee, the trees just might be close enough. He was careful not to make any more noise than possible, and soon had enough boards removed to fit Yankee through. Before exiting he removed all his clothing except his long johns, hoping, *praying* any nearby Rebels would think he was just another drunken comrade making a fool of himself.

Moments later he was astride his all-time favorite horse and flying towards the woods, a very excited Yankee on a dead run. Pete was halfway there when a group of several Rebels finally saw him, so he waved his arms about and whooped at them. "Hurrah fer the Sowth an' Generah Ferrest!" Pete hollered, butchering his attempt at a southern accent but praying his rendition of a drunkard covered it enough. "Hurrah fer nekked ladies an' who-hit-John whiskey!" The men just laughed and shook their heads.

Ten minutes later the three young Rebel soldiers were standing in front of the vacant stall, wondering what horrible fate awaited them. One of them, a large, curly-haired youth came up with an idea. Within a few minutes the boards were in place, albeit haphazardly, and a few minutes after that all three of them had moseyed back midst the prisoners and other guards. Before long they heard the hollering.

"Now that there is one dumb bastard," the curly-haired youth said to the others as he observed the guard Pete had first approached. "What's another Yankee more or less? Jus' remember boys, we ain't seen a damned thing, *no* one *no* how. Forrest's gonna have his hide. That is mos' definitely one dumb bastard."

***

PETE KEPT north for a few miles, dodging branches as Yankee flew through the woods then veered east. The feeling of having Yankee under him was exhilarating, thundering along as if the horse were in tune with all that was at stake. It was as though the magnificent creature understood the significance of escaping the mindless horror of the Fort Pillow Massacre and all it represented.

If anyone was following, Pete wasn't aware of them. He rode through the woods and as usual Yankee showed no signs of letting up, mile after mile. They came to a stream and forded it, stopping in a small clearing surrounded by the dark, ever present forest. Yankee drank and fed on the thick spring grass while Pete kept a close watch, his thoughts closing in around him. He tried to keep them at bay, but the best he could do was create a tenuous, illusory barrier, hoping in vain the miles that separated him from the horror of Fort Pillow were capable of doing so.

There was a good vantage point on a hill just to the southeast, with a thick stand of loblolly pines where he could hide. Pete didn't go up there however; too many images of the past twelve hours had come calling, gaining momentum, regardless of his physical distance from the hellish fort. He again glanced at the hill, but feared once he was inside those claustrophobic loblollies something horrid would rain down on him like so many wailing ghosts.

It was mostly a cloudy, damp night and often very dark. Pete soon began to shiver in a way he couldn't stop no matter how hard he tried. His long johns were saturated from all the forest moisture he had encountered, and his wet, bare feet were so numb they throbbed. Still, a fire was out of the question even if he had possessed the matches to start one.

Chilled as he was, that wasn't the main reason he wanted to be around a reassuring fire as he again glanced at the loblollies when enough clouds moved away and a half moon along with a few stars could be seen. It felt as if entities inside the trees were regaining a confused, panic-stricken consciousness, and amidst their terrified bewilderment felt compelled to lash out at anything or anyone they could find. He decided to keep moving through the night, never able to shake the sensation that something was hovering just out of sight, ever searching, moments away from assailing anything that resembled their existence as they once knew it. Pete could feel their anguished wails cut straight through him, even if the only sounds being made were by Yankee moving along.

He spent most of the following day moving warily or hiding, ever mindful of enemy patrols. He didn't know if any were around, he hadn't spotted any, but he also knew anything was possible. Forrest was most likely on the move, but a few of his other officers may have splintered off from the main body, perhaps in force. It wouldn't take very many to recapture or kill him. He had no weapons, but as far as he was concerned at least he had the fastest horse in either army. Still, he felt uneasy without the cover of darkness while fearing it at the same time - fearing the *wails*.

He was lightheaded from the terror he had endured, as well as the fatigue and starvation he was currently enduring. Although he had gone nearly a day and a half without food at least hunger pangs were no longer clawing at him. The jolts of adrenalin had kept his hunger at bay, and although it appeared as if he were alone with no one of this world after him, by the time the adrenalin rushes had subsided, and then not completely, the length of time without food had allowed his body to react as if food wasn't an urgent requirement. He was weak though, and knew he would only grow weaker. Then he spotted it.

He knew a farm had to be nearby if the small, blossoming apple orchard was any indication. There were some black cherry trees as well, along with a few peach. Too bad it wasn't fall. A dozen or so apples and other fruits would have been mighty useful about then, he imagined. There weren't any apples, but less than a quarter mile from the rolling orchard was a small house and two rude outbuildings. No telling who might be about, he thought, or where their sympathies fell. Not that it would matter; seeing a strange man wearing nothing but long underwear would no doubt be enough to create alarm, and it was highly unlikely the local who owned the small farm didn't also own at least a shotgun.

He tethered Yankee to a tree hidden from sight in the woods and cautiously made his way to the back of a small barn. There was a chicken coup attached to it, but trying to garner a few eggs or perhaps a chicken itself would likely be a noisy affair. A rooster was strutting about, and although there was little chance Pete could catch it perhaps he could hit it with a rock.

Finding a rock suitable for throwing proved to be exasperating. The few around were either too small or too large. Pete finally found one about the size of his fist. He moved towards the cock very carefully then stopped when the bird decided to make its pecking about the ground a lower priority than the odd looking man who had come into view. Pete would get one throw, and if he missed the alarmed bird would likely raise quite a fuss. He hit it square on its side, feathers flying about. He wrung its neck and made his way back to the woods.

Raw rooster wasn't much of a delicacy but it served its purpose. He ate it as fast as he could, devouring the liver and heart as well, then wiped his hands on a patch of damp grass then his underwear. He glanced about as he made his way deeper into the woods.

As evening fell he made a cold camp in a ravine buffered by a ten foot outcropping of rock. He was chilled to his marrow but somewhat protected from the wind. It didn't, however, take much of a breeze to set off another round of uncontrollable shivering. God how he wished he could be next to a fire. The warmth of the day was gone but at least the wind finally did die down.

He didn't know it, but he wasn't very far from a road that ran between the small towns of Brownsville and Jackson. He was near a winding curve in the road that cut through the woods over thirty miles east and a little south of Fort Pillow. He wasn't sure how far away he was from the fort, and of course had no way of knowing General Forrest had sent Colonel W.L. Duckworth along with the 7th Tennessee Cavalry out to conscript men. They had managed to capture none other than Major William Bradford himself.

Bradford had already been captured once near Fort Pillow, but had managed to escape after convincing his captors he be allowed to be held at Confederate Colonel

Bob McCullah's headquarters. Major Bradford had been aware any number of West Tennessee Confederates wanted to kill him hence his desire to be held elsewhere, or so he maintained. After his new captors had fallen into a deep sleep which allowed him to make good his escape, he had been recaptured anyway.

Colonel Duckworth was sending him, along with some newly conscripted men, back to General Forrest. It was the sound of the detachment of men that had alerted Pete he was no longer alone in the woods, if ghosts didn't count. He kept Yankee tethered at the sheltered hiding place and made his way through the trees, and soon found the source of the sounds. He remained hidden, grateful that the Rebels seemed to be just moving along and not, apparently, overtly searching for anyone - searching for *him*.

Even in the moonlight and the lanterns attached to a few of the wagons Pete didn't notice the commander of Fort Pillow was with them, not at first. An argument of some kind broke out between a few Rebels at the rear of the column, and one of the men they were escorting. Pete looked closer and was shocked to see the Rebels were having angry words with Major Bradford of all people. Just how in hell the major had ended up a prisoner, in civilian clothes no less, out there so far from Fort Pillow was a wonderment, Pete concluded. Another of a long series of wonderments, all of them bad except for Pete's escape that now seemed in jeopardy or close to it. He would have to be very careful, and very quiet.

A few minutes later three of the Rebels led Bradford away from the rest of the men on the road, still barking at him. To Pete's alarm they were heading directly towards him. He ducked behind a large oak and moved carefully around it as the men approached, not unlike a treed squirrel might do after spotting a suspected predator. Except Pete couldn't climb like a squirrel, and to make matters worse he managed to step on a twig. It only made a slight snapping sound, but to Pete it sounded near as loud as thunder. Fortunately, although not for Bradford, the Rebels were still jawing at their captive and hadn't heard a thing other than their own posturing.

"Never you mind where we're a'takin you, you no-account nigger lovin' bastard!" One of them said after Major Bradford, obviously unnerved, had said something Pete couldn't make out. "Nough fer you ta know there's a price needs payin'!"

"You ain't so damned high-fullutin' now, is you Yankee?" One of the other soldiers said as he shoved the major in the back. "What kinda white man gives guns an' uniforms to a bunch'a God damned niggers anyways? Ah swear, ain't been fer them lily-livered officers of ourns', includin' Mr. Highpockets Forrest his own damned self, we would'a done seen to it all you curs got what fer!"

"I am the commanding officer of the Union forces at an established military garrison, and demand I be accorded the opportunity to speak with either Colonel Duckworth or General Forrest himself!" Bradford had stopped moving and pulled himself up to his full height, but the fear emitting from him had been impossible to disguise.

"Oh, yoo-hoo, Colonel Ducky, General Forresty, y'all hear the nigger lover?" The third soldier sang in a shrill falsetto voice to the delight of his comrades. "She wants ta have her a little pow-wow with y'all! Oh yoo-*hoo!* Well now, don't appears they's interested in conversin' with no buggerin', God damned nigger lover! Stand right there an' don't you move!" Major Bradford sighed nervously, and did as he was told.

He fought to keep from shaking, determined not to let the Confederate soldiers see him waiver in the pale moonlight that filtered through the tree branches, casting a deathly glow. All hope was apparently gone, but not unlike anyone in his position it still lingered, teasing him as it floated just beyond his grasp.

"He's tryin ta escape!" One of them yelled as Bradford stood there, feigning stoicism, not taking his eyes off the crude man. "The buggerin' nigger lover's a tryin ta git away!"

All three muskets erupted, and the three Minie balls slammed through Major William Bradford's chest, sending some of its contents flying backwards along with an explosive mist of blood. The commander of Fort Pillow, like so many of his soldiers both black and white, fell dead where he stood, having offered no resistance as he died.

Soon other Confederates rushed into the woods. The three soldiers insisted they had shot the Yankee after he had tried to run. Sergeant Kelly Ellis looked at the body then turned and faced the men.

"How come he got hit in the front first, then? An' how come y'all brung him out here to begin with?" Sergeant Ellis asked. The three soldiers appeared dumbstruck by the questions, then one of them, looking around as he spoke, replied.

"Said he had ta take him a shit, then done lit out, turned on us agin like he had him a derned gun or somethin', so we done fired."

The Rebels were less than twenty feet from Pete who had plastered himself against the tree as if he were trying to blend into it. His heart was pounding in his chest with so much urgency he could feel his pulse throbbing throughout his entire body, making him lightheaded. He heard the Rebels as they continued to talk back and forth, and it was obvious the Confederate sergeant knew the three soldiers were lying. Sergeant Ellis ordered the men to take the dead Yankee's body back to the road, and told them he would be giving a full report on what he knew they had done.

An official complaint eventually reached General Forrest, stating the Union commander of Fort Pillow had been killed if not murdered under suspicious circumstances, but he chose to do nothing about it, maintaining the trail had grown too cold. Besides, hadn't the Yankees refused to press charges against the Union's Colonel

Fielding Hurst after Forrest had filed official charges against him? The brutal Yankee colonel's infamous regiment was well known for its murderous and plundering ways, but if the Yankee high command was too arrogant, too intransigent to follow through, how could they expect Forrest to acquiesce to their hypocritical demands? If war was all hell, as their pontificating General Sherman would come to describe it, General Nathan Bedford Forrest certainly wasn't about to shy away from the concept, but had no intention of paying heed to much else Yankee inspired.

***

PETE KEPT himself and Yankee hidden near his campsite long after he was certain the Rebels had moved on. He was still terrified, exhausted and cold, but he was alive. Yankee kept a close watch on his companion, his clear, dark eyes missing nothing. He wanted to move, take flight, anything but simply stand around doing nothing. Yankee began to articulate his concerns, at least in his own mind. It seemed as if his two-legged friend understood him, most of the time anyway, even if he could be a perplexing and often times stubborn creature. Yankee loved him though, loved the odd, unpredictable primate with his variety of smells, sounds, body coverings and movements. Yankee whinnied, arousing Pete from his apparent lethargy.

"Guess now's as good a time as any to tempt fate, so you can quit your belly-achin'." Yankee snorted his reply, as if telling Pete talk was just that.

***

MOST OF the Confederates had left Fort Pillow, but there were still a few around and had been throughout the day of April 13, 1864 after a truce had gone into effect. Union steamships had arrived, and amidst all the horror the men from the ships had discovered, there was the task of transporting the surviving wounded Union soldiers onto the ships; many of them soldiers some of the Confederate officers had saved from their own men.

Dr. Charles Fitch, the garrison's post surgeon, was still limping from a wound he had suffered to his leg. It was rumored he had been the first Union man to get wounded at Fort Pillow, and one of the luckiest since it was a minor flesh wound that nonetheless hurt like hell. He had been too busy to pay it much mind, other than to swear at it from time to time. He was helping the other men load the wounded onto the ships, and tending those still in one of the makeshift hospital tents when a Union corporal approached him.

"What about that big fella over there?" He asked Dr. Fitch, pointing to a huge black soldier unconscious upon a cot, his feet hanging over its end by nearly a yard.

"Leave him there a while longer," the doctor said as he glanced at the dying soldier. "We'll carry him on board last if he's still alive by then. Surprised he isn't dead already. Lost a lot of blood. Don't know what's keeping him alive, but he won't last much longer. Can't operate successfully, not in this hell hole. Couldn't even if we got him to Memphis, not where those bullets are lodged. Take the others and go, Corporal. That big fellow, I'm afraid, isn't long for this world except to be buried under it."

Cusman issued a low moan, moved his head slightly, and was then swallowed again by his fevered, disjointed nightmares...*Where you at, Sedman?*

***

VACANT EYED, damp and starving, Pete presented quite a sight when Yankee brought him to the outskirts of Memphis. He hadn't slept in over seventy hours except towards the end of his journey, when a continuously accelerating delirium that mimicked sleep would engulf him until some sound or movement, real or imagined, jolted him back to a disjointed consciousness infested with haunting images of Fort Pillow. Pete couldn't drive the images away any easier than he could stop breathing, and it didn't matter whether he was awake, asleep or caught up in a diabolic dreamscape so profound he was genuinely concerned for his sanity.

Finally, mercifully, a group of Union soldiers appeared on the road ahead, but at first even that had been unsettling. Pete hadn't noticed them in any conventional way; they hadn't been spotted coming down the road, or exiting one of the houses or buildings he had seen up ahead - they had just *appeared*. He was so addled it wouldn't have come as a complete surprise if they suddenly melted into a mass of uniformed, butchered meat.

He soon had food and a fresh uniform. A short while later he collapsed upon a cot after securing a promise from a sergeant to take good care of Yankee. He slept for nearly eight hours until a nightmare jolted him awake. He was bathed in sweat; even the sheets and his cot were wet. The clutching nightmare, which for the longest time wouldn't let go, had been so graphic even the reality of his present surroundings was suspect, as if *it* were the illusion.

Upon regaining most of his senses, Pete sighed with gratitude. He couldn't recall ever having been so relieved to be back from where the dreams, worthy of a special hell, had held him captive; not even the ones he had endured at Salisbury had been so horrifying. He shook his head to help dissipate their effect, realizing he had been wrong about at least one of the recurring Salisbury nightmares. Still, the ones he had just experienced had been bad enough. "I'm glad *that's* over with," he muttered as he rubbed his eyes, still fairly unhinged from the residue of where his nightmares had taken him. In truth he knew nothing was over in that regard, at least not for long. Outside, the sun was shining.

***

"I WOULD be more than happy to accommodate you, Lieutenant," Colonel Robert Hudkins at headquarters told him. "Just give me the messages and I'll have them wired post haste."

Pete wrote out two of them, one for Delicia and one for his parents. "I've included their addresses of course." Pete told the colonel before departing. "And I can't thank you enough for getting me the three month furlough."

"My pleasure, Lieutenant. That was quite a story. Remember to report to headquarters in Chicago. I've heard some gruesome tales before, this damnable war is rife with them, experienced a few things myself for that matter, but have never heard of anything like what you have just told me, no sir I have not. I say hang 'em, hang 'em all, including that murderous bastard Forrest." Pete just looked at Colonel Hudkins. He didn't want to get involved in that conversation. Besides, he just didn't have the words to describe the paradox that was Nathan Bedford Forrest.

Pete left, heading straight for the train station with Yankee. He was bringing the horse with him all the way to Naperville, and God help any man who tried to stop him. Pete had lost count of how many times that magnificent animal had saved his life, but there would be plenty of time to count them up once he was on the train; the train which would finally be taking him close to Naperville, taking him *home*.

Colonel Hudkins read Pete's wires, feeling a little guilty about having done so. The words were few, but touching. The colonel was still marveling at all Pete had been through, filled with admiration for the brave and determined young officer, and wished he could have done more for him than just a three month furlough. If any soldier deserved an honorable discharge, it was McCabe.

It occurred to him there was one thing he could do. If he sent the wires along with the highest military priority available, one which was generally reserved for the most urgent messages issued by those of highest rank, authority and privilege, McCabe's family and loved ones would not only be sure to receive them, but on a much more timely basis. It was the least Colonel Hudkins felt he could do for such a fine young officer, and the well-meaning man put everything else on hold until the task was completed; until the telegrams had been sent not to the addresses Lieutenant McCabe had furnished but to headquarters in Chicago, to General Phineas Smithington.

***

"THANK YOU, Corporal," the good-humored general said to his subordinate after being handed the sealed telegrams from Memphis. The young corporal had never known his superior officer to be so jolly and his good mood seemed to be mushrooming daily. General Smithington was all but whistling as he opened the first telegram.

He sat in stunned silence. His heart pounded precariously, as did his temples. It wasn't a warm day, April rarely produced those in northern Illinois especially near Lake Michigan, but he had begun to sweat anyway. He tore open the second telegram but read only half of it.

A master at surveying a situation and acting accordingly, his mind raced towards his best, his only, options. He was out of his office immediately and didn't return until every dime he owned was in his possession. Thank God Janeway had paid him, and although nearly $600,000 wasn't the millions he knew he would have eventually ended up with one way or another, it would be enough. It would have to be enough, at least for the time being.

According to the telegrams Lieutenant McCabe was scheduled to arrive in Chicago in three days on the 1:30 train, perhaps a day sooner since the colonel in Memphis had also seen fit to give Pete priority status as far as his travel arrangements were concerned. McCabe *and* his horse as it turned out.

Smithington's first impulse had been to take all his money and simply vanish, as he imagined that scoundrel Baileen had likely done. But what if McCabe made it to Chicago but no farther or thereabouts? That got the general to thinking. It was just as easy to kill someone and get rid of their body in a large city or the surrounding countryside as it was anywhere else, almost anyway, *if* one had the right connections. *Perhaps I can get those millions after all,* the general concluded.

General Smithington had plenty of connections all right, or at least enough. Initially Janeway would be furious, very much so, but if things ended well the general would still be in line for the fortune that he had already spent, if only in his mind. Besides, Smithington realized, he still had all that information; knew where Janeway had buried the body so to speak. Janeway needed to be alerted, but not right away. At least not for twenty-four hours, enough time for the general to call on another of his nefarious acquaintances, Rufus McBride.

***

"ALL I'M prepared to give you, McBride, is five hundred." Smithington told the stocky, heavyset thirty-year-old Irishman as they sat in the man's apartment located on the north side of Chicago on West Cornelia Avenue, a few blocks west of North Lincoln Avenue. It was a fair distance from headquarters located well south of McBride's working class Irish neighborhood, but Smithington had wasted no time getting there. "This Major Janeway fellow will be good for the rest, believe me. By this time tomorrow, perhaps the day after, you will be $9,500 richer if you succeed, which I'm confident you will."

"Well, the money's right," Rufus said, stroking his dark beard, "I'll give ya that General darlin', but how do I *know* this Janeway fella is good for the rest? You cough up another $4,500 and we got us a deal."

"I don't have that kind of money!" Smithington whined as if he had been injured. "The best I can do is the five hundred. If you'd rather forget the whole thing, I'm sure there are others who would jump at this golden opportunity." Rufus McBride kept his sharp blue eyes locked on the general's rheumy ones, mulling things over. He finally poured himself another shot of Bushmills to the brim, spilling nary a drop, nor offering any to Smithington.

"Well, I'll at least be needin' the address of this Janeway fella and directions to his place. I'll not be killin' some Yankee lieutenant only to discover the man with the money is nowhere to be found. And I'll take that other six hundred now, my portly friend."

"That's *five* hundred, Rufus."

"So it t'was, so it t'was. But I'll have me expenses, now won't I, General darlin'. Give me the man's address and the six hundred. With that, Ducky, we have us a deal."

The general grumbled as he counted out the six hundred then produced a photograph taken of the 1st Naperville Cavalry. "That's your man, McBride," the general said as he pointed to Pete standing next to Sackett O'Darcy in the front row. "Study his face well. And remember, he's as resourceful as he is lucky, which too many of you shanty Irish seem to have in common. Figure it takes one to catch one, so don't let me down."

***

IT HAD happened, actually happened, but Pete almost couldn't assimilate the reality as he gazed at the landscape rushing by. His train had made it into Illinois, and although the southern part of the state stood in contrast to the Chicago area still hundreds of miles away it was still Illinois; it was still his home state.

He doubted anyone would be waiting for him when the train arrived at the Central Depot in Chicago but perhaps they would. It seemed so very long ago when he had boarded the train bound for Indianapolis with the other green volunteers from Naperville two and a half years before. They had boarded it from the same depot he was heading towards; a curious mix of architectural styles that would prove to be the precursor of future Chicago train stations.

Pete didn't care about such things, or at that moment little else that didn't involve his imminent arrival home. He would arrive at the Central Depot then board a train to Wheaton. From there he would ride Yankee the eight miles or so to Naperville. What a ride that would be! He and Yankee had ridden over so many perilous miles, traversing what had been nothing short of a hostile foreign country as far as Pete was concerned, that covering those eight miles would feel like heaven on earth, he imagined.

Perhaps they should have simply allowed the South to secede after all, Pete considered. To hell with politics, with *war*. Abe Lincoln may have believed saving his precious Union was worth the hell so many had and were enduring, but Pete wasn't so sure. He stewed on that a while, then chided himself for those thoughts when he remembered Fort Pillow and the other atrocities he had witnessed. Father Benjamin had been right along – *Our boys will be fighting so a mother may no longer fear losing ownership of her child* his father had always said, or words to that effect. That, Pete concluded, was at the heart of it all.

He wondered how those men he had come to know, however briefly, had made out. He assumed they were all dead. He recalled the day he had shared lunch with them, after he had confronted the Union soldiers dressed in Yankee blue no less, soldiers who had demonstrated their contempt for men of color as vehemently as any Southerner he had encountered until Fort Pillow. Those Yankees had never owned other human beings, never massacred them as far as he knew, but the only difference Pete really saw was the color of their uniforms. He could envision any number of white Yankee soldiers who would've reacted in a similar fashion had they been dressed in butternut or gray. War separated men for battle, but it couldn't separate men from what was branded upon their souls, not enough of them anyway.

Another topic invaded, one Pete had troubled over during his months of captivity and other times as well. So much had happened, so much despair, mindless destruction and death. Now that he was safe he found himself contemplating things from a different perspective, one that insisted he pay it heed since he might soon be in a position to do something about it if anything needed doing at all. The more he ruminated the more he wondered if Sackett O'Darcy's murder by Clifton Janeway had ever seen the light of day. He doubted it, even if Janeway had survived the peach orchard. As cunning as that scoundrel had been, Pete still had a hard time believing something hadn't happened to him. Janeway had been dressed as a Rebel the last time Pete had seen him and that group of Yankee soldiers had been shooting directly at Janeway and the small group of Confederates he had joined. Pete knew most of them had been killed. *Janeway is probably dead*, Pete concluded as he had in the past, regardless of perspective. *God help him if he isn't though. Gonna kill him myself. I swear on it.*

Pete had considered mentioning what he had witnessed once he had been able to, but had decided against it. Janeway and his father had a great deal of influence and the money to back it up. It would be his word against Clifton's if the scoundrel was still alive, and he could just picture Janeway maintaining things had been too chaotic that day in the peach orchard for Pete to have been able to ascertain what had really occurred, especially from seventy or eighty yards away through all that smoke and all those trees, not to mention the wanton mayhem. If Pete wanted justice, *requital,* he saw only one way to get it. He concluded it would be pure folly to announce his intentions by accusing Janeway of murder. He also knew what he had every intention of doing would be nothing short of premeditated murder, a hanging offense in Illinois. He knew it all right, and also knew that was exactly what he was going to do. If Janeway was alive, he wouldn't be for long. After dwelling on it for what he knew was too long Pete forced those thoughts from his mind; it was *his* time now, his time to return home.

His mind drifted back to his favorite topic. He could just imagine how beautiful a sobbing Delicia would look, how she would feel once he held her in his arms. He would hold her so tight he would have to make sure he didn't crush her. The scent of her hair, perfume, of *her* would leave him dizzy, and he would have to try very hard to keep his own tears in check. Nonsense, he concluded. Let them come; let the whole damned world see it. If ever a man had reason to do so that would surely be the time.

They would be married within the week. Delicia's parents would protest, especially her mother. She would want time to plan everything, to make it all perfect, but what could be more perfect than being married to Delicia? Hang all the pomp and ceremony. Upon further reflection he realized it would be a losing battle. Besides, Delicia would want those same things, and he wasn't about to deny her anything. What were a few more weeks? Oh, about a lifetime he mused, but he had all the time eternity had to offer, or so it felt at that moment.

They would need their own house, but not a very big one, not at first. For a thousand dollars or so he could easily afford a place in town, in *Naperville.* The very name of his hometown, now that it was getting closer, made him giddy, just like it had eons ago when he had been heading for Chattanooga. The house though, back to the house. It would be white; almost all of the homes in Naperville were white. Perhaps Delicia would want a different color, perhaps red, or yellow. Not gray, however, or anything close to butternut. He'd seen enough of those colors to last him a lifetime. Truth told, he was no longer all that enamored with Yankee blue either. It would have to have a large kitchen and a nice parlor, and a fireplace in at least one of the rooms; perhaps even the bedroom…the bedroom.

Pete sighed at the very thought of it. Could it be true? Would he and Delicia actually be making love in just a matter of weeks? His shoulders slumped as he envisioned them alone in their bedroom that first night and countless nights thereafter, and *days* for that matter. How many times would he tell her how much he loved her, especially while demonstrating the depth of his affections? And how wonderful would it be when Delicia said it to him, right when they were in the middle of their passion?

He discovered those were also images best driven from his mind, at least while sitting in a train crowded with people. All anyone would have to do was look at him and his thoughts would be there for all to see. He could stand upon his seat and yell it at them and not be more obvious; he was all but convinced of that as he glanced around. *The house, the house, the house - no, not the house.* Every time he thought of the house he couldn't stay out of the bedroom. *Yankee! That's more like it, Yankee. Billy will do circus flips when he hears about all the things Yankee and I have been though…*darker images invaded, so Pete quickly put himself and Yankee back in Naperville. *Naperville - why is this infernal train going so slow? Wait until Billy and my other brothers take turns riding him, flying down the road in front of Tin Pan Alley! What a sight that will be! Mother will be worried of course, worried Yankee is running so fast it would be impossible for any of us astride to get enough oxygen.* Certain men of science had warned of such things. They had theorized the more powerful locomotives being developed would cause passengers to pass out, perhaps die from acute hypoxia. *Yankee can run at least that fast Mother Grace will insist, just look at him!*

Pete was smiling, his daydreams taking him places no longer beyond his grasp. How long had it been since he could dare to think of such amazing things on the threshold of coming true? There had been Chattanooga of course, but that had evaporated like a morning mist enshrouding Lookout Mountain after an insistent summer's day had swallowed it up. He was in Illinois now, at least a hundred miles from any existing or impending battles, from *war*.

Night had begun settling in as he rode along, dissolving the dying light from the sky outside the train window. The landscape hadn't disappeared yet, but it was fading into undistinguishable forms as well, but that was all right; it was Illinois, and the next day the train would be chugging to a stop at Central Depot, then another train would do the same in Wheaton. *No really, it will, it really will!* He smiled to himself, fairly tingling with anticipation.

Pete was growing tired, but he wanted to check on Yankee; he wanted to be with a close friend. He got up and started walking through the cars, illuminated by lantern light, steadying himself from time to time by placing a hand on the passenger seats as he moved along, smiling and nodding at the folks attempting sleep with little success, or the ones who had been gazing out the windows into the developing darkness before looking at him. How endearing their smiles felt, their slight nods. He was dressed in crisp Yankee blue, and many of those civilian folks appeared to appreciate all it represented, even if not all of it was still irreproachable in Pete's mind.

"Hey boy," Pete said after making several rather dicey maneuvers, carrying a lantern no less, to get into the boxcar where Yankee was located. "How do you like riding on a train? Don't worry boy, it's okay. We'll be there tomorrow, you'll see. We'll be home, Yankee. We'll be in *Naperville.*"

***

CLIFTON JANEWAY had never walked past his own reflection without lingering, especially now that he was so fit and trim. He had on his favorite silk uniform as he stood in front of the mirror in his bedroom fixing his long blonde hair. The barber had done a good job, not cutting off too much. Clifton had it perfect. The ride over to Delicia's would muss his locks, especially the unavoidable breezes which would hit him at the most annoying of angles, but he wasn't concerned, not really. He was filled with anticipation, happiness and joy as he again touched his perfect hair with the lightest of strokes. Upon further reflection, he sighed, it was a shame his hair wouldn't remain exactly as he had it at that moment.

He had spoken to Delicia the day before at the hospital, and she had promised to have an answer for him about their wedding date by the following afternoon. Not about *whether* they would be married but *when*. That's how Clifton had interpreted her words anyway. Granted, she had turned away when he had tried to kiss her, but no matter. It had been disappointing, frustrating more like it, but once they were married, that very *night*, oh how things would change; Clifton could just picture it... *Delicia naked upon the bed, her long hair flying about, me directly behind her, in total command...I'll see to it my precious little darling's virtue will be lost, and in the most creative of ways...*he was engrossed in his lurid fantasy, one that also imagined her screaming his name. *She's screaming like a sex starved whore, begging me to stop...but not for long... 'No, don't stop Clifton, spank your naughty slut! Oh Clifton, hurt me, punish me you* **animal!'**

"Clifton dear?" His mother called from the hallway just outside his door. *Damn that woman!* He said to himself as he quickly buttoned the front of his dress tunic.

"What *is* it, Mother? Can't a man have a little privacy?"

"Of course, dear. But General Smithton's courier has arrived again. He has another message for my important son the major! Shall I have Charles ask him in?"

"I'll be right there, God damn it! And it's Smith***ing***ton for about the thousandth time, and stop fawning over his God damned delivery boy, will you Mother? You're a big enough embarrassment as is."

Clifton took the sealed letter from the courier and dismissed him with a wave of the hand without looking or speaking to the young soldier.

"More important military matters that need your attention, dear?" His smiling mother asked as she entered the large foyer holding her breakfast, a glass of cream sherry; her third that morning.

Clifton waved her off without a glance or word, then turned away from her and walked outside towards the stable, leaving the door unclosed behind him as if opening it had been a big enough inconvenience. *What does General Lard Ass want now,* he wondered as he snapped several dollops of sealing wax and tore open the envelope as he moved along. *More money, no doubt.* He began to read, then stopped before even finishing the message - Major Clifton Janeway stopped cold in his tracks.

Will this God damned nightmare never end? He was so shocked he still hadn't moved. He started reading it again from the beginning:

There has been an unfortunate development. Our former friend has misinformed us. That acquaintance of yours is on a train as I write, unharmed and heading home. He will be arriving this afternoon, tomorrow afternoon at the latest. I have already secured the services of a man more than qualified to rectify the situation. He will be needing $9,400 from you, in cash after he has accomplished his mission. Fear not, we are still in control. No one else is aware of anything, thanks to me.

***

RUFUS MCBRIDE appeared to be reading a newspaper as he sat in a strategic location inside the Chicago Central Depot station. There was no way anyone could come or go without him spotting them. He had burned McCabe's image into his brain, and thanks to the photograph he even knew his victim's height and approximate weight assuming his war experiences hadn't made him rail-thin. McBride hoped his prey hadn't grown a beard, but since he would likely be wearing a lieutenant's uniform his chances of making it past the part-time professional killer undetected were slim at best.

McBride didn't know if he had the right day, but for what he had already been paid coupled with what he was going to get it didn't matter. If McCabe wasn't on the 1:30 Monday he would be Tuesday. He decided to make his way to the platform as 12:30 dragged towards one. He had already been informed the train was on time but had kept a close watch anyway, in case McCabe had somehow ended up on a different train or the one he was supposed to be on arrived early. Obviously neither had happened.

He hoped to hell McCabe's travel arrangements hadn't been so jumbled that he somehow ended up arriving at the Galena & Chicago Union Station. McBride had taken the precaution of hiring one of his flunkies to keep watch over there, but even if the man did spot McCabe, by the time McBride found out he would be hard pressed to locate his prey in time. His plan was to ride on the same train as Pete to Wheaton where McBride had already seen to it a horse was waiting for him, but if he had to somehow get there with McCabe on a train leaving from a different station at a different time, things would grow hurried at best.

After the 1:30 pulled in and the passengers began to disembark, McBride realized his concerns had been unsubstantiated. His target hadn't grown a beard either, and was indeed wearing a lieutenant's uniform. *Where the hell is he going, though?* McBride wondered as he began to follow.

So that's it, he said to himself. *Got his own horse. Leave it to some cavalryman not to want to part with his damned horse.* It became apparent all Pete was doing was making sure Yankee was on the train for Wheaton, but McBride never let him out of his sight anyway. Ten thousand dollars was a lot of money and a man couldn't take too many precautions…then he reconsidered his earlier concern, now that the game was unfolding. *What if that pimple Janeway decides he doesn't know what I'm talking about concerning the ten thousand?* McBride had already decided the six hundred was for expenses and that Janeway would owe him the full amount. *Or decides what he owes me is a damned sight less?* McBride concluded with more clarity, now that he was so close.

He made his way to a ticket window and inquired about the next train to Wheaton. Just as he had suspected, McCabe would have to be on the one after the next train since that next one was about to depart. *He'll need to give himself enough time to board his nag…*McBride bought a ticket and was soon on the one leaving first, making it just in time with at least a two hour head start.

***

BY THE time Pete was boarding his train McBride was halfway to Naperville, riding hard. Before long his horse was galloping up the oval, crushed limestone entrance way which angled around to the front of the Janeway mansion. His horse was foamy and breathing hard. He dismounted and went to the large front door.

"I have a message for a Major Clifton Janeway, sir." He said when Charles, the butler, opened the door. The distinguished looking though pale man called for Mrs. Janeway.

"May I help you, sir?" Cortance inquired after coming to the door. McBride repeated his request.

Clifton had been in his office, stalking about nervously. He had decided he was in no condition to see Delicia and besides, he definitely had more pressing matters even if he didn't know what to do. When he had been informed of the stranger's arrival Clifton came to the foyer and ushered McBride to his office, closing the door behind them.

"What the hell are you doing here?" Clifton asked, clearly unhinged.

"Simmer down, Major darlin'. There's still time, but not much of it. Your darlin' lieutenant is probably gettin' close to the Wheaton station as we speak, seen him me own self. I have time to head him off, but we have a little business matter to settle before I do anything. I do pray, for your sake, that safe over there has ten thousand dollars in it."

"This is about the God damned *money?*" Jesus damned *Christ!*" He went over and began working the combination, pausing long enough to glare at McBride. No words were needed as the stocky man diverted his gaze. Clifton handed the ten thousand to McBride.

"I'll be'a needin' a fresh mount as well, laddie." McBride said as he put the cash in his inside coat pocket.

"If what you say is true McCabe will be in Naperville in about two hours, perhaps a little longer. What is your plan to see that he doesn't arrive?" Clifton asked.

"He'll no doubt be a takin' the same road I just did, saw me several likely spots for an ambush along the way I did."

"How can you be certain he isn't planning to get off at Aurora? You haven't considered that possibility *have* you, you mindless twit!"

"There's no call to use such words, laddie, I just assumed…"

"You just assumed! Well, while you are *assuming* things in that drunken Mick brain of yours, McCabe may well be on his way to Aurora! Considering where the Aurora station is located he won't likely head east down the road out front that comes from Aurora, but enter town from the north!"

"Will he now, that would be a problem at this late time," McBride answered casually, still offended by Clifton's words. "Since you seem to have all the answers, *Major,* why don't you come up with one now? I already have me money, and in my line I always go well-heeled, so if you are gettin' any notions of seeing *my* money again you can put that to rest."

"I'm not interested in the God damned money! You kill McCabe, or help me do it, and I'll *more* than double it!" That got McBride's attention. The mouthy major could call him all the names he wanted.

"And you, sir, have yourself a most able and willing servant. I do apologize for my oversight, but it was that old bag'a wind Smithington that told me your friend was gettin' off at Wheaton."

"Maybe he is, maybe he isn't. The way things have turned out would you trust the words of that fat bastard? I'll deal with him later. You might well get the opportunity to earn a great deal more!"

"Sir, I am indeed your man. Just tell me what that agile mind of yours is concocting. By the by, exactly how *much* more money might I inquire, for McCabe?"

"If McCabe does get off at Wheaton, he will enter Naperville from Washington Street. If it's Aurora, he'll probably come in from the north and end up on West Street, most likely take Jackson east to Washington, since it takes him to the road leading to his farm. Unless…hell, he'll probably spot the new walking bridge if he comes from Aurora! He'll take that short cut for sure! Unless he comes from Wheaton…here's what we'll do. You position yourself on the road you came in on, the one that led to Washington. If he arrives, kill him and get rid of the body. I'll be under the new walking bridge. If he comes that way I'll get him when he's on it. No way he'll be able to get away, not when I get him with this." Clifton went over to a closet as he spoke and brought out his new weapon. It was a huge double-barreled buck and ball shotgun. McBride's eyebrows went up.

"You plannin' on killin' the man or sendin' him halfway to Wisconsin? By the saints, that is one fearsome lookin' weapon."

"Good questions. Perhaps both. No one will recognize him once this beauty has done her job."

"And the extra money? I believe you were about to offer me *how* much more?"

Clifton glared at McBride, annoyed at being reminded of such a trifling detail. "You kill that bastard or help me do it *and* get rid of the body, another $25,000. Now go!"

***

DOC WYGANT didn't know what was amiss. He had been fidgeting about all day, snapping at his help and even at some of his patients. When he cursed after Delicia had dropped a pan, scattering any number of instruments across the floor in the process, it was all she could do not to storm off; perhaps all the way home. She had never known the old man to act in such a manner, but after she had calmed down her concern for his welfare was all that remained.

She was upset anyway, upset that Clifton had failed to show up. It wouldn't have been so nerve wracking if she had good news for him, but when someone has bad news to deliver it's best to get it over with, let alone have it delayed because the recipient is late in arriving to receive it. Her mind was made up though. She wasn't going to marry Clifton Janeway. If that was going to change it wouldn't likely happen in a few months, or even a few years for that matter.

It had struck her all at once as if it had always been inside her, waiting patiently. It had started innocently enough, not that there was anything to feel guilty about. Delicia did anyway, but that wasn't about to change her mind about anything.

Billy had brought a tintype to the hospital that morning and offered it to Delicia as a keepsake. It had been Father Benjamin's idea after he had found it in a trunk stored in the attic. It was a tintype of Pete and Delicia taken by a professional photographer from Aurora. Hezekiah had hired him back in the summer of 1858 to take some photos of both families at their annual Fourth of July picnic that year. Pete had his arm around Delicia's shoulders as they stood by the pond on the O'Darcy place, and both of them looked so happy, so in love. Delicia remembered when the photo had been taken, how Pete had playfully threatened to grab her and pull both of them into the water just before the photographer told them to stand very still and, of course, to stop smiling; they had ignored his last directive.

It was one thing to look at a photograph one sees every day, a photo which might be on a mantle for instance, and another to see one for the first time that had been taken a long time ago, one that brought everything back with such authority, such detail; it was as if Delicia had been swept back in time. She had been swept back, or at least reminded of how being profoundly in love really felt. Pete was dead, she knew that, but when she saw his likeness again, his warm smile so full of promise, *his arm around her*, she knew no one else's image belonged there and never would.

***

"GOD DAMN son of a bitch!" Doc Wygant hollered after dropping his tobacco pouch. None had even spilled, not very much anyway, but from his reaction one might have thought a scalpel had slipped from his hand and stuck a patient in the eye. Delicia went over to where he was sitting, a familiar, reproachful smile on her lovely face.

"Silas, what is it?" She asked in a voice that could calm the devil himself, or so Doc Wygant liked to assume.

"I don't know my dear, it's similar to my other peculiarities, but I have never had one that felt this intense. I've half a mind to quaff a couple gills of laudanum and drive this from my mind, or from wherever it's lurking."

"Why not drink four gills, and kill yourself twice as quickly?" She said, still smiling as she put her hand on his shoulder. He looked up into her dark blue eyes and returned her smile.

Two hours later Doc Wygant was putting away some vials into their respective drawers. Billy happened by, carrying a chamber pot that needed emptying.

"Give me that, Billy." That was odd. Doc never emptied chamber pots. Billy had never even seen him with an empty one, freshly cleaned. Given the old man's mood that afternoon, Billy handed it over and started to walk away. He had plenty of chores ahead of him and the afternoon was getting on, urging twilight to prepare its arrival.

"William, would you please do me a favor?" *William?* Doc had never called him William, not once in all of Billy's years.

"You all right, Doc?" The youth asked, eyeing the tired looking man carefully.

"Just not myself I guess, but I need a favor from you."

"Sure Doc, what is it?"

"I need you to return the squirrel rifle I borrowed from Hezekiah, would you do that for me son?" Billy looked at him again, closer than before. He had already returned the Remington he had borrowed, and just a few days ago Doc had told him to get it back so they could go rabbit hunting again. Doc had even kept the .22 caliber Henry for that very purpose - now this.

"Well, sure Doc, I'll drop it off on my way home tonight."

"That won't do!" Doc Wygant snapped, as if Billy had perhaps offended, or at least irritated him. "I need you to take it to him now. *Right* now."

"I've still got the other chamber pots," Billy replied, himself somewhat offended. "And all those cracker boxes you want hauled to the cellar, and -"

"*Now* William, take the gun *now*. Somebody else can take care of the God damned chamber pots!"

***

THERE WERE glorious spring afternoons and there was the one Pete was in the midst of enjoying as he and Yankee ambled down the road that led west to Naperville from the Wheaton station. The afternoon was getting on, but no matter. They would be home before dark, or just after, since Pete was going to first stop by Delicia's home. He had half expected her to have been waiting for him at the Wheaton station, but perhaps Delicia thought he was getting in tomorrow. That had to have been it, same with his family. He wondered how many of his brothers would be there, if any, besides Billy of course. He also wondered, as always, if they were all alive or if any of them were, but decided Providence had already made that decision. Such news could wait. He had experienced enough of such dreadful news, witnessed it happening long before the soon-to-be bereaved families were aware of their losses.

"Lookit over there, Yankee." Pete said as he pointed to a grove of budding hard maples surrounding a spring fed pond. The virginal, fresh spring grass had already blanketed the area in a resplendent green that would shame an emerald, Pete imagined. "I've caught me a ton of bass in there over the years. It's a fair piece from where we're headed, but worth the trip if you want bass for supper. Guess you aren't interested in fish, are ya boy. Get you some fresh oats when we get home, promise ya that. Not far now. Come fall, you'll be eatin' the best apples this side of paradise, promise ya that too, Yankee boy."

There was a wide bend in the road Pete knew as well as his own front yard. Once he was around it, the road would angle southwest before straightening out again, right to where it intersected with Washington Street. *No, it certainly won't be long now,* he sighed inwardly.

McBride saw him coming from where he was hiding in some bushes a hundred yards up the road, along its north side. His horse was down in a ravine behind him, content with the untouched grass the mare was eating.

"Another seventy yards or so Lieutenant darlin', and Rufus McBride will be a rich man," he said under his breath. "Just a ways longer me tall ridin' pot'a gold, just a ways more..." Rufus checked his Henry rifle again; the rifle that never missed.

"Hallo you on the horse! Is that you, Pete McCabe? Or have I died and heaven is Naperville after all?" The farmer hollered in his familiar booming voice after having emerged from a field. He was across the road from McBride, perhaps fifty yards closer to Pete. He had his three sons with him, in their early and mid teens, large for their ages.

"Why Richard Ritenour, is that you?" Pete called out, recognizing the man immediately. "And these can't be your sons, can they? What in blazes you been feedin' 'em, Rick?" There were glad tidings all about, especially from the four Napervillians who had been told Pete was long dead.

McBride was beside himself. *If I kill the lieutenant now I'll likely have to kill them all, and the divil to pay as well... best to stay calm and see if those hayseeds don't just go on their way. It's not like McCabe has come all this way to be with them for any length of time...*

"You have to come to the house, Pete!" Ritenour said, louder than necessary as Pete recalled the large, blonde-headed farmer had always done, causing Pete to grin inside and out. "Debbie will faint dead away when she sees you! Come on now, I won't hear otherwise!" The farmer pointed directly towards where McBride was lurking, indicating that was the direction they would soon be heading.

That tore it. McBride had to get away from there. Better to head back to Washington Street and set up an ambush there, since Pete would go that way, he figured, or at least pass close enough so he could be tailed. If he did and the farmer and his sons were still with him, McBride figured he would simply have to deal with it somehow. McCabe couldn't stay with them forever, he again assumed. McBride crept down into the ravine, led his horse due west keeping both of them concealed, then bolted off when he was far enough away.

Pete, of course, begged off the invitation but kept talking to the four farmers a short while. He was soon on his way again, Yankee taking him closer.

When things start to go wrong often times it resembles a growing avalanche, at least that's how McBride felt. There hadn't been a soul around earlier, not very many anyway, especially on the outskirts of town. Not only had the lucky lieutenant avoided McBride's first ambush he avoided the next one as well, and for the same reason. "Must be a popular son of a bitch," McBride muttered as he again saw Pete stop and talk with some people - two old maids, or perhaps widows the frustrated man imagined. "*Now* where the hell ya goin', Lieutenant?" McBride muttered.

Pete had known the Rickert sisters his whole life. In fact, he was related to them. They were his mother's paternal cousins and they were indeed widows. They had begun to cry when they recognized the soldier riding down Washington Street, and had bounded into the road as fast as their old legs could carry them and their long, cumbersome skirts and petticoats would allow.

After the initial reunion they told Pete that Delicia had been working at the new hospital, but they were fairly certain it was her day off. Pete had wanted to go to her home first, so when the Rickert sisters told him about the new walking bridge and how it crossed the river just a stone's throw or two from the O'Darcy place, Pete decided to cut down Franklin Avenue, the first road that would take him west to Eagle Street. Then it would be a left to the river, a little over four blocks away. There he'd find the new bridge - the new walking bridge - where Clifton Janeway was waiting underneath the structure along the south bank, hidden from view.

"Beggin' your pardon ladies," McBride said to the Rickert sisters as he rode up, tipping his hat. Pete's back was in view as he approached Eagle Street, three blocks west. "Can I impose upon your good natures a trifle? I'm not from around here, fear I'm lost, and was wonderin' where this road might lead to?" He pointed at Franklin Avenue, a charming smile on his face and in his bright, blue eyes.

"Oh, just the new hospital is down that way sir, except of course the houses." Fanny Rickert responded. "Anyone particular you are trying to find?"

"Is there bein' a new bridge that way?"

"No," Fanny replied, "not that way. But if you go left on Eagle Street three blocks west of here, that will take you right to it."

"I thank you ma'am, you and your lovely companion. Good day to you now, ladies."

McBride watched as Pete made a lazy left on Eagle Street. He didn't want to ride away too fast from the Rickert sisters but as soon as he was fifty feet away he spurred his horse into a gallop anyway. He could usually get around a city the size of Chicago without much difficulty, so he assumed he could make his way to the bridge ahead of McCabe by cutting south at a dead run. McBride went south on Main Street, the first road that allowed him to do so and spurred his horse. He had been right. Pete was moving slowly as he headed south on Eagle Street. A short time later McBride was already thundering across the wooden walking bridge.

"Janeway, where are ya man?"

"Down here, what news have you?"

"Had me a divil of a time, couldn't get a shot off to save me life. But your man is a headin' down this way as I speak. I have done me part, and will be expectin' that other $25,000."

"Has anyone seen him yet?" Clifton asked, looking around nervously. "Spoke to him?" McBride thought about that, and had his answer ready before any suspicions Clifton might have been close to developing had a chance to grow.

"No sir, not a soul." If any negative ramifications of McCabe's conversations did eventually transpire, it wouldn't be until after McBride had his additional $25,000 or so he reasoned; then it would be the blonde-haired dandy of an officer's problem.

"Now about that money -"

"You'll get your God damned money after he's dead and buried!" Clifton said as he stood almost knee-deep in the river, close to the bridge. "Get over to that high ground, find some cover." Clifton was pointing to a spot northwest of the bridge, perhaps a hundred and fifty feet away. It was elevated and covered with sumac and scrub trees, making it an ideal spot to lay in ambush. "Wait until he is halfway onto the bridge, then shoot. He'll have no way of escaping. I'll finish him off with this." Clifton held out his shotgun, took a quick look around then ducked back under the bridge.

***

BILLY WAS still frustrated with the old man but finally doing what Doc Wygant had requested, after the youth had taken a few of the cracker boxes down to the cellar as if in protest. It had been more of a demand than a request, but given the doctor's mood that day Billy decided it was best to simply follow the old man's instructions and get it over with.

Why Billy was supposed to head down Mill Street, a block west of Eagle made no sense. It hadn't to Doc Wygant either, but he had been adamant: "Just do it, William, and make your way back along the river bank to the new bridge from there. Go with a purpose, but be careful. *Just do it,* promise me you'll just *do* it. God's speed, lad, and keep a careful watch." Billy simply shrugged his shoulders and sighed.

***

PETE SWORE he was in heaven. The sun was getting lower, approaching the horizon, painting shadows that spread easterly across Eagle Street as he made his way south. The shadows coming from the branches of the tallest trees were longest, and had made their way over the small houses on the east side of the road. The other shadows, the ones from the rooftops of the houses to his right, had covered most of Eagle Street but not all of it. The spaces between the houses still allowed angled rays of sunlight through, but there was little warmth to be found when Yankee passed through them. Pete barely noticed and cared even less.

It wasn't a warm afternoon, what was left of it, but it felt comfortable. Everything did. It hadn't been easy before, keeping the thoughts of his recent experiences at bay, especially when he had been on the train. When he had let down his guard then, even for a moment as the train had chugged along, the horror of Fort Pillow had been waiting for him.

Other things had invaded his thoughts as well, all the harrowing things that had occurred during his long odyssey. The screams and butchery of Fort Pillow had always been closest to the surface however, waiting to lunge at him as if nothing could hold back the terror for long. The screams especially, they hadn't floated off while he had been on the train. They had been hovering, not unlike a swarm of ghosts trapped in an unholy maelstrom incapable of, or at least unwilling to accept their fate. Not anymore, at least not at that moment as he rode along in the middle of the one place that had been at the apex of his yearning for so long.

Pete wasn't in a hurry now that the ghosts were at bay. Since he was so close, so very close to the warm embraces, tears of joy and voices choked with emotion, he wanted to savor the moments that preceded everything because that's all they were, mere moments. He was indeed anxious, more than anxious, but that made the final few moments all the more wondrous. They would be with him forever he imagined, just as vivid fifty years later as they were at that moment.

He continued to ride along, immersed in the fading afternoon. He saw himself years later lounging upon the front porch of Tin Pan Alley, pipe in hand like Father Benjamin, watching his children, his grandchild, frolicking in the front yard...and the moment he was presently savoring would cascade over him like a warm spring breeze - of that he had no doubt. Pete sighed as he nudged his boot heels into Yankee's sides.

***

BILLY HAD made his way to the north river bank and began walking along the timeworn, narrow dirt path heading east. The early spring plants, the optimistic ones, had already ventured forth. The buds on the trees were more cautious but had begun to show some color as well. Twilight was coaxing dusk, intermingled as they blanketed themselves across the early evening and along the riverbank where Billy was walking. Bushes and trees were to the left of him, fewer to his right closest to the river. Branches brushed against the youth as he made his way, branches poised to leaf out and grow across the path if left to their own purposes. The air was aromatic and fresh, and although that hadn't escaped Billy he wanted to get his silly task over with and appreciate the spring freshness completely unfettered on his way home.

Two mallard ducks, their wings stark still and spread at a downward angle, glided past him. They were five feet above the middle of the lazy river, perhaps lower, not twenty feet away from Billy as they glided by and landed atop the dark water and came to rest, slowly circling each other. The male, seemingly mindful of his colorful plumage and aware of its allure, contrasted with the brown and beige feathered down of his coy mate with just a swatch of contrasting blue on her wings. They huddled together when they spotted the intruder, wary but fairly certain he would continue on his way.

Billy stifled an urge to say hello, and to ask them if they were anticipating parenthood. He enjoyed doing that, talking to creatures as if they deserved to be treated as at least his equals, always hoping the animals would glance his way from time to time, as if they appreciated or at least acknowledged his tidings.

The rifle felt out of place in his hand, and because he was carrying it he surmised the mallards had every right to view him with distain. He let out a sigh as he recalled his trip to the McDowell property with Doc Wygant. It was a good five miles upriver but perhaps the mallards knew what he had done, how he had killed those rabbits. The rabbits hadn't had a mean bone in their bodies, hadn't ever felt compelled to harm a soul. It was as if they were conduits, a continuation of gentleness passed on for countless millenniums.

Billy kept walking, looking around at the promise spring was issuing forth with all the new, innocent life that was unfolding around him. What had he been trying to prove? What was it he had wanted Doc Wygant, *himself,* to come away with after he had shot those innocent creatures? Well, he wouldn't do it again. He would accept what he had done even if he hadn't felt he'd learned anything from it, other than he too was a killer. Spring was a time for revival, to renew all things capable of being renewed, and since he was part of the wonderment he vowed to renew himself as well. He kept looking around, taking it all in. Suddenly, he stopped. William McCabe stopped cold.

***

WHOMEVER THE man was upon the rise, Billy concluded, he certainly was a man with a purpose. Billy had seen the rifle, and how a kneeling McBride was looking to his left, away from Billy, from behind some bushes. *He's a hunter, he must be,* Billy assumed. He couldn't get a good look at the man's face, barely the right side of it, not enough to recognize him if he happened to be a local. Despite what he was stalking Billy felt an urge to alert the man's prey. That would be a good start he felt more than thought, an affirmation of Billy's reawakened resolve. He looked around for a rock or stick, anything he could use to throw in the general direction of whatever unsuspecting creature the man had in his sights. McBride did have something in his sights; the heavyset man had raised his rifle and was indeed aiming at something, lost in concentration. He would be squeezing the trigger soon, Billy just knew it. The youth would have to act fast.

He considered shooting off his own rifle, startling whatever prey the man had in his sights, but that would be foolish even if he did shoot in the air. Most of Naperville was dead ahead and even if the man was irresponsible enough to fire in that direction Billy wasn't about to do it. Bullets came down easier than they went up. He could fire in another direction; there wouldn't be anyone to the west or south, or would there? Perhaps some farmers working or their children playing outside, Billy considered. He almost shot into the ground at that point but it occurred to him the small pop of a .22 wouldn't likely scare off much of anything, not from his vantage point beneath the rise whose foliage also obscured any view of Billy from beneath the bridge. Besides, there wasn't enough time to find a bullet and load the gun.

Billy looked around and spotted a rock. It was fairly good-sized, not unlike the size and shape of a goose egg. He picked it up and threw it with all he had towards the man, aiming it a good five feet over his head. Billy had a strong arm for such a slight youth and had always prided himself with his accuracy. He missed. He watched in alarm as the rock veered down, heading directly for the man's skull. *Must have been heavier than I thought,* Billy assumed. He almost hollered at the man, but at the last instant the rock appeared as if it would just miss him, fly past, and alert the man's prey. It did neither. It slammed into the side of Rufus McBride's skull.

Minute bolts of high-pitched lightning exploded inside McBride's brain, and when he convulsed his trigger finger did the same. A very alarmed Billy was already sprinting towards the man, dropping his rifle as he ran up the hill. The bushes lashed at his face as the loud report from McBride's Henry shattered the calm.

McBride was an excellent marksman. Pete had been directly in his sights after Yankee had made his way a good twenty feet onto the walking bridge, his hoofs making a hollow, wooden sound that came to a sudden stop when both Yankee and Pete heard the explosion. The bullet had slammed into the railing to their right just ahead of the report, sending a shower of pulverized wood in every direction except backwards.

McBride was stunned but not unconscious as he shook his head in an attempt to chase the bantam yet concentrated lightning bolts from it, and was fumbling with the lever action of his gun as he did so, as if by instinct. Billy had made his way to him by then, surprised at the man's determination to apparently fire again. What on earth could be that important to shoot? Billy glanced at the bridge from his new vantage point. He could not believe his eyes. There was his brother, his brother *Pete,* over a hundred feet away holding onto the reins and glaring towards Billy. McBride had most of his wits about him by that time. He glared at Billy, unimpressed by his age and slight build, and took aim at Pete. He'd deal with the young whelp in a second or two.

"NO!" Billy hollered as he lunged at the man. McBride, still kneeling, turned his head towards Billy just in time to receive the full force of the youth's body blow. Their heads collided and the minute lightning bolts returned, exploding inside McBride's skull. Billy was shaken too, but managed to grab onto the rifle still clutched in McBride's hands. Billy stood as he did so then raised his boot and delivered a crushing blow to the side of McBride's head. Billy had control of the rifle and looked frantically back at his brother.

Clifton had scrambled from beneath the bridge and was making his way along the west side of it, knee deep in water as he sloshed towards Pete. He had his powerful buck and ball shotgun out in front of him, angling for a shot which at that range would blow Pete apart. If Clifton managed a head shot from that short a distance Pete's skull would all but vaporize, and a body shot would likely cut him near in half. Pete didn't see Janeway coming until it was too late. He had, however, heard the urgent sloshing of someone approaching from below on his right, and had instinctively reached for the revolver that wasn't there. His eyes widened in terror when Clifton Janeway appeared, his insane eyes glaring upwards, locked on Pete's face. Clifton quickly started to place the stock of the shotgun on his shoulder.

Billy didn't hesitate. Not for the briefest of moments. He aimed the Henry at Janeway's head and squeezed the trigger. The explosion sent smoke hurling forward from the Henry rifle and the large caliber bullet as well. It slammed into Clifton Janeway's skull just above his left ear with so much force the right side of his skull exploded, sending a rain of blood, bone fragments and brain matter spattering into the river under the bridge - *plop, plop, plop*. There was another explosion, much louder, as Janeway's shotgun went off. The water in front of him erupted as if hit by a boulder which had come from a great height, one that had been hurled down with terrific force.

Billy just stood there shaking, staring at Pete. His brother was looking back, equally shocked, frozen in place. Clifton Janeway was face down in the river, bobbing slightly, his boot caught on a rock that impeded him from drifting downriver. His blood wasn't impeded as it poured from the gaping wound; a crimson stream riding upon the surface, muted to a darker red by the waning light of a dying day.

Billy and Pete just stood frozen in place staring at each other. Suddenly, even from the distance of over a hundred feet, Billy saw what he believed was panic in his brother's eyes. Pete's entire bearing was alive with it. Pete started to scream and point but Billy had heard the rustling of grass and branches just as his brother did so. McBride was up, a large knife in his hand. Again Billy didn't hesitate as he cocked the lever, whirled and fired. The bullet slammed into the center of McBride's chest and through his heart. He looked at Billy, quizzically, as he slumped to the ground.

***

DOC WYGANT dropped the chamber pot on the floor then collapsed. Delicia ran to him, dropping the armload of towels she had been carrying and rushed to the old man's side as he lay upon the floor. She fell to her knees and reached for his face but hesitated, her hand suddenly frozen in mid-air. He was still. He was smiling. He was dead.

***

BILLY WATCHED Pete as he dismounted Yankee on the narrow bridge and came running to his youngest brother. The youth kept watching as his brother sprinted across the walking bridge, his body almost a shadowy figure as he moved along, moved through the gloaming. Pete was moving as fast as he could, but to Billy it resembled slow motion even if that wasn't really it. He could see that his brother was moving with determination though. Billy could see his brother through the dying light, see him as he made his way to the north end of the bridge which was silhouetted against the eastern horizon standing sentinel; stationed as if it had a date with Eternity. The last breath of day had almost drawn in the fading light, but not entirely. Billy could still see the bridge, see it in the deep purple gloaming, see the Gloamin' Bridge.

He dropped the rifle and began to run, heading towards his brother as Pete hurried towards the youth. They met, collided really, and grabbed hold of one another. There words were hurried, staccato sentences as their hearts pounded in their chests. They separated but didn't let go of each other as they marveled at the amazing sight of one another. They looked around briefly, first at the river. They could scarcely make out Clifton Janeway's body, but felt its presence. They looked up where the bridge was still standing sentinel. Its lower portion was barely visible closest to the water, whose own presence was indicated by the gentle sound it made as it moved along, taking a ghost with it. The upper portion of the bridge began to fade into the deep purple gloaming as the two brothers made their way towards the structure.

"I want you to meet a new friend, Billy boy," Pete said in a soft, shaky voice. Both of them were trembling. The enterprising palomino had already turned around and made his way to the north end of the bridge where Yankee was waiting for them.

"Yankee," Pete said, still shaking as he stroked the horse's muzzle, "want you to meet someone very special."

XXXIV

Lieutenant General Phineas Smithington hadn't arrived at his headquarters, and it was already well into the late afternoon. His personal aide, a young sergeant, had already alerted the adjutant major after that officer had returned, telling him the general hadn't been in all day and feared something may have happened to him. The portly old general had been out of sorts lately, which was especially unusual since his spirits had been so high of late. The young sergeant was alone in the general's office and had made his way to the large, mahogany desk. He looked towards the door, and after he was satisfied no one was coming did something highly unusual for him; he began to snoop. It took a while but there they were, right in the center drawer under some other documents - Lieutenant Pete McCabe's opened telegrams that were supposed to have been forwarded to Delicia and his parents, with written instructions not to do so in Smithington's own hand no less. There were copies of all the ones the general had sent to Major Rice, General Sherman, and a few especially incriminating ones to Major Clifton Janeway and Captain Calvin Baileen. The young sergeant began to read. "Yo, *Major*," he hollered into the next room. "Would you please come in here a moment, sir?"

***

DELICIA WAS standing outside, facing the hospital. Two other nurses were inside, staying with Doc Wygant's body. They didn't know why, other than they didn't know what else to do and didn't want to leave him alone. Delicia heard the hoof beats before she could see the galloping horse, the one that was approaching from the south up Eagle Street in the darkness after she turned around. Pete was in the saddle with Billy holding on to him from behind. Two lanterns were aglow on either side of the front door. Delicia had lit them, just before turning around and making her way down the front steps, towards the oncoming horse over half a block away. It was closing fast in the near total darkness beyond the lantern light.

She was still in shock, not having fully comprehended the finality of Doc Wygant's sudden death. She was already balancing her emotions, or trying to, with the rationalizations people often times use when an old person dies: *He had a long life, died doing what he loved even if he had been just carrying a chamber pot. Oh, that was an odd thing to reflect upon…his death had been mercifully swift, no lingering illness, no senility, no feelings of helplessness, no having to suffer the humiliation of relying upon others for the simplest of things…he would have hated that so…*

She began to watch the approaching horse more carefully. It was a large animal. The man astride it was bent forward, riding with determination. She was still in the glow of the lanterns, unable to make out the identity of the rider in the shadowy darkness beyond the light. Pete pulled at the reins and Yankee came to an abrupt halt, its light-colored mane flying as dust swirled around its straightened front legs. Pete dismounted and approached. Delicia still couldn't make out the man's face but his hurried stride looked very familiar…*could it be?* He entered the outer boundary of the lantern light.

"Oh dear God, **Pete!**"

They both began to run and flew into each other's arms. No words were spoken as they embraced each other so tightly it was as if it were the only force on earth. Delicia was sobbing as they began to kiss with a hurried intensity as her warm tears spilled onto their lips. Pete's tears soon joined hers as he brought a hand up the back of her neck and ran it through her long, chestnut hair, the back of her head firmly in his grasp with his other hand. Their lips parted, urgent words barely spoken as their lips met again before either of them could complete a sentence.

Billy had slid off Yankee and held the reins, standing next to the stalwart stallion while it pawed the ground, as if he had long since grown accustomed to the peculiarities of the two-legged creatures. Billy stayed back in the darkness, his own emotions trying to escape.

"Wh, what…how?" Delicia said, kissing Pete before he could say a word. She put both her palms on either side of his face, touching his features as a sightless person might do, her fingers exploring every inch of the miracle she held in her hands.

A carriage moving rapidly came up Eagle Street. Hezekiah O'Darcy had left home earlier to pick up his daughter and had heard the shots when he had exited the carriage house. He bounded from his carriage just as it came to a stop. He rushed towards his daughter but Billy stopped him before the alarmed man could make his way into the light of the lanterns.

"It's Pete, Mr. O'Darcy," was all the youth said. Hezekiah stopped and looked in amazement at the couple still in each other's arms, then at Billy.

"I heard shots. Clifton Janeway is dead." Billy looked at him.

"I know sir, I shot him. Shot the other one too." Hezekiah glared at him, mouth agape.

"Other one? *Why*, Billy? What in the name of God has happened?"

***

DOC WYGANT'S funeral was the largest anyone could remember. It was sad for most people, tempered with admiration for those who knew the man well. Billy felt none of the despondency he had for Linda Marie, far from it; he knew Dr. Silas Wygant better than any of them with the possible exception of Delicia. It was held in a cathedral-like clearing surrounded by old growth oaks near the bend in the DuPage River where it flowed through the McDowell property. Those had been Doc Wygant's wishes - demands more like it:

> *Don't want my body anywhere near the inside of a church, as far away from any God damned organ music as possible. Anyone even plays an organ the day I'm buried and I'll come back and pay them a little visit, and by Jesus I won't be coy about it. I like organ music except in church and find it especially annoying at funerals, so play fiddle music, and it better be merry. If old man Wheeler can stay sober long enough not to fall off his stool later on at the Pre-Emption House, some of his bango pickin' would be appreciated. If Robert McCabe is around I sure would appreciate the happy side of his piano playing. Maybe I'll hear it. Probably not. Just might have my hands full. Looking forward to that little run in. Don't even think about burying me in any God damned church graveyard either, or the cemetery on Washington Street. Ask McDowell, he's a good man, and knows where to plant me. If that old cornhusker up and dies before me or is otherwise indisposed, it's the spot near the bend where Billy McCabe and I found that injured fawn. Sorry to say, it's where Billy and I had to eventually bury that soft creature. If that holy rolling God most of you can't stop yammering about did the right thing, that fawn should be waiting for me on the other side. For those of you who are scoffing at the notion, well, you can go to hell. You are presumptuous and then some to believe the essence of another creature is worth less than any of you thick-headed God damned primates that fancy yourselves superior. If that precious God of yours made us in His image as you keep insisting, well, I want you to remember that the next time you are bent over in agony in some God damned outhouse suffering from the green apple quick step. Some image. Do you suppose He lifts His flowing robes before His gas attack gives way to more substantial discharges? Let me guess - sounds like organ music at a funeral. Anyway, bury me next to the fawn.*
> *Dr. Silas Wygant*

***

PETE WAS assigned permanent duty in Chicago for the duration of the war. Four weeks after his return, Pete and Delicia were married in the Methodist church. Later that night in their two story white house at 815 North Center Street which would soon be painted maroon with black trim, purchased for them by Hezekiah O'Darcy as a wedding gift, Pete and Delicia McCabe shared the most wonderful experience imaginable with countless more to follow. Saying "I love you" in the middle of their passion had been every bit as enchanting as Pete had imagined, as was the sound of Delicia's voice when she responded in kind.

It wasn't Pete's nature to insist his wife come into the bedroom with him as some husbands were apt to do, then pout or grow angry if their spouses weren't so inclined. It wasn't Pete's nature, but if cozy flames were dancing in the bedroom fireplace, Delicia knew her husband's mind wasn't on crops or weather.

***

EVERY SINGLE one of the McCabe boys made it home alive. First Ben, Billy and Pete of course, followed by Robert, Jackie and finally the oldest, Don. Unbeknownst to both Pete and Don, the oldest McCabe son had been on board the *New Era* during the Fort Pillow Massacre. The two brothers were shocked to realize they had been so close to each other while Pete had been hiding by the river; only a few hundred yards had separated them.

All six of Benjamin and Grace McCabe's boys had gone off to the deadliest war for Americans in the history of the nation, all experienced its horrors, and each of them took their turn coming down the road in front of Tin Pan Alley just as they had longed for with all their hearts during the long years they were away. They all returned to Tin Pan Alley, their large family, and the sanity of each other's love. The Golden Circle was flowing around smoothly and would continue to do so for their large family and descendants during the decades, and wars, that followed.

Each time one of them had made it back, everyone knew where Father Benjamin would end up, and everyone would leave him to his sobbing, grateful solitude after he had made his way to the High Hayloft. Mother Grace expressed her gratitude upstairs, kneeling by the southwest window of her bedroom clutching her family Bible. Her tears would flow, warm as they left her blue eyes, and on those occasions would stay that way as they ran down her cheeks. She thanked her God with all her heart as she knelt, thanked Him not only for her sons but for the peculiar light He had allowed to glow inside of her when she had needed it most.

***

ROBERT MCCABE and Ginny O'Darcy were married six months after the war ended. It was a beautiful ceremony held in the Methodist church. Reverend Galloway had managed to obtain a new, custom-built pipe organ made by the Moline Organ Company. Immediately after the ceremony the good reverend had asked Robert to play, unaware the young man hadn't touched an instrument in nearly two years. The war had stolen the joy of music from Robert, especially his desire to express those lost emotions with his amazing talent. The wedding had brought Robert back to life in that regard, and the only person who managed to keep a dry eye during Robert's beautiful rendition of *Amazing Grace* was old man Swensen. No one faulted the old fellow. He may have been able to feel a 24 pound Howitzer go off if he was close by, but he wouldn't have been able to hear it. Even his antiquated ear-horn, the size of a soprano saxophone, was only for adornment. Ginny McCabe took a seat next to her husband as he finished his rendition and looked into Robert's eyes with all the love she had been holding fast for so many years. Old man Swensen's watchful eyes had allowed him to join in the celebration then, and became fountains themselves.

***

WHATEVER THE chemistry was that existed between the McCabe and O'Darcy families it must have been contagious. Three months after the wedding of Robert and Ginny, the Methodist church in Naperville was again filled for the wedding of Jackie McCabe and Beth O'Darcy. Jackie could play guitar, but after the ceremony he contented himself with leaving it in its case. He stood next to his brother Robert who had taken a seat in front of the organ, and the duet the two young men sang, a touching song they had written about a river of golden dreams, again brought out so many handkerchiefs it looked as if a flock of white doves had erupted inside the church. Halfway through the song Billy joined his brothers and lent his clear tenor voice, and if there had been a dry eye inside the sanctuary it didn't stay that way long. Forgetting, or not caring they were indeed inside a church, the crowd erupted in heartfelt applause once the performance ended. Encores were demanded, as they would always be when the brothers serenaded family and friends over the proceeding decades.

***

NOT TO be outdone but having run out of O'Darcy sisters save the youngest, Joyce, Don McCabe married Grace Lanier, a new girl in town who had moved with her family to Naperville from Missouri after the war. They had two children, Michael and Barbara. Mickey, as their son came to be called, followed his Uncle Billy everywhere it seemed, at least when Billy was making his veterinarian calls. Mickey had his uncle's kind and loving heart, even resembled him in appearance, and just like the previous generation of young ladies, the post-war Naperville girls seemed to usually find a reason to be as close to Mickey as propriety, and their ingenuity, would allow.

***

BEN MCCABE, to no one's surprise, married a ravishing young lady from the East named Roxanne Cowles. Ben called her Ricky, even in front of his Eastern in-laws. Although the war had hardened him it didn't take long for Ricky to bring out what had been the essence of Ben before the Calamity had all but smothered its glow. During family gatherings, his quick wit and endearing charm were manifested in ways that gave him a Pied Piper status amongst his numerous nieces and nephews. If they desired a story told in a way that brought out the most enchanting and humorous nuances possible there was no escaping for Uncle Ben, who never tried to elude them anyway. Kind eyes were a given in all the McCabe boys, but Uncle Ben's were the most infectious of all.

***

MOTHER GRACE and Father Benjamin lived to experience the joy of grandchildren, even a fair number of great grandchildren. Although they lived well into their nineties the experiences of their boys returning home from the war, one by one, remained so vivid in both their memories it was as if Time wasn't capable of diminishing the glorious occurrences. For them, it was as if each homecoming had been yesterday, every day, for the rest of their lives. Although the return of all their sons had elicited immeasurable joy it was the return of Pete, the one all but Mother Grace had consigned to an unmarked grave, that created the greatest outflow of emotion…

***

IT WAS close to ten that night when Pete and Yankee, with Billy sitting behind his brother upon the stalwart palomino, made their way down the road to Tin Pan Alley. Pete pulled at the reins when they were out front, stroked Yankee's mane, and gazed at the impressive white house that the moonlight had transformed into an inviting steel-blue. The recent events had left him wholly drained, but if a tonic existed capable of bringing him back, save the one he had experienced earlier with Delicia in his arms, it was directly in front of him. Every sound in the night was familiar, biding him welcome, as did the countryside fragrances of home that to Pete were beyond intoxicating.

Mother Grace and Father Benjamin had been fast asleep for hours. Nothing out of the ordinary had occurred to awaken them, at least nothing that might have usually done so. Still, Mother Grace suddenly bolted upright. Something out of the ordinary had most certainly occurred after all.

"Benjamin!"

Father Benjamin stirred then bolted upright himself, as the urgency in his wife's voice alerted him to full consciousness. He could see her face in the moonlight that was caressing the room, caressing her. One brief look was all it took. He shot out of bed and saw a tall man astride a magnificent horse and a smaller person sitting behind him. Time had shadowed his ability to focus but he didn't need the eyesight of his younger years to recognize the man astride the horse in the moonlight.

"Come here, Grace. Your miracle is home."

Mother Grace didn't come to the window however; she didn't have to. She knew. She even knew he was on a magnificent palomino and Billy was directly behind him, behind *Kee*.

Her tears began to flow as she reached over to the bed stand and caressed the leather cover of her family Bible as she glanced briefly towards the southeast window then concentrated on the one in the southwest corner. Soon the front door could be heard opening, then the hurried footfalls - urgent boot steps bounding upon the hardwood stairs that led to the second floor. Father Benjamin, in his nightgown, bolted into the hallway and embraced his second oldest son. Both men were sobbing, and were soon joined by an overjoyed Ben who also embraced his brother.

"You know where to find her, Kee," was all Father Benjamin said as Ben stepped back, a look of profound happiness emanating from him. Father Benjamin again embraced his son then made his way downstairs, out the rear door and barefoot into the barn, then up to the High Hayloft.

"I'm home, Mother," Pete said as he entered the bedroom. "I'm home."

Her sobs of joy could be heard downstairs. Billy just stood in the darkness as if he were being enthralled by a symphony. All the gut-wrenching emotions that had been pulling at him the last few hours dissipated along with his older demons; Billy had come home as well, and he thanked his God for His unconditional forbearance.

***

LIEUTENANT GENERAL Phineas Smithington was arrested and court-martialed. He was sentenced to prison, but escaped after bribing two guards and lived the rest of his years in luxury across the Atlantic. When he died in 1875, six of the loveliest and most expensive courtesans in Paris were at his side. Word had reached them the old man was gravely ill, and had stayed at his side for the duration - at no charge. Over fifty of their peers attended his funeral, having known little about the man other than his extraordinary generosity when it came to beautiful, uninhibited women.

***

LIEUTENANT PETE McCabe's testimony as it pertained to the murder of Major Sackett O'Darcy, coupled with the evidence from General Smithington's court martial, sealed Clifton Janeway's reputation forever. Word, however, of what Clifton had done had spread quickly through the small town of Naperville. Before two days had passed from the time of the incident at the Gloamin' Bridge, as it came to be called, everyone knew what he had done well before the military inquiries and court proceedings. Only Clifton's mother and father, along with a few of the curious and opportunistic, attended his funeral at the near empty church. Buford Janeway had to replace his son's vandalized headstone six times. After it occurred the seventh time, immediately after the passing of Clifton's mother who had outlived Buford by a few years, it was left that way.

***

PETE AND Delicia's first child was borne less than a year after Pete's return. It was a boy. They named him Sackett. They had a daughter and six other sons - Donald, Keith, Robert, Benjamin, Jackie and William. They called the youngest boy Billy, and the third oldest Kee. The girl, borne last, was named Linda Marie.

***

PETE HAD used some of the nearly $2,400 of Elwood Stalworthy's money to buy an exceptional palomino mare, and wired the rest to Mrs. Desiree Beal in LaFayette, Georgia. There was one condition, however: Some of the money had to be used to buy Ely a horse - a white horse, as white as a cloud, without a speck of any other color anywhere on him. It had to be a boy horse too - *that* was non-negotiable.

He received a letter of thanks, written by someone he had always assumed was illiterate - Porticia. She had left Low Cloud Valley after Janny Beal had died and was herself living with Desiree, Buddy and the children, of which there were now five. Biddy, Buddy's mother, was living with them as well. Before the two old women had left the valley they had divided up the gold equally amongst all the families. It wasn't a fortune but there had been enough to allow any family that so wanted to leave Low Cloud Valley forever.

Yankee was more than impressed with his favorite primate's choice, and the stalwart stallion went on to sire some of the finest horses in the entire Chicago area and points beyond, and Pete never sold any of them. When the families gathered for one of their large picnics at Tin Pan Alley, the affairs were never considered complete until all the palominos were allowed to frolic in the Purple Meadow, much to everyone's delight.

True to his strength of character and amazing physicality, Yankee lived to the ripe old age of forty. By then rendering services were available in Naperville but Pete would have none of it. Yankee was buried in the Purple Meadow near the narrow bend in Brook Creek. All anyone needed was one hand to count the number of tombstones in the Washington Street cemetery that were larger than the one honoring Yankee in the Purple Meadow, upon which Pete had painstakingly chiseled: *Here rests Yankee, the strongest, bravest war horse that ever lived or ever will. He never tired, shirked his duty or displayed anything but unfailing courage in the darkest of days. He will always be missed, and never forgotten.*

***

BILLY FELL in love with Joyce O'Darcy, the youngest sister, and married her in the mid 1870's. She was twenty-four by then, the same age as her sister Delicia had been when she married. Joyce had been in love with Billy all her life. Shawnessy O'Keefe took a train all the way from New York City to stand up for Billy as his best man. The two had kept in touch over the years, and although his successful political career demanded much of his time, there was no way Shawn, honored beyond measure, would have denied Billy's request.

"Well now Saint William," Shawn had said, a broad smile on his face when introduced to Joyce before the wedding, "it appears God and all his precious angels still favor you, judgin' by Miss Joyce's extraordinary beauty, intelligence and poise."

Billy and Joyce's first child, a girl, didn't come into the world alone. She was followed a few minutes later by her twin brother. Their arrival reminded Pete of someone, a huge man of color he had known and respected so many years before, a man who had loved to talk about his own girl and boy twins. Pete could do that by then, talk about those harrowing days at least with his brothers, but rarely did so. None of them usually did. The nightmares never went away for any of the brothers, not completely, but their frequency and thankfully their intensity waned over the years.

When Pete held his infant niece and nephew for the first time and the warmth of their tiny bodies radiating through to his arms, he thought of Cusman Sable. Pete was reminded of what President Abraham Lincoln had said on a dreary day near the small town of Gettysburg on November 19th, 1863; how so many had, like the brave African American man had done, given their last full measure of devotion to the country they loved. And for Cusman Sable, the extraordinary devotion and love he had left to the wife and twin children he would never see again.

Pete allowed himself to dwell upon such thoughts for awhile, longer than he usually allowed himself to do, as he held the babies. Many did that, so many people went back in time with their own memories, back to the war years. So much had happened...

XL

It had been a long trip and Jennifer was exhausted. Memphis was a long way from Amherst, the small town of Fulton farther still and beyond that the old fort, but she had wanted, *needed* to see the military gravesite at Fort Pillow. Missy Nell couldn't go with her, not with the two babies, other responsibilities and her own health having suffered by all that had happened. Still, Jennifer had to see it, had to be close to the final resting place.

When Jennifer arrived back in Amherst she could barely keep her eyes open, but she had to check on Missy Nell, check on her daughter. The coachman pulled up in front of the Sable home and helped the lady in black exit the carriage. Jennifer began walking to the front of the large home. Missy Nell rushed through the screen door and appeared on the long front porch.

"Mother! How are you?" The statuesque, young woman said as she embraced the tired woman. "I thought you weren't due until the day after tomorrow."

"I'm fine, my dear. Tired, but fine. How are you feeling? What has the doctor said?"

"Oh I'm better Mother, as well as can be expected. Doctor Reynolds is a fine man."

"And what of the doctors in Boston, child? Have they stopped by like they said they would?"

"Sure enough have, Mother. Been by every Saturday, just like they promised."

"And what have they told you, my dear? Is everything going to be all right? It was touch and go, and I again beg your forgiveness for departing at such a time. It was just that -"

"I know Mother, I know. You loved Sedman so. Oh! Have you been reading the papers?" Missy Nell asked, wondering how her mother might take the news.

"Precious little else to do on such a journey, I'll be bound. And yes, I read about it. I was hoping General Sherman would have bypassed Beaux Hollow, but once I saw he hadn't avoided the general area I wondered if Whisper Manor had suffered. I harbor no ill will towards Trenton, that is for God to decide, but I doubt he feels the same about me, about us." Missy Nell took a deep breath. Her mother hadn't heard the whole story.

"General Sherman's army did get to Whisper Manor, Mother, and Trenton was there when they arrived. The Yankees burned Grand House then smashed it to the ground. Trenton's dead, Mother." Jennifer's shoulders sagged, and she took a seat on one of the porch chairs.

"He was so determined to get away from it all." Jennifer remarked, her emotions competing with one another. "I fear he was detained by my departure. And my sons? Any word about them?" That question caused Missy Nell to smile.

"They're in Boston, Mother. Alive and well. They even came to visit here, told me what happened in Georgia. Good thing you wrote to your sister, and Harriet, finally, to you. Told your boys where you went I did, even told them why. Neither of them was happy about it, but with all that's happened I s'pect they handled it well enough. They said for you to contact them soon as you got back, and asked me to tell you they love you." Jennifer couldn't stop her tears.

"And the babies, child, how are the babies?"

There were heavy footsteps upon the hardwood floor inside the house. Jennifer turned and looked through the front screen door. Any view of the inside of the house was impossible to see; it was blocked by the huge man standing there, a baby in each of his massive arms.

"Welcome back, Mother," Cusman said as the large grin on his tired face eased into concern for Jennifer's welfare. "Why don't you hold your grandchildren, maybe spell me a bit? Feelin' a might tuckered out, I am."

About the Author

Thomas McCabe grew up in the Fox River Valley area of northern Illinois. He currently resides there with his wife of forty-six years. *Gloamin' Bridge (A Civil War Remembrance)* is his debut novel.